R.SP - 3 great stories!!!

LAWRENCE
· SANDERS ·

THREE COMPLETE NOVELS

LAWRENCE
· SANDERS ·

THREE COMPLETE NOVELS

The Anderson Tapes
·

The Fourth Deadly Sin
· ·

The Tenth Commandment
· · ·

G. P. PUTNAM'S SONS · NEW YORK

G. P. Putnam's Sons
Publishers Since 1838
200 Madison Avenue
New York, NY 10016

Library of Congress Cataloging-in-Publication Data

Sanders, Lawrence, date.
[Novels. Selections]
Three complete novels/Lawrence Sanders.
p. cm.
Contents: The Anderson tapes—The fourth deadly sin—The Tenth
Commandment.
ISBN 0-399-14182-0 (acid-free paper)
1. Detective and mystery stories, American.   2. Delaney, Edward X.
(Fictitious character)—Fiction.   3. Private investigators—New York
(N.Y.)—Fiction.   4. Retirees—New York (N.Y.)—Fiction.
5. New York (N.Y.)—Fiction   I. Title.
PS3569.A5125A6   1996   96-7270 CIP
813'.54—dc20

Printed in the United States of America

1   3   5   7   9   10   8   6   4   2

Book design by Julie Duquet

Contents

•

LAWRENCE
· SANDERS ·

THREE COMPLETE NOVELS

THE ANDERSON TAPES

•

AUTHOR'S NOTE

●

THE FOLLOWING ACCOUNT OF A CRIME COMMITTED IN THE City of New York on the night of 31 August and the early morning hours of 1 September, 1968, has been assembled from a variety of sources, including:

—Eyewitness reports dictated to the author, and eyewitness reports available from official sources, on tape recordings and in transcriptions.

—Records of courts, penal institutions, and investigative agencies.

—Tape recordings and transcriptions made by "bugging" and other electronic surveillance devices, by crime prevention and detection agencies of the City of New York, the State of New York, the U.S. government, and by private investigative agencies.

—Personal correspondence, speeches, and private documents of the individuals involved, made available to the author.

—Newspaper reports.

—Official reports and testimony which are a matter of public record, including deathbed statements.

—The author's personal experiences.

It would be impractical to name all the individuals, official and civilian, who provided valuable assistance to the author. However, I am especially grateful to Louis J. Girardi, Managing Editor of the Newark (N.J.) *Post-Ledger,* who granted me a leave of absence from my crime reporting duties with that newspaper in order that I might research and write the full story of this crime, as part of a continuing investigation into the uses and abuses of electronic surveillance equipment by public and private agencies.

LAWRENCE SANDERS

1

•

THE BUILDING AT 535 EAST SEVENTY-THIRD STREET, NEW YORK City, was erected in 1912 as a city residence for Erwin K. Barthold, a Manhattan merchant who owned Barthold, Inc., a firm that dealt in rope, tar, ships' supplies, and marine gear of all types. On the death of Mr. Barthold in 1931, his widow, Edwina, and his son, Erwin, Jr., lived in the house until 1943. Erwin Barthold, Jr., was killed on 14 July, 1943, while engaged on a bombing mission over Bremen, Germany. This was, incidentally, the city in which his father had been born. Mrs. Barthold died six months after the death of her son, from cancer of the uterus.

The house on Seventy-third Street then passed to a brother of the original owner and builder. He was Emil Barthold, a resident of Palm Beach, Florida, and shortly after the will was probated, Emil Barthold sold the house (16 February, 1946) to Baxter & Bailey, 7456 Park Avenue, New York City.

This investment company then converted the town house into eight separate apartments and two professional suites on the ground floor. A self-service elevator and central air conditioning were installed. The apartments and suites were sold as cooperatives, at prices ranging from $26,768 to $72,359.

The building itself is a handsome structure of gray stone, the architecture generally in the French chateau style. The building has been certified and listed by the New York City Landmark Society. Outside decoration is minimal and chaste; the roof is tarnished copper. The lobby is lined with veined gray marble slabs interspersed with antiqued mirrors. In addition to the main entrance, there is a service entrance reached by a narrow alleyway which stretches from the street to a back door that leads to a wide flight of concrete stairs. The two apartments on the top floor have small terraces. There is a small apartment in the basement occupied by the superintendent. The building is managed by Shovey & White, 1324 Madison Avenue, New York.

Prior to 1 September, 1967, for a period of several years, Apartment 3B at 535 East Seventy-third Street had been occupied by a married couple (childless), Agnes and David Everleigh. On or about that date, they separated, and Mrs. Agnes Everleigh remained in possession of Apartment 3B, while David Everleigh took up residence at the Simeon Club, Twenty-third Street and Madison Avenue.

On approximately 1 March, 1968 (this is an assumption), David Everleigh engaged the services of Peace of Mind, Inc., a private investigation agency located at 983 West Forty-second Street, New York. With David Everleigh's assistance—this is presumed, since he still possessed a key to Apartment 3B and was its legal owner—an electronic device was installed in the base of the telephone in Apartment 3B.

It was a microphone transmitter—an Intel Model MT-146B—capable of picking up and transmitting telephone calls as well as conversations taking place in the apartment. A sum of $25 per month was paid to the superintendent of 534 East Seventy-third Street—the building across the street—to allow Peace of Mind, Inc., to emplace a voice-actuated tape recorder in a broom closet on the third floor of that building.

Thus, it was not necessary for an investigator to be present. The voice-actuated tape recorder recorded all telephone calls and interior conversations taking place in Apartment 3B, 535 East Seventy-third Street. The tape was retrieved each morning by an operative from Peace of Mind, Inc., and a fresh tape installed.

The resulting recordings became the basis of David Everleigh's suit for divorce (Supreme Court, New York County) on the grounds of adultery (*Everleigh v. Everleigh,* NYSC-148532), and transcriptions of the tapes have become a matter of public record, which allows them to be reproduced here. It is of some interest to note that the verdict of the trial judge, in favor of David Everleigh, has been appealed by Mrs. Everleigh's attorneys on the grounds that David Everleigh did not obtain a court order, and had no legal right, to implant an electronic surveillance device in Apartment 3B, despite the fact that he was legal owner of the premises in question.

It is expected this litigation will eventually reach the Supreme Court of the United States and will result in a landmark decision.

The following is an excerpt from the transcription made from the Peace of Mind, Inc., tape recording made at approximately 1:15 A.M. on the morning of 24 March, 1968.

This is tape POM-24MAR68-EVERLEIGH. Those present, Mrs. Agnes Everleigh and John Anderson, have been identified by voice prints and interior evidence.

[Sound of door opening and closing.]
MRS. EVERLEIGH: Here we are ... make yourself at home. Throw your coat anywhere.
ANDERSON: How come a classy place like this don't have a doorman?
MRS. EVERLEIGH: Oh, we have one, but he's probably down in the

basement with the super, sucking on a jug of muscatel. They're both a couple of winos.

ANDERSON: Oh?

[Lapse of seven seconds.]

ANDERSON: Nice place you got here.

MRS. EVERLEIGH: *So* glad you like it. Mix us a drink. The stuff's over there. Ice in the kitchen.

ANDERSON: What'll you have?

MRS. EVERLEIGH: Jameson's. On the rocks. With a little soda. What do you drink?

ANDERSON: Got any cognac? Or brandy?

MRS. EVERLEIGH: I have some Martell.

ANDERSON: That'll do fine.

[Lapse of forty-two seconds.]

ANDERSON: Here you are.

MRS. EVERLEIGH: Cheers.

ANDERSON: Yeah.

[Lapse of six seconds.]

MRS. EVERLEIGH: Sit down and relax. I'm going to take off my girdle.

ANDERSON: Sure.

[Lapse of two minutes sixteen seconds.]

MRS. EVERLEIGH: That's better. Thank God.

ANDERSON: Are all the apartments in the building like this?

MRS. EVERLEIGH: Most of them are larger. Why?

ANDERSON: I like it. Class.

MRS. EVERLEIGH: Class? Jesus, you're too much. What do you do for a living?

ANDERSON: I work on a folding machine in a printing plant. For a supermarket newspaper. A daily. Their specials and things like that.

MRS. EVERLEIGH: Aren't you going to ask me what I do?

ANDERSON: Do you do anything?

MRS. EVERLEIGH: That's a laugh. My husband owns this apartment. We're separated. He doesn't give me a cent. But I do all right. I'm the buyer for a chain of women's lingerie shops.

ANDERSON: That sounds interesting.

MRS. EVERLEIGH: Go to hell.

ANDERSON: Are you lushed?

MRS. EVERLEIGH: Some. Not enough.

[Lapse of seventeen seconds.]

MRS. EVERLEIGH: I hope you don't think I make a habit of picking men up off the street?

ANDERSON: Why me?

MRS. EVERLEIGH: You looked clean and reasonably well dressed. Except for that tie. God, I hate that tie. Are you married?

ANDERSON: No.

MRS. EVERLEIGH: Ever been?

ANDERSON: No.

MRS. EVERLEIGH: Jesus Christ, I don't even know your name. What the hell's your name?

ANDERSON: Another drink?

MRS. EVERLEIGH: Sure.

[Lapse of thirty-four seconds.]

MRS. EVERLEIGH: I thank you. What the hell's your name?

ANDERSON: John Anderson.

MRS. EVERLEIGH: That's a nice, clean, neat name. My name's Agnes Everleigh—Mrs. David Everleigh that was. What do I call you—Jack?

ANDERSON: Mostly I'm called Duke.

MRS. EVERLEIGH: Duke? Royalty, for God's sake. Jesus, I'm sleepy. . . .

[Lapse of four minutes thirteen seconds. At this point there is evidence (not admissible) that Mrs. Everleigh dozed off. Anderson wandered about the apartment (supposition). He inspected the intercom system connected to the bells and the microphone in the lobby. He inspected the locks on the windows. He inspected the lock on the front door.]

MRS. EVERLEIGH: What are you doing?

ANDERSON: Just stretching my legs.

MRS. EVERLEIGH: Would you like to stay the night?

ANDERSON: No. But I don't want to go home yet.

MRS. EVERLEIGH: Thanks a lot, bum.

[Sound of loud slap.]

MRS. EVERLEIGH [gasping]: What did you do that for?

ANDERSON: That's what you wanted, isn't it?

MRS. EVERLEIGH: How did you know?

ANDERSON: A big, beefy lady executive like you . . . it had to be.

MRS. EVERLEIGH: Does it show that plainly?

ANDERSON: No. Unless you're looking for it. Should I use my belt?

MRS. EVERLEIGH: All right.

The following is supposition, supported in part by eyewitness testimony.

When he left Apartment 3B at 3:04 A.M., John Anderson spent a few moments examining the lock on Apartment 3A, across the foyer. He then took the self-service elevator up to the fifth floor, examined the locks, and made his way slowly downward, examining doors and locks. There were no peepholes in apartment doors above the ground floor.

When he exited from the lobby—still unattended by a doorman—he was able to examine the security arrangements of the outside doors and the bell system. He then waited on the corner of East Seventy-third Street and York Avenue for a cab, and rode home to his Brooklyn apartment, arriving there at 4:26 A.M. The lights in his apartment were extinguished at 4:43 A.M. (testimony of eyewitness).

2

•

AT 2:35 P.M., ON THE AFTERNOON OF WEDNESDAY, 17 APRIL, 1968, a black sedan was parked on the north side of Fifty-ninth Street, New York City, between Fifth Avenue and Avenue of the Americas. The vehicle was a 1966 Cadillac Eldorado (with air conditioning), license HGR-45-9159. It was registered as a company car by the Benefix Realty Co., Inc., 6501 Fifth Avenue, New York, New York.

The chauffeur of the car—later identified as Leonard Goldberg, forty-two, a resident of 19778 Grant Parkway, the Bronx, New York—was observed lounging nearby.

The sole occupant of the parked car, seated in the back, was Frederick Simons, vice-president of the Benefix Realty Co., Inc. He was fifty-three years old; approximately 5 feet 7 inches; 190 pounds. He wore a black bowler and a double-breasted tweed topcoat. His hair and mustache were white. He was a graduate of Rawlins Law College, Erskine, Virginia, and was also licensed as a certified public accountant in the State of New York (#41-5G-1943). He had no criminal record, although he had twice been questioned—by the New York Federal District Attorney (Southern District) and by a grand jury convened by Manhattan Supreme Court—regarding the control of the Benefix Realty Co., Inc., by an organized criminal syndicate, and the role Benefix had played in the procurement of liquor licenses for several taverns and restaurants in New York City and Buffalo, New York.

Approximately five months prior to this date, on 14 November, 1967, a court order (MCC-B-189M16) had been obtained for the emplacement of an electronic transmitting device in the vehicle described. Application was made by the Frauds Division, New York State Income Tax Bureau. A Gregory MT-146-GB microphone transmitter was concealed under the dashboard of the aforesaid vehicle. It was implanted in the garage where cars registered to the Benefix Realty Co., Inc., were serviced.

At 2:38 P.M., on the afternoon of Wednesday, 17 April, 1968, a man was seen approaching this car. He was later identified by an eyewitness at the scene and by voice prints.

John "Duke" Anderson, thirty-seven, was a resident of 314 Harrar Street, Brooklyn, New York. He was 5 feet 11 inches; 178 pounds; brown hair and brown eyes; no physical scars; dressed neatly and spoke with a slight Southern accent. Anderson was a professional thief, and four months previously had been paroled after serving twenty-three months at Sing Sing (#562-8491) after his conviction on 21 January, 1966, in Manhattan Criminal Court on a charge of breaking and entering. Although it was the first conviction on his record, he had been arrested twice before in New York State, once for burglary, once for simple assault. Both charges had been dropped with no record of trial.

Tape NYSITB-FD-17APR68-106-1A begins:

SIMONS: Duke! My Lord, it's good to see you. How you been?

ANDERSON: Mr. Simons. Mighty fine to see you. How you been?

SIMONS: Fine, Duke, just fine. You're looking well. A little thinner, maybe.

ANDERSON: I expect so.

SIMONS: Of course, of course! We've got this little refreshment stand here. As you can see, I'm already partaking. Can I offer you something?

ANDERSON: Cognac? Or brandy?

SIMONS: How will Rémy Martin suit you?

ANDERSON: Just right.

SIMONS: Pardon the paper cups, Duke. We find it's easier that way.

ANDERSON: Sure, Mr. Simons.
    [Lapse of five seconds.]

SIMONS: Well . . . here's to crime.
    [Lapse of four seconds.]

ANDERSON: God . . . that's good.

SIMONS: Tell me, Duke—how have things been going for you?

ANDERSON: I got no complaints, Mr. Simons. I appreciate everything you all did for me.

SIMONS: You did a lot for us, too, Duke.

ANDERSON: Yes. But it wasn't much. I got the letters through when I could. Sometimes I couldn't.

SIMONS: We understood, I assure you. We don't expect perfection when you're inside.

ANDERSON: I'll never forget that night I got back to Manhattan. The hotel room. The money. The booze. And that cow you sent over. And the clothes! How did you know my sizes?

SIMONS: We have ways, Duke. You know that. I hope you liked the woman. I picked her out myself.

ANDERSON: Just what the doctor ordered.

SIMONS [laughing]: Exactly right.

   [Lapse of nine seconds.]

ANDERSON: Mr. Simons, since I got out I been walking the arrow. I work nights on a folding machine in a printing plant. We do a daily sheet a chain of supermarkets gets out. You know—special buys for the day, things like that. And I report regular. I don't see any of the old gang.

SIMONS: We know, Duke, we know.

ANDERSON: But something came up I wanted to ask you about. A wild idea. I can't handle it myself. That's why I called.

SIMONS: What is it, Duke?

ANDERSON: You'll probably think I'm nuts, that those twenty-three months scrambled my brains.

SIMONS: We don't think you're nuts, Duke. What is it . . . a campaign?

ANDERSON: Yes. Something I came across about three weeks ago. It's been chewing at me ever since. It might be good.

SIMONS: You say you can't handle it yourself? How many will you need?

ANDERSON: More than five. No more than ten.

SIMONS: I don't like it. It isn't simple.

ANDERSON: It is simple, Mr. Simons. Maybe I could do with five.

SIMONS: Let's have another.

ANDERSON: Sure . . . thanks.

   [Lapse of eleven seconds.]

SIMONS: What income do you anticipate?

ANDERSON: You want me to guess? That's all I can do—guess. I guess a minimum of a hundred thou.

   [Lapse of six seconds.]

SIMONS: And you want to talk to the Doctor?

ANDERSON: Yes. If you can set it up.

SIMONS: You better tell me a little more about it.

ANDERSON: You'll laugh at me.

SIMONS: I won't laugh at you, Duke. I promise.

ANDERSON: There's a house on the East Side. Way over near the river. Used to be a privately owned town house. Now it's apartments. Doctors' offices on the ground floor. Eight apartments on the four floors above. Rich people. Doorman. Self-service elevator.

SIMONS: You want to hit one of the apartments?

ANDERSON: No, Mr. Simons. I want to hit the whole building. I want to take over the entire fucking building and clean it out.

3

•

ANTHONY "DOCTOR" D'MEDICO, FIFTY-FOUR, LEGAL RESIDENCE at 14325 Mulberry Lane, Great Neck, Long Island, was identified before the U.S. Senate Special Subcommittee to Investigate Organized Crime, (Eighty-seventh Congress, first session), on 15 March, 1965 (Report of Hearings, pp. 413–19), as being the third-ranking *capo* (captain) of the Angelo family. The Angelos were one of six families controlling the distribution of illicit drugs, extortion, prostitution, loan-sharking, and other illegal activities in the New York, New Jersey, Connecticut, and eastern Pennsylvania area.

D'Medico was president of the Benefix Realty Co., Inc., 6501 Fifth Avenue, New York City. His other holdings included half-partnership in the Great Frontier Steak House, 106-372 Flatbush Avenue, Brooklyn, New York; full ownership of the New Finnish Sauna and Health Club, 746 West Forty-eighth Street, Manhattan; one-third ownership of Lafferty, Riley, Riley & D'Amato, brokers (twice fined by the Securities and Exchange Commission), of 1441 Wall Street, Manhattan; and suspected but unproved ownership or interest in several small taverns, restaurants, and private clubs on the East Side of Manhattan catering to male homosexuals and lesbians.

D'Medico was a tall man, 6 feet 5 inches, portly, and he dressed conservatively (his suits were made by Quint Riddle, tailor, 1486 Saville Row, London; shirts by Trioni, 142-F Via Veneto, Rome; shoes by B. Halley, Geneva). For many years he had been the victim of a chronic and apparently incurable *tic douloureux,* an extremely painful neuralgia of the facial muscles that resulted in a spasmodic twitching of his right eye and cheek.

His criminal record was minimal. At the age of seventeen he was arrested on a charge of assault with a knife upon a uniformed officer. No injury resulted. The case was dropped by Bronx Juvenile Court on the plea of D'Medico's parents. There is no other record of charges, arrests, or convictions.

On 22 April, 1968, the premises of the Benefix Realty Co., Inc., 6501 Fifth Avenue, New York, were under electronic surveillance by three agencies: the Federal Bureau of Investigation, the Frauds Division of the New York State Income Tax Bureau, and the New York Police Department. Apparently none of these agencies was aware of the others' activities.

The following tape, dated 22 April, 1968, is NYPD-SIS-564-03.

ANDERSON: Mr. D'Medico, please. My name is John Anderson.

RECEPTIONIST: Is Mr. D'Medico expecting you?

ANDERSON: Yes. Mr. Simons set up the appointment.

RECEPTIONIST: Just a moment, please, sir.

    [Lapse of fourteen seconds.]

RECEPTIONIST: You may go right in, sir. Through that door and down the hall. First door on your right.

ANDERSON: Thanks.

RECEPTIONIST: You're quite welcome, sir.

    [Lapse of twenty-three seconds.]

D'MEDICO: Come in.

ANDERSON: Afternoon, Mr. D'Medico.

D'MEDICO: Duke! Good to see you.

ANDERSON: Doc . . . it's fine seeing you again. You're looking well.

D'MEDICO: Too much weight. Look at this. Too much. It's the pasta that does it. But I can't resist it. How have you been, Duke?

ANDERSON: Can't complain. I want to thank you. . . .

D'MEDICO: Of course, of course. Duke, have you ever seen the view from our roof? Suppose we go up and take a look around? Get a breath of fresh air.

ANDERSON: Fine.

    [Lapse of five seconds.]

D'MEDICO: Miss Riley? I'll be out of my office for a few moments. Will you ask Sam to switch on the air conditioner? It's very stuffy in here. Thank you.

    [Lapse of three minutes forty-two seconds. Remainder of recording is garbled and indistinct due to mechanical difficulties.]

D'MEDICO: . . . do we know? A guy comes in every morning . . . the place . . . but . . . You wouldn't believe . . . phones . . . gadgets that. . . . The building over there, across the street . . . windows . . . long-range. . . . We try to keep . . . murder. Don't trust. . . . Over here by the air conditioner. The noise. . . . Cold for you?

ANDERSON: No. It's. . . .

D'MEDICO: Fred told me . . . campaign. . . . Interesting. About five men you figured or . . . me more.

ANDERSON: I know . . . idea . . . still . . . Of course, I haven't even gone . . . it. So I . . . you a package, Mr. D'Medico.

D'MEDICO: [Completely garbled.]

ANDERSON: No. No, I. . . . Two months, I'd say . . . be careful . . . first investigation. Good men . . . be in . . . if we went ahead. So all I got . . . right . . . is a hustle. I hoped . . . might stake . . . piece of the action.

D'MEDICO: I see . . . much do you . . . for this initial. . . .

ANDERSON: Three grand tops I . . . most . . . good men. But no use cutting . . . like this. . . .

D'MEDICO: You've got . . . —stand, is personal. My own funds. If it . . . good, I'll have . . . bring in others. You understand? It will . . . more . . . and also we'll want . . . man in. Ours.

ANDERSON: I understand. And thanks . . . help. I really . . . can bring it. . . .

D'MEDICO: Duke . . . anyone . . . you can. You . . . think . . . Fred Simons will . . . funds . . . from him. Let's . . . downstairs. Cold . . . hell. My face . . . act up. Jesus.

End of recording. It is assumed the two men returned to the Benefix offices, but that Anderson did not reenter D'Medico's private office. He departed from the building at 2:34 P.M.

4

•

PATSY'S DELICIOUS MEAT MARKET, 11901 NINTH AVENUE, NEW York. Four months previously these premises had been placed under electronic surveillance by the Investigative Division, Food and Drug Administration. The following tape recording, labeled FDA-PMM-#198-08, is dated 24 April, 1968. Time: approximately 11:15 A.M.

ANDERSON: Are you Patsy?

PATSY: Yes.

ANDERSON: My name is Simons. I called for three of your best steaks. You said you'd have them ready when I came in.

PATSY: Sure. Here they are, all wrapped.

ANDERSON: Thanks. Add that to my bill, will you?

PATSY: A pleasure.

5

•

THOMAS HASKINS (ALIAS TIMOTHY HAWKINS, TERENCE HALL, etc.); thirty-two; 5 feet 4 inches; 128 pounds; faint white scar on left temple; slight figure; blond hair bleached whiter; a confessed male homosexual. This man's record included two arrests on charges of molesting male juveniles. Charges dropped when parents refused to prosecute. Arrested on 18 March, 1964, during raid on bucket shop operation at 1432 Wall Street, Manhattan. Charge dropped. Arrested on 23 October, 1964, on conspiracy to defraud, complaint of Mrs. Eloise MacLevy, 41105 Central Park West, Manhattan, claiming subject had mulcted her of $10,131.56 while promising her high return on investment in pork-belly futures. Charge dropped. Last known address: 713 West Seventy-sixth Street, New York City. Subject lived with sister (see below).

Cynthia "Snapper" Haskins; thirty-six; 5 feet 8 inches; 148 pounds; red hair (dyed; frequently wore wigs); no physical scars. Four convictions for shoplifting, three for prostitution, and one for fraud, in that she charged $1,061.78 worth of merchandise against a stolen credit card of the Buy-Everything Credit Co., Inc., 4501 Marvella Street, Los Angeles, California. Subject had served a total of four years, seven months, thirteen days in the Women's House of Detention, Manhattan; Barnaby House for Women, Losset, New York; and the McAllister Home for Women, Carburn, New York. Subject was author of *I Was a B-Girl* (Smith & Townsend, published 10 March, 1963) and *Women's Prison: A Story of Lust and Frustration* (Nu-World Publishing Corp., published 26 July, 1964).

The premises at 713 West Seventy-sixth Street, New York, were under surveillance by the Bureau of Narcotics, Department of the Treasury. The following is transcription BN-DT-TH-0018-95GT, from a tape recording of the same number (except that the final digits are 95G). Those present have been identified by voice prints and by internal and external evidence. The date and time have not been determined exactly.

HASKINS: . . . so we're on the old uppers, darling. The sad story of our lives. Would you like a stick?
ANDERSON: No. You go ahead. What about you, Snap?

CYNTHIA: We live. I boost a little, and Tommy hustles his ass. We get by.

ANDERSON: I got something for you.

CYNTHIA: Both of us?

ANDERSON: Yes.

CYNTHIA: How much?

ANDERSON: Five bills. Shouldn't take over a week. No sweat.

HASKINS: Sounds divine.

CYNTHIA: Let's hear it.

ANDERSON: I'll tell you what you need to know. After that . . . no questions.

HASKINS: Wouldn't dream, darling.

ANDERSON: There's this house on the East Side. I'll leave you the address and everything I know about the schedules of the doormen and the super. Tommy, I want a complete list of everyone who lives in the place or who works there. That includes day-only servants, doormen, and super. Anything and everything. Names, ages, businesses they're in, daily schedules—the whole schmear.

HASKINS: A lark, darling.

ANDERSON: Snap, there are two professional offices on the ground floor, one a doctor, one a psychiatrist. I want you to look around. Furnishings? Safes? Maybe paintings on the walls? Shoe boxes in the back closet? These fucking doctors collect a lot in cash and never declare. Look it over and decide how you'll handle it. Then let me know before you move.

CYNTHIA: Like you said—no sweat. How do we contact you, Duke?

ANDERSON: I'll call at noon every Friday until you're set. Is your phone clean?

CYNTHIA: Here . . . I'll write it down. It's a phone booth in a candy store on West End Avenue. I'll be there at twelve o'clock every Friday.

ANDERSON: All right.

CYNTHIA: A little something down?

ANDERSON: Two bills.

CYNTHIA: You're a darling.

HASKINS: He's a sweetheart, a messenger from heaven. How's your love life, Duke?

ANDERSON: All right.

HASKINS: I saw Ingrid the other night. She heard you were out. She asked about you. Do you want to see her?

ANDERSON: I don't know.

HASKINS: She wants to see you.

ANDERSON: Yes? All right. Is she still at the old place?

HASKINS: She is indeed, darling. You don't blame her . . . do you?

ANDERSON: No. It wasn't her fault. I got busted from my own stupidity. How did she look?

HASKINS: The same. The pale, white little mouse made of wire and steel. The essence of bitchery.

ANDERSON: Yes.

6

•

FUN CITY ELECTRONIC SUPPLY & REPAIR CO., INC., 1975 AVENUE D, New York City.

The following tape recording was made by the Federal Trade Commission through a rather unusual set of circumstances. The FTC established electronic surveillance of the aforementioned premises (court order MCC-#198-67BC) following complaints from several large recording companies that the proprietor of the Fun City Electronic Supply & Repair Co., Inc., Ernest Heinrich Mann, was engaged in a criminal activity, in that he purchased expensive commercial LP's and tape recordings of classical music—operas and symphonies—recorded them onto his own tapes, and sold the tapes at a greatly reduced (but profitable) price to a large list of clients.

TAPE FTC-30 APR68-EHM-14.

CLERK: Yes?

ANDERSON: The owner around?

CLERK: Mr. Mann?

ANDERSON: Yes. Could I see him for a minute? I want to complain about an air conditioner you people sold me.

CLERK: I'll get him.

[Lapse of nine seconds.]

ANDERSON: You installed an air conditioner in my place and it conked out after I turned it on. I tested it and it ran a few minutes, then it stopped.

MANN: Would you step into the back office for a few minutes, sir, and we'll try to solve your problem. Al, handle things.

CLERK: Yes, Mr. Mann.

[Lapse of thirteen seconds.]

ANDERSON: Professor . . . you're looking good.

MANN: All goes well. With you, Duke?

ANDERSON: Can't complain. Took me a while to track you down. Nice setup you've got here.

MANN: What I've wanted always. Radio, television, hi-fi equipment, tape recorders, air conditioners. I do good.

ANDERSON: In other words, you're making money?

MANN: Yes, that is true.

ANDERSON: In other words, it will cost me more?

MANN [laughing]: Duke, Duke, you have always been a—how do you say it?—you have always been a very sharp man. Yes, it will now cost you more. What is it?

ANDERSON: There's this house on the East Side. Not too far from here. Five floors. Service entrance to basement. I want the basement washed—telephone system, trunk lines, alarms, whatever is down there. The works.

[Lapse of nine seconds.]

MANN: Difficult. With all these terrible robberies on the East Side recently, everyone is most alert. Doorman?

ANDERSON: Yes.

MANN: Back entrance?

ANDERSON: Yes.

MANN: I would guess closed-circuit TV from the back service entrance to the doorman's cubbyhole in the lobby. He doesn't press the button that releases the service door until he sees who is ringing. Am I correct?

ANDERSON: One hundred percent.

MANN: So. Let me think. . . .

ANDERSON: Do that, Professor.

MANN: "Professor." You are the only man I know who calls me Professor.

ANDERSON: Aren't you a professor?

MANN: I *was* a professor. But please . . . let me think. Now. . . . Yes. . . . We are telephone repairmen. The authentic truck is parked in front where the doorman can see it. Uniforms, equipment, identity cards . . . everything. We are bringing a new trunk line down the block. We must inspect the telephone connections in the basement. Duke? All right so far?

ANDERSON: Yes.

MANN: The doorman insists we pull over to the service entrance. . . .

ANDERSON: It's an alleyway leading to the back of the building.

MANN: Excellent. We pull in after he has inspected my identity card. All is well. The driver stays with the truck. I go in. The doorman sees me on his TV monitor. He releases the lock. Yes, I think so.

ANDERSON: I do, too.

MANN: So? What do you want?

ANDERSON: Everything down there. How the telephone lines come in. Can we break them? How? Is it a one-trunk line? Can it be cut or bypassed? How many phones in the whole building? Extensions? Alarm systems? To the local precinct house or private agencies? I want a blueprint of the whole wiring system. And look around down there. Probably nothing, but you never can tell. Can you operate a Polaroid with flash?

MANN: Of course. Clear, complete views. Every angle. Details. Instructions on what to bridge and what to cut. Satisfaction guaranteed.

ANDERSON: That's why I looked you up.

MANN: The cost will be one thousand dollars with half down in advance.

ANDERSON: The cost will be seven hundred dollars with three in advance.

MANN: The cost will be eight with four ahead.

ANDERSON: All right.

MANN: The cost will not include telephone truck and driver. I have no one I can trust. You must provide. Telephone truck, driver, uniform, and paper. You will pay for this?

   [Lapse of four seconds.]

ANDERSON: All right. You'll get your own?

MANN: Yes.

ANDERSON: I'll let you know when. Thank you, Professor.

MANN: Any time.

7

•

FROM TAPE RECORDING POM-14MAY68-EVERLEIGH, Segment I, approximately 9:45 A.M.

MRS. EVERLEIGH: Jesus, you're too much. I've never met anyone like you. How did you learn to do these things?

ANDERSON: Practice.

MRS. EVERLEIGH: You turn me upside down and inside out. You know all the buttons—just what turns me on. About a half hour ago I was down to one little nerve end, red and raw. You get me out.

ANDERSON: Yes.

MRS. EVERLEIGH: For a moment there I wanted to scream.

ANDERSON: Why didn't you?

MRS. EVERLEIGH: That bitch next door—she'd probably tell the door-man to call the cops.

ANDERSON: What bitch?

MRS. EVERLEIGH: Old Mrs. Horowitz. She and her husband have Apartment Three A, across the foyer.

ANDERSON: She's home during the day?

MRS. EVERLEIGH: Of course. He is, too—most days, when he's not at his broker's. He's retired and plays the market for kicks. Why—I don't know. He's got the first buck he ever earned.

ANDERSON: Loaded?

MRS. EVERLEIGH: Loaded *and* cheap. I've seen her put dog-food cans in the incinerator, and they don't even have a dog. I was in their place once. I don't socialize with them, but he called me in one night when she fainted. He panicked and rang my bell. It was just a faint—nothing to it. But while I was in their bedroom I saw a safe that must date from Year One. I'll bet that thing is bulging. He used to be a wholesale jeweler. Do it again, baby.

ANDERSON: Do what?

MRS. EVERLEIGH: You know. . . . with your finger . . . here . . .

ANDERSON: I know something better than that. Open up a little. More. Yes. Keep your knees up, you stupid cow.

MRS. EVERLEIGH: No. Don't do that. Please.

ANDERSON: I'm just starting. It gets better.

MRS. EVERLEIGH: Please, don't. Please, Duke. You're hurting me.

ANDERSON: That's the name of the game.

MRS. EVERLEIGH: I can't . . . oh Jesus, don't . . . please . . . God . . . Duke, I beg . . . oh, oh, oh . . .

ANDERSON: What a fat slob you are. For Chrissakes, you're crying . . .

8

•

HELMAS JOB PRINTING, 8901 AMSTERDAM AVENUE, NEW YORK; 14 May, 1968; 10:46 A.M. Electronic surveillance by the Internal Revenue Service, using a Teletek Model MT-18-48B, transmitting to a voice-actuated tape recorder in the basement of the delicatessen next door. This is tape IRS-HJB-14MAY68-106.

CLERK: Yeah?

HASKINS: Is your employer about?

CLERK: Smitty? He's in back. Hey, Smitty! Someone to see you! [Lapse of six seconds.]

HASKINS: Hello, Smitty.

SMITTY: Where's my twenty?

HASKINS: Right here, Smitty. Sorry it took so long to pay you. I do apologize. But I assure you, I didn't forget it.

SMITTY: Yeah. Thanks, Tommy.

HASKINS: Could I speak to you for a moment, Smitty?

SMITTY: Well . . . yeah . . . all right. Come on in back. [Lapse of eleven seconds.]

HASKINS: I need some paper, Smitty. I've got the cash. See? Plenty of bread. Cash on delivery.

SMITTY: What do you need?

HASKINS: I typed it all out for you on Snapper's typewriter. One identification card in the name of Sidney Brevoort. I've always loved the name Sidney. The company is the New Urban Reorganization Committee, a nonprofit outfit. Any clean address. Make sure you use this phone number. Here's a snapshot of me to staple on the card. Here is what it should say: "This will identify . . ." and so forth and so forth. Then I'll want about twenty Sidney Brevoort business cards. While you're at it, better make up about ten letterheads and envelopes for the New Urban Reorganization Committee. You never know. Okay so far?

SMITTY: Sure. What else?

HASKINS: Snapper wants twenty cards. Very ladylike and elegant. Script.

Here's the name and address: Mrs. Doreen Margolies, five-eight-five
East Seventy-third Street. Something with taste. You know?

SMITTY: Sure. I got taste. That's it?

HASKINS: Yes, that's everything.

SMITTY: Three o'clock this afternoon. Twenty-five bucks.

HASKINS: Thanks so much, Smitty. You're a sweet. I'll see you at three.

SMITTY: With the loot.

HASKINS: Of course. Have. . . .

[The recording was halted by mechanical failure.]

9

•

TAPE RECORDING POM-14MAY68-EVERLEIGH, SEGMENT II; approximately 11:45 A.M.

MRS. EVERLEIGH: I've got to get to the office. I've been away too long.
God, I feel drained.

ANDERSON: Have another shot; you'll feel better.

MRS. EVERLEIGH: I suppose so. Do you think we should leave together?

ANDERSON: Why not? He knows I'm up here, don't he?

MRS. EVERLEIGH: Yes. He called first. Christ, I hope he doesn't shoot
his mouth off to the other owners.

ANDERSON: Give him a tip. He won't talk.

MRS. EVERLEIGH: How much should I give him?

ANDERSON: Have him call you a cab and slip him two bucks.

MRS. EVERLEIGH: Two dollars? Is that enough?

ANDERSON: Plenty.

MRS. EVERLEIGH: Where are you going when you leave?

ANDERSON: It's a nice day—maybe I'll walk over to Ninth and get a
downtown bus to work.

MRS. EVERLEIGH: I won't be able to see you for a while. For about
two weeks.

ANDERSON: How's that?

MRS. EVERLEIGH: I've got to go to Paris on a buying trip. If you'd
give me your address, I'll send you a dirty French postcard.

ANDERSON: I'll wait till you get back. You go on these trips often?

MRS. EVERLEIGH: Almost every month. Either to Europe or some other place to shoot ads. I'm gone at least a week out of every month.
ANDERSON: Nice. I'd like to travel.
MRS. EVERLEIGH: It's just working in a different place. Will you miss me?
ANDERSON: Sure.
MRS. EVERLEIGH: Oh, my God. . . . Well . . . all ready?
ANDERSON: Yes. Let's go.
MRS. EVERLEIGH: Oh, by the way . . . here's something I bought for you. It's a gold cigarette lighter from Dunhill's. I hope you like it.
ANDERSON: Thanks.
MRS. EVERLEIGH: Oh my God . . .

10

•

APPROXIMATELY THREE WEEKS AFTER THE PAROLE OF JOHN ANderson from Sing Sing Penitentiary, intermittent electronic surveillance was established on his newly rented furnished rooms at 314 Harrar Street, Brooklyn, New York. The device used has not been verified. The following tape is coded NYPD-JDA-146-09. It is not dated. Speakers have been identified by voice prints and internal evidence.

ANDERSON: Ed Brodsky?
BILLY: He ain't here.
ANDERSON: Is that you, Billy?
BILLY: Who's this?
ANDERSON: I'm the guy you went to the Peters-McCoy fight with, at the old Garden.
BILLY: Gee, this is great! Duke, how. . . .
ANDERSON: Shut up and listen to me. Got a pencil?
BILLY: Wait a sec . . . yeah . . . okay, Duke, I got a pencil.
ANDERSON: How long will it take you to get to a pay phone?
BILLY: Five minutes maybe.
ANDERSON: Call me at this number, Billy. Now write it down.
BILLY: Okay, go ahead. I'm ready.
ANDERSON: Five-five-five-six-six-seven-one. Got that?
BILLY: Yeah. Sure.

ANDERSON: Read it back.

BILLY: Five-five-five-six-six-one-seven.

ANDERSON: Seven-one. The last two numbers are seven-one.

BILLY: Seven-one. Yeah, I got it now. Five-five-five, six-six-seven-one. How you been, Duke? I sure been. . . .

ANDERSON: Just hang up and go call, Billy. I'll be here.

BILLY: Oh . . . yeah. Okay, Duke, I'll hang up now.

    [Lapse of three minutes forty-two seconds.]

BILLY: Duke?

ANDERSON: How are you, Billy?

BILLY: Gee, it's good to hear from you, Duke. We heard you was out. Ed was saying just the other. . . .

ANDERSON: Where is Ed?

BILLY: He took a fall, Duke.

ANDERSON: A fall? What the hell for?

BILLY: He was a . . . he was a . . . Duke, what's that word—you know—you got a lot of traffic tickets and you throw them away?

ANDERSON: A scofflaw?

BILLY: Yeah! That's it! Ed was a scofflaw. The judge said Ed was the biggest scofflaw in Brooklyn. How about that! So he got thirty days.

ANDERSON: Beautiful. When's he springing?

BILLY: What's today?

ANDERSON: It's Friday, Billy. The seventeenth of May.

BILLY: Yeah. Let's see . . . eighteen, nineteen, twenty, twenty-one. Yeah. The twenty-oneth. That's Tuesday . . . right?

ANDERSON: That's right, Billy.

BILLY: Ed will be out on Tuesday.

ANDERSON: I'll call late Tuesday or Wednesday morning. Tell him, will you, kid?

BILLY: I sure will. Duke, you got a job for us?

ANDERSON: Something like that.

BILLY: We sure could use a job, Duke. Things ain't been so great for me since Ed's been in the can. Listen, Duke, is it something maybe I could handle? I mean, if it's something right away, I could handle it. No use waiting for Ed to spring.

ANDERSON: Well, it's really a two-man job, Billy. If it was a one-man job, I'd tell you right away because I know you could handle anything I'd give you.

BILLY: I sure could, Duke. You know me.

ANDERSON: But this is really a two-man job so I think maybe we should wait for Ed. Okay?

BILLY: Oh, yeah, sure, Duke . . . if you say so.

ANDERSON: Listen, kid, is it really bad? I mean, if you need a couple of plasters until Ed gets out, tell me right now.

BILLY: Oh, no, Duke, thanks. Gee, no. It's not that bad. I mean I can get by till Ed gets sprung. Gee, thanks, Duke, I really do appreciate it. Hey, when you mentioned about that night at the Garden it really took me back. Hey, what a night that was . . . hey? Remember that guy I decked in the restaurant? Gee, what a night that was . . . hey, Duke?

ANDERSON: A great night, Billy. I remember it. Well, listen, keep out of trouble, will you, kid?

BILLY: Oh sure, Duke. I'll be careful.

ANDERSON: And tell Ed I'll call on Tuesday night or early Wednesday.

BILLY: I won't forget, Duke. Honest I won't. Tuesday night or early Wednesday. Duke will call. When I get back to the room I'll write it down.

ANDERSON: That's a good boy, Billy. Keep your nose clean. I'll be seeing you soon.

BILLY: Sure, Duke, sure. It was real good talking to you. Thank you very much.

11

•

INGRID MACHT, THIRTY-FOUR, A RESIDENT OF 627 WEST TWENTY-fourth Street, New York City, was of German or Polish birth (not determined); 5 feet 5 inches; 112 pounds; black hair usually worn very short. Brown eyes. Healed lash marks on left buttock. Healed knife scar in X pattern on inside of left thigh. Scar of second-degree burns on right forearm. Spoke German, English, French, Spanish, and Italian fluently. (See Interpol file #35S-M49876.) Believed to be Jewish. There is evidence (unsubstantiated) that this woman entered the United States illegally from Cuba in 1964 in a group of authentic refugees. Interpol file (see above) lists arrests in Hamburg for solicitation, prostitution, robbery, and blackmail. Served eighteen months in corrective institution in Munich. Arrested on 16 November, 1964, in Miami, Florida, charged with complicity in a scheme to extort money from Cuban refugees on the promise of getting their relatives to the United States. Charges dropped for lack of evidence. Employed as dance instructor at Fandango Dance Ballroom, 11563 Broadway, New York.

Electronic surveillance of Miss Macht's apartment had been established on 15 January, 1968, by the Investigative Branch, Securities and Exchange Commission, on application in Federal Court, claiming that Miss Macht was involved in the theft and sale of securities, including stock shares, corporate bonds, and U.S. government bonds. On the granting of court order FDC-1719M-89C, a Bottomley 956-MT microphone transmitter was installed, tapping both telephone calls and interior conversations.

By coincidence, an employee of the SEC lived in the apartment directly below Miss Macht's. With his kind permission, a voice-actuated tape recorder was installed in his linen closet.

The following transcription was made from tape SEC-21MAY68-IM-12: 18PM-130C.

ANDERSON: Is your apartment clean?

INGRID: Why not? I have been living a clean life. Duke, I heard you were out. How was it?

ANDERSON: Inside? A lot of faggots. You know how it was. You've been there.

INGRID: Yes. I have been there. A brandy—as usual?

ANDERSON: Yes. I like this place now. It looks different.
    [Lapse of twenty-nine seconds.]

INGRID: Thank you. I have spent much money on it. *Prosit.*
    [Lapse of five seconds.]

INGRID: Frankly, it is a surprise to see you. I did not think you would wish to see me again.

ANDERSON: Why not?

INGRID: I thought you would blame me.

ANDERSON: No. I don't blame you. What could you have done— confessed and taken a fall? What for? How would that have helped?

INGRID: That is what I thought.

ANDERSON: I was stupid and got caught. It happens. You have to pay for stupidity in this world. You did exactly what I would have done.

INGRID: I thank you, Duke. Now . . . that makes me feel better.

ANDERSON: You've put on weight?

INGRID: Perhaps. A little. Here and there.

ANDERSON: You look good, real good. Here, I brought you something. A gold cigarette lighter from Dunhill's. You still smoke as much as ever?

INGRID: Oh, yes—more than ever. Thank you. Very handsome. Expensive—no? Are things going so good for you . . . or did a woman give it to you?

ANDERSON: You guess.

INGRID [laughing]: I don't care how you got it. It was very nice, and you were very sweet to think of me. So . . . what happens now? What do you want?

ANDERSON: I don't know. I really don't know. What do *you* want?

INGRID: Oh, *Schatzie,* I stopped wanting many years ago. Now I just accept. It is easier that way.

ANDERSON: It made no difference to you whether I looked you up or not?

INGRID: No difference . . . no. I was curious, naturally. But it makes no difference either way.

[Lapse of fourteen seconds.]

ANDERSON: You're a cold woman.

INGRID: Yes. I have learned to be cold.

ANDERSON: Tommy Haskins said you wanted to see me.

INGRID: Did he? That's Tommy.

ANDERSON: You didn't want to see me?

INGRID: Did—didn't. What difference does it make?

ANDERSON: What time do you go to work?

INGRID: I leave here at seven. I must be at the hall by eight.

ANDERSON: I'm working. Not too far from here. I've got to be there by four.

INGRID: So?

ANDERSON: So we have three hours. I want you to make love to me.

INGRID: If you wish.

ANDERSON: That's what I like—a hot woman.

INGRID: Oh, Duke. . . . If I was a hot woman you would not bother with me.

ANDERSON: Take off your robe. You know what I like.

INGRID: All right.

ANDERSON: You have gained weight. But it looks good.

INGRID: Thank you. Do you wish to undress?

ANDERSON: Not now. Later.

INGRID: Yes.

[Lapse of seventeen seconds.]

ANDERSON: Oh, God. A week ago a woman asked me where I learned these things. I should have told her.

INGRID: Yes. But you don't know everything, Duke. A few things I have held back. Like this. . . .

ANDERSON: I . . . oh, Jesus, don't . . . I can't. . . .

INGRID: But of course you can. You will not die from this, *Schatzie,* I assure you. It can be endured. I think now you will undress.

ANDERSON: Yes. Can we go in the bedroom?

INGRID: Please, no. I have just changed the bedding. I will get the soiled sheet from the hamper and we will spread it here, on the rug.

ANDERSON: All right.

[Lapse of twenty-three seconds.]

ANDERSON: What is that?

INGRID: A girl at the dance hall told me about it, so I went out and bought one. Less than five dollars at a discount drugstore. It is intended for massage. Would you like to try it?

ANDERSON: All right.

INGRID: Look at this shape. So obvious. It makes a buzzing noise when I switch it on. Do not be startled. You will like it. I use it on myself. [Buzzing sound. Lapse of eighteen seconds.]

ANDERSON: No . . . stop. I can't take that.

INGRID: From me? But Duke, you once said you could take anything from me.

ANDERSON: God . . .

INGRID: Let me get closer to you. Look at me.

ANDERSON: What? I . . . what?

INGRID: In my eyes. At me, Duke. In my eyes . . .

ANDERSON: Oh . . . oh . . .

INGRID: "Oh, oh!" What kind of love talk is that? I must punish you for that. There is a nerve near . . . ah, yes, here. Am I not clever, *Schatzie?*

ANDERSON: Uhh . . .

INGRID: Please do not become unconscious so soon. I have several new things I would like to show you. Some are old things that will be new to you. And some are truly new things I have learned since . . . since you have been away. Open your eyes; you are no longer looking at me. You must look at me, *Schatzie.* You must look into my eyes. That is very important . . .

ANDERSON: Why . . .

INGRID: It is very important to me.

ANDERSON: Ah, ah, ah, ah . . .

INGRID: Just spread yourself a little wider and I will get you out. Watch carefully, Duke, and learn. . . . And who knows? Perhaps she will give you another cigarette lighter. . . .

12

•

RESIDENCE OF THOMAS AND CYNTHIA HASKINS, 713 WEST SEVenty-sixth Street, New York; 24 May, 1968. Excerpt from tape recording BN-DT-TH-0018-96G.

THOMAS: . . . and then the nasty turd stiffed me. He said he only had ten dollars with him. He opened his wallet to show me.

CYNTHIA: Bastard.

THOMAS: And then he laughed and asked if I took credit cards. I swear if I had a razor with me, he'd have been a member of the castrati right then. I was just furious. I thought he was good for at least fifty. Midwesterner, of course. Pillar of the church. PTA. Rotarians. Elks. And all that shit.

CYNTHIA: And Odd Fellows.

THOMAS: You wouldn't *believe!* He said he was in New York on a business trip—but I know better, luv. He probably comes in twice a year to get his ashes hauled. I hope the next time he meets some rough trade from uptown. They'll shove his credit cards right up his hairy ass.

CYNTHIA: Duke called today.

THOMAS: What did you say?

CYNTHIA: I said we were working on it. I said we had the paper and were working it out. He was satisfied.

THOMAS: That's good. I don't think we should appear too anxious . . . do you, luv?

CYNTHIA: No, I guess not. But I really want to do a good job for him, Tommy. Maybe then he'll let us in on it. I got the feeling it's something big.

THOMAS: Why do you think that?

CYNTHIA: He's being so very, very careful. And five bills is a lot of bread for what he wants us to do. Someone is behind him on this. He just got out of the poke a few months ago. He wouldn't have that kind of loot.

THOMAS: We'll do a good job for him. He scares me sometimes. His eyes are so pale and they look right through you.

CYNTHIA: I know. And that Ingrid is no Mother Goose, either.
   [Lapse of seven seconds.]

THOMAS: Tell me something, Snap. Did you ever swing with her?
   [Lapse of five seconds.]

CYNTHIA: Twice. No more.

THOMAS: Bent—isn't she?

CYNTHIA: You have no idea. I couldn't describe it.

THOMAS: I thought so, luv. She's got the look. And I bet I can guess her hang-up. . . .

CYNTHIA: What?

THOMAS: Whips, chains, feathers . . . the whole bit.

CYNTHIA: You're warm.

THOMAS [laughing]: I bet I am. That's what I don't understand—Duke going that route. It's not like him.

CYNTHIA: Every man's got to get out sooner or later. I told him we'd be ready by next Friday. Okay?

THOMAS: Why not? I'm ready now.
> [Lapse of six seconds.]

CYNTHIA: I walked past that house on Seventy-third Street this morning.

THOMAS: My God, you didn't go in, did you?

CYNTHIA: Do you think I've got shit for brains? He told us not to . . .
didn't he? Until we get his go-ahead. . . . I walked by across the
street.

THOMAS: How did it look? Want a stick, luv?

CYNTHIA: Yes, all right, light me one. Good-looking town house. Gray
stone. Black canopy from the doorway to the curb. I saw two brass
plates—the doctors' names. There was a doorman talking to the beat
fuzz out in front. Rich-looking building. Smells like money. I wonder what's on Duke's mind?

THOMAS: One of the apartments, I expect. How are you going to work
it?

CYNTHIA: I'm going to call the doctor-doctor for an appointment,
giving the name on those cards you got me. No one recommended
me; I just moved into the neighborhood and need a doctor and saw
his sign. Before I go to see him, I'll bite all my nails off down to the
quick. I'll ask him for something to keep me from biting my nails.
If he suggests something, I'll tell him I tried all kinds of liquids and
paints and they didn't work. I'll ask if he thinks it might be a mental
or emotional problem. I'll get him to recommend me to the shrink
next door.

THOMAS: Sounds good.

CYNTHIA: I'll stop by the shrink's office and see him or make an appointment. I'll leave another card and tell him the doctor-doctor sent
me. If I don't get enough on the first visits, I'll make some excuse
for going back. How does it sound? Anything wrong?

THOMAS: Well . . . one thing. You got the cards and a good address.
They'll never in a billion years check to see if you actually live
there—until their bills are returned. And then it'll probably be too
late. But you better check with Duke to make sure. Find out how
you should handle the bills. My God, if the doctor-doctor sent out
a bill after the day you visited him, and it was returned, it might fuck
the whole thing. You better ask Duke.

CYNTHIA: Yes, that makes sense, Tommy. Doctors usually send bills
out a few weeks or a month later—but no use taking chances. I didn't
think about how I was going to pay them. You know, you've got
some brains in that tiny, pointed head of yours.

THOMAS: And I worship you, too, luv!

CYNTHIA: This is lousy grass . . . you know? Where did you get it?

THOMAS: I just got it. No like?

CYNTHIA: All twigs and seeds. Didn't you strain it?

THOMAS: He told me it had been strained.

CYNTHIA: Who?

THOMAS: Paul.

CYNTHIA: That little scut? No wonder it's lousy. I'd rather have a Chesterfield. Tommy, how are you going to handle your end?

THOMAS: All front. I waltz in, flash my paper, and get a complete list of everyone in the building. After all, I'm making an informal neighborhood census on behalf of the New Urban Reorganization Committee. And by the way, the day I hit you'll have to sit in that booth in the candy store most of the morning. That's the number on my ID card. In case anyone decides to check.

CYNTHIA: All right.

THOMAS: Shouldn't be more than an hour or so, at the most. I'll call as soon as I leave. After I get the list from him, I'll ask him to call individual tenants and see if they'd be willing to be interviewed. Purely voluntary. No pressure. No hard line. Easy does it. If they don't want to, they don't have to. I might get into two or three apartments. Those rich bitches get lonely in the afternoon. They want to talk to someone.

CYNTHIA: Just one visit?

THOMAS: Yes. Let's not push our luck, luv. I'll get what I can on one visit. If Duke isn't satisfied, screw him.

CYNTHIA: You'd like that, wouldn't you? Or vice versa.

THOMAS: How do you like your vice—versa? I guess I would. Maybe. I'm not sure. I told you he frightens me sometimes. He's so cold and aloof and withdrawn. Someday he's going to kill.

CYNTHIA: Do you really think so?

THOMAS: Oh, yes.

CYNTHIA: He never carries a piece.

THOMAS: I know. But he'll do it someday. Maybe he'll kick someone to death. Or with his hands or whatever is handy. That would be like him—standing there coldly kicking someone in their balls and stomping on them. Until they're dead.

CYNTHIA: Jesus, Tommy!

THOMAS: It's true. You know, I'm very psychic about people. Those are the emanations I get from him.

CYNTHIA: Then I won't even suggest it.

THOMAS: Suggest what?

CYNTHIA: Well . . . the whole deal is so interesting—I mean Duke giving us all that loot for what we're doing. I'm sure it's something big. So I thought. . . .

THOMAS: Yes?

CYNTHIA: Well, I thought that if we . . . if you and me . . . we could discover what it was, maybe we could . . . somehow, you know . . . move first and take. . . .

THOMAS [yelling]: You bloody scut! Forget it! Forget it . . . do you hear? If I ever hear you mention such a thing again I'm going right to Duke and tell him. We're getting paid for what we do. That's it! You understand? That's all we know and all we do unless Duke gives us something more. Do you have that straight?

CYNTHIA: Jesus Christ, Tommy, you don't have to scream at me.

THOMAS: Frigging cunt. You get ideas like that and we're dead. You understand what I'm saying? We're dead.

CYNTHIA: All right, Tommy, *all right*. I won't say any more about it.

THOMAS: Don't even think about it. Don't even let the idea get into your stupid little brain again. I know men better than you and. . . .

CYNTHIA: I'm sure you do, Tommy.

THOMAS: . . . and Duke isn't like you and me. If he found out what you said, he'd do things to us you wouldn't believe. And it wouldn't mean a thing to him. Not a thing. Ignorant slut!

CYNTHIA: All right, Tommy, *all right*.

[Lapse of sixteen seconds.]

CYNTHIA: When Duke calls next Friday, you want me to give him what we've got and get the go-ahead?

THOMAS: Yes. Outline it for him. Ask him how you should handle paying the doctors. He'll come up with something.

CYNTHIA: All right.

[Lapse of six seconds.]

THOMAS: Snap, I'm sorry I yelled at you. But I was frightened at what you said. Please, please, forgive me.

CYNTHIA: Sure.

THOMAS: Would you like a nice hot bath, luv? I'll get it all ready for you. With bath oil.

CYNTHIA: That would. . . .

[End of recording due to tape runout.]

13

•

EDWARD J. BRODSKY; THIRTY-SIX; 5 FEET 9½ INCHES; 178 POUNDS; black, oily hair, center part, worn long. Middle finger of right hand amputated. Faint knife scar on right forearm. Brown eyes. This man had a record of four arrests, one conviction. Arrested on charge of assault, 2 March, 1963. Case dismissed. Arrested for breaking and entering, 31 May, 1964. Case dismissed for lack of evidence. Arrested for conspiracy to defraud, 27 September, 1964. Charges withdrawn. Arrested as scofflaw, 14 April, 1968. Sentenced to thirty days in the Brooklyn jail. Completed sentence and released 21 May, 1968. Member of Brooklyn Longshoremen's Union, Local 418 (Steward, 5 May, 1965, to 6 May, 1966). Questioned in connection with fatal stabbing of union official, BLU, Local 526, 28 December, 1965. No charge. Residence: 124-159 Flatbush Avenue, Brooklyn, New York. Older brother of William K. Brodsky (see below).

William "Billy" K. Brodsky; twenty-seven; 6 feet 5 inches; 215 pounds; fair, wavy hair; blue eyes; no physical scars. Extremely muscular build. Elected "Mr. Young Brooklyn" 1963, 1964, and 1965. Arrested 14 May, 1964, on a charge of molesting a minor (female). Charge dropped. Arrested on 31 October, 1966, for assault with a deadly weapon—namely, his fists. Convicted; suspended sentence. Questioned on 16 July, 1967, in case involving attack and rape of two juveniles (female), Brooklyn, New York. Released for lack of evidence. This man dropped out of school after the seventh grade. The investigator's report leading to the suspended sentence in the assault case of 1966 states he had the mentality of a ten-year-old. Lived with his older brother at address given above.

The following meeting took place at the You-Know-It Bar & Grill, 136-943 Flatbush Avenue, Brooklyn, New York, on the afternoon of 25 May, 1968. At the time, these premises were under electronic surveillance by the New York State Liquor Authority, on the suspicion that the owners of record were selling liquor to minors and that the premises were a gathering place for undesirables, including prostitutes and homosexuals.

This tape is coded SLA-25MAY68-146-JB.

ANDERSON: Wait'll we get our drinks, then we'll talk.
EDWARD: Sure.

BILLY: Duke, gee, it's. . . .

WAITER: Here we are, gents . . . three beers. Call me when you're ready for a refill.

EDWARD: Yeah.

ANDERSON: The old ex-con.

EDWARD: Ah, come on, Duke, don't put me on. Isn't that a pile of crap? After what I've done and I get jugged for parking in the wrong places? Honest to God, I'd laugh . . . if it happened to someone else.

BILLY: The judge said Ed was the biggest scofflaw in Brooklyn. Ain't that right, Ed?

EDWARD: *Isn't* that right. . . . You're absolutely correct, kid. That's what the judge said.

ANDERSON: Beautiful. Got anything on?

EDWARD: Not right now. I got a promise of something in October, but that's a long way away.

BILLY: Duke said he had a job for us . . . didn't you, Duke?

ANDERSON: That's right, Billy.

BILLY: Duke said it was a two-man job or I could have handled it. Ain't that right, Duke? I told him I could handle something while you were away, Edward, but Duke said he'd wait until you got out because it was a two-man job.

ANDERSON: You're right, Billy.

EDWARD: Listen, kid, why don't you drink your beer and keep quiet for a while . . . huh? Duke and I want to talk business. Don't interrupt. Just drink your beer and listen. Okay?

BILLY: Oh, yeah, sure, Edward. Can I have another beer?

EDWARD: Sure you can, kid . . . as soon as you finish that one. You got something, Duke?

ANDERSON: There's this house on the East Side in Manhattan. I need the basement swept. I got a guy to do it—a tech named Ernie Mann. You know him?

EDWARD: No.

ANDERSON: Good, solid guy. Knows his stuff. He'll be the only one to go in. But he needs a driver. He wants a telephone company truck. A Manhattan truck. Clothes and ID cards. All the equipment. I can tell you where to get the paper; you'll have to take care of the rest. It's only for a few hours. Three hours at the most.

EDWARD: Where will I be?

ANDERSON: Outside. In the truck. It's like a small van. You've seen them.

BILLY: It's a two-man job . . . right, Duke?

ANDERSON: That's up to Ed. How about it?

EDWARD: Tell me more.

ANDERSON: Converted town house on a quiet block. Doorman. Alley that leads to the service entrance. You can't get in the back door until the doorman sees you on closed-circuit TV and presses the button. You pull up in front. Ernie goes in the lobby and flashes his potsy. Real good odds that the doorman won't ask to see yours. You're sitting outside in the regulation van where he can see it. Ernie tells the doorman the telephone company is bringing a new trunk line down the block and he's got to examine the connections. All right so far?

EDWARD: So far.

ANDERSON: What could go wrong? The tech just wants to get into the basement; he doesn't want to case the apartments. The doorman says okay, that you should pull into the alley and drive to the back entrance. Like I said, only Ernie goes in. You stay with the truck.

BILLY: Me, too, Duke. Don't forget me.

ANDERSON: Yeah. How does it sound, Ed?

EDWARD: Where do we get the ID cards?

ANDERSON: There's a paper man on Amsterdam Avenue. Helmas. Ever use him?

EDWARD: No.

ANDERSON: The best. He's got the blank cards. Not copies. The real thing. You'll need snapshots to staple on—you know, the kind of four-for-a-quarter shots you get on Forty-second Street.

EDWARD: What about the truck, uniforms, equipment, and all that shit?

ANDERSON: That's your problem.

EDWARD: How much?

ANDERSON: Four bills.

EDWARD: When?

ANDERSON: As soon as you're ready. Then I'll call Ernie, and we'll set it up. This is not a hit, Ed. It's just a wash.

EDWARD: I understand, but still. . . . Can't go to five, can you, Duke?

ANDERSON: I can't, Ed. I'm on a budget. But if it works out, it might be something more for you . . . for all of us. You understand?

EDWARD: Sure.

BILLY: What are you talking about? I don't understand what you're talking about.

EDWARD: Shut up a minute, kid. Let's go over it once more, Duke; I want to be sure I got it right. It's just a wash, not a hit. I don't go inside the building. I pick up a Manhattan telephone company van with all the gear. I have the uniform and crap hanging from my belt. What about the tech?

ANDERSON: He'll bring his own.

EDWARD: Good. I lift the truck. I pick up this Ernie guy somewhere. Right?

ANDERSON: Right.

EDWARD: We drive up in front of the house. He gets out, braces the doorman, and shows his ID. We drive up the alley to the back entrance. This Ernie gets out, shows on the TV, and gets let in. I stick in the truck. Have I got it?

ANDERSON: That's it.

EDWARD: How long do I stick around?

ANDERSON: Three hours tops.

EDWARD: And then . . . ?

ANDERSON: If he's not out by then, take off.

EDWARD: Good. That's what I wanted to hear. So he's out in under three hours. Then what?

ANDERSON: Drop him where he wants to go. Ditch the truck. Change back to your regular clothes. Walk away.

BILLY: Gee, that sounds easy . . . doesn't it, Edward? Doesn't that sound easy?

EDWARD: They all sound easy, kid. How do I contact you, Duke?

ANDERSON: It's on?

EDWARD: Yeah. It's on.

ANDERSON: I'll call you every day at one o'clock in the afternoon. If you miss it, don't worry; I'll call the next day. After you get it set, I'll call the tech and we'll set up a meet. Want two bills?

EDWARD: Jesus, do I? Waiter . . . another round!

14

•

THE PREMISES AT 4678 WEST END AVENUE, NEW YORK CITY, A candy and cigar store, were placed under surveillance on 16 November, 1967, by the New York Police Department, on suspicion that the store was being used as a policy (numbers racket) drop. Taps were installed on the two pay phones in booths in the rear of the store.

The following transcription was made from a tape identified as NYPD-SIS-182-BL. It is not dated definitely but is believed to have been recorded on 31 May, 1968.

CYNTHIA: . . . so that's how it shapes up, Duke. How does it sound?

ANDERSON: All right. It sounds all right.

CYNTHIA: The only hang-up we can see is that business of paying the doctors. You know doctors usually wait a few weeks or a month before they bill. But if the doctor-doctor or the shrink happens to bill within a few days, and the letter comes back from my freak address, it means I couldn't make a second visit.

ANDERSON: What does Tommy say?

CYNTHIA: He says to tell you we could handle it a couple of ways. I can tell them I'm going on a cruise or vacation or something and not to bill for a month at least because I don't want mail piling up in the mailbox because that's a tip-off to crooks that no one is home. Or, Tommy says, we can get me a book of personalized checks from Helmas. I can give them a freak check right then and there. That'll guarantee me at least three or four days before it bounces, and during that time I might be able to arrange another visit.

ANDERSON: Why not just pay cash before you leave?

CYNTHIA: Tommy says it would be out of character.

ANDERSON: Shit. That brother of yours should have been a play actor. Look, let's not get so fucking tricky. This is just a dry run. Don't take chances. Get what you can on your first visit. Pay them in cash. Then you can go back a second time whenever you like.

CYNTHIA: Okay, Duke, if you say so. How does Tommy's campaign sound?

ANDERSON: I can't see any holes, Snap. Both of you go ahead. If anything comes up, play it smart and lay off. Don't push. I'll call you next Friday, same time, and set up a meet.

15

•

TRANSCRIPTION FROM TAPE RECORDING FTC-1JUN68-EHM-29L. Premises of Fun City Electronic Supply & Repair Co., Inc., 1975 Avenue D, New York.

ANDERSON: Professor?

MANN: Yes.

ANDERSON: Duke. Your phone clean?

MANN: Of course.

ANDERSON: I have your drivers.

MANN: Drivers? More than one?

ANDERSON: Two brothers.

MANN: This is necessary?

ANDERSON: They're a team. Professionals. No sweat. They'll sit there for three hours tops.

MANN: Plenty. More than plenty. I'll be out in one.

ANDERSON: Good. When?

MANN: Precisely nine forty-five A.M., on the morning of June fourth.

ANDERSON: That's next Tuesday morning? Correct?

MANN: Correct.

ANDERSON: Where?

MANN: On the northwest corner of Seventy-ninth Street and Lexington Avenue. I shall be wearing a light tan raincoat and carrying a small black suitcase. I shall be wearing no hat. You have that?

ANDERSON: Yes, I have it.

MANN: Duke, the two men . . . is it necessary?

ANDERSON: I told you, they're a team. The old one drives. The young one is strictly muscle.

MANN: Why should muscle be necessary?

ANDERSON: It won't be, Professor. The kid's a little light in the head. His brother takes care of him. The kid needs to be with him. You understand?

MANN: No.

ANDERSON: Professor, the two will sit in the truck and wait for you. There will be no trouble. There will be no need for muscle. Everything will go well.

[Lapse of six seconds.]

MANN: Very well.

ANDERSON: I'll call you on Wednesday, June fifth, and we'll set up a meet.

MANN: As you wish.

16

•

THE FOLLOWING IS A TRANSCRIPTION OF A PERSONAL TAPE RECORDING made by the author on 19 November, 1968. To my knowledge, the testimony it contains is not duplicated in any official recording, transcription, or document now in existence.

AUTHOR: This will be a recording GO-1A. Will you identify yourself, please, and state your place of residence.

RYAN: My name is Kenneth Ryan. I live at one-one-nine-eight West Nineteenth Street, New York.

AUTHOR: And will you please state your occupation and where you work.

RYAN: I'm a doorman. I'm on the door at five-three-five East Seventy-third Street in Manhattan. I'm usually on eight in the morning until four in the afternoon. Sometimes we switch around, you understand. There's three of us, and sometimes we switch around, like when a guy wants to go somewhere, like he's got a family thing to go to. Then we switch around. But generally I'm on eight to four during the day.

AUTHOR: Thank you. Mr. Ryan, as I explained to you previously, this recording will be solely for my own use in preparing a record of a crime that occurred in New York City on the night and morning of August thirty-first and September first, 1968. I am not an officer of any branch of the government—city, state, or federal. I shall not ask you to swear to the testimony you are about to give, nor will it be used in a court of law or in any legal proceeding. The statement you make will be for my personal use only and will not be published without your permission, which can only be granted by a signed statement from you, giving approval of such use. In return, I have paid you the sum of one hundred dollars, this sum paid whether or not you agree to the publication of your statement. In addition, I will furnish you—at my expense—a duplicate recording of this interrogation. Is all that understood?

RYAN: Sure.

AUTHOR: Now then . . . this photograph I showed you. . . . Do you recognize him?

RYAN: Sure. That's the fly who told me his name was Sidney Brevoort.

AUTHOR: Well . . . actually this man's name is Thomas Haskins. But he told you he was Sidney Brevoort?

RYAN: That's right.

AUTHOR: When did this happen?

RYAN: It was early in June. This year. Maybe the third, maybe the fourth, maybe the fifth. Around then. This little guy comes up to me in the lobby where I work. That's five-three-five East Seventy-third Street, like I told you.

AUTHOR: About what time was this?

RYAN: Oh, I don't remember exactly. Maybe nine forty-five in the morning. Maybe ten. Around then. "Good morning," he says, and I say, "Good morning." And he says, "My name is Sidney Brevoort, and I am a field representative of the New Urban Reorganization

Committee. Here is my identification card." And then he shows me his card, and it's just like he says.

AUTHOR: Did the card have his photo on it?

RYAN: Oh, sure. All printed and regular like. Official—know what I mean? So he says, "Sir . . ."—he always called me sir—he says, "Sir, my organization is making an informal census of the dwellings and population of the East Side of Manhattan from Fifth Avenue to the river, and from Twenty-third Street on the south to Eighty-sixth Street on the north. We are trying to get legislation passed by New York State allowing for a bond issue to finance the cost of a Second Avenue subway." That's as near as I can remember to what he says. He's talking very official, you know. Very impressive, it was. So I says, "You're damned right. They had the bonds for that years ago, and then they went and pissed the money away on other things. Right into the politicians' pocket," I tells him. And he says, "I can see you keep up on civic affairs." And I says to him, "I know what's going on." And he says, "I am certain you do, sir. Well, to help convince New York State legislators that this bill should be passed, the New Urban Reorganization Committee is making an actual count of everyone on the East Side of Manhattan in the area I mentioned who might conceivably benefit by a Second Avenue subway. What I'd like from you are the names of people living in this building and the numbers of the apartments they occupy."

AUTHOR: And what did you say to that?

RYAN: I told him to go to hell. Well, I didn't put it in those exact words, you understand. But I told him I couldn't do it.

AUTHOR: What did he say then?

RYAN: He said it would be voluntary. He said that any tenant who wanted to volunteer information—why, that would be confidential, and their names wouldn't be given to anyone. They'd just be—you know, like statistics. What he wanted to know was who lived in what apartment, did they have servants, and how they traveled to work, and what time did they go to work and what time did they come home. Stuff like that. So I said, "Sorry, no can do." I told him Shovey and White at one-three-two-four Madison Avenue managed the house, and all us doors got strict orders not to talk to anyone about the tenants, not to give out no information, and not to let anyone into tenants' apartments unless we get the okay from Shovey and White.

AUTHOR: What was his reaction to that?

RYAN: That little shit. He said he could understand it because of all the robberies on the East Side recently, and would it be all right if he called Shovey and White and asked for permission to talk to me and interview the tenants who would volunteer to talk to him. So I said sure, call Shovey and White, and if they say it's okay, then it's okay with me. He said he'd call them and if it was okay, he'd have them call me to give me the go-ahead. He asks me who he should talk to at Shovey and White, and I told him to talk to Mr. Walsh who handles our building. I even gave him the phone number . . . oh, the filth of him! Then he asks me if I had ever seen Mr. Walsh, and I had to tell him no, I had never set eyes on the guy. I only talked to him twice on the phone. You gotta understand, these managers don't take no personal interest. They just sit on their ass behind a phone.

AUTHOR: What did the man you know as Sidney Brevoort do then?

RYAN: He said he'd call Shovey and White and explain what he wanted and have Mr. Walsh contact me. So I said if it was okay with them, it was okay with me. So he thanked me for my trouble—very polite, you understand—and walked away. The dirty little crud.

AUTHOR: Thank you, Mr. Ryan.

17

•

TAPE NYPD-SIS-196-BL. PREMISES OF CANDY STORE AT 4678 West End Avenue. Approximately 10:28 A.M., 3 June, 1968.

CYNTHIA HASKINS: The New Urban Reorganization Committee. May I help you?

THOMAS: It's me, Snap.

CYNTHIA: What's wrong?

THOMAS: I bombed out. The fucking Irishman on the door won't talk unless he gets a go-ahead from the management agents, Shovey and White, on Madison Avenue.

CYNTHIA: Oh, my God. Duke will kill us.

THOMAS: Don't get your balls in an uproar, luv. I thought of something on the way here. I'm calling from a pay phone on the corner of Seventy-third Street and York Avenue.

CYNTHIA: Jesus' sake, Tommy, take it easy. Duke said not to take any chances. Duke said if anything came up to lay off. Now you say you thought of something. Tommy, don't. . . .

THOMAS: You think he's paying us five bills to lay off? He wants us to use our brains, doesn't he? That's why he looked us up, isn't it? If he wanted a couple of dumdums he could have bought them for a bill. Duke wants results. If we don't blow the whole goddamned thing—whatever it is—he won't care how we did it.

CYNTHIA: Tommy, I. . . .

THOMAS: Shut up and listen. Here's how we'll work it. . . .

18

•

APPROXIMATELY 10:37 A.M., 3 JUNE, 1968.

RYAN: Five thirty-five East Seventy-third Street.

CYNTHIA: Is this the doorman?

RYAN: Yeah. Who's this?

CYNTHIA: This is Ruth David at Shovey and White. Did you just talk to a man named Sidney Brevoort who said he was from the New Urban Reorganization Committee?

RYAN: Yeah. He was here a few minutes ago. He wanted a list of people in the building and wanted to talk to them. I told him to call Mr. Walsh.

CYNTHIA: You did exactly right. But Mr. Walsh is out sick. The flu or something. He was out yesterday and he's out today. I'm handling his buildings while he's gone. How did this Brevoort guy look to you?

RYAN: A mousy little swish. I could chew him up and spit him over the left-field fence.

CYNTHIA: He didn't look like a thief, I mean?

RYAN: No, but that don't mean nothing. What do you want me to do if he comes back?

CYNTHIA: Well, I called the New Urban Reorganization Committee, and it's a legitimate outfit. They said yes, Sidney Brevoort was one of their field representatives. Did he have an identification card?

RYAN: Yeah. He showed it to me.

CYNTHIA: Well, I don't want to take the responsibility of giving him the names of tenants or letting him talk to them.

RYAN: You're right. I don't neither.

CYNTHIA: Tell you what . . . Mr. Walsh told me to call him at home in case something came up I couldn't handle. I've got his home phone number. If he says it's okay, you can talk to Brevoort. If Walsh says no, then to hell with Brevoort and the New Urban Reorganization Committee. Either way, you and I are out of it; we'll leave it up to Walsh.

RYAN: Yeah. That's smart.

CYNTHIA: All right. I'll hang up now and call Walsh. I'll call you back in a few minutes and tell you what he said.

RYAN: I'll be here.

19

•

APPROXIMATELY 10:48 A.M., 3 JUNE, 1968.

CYNTHIA: Doorman? This is Ruth David again.

RYAN: Yeah. You talk to Mr. Walsh?

CYNTHIA: Yes. He said it was perfectly all right. He knows this New Urban Reorganization Committee. He says it's okay to give Brevoort the names of tenants. Also, he can talk to any tenants who voluntarily agree. But you ask them first on the intercom. Don't let Brevoort wander around the house. And make sure he comes down to the lobby after every interview.

RYAN: Don't worry, Miss David. I know how to handle it.

CYNTHIA: Good. Well, that's a load off my mind. I didn't want to take the responsibility.

RYAN: I didn't neither.

CYNTHIA: Mr. Walsh said to tell you that you did exactly right, making Brevoort call us. He said to tell you he won't forget how you handled this.

RYAN: Yeah. Fine. Okay, then I'll talk to Brevoort. Thanks for calling, Miss David.

CYNTHIA: Thank you, sir.

20

•

TRANSCRIPTION FROM TAPE SEC-3JUN68-IM-01:48-PM-142C. Premises of Ingrid Macht, 627 West Twenty-fourth Street, New York.

INGRID: Come in, *Schatzie.*

ANDERSON: Glasses? You're wearing glasses now?

INGRID: For perhaps a year. Only for reading. You like them?

ANDERSON: Yes. You're doing something?

INGRID: I am just finishing my breakfast. I slept late today. Coffee?

ANDERSON: All right. Black.

    [Lapse of one minute thirteen seconds.]

INGRID: A little brandy perhaps?

ANDERSON: Fine. You join me?

INGRID: Thank you, no. I will take a sip of yours.

ANDERSON: Then you'll tell me I drink too much, and meanwhile you're sipping half my booze.

INGRID: Oh, *Schatzie,* when did I ever tell you that you drank too much? When did I ever criticize anything you do?

ANDERSON: Never . . . that I can remember. I was just kidding you. Don't be so serious. You have no sense of humor.

INGRID: That is true. Is something bothering you?

ANDERSON: No. Why?

INGRID: You have a look I recognize. Something in your eyes— faraway. You are thinking very hard about something. Do I guess right?

ANDERSON: Maybe.

INGRID: Please do not tell me. I want to know absolutely nothing. I do not wish to go through all that again. You understand?

ANDERSON: Sure. Sit on my lap. No . . . leave your glasses on.

INGRID: You do like them?

ANDERSON: Yes. When I was down South I had an idea of what a big-city woman was like. I could see her. Very thin. Not too tall. Hard. Bony. Open eyes. Pale lips. And heavy, black-rimmed glasses.

INGRID: A strange dream for a man to have. Usually it is a sweet, plump little blonde with big tits.

ANDERSON: Well, that was my dream. And long, straight black hair that hung to her waist.

INGRID: I have a wig like that.

ANDERSON: I know. I gave it to you.

INGRID: So you did, *Schatzie*. I had forgotten. Shall I put it on?

ANDERSON: Yes.

[Lapse of four minutes fourteen seconds.]

INGRID: So. Am I now your dream?

ANDERSON: Close. Very close. Sit here again.

INGRID: And what have you brought me today, Duke . . . another cigarette lighter?

ANDERSON: No. I brought you a hundred dollars.

INGRID: That is nice. I like money.

ANDERSON: I know. More stocks?

INGRID: Of course. I have been doing very well. My broker tells me I have an instinct for trading.

ANDERSON: I could have told him that. Am I hurting you?

INGRID: No. Perhaps we should go into the bedroom.

[Lapse of two minutes thirty-four seconds.]

INGRID: You are thinner . . . and harder. This scar . . . you told me once but I have forgotten.

ANDERSON: Knife fight.

INGRID: Did you kill him?

ANDERSON: Yes.

INGRID: Why did you fight?

ANDERSON: I forget. At the time it seemed important. Do you want me to give you the money now?

INGRID: Do not be nasty, Duke. It is not like you.

ANDERSON: Then start. Jesus, I need it. I've got to get out.

INGRID: Getting out—that is so important to you?

ANDERSON: I need it. I'm hooked. Slowly. . . .

INGRID: Of course. No . . . I told you, don't close your eyes. Look at me.

ANDERSON: Yes. All right.

INGRID: You know, I think I shall write a book. Relax your muscles, *Schatzie;* you are too tense.

ANDERSON: All right . . . yes. Is that better?

INGRID: Much. See . . . isn't that better?

ANDERSON: Oh, God, yes. Yes. A book about what?

INGRID: About pain and about crime. You know, I think criminals—most criminals—do what they do so that they may cause pain to someone. Also, so that they may be caught and be punished. To cause pain and to feel pain. That is why they lie, cheat, steal, and kill.

ANDERSON: Yes. . . .

INGRID: Look . . . I will tie my long, black hair about you. I will pull it tight and knot it . . . like so. There. How funny you look . . . like a strange Christmas package, a gift. . . .

ANDERSON: It's starting. I can feel it. . . .

INGRID: You are getting out?

ANDERSON: Slowly. You may be right. I don't know about those things. But it makes sense. When I was inside I met a guy who drew a minimum of thirty. He would have gotten eight to ten, but he hurt the people he robbed. He didn't have to. They gave him everything he wanted. They didn't yell. But he hurt them bad. And then he left his prints all over the place

INGRID: Yes, that is understandable. You are tensing up again, *Schatzie*. Relax. Yes, that is better. And now. . . .

ANDERSON: Oh, God, Ingrid, please . . . please don't. . . .

INGRID: First you beg me to start, and then you beg me to stop. But I must help you to get out. Is that not so, Duke?

ANDERSON: You are the only one who can do it . . . the only one. . . .

INGRID: So. . . . Now, bite down hard and try not to scream. There . . . and there . . .

ANDERSON: Your teeth . . . I can't . . . please, I . . . oh God . . .

INGRID: Just a little more. You are getting out . . . I can see it in your eyes. Just a little more. And now . . . so . . . so. . . . Oh, you are getting out now, Duke . . . are you not? Yes, now you have escaped. But not me, Duke . . . not me. . . .

21

•

STARTING ON 12 APRIL, 1968, A NUMBER OF LETTERS—OBVIOUSLY written by a mentally deranged person—were received threatening the personal safety of the President of the United States, Justices of the Supreme Court of the United States, and certain U.S. Senators. Incredibly, the unsigned letters were typed on stationery of the Excalibur Arms Hotel, 14896 Broadway, New York, New York.

On 19 April, 1968, with the cooperation of the owners of record, the U.S. Secret Service established electronic surveillance of the premises. A master tap was placed on the main telephone line coming into the building. In addition, several rooms and suites were equipped with bugs to record interior conversations. All these devices fed into an Emplex 47-83B voice-actuated tape recorder connected to a backup Emplex 47-82B-1 in case two conversations came in simultaneously. These machines were emplaced in the basement of the Excalibur Arms.

The following tape, coded USSS-VS-901KD-432, is dated 5 June, 1968. It was recorded from Room 432. The two men present, John Anderson and Thomas Haskins, have been identified by voice prints and interior evidence.

[Knock on door.]

ANDERSON: Who is it?

HASKINS: Me . . . Tommy.

ANDERSON: Come on in. Everything look all right downstairs?

HASKINS: Clear. What a filthy fleabag, darling.

ANDERSON: I just took the room for our meet. I'm not going to sleep here. Sit down over here. I have some brandy.

HASKINS: Thanks, no. But I do believe I'll have a joint. Join me?

ANDERSON: I'll stick to brandy. How did you make out?

HASKINS: Very well, I think. I hit two days ago. Snapper will hit tomorrow.

ANDERSON: Any beef?

HASKINS: A little difficulty. Nothing important. We handled it.

ANDERSON: Get much?

HASKINS: As much as I could. Not as complete as you'd wish, I'm sure, but interesting.

ANDERSON: Tommy, I won't shit you. You've got brains. You know I can't pay out five bills for a wash if I wasn't planning a hustle. Before you give me your report, give it to me straight—would it be worth it?

HASKINS: Which apartment, darling?

ANDERSON: All of them.

HASKINS: Jesus Christ Almighty.

ANDERSON: Would it be worth it?

HASKINS: My God, yes!

ANDERSON: Guess at the income?

HASKINS: Guess? I'd guess a minimum of a hundred G's. But maybe twice that.

ANDERSON: You and I think alike. That's what I guessed. All right, let's have it.

HASKINS: I typed out a report and one carbon on Snapper's machine, so we could go over it together. Naturally you get both copies.

ANDERSON: Naturally.

HASKINS: All right . . . let's start with the doormen. Three of them: Timothy O'Leary, Kenneth Ryan, Ed Bakely. In order, they're on midnight to eight A.M., eight A.M. to four P.M., four P.M. to midnight. O'Leary, the guy on midnight to eight A.M., is the lush. An ex-cop. When one of them takes his day off, the other two work twelve-hour shifts and get paid double. Occasionally, like around Christmas, two of them are off at once, and the union sends over a temporary. Okay?

ANDERSON: Go ahead.

HASKINS: I have all this in the report in more detail, darling, but I just want to go over the highlights with you in case you have any questions.

ANDERSON: Go ahead.

HASKINS: The super. Ivan Block. A Hungarian, I think, or maybe a Pole. A wino. He lives in the basement. He's there twenty-four hours a day, six days a week. On Mondays he goes to visit his married sister in New Jersey. In case of emergency, the super next door at five-three-seven East Seventy-third Street fills in for him. He also fills in when Block takes his two-week vacation every May. Block is sixty-four years old and blind in one eye. His basement apartment is one room and bath. Ryan hinted that he's a cheap son of a bitch. He may have something under the mattress.

ANDERSON: Maybe. These Old World farts don't believe in banks. Let's get on with it. I don't want to spend too much time here. This place bugs me.

HASKINS: Literally, I'm sure. I just saw one. Suite One A, first floor, off the lobby. Dr. Erwin Leister, MD, an internist.

ANDERSON: What's that?

HASKINS: A doctor who specializes in internal medicine. One nurse, one combination secretary-receptionist. Office hours from about nine A.M. to six P.M. Occasionally he's there later. Usually the nurse and secretary are gone by five thirty. The headshrinker is Dr. Dmitri Rubicoff, Suite One B. He's got one secretary-nurse. Office hours usually from nine to nine. Occasionally later. Snapper will give you a more complete rundown on these doctors after Thursday.

ANDERSON: You're doing fine.

HASKINS: Two apartments on each floor. By the way, the lobby floor is called one. Up one flight and you're on floor two. The top floor is the fifth, where the terraces are.

ANDERSON: I know.

HASKINS: Second floor. Apartment Two A. Eric Sabine. A male interior decorator who sounds divine. His apartment got a big write-up in the *Times* last year. I looked it up. Original Picassos and Klees. A nice collection of pre-Columbian art. A gorgeous nine-by-twelve Oriental carpet that's valued at twenty G's. In the photo in the *Times* he was wearing three rings that looked legit. Not really my type, darling, but obviously loaded. I shouldn't have any trouble finding out more about him if you're interested.

ANDERSON: We'll see.

HASKINS: Apartment Two B. Mr. and Mrs. Aron Rabinowitz. Rich, young Jews. He's in a Wall Street law firm. Junior partner. They're active in opera and ballet and theater groups. Shit like that. Very liberal. This is one of the three apartments I actually cased. She was home, delighted to talk about the proposed Second Avenue subway and the plight of the poor. Modern furnishings. I didn't spot anything except her wedding ring, which looked like it had been hacked out of Mount Rushmore. Seeing he's a lawyer, I'd guess a wall safe somewhere. Good paintings, but too big to fool with. All huge, abstract stuff.

ANDERSON: Silver?

HASKINS: You don't miss a trick, do you, darling? Yes, silver . . . on display and very nice. Antique, I think. Probably a wedding gift. It's on a sideboard in their dining room. Any questions?

ANDERSON: Maid?

HASKINS: Not sleep-in. She comes at noon and leaves after she serves their evening meal and cleans up. She's German. A middle-aged woman. Now then . . . up to the third floor. Apartment Three A. Mr. and Mrs. Max Horowitz. He's retired. Used to be a wholesale jeweler. She's got bad arthritis of the knees and uses a cane to walk with. She's also got three fur coats, including one mink and one sable, and drips with ice. At least, that's what the doorman says. He also says they're cheap bastards—a total of five bucks to all employees at Christmastime. But he thinks they're loaded. Apartment Three B. Mrs. Agnes Everleigh. Separated from her hubby. He owns the apartment, but she's living there. Nothing much interesting. A mink coat, maybe. She's a buyer for a chain of woman's lingerie shops. Travels a lot. Incidentally, I've been mentioning the fur coats—but of course you realize, darling, most of them will be in storage this time of year.

ANDERSON: Sure.

HASKINS: Fourth floor. Apartment Four A. Mr. and Mrs. James T. Sheldon, with three-year-old twin girls. A sleep-in maid who goes out shopping in the neighborhood every day at noon. I got into this apartment, too. I was there when the maid left. West Indian. A dish . . . if I was hungry that way. Lovely accent. Big boobs. Flashing smile. Mrs. James T. Sheldon is a perfect fright: horse face, buck teeth, skin like burlap. She must have the money. And Mr. Sheldon must be pronging the maid. He's a partner in a brokerage house, in charge of their Park Avenue branch. Lots of goodies. I caught a quick look at a wood-paneled study with glass display cases lining the walls.

Then Mrs. Sheldon closed the door. A coin collection, I think. It would fit. Easy to check.

ANDERSON: Yes. You say the maid goes shopping every day at noon?

HASKINS: That's right. Like clockwork. I verified it with the doorman later. Her name's Andronica.

ANDERSON: Andronica?

HASKINS: That's right. It's in the report. Crazy. Apartment Four B. Mrs. Martha Hathway—not Hathaway but Hathway. A ninety-two-year-old widow, with an eighty-two-year-old companion-housekeeper. Somewhat nutty. Kind of a recluse.

ANDERSON: A what?

HASKINS: Recluse. Like a hermit. She rarely goes out. Watches TV all day. Has no visitors. The housekeeper shops by phone. Ryan, the doorman, said her husband was a politician, a big shit in Tammany Hall about a thousand years ago. The apartment is furnished with stuff from the original Hathway town house on East Sixty-second Street. She sold off a lot of stuff after her husband died, but kept the best. It was a big auction, so you could check it out easy enough or I could do it for you.

ANDERSON: What do you figure she's got?

HASKINS: Silver, jewelry, paintings . . . the works. It's just a feeling I have, but I think Apartment Four B might prove to be a treasure house.

ANDERSON: Could be.

HASKINS: Top floor—the fifth. Both apartments have small terraces. Apartment Five A. Mr. and Mrs. Gerald Bingham and their fifteen-year-old son, Gerald junior. The kid uses a wheelchair; he's dead from the hips down. He has a private tutor who comes in every day. Bingham has his own management consultant firm with offices on Madison Avenue. Also, he has his own limousine, chauffeur-driven, which is garaged over on Lex. He's driven to work every morning, driven home every night. Sweet. He's listed all over the place, so he won't be hard to check out. His wife has money, too. I have nothing specific on this apartment—nothing good.

ANDERSON: Go on.

HASKINS: The other is Five B. Ernest Longene and April Clifford. They're married, they say, but use their own names. He's a theatrical producer and she was a famous actress. Hasn't appeared in ten years—but she remembers. God, does she remember! Sleep-in maid. A big, fat mammy type. This was the third apartment I got into. April was on her way to a luncheon at the Plaza and was wearing her daytime diamonds. Very nice. Some good, small paintings on the walls. A very nice collection of rough gemstones in glass display cases.

ANDERSON: There's money there?

HASKINS: He's got two hits on Broadway right now. That's got to mean loose cash around the place, probably in a wall safe. Well, darling, those are just the highlights. I'm sorry I couldn't be more specific.

ANDERSON: You did better than I hoped. Give me your carbon of the report.

HASKINS: Of course. I assure you no other copy was made.

ANDERSON: I believe you. I'll pay you the balance of the five bills when I get Snapper's report.

HASKINS: No rush, no rush. Do you have any questions, or is there anything you want me to dig into further?

ANDERSON: Not right now. This is like a preliminary report. There may be some more work for you later.

HASKINS: Anytime. You know you can trust me.

ANDERSON: Sure.

[Lapse of six seconds.]

HASKINS: Tell me, darling . . . are you seeing Ingrid again?

ANDERSON: Yes.

HASKINS: And how is the dear girl?

ANDERSON: All right. I think you better leave now. I'll wait about half an hour, and then I'll take off. Tell Snapper I'll call on Friday, as usual.

HASKINS: Are you angry with me, Duke?

ANDERSON: Why should I be angry with you? I think you did a good job on this.

HASKINS: I mean because I mentioned Ingrid. . . .

[Lapse of four seconds.]

ANDERSON: Are you jealous, Tommy?

HASKINS: Well . . . maybe. A little. . . .

ANDERSON: Forget it. I don't like the way you smell.

HASKINS: Well, I guess I. . . .

ANDERSON: Yes. Better go. And don't get any ideas.

HASKINS: Ideas, darling? What kind of ideas would I get?

ANDERSON: About what I'm doing.

HASKINS: Don't be silly, darling. I know better than that.

ANDERSON: That's good.

22

•

TAPE NYSITB-FD-6JUN68-106-9H. LOCATION OF CAR: SIXTY-fifth Street near Park Avenue.

ANDERSON: Goddammit, I told the Doctor I'd contact him when I was ready. Well, I'm not ready.

SIMONS: Take it easy, Duke. Good heavens, you have the shortest fuse of any man I've ever known.

ANDERSON: I just don't like to get leaned on, that's all.

SIMONS: No one's leaning on you, Duke. The Doctor has invested three thousand dollars of his personal funds in this campaign, and quite naturally and normally he's interested in your progress.

ANDERSON: What if I told him it was a bust . . . a nothing?

SIMONS: Is that what you want me to tell him?

[Lapse of eleven seconds.]

ANDERSON: No. I'm sorry I blew, Mr. Simons, but I like to move at my own speed. This thing is big, probably the biggest thing I've ever been in. Bigger than that Bensonhurst bank job. I want everything to go right. I want to be sure. Another week or two. Three weeks at the most. I'm keeping a very careful account of those three G's. I'm not making a cent out of this. I can tell the Doctor where every cent went. I'm not trying to con him.

SIMONS: Duke, Duke, it's not the money. I assure you the money has very little to do with it. He can drop that in one day at the dogs and never notice it. But Duke, you must recognize that the Doctor is a very proud man, very jealous of his position. He is where he is today because he picked winners. You understand? He would not like the word to get around that he flushed three G's on a free-lancer and got nothing to show for it. It would hurt his reputation, and it would hurt his self-esteem. Perhaps the younger men might say he is slipping, his judgment is going, he should be replaced. The Doctor must consider these things. So, quite naturally, he is concerned. You understand?

ANDERSON: Ah . . . sure. I understand. It's just that I want to make a big score, a *big* score . . . enough to go somewhere for a long, long time. That's why I'm wound up so tight. This one has got to be just right.

SIMONS: Are you trying to tell me it looks good . . . as of this moment?

ANDERSON: Mr. Simons, as of this moment it looks great, just great.

SIMONS: The Doctor will be pleased.

23

•

ERNEST HEINRICH "PROFESSOR" MANN; FIFTY-THREE; RESIDENT of 529 East Fifty-first Street, New York City. Place of business: Fun City Electronic Supply & Repair Co., 1975 Avenue D, New York City. Five feet six inches tall; 147 pounds; almost completely bald, with gray fringe around scalp; gray eyebrows; small Van Dyke beard, also gray. Walked with slight limp, favoring left leg. Deep scar in calf of left leg (believed to be a knife wound; see Interpol file #96B-J43196). He was a technician, skilled in mechanical, electrical, and electronic engineering. Graduated from Stuttgarter Technische Hochschule, 1938, with highest honors. Assistant professor, mechanical and electrical engineering, Zurich Académie du Mécanique, 1939–46. Emigrated to the United States (with Swiss passport) in 1948. Arrested Stuttgart, 17 June, 1937, on public nuisance charge (exhibiting himself to an elderly woman). Case dismissed with warning. Arrested Paris, 24 October, 1938, for scandalous conduct (urinating on Tomb of Unknown Soldier). Deported, after case was dismissed. In Zurich, a record of three arrests for possession of a dangerous drug (opium), indecent exposure, and illegal possession of a hypodermic needle. Suspended sentences. Extremely intelligent. Speaks German, French, Italian, English, some Spanish. Not believed to be violent. Single. Record indicates intermittent drug addiction (opium, morphine, hashish). FBI file indicates no illegal activities during residence in the United States. Applied for U.S. citizenship 8 May, 1954. Rejected 16 November, 1954. (As of this date, this man's brother was a high official in the finance ministry of West Germany, and his file contained an alert tag: IN CASE OF ARREST, PLEASE CONTACT U.S. STATE DEPARTMENT BEFORE CHARGE.)

The following is the first part of a dictated, sworn, signed, and witnessed statement by Ernest Heinrich Mann. It was obtained after prolonged questioning (the complete transcription numbers fifty-six typewritten pages) from 8 October, 1968, to 17 October, 1968. The interrogator was an assistant district attorney, County of New York. The entire document is coded

NYDA-FHM-101A-108B. The following section is labeled *SEGMENT* 101A.

MANN: My name is Ernest Heinrich Mann. I live at five-two-nine East Fifty-first Street, New York, New York, U.S.A. I also have a business, which I own—the Fun City Electronic Supply and Repair Co., Inc., incorporated under the laws of New York State, at one-nine-seven-five Avenue D, New York City. Am I perhaps speaking too rapidly? Good.

On April thirty, 1968, I was contacted at my place of business by a man I know as John Anderson, also known as Duke Anderson. He stated at this time that he wished to employ me to inspect the basement of a house at five-three-five East Seventy-third Street, New York City. He said he wished me to ascertain the telephone, alarm, and security precautions of this house. At no time did he state the purpose of this.

A price was agreed upon, and it was planned that I would approach the house in the uniform of a New York City telephone repairman, arriving in an authentic truck of the telephone company. Anderson said he would supply truck and driver. I provided my own uniform and identification. May I have a glass of water, please? Thank you.

About a month later Anderson called me and said the arrangements for the telephone truck had been made. There would be two drivers. I objected, but he assured me it would be perfectly safe.

On June fourth, at nine forty-five in the morning, I met the truck at the corner of Seventy-ninth Street and Lexington Avenue. There were two men who introduced themselves to me merely as Ed and Billy. I had never seen them before. They were clad in uniforms of New York Telephone Company repairmen. We spoke very little. The actual driver, the man named Ed, seemed reasonably intelligent and alert. The other one, called Billy, was large and muscular but had a childish mentality. I believe he was mentally retarded.

We drove directly to the house on East Seventy-third Street, pulling up in front. As we had agreed, I alighted, walked into the lobby, and presented my credentials to the doorman. He inspected my identification card, glanced out to the curb where the truck was parked, and told me to pull into the alley that runs alongside the building. Do one of you gentlemen have a cigarette? I would appreciate it. Thank you very much.

[Lapse of four seconds.]

So . . . I was identified on the closed-circuit TV screen in the lobby, and the doorman pressed the button unlocking the service door and allowed me entrance into the basement. Pardon?

No, this was merely to be an inspection. There was no intent to steal or destroy. Anderson merely wanted a complete rundown of the basement plus Polaroid photos of anything interesting. You understand? If I thought there was anything illegal required, I never would have accepted this job.

So. I am now in the basement. I went first to the telephone box. Quite ordinary. I made notes of main phones and extensions. I took instant photos of the entrance of the main trunk line into the basement and where it should be cut to isolate the entire house. This was requested by Anderson, you understand. I also ascertained that there were two separate wiring systems which, by their arrangement, I judged to be alarm systems, one to the local precinct house, perhaps triggered by an ultrasonic or radio-wave alarm, and the other to a private security agency which would be, I guessed, activated by opened doors or windows. Quite unexpectedly, both systems bore small tags with the apartment numbers written on them, so I was able to note that the precinct alarm was attached to Apartment Five B, and the private agency alarm to Apartment Four B. I made notes of this, plus photos. As Anderson had requested.

At this moment a door opened into the basement and a man came in. I learned he was Ivan Block, the superintendent of the building. He asked me what I was doing, and I explained that the telephone company was intending to bring a new line down the street and I was examining the premises to see what new equipment would be required. This was the same explanation I had given to the doorman. Another glass of water, please? I thank you.

[Lapse of six seconds.]

Block appeared satisfied with my explanation. Listening to him speak, I realized he was Hungarian or perhaps a Czech. Since I speak neither of these languages, I spoke to him in German, to which he replied in very bad, heavily accented German. However, he was pleased to speak the language. I believe he was somewhat inebriated. He insisted I come into his apartment for a glass of wine. I followed him, happy at the opportunity of making a further examination.

The super's small apartment was dirty and depressing. However, I took a glass of wine with him while looking around. The only thing of value I saw was an antique triptych on his dresser. I guessed it as being at least three hundred years old, beautifully carved. The value, I estimated, might be as much as two thousand dollars. I made no reference to it.

Block continued to drink wine, and I told him I had to call my office, and I left. I then explored the main basement. The only thing of interest I found was quite odd. . . .

It appeared to be a kind of a box—or rather, a small room—built into one corner of the basement. It was obviously quite old, and I judged it had been built into the basement when the building was constructed. Two walls of the basement formed two sides of the boxlike room; the two walls projecting into the basement at a right angle were constructed of fitted wooden slabs. One wood wall had a flush door, closed by an extremely heavy, old-fashioned brass lever and hasp. The big hinges were also of brass. The door was secured with a large padlock.

Closer inspection revealed that the door was also protected by a rather primitive alarm system obviously added years after the boxlike room had been built. It was a simple contact alarm that might ring a bell or flash a light when the door was opened. I traced the wire and judged it went up into the lobby area where it might alert the doorman.

I took complete Polaroid photos of this strange boxlike affair, and made notes of how the alarm might easily be bridged. Almost as an afterthought, I put my hand to the side of this unusual room and found it quite cold to the touch. It reminded me of a large walk-in refrigerator one might find in a butcher's shop in this country.

I took a final look around and decided I had everything that Anderson, my client, required. I then exited from the basement and got into the truck. The two men, Ed and Billy, had waited quite patiently. We pulled out of the driveway. The doorman was standing on the sidewalk, and I smiled and waved as we pulled away.

They dropped me on the corner of Seventy-ninth Street and Lexington Avenue, and then left. I have no knowledge of what they did after that. The entire operation consumed one hour and twenty-six minutes. John Anderson called me on June fifth. I suggested he come over to my shop on the next day. He did, and I delivered to him the photos I had taken, the diagrams, and a complete report of what I saw—which is exactly what I have reported to you gentlemen. I thank you very much for your courtesy.

24

•

B INKY'S B AR & G RILL, 125TH S TREET AND H ANNOX A VENUE, N EW York City; 12 June, 1968; 1:46 P.M. On this date, these premises were under electronic surveillance by the New York State Liquor Authority, on suspicion that the owners of record were knowingly allowing gambling on the premises. The following is tape SLA-94K-KYM. Anderson's presence was verified by voice print and testimony of an eyewitness.

ANDERSON: Brandy.

BARTENDER: This place for blacks, not for whiteys.

ANDERSON: What you going to do—throw me out?

BARTENDER: You a hardnose?

ANDERSON: Hard as I gotta be. Do I get that brandy?

BARTENDER: You from the South?

ANDERSON: Not deep. Kentucky.

BARTENDER: Lexington?

ANDERSON: Gresham.

BARTENDER: I'm from Lex. Cordon Bleu okay?

ANDERSON: Fine.

   [Lapse of eight seconds.]

BARTENDER: You want a wash?

ANDERSON: Water on the side.

   [Lapse of eleven seconds.]

ANDERSON: There's a guy I want to meet. Light brown. Sam Johnson. Goes by the name of Skeets.

BARTENDER: Never heard of him.

ANDERSON: I know. He's got a razor scar on his left cheek.

BARTENDER: Never saw such a man.

ANDERSON: I know. My name's Duke Anderson. If such a man should come in, I'm going to finish this drink and go across the street and get some knuckles and collards. I'll be there for at least an hour.

BARTENDER: Won't do you no good. Never saw such a man. Never heard of him.

ANDERSON: He might come in . . . unexpected like. Here's a fin for you in case he does.

BARTENDER: I'll take your pound and thank you kindly. But it won't do you no good. I don't know the man. Never saw him.

ANDERSON: I know. The name's Duke Anderson. I'll be across the street in Mama's. Keep the faith, baby.

BARTENDER: Up yours, mother.

25

•

TAPE RECORDING NYSNB (NEW YORK STATE NARCOTICS BUreau) 48B-1061 (continuing). Taped at 2:11 P.M., 12 June, 1968, Mama's Soul Food, 125th Street and Hannox Avenue, New York City.

JOHNSON: Here's my man, and gimme your han'.

ANDERSON: Hello, Skeets. Sit down and order up.

JOHNSON: Now that I'm here, I'll have a beer.

ANDERSON: How you been?

JOHNSON: I get some jive so I'm still alive.

ANDERSON: Things going good for you?

JOHNSON: I do this and that, but I don't get fat.

ANDERSON: Cut the shit and talk straight. You got some time to do a job for me?

JOHNSON: If it's a crime, I've got the time.

ANDERSON: Jesus Christ. Skeets, there's a house on the East Side. If you're interested I'll give you the address. There's a live-in spade maid works one of the apartments. Every day at noon she comes out to do shopping.

JOHNSON: When you talk a chick, you gotta click.

ANDERSON: Light tan. West Indian. Big lungs. Pretty. I want you to get close to her.

JOHNSON: How close, oh, Lord, how close?

ANDERSON: Everything. Whatever she can tell you about her apartment. Her name's Andronica. That's right—Andronica. She's from Apartment Four A. There may be a coin collection there. But I want to know about the rest of the house, too—whatever she'll spill.

JOHNSON: If she won't spill, then her sister will.

ANDERSON: There's a funny room in the basement. A cold room. It's locked. Try to find out what the hell it is.

JOHNSON: If the room is cold, then I'll be bold.
ANDERSON: You on?
JOHNSON: If you've got the loot, I've got to suit.
ANDERSON: A bill?
JOHNSON: Make it two and I'll be true.
ANDERSON: All right—two. But do a job for me. Here's a loner to get you started. I'll be back here a week from today, same time. All right?
JOHNSON: As a man you're mean, but I like your green.

26

•

TRANSCRIPTION OF TAPE RECORDING POM-14JUN68-EVER-LEIGH. Approximately 2:10 A.M.

MRS. EVERLEIGH: Did the doorman see you come in?
ANDERSON: He wasn't there.
MRS. EVERLEIGH: The bastard. We're supposed to get twenty-four-hour doorman service, and this bastard is always down in the basement drinking wine with that drunken super. Brandy?
ANDERSON: Yes.
MRS. EVERLEIGH: Yes, *please.*
ANDERSON: Go fuck yourself.
MRS. EVERLEIGH: My, we're in a pleasant mood tonight. Tired?
ANDERSON: Just my eyes.
MRS. EVERLEIGH: I think it's more than that. You look like a man who's got a lot on his mind. Money problems?
ANDERSON: No.
MRS. EVERLEIGH: If you need some money, I can let you have some.
ANDERSON: No . . . thanks.
MRS. EVERLEIGH: That's better. Drink up. I bought a case of Rémy Martin. What are you smiling about?
ANDERSON: You figure this will last for a case?
MRS. EVERLEIGH: What's that supposed to mean? You want to cut out? Then cut out.
ANDERSON: I didn't want to cut out. I just figured you might get tired of me slamming you around. Are you tired of it?
[Lapse of seven seconds.]

MRS. EVERLEIGH: No. I'm not tired of it. I think about it all the time. When I was in Paris, I missed you. One night I could have screamed, I wanted you so bad. I got a million things on my mind. Business things. Details. Pressure. I'm only as good as my last season. I work for the worst bastards in the business—the *worst*. I only relax when I'm with you. I think about you during the day, when I'm at the office. I think about what we did and what we'll do. I don't suppose I should be telling you these things.

ANDERSON: Why not?

MRS. EVERLEIGH: A girl's supposed to play hard to get.

ANDERSON: Christ, you're a stupid bitch.

  [Lapse of five seconds.]

MRS. EVERLEIGH: Yes. Yes, I am. When it comes to you. You've been in prison, haven't you?

ANDERSON: Reform school. When I was a kid. I stole a car.

MRS. EVERLEIGH: And you haven't been in since?

ANDERSON: No. What makes you think so?

MRS. EVERLEIGH: I don't know. Your eyes, maybe. Those Chinese eyes. The way you talk. Or don't talk. Sometimes you frighten me.

ANDERSON: Do I?

MRS. EVERLEIGH: Here's the bottle. Help yourself. Are you hungry? I can fix you a roast beef sandwich.

ANDERSON: I'm not hungry. You going on another trip?

MRS. EVERLEIGH: Why do you ask?

ANDERSON: Just making conversation.

MRS. EVERLEIGH: I've been invited out to Southampton for the July Fourth weekend. Then, late in August and over the Labor Day weekend I'll be going to Rome. May I sit on the couch next to you?

ANDERSON: No.

MRS. EVERLEIGH: That's what I like—a romantic man.

ANDERSON: If I was a romantic man you wouldn't bother with me.

MRS. EVERLEIGH: I suppose not. Still, it would be nice to know, occasionally, that you're human.

ANDERSON: I'm human. Sit on the floor.

MRS. EVERLEIGH: Here?

ANDERSON: Closer. In front of me.

MRS. EVERLEIGH: Here, darling?

ANDERSON: Yes. Take off my shoes and socks.

  [Lapse of fourteen seconds.]

MRS. EVERLEIGH: I've never seen your feet before. How white they are. Your toes look like white worms.

ANDERSON: Take off that thing.

MRS. EVERLEIGH: What are you going to do?

ANDERSON: I'm going to make you forget the bastards you work for, the business, the details, the pressure. That's what you want . . . isn't it?

MRS. EVERLEIGH: Part of it.

ANDERSON: What's the other part?

MRS. EVERLEIGH: I want to forget who I am and what I am. I want to forget you and what I'm doing with my life.

ANDERSON: You want to get out?

MRS. EVERLEIGH: Get out? Yes. I want to get out.

ANDERSON: You've got a good suntan. Take the robe off.

MRS. EVERLEIGH: Like this?

ANDERSON: Yes. God, you're big. Big tits and big ass.

MRS. EVERLEIGH: Duke . . . be nice to me . . . please.

ANDERSON: Nice to you? Is that what you want?

MRS. EVERLEIGH: Not . . . you know . . . not physically. You can do anything you want. Anything. But be nice to me as a person . . . as a human being.

ANDERSON: I don't know what the hell you're talking about. Spread out.

MRS. EVERLEIGH: Oh God, I think I'm going to be sick.

ANDERSON: Go ahead. Puke all over yourself.

MRS. EVERLEIGH: You're not human. You're not.

ANDERSON: All right. So I'm not. But I'm the only man in the world who can get you out. Spread wider.

MRS. EVERLEIGH: Like this? Is this all right, Duke?

ANDERSON: Yes.

[Lapse of one minute eight seconds.]

MRS. EVERLEIGH: You're hurting me, you're hurting me.

ANDERSON: Sure.

MRS. EVERLEIGH: White worms.

ANDERSON: That's right. Getting out?

MRS. EVERLEIGH: Yes . . . yes . . .

ANDERSON: You've got a body like mush.

MRS. EVERLEIGH: Please, Duke. . . .

ANDERSON: You're a puddle.

MRS. EVERLEIGH: Please, Duke. . . .

ANDERSON: "Please, Duke. Please Duke." Stupid bitch.

MRS. EVERLEIGH: Please, I. . . .

ANDERSON: There. Isn't that nice? Now I'm being nice to you as a person. As a human being. Right?

27

•

THE FOLLOWING IS A XEROX COPY OF A HANDWRITTEN REPORT, identified by Dr. Seymour P. Ernst, president, The New Graphology Institution, 14426 Erskine Avenue, Chicago, Illinois, as being in the true handwriting of Cynthia "Snapper" Haskins (previously identified). The two sheets of unlined paper, inscribed on both sides, revealed latent fingerprints of Cynthia Haskins, Thomas Haskins, and John Anderson. The paper itself—an inexpensive typing paper without watermark—bore miniature serrations on its upper edge (tipped with a red adhesive), indicating the sheets had been torn from a pad. The paper was identified as being a popular brand of typing paper sold in pads of twenty-five sheets. Such pads as available in many stationery and variety stores.

DUKE:

I swept the two offices, you know where. No strain, no pain. I gave both doctors freak checks instead of cash. I won't go back. No point in it.

Both big layouts. I guess they're doing all right. The doctor's got a nurse and a secretary-receptionist. I saw her opening mail. Mostly checks. No safe in outer office. Probably night bank deposits. Two rooms off the doctor's office: examination room and small supply room. Little room has drug safe in corner. Toilet is to left as you walk down corridor to doctor's private office.

Pictures on walls are cheap prints. Doctor has five silver cups in his office—for rowing a scull. Whatever that is.

Sorry I pulled a blank here—but that's all there was.

Headshrinker's office was small outer room with secretary-nurse, big private office and toilet to right of outer room.

Shrink has three nice small paintings: Picasso, Miro, and someone else. Looked like the real thing. I described them to Tommy. He estimates 20 G's for the three, possibly more.

Bottom left of shrink's desk has dial lock. He was putting reel of recording tape in drawer when I came in. When I started to talk, he pressed button in desk well. Everything I said was recorded, I'm sure. Must be some interesting things in that desk safe. Think about it.

He has small lavatory and clothes closet next to his office, at back near windows that overlook garden. Something in closet?

Nurse-secretary is young, about twenty-eight. Shrink is about fifty-five, speaks with accent. Small, fat, tired. I think he's on something. I'd guess Dexies.

That's all I got. Sorry it wasn't more.

Don't forget about those tape recordings. Hot off the couch. Know what I mean?

Rough sketches of both offices on back of this sheet. If there's anything else we can do for you, please let us know.

The rest of the $$$, Duke? We had some expenses and we're hung up. Thanks.

SNAP

28

•

RECORDING NYSNB-1157 (CONTINUING). TAPED AT 2:17 P.M., 19 June, 1968, at Mama's Soul Food, 125th Street and Hannox Avenue, New York City. Participants John Anderson and Samuel Johnson have been identified by a paid informer present at the scene.

Samuel "Skeets" Johnson, thirty-three, was a Negro, light tan, with long black greased hair combed in a high "conk" (pompadour). Approximately 6 feet 2 inches; 178 pounds. Deep razor scar on left cheek. Hearing impairment of 75 percent in left ear. Dressed in expensive clothing of bright hues. Wore light pink polish on fingernails. At last report, drove a 1967 Cadillac convertible (electric blue), New Jersey license plates 4CB6732A, registered to Jane Martha Goody, 149 Hempy Street, Hackensack, New Jersey. Johnson's criminal record included arrests for loitering, petty larceny, committing a public nuisance, resisting arrest, simple assault, assault with intent to kill, threatening bodily harm, breaking parole, breaking and entering, armed robbery, and expectorating on a public sidewalk. He had served a total of six years, eleven months, fourteen days in Dawson School for Boys, Hillcrest Reformatory, and Dannemora. This man had the unusual ability of being able to add a series of as many as twenty dictated numbers of eight digits each in his head and arriving at the correct sum within seconds. Frequently carried a switchblade knife in a small leather sheath strapped to right ankle. Frequently spoke in rhymed slang.

ANDERSON: How you doing, Skeets?

JOHNSON: Slip me five, I'm still alive. Now that you're here, have a beer. If you're in the mood, make it food.

ANDERSON: Just a beer.

JOHNSON: I thought you dug this soul food crap—knuckles and hocks and greens?

ANDERSON: Yeah, I like it. Don't you?

JOHNSON: Shit no, man. I go for a good Chateaubriand or maybe some of them frogs' legs swimming in butter and garlic. That's eating. This stuff sucks. Just a beer? That all you want?

ANDERSON: That's all. What'd you find out?

JOHNSON: Wait for the beer, and then give ear.

[Lapse of twenty-seven seconds.]

JOHNSON: By the way, I'm picking up the knock.

ANDERSON: Thanks.

JOHNSON: I got to thank you, lad, 'cause you made me glad.

ANDERSON: How's that?

JOHNSON: That little Andronica you put me onto. Oh, so sweet and juicy. You spend a night with her, all you need is a spoon and a straw. She's a double-dip strawberry sundae with a big whoosh of white whipped cream on top and then a big red cherry sticking up in the air.

ANDERSON: And the first thing you bit off was that cherry.

JOHNSON: Ask me no questions, and I tell you no lies.

ANDERSON: You pushing her?

JOHNSON: Every chance I get—which ain't often. She gets one night off a week. Then we fly. And we had two matinee sessions. Oh, she so cuddly and wiggly and squirming. I could eat her up.

ANDERSON: And I bet you do.

JOHNSON: On occasion, Great White Father, on occasion.

ANDERSON: How did you make the meet?

JOHNSON: What you want to know for?

ANDERSON: How am I going to learn to operate if you don't tell me things?

JOHNSON: Ah, Duke, Duke . . . you got more shit than a Christmas goose. You forgotten more than I could ever teach you. Well, I got this old family friend. A real coon type. But that's just front. This cat is into everything. I mean, he's a black Billy the Kid. Slick. You dig?

ANDERSON: Sure.

JOHNSON: So I slip him a double Z. He meets this Andronica when she comes out of the supermarket. My pal puts his paws on her. "You dirty sex fiend," I scream at him, "how dare you touch and annoy and defile and molest this dear, sweet, little innocent chick?"

ANDERSON: Beautiful.

JOHNSON: I feed him a knuckle sandwich—which he slips. He takes off down the avenue. Andronica is shook.

ANDERSON: And grateful.

JOHNSON: Yeah—and grateful. So I help her wheel her little wagon of groceries home. One thing leads to another.

ANDERSON: So? What did she spill?

JOHNSON: That coin collection is insured for fifty big ones. There's a wall safe behind a painting of a vase of flowers in the study. That's where Mrs. Sheldon keeps her ice. My baby thinks there's other goodies in there, too. Bonds. Maybe some green. Sound good?

ANDERSON: Not bad. They going to be around all summer?

JOHNSON: I regrets to report, massa, they are not. The family moves out this weekend to Montauk. Old man Sheldon will go out every weekend until after Labor Day. That means no more sweet push for pops for another three months unless we can work something out—like her coming into the city or me going out there.

ANDERSON: You'll work it out.

JOHNSON: I mean to. I really mean to. I must see Andronica so she can blow my harmonica.

ANDERSON: What about the cold room? The room in the basement. Remember?

JOHNSON: I didn't forget, white man who speaks with forked tongue. Guess what it is.

ANDERSON: I been trying to. I can't.

JOHNSON: When the house was built, that's where they kept their fruits and vegetables. Then after they had refrigerators, the old geezer who built the joint kept his wines down there. Those walls are thick.

ANDERSON: And now? What's it used for? Wine?

JOHNSON: No, indeedy. They got a little refrigerator-like in there and a machine that takes the water out of the air. It's cold and it's dry. And everyone who lives in that house—the women, that is—they puts their fur coats in there for storage come warm weather. No extra charge. They got their own fur storage locker right there on the premises. How do you like that?

ANDERSON: I like it. I like it very much.

JOHNSON: Thought you would. Duke, if you planning anything—and notice I say *if*—and you need an extra field hand, you know who's available, don't you?

ANDERSON: I give you your due; it could be you.

JOHNSON: Ah, baby, now you're singing our song!

ANDERSON: Reach under the table; it's your other bill.

JOHNSON: Your gelt I'll take, and that's no fake. But why pay me for just what's due? I should pay you for what I screw.

ANDERSON: See you around.

29

•

TAPE SEC-25JUN68-IM-12:48PM-139H. THIS IS A TELEPHONE TAP.

ANDERSON: Hello? It's me.

INGRID: Yes. Ah. . . .

ANDERSON: Did I wake you up? I'm sorry.

INGRID: What time is it?

ANDERSON: About a quarter to one.

INGRID: You are coming over?

ANDERSON: No. Not today. That's why I called. Is your phone clean?

INGRID: Oh, *Schatzie* . . . why should they bother with me? I am a
    nobody.

ANDERSON: God, how I'd like to come over. But I can't. Not today.
    It would put me to sleep. I have a meet tonight.

INGRID: So.

ANDERSON: It's very important. Very big men. I've got to be awake.
    Sharp. These are the money men.

INGRID: You know what you are doing?

ANDERSON: Yes.

INGRID: I wish you very much good luck.

ANDERSON: I'll probably be through with them by two or three. It's
    in Brooklyn. Can I come back?

INGRID: Regretfully, no, *Schatzie*. I am busy tonight.

ANDERSON: Busy?

INGRID: Yes.

ANDERSON: Important?

INGRID: Let us say—profitable. He flies in from Fort Wayne. That is
    in Indiana. That is something . . . no? To fly to New York from Fort
    Wayne, Indiana, to see poor old Ingrid Macht.

ANDERSON: I'd fly from Hong Kong.

INGRID: Ah! Now that is romantic! I do thank you. But tomorrow
    perhaps?

ANDERSON: Yes. All right. I guess that would be best. I'll tell you about
    it then.

INGRID: As you wish. Duke. . . .

ANDERSON: Yes?

INGRID: Be careful. Be very, very careful.

ANDERSON: I will be.

INGRID: There is something in you that distresses me—a wildness, a strangeness. Think. Duke, promise me you will think . . . very clearly.

ANDERSON: I promise you I will think very clearly.

INGRID: *Das is gut.* And perhaps, tomorrow afternoon, we might get out. Together, Duke. For the first time.

ANDERSON: Together? Yes. I'll get you out. I promise.

INGRID: Good. And now I shall go back to sleep.

30

•

THE FOLLOWING MANUSCRIPT WAS DISCOVERED IN A SEARCH OF the premises of John "Duke" Anderson on 3 September, 1968. It consisted of three sheets of yellow notepaper, ruled horizontally with blue lines, and vertically by a thin triple line (red-blue-red) 1¼ inches from the left-hand margin. The sheets themselves measured approximately 8 by 12⅜ inches, with serrations along the top edge indicating they had been torn from a pad or tablet.

Analysis by experts disclosed that this type of paper is commonly sold in pads in stationery and notion stores and is known as legal notepaper. It is frequently used by students, lawyers, professional writers, etc.

The recovered sheets were apparently a part or section of a longer manuscript. The pages were not numbered. Analysts believe they were written approximately ten years before the date of discovery—that is, about 1958. The handwriting was determined to be definitely that of John Anderson. The writing implement used was a ballpoint pen with green ink.

The three sheets reproduced below were being used as shelf paper in a small closet in the premises of 314 Harrar Street, Brooklyn, New York, when they were discovered and submitted to analysis.

[First sheet]

it could be everything.

In other words, crime is not just a little thing, a small part of society, but is right in there, and it makes up most of what everyone calls normal, right and desent living. Let us list them.

When a woman will not give in to a man unless he marrys her, that could be called extortion or blackmail.

Or a woman who wants a fur coat, and if her husband wont give it to her, and she says no sex if he dont. This also is a kind of a crime, like blackmail.

Maybe a boss lies a secretary because she will loose her job otherwise. Extortion.

A guy says, I know you have been playing around. If you don't give me some, I will tell your husband. Blackmail.

A big grosery store comes in to a neyborhood near a small grosery store. And this big chain cuts there prices and puts the small store out of business. This is mugging. Money mugging but it is mugging all the same.

War. You say to a small country you do what we want or we will blow you up. Extortion or blackmail.

Or a big country like the USA goes into a small country and buys the kind of govt we want. This is criminel bribery.

Or we say we will give you such and so if you do this, and then the country does it, and we say thanks a lot! And dont pay off. That is fraud or conspiracy to defraud.

A busness man or maybe even a professer in a collage thinks the other guy will get the job he wants. So he writes letters he dont sign and sends them to the top man. Poyson pen letters. Nothing he could get busted for but hinting.

There are many other exampels, practicaly endless that I

[Second sheet]
could give here about how much of what we say is common, ordinary human behavior is really crime.

Some of these are personel, like between a man and a woman, or two men or two women, and some are in business and some are in govt.

A man wants to shiv another guy in his company and he spreds the word hes a queer. Slander.

A guy buys gifts for his wife because he knows she won't give out if he dont. Bribery.

We teach young kids in the army what is the best way to kill people. Murder.

The local grosery store or department store jacks up the bill if they can get away with it, or maybe shortchanges. Robbery.

A guy wants to go to a cheap restaurant but his woman wants to go to a fancy joint. And she hints if they dont go where she wants, its no push-push for him that night. Extortion.

A guy gives a dame a string of beads and he says there diamonds but they are really zircons or rinestones and she puts out. Fraud.

A guy in a business is taking and another guy finds out and lets the first guy know. So the first guy gets something on the second guy. Then they grin and let live. Conspiracy.

Maybe a woman likes to get beat. So her guy slaps her around. He likes it too. But whos to know? Its still assault.

A peter keeps another peter on the string by saying he will nark on him if the first guy doesnt keep playing games. Extortion.

Similer to above, anyone who says I will kill myself if you do no do like I want, that is also extortion. Or maybe blackmail

[Third sheet]
depending on how the lawyers and judges decide on it.

What I am saying is this, that crime is not just breaking laws because everyone does it. I do not know if this is something new or has been going on for many years. But we are all criminels.

We are all criminels. It is just a question of degree, like first, second and third degree. But if the laws against criminel acts are right, then almost everyone should be in the poke. If these laws are right and rigid, then it shouldnt matter what degree. The married woman who wont put out unless her husband buys her a fur coat is just as guilty as a guy whos got a million dollar extortion hustle going for him.

And the poor pop who breaks into his kids piggy bank, yes its funny, and takes out enough change to get to work, well how is he so different from a good bank man like Sonny Brooks, he died yesterday, it was in the papers. Jesus I loved that guy, he taught me all I know, he was so great. He got cut down coming out of a bank in West Va. I cant believe it he was so carefull, a real pro. Worked once a year but he planed for 6 mos. Carefull and good. Layed off for 6 mos. every year. Hit a big one once a year he said and then lay off. I worked two jobs with him and learned so much.

Oh shit, its all crime. Everything. The way we live. Everyone. We are all cons, everyone of us. So what I do is just being smart enough to make it pay.

We lie and we cheat and we steal and we kill, and if it isnt money its other people or there love or just to get some push. Whatever we get hung on. Oh Jesus its so dirty.

When I was inside I thaught those inside were cleaner then those outside. At least we were open and did our crimes in the open. But the rest think they are so normal and clean and desent and they are the biggest and dirtiest criminels of them all because they
[End of third sheet]

31

•

THE FOLLOWING IS A TRANSCRIPTION MADE FROM TAPE RECORD-
ings of a conversation that took place in Elvira's, an Italian restaurant at 96352
Hammacher Street, Brooklyn, New York, during the early morning hours
of 26 June, 1968.

At the time, these premises were under electronic surveillance by at least
four, and possibly more, law investigation agencies. Apparently there was no
cooperation between these agencies.

A great variety of miniaturized electronic devices was utilized, including
telephone taps, bugs implanted beneath certain tables, in the bar, and in both
the gents' and the ladies' rooms. In addition, the new Sonex Nailhead 158-
JB microphone transmitters had been surreptitiously installed in the base-
boards of the kitchen.

Elvira's, a popular and successful restaurant in the Flatbush section of
Brooklyn, had for many years been known to law enforcement officers as an
eating and meeting place for members of the Angelo family. The restaurant
was firebombed on 15 October, 1958, during what was apparently a gang
war between the Angelo family and a rival organization known as the Snipes
Brothers. The bombing resulted in the death of a waiter, Pasquale Gardini.

On 3 February, 1959, Anthony "Wopso" Angelo was shot down in the
front phone booth of Elvira's while making a phone call to persons unknown.
His killer entered through the glass door, after apparently seeing Angelo go
into the phone booth from an outside observation post. Four bullets of .32
caliber were fired into Angelo. He died instantly. His killer has not yet been
apprehended.

Present at the meeting in a small, private back room at Elvira's on the
morning of 26 June, 1968, were John "Duke" Anderson, Anthony "Doctor"
D'Medico, and Patrick "Little Pat" Angelo. These men have been positively
identified by voice prints, interior and exterior evidence, and by paid inform-
ers present at the scene.

Patrick "Little Pat" Angelo was born in 1932 in Brooklyn, New York.
His father, Patsy "The Hook" Angelo, was killed in a waterfront fracas two
months before Patrick's birth. Patrick's education was financed by his grandfather, Dominick "Papa" Angelo, don of the Angelo family. Patrick Angelo
was 5 feet 8½ inches tall; 193 pounds; blue eyes; thick gray hair worn long,

combed straight back, no part. Physical scars: scalp wound above right temple (bullet); depressed wound in left calf (shrapnel); and excised third right rib (grenade). Subject was a graduate of Walsham School of Business Administration, and had attended one year at the Rolley Law Academy. Enlisted in U.S. Army in 1950 and after training was sent to Korea with the 361st Assault Battalion, 498th Regiment, 22d Combat Division. At war's end, he had risen to rank of major (battlefield promotions) and had earned the Purple Heart (3), Silver Star, and Distinguished Service Cross, in addition to decorations from the South Korean and Turkish governments.

Subject resigned from the Army in 1954 with letters of commendation. He then organized and became president of Modern Automanagement, 6501 Fifth Avenue, New York City, a management consultant firm. In addition, he was an officer of record for Sweeteeze Linens, 361 Forbisher Street, Brooklyn, New York; vice-president of Wrenchies Bowling Alleys, 1388 Grand Evarts, the Bronx, New York; and secretary-treasurer of the Fifth National Discount and Service Organization, Palm Credit Co., Inc., and the Thomas Jefferson Trading Corp., all of Wilmington, Delaware.

Subject had no criminal record.

Subject was married (to Maria Angelo, a second cousin) and was the father of two teenage sons currently students at Harrington Military Academy in Virginia. He also had a four-year-old daughter, Stella.

Supposition: Patrick Angelo will succeed Dominick "Papa" Angelo as don of the Angelo family upon the death of Dominick, who was ninety-four years old.

Due to mechanical difficulties and heavy external noise, no single tape recording contains the entire conversation given below. This is a transcription of parts of four different tapes made by four law enforcement agencies. (At their request, portions of the transcription have been deleted as they concern investigation currently in progress.) This is the author's transcription GO-110T-26JUN68. The time was 1:43 A.M.

D'MEDICO: . . . don't believe you've met Pat Angelo. Pat, this is Duke Anderson, the man I told you about.

ANDERSON: Pleased to make your acquaintance, Mr. Angelo.

ANGELO: Duke, I don't want you to think I'm giving you a fast shuffle, but I've got another meet tonight. Then I've got to drive home to Teaneck. So you'll understand if I make this as short as we can. Okay?

ANDERSON: Sure.

ANGELO: I'll tell you what the Doc told me. See if I got it straight. If not, you correct me. Then I'll start asking questions. You got a campaign. It's a house on the East Side of Manhattan. You want to take the whole place. He advanced you three G's. That's out of his own pocket. You been looking it over. Now we're at the point where we decide do we go ahead or do we call the whole thing off. Am I right so far?

ANDERSON: That's right, Mr. Angelo. Mr. D'Medico, I have a complete list of my expenses with me, and you have three hundred and fifty-nine dollars and sixteen cents coming back on your advance that wasn't spent.

D'MEDICO: I told you, Pat! Didn't I tell you?

ANGELO: Yes. Let's get on with it. So what have we got, Duke?

ANDERSON: I have a report here. It's a handwritten original. No copies. For you and Mr. D'Medico. I think it looks good.

ANGELO: How much?

ANDERSON: Minimum of a hundred thousand. Closer to quarter of a mil, I'd guess.

ANGELO: You'd guess? What the hell are you talking about? What? Retail value? Wholesale value? Resale value? What we can get from fences? What is it? Spell it out.

ANDERSON: It's jewelry, furs, uncut stones, a valuable coin collection, rugs, maybe drugs from two doctors, cash, negotiable securities. These people are loaded.

    [Lapse of five seconds.]

ANGELO: So you're talking about original retail value?

ANDERSON: Yes.

ANGELO: So take a third of what you estimate. Maybe thirty G's if we can unload it. Or possibly eighty G's tops. Is that right?

ANDERSON: Yes.

ANGELO: Let's figure the bottom—thirty G's. How many men?

ANDERSON: Five.

ANGELO: Five? And one of ours. Six. So you want six men to put out for five G's each?

ANDERSON: No. I want my men to be paid a flat fee. Whatever I can settle for. But no share. I figure I can get the five for a total of eight thou tops. I don't know what you'll pay your man. Maybe he's on salary. But figure ten G's tops for employees. That leaves twenty G's for a split. Absolute minimum. I'm no gambler, but I still think it'll run closer to eighty G's. The total, that is.

ANGELO: Forget what you think. We're working on the minimum. So we have twenty G's left for the split. How do you figure that?

ANDERSON: Seventy-thirty.

ANGELO: Seventy to you, of course?

ANDERSON: Yes.

ANGELO: You're a hardnose, aren't you?

D'MEDICO: Pat, take it easy.

ANDERSON: Yes, I'm a hardnose.

ANGELO: Tennessee?

ANDERSON: Kentucky.

ANGELO: I thought so. Duke, put yourself in my place. You want me to okay this thing. You guarantee us about six or seven thousand if we agree to your terms. All right, all right—it may run as high as twenty G's if the take is as big as you guess it might be. I can't figure with guesses. I got to know. So I'm figuring on six G's. Anything over is gravy. All this for six thousand dollars? We can take that legit in one day from our biggest horse parlor. So what's the percentage?

ANDERSON: So what's the risk? One muscle? He's expendable, isn't he?

[Lapse of eight seconds.]

ANGELO: You're no dumdum, are you?

ANDERSON: No, I'm not. And I got to keep repeating that seven G's is the absolute minimum. It'll run more, much more—I swear it.

ANGELO: Put your cock on the line?

ANDERSON: Goddamned right.

D'MEDICO: Jesus, Pat. . . .

ANGELO: He's a hardnose—like I said. I like you, Duke.

ANDERSON: Thanks.

ANGELO: For nothing. Have you started thinking about operations?

ANDERSON: A little. Just a beginning. It should be on a holiday week-end. Half the people will be gone to the beach or on vacation or at their summer places. July Fourth would have been good, but it's too late for that now. If you say okay, we should aim for the Labor Day weekend. We cut all communications. Isolate the house. We pull up a van. We take our time—three hours, four hours, whatever we need.

ANGELO: But you haven't thought it out?

ANDERSON: No, I haven't. I got this report here. It'll give you a run-down on who lives there and where the stuff is and where we should look and how it can be done. But if you say okay, we'll have to dig a lot deeper.

ANGELO: Like what?

ANDERSON: Habits of people in the building. Schedules of the beat fuzz and squad cars in the sector. Private watchmen. People who walk their dogs late at night. Location of call boxes and telephone booths. Bars that are open late at night. A lot of things. . . .

ANGELO: Were you ever in the military?

ANDERSON: Marine Corps. About eighteen months.

ANGELO: What happened?

ANDERSON: I got a dishonorable discharge.

ANGELO: What for?

ANDERSON: I knocked up a captain's wife—amongst other things.

ANGELO: Yes. What did you do? See any action?

ANDERSON: No. I made corporal. I was an instructor on the range at Paris Island.

ANGELO: You're a good shot?

ANDERSON: Yes.

D'MEDICO: But you've never carried a piece on a job—have you, Duke?

ANDERSON: No. I never have.

ANGELO: Christ, I'm thirsty. Doc, get us another bottle of that Volpolicella, will you? But if this campaign goes through, you'll have to pack a piece. You realize that, don't you, Duke?

ANDERSON: Yes.

ANGELO: You're willing?

ANDERSON: Yes.

ANGELO: When you were a corporal of Marines did you ever get any instructions on the technique of a raid? A quick hit-and-run?

ANDERSON: A little.

ANGELO: Did you ever hear about that campaign in Detroit on. . . . We hit the. . . . We used about. . . . What we did was to create a diversion. It pulled off all the precinct buttons to . . . and while they were. . . . And it worked perfectly. Something like that might work here.

ANDERSON: It might.

ANGELO: You don't sound very enthusiastic.

ANDERSON: I got to think about it.

D'MEDICO: Here's the wine, Pat. Chilled just a little . . . the way you like it.

ANGELO: Fine. Thank you, Doctor. So you want to think about it, do you, Duke?

ANDERSON: Yes. It's *my* cock.

ANGELO: It surely is. All right. Supposing Papa gives the go-ahead. What will you need? Have you thought of that?

ANDERSON: Yes, I thought of that. I'll need another two thousand to complete the sweep.

ANGELO: The reconnaissance?

ANDERSON: That's right. To figure how we'll handle it.

ANGELO: Operations and deployment. And then what?

ANDERSON: You'll get a final shakedown on the whole bit. Then if you okay, I'll need the loot to pay off my five men. Half in advance, half when the job's finished.

D'MEDICO: About two thousand for looking, and then another four or five for your staff?

ANDERSON: That's about it.

D'MEDICO: All advances and expenses out of the take before the split?

ANDERSON: Yes.

ANGELO: I've got to get out of here and over to Manhattan. I'm late as it is. Duke, I want to talk to the Doctor. You understand?

ANDERSON: Sure. I appreciate you giving me this time.

ANGELO: We'll get in touch with you—one way or the other—in a week or so. I've got to talk to Papa and, as you probably know, he's ailing. We should all live to be ninety-four and ailing.

D'MEDICO: Amen.

ANDERSON: Nice to meet you, Mr. Angelo. Thanks, Mr. D'Medico.

D'MEDICO: A pleasure, Duke. We'll be in touch.

  [Lapse of seventeen seconds.]

D'MEDICO: How did you know he was from Kentucky, Tennessee—around there?

ANGELO: I recognized him the minute he walked in. Not him, but the type. A mountain man. God knows I saw enough of them in Korea. Kentucky, Tennessee, West Virginia. Rough boys. As rough as the Southerners . . . but they never bugged out. Sometimes you get some freaky Southerners. I never saw a freaky mountain man. They're all born piss-poor. They got nothing but their pride. I had some mountain men who never had a pair of new shoes until they got in the army. This Anderson . . . Jesus Christ, he reminds me so much of a guy I had. He was from Tennessee. Best shot I ever saw. I was a First Looey then. I had this patrol, and we were going down a dry creek bed. This mountain man was point. The target. We went through three points in three days. They fired on the point and that's how we knew where they were.

D'MEDICO: That's nice.

ANGELO: Yes. So this Tennessee mountain man was point, about twenty yards or so ahead of me. A gook comes out of the bushes and charges at him. The gook has a kitchen knife tied to a long pole with string. He was probably hopped up. He comes charging out screaming. My guy could have shot him dead—one, two, three. Like that. But he didn't. He laughed. I swear to God, he laughed. He had his blade on his rifle, and he waited for the gook to come to him. It was classic. Jesus, it was classic. I had been through all the bayonet stuff: advance, parry, thrust. Book stuff. And this was right out of the book. Classic. They could have taken pictures of it for an army manual. My guy took the position, shuffled forward, and when the gook shoved at him, he parried, got his stick in the gook's stomach, withdrew, stuck again into his balls, turned the blade, withdrew, shoved the bayonet into the ground to clean it, and turned and grinned at me. He liked it. There were guys like that. They liked it. They enjoyed it. War, I mean.

D'MEDICO: What happened to him?

ANGELO: Who?

D'MEDICO: Your guy.

ANGELO: Oh. Well, the company went back to Tokyo on leave. This Tennessee guy got caught raping a nine-year-old Japanese girl. He got racked up.

D'MEDICO: Where is he now?

ANGELO: Still in Leavenworth as far as I know. So tell me about this Anderson. What do you know?

D'MEDICO: He came out of the South about ten years ago. A helluva driver. I think he was driving alky for Solly Benedict down there. Anyway, he sliced someone and had to come north. Solly called me about him. About the same time my cousin Gino had a hustle planned. Did you ever meet Gino?

ANGELO: No, I don't believe I ever did.

D'MEDICO: Christ, my face is killing me. Well, it was a warehouse job. Drugs. Pep pills, I think they were. It was cased perfect, but someone tipped the Safe and Loft Squad. We took care of him later. Anyway, I recommended Anderson as the driver, and Gino says okay. The plan was for Gino and two muscles to pull up in his car, Anderson driving. Park a block away. Anderson is told to stay there until Gino returns. The idea is that they'll break the warehouse, the two dum-dums will drive the truck out, and Gino will return to where Anderson is waiting in the car.

ANGELO: So?

D'MEDICO: So everything goes wrong. Floodlights, sirens, bullhorns, riot guns, barkers . . . the whole bit. The two muscles get cut down. Gino takes a bad one in the gut and staggers around the corner. He's told Anderson to stay there, and with all this going on, Anderson is still there.

ANGELO: A mountain man.

D'MEDICO: Yes. He didn't cut. Well, he gets Gino into the car and gets him to a sawbones. It saved his life.

ANGELO: What's he doing now?

D'MEDICO: Gino? He's got this little candy store in Newark. He takes some numbers, handles a few loans. Penny-ante stuff. He's not too good . . . but he's alive. I feed him what I can. But I never forgot. Duke sitting there while the shit hit the fan. He's some man.

ANGELO: I figured that. Then what happened with him?

D'MEDICO: He didn't want any jobs. He wanted to freelance. He cleared everything with me first, and I gave him the go-ahead. He did very well. He's a smart boy, Pat. He learned fast. He hit some East Side apartments for a bundle. Ice, mostly. Never carried a stick. Got clever. In and out so fast and so smooth they could never figure how. He was doing all right. Maybe three or four jobs a year. Always made his contribution and never screamed. I kept track and found out he was bent, sex-wise.

ANGELO: How do you mean?

D'MEDICO: Whips . . . you know.

ANGELO: Which way is he? This is important.

D'MEDICO: Both ways, from what I hear. Then he pulled this job and was waiting on a corner for this Jew bitch he had to pass the stuff to—it was only about a block away—when some lucky probationary patrolman decided he didn't like his looks and shook him down. That kid is a Dick Two now. So Duke went up. The woman wasn't touched; he never mentioned her. I heard she was late for the meet because she was at her stockbroker's.

ANGELO: Beautiful. You been keeping in touch with her?

D'MEDICO: Oh, sure. Since Duke brought up this campaign we been checking her out. She's got a record, and she's hustling right now— shmeck, tail, abortion—the whole bit. She works in a dance hall Sam Bergman owns. We can lean on her anytime we want to.

ANGELO: Good. How did Anderson get onto this thing on the East Side?

D'MEDICO: He's pronging a woman who lives there. We don't know how he met her. But he's in and out of the place at least twice a week. A big dame who looks like money.

ANGELO: All right. I guess that's about it. Christ, have we finished another bottle? My God, I've *got* to get to Manhattan.

D'MEDICO: Pat, how do you feel about it?

ANGELO: If it was up to me, I'd say no. Look, Doc, we're in restaurants, hotels, banks, linen supply, insurance, trucking, laundromats, garbage disposal—all nice, clean, legit things. And the profits are good. So why do we need this bang-bang stuff?

D'MEDICO: Still . . . you're interested?

ANGELO: Yes . . . I guess I am. It's a military problem. Look at me . . . I'm a businessman, my gut is swelling, my ass is sinking, I've got a wife and three kids, I belong to four clubs, I play golf every good weekend, I go to the PTA with my wife, I worry about crabgrass, I've got a poodle with worms. In other words, I'm a solid citizen. But sometimes I look at myself in the mirror—the belly, the jowls, the fat thighs, the soft cock, and I think I was happier in Korea.

D'MEDICO: Pat, maybe you're one of those guys you were telling me about—the guys who enjoy war.

ANGELO: Maybe. I don't know. All I know is, I hear of something like this and I get all excited. My brain starts working. I'm young again. A campaign. Problems. How to figure it. It's really something. But I wouldn't decide without talking it over with Papa. First of all, I owe it to him. Second of all, he may be bedridden with maybe a fat boy now and then to keep him warm, but his mind is still there—sharp and hard. I'll lay it out for him. He likes to feel he's still needed, still making the decisions. Jesus Christ, we got a thousand lawyers and CPA's making decisions he couldn't even understand—but a problem like this, he can understand. So I'll lay it out for him. If he says no, it's no. If he says yes, it's yes. I'll let you know within a week or so. Is that all right?

D'MEDICO: Of course. Got anyone in mind for the sixth man?

ANGELO: No. Do you?

D'MEDICO: A guy named Sam Heming. A nothing. All muscle, no brains. But he's one of Paul Washington's boys.

ANGELO: A smoke?

D'MEDICO: He is, but he passes.

ANGELO: Why him?

D'MEDICO: I owe Paul a favor.

ANGELO: Linda Curtis?

D'MEDICO: You don't miss much, do you?

ANGELO: No, Doc, not much. Heming is okay with me if he's solid.

D'MEDICO: He's solid.

ANGELO: Good. Papa will want to know. I'll tell him you go for this guy. Okay?

D'MEDICO: Yes . . . if it's necessary.

ANGELO: It's necessary. Jesus Christ, Doc, you're twitching like a maniac. Can't you do anything about that face of yours?

D'MEDICO: No. Not a thing.

ANGELO: Tough shit. I've got to run. Thanks for the dinner and vino.

D'MEDICO: My pleasure. I'll hear from you on this in a week or so?

ANGELO: Sure. Oh . . . by the way, Doc, keep an eye on Fred Simons.

D'MEDICO: Anything wrong?

ANGELO: Not yet. But he's been hitting the sauce hard lately. Maybe talking a little more than he should. Just a friendly tip.

D'MEDICO: Of course. Thanks. I'll call it to his attention.

ANGELO: You do that.

32

•

TAPE RECORDING POM-9JUL68-EVERLEIGH. TIME IS APPROXImately 2:45 P.M.

MRS. EVERLEIGH: Let me get you a big drink. I want you to sit quietly
for a while. I want to show you some pictures—my photo album.

ANDERSON: All right.

[Lapse of sixteen seconds.]

MRS. EVERLEIGH: Here . . . just the way you like it—one ice cube.
Here we go. I bought this album at Mark Cross. It's nice, isn't it?

ANDERSON: Yes.

MRS. EVERLEIGH: Here . . . this tintype. This was my great-grandfather
on my father's side. He was in the Civil War. That's the uniform of
a captain he's wearing. The picture was made when he came home
on leave. Then he lost an arm at Antietam. But they let him keep
his company. They didn't care so much about things like that in
those days.

ANDERSON: I know. My great-grandpappy went through the Second
Wilderness with a wooden leg.

MRS. EVERLEIGH: Then, after the war, he came home and married my
great-grandmother. Here's their wedding photo. Wasn't she the tiniest, sweetest, prettiest thing you've ever seen? Raised seven children in Rockford, Illinois. Now this is the only picture I have of my
mother's parents. He was an older man, had a general store near
Sewickley in Pennsylvania. His wife was a real monster. I remember
her vaguely. I guess I got my size from her. She was huge—and ugly.
My mother was an only child. Here's my mother's graduating class.
She went two years to a teacher's college. The one with the circle is
her. This little fellow is my father at the age of ten. Wasn't he cute?
Then he went to Yale. Look at that hat he's wearing! Isn't that a
scream? He rowed for them. And he was a great swimmer, too. Here
he is in a swimsuit. This was taken during his last year at Yale.

ANDERSON: Looks like he was hung.

MRS. EVERLEIGH: Bastard. Well, I can tell you he was all man. Tall
and muscular. He met my mother at a prom, and they got married

right after he graduated. He started as a junior clerk in Wall Street about three years before World War One. My brother Ernest was born in 1915, but when America got into the war, Daddy enlisted. He went overseas in 1918. I don't think he ever actually saw any action. Here he is in his uniform.

ANDERSON: Those wraparound puttees must have been murder. My mother's first husband got killed with the Marines on the Marne.

MRS. EVERLEIGH: That couldn't have been your father?

ANDERSON: No. My pappy was her third husband.

MRS. EVERLEIGH: Well, here's Mom and Daddy with Ernie and Tom—he was the second-born. He was missing in action in France in World War Two. Then here's Mother holding me in her arms— the first picture ever taken of me. Wasn't I cute?

ANDERSON: Yes.

MRS. EVERLEIGH: Then here are some pictures of me growing up. Bloomers. Gym suit. Bathing suit. We went to a cabin on a lake up in Canada. Here are all the kids—Ernest and Thomas and me and Robert. All of us.

ANDERSON: You were the only girl?

MRS. EVERLEIGH: Yes. But I could keep up with them, and after a while I could outswim them all. Mother got sick and was in bed a lot, and Daddy was busy with his business. So the four of us kids were together a lot. Ernie was the leader because he was oldest, but when he went to Dartmouth, I took over. Tom and Bob never had the authority that Ernie had.

ANDERSON: How old were you when that one was taken?

MRS. EVERLEIGH: About thirteen, I think.

ANDERSON: A great pair of lungs.

MRS. EVERLEIGH: Yes, I matured early. The story of my life. I started bleeding at eleven. Look at the shoulders I had, and those thighs. I could outswim my brothers and all their friends. I think the boys resented it. They liked frail, weak, feminine things. I had this big, strong, muscular body. I thought the boys would like a girl who could swim with them and ride horses with them and wrestle and all that. . . . But when dances came along, I noticed it was the frail, weak, pale feminine things who got invited. Mother insisted I take dancing lessons, but I was never very good at it. I could dive and swim, but on the dance floor I felt like a lump.

ANDERSON: Who copped your cherry?

MRS. EVERLEIGH: My brother Ernie. Does that shock you?

ANDERSON: Why should it? I'm from Kentucky.

MRS. EVERLEIGH: Well, it happened when he was home one Easter vacation from Dartmouth. And he was drunk.

ANDERSON: Sure.

MRS. EVERLEIGH: Here I am at my high school graduation. Don't I look pretty?

ANDERSON: You look like a heifer in a nightgown.

MRS. EVERLEIGH: I guess I do . . . I guess I do. Oh, God, that hat. But then, here, when I started going to Miss Proud's school, I slimmed down. A little. Not much, but a little. I was on the swimming team, captain of the winning intramural field–hockey team, captain of the riding and golf teams, and I played a good game of tennis, too. Not clever, but strong. Here I am with the cup I got for best all–around girl athlete.

ANDERSON: Christ, what a body. I wish I could have stuck you then.

MRS. EVERLEIGH: Plenty of boys did. Maybe I couldn't dance, but I discovered the secret of how to be popular. A very simple secret. I think they called me Miss Round Heels. All you had to do was ask, and I'd roll over. So I had plenty of dates.

ANDERSON: I'd have figured you for a lez.

MRS. EVERLEIGH: Oh . . . I tried it. I never made the first advance, but I had plenty of those sweet, pale, soft, feminine things touching me up. I tried it, but it didn't take. Maybe it was because of the way they smelled. You didn't shower this morning, did you?

ANDERSON: No.

MRS. EVERLEIGH: That horsey, bitter, acid smell. It really turns me on. Then I met David. He was a friend of my youngest brother, Bob. Here's David.

ANDERSON: Looks like a butterfly.

MRS. EVERLEIGH: He was . . . but I didn't discover that until it was too late. And he drank and drank and drank. . . . But he was funny and kind and considerate. He had money, and he made me laugh and held doors open for me, and if he wasn't so great in the sack, well, I could excuse that because he always had too much to drink. You know?

ANDERSON: Yes.

MRS. EVERLEIGH: Lots of money. Cleveland coal and iron and things like that. Sometimes I wondered if he was a little Jewish.

ANDERSON: A little Jewish?

MRS. EVERLEIGH: You know . . . way back. Anyway, here we are at the beach, at the prom, at a horse show, at the engagement party, the wedding pictures, reception, and so forth. I wore low heels because I was just a wee bit taller than he was. He had beautiful hair. Didn't he have beautiful hair?

ANDERSON: Beautiful. Much more of this shit?

MRS. EVERLEIGH: No, not much more. Here we are at our summer place in East Hampton. Some good times. Drunken parties. I walked in on him once when he was getting buggered by a Puerto Rican busboy. I don't have a picture of *that!* And that's about all. Some pictures of me on buying trips—Paris, Rome, London, Geneva, Vienna. . . .

ANDERSON: Who's this guy?

MRS. EVERLEIGH: A kid I bought in Stockholm.

ANDERSON: Good lay?

MRS. EVERLEIGH: Not really.

ANDERSON: What the hell are you crying for?

    [Lapse of seven seconds.]

MRS. EVERLEIGH: These pictures. A hundred years. My great-grandparents. The Civil War. My parents. The world wars. My brothers. I just think of what all these people went through. To produce me. Me. I'm the result. Ah, Jesus, Duke, what happens to us? How did we get to be what we are? I just can't stand thinking about it—it's so awful. So sad.

ANDERSON: Where's your husband now?

MRS. EVERLEIGH: David? The last time I saw him, he was wearing lipstick. That's what I mean. And look at me. Am I any better?

ANDERSON: You want me to go?

MRS. EVERLEIGH: And leave me here counting the walls? Duke, for the love of God, get me out. . . .

33

•

DOMINICK "PAPA" ANGELO, NINETY-FOUR, DON OF THE ANGELO family, was a legal resident of 67825 Flint Road, Deal, New Jersey. Born Mario Dominick Nicola Angelo in Mareno, Sicily, 1874. His family was a "left-side" branch of the Angelo family, and for five generations had been tenant farmers in Sicily. There is no record of Dominick's early schooling.

During a New York State investigation in 1934 (see Records of the Murphy Committee, Vol. I, pp. 432–35) evidence was presented that Dominick Angelo entered the United States illegally in 1891 by swimming ashore from a merchant ship on which he was working as cook. In any event, records are confused—or missing—and Dominick Angelo filed for his first citizenship papers in 1896, and became a U.S. citizen in 1903. At that time he listed his occupation as "waiter."

His criminal record includes an arrest for disturbing the peace in 1904 (no disposition) and assault with intent to kill in 1905 (charge withdrawn). In 1907 he was arrested on a charge of assault with a deadly weapon (knife) with the intent to commit grievous bodily harm (he castrated his victim). He was tried, convicted, and served two years, seven months, and fourteen days at Dannemora (#46783).

Upon his release from prison, there is inconclusive evidence that he became a "button" for the Black Hand, as the Italian criminal organization in this country was then called.

(In their treatise *Origins of American Slang,* Hawley and Butanski, Effrim Publishers Co., Inc., 1958, the authors state [pp. 38–39] that in the period 1890–1910, the term "button" was used to describe a gangland executioner, and may have come from a description of a man who could "button the lip" of an informer or enemy. The authors point out that later, in the 1920's and 1930's, the terms "buttons" or "Mr. Buttons" came into use in criminal circles to describe a uniformed policeman.)

In 1910, Dominick Angelo obtained employment with the Alsotto Sand & Gravel Co., of Brooklyn, New York, ostensibly as a loader. In 1917 he volunteered for service with the American Expeditionary Forces, but because of his age, his services were limited to guard duty on the docks at Bayonne, New Jersey.

In 1920 he secured employment as foreman with the Giovanni Shipping Enterprises, Inc. During this period he married Maria Florence Gabriele Angelo, a distant relative. Their first child, a boy, was born in 1923. He was subsequently killed in action on Guadalcanal Island in 1942.

During World War II, Dominick Angelo volunteered his services to the U.S. government and, according to documents on file, his assistance was "invaluable" in preparing for the invasions of Sicily and Italy. There is in existence a letter from a high official of the OSS attesting to his "magnificent and unique cooperation."

During the period 1948–68, official records reveal his rise to a position of great prominence and power in the Italian-dominated structure controlling organized crime in the United States. From soldier to *capo* to don took him less than ten years, and by 1957 he was recognized as leader of one of the several national "families." His personal fortune was variously estimated as $20,000,000 to $45,000,000.

Students and observers of organized crime in the United States—of what has been described as the Black Hand, the Syndicate, the Mafia, the Cosa Nostra, the Family, etc.—generally agree that Dominick Angelo was the guiding spirit, brain, and power behind the conversion of the violent system to a semilegitimate cartel that increasingly avoided the strong-arm methods of previous years and invested more funds in loan companies, real estate, entertainment enterprises, brokerage houses, garbage collection, banks, linen supply companies, restaurants, laundromats, insurance companies, and advertising agencies.

In 1968,* Dominick Angelo was ninety-four; 124 pounds; 5 feet 6 inches tall; almost totally bald; almost completely bedridden from diabetes, arthritis, and the effects of two severe coronary occlusions. Very dark eyes; extraordinarily long fingers; a habit of stroking his upper lip with one finger (he wore a long mustache until 1946).

His home in Deal, New Jersey, was large, comfortable, and situated in the center of a generous acreage, without being ostentatious. The estate was surrounded by a 12-foot brick wall topped with cement into which pieces of broken glass had been studded. It is believed the staff consisted of several people—housekeeper, two or three groundsmen, a personal valet, butler, a male medical attendant, a female nurse, three maids, and two chauffeurs.

On 16 May, 1966, an explosion occurred at the locked gate leading to the Angelo estate. Officers investigating the incident reported it had been caused by several sticks of dynamite wired to a crude time fuse—a cheap alarm clock. No injuries were reported, and no arrests were made. The investigation is continuing.

Of peripheral interest are two unsubstantiated reports on Dominick Angelo: After his wife's death in 1952, he engaged in homosexual liaisons, preferring the company of very young boys; and he was the inventor of the split-level coffin, although this "credit" has since been given to others. The split-level coffin is a device to get rid of victims of gangland slayings. The coffins are built somewhat deeper than usual, and the victim is buried in a section beneath the legitimate corpse. This scheme, of course, depends upon the cooperation of funeral parlors, in which the family has a substantial financial interest.

The following transcription is from a tape recording made by agents of the New Jersey Special Legislative Subcommittee to investigate Organized Crime. The transcription is labeled NJSLC-DA-#206-IC, and is dated 10 July, 1968. The time was approximately 11:45 P.M., and the recording was made at Dominick Angelo's home at 67825 Flint Road, Deal, New Jersey. The transmitting device was a Socklet MT-Model K.

From internal evidence, the two persons present were Dominick "Papa" Angelo and Patrick "Little Pat" Angelo. Although the tape recording from which this transcription was made ran for slightly less than three hours, portions have been deleted that repeat evidence already presented. In addition, law enforcement agencies of New Jersey, New York, and Las Vegas, Nevada, have requested that certain portions be withheld, since they concern possible criminal prosecutions presently under investigation. All such deletions have been indicated by "lapse of time" notations.

> [Lapse of thirty-two minutes during which Patrick Angelo inquired as to his grandfather's health and was informed that it was "as well as could be expected." Patrick Angelo then reported on the meeting with John Anderson and Anthony D'Medico.]

*Dominick Angelo died on February 19, 1969.

PATRICK: Well, Papa, what do you think?

PAPA: What do *you* think?

PATRICK: I say no. Too many people involved. Too complex, considering the possible profit.

PAPA: But I see your eyes shining. I see you are interested. You say to yourself, this is action! You are excited. You say to yourself, I am getting old and fat. I need action. This is how it was in Korea. I will plan this like a military raid. To me you say no—but in yourself you want this thing.

PATRICK [laughing]: Papa, you're wonderful! You've got it all exactly right. My brain tells me this is nothing. But my blood wants it. I am sorry.

PAPA: Why be sorry? You think it is a good thing to be all brain and no blood? It is as bad as being all blood and no brain. The right mixture—that is what is important. This man Anderson—what is your feeling on him?

PATRICK: A hardnose. He has never carried a piece, but he is hard. And proud. From Kentucky. A mountain man. Everything the Doctor told me about him was good.

PAPA: Anderson? From the South? About ten years ago Gino Belli— he is the Doctor's cousin—had a thing planned. It seemed good but it went sour. He had a driver named Anderson. Is that the man?

PATRICK: The same one. What a memory you've got, Papa!

PAPA: The body grows old; the mind remains young, praise to God. This Anderson brought Gino to a doctor. I remember it all now. I met him, very briefly. Tall and thin. A long, sunken face. Proud. Yes, you are right—a very proud man. I remember.

PATRICK: So what do you want to do, Papa?

PAPA: Be quiet and let me think.

[Lapse of two minutes thirteen seconds.]

PAPA: This Anderson—you say he has his own staff?

PATRICK: Yes. Five men. One's a smoke. One's a tech. Two are drivers, one of them a dumdum.

[Lapse of nine seconds.]

PAPA: That is four. And the other? The fifth man?

[Lapse of sixteen seconds.]

PAPA: Well? The fifth man?

PATRICK: He's fancy. Knows about paintings, rugs, art collections— things like that.

PAPA: I see. Is his name Bailey?

PATRICK: I don't know what his name is, Papa. I can find out.

PAPA: There was a fancy boy named Bailey out in Vegas. We did a....

[Lapse of four minutes thirty-two seconds.]

PAPA: But that is not important. Besides, I suspect it is not Bailey. I suspect Bailey is dead. And who does the Doctor recommend as our representative?

PATRICK: A man named Sam Heming. One of Paul Washington's boys.

PAPA: Another dinge?

PATRICK: Yes.

PAPA: No. That won't do.

PATRICK: Papa? You mean you approve of this campaign?

PAPA: Yes. I approve. Go ahead with it.

PATRICK: But why? The money is. . . .

PAPA: I know. The money is nothing. There are too many people involved. It will end in disaster.

PATRICK: So . . . ?

[Lapse of seventeen seconds.]

PAPA: Little Pat is thinking why should Papa okay something like this? All these years we work hard to get legit. We deal with Wall Street bankers, Madison Avenue advertising agencies, political parties. We are in all good businesses. The profits are good. Everything is clean. We keep trouble down. And now here is Papa, ninety-four years old, and maybe his mind is getting feeble, too—here is Papa saying all right to this silly plan, this *meshugeneh* raid, where people will be hurt and probably killed. Maybe Papa is no longer to be trusted. Is that what Patrick thinks?

PATRICK: I swear to God, Papa, I never. If you say it's okay, it's okay.

PAPA: Little Pat, you will be don soon enough. Soon enough. A year. Two at the most.

PATRICK: Papa, Papa . . . you'll outlive us all.

PAPA: Two years at the most. Probably one. But if you are to be don you must learn to think . . . *think*. Not only must you think should we do this thing, can we profit from this thing, but also, what are the consequences of this thing? What will result from this thing a year, five years, ten years from now? Most men—even big executives in the best American companies—gather all the facts and make a decision. But they fail to consider the consequences of their decision. The long-term consequences. Do you understand me?

PATRICK: I think so, Papa.

PAPA: Suppose there is a man we must put down. We consider what he has done and what a danger he represents to us. On the basis of these facts, we say he must be put down. But we must also consider the consequences of his death. Does he have relatives who will be embittered? Will the blues get upset? What will the papers say? Is there a young, smart, ambitious politician who will take this man's death and get elected on it? You understand? It is not enough to consider the immediate facts. You must also project your mind and consider the future. In the long run, will it help us or hurt us?

PATRICK: Now I understand, Papa. But what has that to do with Anderson's hustle?

PAPA: Remember about four years ago in Buffalo, we. . . .

[Lapse of four minutes nine seconds.]

PAPA: So what did that teach us? The advantage of fear. We first create and then maintain an atmosphere of fear. Why do you think we have been so successful in our legitimate dealings? In real estate and garbage collection and banks and linen service? Because our rates are lower? Ah, you know our rates are higher. Higher! But they fear us. And because of their fear, we do good business. The steel fist in the velvet glove. But if this is to continue, if our legitimate enterprises are to flourish, we must maintain our reputation. We must let businessmen know who we are, of what we are capable. Not frequently, but occasionally, choosing incidents that we know will not be lost on them, we must let the public know that beneath that soft velvet glove is bright, shining steel. Only then will they fear us, and our legitimate enterprises will continue to grow.

PATRICK: And you want to use Anderson's campaign as an example? You feel it will end in failure, but you want the newspapers to play it up as ours? You want people hurt and people killed? You want businessmen who read about it in the papers to shiver, and then call us and say yes, they'll take another million yards of our rayons or use our trucking firms or our insurance business?

PAPA: Yes. That is exactly what I want.

PATRICK: Is that why you okayed Al Petty's job two years ago when. . . .

[Lapse of forty-seven seconds.]

PAPA: Of course. I knew he could never succeed. But it made headlines all over the country, and the men arrested were linked to us. Three people, one a child, were killed on that job, and our collections took a five point two percent jump in the following six months. Fear. Let others—the English and the Americans—use persuasion and business pressure. We use fear. Because we know it always works.

PATRICK: But Anderson, he's not. . . .

PAPA: I know he is not linked closely with us. So we must put a man in who is. Toast came to visit me yesterday.

PATRICK: Toast? I didn't know he was in town. Why didn't he call me?

PAPA: He asked me to apologize to you. He was between flights. He just had time for a quick trip out here by car, and then on to Palm Beach.

PATRICK: How old was she this time?

PAPA: About fifteen. A real beauty. Long blond hair. And blind.

PATRICK: Blind? That's good—for her sake.

PAPA: Yes. But Toast has a problem. Perhaps we can solve it for him with this Anderson thing.

PATRICK: What is the problem?

PAPA: Toast has a man—Vincent Parelli. You know him? They call him Socks.

PATRICK: That idiot? I've read about him.

PAPA: Yes. Parelli has gone crazy. He fights people. He runs them down in his car. He shoots them. He just doesn't care. He is a very great embarrassment to Toast.

PATRICK: I can imagine.

PAPA: Parelli is very closely linked with us, very closely. Toast wants to get him out. You understand?

PATRICK: Yes.

PAPA: But Parelli is not that easy. He has some muscle of his own. They are all crazy . . . crazy. Al Capones. Throwbacks. They cannot think. Toast asked if there is anything I can do.

PATRICK: So . . . ?

PAPA: I owe a favor to Toast. You remember last year he got Paolo's nephew into the university after the boy had been turned down all over? So here is what we do. . . . I will tell Toast to send Parelli in from Detroit to be our man on the Anderson campaign. Toast will tell Parelli that we have definite evidence of at least a million dollars' worth of jewelry in the house. Otherwise Parelli would laugh at us. Toast will tell him we want a good, trustworthy man of our own on the scene to make sure there is no chance of a cross. This Parelli is gun-happy. He will probably blast. At the same time, you tell Anderson that we approve his plan providing he carries a piece and, at the end of the action, he puts Parelli down. That is our price for financing his hustle.

[Lapse of eleven seconds.]

PATRICK: Papa, I don't think Anderson will go for it.

PAPA: I think he will. I know these amateurs. Always the big chance, the big hit, and then retirement to South America or the French Riviera for the rest of their lives. They think crime is one big lottery. They don't know what hard work it is . . . hard, grinding work, year after year. No big hits, no big chances. But a job—just like any other. Maybe the profits are larger, but so are the risks. Anderson will stall a while, but then he will go for it. He will put Parelli down. Anderson has the blood and the pride to keep a bargain. I believe the whole thing will be a madness, with innocent people hurt and killed, and Vincent Parelli, who is so closely linked with us, found dead at the scene of the crime.

PATRICK: And you think that will help us, Papa?

PAPA: It will be in headlines all over the country and, eventually, it will help us.

PATRICK: What if the campaign comes off?

PAPA: So much the better. Parelli will no longer be a nuisance to Toast, we will get credit for the grab, and we will also profit. And maybe Anderson will end up in Mexico after all. Patrick, phone me every day and tell me how this is coming. I am very interested. Explain to the Doctor only as much as he needs to know. You understand?

PATRICK: Yes, Papa.

PAPA: I will take care of Toast, and Toast will make certain that Parelli is here when needed. Do you have any questions?

PATRICK: No, Papa. I know what must be done.

PAPA: You are a good boy, Patrick . . . a good boy.

34

•

ON 12 JULY, 1968, AT 2:06 P.M., A MEETING TOOK PLACE BETWEEN John Anderson and Patrick Angelo in the dispatcher's office of the Jiffy Trucking & Hauling Co., 11098 Tenth Avenue, New York, New York. This company was a subsidiary of the Thomas Jefferson Trading Corp., of which Patrick Angelo was an officer (secretary-treasurer) of record. The premises were under surveillance by the Bureau of Customs, pursuant to Federal Court Order MFC-#189-605HG, on suspicion that they were being used as a drop for smuggled merchandise. The following is tape USBC-1089756738-B2.

ANDERSON: Well?

ANGELO: It looks good. Papa okayed it.
    [Lapse of four seconds.]

ANDERSON [sighing]: Jesus.

ANGELO: But you've got to do something for us.
    [Lapse of six seconds.]

ANDERSON: What?

ANGELO: We've got to put our own man in. You know, that's SOP—Standard Operating Procedure.

ANDERSON: I know. I figured that. Who?

ANGELO: A man from Detroit. Vincent Parelli. They call him Socks. You know him?

ANDERSON: No.

ANGELO: You heard about him?

ANDERSON: No.

ANGELO: A good man. Experienced. He's no punk. But you'll be the boss. That's understood. He'll be told he takes orders from you.

ANDERSON: All right. That sounds all right. What else?

ANGELO: You got a brain.

ANDERSON: What else do I got to do?

ANGELO: We want you to cut down on him.

[Lapse of five seconds.]

ANDERSON: What?

ANGELO: Put him down. After it's all over. When you're ready to leave. You put him down.

[Lapse of eleven seconds.]

ANGELO: You understand?

ANDERSON: Yes.

ANGELO: You knew you'd have to carry a barker on this job?

ANDERSON: Yes.

ANGELO: So . . . you cut this Parelli down. Just before you take off.

ANDERSON: You want me to kill him.

[Lapse of seven seconds.]

ANGELO: Yes.

ANDERSON: Why?

ANGELO: You don't have to know that. It's got nothing to do with you, nothing to do with this hustle. We want him out—that's all. You get him out. That's our price.

[Lapse of sixteen seconds.]

ANGELO: Well?

ANDERSON: You want me to answer now?

ANGELO: No. Take a day or two. We'll be in touch. If it's no, then no hard feelings and we'll forget the whole thing. If it's yes, the Doctor will get the scratch to you and we'll start the operations plan. We can get you the schedules of the beat fuzz and the sector cars. But it's up to you. It's your decision.

ANDERSON: Yes.

ANGELO: You know exactly what you must do? There's no misunderstanding? I've made it plain? In things like this, it's best to make absolutely certain everyone knows what's going to happen.

ANDERSON: I know what's going to happen.

ANGELO: Good. You think about it.

ANDERSON: All right. I'll think about it.

35

•

IN ADDITION TO THE MICROPHONE TRANSMITTER IMPLANTED AT the home of Dominick Angelo, 67825 Flint Road, Deal, New Jersey, a telephone tap had been installed by the Federal Bureau of Narcotics. This portion of tape FBN-DA-10935 is dated 12 July, 1968. The time: 2:48 P.M.

ANGELO: He was shook, Papa . . . really spooked. I think you were right. I think he'll go for it. Now about this thing with Benefici in Hackensack . . . I think we should. . . .

36

•

TAPE SEC-13JUL68-IM-4:24PM-149H. THIS WAS A SATURDAY.

INGRID: So . . . how is it you are here at this hour? You are not working?
ANDERSON: No. I'm off this weekend. I get every other weekend off.
INGRID: You should have called first. I might have been busy.
ANDERSON: Are you busy?
INGRID: No. I have been doing some mending. You would like a drink?
ANDERSON: I brought some Berliner Weisse and raspberry syrup.
INGRID: You darling! How wonderful! You remembered!
ANDERSON: You have big glasses?
INGRID: I will serve it in big brandy snifters I have. How wonderful! You remembered!
   [Lapse of two minutes eighteen seconds.]
INGRID: Here you are. Such a beautiful color. *Prosit.*

ANDERSON: *Prosit.*

[Lapse of fourteen seconds.]

INGRID: Ah. So good, so good. Tell me, Duke—how are things with you?

ANDERSON: All right.

INGRID: That meet you had, the last time I spoke to you . . . that turned out well?

ANDERSON: Yes . . . sort of.

INGRID: You are troubled, *Schatzie?* That is why you came? You want to get out?

ANDERSON: No. But I got to talk. I don't mean that the way it sounds. I got to talk to *you.* You're the smartest one I know. I want your opinion. Your advice.

INGRID: This is a job?

ANDERSON: Yes.

INGRID: I don't want to know about it.

ANDERSON: Please. I don't say please very often. I'm saying please to you.

[Lapse of thirteen seconds.]

INGRID: You know, Duke, I have a feeling about you. A very bad feeling.

ANDERSON: What is that?

INGRID: I have this feeling that through you I will meet my death. Just by knowing you and talking to you, I will die before my time.

ANDERSON: Does that scare you?

INGRID: No.

ANDERSON: No. Nothing scares you. Does it make you sad?

INGRID: Perhaps.

ANDERSON: Do you want me to leave?

[Lapse of twenty-two seconds.]

INGRID: What do you want to tell me? Why is this thing so important you need my advice?

ANDERSON: I have this hustle planned. It's a good one. If I hit, it means a lot of money. A lot of money. If it works out, I can go to Mexico, South America, Europe—anywhere. And live for the rest of my life. I mean, *live.* I would ask you to come with me. But don't think about that. Don't let that influence what you tell me.

INGRID: I won't, *Schatzie.* I have heard that before.

ANDERSON: I know, I know. But for this hustle I need money, ready money. To pay people and plan things. You understand?

INGRID: Yes. You want money from me?

ANDERSON: No, I don't want any money from you.

INGRID: Then the people you will get money from, the people whose cooperation you need—they want something . . . *nein?*

ANDERSON: You're so goddamned smart it scares me.

INGRID: Think of what my life has been. What do they want?

ANDERSON: I have a staff. Five men I can get. But these money people must put their own man in. Okay. This is understandable. I'm
a free-lance. It happens all the time with free-lancers. You get permission to operate but they must put their own man in to make
sure there's no cross, so they know definitely what the take is. You
understand?

INGRID: Of course. So?

ANDERSON: They want to bring a man in from Detroit. I've never met
him. I've never heard of him. They tell me he's a pro. They tell me
he will take orders from me. I will be the boss of this campaign.

INGRID: So?

ANDERSON: They want me to cut down on him. This is their price.
After the hit is finished, I am to burn this man. They won't tell me
why; it isn't my business. But this is their price.

INGRID: Ah. . . .

    [Lapse of one minute twelve seconds.]

INGRID: They know you. They know you so well. They know if you
agree to this, you will do it. Not from fear of what they might do if
you didn't, but because you are John Anderson, and when you say
you will do a thing, you will then do it. Am I right?

ANDERSON: I don't know what they think.

INGRID: You ask me for my advice. I am trying to give it to you. If
you say yes, you will then kill this man. Tell me, *Schatzie,* if you say
no, are you then in trouble?

ANDERSON: Not in trouble . . . no. They won't kill me. Nothing like
that. I'm not worth it. But I couldn't free-lance anymore. I couldn't
get clearance from them. I could operate, if I wanted to, but it would
never be the same again. It would be very bad—penny-ante stuff.
I'd have to go back home. I couldn't operate in this town.

INGRID: Home? Where is home?

ANDERSON: South. Kentucky.

INGRID: And what would you do there?

ANDERSON: Open your robe, will you?

INGRID: Yes. Like this . . . ?

ANDERSON: Yes. Just let me look at you while I'm talking. Christ, I've
got to talk.

INGRID: Is this better?

ANDERSON: Yes . . . better. I don't know what I'd do. Run some alky.
Gas stations maybe. A bank now and then if I could find the right
men.

INGRID: That is all you know?

ANDERSON: Yes, goddammit, that's all I know. Do you think I would become a computer operator in Kentucky, or maybe an insurance salesman?

INGRID: Do not be angry with me, *Schatzie*.

ANDERSON: I'm not angry with you. I told you, I just want your advice. I'm all fucked up.

INGRID: You killed a man before.

ANDERSON: Yes. But that was in blood. I had to. You understand? He said things.

INGRID: So now it is part of a job. How is it different?

ANDERSON: Shit. You foreigners. You don't understand.

INGRID: No, I do not.

ANDERSON: This guy I cut kept pecking at me and pecking at me. We had words. Finally I had to put him down or I couldn't have lived with myself. I *had* to. I was forced into it.

INGRID: You Americans—you are so strange. You "put a man down," or you "cut him," or you "burn him," or you "put him away" or "take him for a ride." But you will never say you killed him. Why is that?

ANDERSON: Yes, you're right. It's funny. I don't know why it is. These people who want me to do this thing I told you about, I finally asked the man, "You want me to kill him?" and he finally admitted that was what they wanted. But I could tell from the way he paused and the way he looked that the word "kill" didn't taste sweet to him. When I was driving for a legger down home we had this old smoke working for us—he could turn out a mighty fine mash—and he said everybody's got to go—everybody. He said this is the one thing all men are fearful of most, and they invent all kinds of words so as not to say it. And preachers come along and say you'll be born again, and you grab at the preacher and give him money, though way down deep in your heart you know he's lying. Catholic, Baptist, Methodist, Jew—I don't care what, they all know nobody's going to be born again. When you're dead, man, you're dead. That's it. That's the end. That's what this old black kept telling me, and boy, was he right. That's the one thing in all of us—you, me, and everyone else in this world—and we're scared of dying, or even thinking about it. Look at you there, almost bare-ass naked with your cousy hanging out, and you think that's going to last forever? Baby, we're all getting out. Finally. We're all getting out. Why do you think I keep coming back to you and grabbing at you to get me out? Because you always get me out for a short time, and I always know I'm coming back. And somehow, and don't ask me how because I can't explain it or understand it, you get me out for a little while and then I come back, and it makes the big getting-out easier to take. The last getting-out. Like I might come back from that, too. I don't know. I can't figure it all—but that's what I think. I want to get out so I can forget the shit I have to eat every day, but also I want to get out like it's practice for what's coming. You know? And this poor, fat, rich East Side bitch I slap around, that's what she's looking for, too. Sure, maybe it's a kick and makes us forget how much crap we wade through every day, but maybe it convinces us that every little time we die— well, then, the big time is no different, and we'll come back from that, too. Which is a laugh. Isn't that a laugh, baby?

INGRID: Yes. That is a laugh.

ANDERSON: I didn't really come here for your advice. I came to tell you what I'm going to do. I'm going to kill this Parelli guy. I don't know who he is or what he is or how bad he needs killing. But whether I do it or a bolt of lightning strikes him tomorrow or twenty years from now, it's going to be done. But I'm going to kill him because maybe I can get a few clean years out of all this. And right now I'm so charged with blood and you sitting there with all your woman hanging out and staring at me, and I can taste the moment when I put that guy down, and what I'm going to do right now is get you out . . . maybe for the first time in your life.

INGRID: And how are you going to do that?

ANDERSON: I'll do it. I don't know how, but I'll do it. You've got all this crazy stuff around for your customers, haven't you? We'll do it with that if we have to. But we'll do it. I'm going to get you out, Ingrid. I swear it. . . .

INGRID: Yes?

37

•

XEROX COPY OF A TELETYPE DATED 6 JUNE, 1968.

TT-68-7946 . . . FR NYPD-PC . . . TO ALL DEP, INS, BOR AND PRNCT CMDRS, CPTS, LTS, SGTS . . . FOR POSTING . . . REPEAT, FOR POSTING . . . AS OF THIS DATE, NEW PCC (POLICE COMMUNICATIONS CENTER) IS IN FULL OPER . . . EMRGNCY NMBR 911 . . . KILL 440-1234 . . . ALL CMPLNTS TO 911 WILL BE FRWRD TO PRNCT VIA TT OR TE . . . CMD OF CARS WITH PCC . . . CNFRM . . . PC . . .

38

•

THIS IS TAPE RECORDING NYSITB-FD-15JUL68-437-6G; 15 JULY, 1968; 12:45 P.M.

SIMONS: Hello, Duke. Close that door quick. Let's not give any of this air conditioning a chance to escape. Good to see you again.

ANDERSON: Hello, Mr. Simons. How you been?

SIMONS: Getting by, Duke, getting by. Can I offer you something?

ANDERSON: Not right now, Mr. Simons.

SIMONS: Well . . . you don't mind if I go ahead, do you? I have a luncheon appointment in about half an hour, and I always find that a martini sharpens the appetite.

ANDERSON: You go right ahead.

SIMONS: Well, now, Duke, what have you decided?

ANDERSON: Yes. It's all right.

SIMONS: You understand completely what you must do in regards to this person from Detroit?

ANDERSON: Yes. I understand.

SIMONS: Excellent. Now then . . . let's get down to the fine print. This person from Detroit will be our responsibility. That is, any payment to him or to his heirs is our responsibility and is not part of any of the financial arrangements which, I trust, you and I will soon agree upon. Is that clear?

ANDERSON: Yes.

SIMONS: All expenses and advances will come off the top. In that connection, if these terms are agreeable to you, I have with me and am authorized to turn over to you the two thousand additional expense funds you requested. Upon approval of the operational plan, we will then turn over to you a sum sufficient for half payment of fees of the men involved which, I understand, you estimated as four to five thousand dollars. Is that correct?

ANDERSON: Yes. That's right. That's half their take.

SIMONS: Now then . . . when the final cash income is determined, all these sums—advances, expenses, and salaries—will come off the top. Clear?

ANDERSON: That includes the final payment to my staff—the other half, about four or five thousand to close them out?

SIMONS: That's correct. All such expenses will be subtracted first. We anticipate no additional expenses other than those you have outlined. In any event, we feel they will be so minor that they need not concern us at this time. Now then . . . we are down to the net income. We propose a fifty-fifty split.

ANDERSON: I asked for seventy-thirty.

SIMONS: I know you did, Duke. But under the circumstances, and considering the take may be considerably less than your most optimistic estimate, we feel a fifty-fifty split is justified. Especially in view of the moneys we have so far advanced.

ANDERSON: It's not right. Not when you figure what I'm going to do for you. I won't go for it.

SIMONS: Duke, we could sit here and argue for hours, but I know you don't want that any more than I do. I was instructed to offer you the fifty-fifty deal because we feel that is a fair and equitable arrangement, considering the risks involved and the cash outlay up to this point. Quite frankly, I must admit that Mr. Angelo—Little Pat, that is—he did not feel you would be satisfied with this. Therefore, I am authorized to propose a sixty-forty division. And that, Duke, I can tell you in all honesty is the best I can do. If that is not satisfactory, then you'll have to take up the entire matter with Mr. D'Medico or Mr. Angelo.

[Lapse of eighteen seconds.]

ANDERSON: Sixty for me, forty for you?

SIMONS: That is correct.

ANDERSON: And for this I put my cock on the line for a murder-one rap?

SIMONS: Duke, Duke . . . I wouldn't attempt to advise you, my boy. It's your decision to make, and you know the factors involved in it much better than I. All I can do is offer you the sixty-forty split. That's my job, and I'm doing it. Please don't be angry with me.

ANDERSON: I'm not angry with you, Mr. Simons. Or with Mr. D'Medico or Mr. Angelo. You got your job to do and I got mine. And I suppose you all got to answer to someone else.

SIMONS: We do indeed, Duke, we do indeed.

[Lapse of four seconds.]

ANDERSON: All right. I'll buy the sixty-forty.

SIMONS: Excellent. I'm sure you won't regret it. Here's the two thousand. Small bills. All clean. We'll make arrangements for Parelli to come in from Detroit. You'll be informed when he's available for planning. We think your idea of a hit on the Labor Day weekend is a good one. Meanwhile we'll see what we can do about getting you schedules of the two fifty-first Precinct and the Sector George cars. When you have your campaign firmed up, get in touch with me and I'll set up a meet for you with Mr. Angelo. I suggest you do this before you make a firm commitment to your staff. You understand? No use bringing them in until the whole thing is laid out. You agree?

ANDERSON: Yes.

SIMONS: Is everything clear now? I mean about money, and personnel, or anything else? If you have any questions, now is the time to ask them.

    [Lapse of six seconds.]

ANDERSON: This Parelli—what did he do?

SIMONS: I don't know and I don't want to know. I suggest you cultivate the same attitude. Would you like something now?

ANDERSON: Yes. All right. A brandy.

SIMONS: Excellent, excellent. . . .

39

•

XEROX COPY OF A LETTER DATED 16 JULY, 1968, FROM UNITED Electronics Kits, Inc., 65378 Michigan Boulevard, Chicago, Illinois, addressed to Mr. Gerald Bingham, Jr., Apartment 5A, 535 East Seventy-third Street, New York, New York.

DEAR MR. BINGHAM:

In reply to your letter of the 5th inst., please be advised that we have found your suggestion of considerable merit. Accordingly, we are modifying our Amplifier Kit 57-68A so that the back plate is easily removed (via screws) rather than soldered as at present. We are sure, as you suggest, that this will aid construction and servicing of the completed unit.

We wish to express our appreciation for your interest, and we are, frankly, somewhat chagrined that our engineers did not spot this drawback to the 57-68A kit prior to its distribution. The fact that you are, as you say, fifteen years old, makes our chagrin more understandable!

In any event, to express our appreciation for your suggestion in a more tangible form, we are forwarding to you (this date) a complimentary gift of our Deluxe 32-16895 Three-Speed Stereo Tape Deck Kit (no charge).

Again—thank you for your kind interest in our products.

Sincerely,

[signed] DAVID K. DAVIDSON,
Director, Public Relations

40

•

TAPE RECORDING FBN-DA-11036. TUESDAY, 16 JULY, 1968, 2:36 P.M.

OPERATOR: I have a person-to-person call, Detroit. From Mr. Dominick Angelo of Deal, New Jersey, to Mr. Nicola D'Agostino at three-one-one, one-five-eight, eight-nine-seven-three.

OPERATOR: Just a moment, Operator.

OPERATOR: Thank you.

[Lapse of fourteen seconds.]

OPERATOR: Is this three-one-one, one-five-eight, eight-nine-seven-three?

MALE VOICE: Yes.

OPERATOR: I have a person-to-person call for a Mr. Nicola D'Agostino from Mr. Dominick Angelo of Deal, New Jersey. Is Mr. D'Agostino there?

MALE VOICE: Just a minute, Operator.

OPERATOR: Thank you. Are you there, New Jersey?

OPERATOR: Yes, dear.

OPERATOR: Thank you. They're trying to find Mr. D'Agostino.

[Lapse of eleven seconds.]

D'AGOSTINO: Hello?

OPERATOR: Mr. Nicola D'Agostino?

D'AGOSTINO: Yes.

OPERATOR: Just a moment, please, sir. Deal, New Jersey, calling. Go ahead, New Jersey. Mr. D'Agostino is on the line.

OPERATOR: Thank you, dear. Go ahead, Mr. Angelo. Mr. D'Agostino is on the line.

ANGELO: Hello? Hello, Toast?

D'AGOSTINO: Papa—is that you? How *nice* to hear your voice! How are you, Papa?

ANGELO: Getting along. Getting along. And how was Florida?

D'AGOSTINO: Magnificent, Papa. Gorgeous. You should move there. You'd live another hundred years.

ANGELO: God forbid. And the family?

D'AGOSTINO: Couldn't be better, Papa. Angelica asked about you. I told her you'd outlive us all.

ANGELO: And the children?

D'AGOSTINO: Fine, Papa, fine. Everyone is fine. Tony fell off his bike yesterday and broke his tooth—but it's nothing.

ANGELO: My God. You need a good dentist? I'll fly him out.

D'AGOSTINO: No, no, Papa. It's a baby tooth. We got a good dentist. He said it's nothing. Don't worry yourself.

ANGELO: Good. You have any trouble, you let me know.

D'AGOSTINO: I will, Papa, I will. Thank you for your interest. Believe me, Angelica and I, we appreciate it.

ANGELO: Toast, you remember when you were here, we discussed your problem?

D'AGOSTINO: Yes, Papa, I remember.

ANGELO: This problem, Toast—I think we can help you with it. I think we can solve it.

D'AGOSTINO: Believe me, I would appreciate that, Papa.

ANGELO: It would be a permanent solution. You understand, Toast?

D'AGOSTINO: I understand, Papa.

ANGELO: That is what you want?

D'AGOSTINO: That is what I want.

ANGELO: Good. It will work out well. You will send him to me as soon as possible. Within a week. Is that possible, Toast?

D'AGOSTINO: Of course.

ANGELO: Tell him only that it is a big job. You understand?

D'AGOSTINO: I understand, Papa. You will have him by Friday.

ANGELO: Good. Please give my love to Angelica. And to Auntie and Nick. And tell Tony I will send him a new bicycle. This one won't throw him off and break his tooth.

D'AGOSTINO [laughing]: Papa, you're too much! I love you. We all love you.

ANGELO: You keep well.

D'AGOSTINO: You too, Papa. You keep well—forever.

41

•

TRANSCRIPTION OF TAPE RECORDING POM-20JUL68-EVER-
LEIGH. This recording began at 1:14 P.M., 20 July, 1968, and ended at 2:06
P.M., 21 July. It was recorded at Apartment 3B, 535 East Seventy-third Street.
This tape has been heavily edited to eliminate extraneous conversations,
names of innocent persons, and repetition of information already obtained
from other sources. During the more than twenty-four-hour period mentioned above, it is not believed that Mrs. Agnes Everleigh and John Anderson
left Apartment 3B.

SEGMENT I.20JUL-1:48PM.
ANDERSON: . . . can't. I had last weekend off.
MRS. EVERLEIGH: You can call in sick, can't you? It's not the whole
    weekend. It's just tonight. You can be back at work tomorrow night.
    You get sick leave, don't you?
ANDERSON: Yes. Ten days a year.
MRS. EVERLEIGH: Have you taken any?
ANDERSON: No. Not since I been working there.
MRS. EVERLEIGH: So take tonight off. I'll give you fifty dollars.
ANDERSON: All right.
MRS. EVERLEIGH: You'll take the fifty?
ANDERSON: Yes.
MRS. EVERLEIGH: This is the first time you've ever taken money from
    me.
ANDERSON: How does it make you feel?
MRS. EVERLEIGH: You know . . . don't you?
ANDERSON: Yes. Go get the fifty. I'll make a call and tell them I'm
    sick.
MRS. EVERLEIGH: You'll stay with me? All night?
ANDERSON: Sure.

SEGMENT II. 20JUL-2:13PM.
MRS. EVERLEIGH: I love you when you're like this—relaxed and nice
    and good to me.
ANDERSON: Am I good to you?

MRS. EVERLEIGH: So far. So far you've been a perfect gentleman.

ANDERSON: Like this?

MRS. EVERLEIGH: Must you? Must you do that?

ANDERSON: Sure. If I want to earn my fifty bucks.

MRS. EVERLEIGH: You're such a bastard.

ANDERSON: Honest. I'm honest.

SEGMENT III. 20JUL-5:26PM.

MRS. EVERLEIGH: . . . at least forty percent. How do you like that?

ANDERSON: Can they do it?

MRS. EVERLEIGH: You idiot, of course they can do it. This apartment is a cooperative. I'm not on the board. After my husband moved out, our lawyers got together and I agreed to pay the maintenance and he agreed to keep paying the mortgage. The apartment is in his name. Now they're going to increase the maintenance by at least forty percent.

ANDERSON: What are you going to do?

MRS. EVERLEIGH: I haven't decided yet. I'd move out tomorrow if I could find something better. But go look for an apartment on the East Side of Manhattan. These new places charge one hundred and eighty-five dollars for one room. I'll probably give them what they want and stay right here. Roll over.

ANDERSON: I've had enough.

MRS. EVERLEIGH: No you haven't.

SEGMENT IV. 20JUL-6:32PM.

MRS. EVERLEIGH: It depends on what you want. Feraccis has barbecued chicken or short ribs—stuff like that. It's a kind of a delicatessen. If we're going to cook, we can order up from Ernesto Brothers. We can get frozen TV dinners or Rock Cornish hens or we can get a steak and pan-fry it or broil it—whatever you want.

ANDERSON: Let's have a chicken—a big chicken. Three pounds if they've got a fryer-broiler that size. We'll fry it. And maybe some French fried potatoes and greens.

MRS. EVERLEIGH: What kind of greens?

ANDERSON: Collards? They got collards?

MRS. EVERLEIGH: What are collards?

ANDERSON: Forget it. Just get us a big chicken we can fry and a lot of cold beer. How does that sound?

MRS. EVERLEIGH: That sounds scrumptious.

ANDERSON: Order it up. I'll pay for it. Here's fifty.

MRS. EVERLEIGH: You sonofabitch.

SEGMENT V. 20JUL-9:14PM.

ANDERSON: What are you going to do in Rome?

MRS. EVERLEIGH: The usual . . . see the new fall collections . . . visit some fag boutiques . . . buy some stuff . . . it's a drag.

ANDERSON: Like I said, I wish I could travel. All you need is money. Like this apartment house. You're going to Rome. Your neighbors are going down to the Jersey shore. I bet everyone in the house will be going somewhere on the Labor Day weekend—Rome, Jersey, Florida, France . . . somewhere. . . .

MRS. EVERLEIGH: Oh, sure. The Sheldons—they're up in Four A—they're already out in their place on Montauk. The people below me, a lawyer and his wife, will be out in East Hampton. Up on top in Five B, Longene and that bitch who's living with him—they're not married, you know—are sure to be invited someplace for the Labor Day weekend. So the house will probably be about half full. That fag in Two A will probably be gone, too. What are you going to do?

ANDERSON: Work, probably. I get triple-time when I work nights on a holiday. I can make a lot of loot if I work over the Labor Day weekend.

MRS. EVERLEIGH: Will you think of me?

ANDERSON: Sure. There's one drumstick left. You want it?

MRS. EVERLEIGH: No, darling. You finish it.

ANDERSON: All right. I like drumsticks and wings and the Pope's nose. More than I do the breast. Dark meat got more flavor.

MRS. EVERLEIGH: Don't you like white meat at all?

ANDERSON: Maybe. Later.

SEGMENT VI. 21JUL-6:14AM.

ANDERSON [groaning]: Mammy . . . Mammy. . . .

MRS. EVERLEIGH: Duke? Duke? What is it, Duke?

ANDERSON: Mammy?

MRS. EVERLEIGH: Hush . . . hush. You're having a nightmare. I'm here, Duke.

ANDERSON: Mammy . . . Mammy. . . .

SEGMENT VII. 21JUL-8:56AM.

ANDERSON: Shit. You got a cigarette?

MRS. EVERLEIGH: There.

ANDERSON: Filters? Christ. These places around here—they're open on Sundays?

MRS. EVERLEIGH: Ernesto's is. What do you want?

ANDERSON: Cigarettes—to begin with. You mean this place is open on Sundays?

MRS. EVERLEIGH: Sure.

ANDERSON: Holidays too?

MRS. EVERLEIGH: They're open every day in the year, twenty-four hours a day. That's their brag. They have a sign in the window that says so. If you're pregnant, you can get a dill pickle at three in the morning from Ernesto's. That's how they stay in business. They can't compete with the big supermarkets on First Avenue, like Lambreta Brothers. So they stay open every minute of the day and night.

ANDERSON: My God, don't they get held up?

MRS. EVERLEIGH: They sure do . . . about two or three times a month. But they keep open. It must pay off. Besides, doesn't insurance pay when you get robbed?

ANDERSON: I guess so. I don't know much about these things.

MRS. EVERLEIGH: Well, I'll call and have them deliver some cigarettes. It's about nine now. When do you have to go?

ANDERSON: Around two o'clock. Something like that.

MRS. EVERLEIGH: Well, suppose I order up some food for a little breakfast and some food for a dinner about noon. Like a steak and baked potatoes. How does that sound?

ANDERSON: That sounds all right.

MRS. EVERLEIGH: You're the most bubbling, enthusiastic man I've ever met.

ANDERSON: I don't understand that.

MRS. EVERLEIGH: Forget it.

42

•

THE FOLLOWING IS LABELED SEGMENT 101-B OF DOCUMENT NYDA-EHM-101A-108B, a dictated, sworn, signed, and witnessed statement by Ernest Heinrich Mann.

MANN: So . . . we are now up to twenty-sixth July. I remember it was on a Friday. On this date the man I know as John Anderson came to my shop and. . . .

QUESTION: What time was this?

MANN: It was perhaps one o'clock. Definitely after lunch. He came to my shop and asked to speak with me. So we went into the back room. There is a door there I can close and lock; we would not be disturbed. At this time, Anderson asked if I would be available for a job he had in mind.

QUESTION: What kind of a job?

MANN: He was most evasive. Very vague. Deliberately so, you understand. But I knew that it was to be in the apartment house I had already investigated for him. When I learned that, I asked him if he had determined the purpose of the cold room I had discovered in the basement of the house.

QUESTION: What did he say?

MANN: He said yes, he had discovered the purpose of the cold room.

QUESTION: Did he tell you what it was used for?

MANN: At this time, no. Later he told me. But at this meeting on July twenty-sixth he did not tell me and I did not ask further.

QUESTION: What kind of a job did John Anderson ask you to do for him?

MANN: Well . . . he did not actually ask me to do it. At this date he merely wanted to know if I was interested, if I would be available. He said the job would consist of cutting all telephone and alarm connections of the entire apartment house.

QUESTION: What else?

MANN: Well . . . of cutting the power supply to the self-service elevator.

QUESTION: What else?

MANN: Well . . . uh. . . .

QUESTION: Mr. Mann, you promised us complete cooperation. On the basis of that promise we agreed to offer you what assistance we could under the law. You understand, of course, we cannot offer you complete immunity?

MANN: Yes. I understand. Of course.

QUESTION: A great deal depends upon your attitude. What else did John Anderson ask you to do at this meeting on July twenty-six?

MANN: Well, as I told you, he did not actually ask. He was outlining a hypothetical situation, you understand. He was feeling me out, I believe you say. Determining my interest in an assignment.

QUESTION: Yes, yes, you've already said that. The assignment would include cutting all telephone and alarm connections of the apartment house in question, and perhaps cutting the power supply to the self-service elevator.

MANN: Yes. This is correct.

QUESTION: All right. Mr. Mann. You have now admitted to destruction of private property, a relatively minor offense. And perhaps breaking and entering. . . .

MANN: Oh no! No, no, no! Not breaking and entering. The premises were to be quite open when I arrived. I was to have nothing to do with that.

QUESTION: I see. And how much money were you offered for cutting the telephone and alarm connections, and for cutting the elevator power supply?

MANN: Well . . . we came to no definite agreement. You must realize we were talking generalities. There was no definite job, no definite assignment. This man Anderson merely wished to discover if I was interested and what my charge would be.

QUESTION: And what did you tell him your charge would be?

MANN: I suggested five thousand dollars.

QUESTION: Five thousand dollars? Mr. Mann, isn't that a rather large sum for cutting a few wires?

MANN: Well . . . perhaps . . . yes. . . .

QUESTION: All right. We've got as much time as you have. We'll try again. What else were you asked to do on this hypothetical assignment?

MANN: Well, you understand it was very indefinite. No arrangement was made.

QUESTION: Yes, yes, we understand that. What else did Anderson want you to do?

MANN: Well, there were, perhaps, some doors that would require unlocking. Also, perhaps, an upright safe and perhaps a wall safe. He wanted a technically trained man who understood those things.

QUESTION: Of course, Mr. Mann. And you understood those things?

MANN: But naturally! I am a graduate of the Stuttgarter Technische Hochschule, and served as assistant professor in mechanical and electrical engineering at the Zurich Académie du Mécanique. I assure you, I am quite competent in my fields.

QUESTION: We are quite aware of that, sir. Now let's see if we've got all this straight. On July twenty-six, at about one P.M., John Anderson came to your shop at one-nine-seven-five Avenue D, New York City, and asked if you would be available for a job that might or might not materialize. This job would consist, on your part, of cutting telephone and alarm systems in a certain apartment house— location unspecified—of cutting the power supply to the self-service elevator in that house, of forcing open doors or picking the locks of doors in that house, and of opening safes of various types in the apartments of that house. Is that correct?

MANN: Well, I. . . .

QUESTION: Is that correct?

MANN: Please, may I have a glass of water?

QUESTION: Certainly. Help yourself.

MANN: Thank you. My throat is quite dry. I smoke so much. You have a cigarette perhaps?

QUESTION: Here.

MANN: Thank you again.

QUESTION: The statement I just repeated to you—is that correct?

MANN: Yes. That is correct. That is what John Anderson wanted me to do.

QUESTION: And for this you requested five thousand dollars?

MANN: Yes.

QUESTION: What was Anderson's reaction?

MANN: He said he could not pay that much, that his operating budget would not allow it. But he said, if the campaign was finalized, he was sure that he and I could get together in a mutually profitable agreement.

QUESTION: You used the term "if the campaign was finalized." Let me get this straight. Your impression is that on this date, the twenty-sixth of July, it had not yet been decided whether or not this job was actually on?

MANN: Yes, that was and is my impression.

QUESTION: Thank you. I think that's enough for today, Mr. Mann. I appreciate your cooperation.

MANN: I appreciate your kindness, sir.

QUESTION: We have much more to discuss about this affair. I'll be seeing you again, Mr. Mann.

MANN: I am at your service, sir.

QUESTION: Fine. Guard!

43

•

XEROX COPY OF A LETTER DATED 29 JULY, 1968, FROM THE PUBLIC Information Officer, Department of Research & Development, National Office of Space Studies, Washington, D.C. 20036, addressed to Mr. Gerald Bingham, Jr., Apartment 5A, 535 East Seventy-third Street, New York, New York.

DEAR SIR:

Re your letter of 16, May 1968, I have been instructed by the Director of the Department of Research & Development, National Office of Space Studies, to thank you for your interest in our activities, and for your suggestion of the use of solidified carbon dioxide ("dry ice") as an ablative material on the nose cones of rockets, space probes, and manned space vehicles during reentry into the Earth's atmosphere.

As you doubtlessly know, Mr. Bingham, a great deal of expensive research has been conducted in this area, and a wide variety of materials has been tested, ranging from metals and metal alloys to ceramics and ceramic-metal alloys. The material currently in use has been tested successfully in our Mercury, Gemini and Apollo programs.

I have been instructed to inform you that "dry ice" could not withstand the extremely high temperatures encountered during the reentry of heavy rockets and manned space vehicles.

However, your letter revealed a very high level of sophisticated scientific expertise, and the fact that you are, as you say, fifteen years old, is of great interest to us. As you probably know, the National Office of Space Studies has a number of college and university scholarship awards at its disposal. Within the next six months, a representative of our Scholarship Award Department will call upon you personally to determine your interest in this area.

Meanwhile, we wish to thank you again for your interest in our activities and your country's space program.

Cordially,
[signed]CYRUS ABERNATHY,
PIO, R&D

44

•

THE FOLLOWING TAPE RECORDING WAS MADE ON 13 AUGUST, 1968, beginning at 8:42 P.M. The participants, Patrick Angelo and John Anderson, have been identified by voice prints. The meeting was held in the upstairs study of Angelo's home at 10543 Foxberry Lane, a few miles north of Teaneck, New Jersey.

These premises were under electronic surveillance by the Federal Trade Commission, and had been for several months, in a continuing investigation of the interlocking business holdings of Patrick Angelo. The investigation concerned possible violations of the Sherman Anti-Trust Act.

There were several time gaps during the course of this recording, which technicians were unable to explain. The tape recording mechanism checked out; the experts were inclined to believe the fault lay with the SC-7, Mk. II M-T, a relatively new device that may possibly have been affected by atmospheric conditions. It had rained heavily prior to the meeting recorded below, and during the meeting the skies were overcast and humidity was very high.

This is recording FTC-KLL-13AUG68-1701.

ANGELO: . . . like cognac?

ANDERSON: Yes. That's all I drink—brandy.

ANGELO: Then you're going to like this. It's a small importer, maybe a thousand cases a year. I must buy two hundred of them. I drink a lot of the stuff and I give it for gifts. A guy in Teaneck orders it for me. Close to twenty a bottle. There you are. Want a wash?

ANDERSON: No. This is fine.

    [Lapse of four seconds.]

ANDERSON: Jesus, that's good. I don't know whether to drink it or breathe it. That's really good.

ANGELO: Glad you like it. And no head in the morning. I keep Papa supplied. He drinks maybe a bottle a month. A thimbleful before he goes to sleep.

ANDERSON: Better than pills.

ANGELO: That's for sure. You met Parelli?

ANDERSON: Yes.

ANGELO: What do you think of him?

ANDERSON: I hardly talked to him. I hardly *saw* him. We were in the steam room of that health club the Doc's got on West Forty-eighth Street.

ANGELO: I know, I know. What do you think of him?

ANDERSON: Heavy muscle. A mutt.

ANGELO: A mutt? Yeah, he's that all right. Not too much brains.

ANDERSON: I figured that.

ANGELO: Look, Duke, you're doing us a favor. So I'll do you one. The guy's crazy. Know what I mean? He likes to blast, to hurt people. He packs one of these big army automatics. What does it weigh— about ten pounds?

ANDERSON: Not that much. But it's heavy.

ANGELO: Yes, and big and mean. He loves it. You've met guys like that before. It's their cock.

ANDERSON: Yes.

ANGELO: Well, don't turn your back on him . . . you know?

ANDERSON: I know. Thanks.

ANGELO: All right . . . now what have you got for me?

ANDERSON: I got this report here. Handwritten. Just this one copy. It's how we should do it. I'm not saying it's final, but we got to start someplace. This includes what I learned since I saw you last. I've had my guys working. I know there will be changes—you'll probably want to change things—and we'll be changing things right up to the last minute . . . you know, little adjustments like. But I think the main plan is strong.

ANGELO: Did the Doctor get those police schedules to you?

ANDERSON: Yes, he did. Thanks. I had the Brodsky boys checking out the beat fuzz on my own. Everything cleared. It's all worked into this report. You want to read it now, or you want me to leave it and come back in a day or so?

ANGELO: I'll read it now. Time's getting short. We got less than three weeks.

ANDERSON: Yes.

ANGELO: Help yourself to the cognac while I read this thing. You write a nice, clear, plain hand.

ANDERSON: Thanks. Maybe my spelling ain't so great. . . .

ANGELO: It's all right. No problem. . . .

[Lapse of seven minutes twenty-three seconds, followed by sound of door opening.]

MRS. ANGELO: Pat? Oh, I'm sorry; you're busy.

ANGELO: That's all right, Maria . . . Come in, come in. Darling, this is John Anderson, a business associate. Duke, this is my wife.

MRS. ANGELO: How do you do, Mr. Anderson.

ANDERSON: Pleased to make your acquaintance, ma'am.

MRS. ANGELO: Is my husband taking care of you? I see you have a little drink. Would you like something to eat? Are you hungry? We have some cold chicken. Perhaps a sandwich?

ANDERSON: Oh, no thank you, ma'am. I'm fine.

MRS. ANGELO: Some short cookies. We have some delicious butter cookies.

ANDERSON: Ma'am, thank you kindly, I do appreciate it, but I'll just stick with this drink.

MRS. ANGELO: Pat, Stella is in bed. You want to say good night?

ANGELO: Of course. Duke, excuse me a moment, please.

ANDERSON: Sure, Mr. Angelo.

ANGELO: And when I come back, I'm bringing some of those butter cookies. My wife makes them herself. You couldn't buy them.

[Lapse of four minutes thirteen seconds.]

ANGELO: Here . . . help yourself. They're delicious. Look at the gut I got, you'll realize how many I eat.

ANDERSON: Thanks.

ANGELO: Now let's see . . . where was I. . . . Yeah, here we are. Duke, you got nice manners. I appreciate that. Now let's see. . . .

[Lapse of six minutes eighteen seconds.]

ANGELO: Duke, I got to hand it to you. Generally, I think . . . my God, no more cognac? Well, let's get rid of this dead soldier. Then we'll go over your operational plan step by step and. . . .

[Lapse of eighteen minutes nine seconds.]

ANGELO: . . . we are. Just take a sniff of that bottle.

ANDERSON: Great.

ANGELO: You're ready for another? I can see you are. So all we got is a lot of little disagreements and small details that really don't amount to much. Am I right?

ANDERSON: As long as you okay the main plan.

ANGELO: Sure. It's strong. Like I said, we can help you out with the truck. That's no problem. About the diversions—you may be right. They got these tactical squads of buttons these days—they load them into buses and before you know it, *bam!* Maybe we'd be asking for trouble. Let me talk to Papa about it.

ANDERSON: But otherwise it sounds good?

ANGELO: Yes, it sounds good. I like the idea of half the people being away on that weekend. How many on your staff?

ANDERSON: Five. With me, six. With Parelli, seven.

ANGELO: My God, you'll have them outnumbered!

ANDERSON: Just about.

ANGELO: Well, go ahead. Contact Fred Simons tomorrow and arrange to get the first half of the emolument for your personnel.

ANDERSON: Emolument?

ANGELO: It means fees or salary.

ANDERSON: Oh . . . yeah.

ANGELO: So now you can have your first real recruiting meeting. Right? You can bring them all together and get down to business. Right? This has got to include Parelli. You know how to get in touch with him?

ANDERSON: Through Simons or the Doctor. Not directly.

ANGELO: That's right. Fred will keep you in touch with him. I would also like to talk to you about once a week, at least, until D-Day. Out here. Is that a problem?

ANDERSON: I rented a car. I shouldn't be leaving the state, but I don't figure the risk is too much.

ANGELO: I agree. All right. You get the money from Simons. At the same time you contact Parelli through him and set up a meet with your other people. I'll start working on the truck. I'll talk to Papa about the diversions. You get that map to me—the one the Brodsky boys made. Come on . . . let's get rolling on this thing!

ANDERSON: Yes. We're coming down to the line. . . .

ANGELO: Jesus Christ, I'm really getting excited! Duke, I think you can pull it off.

ANDERSON: Mr. Angelo, I've been living with this thing for four months now, and I just can't see what could go wrong.

45

•

TAPE SEC-16AUG68-IM-11:43AM-198C. NEW YORK CITY. THIS is a telephone interception.

ANDERSON: Hello? Ingrid?

INGRID: Yes. Duke? Is that you?

ANDERSON: Can I talk?

INGRID: Of course.

ANDERSON: I got your card.

INGRID: It was a silly idea. A little-girl idea. You will laugh at me.

ANDERSON: What is it?

INGRID: Tomorrow, Saturday, do you work?

ANDERSON: Yes.

INGRID: You must be there by four o'clock, you said?

ANDERSON: About.

INGRID: I would like . . . what I would like. . . . You will laugh at me, Duke.

ANDERSON: For Jesus' sake, will you tell me what it is?

INGRID: I would like us to go on a picnic.

ANDERSON: A *picnic?*

INGRID: Yes. Tomorrow. In Central Park. If the weather is nice. The radio states the weather will be nice. I will bring some cold fried chicken, potato salad, tomatoes, peaches, grapes—things like that. You will bring a bottle of wine for me and perhaps a bottle of brandy for yourself, if you so desire. Duke? What do you think?

[Lapse of five seconds.]

INGRID: Duke?

ANDERSON: That's fine. A good idea. Let's do it. I'll bring the stuff to drink. When should I pick you up—about eleven?

INGRID: Excellent. Yes, about eleven. Then we can stay in the park and have our lunch until you must leave. You know a good place?

ANDERSON: Yes. There's a little spit of land that sticks out into the lake at Seventy-second Street. Not too crowded but easy to get to. It's really a turn-around for cars, but the grass slopes down to the lake. It's nice.

INGRID: Good. Duke, if you bring a bottle of wine for me, I would like something chilled.

ANDERSON: All right.

INGRID: And please, do not forget the corkscrew.

ANDERSON: And please, do not forget the salt.

INGRID [laughing]: Duke, it will be fun for us. I have not been on a picnic in many years.

ANDERSON: Yes. I'll see you tomorrow at eleven.

46

•

ACTING ON INTERNAL EVIDENCE CONTAINED IN THE PRECEDING recording, the SEC requested the cooperation of the New York Parks, Recreation and Cultural Affairs Administration. With the help of this agency, a Borkgunst Telemike Mk. IV (a telescopic microphone) was concealed in wooded high ground overlooking the site of the proposed picnic of John Anderson and Ingrid Macht on 17 August, 1968.

The following recording is SEC-17AUG68-#146-37A. It has been heavily edited to eliminate extraneous material and evidence currently under adjudication.

SEGMENT I. 17AUG-11:37AM.

ANDERSON: This was a great idea. Beautiful day. Clear for a change. Not too hot. Look at that sky! Looks like someone washed it and hung it out to dry.

INGRID: I remember a day like this. I was just a little girl. Eight, perhaps, or nine. An uncle took me on a picnic. My father was dead. My mother was working. So this uncle offered to take me to the country for the day. A Saturday, just like this. Sunshine. Blue sky. Cool breeze. Sweet smells. He gave me some schnapps, and then he pulled my pants down.

ANDERSON: Some uncle.

INGRID: He was all right. A widower. In his late forties. Perhaps fifty. He had a great Kaiser Wilhelm mustache. I remember it tickled.

ANDERSON: Did you like it?

INGRID: It meant nothing to me. Nothing.

ANDERSON: Did he give you something, a gift, so you wouldn't talk?

INGRID: Money. He gave me money.

ANDERSON: Was that his idea or yours?

INGRID: That was my idea. My mother and I, we were always hungry.

ANDERSON: Smart kid.

INGRID: Yes. I was a smart kid.

ANDERSON: How long did that go on?

INGRID: A few years. I took him for much.

ANDERSON: Sure. Did your mother know?

INGRID: Perhaps. Perhaps not. I think she did.

ANDERSON: What happened?

INGRID: To my uncle?

ANDERSON: Yes.

INGRID: A horse kicked him and he died.

ANDERSON: That's funny.

INGRID: Yes. But it made no difference. I was then ten, perhaps eleven. I knew then how it was done. There were others. *Schatzie,* the wine! It will be getting warm.

SEGMENT II. 17AUG-12:02PM.

ANDERSON: What then?

INGRID: You will not believe.

ANDERSON: I'll believe it.

INGRID: For an example, there was this man in Bavaria. Very rich. Very important. If I said his name, you would recognize it. Once a month, on a Friday night, his butler would assemble perhaps six, perhaps ten young girls. I was just thirteen. We would be naked. The butler would put feathers in our hair and tie belts of feathers about our waists and make us wear bracelets of feathers around our wrists and ankles. Then this man, this very important man, would sit on a chair, quite naked, and he would play with himself. You understand? And we would dance around him in a circle. We would flap our arms and caw and make bird sounds. Like chickens. You understand? And this funny butler with gray whiskers would clap his hands to mark time and chant, "One and two, and one and two," and we would dance around and caw, and this old man would look at us and our feathers and play with himself.

ANDERSON: Did he ever touch you?

INGRID: Never. When he was finished with himself, he rose and stalked out. We would remove our feathers, and we would dress. The butler stood by the door and paid us our money as we walked out. Very good money. The next month we'd be back again. Perhaps the same girls, perhaps a few new ones. Same thing.

ANDERSON: How do you figure his hang-up?

INGRID: I don't. I gave up trying many years ago. People are what they are. This I can accept. But I cannot accept what they pretend to be. This man who fondled himself while I pranced about him clad in chicken feathers, this man attended church every Sunday, contributed to charities, and was—still is—considered one of the leading citizens of his city and his country. His son is also now very important. At first it all sickened me.

ANDERSON: The chicken feathers?

INGRID: The filth! The filth! Then I learned how the world is run. Who has the power. What money can do. So I declared war on the world. My own personal war.

ANDERSON: Have you won?

INGRID: I am winning, *Schatzie.*

SEGMENT III. 17AUG-12:41PM.

ANDERSON: It could have been different.

INGRID: Perhaps. But we are mostly what has happened to us, what the world has done to us. We cannot always make the choice. By the time I was fifteen I was an accomplished whore. I had stolen, blackmailed, had been terribly beaten several times, and I had marked a pimp. Still, I was a child. I had no education. I tried only to survive, to have food, a place to sleep. At that time I wanted very little. Perhaps that is why we are so *simpatico.* You were poor also . . . *nein?*

ANDERSON: Yes. My family was white niggers.

INGRID: Understand, *Schatzie,* I make no excuses. I did what I had to do.

ANDERSON: Sure. But after you got older . . . ?

INGRID: I learned very quickly. As I told you, I learned where the money was and where the power was. Then there was nothing I would not do. It was war—total war. I hit back. Then I hit first. That is very important. The only crime in this world is to be poor. That is the only crime. If you are not poor, you can do anything.

SEGMENT IV. 17AUG-12:08PM.

ANDERSON: Sometimes you scare me.

INGRID: Why is that, *Schatzie?* I mean no bad to you.

ANDERSON: I know, I know. But you never get out. You live with it every minute.

INGRID: I have tried everything—alcohol, drugs, sex. Nothing works for me. I must live with it every minute—so I do. Now I live quietly. I have a warm home. Food. I have money invested. Safe money. Men pay me. You know that?

ANDERSON: Yes.

INGRID: I have stopped wanting. It is very important to know when to stop wanting.

ANDERSON: Don't you ever want to get out?

INGRID: It would be nice—but if I cannot, I cannot.

    [Lapse of seven seconds.]

ANDERSON: You're some woman.

INGRID: It is my occupation, *Schatzie*. It is not my sex.

SEGMENT V. 17AUG-2:14PM.

INGRID: It has been a beautiful afternoon. Are you drunk?

ANDERSON: A little.

INGRID: We must go soon. You must go to work.

ANDERSON: Yes.

INGRID: Are you sleeping?

ANDERSON: Some. . . .

INGRID: Shall I talk to you . . . the way you like?

ANDERSON: Yes. Do *you* like it?

INGRID: Of course.

SEGMENT VI. 17AUG-3:03PM.

INGRID: Please, *Schatzie,* we must go. You will be late.

ANDERSON: Sure. All right. I'll clean up. You finish the wine; I'll finish the brandy.

INGRID: Very well.

ANDERSON: I would like to tell you what I am doing.

INGRID: Please . . . no.

ANDERSON: You're the smartest woman I ever knew. I'd like to get your opinion, what you think of it.

INGRID: No . . . nothing. Tell me nothing. I do not wish to know.

ANDERSON: It's big.

INGRID: It is always big. It will do no good to tell you to be careful, I know. Just do what you must do.

ANDERSON: I can't pull out now.

INGRID: I understand.

ANDERSON: Will you kiss me?

INGRID: Now? Yes. On the lips?

47

•

TAPE BN–DT–TH–0018–98G; 19 AUGUST, 1968; 11:46 A.M.

HASKINS: Was that what you wanted?

ANDERSON: Fine. It was fine, Tommy. More than I expected.

HASKINS: Good. Someday I'll tell you how I got those floor plans. It was a gas!

ANDERSON: You want in?

HASKINS: In? On the whole hype?

ANDERSON: Yes.

    [Lapse of five seconds.]

HASKINS: How much?

ANDERSON: A fee. Two big ones.

HASKINS: Two? That's a bit skimpy, isn't it, darling?

ANDERSON: It's what I can go. I got six guys to think about.

HASKINS: Are you including Snapper?

ANDERSON: No.

HASKINS: I don't know . . . I don't know. . . .

ANDERSON: Make up your mind.

HASKINS: Are you anticipating . . . well, you know . . . violence?

ANDERSON: No. More than half will be out of the house.

HASKINS: You don't want me to carry . . . ?

ANDERSON: No. Just to spot for me. Finger what to take and what to leave. The paintings, the rugs, the silver—shit like that.

    [Lapse of four seconds.]

HASKINS: When would I be paid?

ANDERSON: Half before, half after.

HASKINS: I've never done anything like this before.

ANDERSON: A piece of cheese. Nothing to worry about. We'll take our time. The whole fucking place will be ours. Two, three hours . . . whatever it takes.

HASKINS: Will we wear masks?

ANDERSON: Are you in?

HASKINS: Yes.

ANDERSON: All right. I'll let you know later this week when we all get together. It's going to be all right, Tommy.

HASKINS: Oh, God. Oh, Jesus.

48

•

21 AUGUST, 1968; 12:15 P.M. TAPE NYSNB-49B-767 (CONTINU-ing).

ANDERSON: You want in?

JOHNSON: Who do I bash and what's the cash?

ANDERSON: Two big ones, half in advance.

JOHNSON: Gimme your han' 'cause you're my man.

ANDERSON: I'll be in touch to tell you where and when. Keep clean for the next two weeks. Can you do that?

JOHNSON: You gotta know. Like the driven snow.

ANDERSON: Don't fuck me up, Skeets. Or I'll have to come looking for you. You know?

JOHNSON: Aw, now, Massa Anderson, you wouldn't be trying to skeer this pore, ignorant ole nigguh, would you now?

49

•

TRANSCRIPTION NYPD-JDA-154-11; 22 AUGUST, 1968; 1:36 P.M. A telephone interception.

ANDERSON: Ed?

BRODSKY: Duke?

ANDERSON: Yes.

BRODSKY: Was everything all right? Was that what you wanted?

ANDERSON: Fine, Ed. Just right. The map was great.

BRODSKY: Jesus, that's good to hear. I mean we worked, Duke. We really sweat.

ANDERSON: I know you did, Ed. I liked it. The man liked it. Everything is set. You want in?

BRODSKY: Me? Or me and Billy?

ANDERSON: Both of you. Two G's. No shares. Just a fee. Half in advance.

BRODSKY: Yes. Christ, yes! I need it, Duke. You got no idea how I need it. The sharks are at me.

ANDERSON: I'll be in touch.

BRODSKY: Thank you very much, Duke.

50

•

ANDERSON'S APARTMENT; AN INTERIOR CONVERSATION. TRAN-
scription NYPD-JDA-155-23; 23 August, 1968. Participants John Anderson
and Vincent "Socks" Parelli have been identified by voice prints.

PARELLI: Jesus Christ, a guy could get a heart attack climbing those fucking stairs. You really live in this shit-house?

ANDERSON: That's right.

PARELLI: And you got to make a meet here? It couldn't be a nice restaurant in Times Square? A hotel room maybe?

ANDERSON: This place is clean.

PARELLI: How do you know? How does anyone know? Maybe one of your rats is wired. Maybe your cockroaches been trained. Hey! How about that! Trained bugs! Not bad, huh?

ANDERSON: Not bad.

PARELLI: What I'm saying is, why have me drag my ass all the way over here? What's so important?

ANDERSON: This is the way I wanted it.

PARELLI: All right, all right. So you're the boss. Big deal. We agreed. I take orders. Okay, boss, what's the setup?

[Lapse of six seconds.]

ANDERSON: We have our first meet tomorrow night, eight thirty. Here's the address. Don't lose it.

PARELLI: Tomorrow? Eight thirty? For Christ's sake, tomorrow's Saturday. Who the hell works on Saturday?

ANDERSON: We meet tomorrow, like I said.

PARELLI: Not me, buster. I can't make it. I'm getting a blow job at eight. Include me out.

ANDERSON: You want out of the whole thing?

PARELLI: No, I don't want out of the whole thing. But I. . . .

ANDERSON: I'll tell Mr. Angelo you can't make the meet tomorrow because some quiff is going to give you head. Okay?

PARELLI: You suck, you bastard. When this is all over, you and me, we'll have our own meet. Somewhere. Someday.

ANDERSON: Sure. But you be at that meet tomorrow.

PARELLI: All right, all right . . . I'll be there.

ANDERSON: I got five guys, plus you and me. There's a smart fag who can finger the good stuff. He knows paintings and jewelry and silver. His name's Haskins. I got a tech named Ernest Mann. He'll cut off the telephones and alarms, open the doors and boxes—whatever we need. Then there's a spade named Johnson, a muscle, but smart. He's no hooligan. Then there's two brothers—Ed and Billy Brodsky. Ed is an all-around man, a good driver. His young brother Billy, he's a wet-brain but he's a powerhouse. We need a guy for lifting and carrying. Billy will do what he's told.

PARELLI: Any of them panic guys?

ANDERSON: Tommy Haskins maybe. The others are solid—real pros.

PARELLI: I'll keep my eye on Haskins.

ANDERSON: You do that. Socks, I don't want no blasting. There's no need. Half the families will be gone. No one left but old women and kids. We got a plan that's been figured four ways from the middle. You'll hear it tomorrow. Everything will go like silk.

PARELLI: I carry a stick. That's definite.

ANDERSON: All right, you carry a stick. Just don't use it—that's all I'm saying.

PARELLI: I hear you work clean.

ANDERSON: That's right.

PARELLI: I still carry.

ANDERSON: I told you, that's up to you—but you'll have no call to use it. You won't need it.

PARELLI: We'll see.

ANDERSON: Another thing—I don't want these people slammed around. You understand?

PARELLI: Oh, I'll be very polite, boss.

[Lapse of five seconds.]

ANDERSON: And I don't like you, prick-nose. But I'm stuck with you. I needed another body and they gave me a sack of shit like you.

PARELLI: You fuck! You fuck! I could burn you! I should burn you right now!

ANDERSON: Go ahead, prick-nose. You're the guy who carries a stick. I got nothing. Go ahead, burn me.

PARELLI: Oh, you lousy fuck! You piece of funk! I swear to Christ, when this is over I'll get you good. But good! Nice and slow. That's what you'll get, cracker. Something nice and slow, right through the balls. Oh, are you going to get it! I can taste it. I can taste it!

ANDERSON: Sure, you can taste it. You got a big, fucking mouth— and that's all you've got. Just you be at that meet tomorrow, and at the other meets until next Saturday.

PARELLI: And after that, white trash, it'll be you and me . . . just you and me.

ANDERSON: That's right, prick-nose. How many women you screwed with that snout? Now get your ass out of here. Be careful getting a cab. We got some punks in this neighborhood—oh, maybe ten years old or so—who might take your piece away from you.

PARELLI: You mother. . . .

51

•

THE DRIVEWAY OUTSIDE PATRICK ANGELO'S HOME, 10543 Fox-berry Lane, Teaneck, New Jersey; 25 August, 1968; 8:36 P.M. On this date, Angelo's "personal" car (he owned three) was under electronic surveillance by an investigative agency of the U.S. government, which cannot be named at this time, using a device which cannot be revealed. The car was a black Continental, license LPA-46B-8935K. Patrick Angelo and John Anderson sat in the backseat of the parked car.

ANGELO: Sorry I can't ask you into the house, Duke. The wife's got some neighbors in tonight for bridge. I figured we could talk better out here.

ANDERSON: Sure, Mr. Angelo. This is okay.

ANGELO: But I brought out some of this cognac you like and a couple of glasses. We might as well be comfortable. Here you are. . . .

ANDERSON: Thanks.

ANGELO: Success.

ANDERSON: Luck.

[Lapse of four seconds.]

ANGELO: Beautiful. Jesus, that's like music on the tongue. Duke, I heard you leaned on our boy the other day.

ANDERSON: Parelli? Yes, I leaned on him. He tell you?

ANGELO: He told D'Medico. The Doc told me. What are you doing—setting him up?

ANDERSON: Something like that.

ANGELO: You figured he's got a short fuse as it is—and not too much brains—so you'll psych him. Now he's so sore at you he's not even using the little brains he's got. So you're that much more on top of him.

ANDERSON: I guess that's it.

[Lapse of seven seconds.]

ANGELO: Or was it you wanted to hate his guts so it would be easier to spoil him?

ANDERSON: What difference does it make?

ANGELO: None, Duke. None at all. I'm just running off at the mouth. You had your first meet yesterday?

ANDERSON: That's right.

ANGELO: How did it go?

ANDERSON: It went fine.

ANGELO: Any weak spots?

ANDERSON: The faggot, Tommy Haskins, has never done a hard job before. He's been on the con or hustling his ass or pulling paper hypes. But his job is easy. I'll keep an eye on him. Johnson—he's the dinge—and the two Brodsky boys are true blue. Hard. The tech, Ernest Mann, is so money hungry he'll do what I tell him. If he's caught, he'll spill, of course. All they'll have to do is threaten to take his cigarettes away.

ANGELO: But he's not going to be caught . . . is he?

ANDERSON: No. Parelli is stupid and vicious and kill-crazy. A bad combination.

ANGELO: You'll have to play that guy by ear. I told you . . . don't turn your back.

ANDERSON: I don't figure to. I gave my boys their advances.

ANGELO: Do they know what everyone is getting?

ANDERSON: No. I gave them sealed envelopes separately. I told each guy he was getting more than the others and to keep his mouth shut.

ANGELO: Good.

ANDERSON: Did you ask about the diversions?

ANGELO: Papa says forget it. Keep it as simple as possible. He says it's tricky enough as it is.

ANDERSON: He's right. I'm glad about that. Can you tell me about the truck now?

ANGELO: Not now. When we meet on Thursday.

ANDERSON: All right. The Brodsky boys will pick it up wherever you say. It'll be in New York, won't it?

ANGELO: Yes. In Manhattan.

ANDERSON: Fine. Then we can figure out our final timing. What about the drop?

ANGELO: I'll give you that on Thursday, too. How many men will make the drop?

ANDERSON: I was figuring on me and the Brodsky boys.

ANGELO: All right. Now let's see . . . what else did I want to ask. . . . Oh, yes . . . do you need a piece?

ANDERSON: I can get one. I don't know how good it will be.

ANGELO: Let me get you a good one. Right off the docks. When your boys pick up the truck, it'll be in the glove compartment or taped under the dash. Loaded. How does that sound?

ANDERSON: That sounds all right.

ANGELO: A .38 okay?

ANDERSON: Yes.

ANGELO: I'll see it's taken care of. Now let's see . . . oh, yes, the masks. You got all that fixed? Gloves . . . shit like that?

ANDERSON: It's all arranged, Mr. Angelo.

ANGELO: Good. Well, I can't think of anything else. I'll see you on Thursday, then. Your second meet is on Wednesday and your last on Friday?

ANDERSON: Yes.

ANGELO: How do you feel?

ANDERSON: I feel great. I'm hot with this thing but I got no doubts.

ANGELO: Duke . . . remember one thing. This is like war. Your reconnaissance and intelligence and operations plan can be the best in the world. But things go wrong. Unexpected things come up. Somebody screams. A rabbit becomes a lion. The fuzz drops by unexpected because one of them has to take a pee. Sometimes crazy things happen—things you never counted on. You know?

ANDERSON: Yes.

ANGELO: So you've got to stay loose in there. You got a good plan, but be ready to improvise, to deal with these unexpected things as they come up. Don't get spooked when something happens you didn't figure on.

ANDERSON: I won't get spooked.

ANGELO: I know you won't. You're a pro, Duke. That's why we're going along with you on this. We trust you.

ANDERSON: Thanks.

52

•

DICTATED, SIGNED, SWORN, AND WITNESSED STATEMENT BY TIM-othy O'Leary, 648 Halverston Drive, Roslyn, New York. This is transcription NYPD-SIS-#146-11, dated 7 September, 1968.

"On the night of thirty-one August of this year—that is, the night it was between the last day of August and the first of September, with Labor Day to come, it was that weekend—I come on duty at 535 East Seventy-third Street where I am doorman from midnight until eight in the morning.

"Being my usual custom, I arrived on the premises about ten minutes early, stopped to exchange the time of night with Ed Bakely, the lad I was relieving, and then I went down into the basement. There we have three lockers in the hallway that leads from the super's apartment to the back basement rooms where are the boilers and such. I changed to my uniform which, in the summer, is merely a tan cotton jacket, and as I was wearing black pants, white shirt, and a black bow tie, the time was nothing.

"I come back upstairs and Ed goes down, to change back. Whilst he was gone, I took a look at the board where it is we keep messages and such. I saw that Dr. Rubicoff, he's One B, was in his office and working late. And also there would be two friends of Eric Sabine, he's Two A, staying in his apartment for the Labor Day weekend. Ed, then, came up—he was carrying his bowling ball in a little bag—and said he was off to his alley, and would be able to get in a few games with his mates before the alleys closed.

"No sooner was he gone, with me out on the street taking a breath of air, when a truck come slowly down the street—yes, from East End Avenue since that is how the street runs. Much to my surprise it made a slow turn and pulled into our service entrance, going all the way to the back where it stopped, and turned off motor and lights. As it went past me I saw it was a moving van of some kind—I remember seeing the word 'moving' painted on the side and surmised it either had the wrong address or perhaps some of my tenants was moving or was expecting a furniture delivery of some kind which struck me as strange considering the time of night it was and also, you understand, we would have it on the board if some tenant was expecting a night delivery.

"So I strolled back to where the truck was now parked and dark, and I says, 'And what the hell do you think you are doing in my driveway?'

"No sooner was these words out of my mouth when I felt something on the back of my neck. Cool it was, metal and round. It could have been a piece of pipe, I suppose, but I surmised it was a gun. I was twenty years on the Force, and I am no stranger to guns.

"At the same time I felt the muzzle on my neck—a crawly feeling it was— the man holding the gun says, very cool, 'Do you want to die?'

" 'No,' I tells him, 'I do not want to die.' I was calm, you understand, but I was honest.

" 'Then you will do just what I tell you,' he says, 'and you will not die.'

"With that he walks me back to the service door, kind of prodding me with the muzzle of the gun, if that's what it was, and I think it was, but not hurting me, you understand. All this time the truck was dark and quiet and I saw no other men. In fact, up to this time I had actually seen no one. Just felt the gun and heard the voice.

"He had me stand pressed faceup against the wall by the service door, the muzzle of the gun still in the middle of my neck. 'Not a sound from you,' he says.

" 'Not a sound you'll get,' I whispers to him.

" 'All right,' he calls, and I hear the doors of the truck opening. Two doors open. In a minute I hear a rattle of chain and the sound of a tailgate flopping down. I saw nothing, nothing at all. I stared at the wall and said 'Hail, Marys.' I had the feeling others were standing about, but I turned my head neither to the right nor to the left. I heard footsteps walking away. All was quiet. No one spoke. In a moment I heard the buzzer and knew that someone inside the lobby was pressing the button that released the lock on the service door.

"I was prodded forward into the service entrance, the gun still at my neck, and told to lay on the concrete floor, which I did although I was sorry for soiling my uniform jacket and my trousers which my wife Grace had pressed that very afternoon. I was told to cross my ankles and cross my wrists behind me. I did all this, just as I was told, but at this time I switched to 'Our Father, Who art in Heavens. . . .'

"They used what I guess was a wide strip of adhesive tape. I could hear that sound of sticking as it came off the reel. They taped my ankles and my wrists, and then a strip was put across my mouth.

"At this time, the man—I think he was the man with the gun—he says to me, 'Can you breathe okay? If you can breathe okay, nod your head.'

"So I nodded my head and blessed him for his consideration.''

53

•

THE FOLLOWING IS FROM A DICTATED, SWORN, SIGNED, AND WIT-
nessed statement by Ernest Heinrich Mann. This is Segment NYDA-EHM-
105A.

MANN: So . . . now we are at the night of August thirty-first and the
   morning hours of September first. The truck picked me up at the
   appointed place and I. . . .

QUESTION: Pardon me a moment. I believe you told us previously that
   the truck was to pick you up on the southeast corner of Lexington
   Avenue and Sixty-fifth Street. Is that correct?

MANN: Yes. Correct.

QUESTION: And that was, in fact, where you joined the others?

MANN: Yes.

QUESTION: What time was this?

MANN: It was eleven forty P.M. This was the time agreed upon. I was
   on time and so also was the truck.

QUESTION: Will you describe this truck for us.

MANN: It was, I would say, a medium-sized moving van. In addition
   to the doors to the cab, there were two large rear doors fastened with
   a chained tailgate, as well as a door in the middle of each side. It was
   by one of these doors that I entered the truck, the men inside assisting
   me to climb up.

QUESTION: How many men were in the truck at this time?

MANN: Everyone was there—everyone I have described to you who
   was at the planning meetings. The man I know as Anderson and the
   two men I know as Ed and Billy were in the cab. Ed was driving.
   The others were in the body of the truck.

QUESTION: What was painted on the side of the truck? Did you notice
   any words or markings?

MANN: I saw only the word "Moving." There were also several markings that appeared to be license numbers and maximum load
   weights—things of that sort.

QUESTION: After you boarded the truck, what happened?

MANN: The truck began to move. I assumed we were heading for the apartment house.

QUESTION: Were you standing inside the truck or were you seated?

MANN: We were seated, but not on the floor. A rough wooden bench had been provided on one side of the truck. We sat on that. Also, there was a light inside the truck body.

QUESTION: What happened then?

MANN: The man I know as John Anderson opened the sliding wooden panel between the cab and the body of the truck. He told us to put on our masks and gloves.

QUESTION: These had been provided for you?

MANN: Yes. There was a set for each of us, plus two extra sets in case of accident . . . in case the stocking masks might perhaps tear while we were putting them on.

QUESTION: And you all put them on?

MANN: Yes.

QUESTION: The men in the cab, too?

MANN: That I do not know. Anderson closed the sliding panel. I could not see what was happening up there.

QUESTION: Then what?

MANN: We drove. Then we stopped. I heard the cab door open and slam. I assumed that was Anderson getting out. As I told you, the plan required him to be waiting across the street from the apartment house when the truck arrived.

QUESTION: And then?

MANN: The truck drove on. We went around a few blocks to give Anderson time to get into position.

QUESTION: What time was this?

MANN: It was perhaps ten minutes after midnight, give or take a minute either way. Everything was precisely timed. It was an admirable plan.

QUESTION: Then what?

MANN: The truck picked up a little speed. We were all quiet. We made a very sharp turn, up a small rise. I knew we were then pulling into the driveway of the apartment house. The truck engine was switched off and the lights also.

QUESTION: Including the light in the body of the truck, where you were?

MANN: Yes. There were no lights whatsoever. In addition, we did not speak. This had been made very clear. We made no noise whatsoever.

QUESTION: Then what happened?

MANN: I heard voices outside the truck, but so low that I could not hear what was being said. Then, in a minute or two, Anderson called, "All right." At this time the side door of the truck was opened, and we all got out. Also Ed and Billy from the cab. I was assisted to descend from the truck by the man I know as Skeets, the Negro. He was very polite and helpful.

QUESTION: Go on.

MANN: The one named Tommy, the slight, boyish one, went immediately around to the front of the building. I watched him. He paused a moment to make certain there was no one on the street, no one observing—he was wearing mask and gloves, you understand—and then he slipped around to the front entrance. In a moment the release button sounded on the outside service door, and the man I know as Socks—the uncouth man I described to you before—entered first, his hand in his jacket pocket. I believe he was carrying a weapon. He went directly down to the basement. I waited until Anderson had bound and gagged the doorman, then I followed Socks down into the basement, as we had planned. Every move had been planned.

QUESTION: What was the purpose of your waiting until the doorman was tied up before following Socks down to the basement?

MANN: I don't know precisely why I was to wait, but this is what I was told to do—so I did it. I think perhaps it was to give Socks time to immobilize the superintendent. Also, it was to give Anderson time to follow me and check on my work. In any event, as I went down into the basement, Anderson was right behind me.

QUESTION: Then what?

MANN: As we entered the basement, Socks came toward us from the superintendent's apartment. He said, "What a pigsty. The slob is out cold. The place smells like a brewery. He won't wake up till Monday." Anderson said, "Good." Then he turned to me. "All right, Professor," he said. So I set to work.

QUESTION: The lights in the basement were on at this time?

MANN: One dim overhead light, yes. But it was insufficient, and flashlights and a flood lantern were used in the area of my work.

QUESTION: You had brought your tools with you.

MANN: That is correct. My own personal hand and power tools. The heavy equipment, as I explained to you—the torches and the gas cylinders—had been provided and were still inside the body of the truck. So . . . I set to work on the schedule we had planned. Anderson and Socks held the lights. First of all, I cut all telephonic communication, isolating the entire building. I then bridged the alarms in a manner which I have described to your technician, Mr. Browder. This was in case the alarm would sound if the current was interrupted. I then cut the power to the self-service elevator. This was simply a matter of throwing a switch. Finally, I cut the alarm to the cold box and picked the lock. I opened the door. At this time the men I know as Ed and Billy had joined us. Anderson motioned at the furs hanging inside the cold box and said to Ed and Billy, "Start loading. Every-thing. Clean it out. And don't forget the super's apartment." I then went back to the service entrance on the ground level and picked the lock of the door connecting the service entrance with the lobby. The Negro, Skeets, and Anderson went into the lobby. Myself and Tommy, we waited. We watched Ed and Billy carry up armloads of fur coats and put them in the truck.

54

•

DICTATED, SIGNED, SWORN, AND WITNESSED STATEMENT BY DR. Dmitri Rubicoff, Suite 1B, 535 East Seventy-third Street, New York City. NYPD-SIS-#146-8, dated 6 September, 1968.

"It had been my intention to spend the entire Labor Day weekend with my wife and my daughter, her husband and child, at our summer home in East Hampton. However, early Friday morning I realized the press of work facing me was so great that I could not afford the luxury of taking four or five days off away from my desk.

"Accordingly, I sent my family on ahead—they took the station wagon, my wife driving—and I told them I would be out late Saturday night or perhaps early Sunday morning. I said I would keep them informed by phone as to my plans.

"My secretary I allowed to leave early on Friday as she was planning a five-day holiday at Nassau. I worked alone in the office all day Saturday, but realized I was too tired to drive out Saturday night in the Corvair. So I determined to work late Saturday night and sleep at home—I live on East Seventy-ninth Street—and then drive out on Sunday morning. I called my wife and informed her of my plans.

"I had a sandwich sent in at noon on Saturday. In the evening I dined at a nearby French restaurant, the Le Claire. I had an excellent poached filet of sole that was, perhaps, a trifle too salty. I returned to my office at about nine in the evening to finish up as much as I could. As usual when I am working alone in the office at night, I locked the door to the lobby and put on the chain. I then turned on my hi-fi. I believe it was something by Von Weber.

"It was perhaps twelve thirty or a little later when the lobby door chimed. I was in the process of straightening my desk and packing a briefcase with professional journals I wished to take to East Hampton with me. I went to the door and opened the peephole. The man standing there was off to one side; all I could see was his shoulder and half of his body.

" 'Yes?' I said.

" 'Doctor Rubicoff,' he said, 'I'm the relief doorman for the Labor Day weekend. I have a special-delivery, registered letter for you.'

"I must admit I reacted foolishly. But in my own defense, I should tell you this: First—I was ready to leave, I was about to unlock the door, and it seemed ridiculous to ask this man to slide the letter under the door. Second— frequently, you understand, on holidays and during vacations, we have relief doormen take the place of our regular employees. So I was not concerned that, on the Labor Day weekend, this was a man whose voice I did not recognize. Third—the fact that he had a special-delivery, registered letter for me—or claimed he had—did not alarm me. You understand, psychiatrists are quite used to receiving letters, telegrams, and phone calls from patients, in unusual forms and at unusual hours.

"I suspected nothing. I slipped the chain and unlocked the door.

"The two men who pushed the door forcibly aside and entered were both wearing head coverings that appeared to be semiopaque women's stockings. The bottom half of the stocking had been cut off. The top half was pulled over the man's head and tied in a knot at the top. Presumably so it could not slip down or be pulled down. One of the men, I should say, was slightly under six feet tall. The other was perhaps three inches taller, and I had the feeling this man was a Negro. It was extremely difficult to judge, as only a vague shape of their features came through their masks, and both men wore white cotton gloves.

" 'Is your secretary here?' the shorter man asked me. This was the first thing he said.

"I am quite used to dealing with disturbed people, and I think I handled the situation quite calmly.

" 'No,' I told him. 'She has left for a five-day vacation. I am alone.'

" 'Good,' the man said. 'Doctor, we don't want to hurt you. Please lay down on the floor, your wrists and ankles crossed behind you.'

"Frankly, I was impressed by his air of quiet authority. I knew at once of course that this was a robbery. I thought perhaps they had come for my drugs. I had been the victim twice before of robberies in which the thieves only wanted my drugs. Incidentally, I keep an extremely small supply of narcotics in my safe. I did as the man requested. My ankles and wrists were taped, and then a strip of wide tape was put across my mouth. Very painful to remove later, I might add, because of my mustache. The man asked me if I could breathe comfortably, and I nodded. I was quite impressed with him—in fact, with the whole operation. It was very professional."

55

•

NYPD-SIS RECORDING #146-83C; INTERROGATION OF THOMAS Haskins; Segment IA, dated 4 September, 1968. The following tape has been heavily edited to avoid repetition of material already presented and to eliminate material currently under adjudication.

QUESTION: Mr. Haskins, my name is Thomas K. Brody, and I am a detective, second grade, in the Police Department of the City of New York. It is my duty. . . .

HASKINS: Thomas! My name is Thomas, too. Isn't that sweet?

QUESTION: It is my duty to make absolutely certain that you are aware of your rights and privileges, under the laws of the United States of America, as a person accused of a crime constituting a felony under the laws of the State of New York. Now, you are. . . .

HASKINS: Oh, I'm aware, Tommy. I'm really aware! I know all that jazz about lawyers and such. You can skip it.

QUESTION: You are not required at this time to answer any questions whatsoever that may be put to you by law enforcement officials. You may request legal counsel of your choice. If you are unable to afford legal counsel, or if you have no personal counsel of your own, the court will suggest such counsel, subject to your approval. In addition, you. . . .

HASKINS: All right already! I'm willing to spiel. I want to talk! I know my rights better than you. Can't we just start talking—just you and me, two Tommies?

QUESTION: Whatever statements you may make at this time, without the presence of counsel, are of your own free will and volition. And anything you say—I repeat, *anything* you say—even that which may seem to you of an innocent nature—may possibly, in the future, be used against you. Do you understand?

HASKINS: Of course I understand.

QUESTION: Is everything clear to you?

HASKINS: Yes, Tommy baby, everything is clear to me.

QUESTION: In addition. . . .

HASKINS: Oh, Jesus Christ!

QUESTION: In addition, I have this printed statement I would like you to sign in the presence of Policewoman Alice H. Hilkins, here as witness, that you fully understand your rights and privileges as an accused person under the laws already cited, and that whatever statements you make are made with full and complete comprehension of those rights and privileges.

HASKINS: Look, Dick Two, I want to talk, I'm willing to talk, I'm eager to talk. So let's. . . .

QUESTION: Will you sign this statement?

HASKINS: Gladly, gladly. Gimme the goddamn thing.

[Lapse of four seconds.]

QUESTION: In addition, I have a second statement that. . . .

HASKINS: Oh, oh, oh. Tommy, I just. . . .

QUESTION: This second printed statement declares that you have not been physically threatened into signing the first statement, that you signed it of your own free will and desire, that no promises have been made to you as to the extent or punishment for the accused crime. In addition, you do say, affirm, and swear that. . . .

HASKINS: Tommy, how the fuck does a guy confess these days?

[Lapse of seven minutes thirteen seconds.]

HASKINS: . . . so that the one thing that really stuck in my mind was something Duke said at our last meeting. He said crime was just war during peacetime. He said the most important thing we could learn from war was that no matter how good a plan was, it was just not humanly possible to plan *everything*. He said things can go wrong or unexpected things happen, and you must be ready to cope with them. He said—this is Duke talking, you understand—he said that he and others—that's what he said, "others"—had made our plan as foolproof as they could, but he knew unexpected things would happen they hadn't counted on. Maybe a squad car would stop by. Maybe a beat fuzz would come into the lobby to rap a little with the doorman. Maybe one of the tenants would pull a gun. He said to expect the unexpected and not get spooked by it. He said the plan was good, but things could happen that hadn't been planned for. . . .

So after we got there, I went around into the lobby and pressed the release button for the outside service door. It was right where Duke had told me it would be. While I was there, I took a look at a clipboard the doormen keep. It tells them what deliveries to expect and what tenants were away for the weekend—things like that. I saw right away that the headshrinker was in his office and working late. Also, there were two guests staying in Two A. Those were two of the unexpected things Duke had warned us about. So the moment he came through the opened door to the service entrance, I told him about them. He patted my arm. That's the first time he ever touched me. . . .

So he and the smoke took care of the doctor, just like that, and we went ahead with the plan. You see, we knew there would be several tenants still in the building who hadn't gone away for the Labor Day weekend. The idea was, instead of tying them all up in their apartments or keeping a watch on them, which we didn't have enough people to do, the idea was to assemble everyone in the building in Apartment Four B where the old widow Mrs. Hathway lived with her housekeeper. These were two really ancient dames, and Duke didn't want to risk taping them up. So it was decided we'd bring everyone in the building to Apartment Four B, scare the hell out of them, and Skeets or Socks would keep an eye on them all together. After all, what could they do? The phones were cut. They didn't know if we had guns or knives or whatever. And we had them all in one place and one guy could keep them quiet while the rest of us cleaned out the whole fucking apartment house.

It was a marvelous plan. . . .

56

•

THE FOLLOWING IS A PORTION OF A LENGTHY LETTER ADDRESSED to the author from Ernest Heinrich Mann, dated 28 March, 1969.

MY DEAR SIR:

I wish to thank you for your kind inquiries as to my physical health and mental stamina, as expressed in your recent missive. I am happy to tell you that, God willing, I am in good health and spirits. The food is plain but plentiful. The exercise—outdoors, that is—is sufficient, and my work in the library I find very rewarding.

You may be interested to learn that I have recently taken up the Yoga regimen, insofar as it relates to physical exercise. The philosophy does not concern me. But the physical program interests me as it requires no equipment, so that I am able to practice it in my cell, at any time. Needless to say, this is much to the amusement of my cellmate whose main exercise is turning the pages of the latest comic book, detailing the adventures of Cosmic Man!

I thank you for your recent gift of books and cigarettes which arrived in good order. You ask if there is any special printed matter which you may supply that is not available in the prison library. Sir, there is. Some months ago, in an issue of the New York *Times,* I read that, for the first time, scientists had succeeded in the synthetic reproduction of an enzyme in the laboratory. This is a subject that interests me greatly, and I would be much obliged if you could obtain for me copies of the scientific papers describing this discovery. I thank you.

Now then . . . you ask me about the personality and the character traits of the man I called John Anderson.

I can tell you he was a most complex man. As you may have surmised, I had several dealings with him prior to the events of 31 August–1 September, 1968. In all our dealings, I found him a man of the highest probity, of exceptional honesty, trustworthiness, and steadfastness. I would never hesitate in giving him a character reference, if such was requested of me.

A man of very little education and very much intelligence. And the two have little in common as, I am certain, you recognize. In all our personal and business relations he radiated strength and purposefulness. As is understandable in such a relationship, I was, perhaps, a little frightened of him. Not because he ever threatened me physical harm. Not at all! But I was frightened as we all poor mortals become frightened in the presence of one we feel and sense and know is of, perhaps, almost superhuman strength and resolve. Let me say only that I felt inferior to him.

I believe that, directed into more constructive channels, his intelligence and native wit could have taken him very far. Very far indeed. Let me give you an example. . . .

Following our second planning meeting—I believe it was on August 28th—I walked with him to the subway after the meeting was concluded. Everything had gone very well. I congratulated him on the detailed planning, which I thought was superb. I told him I thought it must have taken much thought on his part. He smiled, and this is what he said—as nearly as I can remember. . . .

"Yes, I have been living with this thing for some months now, thinking of it every waking minute and even dreaming of it. You know, there is nothing like thinking. You have a problem that worries you and nags you and keeps you awake. The thing to do then is to get to the very rock bottom of that problem. First, you figure out *why* it is a problem. Once you have done that, it is half solved. For instance, what do you think was the most difficult problem in making up the plan you heard tonight?"

I suggested it might be how to handle the doorman when the truck first pulled into the driveway.

"No," he said, "there are several good ways we could handle that. The big problem, as I saw it, was how to handle the tenants who were still at home. That is, how could we get into their apartments? I figured they all had locked doors and chains also. In addition, it would be after midnight and I could figure most of them—particularly the old ladies in Four B and the family with the crippled boy in Five A—would be asleep. I thought of our possibilities. We could force the doors, of course. But even if their phones were cut, they could still scream before we broke in and maybe alert the people in the house next door. I could ask you to pick the locks—but I had no guarantee that *everyone* would be asleep at that hour. They might hear you working and start screaming. It was a problem to know exactly what we should do. I wrestled with this thing for three days, coming up with a dozen solutions. I threw them all out because they didn't *feel* right to me. So then I went to the rock-bottom basic of the problem, just like I told you. I asked myself, Why do all these people have locks and chains on their doors? The answer was easy—because they were scared of guys like me—crooks and burglars and muggers. So then I thought, if they keep their doors locked from *fear,* what can make them open up? I remembered from the first time I was in that house that the doors above the lobby floor didn't have peepholes. The doctors' offices on the lobby floor did, but the doors above were blind. Who needs peepholes when they have twenty-four-hour doorman service and a locked service door and all that shit? So then I thought, if *fear* makes them keep their doors locked, then a *bigger* fear will make them unlock them. And what's a bigger fear than being robbed? That was easy. It was fire."

And that, my dear sir, is something I can tell you about the man I knew as John Anderson and how intelligent he was at his job, although he was, as I have told you, uneducated. . . .

57

•

FOLLOWING THE EVENTS RELATED HEREIN, ATTEMPTS WERE
made to obtain sworn statements from all the principals involved as soon as
possible, while the details were fresh in their minds. Individuals interrogated
included the victims and the alleged lawbreakers. It soon became apparent
that the key to the proposed plan to loot the apartment house at 535 East
Seventy-third Street was Apartment 4B, owned by Mrs. Martha Hathway,
widow, and occupied by her and her companion-housekeeper, Miss Jane
Kaler, a spinster.

Mrs. Hathway was ninety-one at the time of the crime. Miss Kaler was
eighty-two. Both ladies refused to be interviewed or to make statements
individually; each insisted the other be present—a rather surprising request
in view of the results of their interrogation.

In any event, the statements of both ladies were taken at the same time.
The following is an edited transcription of NYPD-SIS recording #146-91A.

MRS. HATHWAY: Very well. I will tell you exactly what happened. Are
   you taking all this down, young man?
QUESTION: The machine is, ma'am. It's recording everything we say.
MRS. HATHWAY: Hmph. Well . . . it was the morning of September
   first. Sunday morning. I'd say it was about one o'clock in the morn-
   ing.
MISS KALER: It was about fifteen minutes to one.
MRS. HATHWAY: You shut your mouth. I'm telling this.
MISS KALER: You're not telling it right.
QUESTION: Ladies. . . .
MRS. HATHWAY: It was about one o'clock. We had been asleep for,
   oh, about two hours or so.
MISS KALER: You might have been asleep. I was wide awake.
MRS. HATHWAY: Oh, you were indeed! I could hear the snores!
QUESTION: Ladies, please. . . .
MRS. HATHWAY: Suddenly I woke up. There was this pounding on
   our front door. A man was shouting, "Fire! Fire! There is a fire in
   the building and everyone must vacate the premises!"
QUESTION: Were those the exact words you heard?

MRS. HATHWAY: Something like that. But of course all I heard was "Fire! Fire!" so I immediately rose and donned my dressing gown.

MISS KALER: Naturally, being awake, I was already suitably clad and standing near the front door. "Where is the fire?" I asked through the door. "In the basement, ma'am," this man said, "but it is spreading rapidly throughout the entire building and we must ask you to leave the premises until the fire is under control." So I said to him, "And who might you be?" And he said, "I am Fireman Robert Burns of the New York Fire Department, and I would—"

MRS. HATHWAY: Will you stop gabbling for just a minute? I own this apartment, and it is my right to tell what happened. Isn't that correct, young man?

QUESTION: Well, ma'am, we'd like to get both. . . .

MISS KALER: "And I would like all the occupants of this apartment to leave immediately," he said. So I said, "Is it serious?" And he said— all this was through our locked door, you understand—he said, "Well, ma'am, we hope it won't be, but for your own safety we suggest you come down to the lobby while we get the fire under control." So I said, "Well, if you're—"

MRS. HATHWAY: Will you shut your mouth, you silly, blathering creature? Just be quiet and let me tell this nice young man what happened. So, seeing we were both perfectly covered in our dressing gowns and we had on our carpet slippers, I told the girl to open the door. . . .

MISS KALER: Mrs. Hathway, I've asked you times without end not to refer to me as "the girl." If you remember, you promised to. . . .

MRS. HATHWAY: So she opened the door. . . .

QUESTION: It was locked at the time?

MRS. HATHWAY: Oh, my, yes. We have the regular lock, always double-locked whenever we're in the apartment. Then we have a chain lock which allows the door to be opened slightly but held with a powerful chain. And we also have something called a policeman's lock which had been recommended to me by Sergeant Tim Sullivan, retired now but formerly of the Twenty-first Precinct. Do you know him?

QUESTION: I'm afraid not, ma'am.

MRS. HATHWAY: A wonderful man—a very good friend of my late husband's. Sergeant Sullivan was forced to retire at an early age because of a hernia. After we had so many robberies on the East Side, I called him and he suggested we have this policeman's lock installed, which is really a steel rod that fits into the floor and is shoved against the door, and it's impossible to break in.

MISS KALER: Ask her how this "wonderful man" got his hernia.

MRS. HATHWAY: That is of no importance, I'm sure. So the man outside kept shouting, "Fire! Fire!" and naturally we were quite upset, so we opened the three locks and threw open the door. And much . . .

MISS KALER: And there he was! A monster! He must have been seven feet tall, with this terrible mask and a big gun in his hand. And he snarled at us, "If you—"

MRS. HATHWAY: He was, perhaps, six feet tall, and he had no gun that I could see, although I believe one hand was in his pocket so he might have had a weapon. But really, he was quite polite and said, "Ladies, we must use your apartment for a short while, but if you are quiet and offer us no resistance, then we can—"

MISS KALER: And right behind him were two other monsters—sex fiends, all of them! And they had masks and revolvers. And they pushed us back into the apartment, and I said, "Then there is no fire?" And the first man to come in said, "No, ma'am, there is no fire, but we must request the use of your apartment for a while. And if you don't scream or carry on, it won't be necessary to tie you up or tape your mouth shut. And we will not tape your mouth shut if you act intelligently." And I said, "I will act intelligently." And then the first man said, "Keep an eye on them, Killer, and if they scream or act up, you may destroy them." And the second man—who, I am sure, was a darkie—he said, "Yes, Butch, if they scream or act up, I will destroy them." And then the darkie stayed and watched us through his mask, and the other two men. . . .

MRS. HATHWAY: Will you shut up? Will you just shut your mouth?

QUESTION: Ladies, ladies. . . .

58

•

RECORDING NYDA-#146-98B. SEE NYDA-#146-98BT FOR CORrected and edited transcription.

QUESTION: The recorder has now started, Mrs. Bingham. My name is Roger Leibnitz. I am an assistant in the office of the District Attorney, County of New York, State of New York. It is the eleventh day of September, 1968. I wish to question you about events occurring during the period August thirty-first to September first of this year at your residence. If for any reason you do not wish to make a statement, or if you wish counsel of your choice to be present during this interview, or if you wish the court to appoint such counsel, will you please so state at this time?

MRS. BINGHAM: No . . . that's all right.

QUESTION: Very well. You understand, it is my duty to notify you of your rights under law?

MRS. BINGHAM: Yes. I understand.

QUESTION: For the record, will you please identify yourself—your full name and your place of residence.

MRS. BINGHAM: My name is Mrs. Gerald Bingham, and I live in Apartment Five A, five-three-five East Seventy-third Street, Manhattan, New York.

QUESTION: Thank you. Before we get started—may I inquire about your husband's condition?

MRS. BINGHAM: Well . . . I feel a lot better now. At first they thought he might lose the sight of his right eye. Now they say he will be able to see, but the sight may be impaired. But he's going to be all right.

QUESTION: I'm very happy to hear that, ma'am. Your husband is a very brave man.

MRS. BINGHAM: Yes. Very brave.

QUESTION: Are you all right, Mrs. Bingham?

MRS. BINGHAM: Yes . . . I'm all right.

QUESTION: If you wish to put this questioning over to another day, or if you'd like to rest at any time, please tell me. Would you like coffee . . . a cup of tea?

MRS. BINGHAM: No . . . I'll be all right.

QUESTION: Fine. Now I want you to state in your own words exactly what happened during the period in question. I'll try to avoid interrupting. Just take your time and tell me what happened in your own words. . . .

MRS. BINGHAM: It was the thirty-first of August. Most of the people in the house had left for the Labor Day weekend. We rarely go away because of my son. His name is Gerry—Gerald junior. He is fifteen years old. He was in an accident at the age of ten—he was hit by a truck—and he has lost the use of his legs. The doctors say there is no hope he will ever walk normally again. He is a good boy, very intelligent, but he must be helped. He uses a wheelchair and sometimes crutches for short periods. From the waist up he is very strong, but he can't walk without help. So we very rarely go anywhere.

QUESTION: You have no other children?

MRS. BINGHAM: No. On the night of August thirty-first, my son went to bed about midnight. He read awhile, and I brought him a Coca-Cola, which he dearly loves, and then he turned out his bed lamp and went to sleep. My husband and I were in the living room. I was working on a petit point cover for a footstool, and my husband was reading something by Trollope. He dearly loves Trollope. I think it was about fifteen minutes after one. I'm not sure. It could have been fifteen minutes either way. Suddenly there was a pounding at the front door. A man's voice shouted, "Fire! Fire!" It was a very cruel thing to do.

QUESTION: Yes, Mrs. Bingham, it was.

MRS. BINGHAM: My husband said, "My God!" and jumped to his feet. He dropped his book on the floor. He rushed over to the door and unlocked it and took off the chain and opened it. There were two men standing there with masks on their faces. I could see them from where I sat. I was still in the easy chair. I hadn't reacted as fast as my husband. I could see these two men. The one in front had his hand in his jacket pocket. They were wearing these strange masks that came to a knot on the tops of their heads. I didn't know at first, but later I realized they were stockings—women's stockings. My husband looked at them and he said again, "My God!" Then he . . . he struck at the man in front. He reacted very quickly. I was so proud of him, thinking about it later. He knew at once what it was and he reacted so quickly. I was just sitting there, stunned.

QUESTION: A very brave man.

MRS. BINGHAM: Yes. He is. So he hit out at this man, and this man laughed and moved his head so that my husband didn't really hit him. Then this man took a gun out of his pocket and hit my husband in the face with it. He just smashed him with it. We found out later it had broken the bones above and below my husband's right eye. My husband fell to the floor and I saw the blood. The blood just gushed out. Then this man kicked my husband. He kicked him in the stomach and in the . . . in the groin. And I just sat there. I just sat there. . . .

QUESTION: Please, Mrs. Bingham . . . please. . . . Would you like to put this over to another day?

MRS. BINGHAM: No . . . no . . . that's all right . . . no. . . .

QUESTION: Let's take a little break. What I would like you to do, if you feel you are capable of it at this time, is to come with me downstairs to another office. There we have an exhibit of many types of guns used by lawbreakers. I would like you, if you can, to identify the gun the man used when he hit your husband. Will you do that for us?

MRS. BINGHAM: It was a very big gun, very heavy. I think it was black or maybe. . . .

QUESTION: Just come with me, and let's see if you can identify the gun from our collection. I'll take the machine with us.

[Lapse of four minutes thirty-eight seconds.]

QUESTION: This is NYDA Number one-four-six, nine-eight-B, two. We are now in the gun room. Now, Mrs. Bingham, as you can see, these are cases of weapons that have been used in crimes. What I would like you to do is to examine these weapons—take all the time you need; don't hurry—and try to pick out the weapon you think that first masked man used to strike your husband.

MRS. BINGHAM: There are so many!

QUESTION: Yes . . . many. But take your time. Look at all of them and try to identify the gun the man used.

[Lapse of one minute thirty-seven seconds.]

MRS. BINGHAM: I don't see it.

QUESTION: Take your time. No hurry.

MRS. BINGHAM: It was black, or maybe dark blue. It was square.

QUESTION: Square? Come over to this case, ma'am. Something like this?

MRS. BINGHAM: Yes . . . these look more like it . . . Yes . . . yes . . . there it is! That's the one.

QUESTION: Which one is that?

MRS. BINGHAM: There it is . . . that second one from the top.

QUESTION: You're sure of that, ma'am?

MRS. BINGHAM: Absolutely. No question about it.

QUESTION: The witness has just identified a U.S. pistol, caliber .45, 1917, Colt automatic, Code Number nineteen seventeen, C-A, three-seven-one-B. Thank you, Mrs. Bingham. Shall we go upstairs now? Perhaps I'll order in some coffee or tea?

MRS. BINGHAM: A cup of tea would be nice.

QUESTION: Of course.

[Lapse of seven minutes, sixteen seconds.]

MRS. BINGHAM: I feel better now.

QUESTION: Good. This is NYDA Number one-four-six, nine-eight-B, three. Ma'am, do you think you'd like to finish up today—or should we put it off?

MRS. BINGHAM: Let's finish now.

QUESTION: Fine. Now then . . . you said your husband hit out at the masked man. The masked man drew a weapon from his pocket and struck your husband. Your husband fell to the floor. The masked man then kicked him in the stomach and in the groin. Is that correct?

MRS. BINGHAM: Yes.

QUESTION: Then what happened?

MRS. BINGHAM: It's all very hazy. I'm not sure. I think I was out of my chair by this time and moving toward the door. But I distinctly saw the second masked man push the first one aside. And the second man said, "That's enough." I remember that very clearly because it was exactly what I was thinking at the time. The second masked man shouldered the first one aside so he couldn't kick my husband anymore, and he said, "That's enough."

QUESTION: And then?

MRS. BINGHAM: I'm afraid I don't remember in what sequence things took place. I'm very hazy about it all. . . .

QUESTION: Just tell it in your own words. Don't worry about the sequence.

MRS. BINGHAM: Well, I ran over to my husband. I think I got down on my knees alongside him. I could see his eye was very bad. There was a lot of blood, and he was groaning. One of the men said, "Where's the kid?"

QUESTION: Do you remember which man said that?

MRS. BINGHAM: I'm not sure, but I think it was the second one—the one who told the first man to stop kicking my husband.

QUESTION: He said, "Where's the kid?"

MRS. BINGHAM: Yes.

QUESTION: So he knew about your son?

MRS. BINGHAM: Yes. I asked him please, not to hurt Gerry. I told him Gerry was asleep in his bedroom and that he was crippled and could only move in his wheelchair or for short distances on crutches. I asked him again, please not to hurt Gerry, and he said he wouldn't hurt him.

QUESTION: This is still the second man you're talking about?

MRS. BINGHAM: Yes. Then he went into my son's bedroom. The first man, the one who kicked my husband, stayed in the living room. After a while the second man came out of the bedroom. He was pushing my son's empty wheelchair and carrying his aluminum crutches. The first man said to him, "Where's the kid?" The other one said, "He's pretending he's asleep, but he's awake all right. I told him if he yelled I'd come back and break his neck. As long as we've got his chair and crutches, he can't move. He's a gimp. We checked this out." And the first man said, "I think we should take him." And then the second man said, "The elevator is stopped. You want to carry him down? How we going to get him down?" And then they argued a while about whether they should take the boy. Finally they agreed they would leave him in bed but they would gag him and look in on him every ten minutes or so. I asked them please not to do that. I told them that Gerry has sinus trouble, and I was afraid if they'd gag him, perhaps he wouldn't be able to breathe. The second man said they were taking my husband and me down to Mrs. Hathway's apartment on the fourth floor, and they couldn't take the chance of leaving Gerry alone in the apartment, even if he couldn't move. I told them I would make Gerry promise to keep quiet if they would let me talk to him. They argued about this for a while, and then the second man said he would come into the bedroom with me and listen to what I said to Gerry. So we went into the bedroom. I snapped on the light. Gerry was lying on his back, under the covers. His face was very white. His eyes were open. I asked him if he knew what was going on, and he said yes, he had heard us talking. My son is very intelligent.

QUESTION: Yes, ma'am. We know that now.

MRS. BINGHAM: I told him they had taken his chair and crutches, but if he promised not to yell or make any sounds, they had agreed not to tie him up. He said he wouldn't make any sounds. The man went over to the bed and looked down at Gerry. "That's a bad man out there, boy," he said to Gerry. "I think he's already put your pappy's eye out. You behave yourself or I'll have to turn him loose on your pappy again. You understand?" Gerry said yes, he understood. Then the man said there would be someone looking in on him every few minutes so not to get wise-ass. That was the expression he used. He said, "Don't get wise-ass, kid." Gerry nodded. Then we went back into the living room.

QUESTION: Did you leave the light on in the bedroom?

MRS. BINGHAM: Well, I turned it off, but the masked man turned it on again and said to leave it on. So we went back into the living room. My husband was on his feet, swaying a little. He had gotten a towel from the bathroom and was holding it to his eye. I don't know why I hadn't thought of that before. I'm afraid I wasn't behaving very well.

QUESTION: You were doing just fine.

MRS. BINGHAM: Well . . . I don't know. . . . I don't think I'm very brave. I know I was crying. I started crying when I saw my husband on the floor and the man was kicking him, and somehow I just couldn't stop. I couldn't stop. . . . I tried to stop but I just. . . .

QUESTION: Let's leave the rest of this for another day, shall we? I think we've done enough for one day.

MRS. BINGHAM: Yes . . . all right. Well, they just took us down the service staircase to the fourth floor, to Mrs. Hathway's apartment. I imagine you know what happened after that. I helped support my husband on the way down the stairs; he was still very shaky. But in Mrs. Hathway's apartment we could take care of him. They had brought everyone there, including Dr. Rubicoff, and he helped me bathe my husband's eye and put a clean towel on it. Everyone was very . . . everyone was very . . . everyone . . . oh, my God, my God!

QUESTION: Yes, Mrs. Bingham . . . yes, yes. Just relax a moment. Just sit quietly and relax. It's all over. It's all completely over.

59

•

THE FOLLOWING IS A PERSONAL LETTER TO THE AUTHOR, DATED 3 January, 1969, from Mr. Jeremy Marrin, 43-580 Buena Vista Drive, Arlington, Virginia.

DEAR SIR:

In reply to your letter of recent date, requesting my personal recollections and reactions to what happened in New York City last year on Labor Day weekend, please be advised that both myself and John Burlingame have made very complete statements to the New York City police anent these events, and I'm sure our statements are a matter of public record and you may consult them. However, as a matter of common courtesy (called common, no doubt, because it is so *un*common) I will pen this very short note to you as you say it is of importance to you.

John Burlingame, a chum of mine, and I planned to spend the Labor Day weekend in New York, seeing a few shows and visiting companions. We wrote to Eric Sabine, a very dear friend of ours, who occupies Apartment 2A at 535 East Seventy-third Street, hoping to spend some time with him and his very groovy circle of acquaintances. Eric wrote back that he would be out of the city for the weekend. Fire Island, I believe he said. But he put his gorgeous apartment completely at our disposal, mailed us the key, and said he would leave instructions with the doormen that we would be staying for the weekend. Naturally, we were delighted and very grateful to kindhearted Eric.

We started out very early Saturday morning, driving up, but with one thing and another, we did not arrive until 10:30 or so, quite worn out with the trip. The traffic was simply murder. So we bought the Sunday papers and just locked ourselves in for the night. Dear Eric had left a full refrigerator (fresh salmon in aspic, no less!) and, of course, he's got the best bar in New York—or anywhere else, for that matter. Some of his liqueurs are simply incredible. So John and I had a few drinks, soaked awhile in a warm tub, and then went to bed—oh, I'd say it was 12:15, 12:30, around then. We were awake, you understand, just lying in bed and drinking and reading the papers. It was a very groovy experience.

It was about—oh, I'd say fifteen minutes after one o'clock or so, when we heard this terrible banging on the front door, and a man's voice shouted, "Fire! Fire! Everybody out! The whole house is on fire!"

So naturally, we just leaped out of bed. We had brought pj's, but neither of us had thought to bring robes. Fortunately, dear Eric has this groovy collection of dressing gowns, so we borrowed two of his gowns (I had this lovely thing in crimson jacquard silk), put them on, rushed into the living room, unlocked the door . . . and here were these two horrid men with masks over their heads. One was quite short and one quite tall. The tall one, whom I am absolutely certain was a jigaboo, said, "Let's go. You come with us and no one get hurt."

Well, we almost fainted, as you can well imagine. John shouted, "Don't hurt my face, don't hurt my face!" John is in the theater, you know—a very handsome boy. But they didn't hurt us or even touch us. They had their hands in their pockets and I suspect they had weapons. They took us up the service stairway at the back of the building. We went into Apartment 4B where there were several other people assembled. I gathered that everyone in the building, including the doorman, had been brought there. One man was wounded and bleeding very badly from his eye. His wife, the poor thing, was weeping. But as far as I could see, no one else had been physically harmed.

We were told to make ourselves comfortable, which was a laugh as this was the most old-fashioned, campy apartment I have ever seen in my life. John said it would have made a perfect set for *Arsenic and Old Lace*. They told us not to scream or make any noise or attempt to resist in any way, as they merely wished to rob the apartments and not to hurt anyone. They were polite, in a way, but still you felt that if the desire came over them, they would simply slit your throat wide open.

After a while they all left except for the man who was, I'm sure, a spade. He stood by the door with his hand in his pocket, and I believe he was armed.

I'm sure you know the rest better than I can tell it. It was a very shattering experience, and in spite of the many groovy times I have had in New York, I can assure you it will be a long time before I visit Fun City again.

I do hope this may be of help to you in assembling your account of what happened, and if you're ever down this way, do look me up.

Very cordially,
[signed] JEREMY MARRIN

60

•

STATEMENT NYDA-EHM-106A.

MANN: It was now twenty minutes after one. Perhaps one thirty. Everything was going very well. Everyone had been assembled in Apartment Four B except for the superintendent, drunk and asleep in his basement apartment, and the crippled boy in Apartment Five A. So then, the building secured, we moved into the second phase of the operation in which we were divided into three teams.

QUESTION: Teams?

MANN: Yes. The man I knew as John Anderson and I constituted the first team. We worked from the basement upward. He had a checklist. We would move to an apartment. I would unlock the door and. . . .

QUESTION: Pick the lock?

MANN: Well . . . ah . . . my assignment was purely technical, you understand. Then we would enter the apartment. Anderson, who carried the checklist, would point out to me what he wished me to do.

QUESTION: What did that entail?

MANN: Well . . . you understand . . . perhaps a box safe, a wall safe. Perhaps a locked closet or cabinet. Things of that sort. Then, as we left the apartment, the second team would enter. This was the very short man, Tommy—effeminate, I believe—and the two men I knew as Ed and Billy. Tommy, who apparently knew the value of things, carried a copy of Anderson's checklist. He would direct the two brothers as to what should be removed and carried down to the truck. They were merely laborers, you understand.

QUESTION: What did they remove and carry to the truck?

MANN: What did they *not* remove! Furs, the triptych from the super's apartment, a small narcotics safe from one of the doctor's offices, jewelry, paintings, silver, unset gems, *objets d'art,* even rugs and small pieces of furniture from the decorator's apartment in Two A. One unexpected treasure was discovered in the medical doctor's suite on the lobby floor. There, this man Anderson, after I had opened the door, went directly to a closet in the doctor's office and there, on a back shelf of the closet, he discovered a cardboard shoe box containing a great deal of cash. I would say at least ten thousand dollars. Perhaps more. The Internal Revenue Service will be interested in that . . . *nein?*

QUESTION: Perhaps. You had no problems opening the doors or safes?

MANN: None. Very inferior. After we gained the third floor, I was confident I would have no need for the torches and tanks in the truck. Quite frankly, it was not a challenge to me. Simple. Everything went well.

QUESTION: You mentioned three teams. Who were on the third team?

MANN: They were the Negro and the uncouth man. They were detailed to guard the people assembled in Apartment Four B, and to look in on the sleeping super in the basement and the crippled boy in Apartment Five A. They were what is called muscle. They took no actual part in removing objects from the house—and, of course, I didn't either, you understand. Their duties were merely to keep the building quiet while it was being emptied.

QUESTION: And everything went well?

MANN: Beautiful. It was beautiful! A remarkable job of organization. I admired the man I knew as John Anderson.

61

•

THE FOLLOWING IS A PORTION OF A STATEMENT DICTATED TO A representative of the District Attorney's Office, County of New York, by Gerald Bingham, Jr., a minor, resident of Apartment 5A, 535 East Seventy-third Street, New York, New York. His entire statement is on recordings NYDA-#145-113A-113G, and as transcribed (NYDA-#146-113AT-113GT) consists of forty-three typewritten pages.

The following is an excerpt covering the most crucial period of the witness's activities. Material covered in previous testimony, and that to be covered in following testimony, has been deleted.

WITNESS: I heard the front door close, and I looked at my watch on the bedside table. It was nine minutes, thirty-seven seconds past one. My watch was an Omega chronometer. I never got it back. It was a very fine machine. Very accurate. I don't believe it gained more than three minutes a year. That's very good for a wristwatch, you know. In any event, I noted the time. Of course, I wasn't certain both the thieves had left the apartment with my parents. But my hearing is very acute—possibly because of my physical debility. That is an interesting avenue for research—whether paralyzed legs might affect other senses, the way a blind man hears and smells with such sensitivity. Well, some day. . . .

I judged they would come back to check on me within ten minutes. Actually, I heard the living room door open about seven minutes after they had left. A masked man came into the apartment, came into my bedroom, and looked at me. He was not the man who had spoken to me before. This man was somewhat shorter and heavier. He just looked at me, without saying anything. Then he saw my Omega chronometer on the bedside table, picked it up, put it in his pocket, and walked out. This angered me. I was already resolved to foil their plans, but this gave me an added incentive. I do not like people to touch my personal belongings. My parents know this and respect my wishes.

I heard the living room door close, and I began counting, using the professional photographers' method of ticking off seconds: "One hundred and one, one hundred and two . . ." and so forth. While I was counting, I picked up my bedside phone extension. As I suspected, it was completely dead, and I judged they had cut the main trunk line in the basement. This did not alarm me.

I judged they would check me every ten minutes or so for one or two times. Then, when they saw I was making no effort to escape or to raise an alarm, their visits would become more infrequent. Such proved to be the case. Their first visit, as I have said, occurred about seven minutes after their initial departure from the apartment. The second visit, by the same man, was eleven minutes and thirty-seven seconds after the first. The third visit—this was by a taller, more slender, masked man—came sixteen minutes and eight seconds after the second visit.

I judged the fourth visit would be approximately twenty minutes after the third. I estimated that, conservatively speaking, I had ten minutes in which I would not be disturbed. I did not wish to take the full twenty minutes as I did not wish to endanger my parents or the other tenants of the building who endeavor to be pleasant to me.

You must understand that although the lower half of my body is paralyzed and without control, I am very well developed from the waist up. My father takes me to a private health club three times a week. I am a very good swimmer, I can perform on the horizontal bars, and Paul—he's the trainer—says he has never seen anyone as fast as I am on the rope climb. My shoulders and arms are very well muscled.

The moment I heard the outside door close, after the third visit by one of the miscreants, I threw back the sheet and began to slide to the floor. Naturally, I wanted to be as quiet as possible. I didn't want to make any heavy thumps that might alert the thieves if they happened to be in Apartment Four A, directly below. So I got my upper body onto the floor and then, lying on my shoulders and back, I lifted my legs down with my hands. All this time I was counting, you understand. I wished to accomplish everything within the ten minutes I had allotted myself and be back in bed before the next inspection.

I moved by reaching out my arms, placing my forearms flat on the floor, and dragging my body forward with my biceps and shoulder muscles. I weigh almost one hundred and seventy-five pounds, and it was slow going. I remember trying to estimate the physical coefficients involved—angles, muscles involved, power required, the friction of the rug—things like that. But that's of no importance. Within three minutes I had reached the door of my closet—the walk-in closet on the north side of my bedroom, not the clothes closet on the south side.

After I became interested in electronics, my father had the walk-in closet cleared of hooks, hangers, and poles. He had a carpenter install shelves and a desk at the right height for me when I was seated in my wheelchair. It was in this closet that I installed all my electronic equipment. This not only included my shortwave transmitter and receiver, but also hi-fi equipment wired to speakers in my bedroom and in the living room and in my parents' bedroom. I had two separate turntables so my parents could listen to one LP while I listened to another, or we could even listen to separate tapes, if so desired. This was a wise arrangement as they enjoy Broadway show tunes—original-cast recordings—while I like Beethoven, Bach, and also Gilbert and Sullivan.

You may be interested to know that I had personally assembled every unit in that closet from do-it-yourself kits. If I told you how many junctions I had soldered, you wouldn't believe me. But not only were the savings considerable—over what the cost of the completed units would be—but as I went along I was able to make certain improvements—minor ones, to be sure—they gave us excellent stereo reproduction from tape and LPs and FM radio. I am currently assembling a cassette player on the worktable to the left of the control board. Well, enough of that. . . .

I opened the closet door by reaching up. However, the worktable and controls of my shortwave transmitter seemed impossibly high. But fortunately, the carpenter who installed the table had built sturdily, and I was able to pull myself up by fingers, wrists, arms, and shoulders. It was somewhat painful but not unendurable. I should mention here that my antenna was on the roof of the building next door. It is an eighteen-story apartment house and towers over our five-story building. My father paid for the installation of an antenna and also pays ten dollars a month fee. The lead-in comes down the side of the tall building and into my bedroom window. It is not a perfect arrangement, but obviously better than having the antenna on our terrace, blocked by surrounding buildings.

Supporting myself on my arms, I turned on my equipment and waited patiently for the warm-up. I was still counting, of course, and figured five minutes had elapsed since I crawled out of bed. About thirty seconds later I began broadcasting. I gave my call signal, of course, and stated that a robbery was taking place at five-three-five East Seventy-third Street, New York, New York, and please, notify the New York Police Department. I didn't have time to switch on my receiver and wait for acknowledgments. I merely broadcast steadily for two minutes, repeating the same thing over and over, hoping that someone might be on my wavelength.

When I calculated that seven minutes had elapsed from the time I got out of bed, I switched off my equipment, let myself drop to the floor, closed the closet door, dragged myself back to my bed, hauled myself up, and got beneath the sheet. I was somewhat tired.

I was glad I had not taken the full twenty minutes I had estimated I had before the fourth visit because one of the thieves came into my bedroom sixteen minutes and thirteen seconds after the third visit. It was the same tall, slender man who had made the previous inspection.

"Behaving yourself?" he asked pleasantly. Actually, he said, "Behavin' yoself," from which I judged he was colored. "Yes," I said, "I can't move, anyhow." He nodded and said, "We all got troubles." Then he left and I never saw him again.

I lay there and thought back on what I had just done. I tried to analyze the problem to see if there was anything more I could do, but I couldn't think of what it might be—without endangering my parents or the other tenants. I hoped someone had heard me, and I felt that, with luck, someone had. Luck is very important, you know. In many ways I know I am very lucky.

Also, to be quite frank, I thought these robbers were very stupid. They had obviously investigated our apartment house very well, but they had missed the one thing that might possibly negate all their efforts.

I could plan a crime much better than that.

62

•

NYPD-SIS RECORDING #146-83C.

HASKINS: Oh, God, Tommy, it was beautiful. Beautiful! It's about two o'clock now, maybe a little later. The first team is working the third floor. The second team, with me in charge, is finishing up Two A and Two B. And what we got in those places you wouldn't believe! From the fruit's apartment we took his paintings, small rugs, a few small pieces of antique furniture, his collection of unset gemstones, two original Picassos, and a Klee. From Two B, from the wall safe the tech had opened, we got a gorgeous tiara, a pearl necklace, and also a very chaste ruby choker I slipped into my pocket, figuring Snapper would flip over it. After all, she worked on this thing, too— even if the orders were that everything went into the truck. I knew we were already over our estimate when we hit the third floor. That retired jeweler in Three A had bags and bags of unset diamonds— most of them industrial but some very nice rocks as well. His little hedge against inflation. It took the tech less than three minutes to open the can—and without a torch. I was sure we'd hit a quarter of a mil at least. Maybe more. From the third, we were going to move up to the fifth, clean that out, and then come back down to the fourth where all the tenants were being held. But already I knew it was going to be great—much better than we had estimated. I knew the old biddies' apartment, Four B, would be a treasure-house. I was thinking we might hit half a million. Jesus, what luck! Everything was coming up roses!

63

•

THE FOLLOWING ARE THE INTRODUCTORY PARAGRAPHS OF AN AR-
ticle appearing in *The New York Times,* Tuesday, 2 July, 1968. The story was
published on the first page of the second section of that day's newspaper, was
bylined by David Burnham, and is copyrighted by *The New York Times.*
The article was entitled "Police Emergency Center Dedicated By Mayor."

Mayor Lindsay yesterday dedicated a $1.3-million police commu-
nications center that cuts in half the average time it takes the police to
dispatch emergency help to the citizen.

"The miraculous new electronic communication system we inau-
gurate this morning will affect the life of every New Yorker in every
part of our city, every hour of the day," Mr. Lindsay said during a
ceremony staged in the vast, windowless, air-conditioned communications center on the fourth floor of the ponderous old Police Headquarters building at 240 Centre Street.

"This is, perhaps, the most important event of my administration as
Mayor," Mr. Lindsay said. "No longer will a citizen in distress risk
injury to life or property because of an archaic communications system."

The Mayor dedicated the new system about four weeks after it went
into operation.

In that period the police response time to emergency calls was reduced to 55 seconds from about two minutes through a number of
complex inter-related changes in the police communication chain.

First, the time it takes to dial the police has been shortened by changing the old seven-digit emergency number—440-1234—to a new
three-digit number, 911.

Second, the time it takes the police to answer an emergency call has
been reduced by increasing the maximum number of policemen receiving calls during critical periods to 48 from 38 and by putting them
in one room where all are available to handle any emergency that might
occur in one area. Under the old system, when a citizen dialed 440-
1234, his call went to a separate communications center situated in the
borough from which he was calling.

64

•

THE FOLLOWING SECTION—AND THOSE OF A SIMILAR NATURE BE-
low—are excerpts from the twenty-four-hour tape kept during the period
12:00 midnight, 31 August, 1968, to 12:00 midnight, 1 September, 1968, at
the New York Police Communications Center at 240 Centre Street, Manhattan.
   Tape NYPDCC-31AUG-1SEP. Time: 2:14:03 A.M.

OFFICER: New York Police Department. May I help you?
OPERATOR: Is this the New York City Police Department?
OFFICER: Yes, ma'am. May I help you?
OPERATOR: This is New York Telephone Company Operator four-
   one-five-six. Will you hold on a moment, please?
OFFICER: Yes.
   [Lapse of fourteen seconds.]
NEW YORK OPERATOR: I have the New York City Police Depart-
   ment for you, Maine. Will you go ahead, please.
MAINE OPERATOR: Thank you, New York. Hello? Is this the New
   York City Police Department?
OFFICER: Yes, ma'am. May I help you?
MAINE OPERATOR: This is the operator in Gresham, Maine. I have a
   collect call for anyone in the New York City Police Department
   from Sheriff Jonathon Preebles of County Corners, Maine. Will you
   accept the charges, sir?
OFFICER: Pardon? I didn't get that.
MAINE OPERATOR: I have a call for anyone in the New York City
   Police Department from Sheriff Jonathon Preebles of County Cor-
   ners, Maine. It is a collect call. Will you accept the charges, sir?
OFFICER: What's it about?
MAINE OPERATOR: Will you accept the charges, sir?
OFFICER: Can you hang on a minute?
MAINE OPERATOR: Yes, sir.
   [Lapse of sixteen seconds.]
O'NUSKA: Sergeant O'Nuska.

OFFICER: Sarge, this is Jameson. I've got a collect call from a sheriff up in Maine. They want to know if we'll accept the charges.

O'NUSKA: A collect call?

OFFICER: That's right.

O'NUSKA: What's it about?

OFFICER: They won't tell unless we accept the charges.

O'NUSKA: Jesus Christ. Hang on a minute—I'll be right over.

OFFICER: Okay, Sarge.

[Lapse of forty-seven seconds.]

O'NUSKA: Hello? Hello? This is Sergeant Adrian O'Nuska of the New York Police Department. Who's calling?

MAINE OPERATOR: Sir, this is the operator in Gresham, Maine. I have a collect call for anyone in the New York City Police Department from Sheriff Jonathon Preebles of County Corners, Maine. Will you accept the charges, sir?

O'NUSKA: What's it about?

MAINE OPERATOR: Will you accept the charges, sir?

O'NUSKA: Hang on a minute. . . . Jameson, what can it cost to call from Maine?

JAMESON: A couple of bucks maybe. Depends on how long you talk. I call my folks down in Lakeland, Florida, every month. Costs me maybe two, three bucks, depending on how long we talk.

O'NUSKA: I'll never get it back. I'll get stuck for it. You mark my words, I'll get stuck for it. . . . Okay, Operator, put the sheriff on the line.

OPERATOR: Go ahead, sir. Sergeant Adrian O'Nuska of the New York City Police Department is on the line.

SHERIFF: Hello there! You there, Sergeant?

O'NUSKA: I'm here.

SHERIFF: Well . . . good to talk to you. What kind of weather you folks been having?

O'NUSKA: Sheriff, I. . . .

SHERIFF: I tell you, we had a rainy spell last week. Four solid days like a cow pissing on a flat rock. Let up yesterday though. Sky nice and clear tonight. Stars out.

O'NUSKA: Sheriff, I. . . .

SHERIFF: But that ain't what I called to tell you about.

O'NUSKA: I'm glad to hear that, Sheriff.

SHERIFF: Sergeant, we got a boy down the road. Smart as a whip. Willie Dunston. He's the son—the second son—of old Sam Dunston. Sam's been farming in these parts for two hundred years. His folks has, anyways. Well, Willie is the smartest kid we've had in these parts since I can remember. We're right proud of Willie. Wins all the prizes. Had a writing of his published in this here scientific journal. The kids these days—I tell you!

O'NUSKA: Sheriff, I. . . .

SHERIFF: Willie's in his last year in high school over in Gresham. He's interested in all things scientific like. He's got himself this telescope, and I saw with my own eyes this little weather station he built with his own hands. You want to know what kind of weather you'll have tomorrow down there in New York, you just ask Willie.

O'NUSKA: I'll do that. I'll surely do that. But Sheriff, I. . . .

SHERIFF: And Willie's got this ham radio setup he built in a corner of the barn old Sam let him have. You know about this shortwave radio, Sergeant?

O'NUSKA: Yes, I know. I know.

SHERIFF: Well, maybe about fifteen-twenty minutes ago, I got this call from Willie on the telephone. He said on account of it was Saturday night and he could sleep late Sunday morning, he said he was out there in his corner there in the barn, listening in and talking to folks. You know how these shortwave radio folks do.

O'NUSKA: Yes. Go on.

SHERIFF: Willie said he picked up a call from New York City. He said he logged it in real careful and he figures it was about two minutes after two o'clock. You got that, Sergeant?

O'NUSKA: I got it.

SHERIFF: He said it was from a real smart kid in New York City he had talked to before. This kid said a robbery was going on right then and there in the apartment house where he lived. The address is five-three-five East Seventy-third Street. You got that, Sergeant?

O'NUSKA: I've got it. It's five-three-five East Seventy-third Street.

SHERIFF: That's right. Well, Willie said the kid wasn't receiving and didn't answer any questions. All he said was that there was a robbery going on in his house and if anyone heard him they should call the New York City Police and tell them. So then Willie called me. Got me up. I'm standing here in my skin. I figure it's probably nothing. You know how kids like to fun. But I figured I better call you anyhow and let you know.

O'NUSKA: Sheriff, thank you very much. You did exactly right, and we appreciate it.

SHERIFF: Let me know how it comes out, will you?

O'NUSKA: I'll surely do that. Thanks, Sheriff. Good-bye.

SHERIFF: Good-bye. You take care now.

　　　[Lapse of six seconds.]

JAMESON: For God's sakes.

O'NUSKA: Were you listening in on that?

JAMESON: I sure was. That's pretty nutty—to have a Maine sheriff call us and tell us we got a crime in progress.

O'NUSKA: I think it's a lot of shit, but with all this stuff on tape, who can take a chance? Send a car. That's Sector George, isn't it? Tell them to cruise five-three-five East Seventy-third Street. Tell them not to stop—just cruise the place, take a look, and call back.

JAMESON: Will do. That was some long-winded sheriff . . . wasn't he, Sarge?

O'NUSKA: Was he? I guess so. Toward the end there he was getting to me.

2:23:41AM.
DISPATCHER: Car George Three, car George Three.
GEORGE THREE: George Three here.
DISPATCHER: Proceed five-three-five East Seventy-three. Signal nine-five. Proceed five-three-five East Seventy-three. Signal nine-five. Extreme caution. Report A-sap.
GEORGE THREE: Rodge.

2:24:13AM.
OFFICER: New York Police Department. May I help you?
VOICE: This is the Wichita, Kansas, Police Department Crime Communications Center. We got a phone call from a ham radio operator stating that he tuned in a call from New York stating that a robbery. . . .

2:25:01AM.
OFFICER: New York Police Department. May I help you?
VOICE: My name is Everett Wilkins, Junior. I live in Tulsa, Oklahoma, where I'm calling from. I'm a ham radio operator, and a little while ago I got a. . . .

2:27:23AM.
OFFICER: New York Police Department. May I help you?
VOICE: Hiya, there! This here's the chief of police down in Orange Center, Florida. We got this little old boy here who's like a nut about electronics and shortwave radio, and he says. . . .

2:28:12AM.
SERGEANT O'NUSKA: Jesus Christ!

2:34:41AM.
GEORGE THREE: Car George Three reporting.
DISPATCHER: Go ahead, Three.

GEORGE THREE: On your signal nine-five. Five-story apartment house. Lobby is lighted but we couldn't see anyone in it. There's a truck pulled up in the service alley. We saw two men loading what appeared to be a rug into the truck. The men appeared to be wearing some kind of masks.

DISPATCHER: Stand by. Out of sight around the corner or some place.

GEORGE THREE: Will do.

2:35:00AM.

JAMESON: Sarge, the car says it's a five-story apartment house. No one in the lobby. Truck parked in the service entrance. Two men, maybe masked, loading what appeared to be a rug into the truck.

O'NUSKA: Yes. Who's on duty—Liebman?

JAMESON: No, Sarge, his son was Bar-Mitzvahed today—or yesterday rather. He switched with Lieutenant Fineally.

O'NUSKA: Better get Fineally down here.

JAMESON: I think he went across the street to Ready's.

O'NUSKA: Well, get him over here, God damn it! And call the phone company. Get the lobby number of that address.

2:46:15AM.

OFFICER: New York Police Department. May I help you?

VOICE: My name is Ronald Trigere, and I live at four-one-three-two East St. Louis Street, Baltimore, Maryland. I am a ham radio operator, and I heard. . . .

2:48:08AM.

OFFICER: New York Police Department. May I help you?

VOICE: This is Lieutenant Donald Brannon, Chicago. We picked up a call from New York that stated. . . .

2:49:32AM.

JAMESON: Sarge, the phone company says the lobby number of that apartment house is five-five-five, nine-oh-seven-eight.

O'NUSKA: Call it.

JAMESON: Yes, sir.

2:49:53AM.

LIEUTENANT FINEALLY: What the fuck's going on here?

65

•

NYPD-SIS RECORDING #146-83C.

HASKINS: Now it's a quarter to three. Maybe a smidgen before. We were all in Five B. The second team had caught up with the first. The tech was having trouble with a wall safe. This was the apartment of Longene, the theatrical producer. We already had his collection of gemstones, and the brothers had taken a very nice Kurdistan down to the truck. We figured the wall safe for Longene's cash and his wife's jewels—if she *was* his wife which I, for one, am inclined to doubt. Then Ed Brodsky came running in, breathing hard. He had just pounded up all the stairs. He told Duke a squad car had cruised by, just as he and his brother were loading the rug into the truck. Duke cursed horribly and said the cruise car for that street was supposed to be in the coop at that hour.

QUESTION: Is that the term he used—"In the coop?"

HASKINS: Yes, Tommy, it was. Definitely. Duke then asked Brodsky if he thought the fuzz had seen him. Brodsky said he couldn't tell for sure, but he thought they had. Just as the car came past, Ed and his brother were carrying the rug out the service entrance. The inside of the service staircase was lighted. We had to keep the lights on so the brothers wouldn't break their necks coming downstairs with the stuff. Brodsky said he thought he saw a white blur as the face of the driver turned toward him. Ed and his brother were still wearing their masks, of course.

QUESTION: What did Anderson say to this?

HASKINS: He just stood there awhile, thinking. Then he called me over to a corner, and he said he had decided to cut the whole thing short. We would just hit the things we were sure of. So he and I went over our checklists together. We decided to do the wall safe in Five B, which the tech was still working on. We'd skip Five A completely. This was where the crippled boy was in his bedroom, but there was really nothing worth risking our necks for. Then we'd go down to Four A and get Sheldon's coin collection and also spring his wall safe. That's all we'd do there. Then we'd move all the tenants from Four

B to Four A, and then we'd do as much as we could in Mrs. Hathway's Four B apartment as I anticipated a veritable treasure trove there. So we agreed on this, and Duke told everyone to move faster—we were getting out. About this time he also sent the spade down to the lobby and told him to stay there, out of sight, but to report any police activity in the street outside. That maniac from Detroit would guard the people in Four A. Just then the tech sprung Longene's wall safe, and we got a nice box of ice, some bonds, and at least twenty G's in cash. I took this as a good omen, although I didn't like the idea of a prowl car going by outside.

66

•

CONTINUING EXCERPTS FROM TWENTY-FOUR-HOUR TAPE, NYPDCC–31AUG–1SEP.

2:52:21AM.

JAMESON: Sir, there's no answer from the lobby phone at five-three-five East Seventy-third Street. It's not even ringing.

LIEUTENANT FINEALLY: Get back to the phone company. Ask them if they know what's wrong. Sergeant.

O'NUSKA: Sir?

FINEALLY: The captain picked a good weekend to go to Atlantic City.

O'NUSKA: Yes, sir.

FINEALLY: Who's the standby inspector?

O'NUSKA: Abrahamson, sir.

FINEALLY: Get him up. Tell him what's happening. We'll call him as soon as we know.

O'NUSKA: Yes, sir.

FINEALLY: You . . . what's your name?

OFFICER: Bailey, sir.

FINEALLY: Bailey, get out the block map for the Two fifty-first Precinct. Find out what address is back-to-back with five-three-five East Seventy-third Street. That's on the north side of Seventy-third, so the house backing it will be on the south side of Seventy-fourth. Probably five-three-four or five-three-six. Get a description of it.

BAILEY: Yes, sir.

2:52:49AM.

FINEALLY: You want me?

JAMESON: The phone company says the lobby line is completely dead, sir. They don't know why. And they get no answer from any other phone at that address.

FINEALLY: Who told them to try the other numbers at that address?

JAMESON: I did, sir.

FINEALLY: What's your name?

JAMESON: Marvin Jameson, sir.

FINEALLY: College?

JAMESON: Two years, sir.

FINEALLY: You're doing all right, Jameson. I won't forget it.

JAMESON: Thank you, sir.

2:59:03AM.

BAILEY: Lieutenant, the house backing on five-three-five East Seventy-third Street is five-three-six East Seventy-fourth Street. It's a ten-story apartment house with a small open paved space in back.

FINEALLY: All right. Who talked to the car that saw the masked men— or thought they saw masked men?

JAMESON: I talked to the dispatcher, sir.

FINEALLY: You again? What number was it?

JAMESON: George Three, sir.

FINEALLY: Where are they now?

JAMESON: I'll find out, sir.

FINEALLY: Fast. Sergeant.

O'NUSKA: Sir?

FINEALLY: You think we ought to bring in the inspector?

O'NUSKA: Yes, sir.

FINEALLY: So do I. Call him and alert his driver.

3:01:26AM.

JAMESON: Lieutenant.

FINEALLY: Yes?

JAMESON: Car George Three is standing by on East Seventy-second Street.

FINEALLY: Tell them to proceed to five-three-six East Seventy-fourth Street. No siren. Get on the roof or any floor where they can see down onto five-three-five East Seventy-third Street. Tell them to report any activity A-sap. You got that?

JAMESON: Yes, sir.

O'NUSKA: Lieutenant, the inspector's on his way. But he's got to come in from Queens. It'll be half an hour at least.

FINEALLY: All right. It may still be nothing. Better call the Two fifty-

first and talk to the duty sergeant. Tell him what's going on. Find
out where his nearest beat men are. You better send three more cars.
Have them stand by on East Seventy-second Street. No sirens or
lights. Tell the duty sergeant of the Two fifty-first that we'll pull in
two cars from Sector Harry to fill in. You take care of it. And we'll
keep him informed. Now let's see—have we forgotten anything?

O'NUSKA: Tactical Patrol Force, sir?

FINEALLY: God bless you. But what have they got on for tonight? It's
a holiday weekend.

O'NUSKA: One bus. Twenty men. I put them on Blue Alert.

FINEALLY: Good. Good.

O'NUSKA: And I didn't even go to college.

67

•

THE FOLLOWING IS AN ADDITIONAL PORTION OF THE STATEMENT
dictated to a representative of the District Attorney's Office, County of New
York, by Gerald Bingham, Jr., a minor, resident of Apartment 5A, 535 East
Seventy-third Street, New York, New York, excerpted from recordings
NYDA-#146-113A-113G, and as transcribed (NYDA-#146-113AT-
113GT).

WITNESS: I estimated it was now approximately three in the morning.
I heard voices and sounds of activity coming from across the hall. I
judged that the thieves were ransacking Apartment Five B and would
soon be into our apartment. This caused me some trepidation, as I
felt certain they would discover the electronic equipment in the
closet in my bedroom. However, I took comfort from the fact that
it might be possible they would not recognize the nature of the
equipment. They would not realize it was a shortwave transmitter.
Perhaps I could convince them it was part of our hi-fi system.

In any event, you understand, although I felt some fear—I realized
that my body was covered with perspiration—I did not really care
what they did to me. They could not know I had used the equipment. And I did not really believe they would kill me. I felt they
might hurt me if they recognized the equipment and thought I might
have used it. But I am no stranger to pain, and the prospect did not

alarm me unduly. But I was disturbed by the realization that they might hurt my mother and father.

However, all my fears were groundless. For reasons I did not comprehend at the time, they skipped our apartment completely. The only man who came in was the tall, slender one who had removed my wheelchair and crutches earlier. He came in, stood alongside my bed and said, "Behaving yourself, boy?"

I said, "Yes, sir."

As soon as I said it, I wondered why I called him Sir. I do not call my father Sir. But there was something about this masked man. I have thought a great deal about him since the events of that night, and I have decided that somehow—I don't know quite how—he had an air and bearing of authority. Somehow, I don't know how, he demanded respect.

In any event, he nodded and looked about. "Your room?" he asked me.

"Yes," I said.

"All yours." He nodded again. "When I was your age, I lived in a room not much bigger than this with my mammy and pappy and five brothers and sisters."

"The late John F. Kennedy said that life is unfair," I told him.

He laughed and said, "Yes, that is so. And anyone over the age of four who don't realize it ain't got much of a brain in him. What you want to be, boy?"

"A research scientist," I said promptly. "Perhaps in medicine, perhaps in electronics, maybe in space technology. I haven't decided yet."

"A research scientist?" he asked, and by the way he said it, I knew he didn't have a very clear idea of what that was. I was going to explain to him but then I thought better of it.

"A research scientist?" he repeated. "Is there money in it?"

I told him there was, that I'd already had offers from two companies and that if you discovered something really important, you could become a multimillionaire. I don't know why I was telling him these things except that he seemed genuinely interested. At least, that's the impression I received.

"A multimillionaire," he repeated. He said, "Mult-*eye*."

Then he looked around the room—at my books, my worktable, the space maps I had pinned to the walls.

"I could—" he started to say, but then he stopped and didn't go on.

"Sir?" I said.

"I could never understand any of this shit," he said finally and laughed. Then he said, "You keep behaving yourself, y'hear? We'll be out of here soon. Try to get some sleep."

He turned around and walked out. I only saw him once after that, very briefly. I felt that if he. . . . I felt that maybe I could have been a good. . . . I felt that maybe he and I might. . . . I am afraid I am not being very precise. I do not know exactly what I felt at that moment.

68

•

CONTINUING EXCERPTS FROM THE TWENTY-FOUR-HOUR TAPE, NYPDCC–31AUG–1SEP.

3:14:32AM.

O'NUSKA: Lieutenant, we have a report from Officer Meyer in car George Three. He got onto the roof of the building at five-three-six East Seventy-fourth Street. He says shades are drawn in all the apartments at five-three-five East Seventy-third. Lights are on in several apartments. The service staircase in the rear of the building is also lighted. There is an unshaded window on the service staircase at each floor. Meyer says he saw masked men carrying objects down the stairs and placing them in the truck parked in the service alley.

FINEALLY: How many men did he see?

O'NUSKA: He says at least five different men, maybe more.

FINEALLY: Five men? My God, what's this going to be—the shoot-out at the O.K. Corral? Get the tactical squad moving. Red Alert. Tell them to park on Seventy-second near the river and wait further instructions. You got those three other cars?

O'NUSKA: Yes, sir. Standing by, within a block or so.

FINEALLY: Seal off East Seventy-third Street. Put one car across the street at East End Avenue and another at York Avenue.

O'NUSKA: Got it.

FINEALLY: Tell George Three to stay where they are. Send the third car around to join them.

O'NUSKA: Right.

FINEALLY: Let's see now—there's got to be tenants in there.

O'NUSKA: Yes, sir. It's the holiday weekend and some of them'll be gone, but there's got to be someone—the super, the doorman, the kid who sent out the shortwave call. Others probably.

FINEALLY: Get me the duty sergeant at the Two fifty-first. You know who he is?

O'NUSKA: Yes, sir. He's my brother.

FINEALLY: You kidding?

O'NUSKA: No, sir. He really is my brother.

FINEALLY: What kind of a precinct is it?

O'NUSKA: Very tight. Captain Delaney lives right next door in a converted brownstone. He's in and out all the time, even when he's not on duty.

FINEALLY: Don't tell me that's "Iron Balls" Delaney?

O'NUSKA: That's the man.

FINEALLY: Well, well, well. Will wonders never cease? Get him for me, will you? We need a commander on the scene.

O'NUSKA: Right away, Lieutenant.

3:19:26AM.

DELANEY: I see. . . . What is your name?

FINEALLY: Lieutenant John K. Fineally, sir.

DELANEY: Lieutenant Fineally, I shall now repeat what you have told me. If I am incorrect in any detail, please do not interrupt but correct me when I have finished. Is that understood?

FINEALLY: Yes, sir.

DELANEY: You have reason to believe that a breaking and entering, and a burglary and/or armed robbery is presently taking place at five-three-five East Seventy-third Street. A minimum of five masked men have been observed removing objects from this residence and placing them in a truck presently located in the service alleyway alongside the apartment house. Four Sector George cars are presently in the area. One is blocking Seventy-third Street at East End Avenue, and one is blocking the street at York Avenue. Two cars with four officers are on Seventy-fourth Street, in the rear of the building in question. The duty sergeant of this precinct has alerted two patrolmen to stand by their telephones and await further instructions. The Tactical Patrol Force bus is presently on its way with a complement of twenty men, under Red Alert, and has been instructed to stand by on Seventy-second Street to await further orders. Inspector Walter Abrahamson has been alerted and is on his way to the scene of the suspected crime. I will proceed to the scene and take command of the forces at my disposal until such time as the inspector arrives. I will enter the premises with the forces at my disposal and, with proper care for the life and well-being of innocent bystanders, forestall the alleged thieves from escaping, place them under arrest, and recover the reportedly stolen objects. Is that correct in every detail?

FINEALLY: You've got it right, sir. In every detail.

DELANEY: Is a tape being made of this conversation, Lieutenant?

FINEALLY: Yes, sir, it is.

DELANEY: This is Captain Edward X. Delaney signing off. I am now departing to take command of the forces available to me at the scene of the reported crime.

    [Lapse of six seconds.]

FINEALLY: Jesus Christ. I don't believe it. I heard it but I don't believe it. Were you listening to that, Sergeant?

O'NUSKA: Yes, sir.

FINEALLY: I've heard stories about that guy but I never believed them.

O'NUSKA: They're all true. He's had more commendations than I've had hangovers.

FINEALLY: I still don't believe it. He's something else again.

O'NUSKA: That's what my brother says.

69

•

THE FOLLOWING IS A TYPED TRANSCRIPTION (NYDA-#146-121AT) from an original recording (NYDA-#146-121A) made on 11 September, 1968, at Mother of Mercy Hospital, New York City. The witness is Gerald Bingham, Sr., resident of Apartment 5A, 535 East Seventy-third Street, New York, New York.

QUESTION: Glad to see you looking better, Mr. Bingham. How do you feel?

BINGHAM: Oh, I feel a lot better. The swelling is down, and I received some good news this morning. The doctors say I won't lose the sight of my right eye. They say the sight may be slightly impaired, but I'll be able to see out of it.

QUESTION: Mr. Bingham, I'm glad to hear that . . . real glad. I can imagine how you felt.

BINGHAM: Yes . . . well . . . you know. . . .

QUESTION: Mr. Bingham, there are just a few details in your previous statement we'd like to get cleared up—if you feel you're up to it.

BINGHAM: Oh, yes. I feel fine. As a matter of fact, I welcome your visit. Very boring—just lying here.

QUESTION: I can imagine. Well, what we wanted to clear up was the period around three thirty on the morning of 1 September, 1968. According to your previous statement, you were at that time in Apartment Four B with the other tenants and the doorman. You were being guarded by the man who struck you in the face and kicked you earlier in your own apartment. This man was carrying a weapon. Is that correct?

BINGHAM: Yes, that's right.

QUESTION: Do you know anything about handguns, Mr. Bingham?

BINGHAM: Yes . . . a little. I served with the Marines in Korea.

QUESTION: Can you identify the weapon the man was carrying?

BINGHAM: It looked to me like a government-issue Colt .45 automatic pistol of the 1917 series.

QUESTION: Are you certain?

BINGHAM: Fairly certain, yes. I had range training with a gun like that.

QUESTION: At the time in question—that is, three thirty on the morning of first September—what was your physical condition?

BINGHAM: You mean was I fully conscious and alert?

QUESTION: Well . . . yes. Were you?

BINGHAM: No. My eye was quite painful, and I was getting this throbbing ache from where he had kicked me. They had put me on the couch in Mrs. Hathway's living room—it was really a Victorian love seat covered with red velvet. My wife was holding a cold, wet towel to my eye, and Dr. Rubicoff from downstairs was helping also. I think I was a little hazy at the time. Perhaps I was in mild shock. You know, it was the first time in my life I had been struck in anger. I mean, it was the first time I had ever been physically assaulted. It was a very unsettling experience.

QUESTION: Yes, Mr. Bingham, I know.

BINGHAM: The idea that a man I didn't know had struck me and injured me, and then had kicked me . . . to tell you the truth, I felt so ashamed of myself. I know this was probably a strange reaction to have, but that's the way I felt.

QUESTION: You were ashamed?

BINGHAM: Yes. That's the feeling I had.

QUESTION: But why should you feel ashamed? You had done all you could—which was, incidentally, much more than many other men would have done. You reacted very quickly. You tried to defend your family. There was no reason why you should have been ashamed of yourself.

BINGHAM: Well, that's the way I felt. Perhaps it was because the man with the gun treated me—and the others, too—with such utter, brutal contempt. The way he waved that gun around. The way he laughed. I could see he was enjoying it. He shoved us around. When he wanted the doorman to get away from the window, he didn't tell him to get away; he shoved him so that poor Tim O'Leary fell down. Then the man laughed again. I think I was afraid of him. Maybe that's why I felt ashamed.

QUESTION: The man was threatening you with a loaded gun. There was good reason to be frightened.

BINGHAM: Well . . . I don't know. I was in action in Korea. Small-scale infantry action. I was frightened then, too, but I wasn't ashamed. There's a difference but it's hard to explain. I knew this man was very sick and very brutal and very dangerous.

QUESTION: Well, let's drop that and get on. . . . Now, you said that at about three thirty—maybe a little later—four of the others came in and moved all of you to Apartment Four A across the hall.

BINGHAM: That's correct. I was able to walk, supported by my wife and Dr. Rubicoff, and they got us all out of Apartment Four B and into Four A.

QUESTION: Did they tell you why they were moving you?

BINGHAM: No. The man who seemed to be the leader just came in and said, "Everyone across the hall. Make it fast. Move." Or something like that.

QUESTION: He told you to make it fast?

BINGHAM: Yes. Perhaps I was imagining things—I was still shaky, you understand—but I thought there was a tension there. They prodded us to move faster. They seemed to be in a big hurry now. When they first came to my apartment earlier in the evening they were more controlled, more deliberate. Now they were hurrying and pushing people.

QUESTION: Why did you think that was?

BINGHAM: I thought they seemed frightened, that something was threatening them and they wanted to wind up everything and get out in a hurry. That's the impression I got.

QUESTION: You thought *they* were frightened? Didn't that make you feel better?

BINGHAM: No. I was still ashamed of myself.

70

•

THE FOLLOWING SECTION (AND SEVERAL BELOW) IS EXCERPTED from the final report of Captain Edward X. Delaney—a document that has become something of a classic in the literature of the New York Police Department, and that has been reprinted in the police journals of seven countries, including Russia. It's official file number is NYPD-EXD-1SEP1968.

"I arrived at the corner of East Seventy-third Street and York Avenue at approximately 3:24 A.M. I had driven over from the 251st Precinct house. My driver was Officer Aloysius McClaire. I immediately saw the squad car that had been parked across Seventy-third Street, supposedly blocking exit from the street. However, it was improperly situated. This was car George Twenty-four (See Appendix IV for complete list of personnel involved.) After identifying myself, I directed that the car be parked slightly toward the middle of the block at a point where private cars were parked on both sides of the street, thus more effectively blocking exit from the street.

"There is a public phone booth located on the northwest corner of East Seventy-third Street and York Avenue. My investigation proved this phone to be out of order. (N.B. Subsequent investigation proved all the public phone booths within a ten-block area of the crime had been deliberately damaged, apparent evidence of the careful and detailed planning of this extremely well-organized crime.)

"I thereupon directed Officer McClaire to force open the door of a cigar shop located on the northwest corner of East Seventy-third Street and York Avenue. He did so, without breaking the glass, and I entered, switched on the lights, and located the proprietor's phone. (I was careful to respect his property, although recompense should be made by the City of New York for his broken lock.)

"I then called Communications Center and spoke to Lieutenant John K. Fineally. I informed him of the location of my command post and requested that the telephone line on which I was speaking be kept open and manned every minute. He agreed. I also requested that Inspector Walter Abrahamson, on his way in from Queens, be directed to my command post. Lieutenant Fineally acknowledged. I then directed my driver, Officer McClaire, to remain at the open phone line until relieved. He acknowledged this order.

"I was dressed in civilian clothes at this time, being technically off duty. I divested myself of my jacket and carried it over one arm, after rolling up my shirtsleeves. I left my straw hat in the cigar store. I borrowed a Sunday morning newspaper from one of the officers in the car blockading Seventy-third Street. I placed the folded newspaper under my arm. Then I strolled along the south side of East Seventy-third Street, from York Avenue to East End Avenue. As I passed 535 East Seventy-third Street, across the street, I could see, without turning my head, the truck parked in the service entrance. The side doors of the truck were open, but there was no sign of human activity.

"I saw immediately that it was a very poor tactical situation for a frontal assault. The houses facing the beleaguered building offered very little in the way of cover and/or concealment. Most were of the same height as 535, being town houses or converted brownstones. A frontal assault would be possible, but not within the directives stated in NYPD-SIS-DIR-#64, dated 19 January, 1967, which states: 'In any action, the commanding officer's first consideration must be for the safety of innocent bystanders and, secondly, for the safety and well-being of police personnel under his command.'

"When I reached the corner of East Seventy-third Street and East End Avenue, I identified myself to the officers in car George Nineteen, blocking the street at this corner. Again, the car was improperly parked. After pointing out to the driver how I wished the car to be placed, I had him drive me around the block, back to my command post on York Avenue, and then directed him to return to his original post and block the street at that end in the manner in which I had directed. I then returned the newspaper to the officer from whom I had borrowed it.

"In the short drive around the block to my command post, I had formulated my plan of attack. I contacted Lieutenant Fineally at Communications Center via the open telephone line in the cigar store. (May I say at this time that the cooperation of all personnel at Communications Center during this entire episode was exemplary, and my only suggestion for improvement might be a more formalized system of communication with more code words and numbers utilized. Without these, communications tend to become personalized and informal, which just wastes valuable time.)

"I ordered Lieutenant Fineally to send to my command post five more two-man squad cars. I also requested an emergency squad—to be supplied with at least two sets of walkie-talkies; a weapons carrier, with tear gas and riot guns; two searchlight cars; and an ambulance. Lieutenant Fineally stated he would consult his on-duty roster and supply whatever was available as soon as possible. At this time—I estimate it was perhaps 3:40 or 3:45 A.M.— I also asked Lieutenant Fineally to inform Deputy Arthur C. Beatem, the standby deputy of that date, of what was going on and leave it to Deputy Beatem's judgment as to whether or not to inform the commissioner and/or the mayor.

"I then began to organize my forces. . . ."

71

•

NYPD-SIS RECORDING #146-83C.

HASKINS: About this time, Duke told. . . .

QUESTION: What time was it?

HASKINS: Oh, I don't know exactly, Tommy. It was getting late—or rather early in the morning. I thought the sky was getting light, or perhaps I was imagining it. In any event, I had pointed out to the Brodsky brothers what was to be taken from Apartment Four B. As I had suspected, it was a veritable treasure trove. The tech sprung a huge old-fashioned trunk, brass-bound, with a hasp and padlock on it. And he also opened a few odds and ends like jewel boxes, file cases, and even a GI ammunition box that had been fitted with a hasp and padlock. It was really hilarious what those old biddies had squirreled away. Quite obviously, they did not trust banks! There was one diamond pendant and a ruby choker—all their jewels were incredibly filthy, incidentally—and I judged those two pieces alone would bring close to fifty G's. In addition, there was cash—even some of the old-style large bills that I hadn't seen for years and years. There were negotiable bonds, scads and scads of things like Victorian tiaras, bracelets, "dog collars," headache bands, pins, brooches, a small collection of jeweled snuffboxes, loops and loops of pearls, earrings, men's stickpins—and all of it good, even if it did need a cleaning. My God, Tommy, it was like being let loose in Tiffany's about seventy-five years ago. There were also some simply yummy original glass, enamel, and cloisonné pieces that I couldn't bear to leave behind. Duke had told us to hurry it up, so we disregarded the rugs and furniture, although I saw a Sheraton table—a small one—that any museum in the city would have given an absolute fortune for, and there was a tiny little Kurdistan, no bigger than three by five, that was simply exquisite. I just couldn't bear to leave that behind, so I had Billy Brodsky—the one who had the wet brain—tuck it under his arm and take it down to the truck.

QUESTION: Where was Anderson while all this was going on?

HASKINS: Oh, he was—you know—here, there, and everywhere. He checked on the crippled boy in Apartment Five A, and then he went out on the terrace of Five B to look around. Then he checked how that monster from Detroit was doing with the tenants who had been moved across the hall to Four A, and then he helped the Brodsky boys carry some things down to the truck, and then he prowled through some of the empty apartments. Just checking, you know. He was very good, very alert. Then, after I had finished in Apartment Four B, he told me to go down to the basement and see if the super was still sleeping and also check with the spade who had been stationed in the lobby. So I went down to the basement, and the super was still snoring.

QUESTION: Did you take anything from his apartment?

HASKINS: Oh no. It had been cleaned out earlier. The only thing we got was an antique triptych.

QUESTION: The super claims he had just been paid, he had almost a hundred dollars in his wallet, and this money was taken. Did you take it?

HASKINS: Tommy, that hurts! I may be many things, but I am not a cheap little sneak thief.

QUESTION: When they searched you at the station house you had about forty dollars in a money clip. And you also had almost a hundred dollars folded into a wad and tucked into your inside jacket pocket. Was that the super's money?

HASKINS: Tommy! How could you?

QUESTION: All right. What happened next—after you checked on the super and found he was still sleeping?

HASKINS: Duke had told me to check with Skeets Johnson in the lobby on the way up. He was in the doormen's booth in the rear of the lobby so no one could see him from the street. I asked him if everything was all right.

QUESTION: And what did he say?

HASKINS: He said he hadn't seen any beat fuzz or squad cars. He said the only person he had seen was a man carrying a newspaper with his jacket over his arm go humping by on the other side of the street. He said the man hadn't turned his head when he went by so he didn't think that was anything. But I could tell something was bothering him.

QUESTION: Why do you say that?

HASKINS: Well, everything he had said up to now had been in rhymes, some of them quite clever and amusing. The man was obviously talented. But now he was speaking normally, just as you or I, and he didn't seem to have the high spirits he had earlier in the evening. Like when we were in the truck, on the way to the apartment house, he kept us laughing and relaxed. But now I could tell he was down, so I asked him why. And he said he didn't know why he was down, but he said—and I remember his exact words—he said, "Something don't smell right." I left him there and went back upstairs and reported to Duke that Skeets hadn't seen any fuzz or cars but that he was troubled. Duke nodded and hurried the Brodsky boys along. We were about ready to leave. I figured another half hour at the most and we'd be gone. I wasn't feeling down. I was feeling up. I thought it had been a very successful evening, far beyond our wildest hopes. Even though I was working for a fixed fee, I wanted the whole thing to come off because it was very exciting—I had never done anything like that before—and I thought Duke might give me some more work. Also, you know, I had pocketed a few little things—trinkets . . . really nothing of value—but the whole evening would prove very profitable for me.

72

•

EXCERPT FROM THE FINAL REPORT OF CAPTAIN EDWARD X. DELANEY, NYPD-EXD-1SEP1968.

"See my memorandum No. 563 dated 21 December, 1966, in which I strongly urged that every commanding officer of the NYPD of the rank of lieutenant and above be required to attend a course in the tactics of small infantry units (up to company strength), as taught at several bases of the U.S. Army and at Quantico, Virginia, where officer candidates of the U.S. Marine corps are trained.

"During my service as patrolman in the period 1946–49, the great majority of crimes were committed by individuals, and the strategy and tactics of the NYPD were, in a large part, directed toward thwarting and frustrating the activities of individual criminals. In recent years, however, the nature of crime in our city (and, indeed, the nation—if not the world) has changed radically.

"We are now faced, not with individual criminals, but with organized bands, gangs, national and international organizations. Most of these are paramilitary or military-type organizations, be they groups of militant college students or hijackers in the garment center. Indeed, the organization variously known as Cosa Nostra, Syndicate, Mafia, etc., even has military titles for its members—don for general or colonel, *capo* for major or captain, soldier for men in the ranks, etc.

"The realization of the organized military character of crime today led to my memo cited above in which I urged that police officers be given military training in infantry tactics, and also be required to take a two-week refresher course each year to keep abreast of the latest developments. I myself have taken such courses on a volunteer basis since my appointment as lieutenant in 1953.

"Hence, I saw the situation at 535 East Seventy-third Street, in the early morning hours of 1 September, 1968, as a classic military problem. My forces, gathered and gathering (it was now approximately 3:45 A.M.), occupied the low ground—on the street—while the enemy occupied the high ground—in a five-story apartment house. ('War is geography.') Of particular relevance to such a situation are the U.S. Army handbooks—USA-45617990-416 *(House-to-House Combat)* and USA-917835190-017 (*Tactics of Street Fighting*).

"I decided that, although a direct, frontal assault was possible (such an assault is *always* possible if casualties may be disregarded), the best solution would be vertical envelopment. This is a technique developed by the Germans in World War II with the dropping of paratroopers behind the enemy's lines. It was further refined during the Korean Police Action by the use of helicopters. Attack, up to this time, had been largely a two-dimensional problem. It now became three-dimensional.

"During my reconnaissance along East Seventy-third Street, I had noted that the building immediately adjacent to 535 was what I judged to be a 16- to 18-story apartment house. It was flush against the east side of the beleaguered building. I realized at once that a vertical envelopment was possible. That is, I could have combat personnel lowered from the roof of the higher building or, with luck (a very important consideration in all human activities), I could have police officers exit through the windows of the higher building at perhaps the sixth or seventh floor and merely drop or jump to the terraces of the building occupied by the enemy.

"With a noisy display of force, I judged, the police personnel on the top floors of 535 could 'spook' the criminals and drive them down onto the street. I did not desire the police personnel on the upper floor (I estimated five would be an adequate number) to enter into combat with the enemy. Their sole duty would be to frighten the criminals down to the street level without endangering any tenants of the building who might be present.

"At that time the enemy would no longer enjoy the advantage of holding the upper ground. By careful, calculated timing, I would then have emplaced in a semicircle about the front of 535, four two-man squad cars and two searchlight cars, all personnel instructed to keep behind the cover and concealment offered by their vehicles as much as possible, and not to fire until fired upon. In addition, I intended to position a force of six men in the rear of 535—that is, in the cemented open space in the rear of the Seventy-fourth Street building that backed onto 535 East Seventy-third Street. This force, I felt, would be sufficient to block a rearward escape by the enemy. The fact that one, indeed, by his extraordinary ability and good fortune, did escape (temporarily), does not, in my opinion, negate the virtues of my plan of operations.

"By this time, the tactical squad (Tactical Patrol Force) had reported to me at my command post. This unit consisted of twenty men, in a bus, commanded by a Negro sergeant. There were two additional Negroes in the squad.

"The following comments may be considered by some to be unnecessary—if not foolhardy—considering the current state of ethnic and racial unrest in New York City. However, I feel my judgments—based on twenty-two years of service in the NYPD—may be of value to other officers faced with a comparable situation, and I am determined to make them. . . .

"It is said that all men are created equal—and this may be correct, in the sight of God and frequently—but not always—under the law. However, all men are *not* created equal as to their ethnic and racial origins, their intelligence, their physical strength, and their moral commitment. Specifically, ethnic and racial groups, whatever they may be—Negro, Irish, Polish, Jewish, Italian, etc.—have certain inborn characteristics. Some of these characteristics can be an advantage to a commanding officer; some may be a disadvantage. But if the commanding officer disregards them—through a misguided belief in total equality—he is guilty of dereliction of duty, in my opinion, since his sole duty is to solve the problem at hand, using the best equipment and personnel under his command, with due regard to the potential of his men.

"It has been my experience that Negro personnel are particularly valuable when the situation calls for a large measure of élan and derring-do. And they are especially valuable when they operate as units—that is, when several Negro officers are operating together. Hence, I ordered the Negro sergeant commanding the tactical squad to select the two other Negroes in his squad, augment them by two white officers, and execute the vertical envelopment. This would be the unit that would drop onto the terrace of 535 and flush the enemy down to the street.

"He acknowledged my order, and after a short discussion we agreed his men would be armed with one Thompson submachine gun, two riot guns, service revolvers, smoke, and concussion grenades. In addition, his squad of five men (including himself) would carry a walkie-talkie radio, and they would inform me the moment they had made their drop onto the terrace of 535. The officer's name is Sergeant James L. Everson, Shield 72897537, and I hereby recommend him for a commendation. (See attached form NYPD-RC-EXD-109FGC-1968.)"

73

•

FROM THE OFFICIAL REPORT OF SERGEANT JAMES L. EVERSON, Shield 72897537. This is coded NYPD-JLE-1SEP68.

"I received my orders from Captain Edward X. Delaney at his command post in a cigar store on the corner of East Seventy-third Street and York Avenue. I selected the four additional officers from my squad and proceeded to the corner of East Seventy-third Street and East End Avenue. Transportation was by squad car, as directed by Captain Delaney.

"Upon arrival at the aforesaid corner, I determined it would be best if we went one at a time into the building adjoining 535 East Seventy-third Street. Therefore I ordered my men to follow me at counted intervals of sixty seconds. I went first.

"I entered the lobby of the adjoining building and found the man on duty was not the regular doorman but was the super filling in for the doorman because of the holiday weekend. He was sleeping. I awakened him and explained the situation. By the time the other four men of my squad had joined me, he had told me he thought we could drop onto the terrace of 535 by going out the windows of Apartment 6C which overlooked the apartment house where the criminals were located and operating. We had service revolvers, a submachine gun, riot guns, and grenades. The super escorted us to Apartment 6C.

"This apartment was occupied by Irving K. Mandelbaum, a single man. At the time, there was also present in the apartment a single female, Gretchen K. Strobel. I believe, if desired, a charge of unlawful fornication could be brought against Irving K. Mandelbaum under the civil laws of the City of New York. But because of the cooperation Mr. Mandelbaum offered and provided to officers of the New York Police Department, I do not suggest this.

"Miss Strobel went into the bathroom, and me and the squad went through the bedroom window which directly overlooks the terrace at 535. It was only a two- or three-foot drop. The moment we were all on the terrace, I contacted Captain Delaney via walkie-talkie. Reception was very good. I told him we were in position, and he told me to wait two minutes, then go ahead."

74

•

FROM CAPTAIN EDWARD X. DELANEY'S REPORT NYPD-EXD-1SEP1968.

"It was approximately 4:14 A.M. when Sergeant Everson got through to me. I should mention here that the operation of the new 415X16C radios was excellent. Everson said he and his squad were on the terrace of 535 East Seventy-third Street. We agreed he would wait two minutes before commencing his spooking operation.

"Not all the men and equipment I had requisitioned had arrived by this time. However, I felt it better to proceed with what I had rather than await optimum conditions which rarely, if ever, seem to arrive. Hence, I directed cars George Six and George Fourteen (two officers each) to approach from York Avenue toward 535, and cars George Twenty-four and George Eight to approach from East End Avenue. Leading the two approaching from East End would be Searchlight Car SC-147 (the single one that had arrived by this time). The five vehicles would then park in a semicircle around the entrance of 535. The searchlight car would illuminate the building after all personnel had taken cover behind their vehicles. The arrival of additional squad cars, provided by the efficiency of Lieutenant John K. Fineally, NYPDCC, enabled me to station blocking cars at the exits from East Seventy-third Street at York Avenue and East End Avenue. Car George Nineteen was stationed at East End Avenue, and car George Thirty-two at York Avenue.

"I was in the first car (George Six) approaching the apartment house from York Avenue. My order, repeated several times, was that there was to be no firing until I gave the command."

75

•

RECORDING   NYDA-#146-114A-114G.   INTERROGATION   OF
Gerald Bingham, Jr.

QUESTION: What time was it then?

WITNESS: I don't know exactly. It was after four in the morning.

QUESTION: What happened then?

WITNESS: Suddenly five policemen burst into my bedroom. They came
in through the French doors leading to the terrace. Three of them
were colored. The man in front was colored. They were all carrying
weapons. The first man had a machine gun in his hands, and he said
to me, "Who are you?"

I said, "I am Gerald Bingham junior, and I live in this apartment."

He looked at me and said, "You the kid that sent out the report?"

"Yes," I said, "I sent out a shortwave transmission."

He grinned at me and said, "You get yourself out on that terrace."

I told him I was crippled and couldn't move because they had
taken away my wheelchair and my crutches.

He said, "Okay, you stay right where you're at. Where *they* at?"

"Down on the fourth floor," I told him. "I think they're all on
the fourth floor, right below us."

"Okay," he said, "we'll take care of them. You stay right where
you're at and don't make no noise."

They all started out of the apartment. I called after them, "Please
don't kill him," but I don't think they heard me.

76

•

NYPD-SIS RECORDING #146-83C.

HASKINS: We were finishing up Apartment Four B. We were close to finishing. God, we were so *close!* Then everything came apart. Shouts from upstairs. Noise. Gunshots. A big explosion. Smoke pouring down the stairway. Men shouting, "You're surrounded! Hands up! Throw down your guns! You're dead! We've got you!" Silly things like that. I wet my pants. Yes, Tommy, I admit it freely—I soiled myself. Then we started moving. The tech went pounding down the back stairs, then the two Brodsky boys, and then me following. But before I left I saw the Detroit hooligan rush to the front window of Four A and fire his gun through the glass.

QUESTION: Was there return fire?

HASKINS: No. Well . . . I don't know for sure. I had turned away from the foyer between the two apartments. I was on my way down the service staircase. I saw and heard him fire through the window of Four A. But I didn't see or hear any return fire from the street.

QUESTION: Where was Anderson while all this was going on?

HASKINS: He was standing there in the foyer between the two apartments. He was just standing still. He just didn't move.

77

•

FROM THE FINAL REPORT OF CAPTAIN EDWARD X. DELANEY, NYPD-EXD-1SEP1968.

"My assault forces were in position. The moment I heard the envelopment squad start their mission, the searchlight car—as per my previous orders—illuminated the front of the building. We were almost immediately fired upon from a fourth-floor window. I shouted to my men to hold their fire."

78

•

NYDA-EHM-108B, DICTATED, SWORN, SIGNED, AND WITNESSED statement by Ernest Heinrich Mann.

"The moment the noise began, I realized it was all over. Therefore I walked slowly and quietly down the service staircase, took the door into the lobby, removed my mask and gloves, and seated myself on the marble floor, well out of range of the front doors. I then put my back against the wall, raised my arms above my head, and waited. I detest violence."

79

•

FROM THE FINAL REPORT OF CAPTAIN EDWARD X. DELANEY, NYPD-EXD-1SEP1968.

"We still had not yet fired a shot. Then suddenly a masked man burst through the front doors of the house, firing a revolver at the assembled cars. I thereupon gave the command to open fire, and he was cut down in short order."

80

•

EXCERPT FROM NYPD-SIS RECORDING #146-83C, INTERROGA- tion of Thomas Haskins by Thomas K. Brody, detective, second grade.

HASKINS: When we got down to the ground floor, the two Brodsky boys headed out to the truck through the back entrance. I took the door into the lobby. And there was the tech, sitting on the floor against the wall, without his mask, his hands raised over his head. I felt sick. Then I saw the smoke draw his gun and dash out through the front doors. I heard him say "Shit," and then he was gone out through the doors. Then I heard the guns and I knew he was dead. Frankly, I didn't know what to do. I believe I might have been somewhat hysterical. You understand, don't you, Tommy?

QUESTION: Yes. But what *did* you do?

HASKINS: Well, silly as it may seem—I wasn't thinking quite right, you understand—I turned and went back to the service staircase and started to go up. And there, at the second-floor landing, was Duke Anderson.

QUESTION: What was he doing?

HASKINS: Just standing there. Very calm. I said, "Duke, we've got—"
And he said, very quiet, "Yes, I know. Don't do a thing right now.
Stay right where you are. Just stand here. I've got something to do,
but I'll be right down and we'll be getting out together."

QUESTION: Are those his exact words?

HASKINS: As near as I can remember.

QUESTION: And what did you do then?

HASKINS: I did exactly what he told me. I just stood there on the stairs.

QUESTION: What did he do?

HASKINS: Duke? He turned around and went back up the stairs.

81

•

FROM THE FINAL REPORT OF CAPTAIN EDWARD X. DELANEY,
NYPD-EXD-1SEP1968.

"We were still receiving intermittent fire from the fourth-floor window
from what, I judged, was a single gunman. I instructed my men not to return
his fire. Discipline, I should say at this time, under these difficult and aggra-
vating circumstances was excellent. At approximately three minutes after the
start of the action, two men dashed from the rear service entrance, climbed
aboard the truck, and began to back the truck from the service alley at high
speed.

"This was, of course, a move of desperation, doomed to failure as I had
arranged my cordon of squad cars to forestall such a move. As the truck
backed, one man leaned from the window and fired a revolver at us as the
other drove. We returned his fire.

"The truck crashed into car George Fourteen and stopped there. In the
crash, Officer Simon Legrange, Shield 67935429, suffered a broken leg, and
Officer Marvin Finkelstein, Shield 45670985, was slightly wounded in the
upper arm by a bullet fired by the gunman in the truck. Up to this time, this
was the extent of our casualties.

"When I ordered, 'Cease fire!', we determined that the gunman in the
truck was dead (later certified as Edward J. Brodsky) and the driver of the
truck (later certified as William K. Brodsky) suffered a broken shoulder as a
result of the crash."

82

•

NYPD-SIS-#146-92A.

MRS. HATHWAY: Well, we were all across the hall in Apartment Four A when suddenly the shooting started. I would say it was about fifteen minutes after four in the morning.

MISS KALER: Closer to four thirty.

MRS. HATHWAY: I had my brooch watch, you silly thing, and it was almost four fifteen.

MISS KALER: Four thirty.

QUESTION: Ladies, please. What happened then?

MRS. HATHWAY: Well, this masked man who had been so mean and cruel rushed to the window and began firing his weapon. He broke the glass—and what a mess it made on the rug. And he fired his gun down into the street. And then. . . .

MISS KALER: And then there were these terrible explosions on the stairs and men shouting and everyone wondered what was happening. So I said we should all sit right where we were and not move, and that would be the best thing, and this ruffian kept shooting his gun out the window, and I was thankful we were not in our own apartment as I feared the policemen might fire an atomic rocket through the window and destroy just everything. And just about then this other masked man came through the door and he was drawing a gun from his pocket and I thought he would also fire down through the window but he didn't. . . .

83

•

NYDA-#146-121AT.

BINGHAM: When the firing started, I suggested everyone get down on the floor. We all did except for the old ladies from across the hall who said they wouldn't—or perhaps they couldn't. In any event, they slumped in their chairs. The man who was guarding us fired his pistol out the window.

QUESTION: Was there any return fire, Mr. Bingham?

BINGHAM: No, sir, I do not believe there was. None that I was aware of. The man just kept firing his gun and cursing. I saw him reload at least once from a clip he took from his pocket. And then a few minutes later another masked man came into the apartment. I recognized him as the second man who had been in my apartment.

QUESTION: The man who told the first masked man to stop kicking you?

BINGHAM: Yes, that's the one. Well, he came into the apartment right then and he was drawing a gun from his pocket.

QUESTION: What kind of a gun? Did you recognize it?

BINGHAM: It was a revolver, not a pistol. Big. I'd guess a .38. I couldn't recognize the make.

QUESTION: All right. Then what?

BINGHAM: The second man, the man with the revolver who came in the door, said, "Socks."

QUESTION: Socks? That's all he said?

BINGHAM: Yes. He said, "Socks," and the man at the window turned around. And the second man shot him.

QUESTION: Shot him? How many times?

BINGHAM: Twice. I was watching this very closely and I'm sure of this. He came through the door, taking his gun from his pocket. He said, "Socks," and the man at the window turned around. And then the man coming in walked toward him and shot him twice. I could see the bullets going in. They plucked at his jacket. I think he shot him in the stomach and the chest. That's where it looked to me where the bullets went in. The man at the window dropped his own gun and went down. He went down very slowly. As a matter of fact, he grabbed at the drapes at the window and pulled down a drape and the rod. I think he said "What?"—or maybe it was something else. It sounded like "Wha" or something like that. Then he was on the floor and this maroon drape was across him and he was bleeding and twisting. Jesus. . . .

QUESTION: Shall we take a break for a few minutes, Mr. Bingham?

BINGHAM: No. I'm all right. And then my wife was sick; she up-chucked. And one of the old ladies from across the hall fainted and one screamed, and the two faggots I didn't know and had never seen before hugged each other, and Dr. Rubicoff looked like someone had sapped him. Holy God, what a moment that was.

QUESTION: And what did the killer do then?

BINGHAM: He looked at the man on the floor for a very brief moment. Then he put the gun back in his pocket, turned around, and walked out of the apartment. I never saw him again. Strange you should call him a killer.

QUESTION: That's what he was—wasn't he?

BINGHAM: Of course. But at the moment I got the feeling he was an executioner. That's the feeling I got—this man is an executioner, doing his job.

QUESTION: Then what happened?

BINGHAM: After he left? Dr. Rubicoff went over and knelt by the man who had been shot and examined his wounds and felt his pulse. "Alive," he said, "but not for long. This is very bad."

QUESTION: Thank you, Mr. Bingham.

BINGHAM: You're welcome.

84

•

NYPD-SIS RECORDING #146-83C.

HASKINS: It was a lifetime, an eternity. All that noise and gunfire and confusion. But I did what Duke told me and stood there on the second-floor landing.

QUESTION: You trusted him?

HASKINS: Of course, you silly! If you can't trust a man like Duke, who can you trust? So of course he came back down from the fourth floor, as I knew he would, and he said to me, "Better take your mask off, put your hands up, and go down slowly out the front door."

QUESTION: Why didn't you do that? It was good advice.

HASKINS: I know it was, I know it was. I knew it was then. But I can't explain to you how this man Anderson made me feel. He made me forget caution and made me willing to take a chance. Do you understand?

QUESTION: I'm afraid not.

HASKINS: Oh, Tommy, Tommy—he gave me balls! Well, anyway, when I didn't move, I could see him grin, and he said, "Out the back." So we took off our masks and gloves, dashed down the stairs, out the service entrance, started climbing the back wall . . . and suddenly there were eighteen million screws with flashlights in our faces and guns firing, and then I had my hands in the air as far as I could reach and I was screaming, "I surrender! I surrender!" Oh, God, Tommy, it was so *dramatic!*

QUESTION: And what happened to Anderson?

HASKINS: I really don't know. One moment he was there beside me, and the next moment he was gone. He just simply disappeared.

QUESTION: But you trusted him?

HASKINS: Of course.

85

•

NYDA-#146-113A-114G, INTERROGATION OF GERALD BINGham, Jr.

WITNESS: The noise suddenly stopped. There was no more gunfire or shouts. It was very quiet. I thought it was all over. I was still lying in bed. I was very wet, sweating. . . . Then suddenly the front door slammed. He came running through the apartment, through my bedroom, and out onto the terrace. He didn't say anything. He didn't even look at me. But I knew it was him. . . .

86

•

STATEMENT OF IRVING K. MANDELBAUM, RESIDENT OF APART-
ment 6C, 537 East Seventy-third Street, New York, New York. This transcription is coded NYPD-#146-IKM-123GT.

WITNESS: What a night. What a *night!* I mean, we didn't go away for
the weekend. We'll stay in the city, I figured. We'll have a nice,
quiet weekend. No traffic. No hang-ups. No crowds. Everything
will be nice and quiet. So we're in bed. You understand? Five cops
armed like the invasion of Normandy come through the bedroom
and go out the window. Okay. I'm a good, law-abiding citizen. I'm
with them. We get out of bed. Gretch, she goes into the bathroom
while the cops pile through the window. At least one of the *shvartzes*
has the decency to say, "Sorry about this, pal." So then Gretch comes
out of the bathroom and says, "Back to bed." So then the fireworks
start. Guns, lights, screams—the whole thing is right out of a Warner
Brothers movie of the late 1930s, which I really dig—you know,
something with James Cagney and Chester Morris. We get out of
bed. We're watching all this from the front windows, you understand. It's very exciting. What a weekend! Then everything dies
down. No more guns. No more yells. So Gretch says, "Back to bed!"
So we go. About five minutes later a guy comes through the bedroom window, hoisting himself up and climbing in. He's got a gun
in his hand. Gretch and I get out of bed. He says, "One word out
of you and you're dead." So naturally I didn't even agree with him.
A second later and he's gone. Gretch says, "Back to bed?" And I
said, "No, dear. I think at this moment I will drink a quart of
Scotch." Oh boy.

87

•

STATEMENT OF OFFICER JOHN SIMILAR, SHIELD 35674262, DRIVER of car George Nineteen. Document NYPD-#146-332S.

"I was stationed with my partner, Officer Percy H. Illingham, 45768392, in car George Nineteen closing the exit at East Seventy-third Street and East End Avenue. We had been ordered to place our car across Seventy-third Street to prevent exit from or entrance to the street. We had been informed of the action that was taking place.

"At approximately thirty minutes after four A.M. on the morning of 1 September, 1968, a male (white, about six feet, 180 pounds, black jacket and pants) approached us, walking on the sidewalk, the south sidewalk of East Seventy-third Street. Percy said, 'I better check him out.' He opened the door on his side of the car. As he emerged onto the street, the man drew a weapon from his pocket and fired directly at Officer Illingham. Officer Illingham dropped to the pavement. Later investigation proved that he had been killed.

"I thereupon got out of the car on my side and fired three times at the suspect with my service revolver (Serial Number 17189653) as he fired one shot at me which hit me in the thigh and caused me to fall to the pavement. He then began to run, and while I was trying to line up another shot at him, he disappeared around the corner of Seventy-third Street and East End Avenue.

"I did what I could."

88

•

THE FOLLOWING MANUSCRIPT HAS BEEN MADE AVAILABLE through the cooperation of its author, Dr. Dmitri Rubicoff, psychiatrist, with offices at 535 East Seventy-third Street, New York City. It is a portion of a speech Dr. Rubicoff delivered on the evening of 13 December, 1968, at a meeting of the Psychopathology Society of New York. This is an informal association of psychiatrists and psychologists in the New York area, which meets at irregular intervals to dine at one of the larger Manhattan hotels, to exchange "shop talk," and to hear an address by one of its members which then becomes the subject of a roundtable discussion.

The speech from which the following remarks are excerpted (with the permission of Dr. Rubicoff) was delivered by him at the meeting of the society held in the Hunt Room of the President Fillmore Hotel. It is quoted exactly from the typed transcript of the speech made available to the author by Dr. Rubicoff.

"Madam Chairman—although I have long thought that title something of a sexual anomaly!

(Pause for laughter)

"Fellow members, and ladies and gentlemen. After such a dinner, a belch might be more in order than a speech!

(Pause for laughter)

"May I interject at this time that I feel we all owe a vote of thanks to the Entertainment Committee which arranged such a Lucullan feast.

(Pause for applause)

"Indeed, I'm certain you'll sympathize with me if I question whether their motive was to feed you well or to dull your sensibilities to my remarks that follow!

(Pause for small laughter)

"In any event, it is now my turn to offer the intellectual dessert to such a delightfully physical meal, and I shall do my best.

"As some of you, I'm sure, are aware, I was recently one of the victims of a crime which took place in the City of New York during the late evening and early morning of August 31 and September 1 of this year. My remarks this evening shall concern my thoughts about that crime, about crime in general, and what our profession can contribute to the amelioration of crime in our society.

"I can assure you my remarks will be brief—very brief!

(Possible pause for applause)

"These thoughts I offer to you are pure theory. I have done no research on the subject. I have consulted no hallowed authorities. I merely offer them as what I feel are original ideas—reactions to my experience, if you will— that will serve as subject for the discussion to follow. Needless to say, I shall be extremely interested in your reactions.

"First, let me say that it is hardly new to suggest that sexual aberrations are the underlying motivations for criminal behavior. What I would like to suggest at this time is a much closer relationship between sex and crime. In fact, I suggest that crime—in modern society—has become a substitute for sex.

"What is crime? What is sex? What have they in common? I suggest to you that both share a common characteristic—a *main* characteristic—of penetration. The bank robber forces his way into a vault. The housebreaker forces his way into a house or apartment. The mugger forces his way into your wallet or purse. Is it his intention to penetrate your body—your privacy?

"Even the more complex crimes include this motive of penetration. The confidence man invades his victim's wealth—be it wall safe or savings account. The criminal accountant rapes the firm for which he works. The public servant bent on fraud invades the body of society.

"Indeed, a term used for the most common of crimes—breaking and entering—is a perfect description of the deflowering of a virgin.

"So I suggest to you this evening that the commission of a crime is a substitute for the sexual act, committed by persons who consciously, unconsciously, or subconsciously derive extreme pleasure from this quasi-sexual activity.

"The crime having been committed—what then? The sex act having been finished—what then? In both cases, what follows the penetration is similar. Escape and withdrawal. Getting out. Frantic departure and sometimes a difficult disentangling, be it physical or emotional.

"I suggest to you that the *commission* of the sex crime—and I am convinced that *all* crimes are sex crimes—is easiest for the disturbed protagonist. The *withdrawal,* the escape, is much more difficult.

"For, considering the puritanical hang-up of most Americans, the withdrawal or escape involves recognition of guilt, an emotional desire for punishment, a terrible, nagging wish to be caught and publicly exposed.

"Sex and crime. Penetration and withdrawal. It seems to me they are all ineradicably wedded. Now, if you will allow me, I would like to expand upon. . . ."

89

•

FROM THE FINAL REPORT OF CAPTAIN EDWARD X. DELANEY,
NYPD-EXD-1SEP1968.

"It was now, I would judge, approximately 4:45 A.M. We were no longer
under fire from the fourth floor window. Suddenly we heard the sound of
several gunshots from the vicinity of East Seventy-third Street and East End
Avenue. I immediately dispatched officers Oliver J. Kronen (Shield
76398542) and Robert L. Breech (Shield 92356762) to investigate. Officer
Kronen returned in a few moments to report that an officer had been slain,
another wounded in the thigh. Both had been in car George Nineteen, blocking exit from Seventy-third Street at that corner.

"I thereupon contacted my command post via walkie-talkie. I instructed
my driver, Officer McClaire, to send the standby ambulance around to the
East End Avenue corner. He acknowledged. I also instructed him at this time
to report the situation to Communications Center and request them to pass
on the information to Inspector Abrahamson and Deputy Beatem. He acknowledged.

"I immediately led a squad of six armed men into the building at 535 East
Seventy-third Street. We passed the body of the masked man who had been
killed while trying to escape. Later investigation proved him to be Samuel
'Skeets' Johnson, a Negro. We then entered the lobby where we found a
white man seated on the floor of the lobby, his back against the wall, his
hands raised. He was taken into custody. Later investigation proved him to
be Ernest Heinrich Mann.

"At that time my squad joined forces with the men from the Tactical Patrol
Force coming down from the terrace and the men who had been stationed
at the rear of the building. These men had taken an additional suspect, Thomas J. Haskins, into custody.

"We searched the building thoroughly and found the super asleep in his
basement apartment. We also found some of the tenants and the doorman
present in Apartment 4A. One of the tenants, Gerald Bingham, Sr., was
wounded and apparently in shock. His right eye was bleeding badly. In addition to the people who had been held captive in this apartment, there was
also a masked man lying on the floor, seriously wounded. I was told by
eyewitnesses that he had been shot twice by another masked man.

"I thereupon instructed an officer to go outside and call for three more ambulances to facilitate the removal of the dead and wounded—officers, criminals, and innocent victims.

"Preliminary questioning of the victims revealed there had been another man (later identified as John 'Duke' Anderson) who had been present during the crime and had apparently escaped. I judged he was the man responsible for the killing of Officer Illingham and the wounding of Officer Similar of car George Nineteen at the corner of Seventy-third Street and East End Avenue. I thereupon left the apartment house and, using a walkie-talkie, dictated an alert to Officer McClaire for relay to Communications Center. I described the suspect as the witness had described him to me. Officer McClaire acknowledged, and I stayed on the radio until he could report that Communications Center—Lieutenant Finally in command—had acknowledged and was alerting all precincts and sectors.

"When the ambulances arrived, I sent off the wounded immediately—and later the dead. It so happened that Gerald Bingham, Sr., the wounded tenant, and the wounded suspect (later identified as Vincent 'Socks' Parelli, of Detroit) shared the ambulance going to Mother of Mercy Hospital.

"I then returned to my command post at the corner of York Avenue and East Seventy-third Street. Via Communications Center, I alerted Homicide East, the Police Laboratory, the Manhattan District Attorney's Office, and the Public Relations Division. At this time—it was shortly after 5:00 A.M.—there had been no reports on the whereabouts of the escaped suspect, John Anderson."

90

•

THE FOLLOWING IS A TRANSCRIPTION OF A PERSONAL TAPE RE-cording made by the author on 6 November, 1968. To my knowledge, the testimony it contains is not duplicated in any official recording, statement, or transcription now on record.

AUTHOR: This will be recording GO-2B. Will you identify yourself, please, and state your place of residence.
WITNESS: My name is Ira P. Mayer and I live at twelve hundred sixty East Second Street, New York.
AUTHOR: Thank you. Mr. Mayer, as I explained to you previously,

this recording will be solely for my own use in preparing a record of a crime that occurred in New York City on the night and morning of August thirty-first to September first, 1968. I am not an officer of any branch of the government—city, state, or federal. I shall not ask you to swear to the testimony you are about to give, nor will it be used in a court of law or in any legal proceeding. The statement you make will be for my personal use only, and will not be published without your permission which can only be granted by a signed statement from you, giving approval of such use. In return, I have paid you the sum of fifty dollars, the sum paid whether or not you agree to the publication of your statement. Is all that understood?

WITNESS: Yes.

AUTHOR: Good. Now then, Mr. Mayer, where were you at about five o'clock on the morning of September first, 1968?

WITNESS: I was driving home. Down East End Avenue.

AUTHOR: And where had you been prior to this time?

WITNESS: Well, I was working. Ordinarily I wouldn't be working a holiday weekend, you understand, but so many of the men were off or on vacation—taking the Labor Day weekend off, you understand—that the boss asked me to work the night shift. I'm a master baker, and I work in the Leibnitz Bakery at one-nine-seven-four-oh East End Avenue. That's at One hundred fifteenth Street. My wife was expecting her seventh, and my second-youngest daughter—there was this big dental bill for her. So I needed the money, you understand, so I said I'd work. The union says we get triple time for working nights on a holiday, and also the boss said he'd slip me an extra twenty. So that's why I was working from four o'clock on August thirty-first to four o'clock the next morning.

AUTHOR: You say you're a master baker. What do you bake?

WITNESS: Bagels, bialies, onion rolls—things like that.

AUTHOR: And what did you do after you got off work at four on the morning of September first?

WITNESS: I got cleaned up and changed into my street clothes. I stopped for a beer with the boys in the locker room. No bars are open at that time, you understand, but we got a refrigerator and we keep beer in there. In the locker room. We chip in a dollar a week a man. The boss knows about it, but he don't care providing nobody gets loaded. Nobody ever does. We just have a beer or two before heading home. To relax like. You understand? So then I had one beer and got into my car and headed south on East End Avenue. I usually take First Avenue when I go uptown to work, and East End when I go downtown after work.

AUTHOR: And what happened at approximately five A.M. on the morning of September first?

WITNESS: I stopped for a red light on the corner of Seventy-fourth Street. I started to light a cigar. Then suddenly the door opened on the passenger side, and a guy was standing there. He had a gun, and he poked this gun at me. He held the gun in his right hand, and his left arm was across the front of him, like he was holding his belly.

AUTHOR: Can you describe this man?

WITNESS: Maybe six feet tall. Thin. No hat. His hair was short—like a crew cut. Sharp features. Mean looking. You understand?

AUTHOR: What was he wearing?

WITNESS: It was mostly black. A black jacket, black turtleneck sweater, black pants, black shoes. But he was a white man. You understand?

AUTHOR: And he opened the door on the passengers' side of the front seat and shoved a gun at you?

WITNESS: That's right.

AUTHOR: This was on the corner of Seventy-fourth Street and East End Avenue, while you were stopped for a light?

WITNESS: That's right. I was just lighting a cigar.

AUTHOR: And what was your reaction?

WITNESS: My reaction? Well, right away I thought it was a stickup. Why else would a guy jerk open the door of my car and point a gun at me?

AUTHOR: And how did you react?

WITNESS: How did I react? I felt sick. I had just been paid. With triple-time and the bonus I had almost four hundred bucks on me. I needed that dough. It was spent already. And I thought this guy was going to take it away from me.

AUTHOR: Would you have given it to him? If he had asked for your money?

WITNESS: Sure, I'd have given it to him. What else?

AUTHOR: But he didn't ask for your money?

WITNESS: No. He got in alongside of me and poked the gun in my side. With his left hand he slammed the door on his side, then went back to holding his belly.

AUTHOR: What did he say?

WITNESS: He said, "When the light changes, you drive south just the way you're going. Don't drive too fast and don't jump any lights. I'll tell you when to turn off." That's what he said.

AUTHOR: And what did you say?

WITNESS: I said, "You want my money? You want my car? Take them and let me go." And he said, "No, you gotta drive. I can't drive. I'm hurt." And I said, "You wanta go to a hospital? Mother of Mercy is back only five blocks. I'll drive you there." And he said, "No, you just drive where I tell you." And I said, "You gonna kill me?" And he said, "No, I won't kill you if you do what I say."

AUTHOR: And did you believe him?

WITNESS: Of course I believed him. What else am I going to do in a situation like that? You understand? Sure I believed him.

AUTHOR: What happened then?

WITNESS: I did like he said. When the light changed I headed south. I drove at the legal limit so we made all the lights.

AUTHOR: I don't imagine there was much traffic at that time on a Sunday?

WITNESS: Traffic? There was no traffic. We had the city to ourself.

AUTHOR: Did he say anything while you were driving?

WITNESS: Once. It was maybe around the Sixties. He asked me what my name was and I told him. He asked me if I was married, and I told him I was and had six kids and one on the way. I thought maybe he'd feel sorry for me and wouldn't kill me. You understand?

AUTHOR: That's all he said?

WITNESS: Yes, that's all he said. But once he kinda groaned. I looked sideways at him, just for a second, and blood was coming out from between his fingers. Where he had his left hand clamped across his belly. I could see blood coming out from between his fingers. I knew he was hurt bad, and I felt sorry for him.

AUTHOR: Then what happened?

WITNESS: At Fifty-seventh Street he told me to take a right and drive west on Fifty-seventh Street, so I did.

AUTHOR: Was his voice steady?

WITNESS: Steady? Sure, it was steady. Low, maybe, but steady. And that gun in my ribs was steady, too. So we drove across town on Fifty-seventh Street. When we got to Ninth Avenue he told me to take a left and drive downtown. So I did.

AUTHOR: What time was this?

WITNESS: Time? Oh, five thirty. About. Something like that. It was getting light.

AUTHOR: What happened then?

WITNESS: I drove very, very carefully, so I made all the signals. He told me to stop at Twenty-fourth Street.

AUTHOR: Which side?

WITNESS: The west side. On the right. I pulled over to the curb. It was on his side. He opened the door using his right hand, the hand with the gun in it.

AUTHOR: You didn't think of jumping him at this moment?

WITNESS: You crazy? Of course not. He got out, closed the door. He leaned through the window. He said, "Just keep driving. I will stand here and watch to make sure that you keep driving."

AUTHOR: And what did you do then?

WITNESS: What do you think? I kept driving. I went on south to Sixteenth Street, and I figured he couldn't see me anymore. So I stopped and went into a corner phone booth on the sidewalk. There was a sign saying you could call nine-one-one, the police emergency number, without putting a dime in. So I called the cops. When they answered, I told them what had happened. They asked me for my name and address, which I gave them. They asked where I was, which I told them. They told me to stay right where I was and a car would be right there.

AUTHOR: Then what?

WITNESS: I went back to my car. I figured I'd sit in my car and try to calm down until the cops came. I was shaky—you understand? I tried to light my cigar again—I never had got it lighted—but then I saw the seat where he had been. There was a pool of blood on the seat and it was dripping down onto the mat. I got out of the car and waited on the sidewalk. I threw my cigar away.

91

•

VINCENT "SOCKS" PARELLI WAS ADMITTED TO EMERGENCY AT Mother of Mercy Hospital, Seventy-ninth Street and East End Avenue, at 5:23 A.M., 1 September, 1968. He was first declared DOA (Dead On Arrival) but a subsequent examination by Dr. Samuel Nathan revealed a faint pulse and heartbeat. Stimulants and plasma were immediately administered, and Parelli was taken to the Maximum Security Ward on the second floor. After further examination, Dr. Nathan declared the prognosis was negative. Parelli had been shot twice, one bullet apparently entering the lungs and the other rupturing the spleen.

By 5:45 A.M., the bed occupied by Parelli was surrounded by screens. In this enclosure, in addition to Dr. Nathan, were Dr. Everett Brisling (intern) and Nurse Sarah Pagent, both of the Mother of Mercy staff; Assistant District Attorney Ralph Gimble of the New York District Attorney's Office; Detective, First Grade, Robert C. Lefferts of Homicide East; Detective, Second Grade, Stanley Brown of the 251st Precinct; Officer Ephraim Sanders (no relation to the author) of the 251st Precinct; and Security Guard Barton McCleary, also of the Mother of Mercy staff.

The following recording, made by the New York District Attorney's Office, is coded NYDA-VP-DeBeST. It is dated 6:00 A.M., 1 September, 1968.

GIMBLE: What's happening?

NATHAN: He's dying. By all rights he should be dead now.

LEFFERTS: Can you do anything?

NATHAN: No. We've already done all we can.

GIMBLE: Will he regain consciousness?

NATHAN: Brisling?

BRISLING: Maybe. I doubt it.

GIMBLE: We've got to question him.

NATHAN: What do you want from me? I'm not God.

BRISLING: Let the man die in peace.

BROWN: No, goddamn it. An officer was killed. Get him up. Get him awake. We've got to find out what all this was about, why he was shot. This is important.

BRISLING: Doctor?

    [Lapse of seven seconds.]

NATHAN: All right. Nurse?

PAGENT: Yes, Doctor?

NATHAN: Fifty cc's. You've got it?

PAGENT: Yes, Doctor.

NATHAN: Administer it.

    [Lapse of twenty-three seconds.]

NATHAN: Pulse?

BRISLING: Maybe a little stronger. Heart is still fluttering.

GIMBLE: His eyelids moved. I saw them move.

LEFFERTS: Parelli? Parelli?

NATHAN: Don't shove him.

BROWN: He's dying, isn't he?

NATHAN: Just don't touch him. He's a patient in this hospital under my care.

PARELLI: Guh . . . guh. . . .

GIMBLE: He said something. I heard him say something.

LEFFERTS: It didn't make sense. Sanders, move the mike closer to his mouth.

PARELLI: Ah . . . ah. . . .

BROWN: His eyes are open.

GIMBLE: Parelli. Parelli, who shot you? Who was it, Parelli? Why did they shoot you?

PARELLI: Guh . . . guh. . . .

BRISLING: This is obscene.

LEFFERTS: Who planned it, Parelli? Who put up the money? Who was behind it, Parelli? Can you hear me?

PARELLI: Climb planging. No man can ever the building. I said to bicycle of no lad can be to mother.

GIMBLE: What? What?

PARELLI: Or sake to make a lake. We see today not by gun if she does.

LEFFERTS: Can you give him another shot, Doc?

NATHAN: No.

PARELLI: Guh . . . guh. . . .

BRISLING: Fibrillations.

PAGENT: Pulse weakening and intermittent.

NATHAN: He's going.

BROWN: Parelli, listen to me. Parelli, can you hear me? Who shot you, Parelli? Who put up the money? Who brought you here from Detroit? Parelli?

PARELLI: I never thought to. And then I was on the street where. Louise? We saw the car sky and what. Momma. In the sky. It was in. Never a clutch could. Some day she. Fucking bastard. I think that I should.

GIMBLE: Who, Parelli? Who did it?

PARELLI: A bird at song if even wing, the girl herself shall never sing.

NATHAN: Nurse?

PAGENT: No pulse.

NATHAN: Brisling?

BRISLING: No heartbeat.

    [Lapse of nine seconds.]

NATHAN: He's gone.

LEFFERTS: Shit.

92

•

MEMORANDUM (CONFIDENTIAL) EXD-794, DATED 14 DECEMBER, 1968, from Edward X. Delaney, Captain, NYPD, to Police Commissioner, NYPD, with confidential copies to Deputy Arthur C. Beatem and Chief Inspector L. David Whichcote.

"This document should be considered Addendum 19-B to my final report NYPD-EXD-1SEP-1968.

"It has been brought to my attention that the attempted robbery of the premises at 535 East Seventy-third Street, New York City, on 31 August-1 September, 1968, might have been prevented if there had been closer cooperation between agencies of the city, state, and federal governments, and private investigative agencies. A list of agencies involved is attached (see EXD-794-A).

"While I cannot reveal the identity of my informant *at this time,* I can state without fear of serious contradiction that for several months prior to the commission of the crime, the aforesaid agencies were in possession of certain facts (on tape recordings and in transcriptions) relating to the planned crime, obtained via bugging and other electronic surveillance devices.

"Admittedly, no *one* agency was in possession of *all* the facts or all the details regarding the proposed crime—such as address, time, personnel involved, etc. And yet, if a central pool or clearing house (computerized, perhaps?) for electronic surveillance had been in existence, I have little doubt but that the crime in question could have been forestalled.

"I strongly urge that a meeting of representatives of law-enforcement agencies of city, state, and federal governments be convened immediately to consider how such a clearing house for the results of electronic surveillance can be established. I shall hold myself ready to assist in any way I can to help organize such a project, as I have a number of very definite ideas on how it should be structured."

93

•

APPROXIMATELY 5:45 A.M. THE APARTMENT OF INGRID MACHT, 627 West Twenty-fourth Street, New York, New York. This is tape recording SEC-1SEP68-IM-5:45AM-196L.

> [Sound of doorbell.]
> [Lapse of eleven seconds.]
> [Sound of doorbell.]
> [Lapse of eight seconds.]

INGRID: Yes?

ANDERSON: Duke.

INGRID: Duke, I am sleeping. I am very tired. Please call me later in the day.

ANDERSON: You want me to shoot the lock off?

INGRID: What? What are you saying, Duke?

[Lapse of six seconds.]

INGRID: Oh, my God.

ANDERSON: Yes. Close and lock the door. Put the chain on. Are the shades down?

INGRID: Yes.

ANDERSON: Get me something—some towels. I don't want to drip on your white rug.

INGRID: Oh, *Schatzie, Schatzie.* . . .

[Lapse of nine seconds.]

INGRID: My God, you're soaked. Here . . . let. . . .

ANDERSON: Not so bad now. It's inside now. . . .

INGRID: Gun or knife?

ANDERSON: Gun.

INGRID: How many?

ANDERSON: Two. One high up, just below my wishbone. The other is down and on the side.

INGRID: Did they come out?

ANDERSON: What? I don't think so. Brandy. Get me some brandy.

INGRID: Yes . . . let me help you to the chair. All right. Don't move.

[Lapse of fourteen seconds.]

INGRID: Here. Shall I hold it?

ANDERSON: I can manage. Ah Jesus . . . that helps.

INGRID: Is it bad?

ANDERSON: At first, I wanted to scream. Now it's just dull. A big blackness in there. I'm bleeding in there. I can feel it all going out . . . spreading. . . .

INGRID: I know a doctor. . . .

ANDERSON: Forget it. No use. I'm getting out. . . .

INGRID: And you had to come here. . . .

ANDERSON: Yes. Ah . . . God! Yes, like a hound dragging hisself so he can die at home.

INGRID: You had to come here. Why? To pay me back for what I did?

ANDERSON: For what you did? Oh. No, I forgot that a long time ago. It was nothing.

INGRID: But you had to come here. . . .

ANDERSON: Yes. I came to kill you. See? Here . . . look. . . . Two left. I told you I'd get you out someday. I promised you. . . .

INGRID: Duke, you are not making sense.

ANDERSON: Oh, yes. Oh, yes. If I say. . . . Ah, Jesus . . . the blackness. . . . I can hear the wind. Do you want to yell? Do you want to run into the other room, maybe jump out the window?

INGRID: Ah, *Schatzie, Schatzie* . . . you know me better than that. . . .

ANDERSON: I know you better . . . better than that. . . .

INGRID: It's worse now?

ANDERSON: It's coming in waves, like black waves. It's like the sea. I'm really getting out, I'm getting out. Ah, Jesus. . . .

INGRID: It all went bad?

ANDERSON: Yes. We were so close . . . so close. . . . But it went sour. I don't know why. . . . But for a minute there I had it. I had it all.

INGRID: Yes. You had it all. . . . Duke, I have some drugs. Some shmeck. Do you want a shot? It will make it easier.

ANDERSON: No. No, I can handle this. This isn't so bad.

INGRID: Give me the gun, *Schatzie.*

ANDERSON: I meant what I said.

INGRID: What will that do? How will that help?

ANDERSON: I promised. I gave my word. I promised you. . . .

    [Lapse of seven seconds.]

INGRID: All right. If that is what you must do. It is all over for me, anyway. Even if you died here this instant, it is all over for me.

ANDERSON: Died? Is this the end of me then? Nothing anymore?

INGRID: Yes. The end of John Anderson. Nothing anymore. And the end of Ingrid Macht. And Gertrude Heller. And Bertha Knobel. And all the other women I have been in my life. The end of all of us. Nothing anymore.

ANDERSON: Are you scared?

INGRID: No. This is best. You are right. This is best. I am tired, and I haven't been sleeping lately. This will be a good sleep. You won't hurt me, *Schatzie?*

ANDERSON: I'll make it quick.

INGRID: Yes. Quick. In the head, I think. Here . . . see . . . I will kneel before you. You will be steady?

ANDERSON: I will be steady. You can depend on me.

INGRID: I could always depend on you. Duke, do you remember that day in the park? The picnic we had?

ANDERSON: I remember.

INGRID: For a moment there . . . for a moment. . . .

ANDERSON: I know . . . I know. . . .

INGRID: I think I will turn around now, *Schatzie.* I will turn my back to you. I find I am not as brave as I thought. I will kneel here, my back to you, and I will talk. I will just say anything that comes into my mind. And I will keep talking, and then you will. . . . You understand?

ANDERSON: I understand.

INGRID: What was it all about, Duke? Once I thought I knew. But now I am not sure. You know, the Hungarians have a saying— "Before you have a chance to look around, the picnic is over." It has all gone so fast, Duke. Like a dream. How is it the days crawl by and yet the years fly? Life for me has been a bone caught in my throat. There were little moments, like that afternoon in the park. But mostly it was hurt . . . it was hurt. . . . Duke, please . . . now . . . don't wait any longer. Please. Duke? *Schatzie?* Duke, I. . . .

    [Lapse of five seconds.]

INGRID: Ah. Ah. You are gone, Duke? You are finally out? But I am here. I am here. . . .

    [Lapse of one minute fourteen seconds.]

    [Sound of phone being dialed.]

VOICE: New York Police Department. May I help you?

94

•

THE BODY OF JOHN "DUKE" ANDERSON WAS REMOVED TO THE New York City Morgue at about 7:00 A.M., 1 September, 1968. Ingrid Macht was taken to the House of Detention for Women, 10 Greenwich Avenue. The premises at 627 West Twenty-fourth Street were then sealed and a police guard placed at the door.

On the morning of 2 September, 1968, at Police Headquarters, 240 Centre Street, at approximately 10:00 A.M., a meeting was held of representatives of interested authorities, including the New York Police Department; the District Attorney's Office, County of New York; the Federal Bureau of Investigation; the Internal Revenue Service; the Federal Narcotics Bureau; and the Securities and Exchange Commission. Representatives of the New York Police Department included men from the 251st Precinct, Narcotics Squad, Homicide East, Homicide West, the Police Laboratory, and the Communications Center. There was also a representative from Interpol. The author was allowed to be present at this meeting as an observer.

At this time a squad of ten men was organized and directed to search the apartment of Ingrid Macht at 627 West Twenty-fourth Street, the toss to commence at 3:00 P.M., 2 September, 1968, and to be terminated upon agreement of all representatives present. The author was allowed to attend as an observer but not active participant in the search.

The toss of the aforesaid premises commenced at approximately 3:20 P.M., and was, to my satisfaction, conducted with professional skill, speed, and thoroughness. Evidence was uncovered definitely linking Ingrid Macht with the smuggling of illicit narcotics into this country. There was also some evidence (supposition) that she had been involved in prostitution in the City of New York. In addition, there was evidence (not conclusive) that Ingrid Macht had also been involved in the theft and sale of securities, including stock shares, corporate bonds, and U.S. government bonds.

Also, there was some evidence that Ingrid Macht was operating a loan-shark operation, lending sums to persons she met on her job at the dance hall, to pushers of narcotics, and other individuals known to law enforcement officials. In addition to all this, evidence was uncovered (not sufficient for prosecution) that she was a steerer for an abortion ring, with headquarters in a small New Jersey motel.

During the extremely painstaking search of the premises, a detective from the 251st Precinct discovered a small book concealed beneath the lowest drawer of a five-drawer chest in the bedroom. On first examination, it appeared to be merely a diary. In fact, it was a volume bound in imitation leather (in red; imprinted on the front cover: FIVE-YEAR DIARY). Closer examination proved it to be more in the nature of a commercial ledger, detailing Ingrid Macht's personal dealings in stocks and other securities.

Cursory examination of the entries, which included investments (amounts and dates) and sales (amounts, dates, and profits), showed immediately that Ingrid Macht had been successful in her financial dealings. (In a statement to the press, one of her defense attorneys has estimated her personal wealth as being "in excess of $100,000.")

The author was present when the "diary" was discovered and had an opportunity to leaf through it briefly.

On the inside back cover, in the same handwriting as the other entries in the journal, was this inscription: "Crime is the truth. Law is the hypocrisy."

THE FOURTH DEADLY SIN

•

1

•

THE NOVEMBER SKY OVER MANHATTAN WAS CHAIN MAIL, RAVEL-
ing into steely rain. A black night with coughs of thunder, lightning stabs
that made abrupt days. Dr. Simon Ellerbee, standing at his office window,
peered out to look at life on the street below. He saw only the reflection of
his own haunted face.

He could not have said how it started, or why. He, who had always been
so certain, now buffeted and trembling . . .

All hearts have dark corners, where the death of a loved one is occasionally
wished, laughter offends, and even beauty becomes a rebuke.

He turned back to his desk. It was strewn with files and tape cassettes:
records of his analysands. He stared at that litter of fears, angers, passions,
dreads. Now his own life belonged there, part of the untidiness, where once
it had been ordered and serene.

He stalked about, hands thrust deep into pockets, head bowed. He pondered his predicament and dwindling choices. Mordant thought: How does
one seek "professional help" when one is a professional?

The soul longs for purity, but we are all hungry for the spiced and exotic.
Evil is just a word, and what no one sees, no one knows. Unless God truly
is a busybody.

He lay full-length on the couch some of his patients insisted on using,
though he thought this classic prop of psychiatry was flimflam and often
counterproductive. But there he was, stretched out tautly, trying to still his
churning thoughts and succeeding no better than all the agitated who had
occupied that same procrustean bed.

Groaning, he rose from the couch to resume his pacing. He paused again
to stare through the front window. He saw only a rain-whipped darkness.

The problem, he decided, was learning to acknowledge uncertainty. He,
the most rational of men, must adjust to the variableness of a world in which
nothing is sure, and the chuckles belong to chance and accident. There could
be satisfaction in living with that—fumbling toward a dimly glimpsed end.
For if that isn't art, what is?

The downstairs bell rang three times—the agreed-upon signal for all late-night visitors. He started, then hurried into the receptionist's office to press the buzzer unlocking the entrance from the street. He then unchained and unbolted the door leading from the office suite to the corridor.

He ducked into the bathroom to look in the mirror, adjust his tie, smooth his sandy hair with damp palms. He came back to stand before the outer door and greet his guest with a smile.

But when the door opened, and he saw who it was, he made a thick, strangled sound deep in his throat. His hands flew to cover his face and hide his dismay. He turned away, shoulders slumping.

The first heavy blow landed high on the crown of his head. It sent him stumbling forward, knees buckling. A second blow put him down, biting at the thick pile carpeting.

The weapon continued to rise and fall, crushing his skull. But by that time Dr. Simon Ellerbee was dead, all dreams gone, doubts fled, all questions answered.

2

•

BY MONDAY MORNING THE SKY HAD BEEN RINSED; A CASABA SUN loomed; and pedestrians strode with opened coats flapping. A chill breeze nipped, but New York had the lift of early winter, with stores preparing for Christmas, and street vendors hawking hot pretzels and roasted chestnuts.

Former Chief of Detectives Edward X. Delaney sensed the acceleration. The city, *his* city, was moving faster, tempo changing from andante to con anima. The scent of money was in the air. It was the spending season—and if the boosters didn't make it in the next six weeks, they never would.

He lumbered down Second Avenue, heavy overcoat hanging from his machine-gunner's shoulders. Hard homburg set solidly, squarely, atop his head. Big, flat feet encased in ankle-high shoes of black kangaroo leather. A serious man who looked more like a monsignor than an ex-cop. Except that cops are never ex-.

The sharp weather delighted him, and so did the food shops opening so rapidly in Manhattan. Every day seemed to bring a new Korean greengrocer, a French patisserie, a Japanese take-out. And good stuff, too—delicate mushrooms, tangy fruits, spicy meats.

And the breads! That's what Edward X. Delaney appreciated most. He suffered, as his wife, Monica, said, from "sandwich senility," and this sudden bonanza of freshly baked breads was a challenge to his inventiveness.

Pita, brioche, muffins, light challah and heavy pumpernickel. Loaves no larger than your fist, and loaves of coarse German rye as big as a five-inch shell. Flaky stuff that dissolved on the tongue, and some grainy doughs that hit the stomach with a thud.

He stopped in a half-dozen shops, buying this and that, filling his net shopping bag. Then, fearful of his wife's reaction to his spree, he trundled his way homeward. He had a vision of something new: smoked chub tucked into a split croissant—with maybe a thin slice of Vidalia onion and a dab of mayonnaise, for fun.

This hunched, ponderous man, weighty shoes thumping the pavement, seemed to look at nothing, but he saw everything. As he passed the 251st Precinct house—*his* old precinct—and came to his brownstone, he noted the unmarked black Buick illegally parked in front. Two uniformed cops in the front seat. They glanced at him without interest.

Monica was perched on a stool at the kitchen counter, going through her recipe file.

"You have a visitor," she said.

"Ivar," he said. "I saw his car. Where'd you put him?"

"In the study. I offered a drink or coffee, but he didn't want anything. Said he'd wait for you."

"He might have called first," Delaney grumbled, hoisting his shopping bag onto the counter.

"What's all that stuff?" she demanded.

"Odds and ends. Little things."

She leaned forward to sniff. "Phew! What's that smell?"

"Maybe the blood sausage."

"Blood sausage? Yuck!"

"Don't knock it unless you've tried it."

He bent to kiss the back of her neck. "Put this stuff away, will you, hon? I'll go in and see what Ivar wants."

"How do you know he wants anything?"

"He didn't come by just to say hello—that I know."

He hung his hat and coat in the hall closet, then went through the living room to the study at the rear of the house. He opened and closed the door quietly, and for a moment thought that First Deputy Commissioner Ivar Thorsen might be dozing.

"Ivar," Delaney said loudly, "good to see you."

The Deputy—known in the Department as the "Admiral"—opened his eyes and rose from the club chair alongside the desk. He smiled wanly and held out his hand.

"Edward," he said, "you're looking well."

"I wish I could say the same about you," Delaney said, eyeing the other man critically. "You look like something the cat dragged in."

"I suppose," Thorsen said, sighing. "You know what it's like downtown, and I haven't been sleeping all that much lately."

"Take a glass of stout or port before you go to bed. Best thing in the world for insomnia. And speaking of the old nasty—it's past noon, and you could use some plasma."

"Thank you, Edward," Thorsen said gratefully. "A small scotch would do me fine."

Delaney brought two glasses and a bottle of Glenfiddich from the cellarette. He sat in the swivel chair behind his desk and poured them both tots of the single malt. They tinked glass rims and sipped.

"Ahh," the Admiral said, settling into his armchair. "I could get hooked on this."

He was a neat, precise man. Fine, silvery hair was brushed sideways. Ice-blue eyes pierced the world from under white brows. Ordinarily he had a baby's complexion and a sharp nose and jaw that could have been snipped from sheet metal. But now there were stress lines, sags, pouches.

"Monica had lunch with Karen the other day," Delaney mentioned. "Said she's looking fine."

"What?" Thorsen said, looking up distractedly.

"Karen," Delaney said gently. "Your wife."

"Oh . . . yes," Thorsen said with a confused laugh. "I'm sorry; I wasn't listening."

Delaney leaned toward his guest, concerned. "Ivar, is everything all right?"

"Between Karen and me? Couldn't be better. Downtown? Couldn't be worse."

"More political bullshit?"

"Yes. But this time it's not from the Mayor's office; it's the Department's own bullshit. Want to hear about it?"

Delaney really didn't want to. Political infighting in the upper echelons of the New York Police Department was the reason he had filed for early retirement. He could cope with thieves and killers; he wasn't interested in threading the Byzantine maze of Departmental cliques and cabals. All those intrigues. All those naked ambitions and steamy hatreds.

In the lower, civil service ranks of sergeant, lieutenant, captain, he had known the stress of political pressure—from inside and outside the Department. He had been able to live with it, rejecting it when he could, compromising when he had to.

But nothing had prepared him for the hardball games they played in the appointive ranks. When he got his oak leaves as a Deputy Inspector, he was thrown into a cockpit where the competition was fierce, a single, minor misstep could mean the end of a twenty-year career, and combatants swigged Maalox like fine Beaujolais.

And as he went up the ladder to the two stars of an Assistant Chief, the tension increased with the responsibility. You not only had to do your work, and do it superbly well, but you had constantly to look over your shoulder to see who stood close behind you with a knife and a smirk.

Then he had the three stars of Chief of Detectives, and wanted only to be left alone to do the job he knew he could do. But he was forced to spend too much time soothing his nervous superiors and civilian politicos with enough clout to make life miserable for him if he didn't find out who mugged their nephew.

He couldn't take that kind of constraint, and so Edward X. Delaney turned in his badge. The fault, he acknowledged later, was probably his. He was mentally and emotionally incapable of "going along." He had a hair-trigger temper, a strong sense of his own dignity, and absolute faith in his detective talents and methods of working a case.

He couldn't change himself, and he couldn't change the Department. So he got out before the ulcers popped up, and tried to keep busy, tried to forget what might have been. But still . . .

"Sure, Ivar," he said with a set smile, "I'd like to hear about it."

Thorsen took a sip of his scotch. "You know Chief of Detectives Murphy?"

"Bill Murphy? Of course I know him. We came through the Academy together. Good man. A little plodding maybe, but he thinks straight."

"He's put in his papers. As of the first of the year. He's got cancer of the prostate."

"Ahh, Jesus," Delaney said. "That's a crying shame. I'll have to go see him."

"Well . . ." the Admiral said, peering down at his drink, "Bill thought he could last until the first of the year, but I don't think he's going to make it. He's been out so much we've had to put in an Acting Chief of Detectives to keep the bureau running. The Commish says he'll appoint a permanent late in December."

"Who's the Acting Chief?" Delaney asked, beginning to get interested.

Thorsen looked up at him. "Edward, you remember when they used to say that in New York, the Irish had the cops, the Jews had the schools, and the Italians had the Sanitation Department? Well, things have changed—but not all that much. There's still an Old Guard of the Irish in the Department, and they take care of their own. They just refuse to accept the demographic changes that have taken place in this city—the number of blacks, Hispanics, Orientals. When it came to getting the PC to appoint an Acting Chief of Detectives, I wanted a two-star named Michael Ramon Suarez, figuring it would help community relations. Suarez is a Puerto Rican, and he's been running five precincts in the Bronx and doing a hell of a job. The Chief of Operations, Jimmy Conklin, wanted the Commissioner to pick Terence J. Riordan, who's got nine Brooklyn precincts. So we had quite a tussle."

"I can imagine," Delaney said, pouring them more whiskey. "Who won?"

"I did," Thorsen said. "I got Suarez in as Acting Chief. I figured he'd do a good job, and when the time came, the PC would give him his third star and appoint him permanent Chief of Detectives. A big boost for the Hispanics. And the Mayor would love it."

"Ivar, you should have gone into politics."

"I did," Thorsen said with a crooked grin.

"So? You didn't stop by just to tell me how you creamed the Irish. What's the problem?"

"Edward, did you read the papers over the weekend? Or watch the local TV? That psychiatrist who got wasted—Dr. Ellerbee?"

Delaney looked at him. "I read about it. Got snuffed in his own office, didn't he? And not too far from here. I figured it was a junkie looking for drugs."

"Sure," Thorsen said, nodding. "That was everyone's guess. God knows it happens often enough. But Ellerbee didn't keep any drugs in his office. And there was no sign of forced entry, either at the street entrance or his office door. I don't know all the details, but it looks like he let someone in he knew and expected."

Delaney leaned forward, staring at the other man. "Ivar, what's this all about—your interest in the Ellerbee homicide? It happens four or five times a day in the Big Apple. I didn't think you got all that concerned about one kill."

Thorsen rose and began to pace nervously about the room. "It isn't just another kill, Edward. It could be big trouble. For many reasons. Ellerbee was a wealthy, educated man who had a lot of friends in what they call 'high places.' He was civic-minded—did free work in clinics, for example. His wife—who's a practicing psychologist, by the way—is one of the most beautiful women I've ever seen, and she's been raising holy hell with us. And to top that, Ellerbee's father is Henry Ellerbee, the guy who built Ellerbee Towers on Fifth Avenue and owns more Manhattan real estate than you and I own socks. He's been screaming his head off to everyone from the Governor on down."

"Yes, I'd say you have a few problems."

"And the clincher," Thorsen went on, still pacing, "the clincher is that this is the first big homicide Acting Chief of Detectives Michael Ramon Suarez has had to handle."

"Oh-ho," Delaney said, leaning back in his swivel chair and swinging gently back and forth. "Now we get down to the nitty-gritty."

"Right," the Admiral said, almost angrily. "The nitty-gritty. If Suarez muffs this one, there is no way on God's green earth he's going to get a third star and permanent appointment."

"And you'll look like a shithead for backing him in the first place."

"Right," Thorsen said again. "He'd better clear this one fast or he's in the soup, and I'm in there with him."

"All very interesting," Delaney said. "So?"

The Admiral groaned, slumped into the armchair again. "Edward, you're not making this any easier for me."

"Making what easier?" Delaney said innocently.

Then it all came out in a rush.

"I want you to get involved in the Ellerbee case," the First Deputy Commissioner said. "I haven't even thought about how it can be worked; I wanted to discuss it with you first. Edward, you've saved my ass before—at least twice. I know I gave you a lot of bullshit about doing it for the Department, or doing it just to keep active and not becoming a wet-brained retiree. But this time I'm asking you on the basis of our friendship. I'm asking for a favor— one old friend to another."

"You're calling in your chits, Ivar," Delaney said slowly. "I would never have gone as far as I did without your clout. I know that, and you know I know it."

Thorsen made a waving gesture. "Put it any way you like. The bottom line is that I need your help, and I'm asking for it."

Delaney was silent a moment, looking down at his big hands spread on the desk top.

"I'm getting liver spots," he said absently. "Ivar, have you talked to Suarez about this?"

"Yes, I talked to him. He'll cooperate one hundred percent. He's out of his depth on this case and he knows it. He's got some good men, but no one with your experience and know-how. He'll take help anywhere he can get it."

"Is he working the Ellerbee case personally?"

"After the flak started, he got personally involved. He had to. But from what he told me, so far they've got a dead body, and that's all they've got."

"It happened Friday night?"

"Yes. He was killed about nine P.M. Approximately. According to the ME."

"More than forty-eight hours ago," Delaney said reflectively. "And getting colder by the minute. That means the solution probability is going down."

"I know."

"What was the murder weapon?"

"Some kind of a hammer."

"A hammer?" Delaney said, surprised. "Not a knife, not a gun? Someone brought a hammer to his office?"

"Looks like it. And crushed his skull."

"A hammer is usually a man's weapon," Delaney said. "Women prefer knives or poison. But you never know."

"Well, Edward? Will you help us?"

Delaney shifted his heavy bulk uncomfortably. "If I do—and you notice I say *if*—I don't know how it could be done. I don't have a shield. I can't go around questioning people or rousting them. For God's sake, Ivar, I'm a lousy *civilian*."

"It can be worked out," Thorsen said stubbornly. "The first thing is to persuade you to take the case."

Delaney drew a deep breath, then blew it out. "Tell you what," he said. "Before I give you a yes or no, let me talk to Suarez. If we can't get along, then forget it. If we hit it off, then I'll consider it. I know that's not the answer you want, but it's all you're going to get at the moment."

"It's good enough for me," the Deputy said promptly. "I'll call Suarez, set up the meet, and get back to you. Thank you, Edward."

"For what?"

"For the scotch," Thorsen said. "What else?"

After the Admiral left, Delaney went back into the kitchen. Monica had gone, but there was a note on the refrigerator door, held in place with a little magnetic pig. "Roast duck with walnuts and cassis for dinner. Be back in two hours. Don't eat too many sandwiches."

He smiled at that. But they usually dined at 7:00 P.M., and it was then barely 1:30. One sandwich was certainly not going to spoil his appetite for roast duck. Or even two sandwiches, for that matter.

But he settled for one—which he called his U.N. Special: Norwegian brisling sardines in Italian olive oil heaped on German schwarzbrot, with a layer of thinly sliced Spanish onion and a dollop of French dressing.

He ate this construction while leaning over the sink so it would be easy to rinse the drippings away. And with the sandwich, to preserve the international flavor, he had a bottle of Canadian Molson ale. Finished, the kitchen restored to neatness, he went down into the basement to find the newspapers of the last two days and read again about the murder of Dr. Simon Ellerbee.

Shortly after midnight, Monica went up to their second-floor bedroom. Delaney made his customary rounds, turning off lights and checking window and door locks. Even those in the empty bedrooms where his children by his first wife, Barbara (now deceased), had slept—rooms later occupied by Monica's two daughters.

Then he returned to the master bedroom. Monica, naked, was seated at the dresser, brushing her thick black hair. Delaney perched on the edge of his bed, finished his cigar, and watched her, smiling with pleasure. They conversed in an intimate shorthand:

"Hear from the girls?" he asked.

"Maybe tomorrow."

"Should we call?"

"Not yet."

"We've got to start thinking about Christmas."

"I'll buy the cards if you'll write the notes."

"You want to shower first?"

"Go ahead."

"Rub my back?"

"Later. Leave me a dry towel."

The only light in the room came from a lamp on the bedside table. The tinted silk shade gave the illumination a rosy glow. Delaney watched the play of light on his wife's strong back as she raised her arms to brush, religiously, one hundred times.

She was a stalwart woman with a no-nonsense body: wide shoulders and hips, heavy bosom, and a respectable waist. Muscular legs tapered to slender ankles. There was a warm solidity about her that Delaney cherished. He reflected, not for the first time, how lucky he had been with women: first Barbara and now Monica—two joys.

She took up her flannel robe and went into the bathroom, pausing to glance over her shoulder and wink at him. When he heard the shower start, he began to undress, slowly. He unlaced his high shoes, peeled off the white cotton socks. He removed the heavy gold chain and hunter from his vest. The chunky chain had been his grandfather's, the pocket watch his father's. It had stopped fifty years ago; Delaney had no desire to have it started again.

Off came the dark suit of cheviot as coarse as an army blanket. White shirt with starched collar. Silk rep tie in a muted purple, like a dusty stained-glass window. He hung everything carefully away, moving about the bedroom in underdrawers as long as Bermuda shorts and balbriggan undershirt with cap sleeves.

Monica called him a mastodon, and he supposed he was. There was a belly now—not big, but it was there. There was a layer of new fat over old muscle. But the legs were still strong enough to run, and the shoulders and arms powerful enough to deal a killing blow.

He had come to an acceptance of age. Not what it did to his mind, for he was convinced that was as sharp as ever. Sharper. Honed by experience and reflection. But the body, undeniably, was going. Still, it was no good re-membering when he was a young cop and could scamper up a fire escape, leap an airshaft, or punch out some gorilla who wanted to remake his face.

His face . . . The lines were deeper now, the features ruder—everything beginning to look like it had been hacked from an oak stump with a dull hatchet. But the gray hair, cut *en brosse,* was still thick, and Doc Hagstrom assured him once a year that the ticker was still pumping away sturdily.

Monica came out of the bathroom in her robe, sat again at the dresser, and began to cream her face. He headed for the shower, pausing to touch her shoulder with one finger. Just a touch.

He bathed swiftly, shampooed his stiff hair. Then he put on his pajamas— light cotton flannel, the pants with a drawstring waist, the coat buttoned as precisely as a Norfolk jacket.

When he came out, Monica was already in her bed, sitting up, back propped with pillows. She had taken the bottle of Rémy from the bedside table and poured them each a whack of the cognac in small crystal snifters.

"Bless you," he said.

"You smell nice," she said.

"Nothing but soap."

He turned down the thermostat, opened the window a few inches. Then he got into his own bed, propping himself up as she had done.

"So tell me," she said.

"Tell me what?" he asked, wide-eyed.

"Bastard," she said. "You know very well. What did Ivar Thorsen want?"

He told her. She listened intently.

"Ivar's done a lot for me," he concluded.

"And you've done a lot for him."

"We're friends," he said. "Who keeps score?"

"Diane Ellerbee," she said. "The wife—the widow of the man who was killed—I know her."

"You *know* her?" he said, astonished.

"Well, maybe not know—but I met her. She addressed one of my groups. Her subject was the attraction between young girls and horses."

"Horses?"

"Edward, it's not a joke. Young girls *are* attracted to horses. They love to ride and groom them."

"And how did Mrs. Diane Ellerbee explain this?"

"*Dr.* Diane Ellerbee. There was a lot of Freud in it—and other things. I'll dig out my notes if you're interested."

"Not really. What did you think of her?"

"Very intelligent, very eloquent. And possibly the most beautiful woman I've ever seen. Breathtaking."

"That's what Ivar said."

They were silent a few moments, sipping their cognacs, reflecting.

"You're going to do it?" she asked finally.

"Well, as I said, I want to talk to Suarez first. If we can get along, and work out a way I can act like a, uh, consultant, maybe I will. It might be interesting. What do you think?"

She turned onto her side to look at him. "Edward, if it was a poor nobody who got murdered, would Ivar and the Department be going to all this trouble?"

"Probably not," he admitted. "The victim was a white male WASP. Wealthy, educated, influential. His widow has been raising hell with the Department, and his father, who has mucho clout, has been raising double-hell. So the Department is calling up all the troops."

"Do you think that's fair?"

"Monica," he said patiently, "suppose a junkie with a snootful of shit is found murdered in an alley. The clunk has a sheet as long as your arm, and he's a prime suspect in muggings, robberies, rapes, and God knows what else. Do you really want the Department to spend valuable man-hours trying to find out who burned him? Come on! They're delighted that garbage like that is off the streets."

"I suppose . . ." she said slowly. "But it just doesn't seem right that the rich and influential get all the attention."

"Go change the world," he said. "It's always been like that, and always will. I know you think everyone is equal. Maybe we all are—in God's eyes and under the law. But it's not as clear-cut as that. Some people try to be good, decent human beings, and some are evil scum. The cops, with limited budgets and limited personnel, recognize that. Is it so unusual or outrageous that they'll spend more time and effort protecting the angels than the devils?"

"I don't know," she said, troubled. "It sounds like elitism to me. Besides, how do you know Dr. Simon Ellerbee was an angel?"

"I don't. But he doesn't sound like a devil, either."

"You're really fascinated by all this, aren't you?"

"Just something to do," he said casually.

"I have a better idea of something to do," she said, fluttering her eyes.

"I'm game," he said, smiling.

3

•

THE SMALL, NARROW TOWNHOUSE ON EAST 84TH STREET, BE-tween York and East End avenues, was jointly owned by Drs. Diane and Simon Ellerbee. After its purchase in 1976, they had spent more than $100,000 on renovations, stripping the pine paneling of eleven layers of paint, restoring the handsome staircase, and redesigning the interior to provide four useful floor-throughs.

The first level, up three stone steps from the sidewalk, was occupied by the Piedmont Gallery. It exhibited and sold handwoven fabrics, quilts, and primitive American pottery. It was not a profitable enterprise, but was operated almost as a hobby by two prim, elderly ladies who obviously didn't need income from this commercial venture.

The offices of Dr. Diane Ellerbee were on the second floor, and those of

Dr. Simon Ellerbee on the third. Both floors had been remodeled to include living quarters. Living room, dining room, and kitchen were on the second; two bedrooms and sitting room on the third. Each floor had two bathrooms.

The professional suites on both floors were almost identical: a small outer office for a receptionist and a large, roomy inner office for the doctor. The offices of Drs. Diane and Simon Ellerbee were connected by intercom.

The fourth and top floor of the townhouse was a private apartment, leased as a pied-à-terre by a West Coast filmmaker who was rarely in residence.

In addition to the townhouse, the Ellerbees owned a country home near Brewster, New York. It was a brick and stucco Tudor on 4.5 wooded acres bisected by a swift-running stream. The main house had two master bedrooms on the ground floor and two guest bedrooms on the second. A three-car garage was attached. In the rear of the house was a tiled patio and heated swimming pool.

Both the Ellerbees were avid gardeners, and their English garden was one of the showplaces of the neighborhood. They employed a married couple, Polish immigrants, who lived out. The husband served as groundsman and did maintenance. The wife worked as housekeeper and, occasionally, cook.

It was the Ellerbees' custom to stay in their East 84th Street townhouse weekdays—and, on rare occasions, on Saturday. They usually left for Brewster on Friday evening and returned to Manhattan on Sunday night. Both spent the entire month of August at their country home.

The Ellerbees owned three cars. Dr. Simon drove a new bottle-green Jaguar XJ6 sedan, Dr. Diane a 1971 silver and black Mercedes-Benz SEL 3.5. Both these cars were customarily garaged in Manhattan. The third vehicle, a Jeep station wagon, was kept at their Brewster home.

On the Friday Dr. Simon Ellerbee was murdered, he told his wife—according to her statement to the police—that he had scheduled an evening patient. He suggested she drive back to Brewster as soon as she was free, and he would follow later. He said he planned to leave by 9:00 P.M. at the latest.

Dr. Diane said she left Manhattan at approximately 6:30 P.M. She described the drive north as "ferocious" because of the 40 mph wind and heavy rain. She arrived at their country home about 8:00 P.M. Because of the storm, she guessed her husband would be delayed, but expected him by 10:30 or 11:00.

By 11:30, she stated she was concerned by his absence and called his office. There was no reply. She called two more times with the same result. Around midnight, she called the Brewster police station, asking if they had any report of a car accident involving a Jaguar XJ6 sedan. They had not.

Becoming increasingly worried, she phoned the Manhattan garage where the Ellerbees kept their cars. After a wait of several minutes, the night attendant reported that Dr. Simon Ellerbee's Jaguar had not been taken out; it was still in its slot.

"I was getting frantic," she later told detectives. "I thought he might have been mugged walking to the garage. It happened once before."

So, at approximately 1:15 A.M., Dr. Diane called Dr. Julius K. Samuelson. He was also a psychiatrist, a widower, and close friend and frequent house-guest of the Ellerbees. Dr. Samuelson was also president of the Greater New York Psychiatric Association. He lived in a cooperative apartment at 79th Street and Madison Avenue.

Samuelson was not awakened by Diane Ellerbee's phone call, having recently returned from a concert by the Stuttgart String Ensemble at Carnegie Hall. When Dr. Diane explained the situation, he immediately agreed to taxi to the Ellerbees' house and try to find Dr. Simon or see if anything was amiss.

Samuelson stated he arrived at the East 84th Street townhouse at about 1:45 A.M. He asked the cabdriver to wait. It was still raining heavily. He stepped from the cab into a streaming gutter, then hurried across the sidewalk and up the three steps to the front entrance. He found the door ajar.

"Not wide open," he told detectives. "Maybe two or three inches."

Samuelson was fifty-six, a short, slender man, but not lacking in physical courage. He tramped determinedly up the dimly lighted, carpeted staircase to the offices of Dr. Simon on the third floor. He found the office door wide open. Within, he found the battered body.

He checked first to make certain that Ellerbee was indeed dead. Then, using the phone on the receptionist's desk, he dialed 911. The call was logged in at 1:54 A.M.

All the above facts were included in New York City newspaper reports and on local TV newscasts following the murder.

4

•

DELANEY PLANTED HIMSELF ACROSS THE STREET FROM ACTING Chief Suarez's house on East 87th, off Lexington Avenue. He squinted at it, knowing exactly how it was laid out; he had grown up in a building much like that one.

It was a six-story brownstone, with a flight of eight stone steps, called a stoop, leading to the front entrance. Originally, such a building was an old-law tenement with two railroad flats on each floor, running front to back, with almost every room opening onto a long hallway.

"Cold-water flats," they were sometimes called. Not because there was no hot water; there was if you had a humane landlord. But the covered bathtub was in a corner of the kitchen, and the toilet was out in the hall, serving the two apartments.

Not too many brownstones like that left in Manhattan. They were being demolished for glass and concrete high-rise co-ops or being purchased at horrendous prices in the process called "gentrification," and converted into something that would warrant a six-page, four-color spread in *Architectural Digest*.

Edward X. Delaney wasn't certain that was progress—but it sure as hell was change. And if you were against change, you had to mourn for the dear, departed days when all of Manhattan was a cow pasture. Still, he allowed himself a small pang of nostalgia, remembering his boyhood in a building much like the one across the street.

He saw immediately that the people who lived there were waging a valiant battle against the city's blight. No graffiti. Washed windows and clean curtains. Potted ivy at the top of the stoop (the pots chained to the railing). The plastic garbage cans in the areaway were clean and had lids. All in all, a neat, snug building with an air of modest prosperity.

Delaney lumbered across the street, thinking it was an offbeat home for an Acting Chief of the NYPD. Most of the Department's brass lived in Queens, or maybe Staten Island.

The bell plate was polished and the intercom actually worked. When he pressed the 3-B button alongside the neatly typed name, M.R. SUAREZ, a childish voice piped, "Who is it?"

"Edward X. Delaney here," he said, leaning forward to speak into the little round grille.

There was static, the sound of thumps, then the inner door lock buzzed, and he pushed his way in. He tramped up to the third floor.

The man waiting for him at the opened apartment door was a Don Quixote figure: tall, thin, splintery, with an expression at once shy, deprecatory, rueful.

"Mr. Delaney?" he said, holding out a bony hand. "I am Michael Ramon Suarez."

"Chief," Delaney said. "Happy to make your acquaintance. I appreciate your letting me stop by; I know how busy you must be."

"It is an honor to have you visit my home, sir," Suarez said with formal courtesy. "I hope it is no inconvenience for you. I would have come to you gladly."

Delaney knew that; in fact, Deputy Commissioner Thorsen had suggested it. But Delaney wanted to meet with the Acting Chief in his own home and get an idea of his life outside the Department: as good a way to judge a man as any.

The apartment seemed mobbed with children—five of them ranging in age from three to ten. Delaney was introduced to them all: Michael, Jr.,

Maria, Joseph, Carlo, and Vita. And when Mrs. Rosa Suarez entered, she was carrying a baby, Thomas, in her arms.

"Your own basketball team," Delaney said, smiling. "With one substitute."

"Rosa wishes to try for a football team," Suarez said dryly. "But there I draw the line."

They made their guest sit in the best chair, and, despite his protests that he had just dined, brought coffee and a platter of crisp pastries dusted with powdered sugar. The entire family, baby included, had coffee laced with condensed milk. Delaney took his black.

"Delicious," he pronounced after his first cup. "Chicory, Mrs. Suarez?"

"A little," she said faintly, lowering her eyes and blushing at his praise.

"And these," he said, raising one of the sweetmeats aloft. "Homemade?"
She nodded.

"I love them," he said. "You know, the Italians and French and Polish make things very similar."

"Just fried dough," Suarez said. "But Rosa makes the best."

"I concur," Delaney said, reaching for another.

He got the kids talking about their schools, and while they chattered away he had a chance to look around.

Not a luxurious apartment—but spotless. Walls a tenement green. A large crucifix. One hanging of black velvet painted with what appeared to be a view of Waikiki Beach. Patterned linoleum on the floor. Furniture of orange maple that had obviously been purchased as a five-piece set.

None of it to Delaney's taste, but that was neither here nor there. Any honest cop with six children wasn't about to buy Louis Quatorze chairs or Aubusson carpets. The important thing was that the home was warm and clean, the kids were well fed and well dressed. Delaney's initial impression was of a happy family with love enough to go around.

The kids begged to watch an hour of TV—a comedy special—and then promised to go to their rooms, the younger to sleep, the older to do their homework. Suarez gave his permission, then led his visitor to the large kitchen at the rear of the apartment and closed the door.

"We shall have a little peace and quiet in here," he said.

"Kids don't bother me," Delaney said. "I have two of my own and two stepdaughters. I like kids."

"Yes," the Chief said, "I could see that. Please sit here."

The kitchen was large enough to accommodate a long trestle table that could seat the entire family. Delaney noted a big gas range and microwave oven, a food processor, and enough pots, pans, and utensils to handle a company of Marines. He figured good food ranked high on the Suarez family's priority list.

He sat on one of the sturdy wooden chairs. The Chief suddenly turned.

"I called you Mr. Delaney," he said. "Did I offend?"

"Of course not. That's what I am—a mister. No title."

"Well . . . you know," Suarez said with his wry smile, "some retired cops prefer to be addressed by their former rank—captain, chief, deputy . . . whatever."

"Mister will do me fine," Delaney said cheerfully. "I'm just another civilian."

"Not quite."

They sat across the table from each other. Delaney saw a long-faced man with coarse black hair combed back from a high forehead. A thick mustache drooped. Olive skin and eyes as dark and shiny as washed coal. A mouthful of strong white teeth.

He also saw the sad, troubled smile and the signs of stress: an occasional tic at the left of the mouth, bagged shadows under the eyes, furrows etched in the brow. Suarez was a man under pressure—and beginning to show it. Delaney wondered how he was sleeping—or if he was sleeping.

"Chief," he said, "when I was on active duty, they used to call me Iron Balls. I never could figure out exactly what that meant, except maybe I was a hard-nosed, blunt-talking bastard. I insisted on doing things my way. I made a lot of enemies."

"So I have heard," Suarez said softly.

"But I always tried to be up-front in what I said and what I did. So now I want to tell you this: On the Ellerbee case, forget what Deputy Commissioner Thorsen told you. I don't know how heavily he's been leaning on you, but if you don't want me in, just say so right now. I won't be offended. I won't be insulted. Just tell me you want to work the case yourself, and I'll thank you for a pleasant evening and the chance to meet you and your beautiful family. Then I'll get out of your hair."

"Deputy Thorsen has been very kind to me," he said. "Kinder than you can ever know."

"Bullshit!" Delaney said angrily. "Thorsen is trying to save his own ass and you know it."

"Yes," Suarez said earnestly, "that is true. But there is more to it than that. How long has it been since you turned in your tin, Mr. Delaney—five years?"

"A little more than that."

"Then you cannot be completely aware of the changes that have taken place in the Department, and are taking place. A third of all the cops on duty have less than five years' experience. The old height requirement has been junked. Now we have short cops, black cops, female cops, Hispanic cops, Oriental cops, gay cops. At the same time we have more and more cops with a college education. And men and women who speak foreign languages. It is a revolution, and I am all for it."

Delaney was silent.

"These kids are motivated," Suarez went on. "They study law and take courses in sociology and psychology and human relations. It has to help the Department—don't you think?"

"It can't hurt," Delaney said. "The city is changing. If the Department doesn't change along with it, the Department will go down the tube."

"Yes," the Chief said, leaning back. "Exactly. Thorsen realizes that also. So he has been doing whatever he can whenever he can to remake the Department so that it reflects the new city. He has been pushing for more minority cops on the street and for advancement of minorities to higher ranks. Especially appointive ranks. You think I would have two stars today if it was not for Thorsen's clout? No way! So when you tell me he is trying to save his own ass by bringing you in on the Ellerbee case, I say yes, that is true. But it is also to protect something in which he believes deeply."

"Thorsen is a survivor," Delaney said harshly. "And a shrewd infighter. Don't worry about Thorsen. I owe him as much as you do. I know damned well what he's up against. He's fighting the Irish Mafia every day he goes downtown. Those guys remember the way the Department was thirty years ago, and that's the way they want it to be today—an Irish kingdom. I can say that because I'm a mick myself, but I had my own fights with harps in high places. I agree with everything you've said. I'm just telling you to be your own man. Screw Thorsen and screw me. If you want to work on the Ellerbee case on your own, say so. You'll break it or you won't. Either way, it'll be *your* way. And God knows if I do come in, there's absolutely no guarantee that I can do a damned bit of good—for you, for Thorsen, or for the Department."

There was silence, then Suarez said in a low voice, "I admit that when Deputy Thorsen first suggested that he bring you into the investigation, I was insulted. I know your reputation, of course. Your record of closed files. Still, I thought Thorsen was saying, in effect, that he did not trust me. I almost told him right off that I wanted no help from you or anyone else; I would handle the Ellerbee homicide by myself. Fortunately, I held my tongue, came home, thought about it, and talked it over with Rosa."

"That was smart," Delaney said. "Women may know shit-all about Department politics, but they sure know a hell of a lot about people—and that's what the Department is."

"Well . . ." Suarez said, sighing, "Rosa made me see that it was an ego thing for me. She said that if I failed on the Ellerbee case, everyone in the city would say, 'See, the spic can't cut the mustard.' She said I should accept help anywhere I could get it. Also, there is another thing. If the Ellerbee crime is solved, Thorsen will try to get me a third star and permanent appointment as Chief of Detectives when Murphy retires. Did you know that?"

"Yes. Thorsen told me."

"So there are a lot of motives involved—political, ethnic, personal. I cannot honestly tell you which is the strongest. So I gave the whole matter many hours of very heavy thought."

"I'll bet you did," Delaney said. "It's a tough decision to make."

"Another factor . . ." Suarez said. "I have some very good men in my bureau."

"I trained a lot of them myself."

"I know that. But none have your talent and experience. I don't say that to butter you up; it is the truth. I spoke to several detectives who worked with you on various cases. They all said the same thing: If you can get Delaney, *get him!* So that finally made up my mind. If you would be willing to help me on the Ellerbee homicide, I will welcome your help with deep gratitude and give you all the cooperation I possibly can."

Delaney leaned forward to look at him. "You're sure about this?"

"Absolutely sure."

"You realize I might strike out? Believe me, it wouldn't be the first time I failed. Far from it."

"I realize that."

"All right, let's get down to nuts and bolts. I've been following the case in the papers. Reading between the lines, I'd say you haven't got much."

"Much?" Suarez cried. "We have nothing!"

"Let me tell you what I know about it. Then you tell me what I've got wrong."

Speaking rapidly, Delaney summarized what he had read in newspaper accounts and heard on TV newscasts. Suarez listened intently, not interrupting. When Delaney finished, the Chief said, "Yes, that is about it. Some of the times you mentioned are a little off, but not enough to make any big difference."

Delaney nodded. "Now tell me what you *didn't* give to the reporters."

"Several things," Suarez said. "They may or may not mean anything. First of all, the victim told his wife he was staying in Manhattan because he was expecting a patient late on Friday evening. We found his appointment book on his desk. The last patient listed was for five P.M. No one listed after five. The receptionist says that was not unusual. Sometimes the doctor got what they called 'crisis screams.' A patient who is really disturbed phones and says he must see the shrink immediately. The doctor makes the appointment and neglects to tell the receptionist. She left at five o'clock anyway, right after the last patient listed in the appointment book arrived."

"Uh-huh," Delaney said. "Could happen . . ."

"The second thing is this. The Medical Examiner thinks the murder weapon was a ball peen hammer. You know what that is?"

"A ball peen? Sure. It's got a little rounded knob on one side of the head."

"Correct. I asked, and found that such a hammer is used to shape metal— like taking a dent out of a fender. Ellerbee was struck multiple blows on the top and back of his skull with the ball peen. They found many round wounds, like punctures."

"Multiple blows? Someone hammering away even after he was a clunk?"

"Yes. The ME calls the attack 'frenzied.' Many more blows than were needed to kill him. But that is not all. After Ellerbee was dead, the killer apparently rolled him over onto his back and struck him two more times. In his eyes. One blow to each eye."

"That's nice," Delaney said. "Was the rounded knob of the ball peen used on the eyes?"

"It was. When Dr. Samuelson found the corpse, it was on its back, the eyes a mess."

"All right," Delaney said. "Anything else you didn't give the press?"

"Yes. When Samuelson discovered the body, he called nine-eleven, then went back downstairs to wait for the cops. A car with two uniforms responded. Here is where we got a little lucky—I think. Because those two blues, first on the scene, did everything by the book. One of them hung on to Samuelson and his cabdriver, making sure they would not take off. Meanwhile, he called in for backup, saying they had a reported homicide. The second blue went upstairs to confirm the kill. You remember how hard it was raining Friday night? Well, the uniform who went upstairs saw soaked tracks on the carpet of the hall and the staircase leading to the third floor. So he was careful to step as close to the wall as he could to preserve the prints."

"That was smart," Delaney said. "Who was he?"

"A big, big black," Suarez said. "I talked with him, and he made me feel like a midget."

"My God!" Delaney said, astonished. "Don't tell me his name is Jason T. Jason?"

It was Suarez's turn to be astonished. "That is who it was. You know him?"

"Oh, hell yes. We worked together. They call him Jason Two. A brainy lad. There's detective material if ever I saw it. He'd never go trampling over everything."

"Well, he did not. So when the Crime Scene Unit arrived, they were able to eliminate his wet prints on the carpet of the staircase and in the receptionist's office where the body was found. A day later, they had also eliminated Dr. Samuelson's footprints. He was wearing street shoes and has very small feet. The kicker is this: That left *two* sets of unidentified wet prints on the carpet."

"*Two* sets?"

"Absolutely. The photos prove it. Ellerbee had two visitors that night. Both were wearing rubbers or galoshes. Indistinct blots, but there is no doubt they were made by two different people."

"Son of a bitch," Delaney said. "Male or female?"

Suarez shrugged. "With rubbers or boots, who knows? But there were two sets of prints left after Samuelson's and Jason's were eliminated."

"Two sets of prints," Delaney repeated thoughtfully. "How do you figure that?"

"I do not. Do you?"

"No."

"Well," Suarez said, "that's all the information that has not yet been released. Now let us discuss how we are going to manage your assistance in this investigation. You tell me what you would like and I will make every effort to provide what I can."

They talked for another half hour. They agreed it would be counterproductive to run two separate investigations of the same crime.

"We'd be walking up each other's heels," Delaney said.

So they would try to coordinate their efforts, with Suarez in command and Delaney offering suggestions and consulting with Suarez as frequently as developments warranted.

"Here's what I'll need," Delaney said. "First of all, a Department car, unmarked. Then I want Sergeant Abner Boone as an assistant to serve as liaison officer with you and your crew. Right now he's heading a Major Crime Unit in Manhattan North. I want him."

"No problem," Suarez said. "I know Boone. Good man. But he . . ."

His voice trailed away. Delaney looked at him steadily.

"Yes," he said, "Boone was on the sauce. But he straightened himself out. Getting married helped. He hasn't had a drink in more than two years. My wife and I see him and his wife two or three times a month, and believe me, I know: the man is clean."

"If you say so," Suarez said apologetically. "Then by all means let us have Sergeant Boone."

"And Jason Two," Delaney said. "I want to give that guy a chance; he deserves it."

"In uniform?"

Delaney thought a moment. "No. Plainclothes. I need Boone and Jason because they've got shields. They can flash their potzies and get me in places I couldn't go as a civilian. Also, I'll want to see copies of everything you've got on the case—reports, memos, photos, the PM, fake confessions, tips, the whole schmear."

"It can be done," Suarez said, nodding. "But you realize of course I will have to clear all this with Deputy Thorsen."

"Sure. Keep him in the picture. That'll keep him off my back."

"Yes," Suarez said sadly, "and on mine."

Delaney laughed. "It comes with the territory," he said.

They sat back and relaxed.

"Tell me, Chief, what have you done so far?"

"At first," Suarez said, "we thought it was a junkie looking to score. So we leaned on all our snitches. No results. We searched every garbage can and sewer basin in a ten-block area for the murder weapon. Nothing. We canvassed every house on the street, and then spread out to the whole area. No one had seen anything—they said. We checked out the license plates of all parked cars near the scene of the crime and contacted the owners. Again, nothing. We have more or less eliminated the wife and Dr. Samuelson; their alibis hold up. Now we are attempting to question every one of his patients. And former patients. Almost a hundred of them. It is a long, hard job."

"It's got to be done," Delaney said grimly. "And his friends and professional associates?"

"Yes, them also. So far we have drawn a blank. You will see all this from the reports. Sometimes I think it is hopeless."

"No," Delaney said, "it's never hopeless. Occasionally you get a break when you least expect it. I remember a case I worked when I was a dick two. This young woman got offed in Central Park. The crazy thing was that she was almost bald. We couldn't figure it until we talked to her friends and found out she had cancer and was on chemotherapy. The friends said she usually wore a blond wig. We were nowhere on this case, but three weeks later the One-oh Precinct raided an after-hours joint and picked up a transvestite wearing a blond wig. One of the arresting cops remembered the Central Park killing and called up. Same wig. It had the maker's name on a tiny label inside. So we leaned on the transvestite. He hadn't chilled the woman, but he told us who he had bought the wig from, and eventually we got the perp. It was luck—just dumb luck. All I'm saying is that the same thing could happen on this Ellerbee kill."

"Let us pray," Michael Ramon Suarez said mournfully.

After a while Delaney rose to leave. The two men shook hands. Suarez said he would check everything with Deputy Thorsen immediately and call Delaney the following morning.

"I thank you," he said solemnly. "For your honesty and for your kindness. I believe we can work well together."

"Sure we can," Delaney said heartily. "We may scream at one another now and then, but we both want the same thing."

In the living room, Mrs. Rosa Suarez was seated before the darkened television set, placidly knitting. Delaney thanked her for her hospitality, and suggested that she and her husband might like to visit his home.

"That would be nice," she said, smiling shyly. "But with the children and the baby . . . Well, perhaps we can arrange it."

"Try," he urged. "I have a feeling you and my wife would hit it off."

She looked at her husband. If a signal passed between them, Delaney didn't catch it.

At the door, she put a hand on his arm. "Thank you for helping," she said in a low voice. "You are a good man."

"I'm not so sure about that," he said.

"I am," she said softly.

5

.

THEY WERE HAVING A BREAKFAST OF EGGS SCRAMBLED WITH onions and lox. Delaney was chomping a buttered bagel.

"What are your plans for today?" he asked idly.

"Shopping," Monica said promptly. "With Rebecca. All day. We'll have lunch somewhere. I'll buy the Christmas cards and gifts for the children."

"Good."

"What would you like for Christmas?"

"Me? I'm the man who's got everything."

"That's what *you* think, buster. How about a nice cigar case from Dunhill?"

He considered that. "Not bad," he admitted. "That old one I've got is falling apart. A dark morocco would be nice. What would you like?"

"Please," she said, "no more drugstore perfume. Surprise me. Are you going shopping?"

"No, I'll hang around awhile. Suarez said he'd call, and I want to be here."

"What would you like for dinner?"

"You know what we haven't had for a long time? Creamed chicken on buttermilk biscuits with—"

"With mashed potatoes and peas," she finished, laughing. "A real goyish meal. A good Jew wouldn't be caught dead eating that stuff."

"Force yourself," he told her. "I just suffered through a Jewish breakfast, didn't I?"

"Some suffering," she jeered. "You gobbled that—"

But then the phone rang, and he rose to answer it.

"Edward X. Delaney here," he said. "Yes, Chief . . . Good morning . . . You did? And what was his reaction? Fine. Fine. I thought he'd go for it. Yes, I'll wait for them. Thank you, Chief. I'll be in touch."

He hung up and turned to Monica.

"Thorsen okayed everything. I'm getting the car, and Boone and Jason T. Jason will be delegated to me, through Suarez, on temporary assignment. They're copying the files now and will probably be here before noon."

"Can I tell Rebecca about Abner?"

"Sure. He's probably told her already."

"Are you happy about this, Edward?"

"Happy?" he said, surprised at the word. "Well, I'm satisfied. Yes, I guess I'm happy. It's nice to be asked to do a job."

"They need you," she said stoutly.

"No guarantees. I warned Thorsen and I warned Suarez."

"But the challenge really excites you."

He shrugged.

"You'll crack it," she assured him.

"*Crack* it?" he said, smiling. "You're showing your age, dear. Cops don't crack cases anymore, and reporters don't get scoops. That was all long ago."

"Goodbye, then," she said, "if I'm so dated. You clean up. I'm going shopping."

"Spend money," he said. "Enjoy."

He did clean up, scraps and dishes and coffeemaker. He shouted a farewell to Monica when she departed, then went into the study to read the morning *Times* and smoke a cigar. But then he put the paper aside a moment to reflect.

You just couldn't call it a challenge—as Monica had; there was more to it than that.

Every day hundreds—thousands—of people were dying in wars, revolutions, terrorist bombings, religious feuds; on highways, in their homes, walking down the street, in their beds. Unavoidable deaths, some of them—just accidents. But too many the result of deliberate violence.

So why be so concerned with the killing of a single human being? Just another cipher in a long parade of ciphers. Not so. Edward X. Delaney could do little about wars; he could not end mass slaughter. His particular talent was individual homicide. Event and avenger were evenly matched.

A life should not be stopped before its time by murder. That's what it came down to.

He took up his newspaper again, wondering if he was spinning fantastical reasons that had no relation to the truth. His motives might be as complex as those of Michael Ramon Suarez in seeking his help.

Finally, common sense made him mistrust all these soft philosophical musings and he came back to essentials: A guy had been chilled, Delaney was a cop, his job was to find the killer. That defined his role as something of value: hard, simple, and understandable. He could be content with that.

He finished his newspaper and cigar at about the same time, and put both aside. The *Times* carried a one-column story on the Ellerbee homicide in the Metropolitan Section. It was mostly indignant tirades from Henry Ellerbee and Dr. Diane Ellerbee, denouncing the NYPD for lack of progress in solving the murder.

Acting Chief of Detectives Suarez was quoted as saying that the Department was investigating several "promising leads," and "significant developments" were expected shortly. Which was, as Delaney well knew, police horseshit for "We ain't got a thing and don't know where to turn next."

• • •

THE TWO OFFICERS arrived a little after noon, lugging four cartons tied with twine. Delaney led them directly into the study, where they piled the boxes in a high stack. Then they all had a chance to shake hands, grinning at each other. The two cops were wearing mufti, and Delaney took their anoraks and caps to the hall closet. They were still standing when he returned to the study.

"Sit down, for God's sake," he said. "Sergeant, I saw you ten days ago, so I know how *you* are. Monica's out with Rebecca today, by the way, spending our money. Jason, I haven't seen you in—what's it been?—almost two years. Don't tell me you've lost some weight?"

"Maybe a few pounds, sir. I didn't think it showed."

"Well, you're looking great. Family okay?"

"Couldn't be better, thank you. My two boys are sprouting up like weeds. All they talk about is basketball."

"Don't knock it," Delaney advised. "Good bucks there."

The two officers didn't ask any questions about what the deal was and what they were doing there—and Delaney knew they wouldn't. But he felt he owed them a reason for their presence.

Briefly, he told them that Acting Chief of Detectives Suarez had more on his plate than he could handle, and Deputy Commissioner Thorsen had asked Delaney to help out on the Ellerbee homicide because the Department was getting so much flak from the victim's widow and father—both people of influence.

Delaney said nothing about the cutthroat ethnic and political wars being waged in the top ranks of the NYPD. Boone and Jason seemed to accept his censored explanation readily enough.

"Sergeant," Delaney said, "you'll assist in my investigation and liaise with Suarez's crew. Remember, he's in command; I'm just a civilian consultant. Jason, you'll be here, there, everywhere you're needed. These are temporary assignments. If the case is cleared, or I get bounced, the two of you go back to your regular duties. Okay?"

"Suits me just fine," Jason Two said.

"It'll be a vacation," Sergeant Boone said. "Working just one case."

"Vacation, hell!" Delaney said. "I'm going to run your ass off. Now the first thing the three of us are going to do is go through all the paper on the Ellerbee kill. We'll read every scrap, look at every photo. We'll take a break in an hour or so. I've got some sandwiches and drinks. Then we'll get back to it until we've emptied the cartons. Then we'll sit around and gas and decide what we do first."

They set to work, opening the cartons, piling the photocopied documents on Delaney's desk. He read each statement first, then handed it to Boone, who scanned it and passed it along to Officer Jason. Most of the stuff was short memos, and those went swiftly. But the Medical Examiner's postmortem and the reports of the Crime Scene Unit were longer and took time to digest.

Delaney smoked another cigar, and the two cops chain-smoked cigarettes. The study fogged up, and Delaney rose to switch on an exhaust fan set in the back window. But there was no conversation; they worked steadily for more than an hour. Then they broke for lunch. Delaney brought in a platter of sandwiches he'd prepared earlier and cans of Heineken for Jason and himself. Abner Boone had a bottle of club soda.

Delaney parked his feet up on his desk.

"Jason," he said, "you did a hell of a job keeping clear of those wet tracks on the carpet."

"Thank you, sir."

"I think your report covered just about everything. Nothing you left out, was there?"

"Nooo," the officer said slowly, "not to my remembrance."

"When you went up the stairs," Delaney persisted, "and into the receptionist's office, did you smell anything?"

"Smell? Well, that was a damned wet night. The inside of that house smelled damp. Almost moldy."

"But nothing unusual? Perfume, incense, cooking odors—something like that?"

The big black frowned. "Can't recall anything unusual. Just the wet."

"That art gallery on the first floor—the door was locked?"

"Yes, sir. And so was the door to Dr. Diane Ellerbee's office on the second floor. And so was that private apartment on the fourth. The victim's office was the only one open."

"He was lying on his back?"

"Yes, sir. Not a pretty sight."

"Sergeant," Delaney said, swinging his swivel chair to face Boone, "how do you figure those two hammer blows to the eyes? After the poor guy was dead."

"That seems plain enough. Symbolic stuff. The killer wanted to blind him."

"Sure," Delaney agreed. "But after he was dead? That's heavy."

"Well, Ellerbee was a psychiatrist dealing with a lot of crazies. It could have been a patient who thought the doctor was seeing too much."

Delaney stared at him. "That's interesting—and plausible. Listen, there are three sandwiches left, and I've got more beer and soda. Why don't we finish eating and work at the same time?"

They were done a little after 3:00 P.M., and stuffed everything back in the cartons. Then they all sat back and stared at each other.

"Well?" Delaney demanded. "What do you think of the investigation so far?"

Boone drew a deep breath. "I don't like to put the knock on anyone," he said hesitantly, "but it appears to me that Chief Suarez hasn't been riding herd on his guys. For instance, in her statement Dr. Diane Ellerbee says she called Dr. Julius Samuelson about one-fifteen in the morning. The guy who's supposed to check it out goes to Samuelson and asks, 'Did Dr. Diane call you at one-fifteen?' And Samuelson says, 'Yes, she did.' Now what kind of garbage is that? Maybe the two of them were in it together and protecting each other's ass. She says she called from their Brewster home. That's a toll call to Manhattan. So why didn't someone check phone company records to make sure the call was actually made?"

"Right!" Jason T. Jason said loudly. "Ditto her call to the Ellerbees' garage. The night attendant says, 'Yeah, she called,' but no one checked to make sure the call was made from Brewster. Sloppy, sloppy work."

"I concur," Delaney said approvingly. "And Samuelson said he was at a concert in Carnegie Hall when Ellerbee was offed. But I didn't see a damned thing in those four cartons that shows anyone checked that out. Was he at the concert with someone or was he alone? And if he was alone, did anyone see him there? Does he have a ticket stub? Can the Carnegie Hall people place him there that night? Chief Suarez said he had more or less eliminated the widow and Samuelson as suspects. *Bullshit!* We've got a way to go before I'll clear them. Don't blame Suarez; he's got a zillion other things on his mind besides this Ellerbee kill. But I agree; so far it's been a half-ass investigation."

"So?" Boone said. "Where do we go from here?"

"Jason," Delaney said, pointing a thick forefinger at him, "you take the widow. Check out those two calls she says she made from Brewster. And while you're at it, talk to the Brewster cop she says she phoned to ask if there was a highway accident. Make sure she *did* call, and ask the cop how she sounded. Was she hysterical, cool, angry—whatever. Boone, you take Samuelson and his alibi. See if you can find out if anyone can actually place him at Carnegie Hall at the time Ellerbee was killed."

"You think the widow and Samuelson might be lying?" Jason said.

"Oh, Jesus," Delaney said. "I lie, you lie, Boone lies, everyone lies. It's part of the human condition. Mostly it's innocent stuff—just to help us all get through life a little easier. But in this case we've got a stiff on our hands. Yes, the widow and Samuelson might be lying—even if they're not the perps. Maybe they have other reasons. Let's find out."

"What do *you* plan on doing, sir?" Sergeant Boone asked curiously.

"Me? I want to study those statements about the hassle Dr. Samuelson had with the Department's legal eagles. The argument was about the doctor-patient relationship, which is supposed to be sacred under the law. Ha-ha. But here we have a case where a doctor has been knocked off and the Crime Scene Unit guys grabbed his appointment book. So now we know the names of his patients, but Samuelson claimed the files were confidential. The Department's attorneys said not so; a murder was committed and the public good required that patients be questioned. As I understand it, they came to a compromise. The patients can be investigated, but they cannot be *questioned* unless they agree to it, because the questioning might involve their illness— the reason they were consulting Ellerbee in the first place. It's a nice legal point, and could keep a platoon of lawyers busy for a year. But as things stand now, we can check the whereabouts of every patient at the time of Ellerbee's death, but we can't question the patients or examine their files unless they agree to it. Now isn't that as fucked up as a Chinese fire drill?"

"You think the patients will agree to answer questions?" Boone said.

"I think if one of his patients chilled Ellerbee, he or she will agree to be questioned, figuring that if they refuse, they'll be automatically suspected by the cops."

"Oh, wow," Jason Two said, laughing. "You figure crazies can reason like that?"

"First of all we don't know yet just how nutty his patients are. Second, you can be a complete whacko and still be able to think as rationally as any so-called normal man or woman. I remember a guy we racked up who was a computer whiz. I mean a genius. All his work involved mathematical logic. But he had one quirk: He liked to rape little girls. Except for that, he was an intellectual giant. So don't get the idea that all of Ellerbee's patients are dummies."

"When are we going to get started on the patient list, sir?" Jason asked.

"Another thing," Delaney said, ignoring Jason's question. "I saw nothing in those cartons to indicate that anyone had thought to run the victim, his widow, his father, and Dr. Samuelson through Records."

"My God," Boone said, "you don't think people like that have jackets, do you?"

"No, I don't—but you never know, do you, and it's got to be done. Ditto the Ellerbees' two receptionists, the old ladies who own the art gallery, and the guy who leases the apartment on the top floor. Sergeant, you do that. Run them all through Records. For the time being let's concentrate on the people who live and work in that townhouse. Plus Samuelson and Ellerbee's father. After we've cleared them, we'll spread out to friends, acquaintances, and Ellerbee's patients."

They talked a while longer, discussing how they'd divide up use of the Department car and how they'd keep in touch with each other. Delaney urged both men to call him any hour of the day or night if they had any problems or anything to report.

Then the two officers left, and Delaney returned to his study. He called Deputy Commissioner Thorsen and was put through immediately.

"All right, Ivar," Delaney said. "We've started."

"Thank God," the Admiral said. "If there's anything I can do to help, just let me know."

"There is something," Delaney said. "The Department has a house shrink, doesn't it?"

"Sure," Thorsen said. "Dr. Murray Walden. He set up alcohol and drug rehabilitation programs. And he's got a family counseling service. A very active, innovative man."

"Dr. Murray Walden," Delaney repeated, jotting the name on his desk calendar. "Would you phone him and tell him to expect a call from me?"

"Of course."

"He'll cooperate?"

"Absolutely. Did you go through the files, Edward?"

"I did. Once."

"See anything?"

"A lot of holes."

"That's what I was afraid of. You'll plug them, won't you?"

"That's what I'm getting paid for. By the way, Ivar, what *am* I getting paid?"

"A case of Glenfiddich," Thorsen said. "And maybe a medal from the Mayor."

"Screw the medal," Delaney said. "I'll take the scotch."

He hung up after promising the Deputy he'd keep him informed of any developments. Then he tidied up, returning the emptied sandwich platter, beer cans, and soda bottles to the kitchen.

Back in the study, he eyed the cartons of Ellerbee records with some distaste. He knew that eventually all that bumf would have to be divided logically and neatly into separate file folders. He could have told Boone or Jason to do it, but it was donkey labor, and he didn't want their enthusiasm dulled by paperwork.

It took him five minutes to find the two documents he was looking for: the exchange of correspondence and memos between Dr. Julius K. Samuelson and the Department's attorneys regarding the issue of doctor-patient confidentiality, and the photocopies of Dr. Simon Ellerbee's appointment book.

After rereading the papers, Delaney was definitely convinced that their so-called compromise was ridiculous and unworkable. No way could a detective investigate a possible suspect without direct questioning. He decided to ignore the whole muddle, and if he stepped on toes and someone screamed, he'd face that problem when it arose.

What interested him was that Samuelson had made his argument for the inviolability of Ellerbee's files as president of the Greater New York Psychiatric Association. He was, in effect, a professional upholding professional ethics.

But Samuelson was also a witness involved in a murder case and a friend of the victim. Nowhere in his correspondence did he state his personal views about investigating Ellerbee's patients to find the killer.

Even more intriguing, the opinions of Dr. Diane Ellerbee on the subject were never mentioned. Granted that the lady was a psychologist, not a psychiatrist, still the absence of her objection suggested that she was willing to see her husband's patients interrogated.

Delaney pushed the papers away and leaned back in his swivel chair, hands clasped behind his head. He admitted to an unreasonable impatience with lawyers and doctors. In his long career as a detective, they had too often obstructed, sometimes stymied, his investigations. He recalled he had spoken about it to his first wife, Barbara.

"Goddamn it! How can a guy become a lawyer, doctor—or even an undertaker, for that matter. All three are making a living on other people's miseries—isn't that so? I mean, they only get paid when other people are in a legal bind, sick, or dead."

She had looked at him steadily. "You're a cop, Edward," she said. "That's the way you make your living, isn't it?"

He stared at her, then laughed contritely. "You're so right," he said, "and I'm an idiot."

But still, lawyers and doctors weren't his favorite people. "Carrion birds," he called them.

Closer inspection of Ellerbee's appointment book proved more rewarding. It was an annual ledger, and, starting at the first of the year, Delaney attempted to list the name of every patient who had consulted the doctor. He used a long, yellow legal pad which he ruled into neat columns, writing in names, frequency of visits, and canceled appointments.

It was an arduous task, and when he finished, more than an hour later, he peered at the yellow pages through his reading glasses and wasn't sure what in hell he had.

Some patients consulted Ellerbee at irregular intervals. Some every two or three months. Some once a month. Some every two weeks. Some weekly. Many twice or thrice a week. Two patients five times a week!

In addition, a few patients' names appeared in the appointment book one or two times and then disappeared. And there were entries that read simply: "Clinic." The doctor's hours were generally from 7:00 A.M. to 6:00 P.M., five days a week. But sometimes he worked later, and sometimes he worked Saturdays.

No wonder the whole month of August was lined through and marked exultantly: VACATION!

Delaney knew from other reports that Dr. Simon had charged a hundred dollars for a forty-five-minute session. A break of fifteen minutes to recuperate, then on to the next patient. Dr. Diane Ellerbee charged seventy-five dollars for the same period.

He did some rough figuring. Assuming fifty consultations a week for both

Dr. Simon and Dr. Diane Ellerbee, the two were hauling in an annual take of about $420,000. A sweet sum, but it didn't completely explain the townhouse, the Brewster country home, the three cars.

But the victim had been the son of Henry Ellerbee, who owned a nice chunk of Manhattan. Maybe Daddy was coming up with an allowance or there was a trust involved. And maybe Dr. Diane was independently wealthy. Delaney knew nothing about her background.

He remembered an old detective, Alberto Di Lucca, a pasta fiend, who had taught him a lot. That was years ago, and Big Al and he were working Little Italy. One day they were strolling up Mott Street, picking their teeth after too much linguine with white clam sauce at Umberto's, and Delaney expressed sympathy for the shabbily dressed people he saw around him.

"They look like they haven't got a pot to piss in," he said.

Big Al laughed. "You think so, do you? See the old gink leaning in the doorway of that bakery across the street? You could read the *News* through his pants, they're so thin. Well, he owns that bakery, which just shits money. I also happen to know he owns three mil of AT&T."

"You're kidding!"

"I'm not," Di Lucca said, shaking his head. "Don't judge by appearances, kiddo. You never know."

Big Al had been right. When it came to money, you never knew. A beggar could be a millionaire, and a dude hosting a party of eight at Lutèce could be teetering on the edge of bankruptcy.

So maybe the Drs. Ellerbee had sources of income Suarez's men hadn't gotten around to investigating. Another hole that had to be plugged.

Edward X. Delaney liked Michael Ramon Suarez, liked his wife, liked his children and his home. But so far the Acting Chief of Detectives's investigation had been a disaster.

It offended Delaney's sense of order. He realized that he and his two assistants would really have to start from scratch.

He finished the warm dregs of his ale, then went into the kitchen to set the table. He hoped Monica wouldn't forget the buttermilk biscuits.

6

•

"EDWARD X. DELANEY HERE," HE SAID.

There was an amused grunt. "And Doctor Murray Walden here," a raspy voice said. "Thorsen told me you'd be calling. What can I do for you, Delaney?"

"An hour of your time?"

"I'd rather lend you money—and I don't even *know* you. I suppose you want it today?"

"If possible, doctor."

There was a silence for a moment, then: "Tell you what—I've got to come uptown for a hearing. It's supposed to adjourn at one o'clock, which means it'll break up around two, which means I'll be so hungry I won't be able to see straight. This business of yours—can we talk about it over lunch?"

"Sure we can," Delaney said, preferring not to.

"Delaney—that's Irish. Right?"

"Yes."

"You like Irish food?" the psychiatrist asked.

"Some of it," Delaney said cautiously. "I'm allergic to corned beef and cabbage."

"Who isn't?" Walden said. "There's an Irish pub on the East Side—Eamonn Doran's. You know it?"

"Know it and love it. They've got J.C. ale and Bushmill's Black Label—if the bartender knows you."

"Well, can you meet me there at two-thirty? I figure the lunch crowd will be cleared out by then and we'll be able to get a table and talk."

"Sounds fine. Thank you, doctor."

"You'll have no trouble spotting me," Walden said cheerfully. "I'll be the only guy in the place with no hair."

He wasn't joking. When Delaney walked through the bar into the back room of Eamonn Doran's and looked around, he spotted a lean man seated alone at a table for two. The guy's pate was completely naked. A black mustache, no larger than a typewriter brush, didn't make up for it.

"Doctor Walden?" he asked.

"Edward X. Delaney?" the man said, rising and holding out a hand. "Pleasure to meet you. Sit. I just ordered two of those J.C. ales you mentioned. Okay?"

"Couldn't be better."

Seated, they inspected each other. Walden suddenly grinned, displaying a mouthful of teeth too good to be true. Then he ran a palm over his shiny scalp.

"Yul Brynner or Telly Savalas I'm not," he said. "But I had so little fringe left, I figured the hell with it and shaved it all off."

"A rug?" Delaney suggested.

"Nah, who needs it? A sign of insecurity. I'm happy with a head of skin. People remember me."

The waitress brought their ales and menus. The police psychiatrist peered at his digital wristwatch, bringing it up close to his eyes.

"I promised you an hour," he said, "and that's what you're going to get; no more, no less. So let's order right now and start talking."

"Suits me," Delaney said. "I'll have the sliced steak rare with home fries and a side order of tomatoes and onions."

"Make that two, please," Walden told the waitress. "Now then," he said to Delaney, "what's this all about? Thorsen sounded antsy."

"It's about the murder of Doctor Simon Ellerbee. Did you know the man?"

"We weren't personal friends, but I met him two or three times professionally."

"What was your take?"

"Very, very talented. A gifted man. Heavy thinker. The last time I met him, I got the feeling he had problems—but who hasn't?"

"Problems? Any idea what kind?"

"No. But he was quiet and broody. Not as outgoing as the other times I met him. But maybe he'd just had a bad day. We all do."

"It must be a strain dealing with, uh, disturbed people every day."

"Disturbed people?" Dr. Walden said, showing his teeth again. "You weren't about to say 'nuts,' or 'crazies,' or 'whackos,' were you?"

"Yes," Delaney admitted, "I was."

"Tell me something," Walden said as the waitress set down their food, "have you ever felt guilt, depression, grief, panic, fear, or hatred?"

Delaney looked at him. "Sure I have."

The psychiatrist nodded. "You have, I have, everyone has. Laymen think psychotherapists deal with raving lunatics. Actually, the huge majority of our patients are very ordinary people who are experiencing those same emotions you've felt—but to an exaggerated degree. So exaggerated that they can't cope. That's why, if they've got the money, they go to a therapist. But nuts and crazies and whackos they're not."

"You think most of Ellerbee's patients were like that—essentially ordinary people?"

"Well, I haven't seen his files," Dr. Walden said cautiously, "but I'd almost bet on it. Oh, sure, he might have had some heavy cases—schizoids, patients with psychosexual dysfunctions, multiple personalities: exotic stuff like that. But I'd guess that most of his caseload consisted of the kind of people I just described: the ones with emotional traumata they couldn't handle by themselves."

"Tell me something, doctor," Delaney said. "Simon Ellerbee was a psychiatrist, and his wife—his widow—is a psychologist. What's the difference?"

"He had an MD degree; his widow doesn't. And I expect their education and training were different. As I understand it, she specializes in children's problems and runs group therapy sessions for parents. He was your classical analyst. Not strictly Freudian, but analytically oriented. You've got to understand that there are dozens of therapeutic techniques. The psychiatrist may select one and never deviate or he may gradually develop a mix of his own that he feels yields the best results. This is a very personal business. I really don't know exactly how Ellerbee worked."

"By the way," Delaney said when the waitress presented the bill, "this lunch is on me."

"Never doubted it for a minute," Walden said cheerily.

"You said before that most of Ellerbee's patients were probably ordinary people. You think any of them are capable of violence? I mean against the analyst."

Dr. Walden sat back, took a silver cigarette case from his inside jacket pocket, and snapped it open.

"It doesn't happen too often," he said, "but it does happen. The threat is always there. Back in 1981 four psychiatrists were murdered by their patients in a six-week period. Scary. There are a lot of reasons for it. Psychoanalysis can be a very painful experience—worse than a root canal job, believe me! The therapist probes and probes. The patient resists. That guy behind the desk is trying to get him to reveal awful things that have been kept buried for years. Sometimes the patient attacks the doctor for hurting him. That's one reason. Another is that the patient fears the therapist is learning too much, peering into the patient's secret soul."

"I'm telling you this in confidence," Delaney said sternly, "because it hasn't been released to the press. After Ellerbee was dead, the killer rolled him over and hit him two or more times in the eyes with a ball peen hammer. One of my assistants suggested it might have been an attempt to blind the doctor because he saw, or was seeing, too much. What do you think of that theory?"

"Very perceptive. And quite possible. I think that most assaults on therapists are made by out-and-out psychotics. In fact, most of the attacks are made in prisons and hospital wards for the criminally insane. Still, a number do occur in the offices of high-priced Park Avenue shrinks. What's worse, the psychiatrist's family is sometimes threatened and occasionally attacked."

"Could you estimate the percentage of therapists who have been assaulted by patients?"

"I can give you a guess. Between one-quarter and one-third. Just a guess."

"Have you ever been attacked, doctor?"

"Once. A man came at me with a hunting knife."

"How do you handle something like that?"

"I pack a handgun. You'd be surprised at how many psychiatrists do. Or keep it in the top drawer of their desk. Usually slow, soft talk can defuse a dangerous situation—but not always."

"Why did the guy come at you with a knife?"

"We were at the breaking point in his therapy. He had a lech for his fifteen-year-old daughter and couldn't or wouldn't acknowledge it. But he was taking her clothes to prostitutes and making them dress like the daughter. Sad, sad, sad."

"Did he finally admit it?" Delaney asked, fascinated.

"Eventually. I thought he was coming along fine; we were talking it out. But then, about three weeks later, he left my office, went home, and blew his brains out with a shotgun. I don't think of that case very often—not more than two or three times a day."

"Jesus," Delaney said wonderingly. "How can you stand that kind of pressure?"

"How can a man do open-heart surgery? You go in, pray, and hope for the best. Oh, there's another reason patients sometimes assault their therapists. It involves a type of transference. The analysand may have been an abused child or hate his parents for one reason or another. He transfers his hostility to the therapist, who is making him dredge up his anger and talk about it. The doctor becomes the abusive parent. Conversely, the patient may identify with the aggressive parent and try to treat the psychiatrist as a helpless child. As I told you, there are many reasons patients might attack their therapists. And to confuse you further, I should add that some assaults have been made for no discernible reason at all."

"But the main point," Delaney insisted, "is that murderous attacks on psychiatrists are not all that uncommon, and it's very possible that Doctor Ellerbee was killed by one of his patients."

"It's possible," Walden agreed.

Then, when Delaney saw the doctor glance at his watch, he said, "I should warn you, I may bother you again if I need the benefit of your advice."

"Anytime. You keep buying me steak and I'm all yours."

They rose from the table and shook hands.

"Thank you," Delaney said. "You've been a big help."

"I have?" Dr. Murray Walden said, stroking his bald pate. "That's nice. One final word of caution. If you're thinking of questioning Ellerbee's patients, don't come on strong. Play it very low-key. Speak softly. These people feel threatened enough without being leaned on by a stranger."

"I'll remember that."

"Of course," Walden said thoughtfully, "there may be some from whom you'll get the best results by coming on strong, shouting and browbeating them."

"My God!" Edward X. Delaney cried. "Isn't there anything definite in your business?"

"Definitely not," Walden said.

7

•

THE THREE SAT IN THE STUDY, HUNCHED FORWARD, INTENT.

"All right, Jason," Delaney said, "you go first."

The black officer flipped through his pocket notebook to find the pages he wanted. "The widow lady is clean as far as those Brewster calls go. She did phone the Manhattan garage at the time she says she did. Ditto the call later to Doctor Samuelson. The phone company's got a record. I talked to the Brewster cop who took her call when she asked about an accident involving her husband's car. He says she wasn't hysterical, but she sounded worried and anxious. So much for that. Then, just for fun, I dropped by that Manhattan garage to ask when the lady claimed her car on that Friday night."

"Smart," Delaney said, nodding.

"Well, she checked her car out at six twenty-two in the evening, which fits pretty close to her statement. No holes that I could find."

"Nice job," Delaney said. "Sergeant?"

Boone peered down at his own notebook. "Samuelson seems to be clean, too. Before the concert he had dinner with two friends at the Russian Tea Room. They swear he was there. He picked up the tab and paid with a credit card. I got a look at his signed check and the restaurant's copy of his credit card bill. Everything looks kosher. Then Samuelson and his friends went to the concert. They say he never left, which is probably true because after the concert was over, the three of them dropped by the St. Moritz for a nightcap. All this covers Ellerbee's time of death, so I guess we can scratch Doctor Samuelson."

Delaney didn't say anything.

"Now, about Records . . ." the Sergeant continued. "I checked out Ellerbee, his widow, his father, the two receptionists, the two old dames who own the art gallery on the first floor, the part-time super who takes care of the building, and the guy who leases the top floor. The only one with a jacket is the last—the West Coast movie producer who keeps that fourth-floor apartment to use when he's in town. His name is J. Scott Hergetson, and his sheet is minor stuff: traffic violations, committing a public nuisance—he peed on the sidewalk while drunk—and one drug bust. This disco was raided and he was pulled in with fifty other people. No big deal. Charges dropped."

"So that's it?" Delaney asked.

"Not all of it," Boone said, flipping his notebook. "The ME says Ellerbee died about nine P.M. This is where all these people claim they were at that time . . .

"Doctor Diane Ellerbee was up in Brewster, waiting for her husband to arrive.

"Henry Ellerbee was at a charity dinner at the Plaza Hotel. I confirmed his presence there at nine o'clock.

"Doctor Samuelson was at the Carnegie Hall concert. Confirmed.

"One of the receptionists was home watching television with her mother. Mommy says yes, she was. Who knows?

"The other receptionist says she was shacked up with her boyfriend in his apartment. He says yes, she was. Who knows?

"The super was playing pinochle at his basement social club. The other guys in the game say yeah, he was there.

"The two ladies who run the art gallery were at a private dinner with eight other people of the Medicare set. Their presence is confirmed. Besides, the two of them are so frail I don't think they could *lift* a ball peen hammer.

"The top-floor movie producer was at a film festival in the south of France. His presence there is confirmed by news reports and photographs. Scratch him.

"And that's it."

Delaney looked admiringly from Boone to Jason and back again. "What the hell does Suarez need me for? You two guys can break this thing on your own. Well, here's what I've got. It isn't much."

He gave them a précis of his conversation with the police psychiatrist and told them what Dr. Walden had said about the incidence of attacks on therapists by their patients.

"He guessed about one-quarter to one-third of all psychiatrists have been assaulted. Those percentages look good. After what you've just told me, I'm beginning to think Ellerbee's patient list may be our best bet."

Then he said that Walden had agreed with Boone's theory about those hammer blows to the eyes: It could be a symbolic effort to blind the doctor.

"After he was dead?" Jason said.

"Well, Walden thinks most attacks on therapists are made by psychotics. I didn't tell him about the two sets of unidentified footprints. That could mean there were two psychotics working together, or Ellerbee had two visitors that night at different times. Any ideas?"

Jason and Boone looked at each other, then shook their heads.

"All right," Delaney said briskly. "Here's where we go from here. I want to see that townhouse and I want to meet Doctor Diane Ellerbee. Maybe we can do both at the same time. Sergeant, suppose you call her right now. Tell her you'd like to see her as soon as possible, as part of the investigation into her husband's death. Don't mention that I'll be with you."

Rather than dig through the records in the cartons for Diane Ellerbee's phone number, Boone looked it up in the Manhattan directory. He identified himself and asked to speak to the doctor. He ended by giving Delaney's phone number. Then he hung up.

"She's with a patient," he reported. "The receptionist said she'll give the doctor my message and she'll probably call back as soon as she's free."

"We'll wait," Delaney said. "It shouldn't be more than forty-five minutes. Meanwhile, there's something else I want to know more about. Boone, do you know a dick one named Parnell? I think his first name is Charles."

"Oh, hell, yes," the Sergeant said, smiling. "I know him. They call him Daddy Warbucks. He's still on active duty."

"That's the guy," Delaney said. He turned to Jason. "You've got to realize that some detectives make a good career for themselves by specializing. Now this Parnell, he's a financial whiz. You want a money picture on someone and he can come up with it. He's got good contacts with banks, stockbrokers, credit agencies, accountants, and for all I know, the IRS. He knows how to read wills, trusts, and reports of probate. He's just the guy we need to get a rundown on the financial status of the deceased and his widow. Sergeant, tell Chief Suarez everything we've done so far—don't leave anything out—and then ask him to have Daddy Warbucks check out the net worth of the dead guy and Doctor Diane Ellerbee." He paused a moment, pondering. Then: "And throw in Doctor Julius K. Samuelson for good measure. Let's find out how fat his bank account is."

"Will do," Boone said, making some quick jottings in his notebook.

"Sir," Jason T. Jason said hesitantly, "would you mind telling me the reason for this?"

"*Cui bono,*" Delaney said promptly. "Who benefits? In this case, who stands to gain from the death of Simon Ellerbee? I'm not saying money was the motive here, but it might have been. It sure as hell has been in a lot of homicides where the perp turns out to be a member of the family or a beneficiary. It's something that's got to be checked out."

"I'll get on it right—" Boone started to say, but then the phone rang.

"That may be Doctor Diane," Delaney said. "You better answer, Sergeant."

He talked briefly, then hung up and turned to them.

"Six o'clock tonight," he said. "She'll be finished with her patients by then."

"How did she sound?" Delaney asked.

"Furious. Trying to keep her cool. I'm not looking forward to that meeting, sir."

"Has to be done," Delaney said stubbornly. "The lady is said to be a real beauty—if that's any consolation. Well, we've got about eight hours. Boone, why don't you contact Suarez and get Charlie Parnell working on the financial reports. Jason, you take the car and go up to Brewster. The Ellerbees have a married couple who take care of their place. The man does maintenance and works around the grounds. Talk to him. He may have a toolshed or workshop on the premises."

"Oh-ho," Jason T. Jason said. "You want to know if he owns a ball peen hammer—right?"

"Right. And if he does, has he still got it? And if he has, you grab it."

"Oh, yeah," Jason said.

"And while you're at it, get a look at the house and grounds. I'd like your take on it."

"I'm on my way."

"And so am I," Boone said, as both officers rose.

"Sergeant, I'll meet you at the Ellerbees' townhouse at five-thirty. It'll give us a chance to look around the neighborhood before we brace the widow."

"I'll be there," Abner Boone promised.

After they left, Delaney returned to his study and looked at the cartons of files with dread. It had to be done, but he didn't relish the task.

He set to work, dividing the records into separate folders: the victim, Dr. Diane Ellerbee, Dr. Julius Samuelson, the ME's reports and photographs, the reports, photos, and map of the Crime Scene Unit, statements of everyone questioned. Then he added notes of his conversation with Dr. Murray Walden, and what Sergeant Boone and Jason T. Jason had just told him.

It went faster than he had anticipated, and by 12:30 he had a satisfyingly neat stack of labeled file folders that included all the known facts concerning the murder of Dr. Simon Ellerbee. It was time, he decided, for a sandwich.

He went into the kitchen, opened the refrigerator, and inspected the possibilities. There was a single onion roll in there, hard as a rock, but it could be toasted. And there were a few slices of pork left over from a roast loin. Some German potato salad. Scallions he could slice. Maybe a wee bit of horseradish.

He slapped it all together and ate it leaning over the sink. Monica would have been outraged, but she was gone, doing volunteer work at a local hospital. She kept nagging him about his addiction, and she was right; he was too heavy in the gut. It was hard to convince her that the Earl of Sandwich had been one of civilization's great benefactors.

He returned to the study and stared at the stack of Ellerbee file folders.

He had a disturbing hunch that this was going to be a "loose-ends case."

That's what he called investigations in which nothing was certain, nothing could be pinned down. A hundred suspects, a hundred alibis, and no one could say yes or no.

You had to live with that confusion and, if you were lucky, discard the meaningless and zero in on the significant. But how to tell one from the other? False trails and time wasted chasing leads that dribbled away. Meanwhile, Thorsen was sweating to have a murder cleaned up, neat and clean, by the holidays. So his man could be promoted.

Two sets of unidentified footprints and two blows to the victim's eyes. Was there any meaning in that? Or in Ellerbee telling his wife he had scheduled a late patient, presumably meaning someone after 6:00 P.M. But he had died at approximately nine o'clock. Would he have waited that long for a late patient? Someone who would arrive, say, at 8:00 P.M.

No signs of forced entry. So Ellerbee buzzed someone in, someone he was expecting. One person or two? And why leave that street door open when they left?

"The butler did it," Delaney said aloud, and then pulled his yellow legal pad toward him, put on his reading glasses, and began making notes on how much he didn't know. It was a long, depressing list. He stared at it and had an uneasy feeling that he might be missing the obvious.

He remembered a case he had worked years ago. There had been a string of armed robberies on Amsterdam Avenue; six small stores had been hit in a period of two months. Apparently the same cowboy was pulling all of them— a young punk with a Fu Manchu mustache, waving a nickel-plated pistol.

One of the six places allegedly robbed at gunpoint was a mom-and-pop grocery store near 78th Street. The owners lived in a rear apartment. The old lady opened the store every morning at 7:30. Her husband, who had a weakness for slivovitz, usually joined her behind the counter a half hour or hour later.

On this particular morning, the old man said, his wife had gone into the store to open up as usual. He was dressing when he heard a gunshot, rushed out, and found her lying behind the counter. The cash register was open, he said, and about thirty dollars' worth of bills and coin were gone.

The old lady was dead, hit in the chest with what turned out to be a .38 slug. Delaney and his partner, a Detective second grade named Loren Pierce, chalked it up to the Fu Manchu punk with the shiny pistol. They couldn't stake out every little shop on Amsterdam Avenue, but they haunted the neighborhood, spending a lot of their off-hours walking the streets and eyeballing every guy with a mustache.

They finally got lucky. The robber tried to rip off a deli, not knowing the owner's son was on his knees, out of sight behind a pile of cartons, putting stock on the shelves. The son rose up and hit Fu Manchu over the head with a five-pound canned ham. That was the end of that crime wave.

It turned out the punk was snorting coke and robbing to support a $500-a-day habit. Even more interesting, his nickel-plated weapon was a .22, the barrel so dirty it would have blown his hand off if he had ever fired it.

Detectives Delaney and Pierce looked at each other and cursed. Then they went back to the mom-and-pop grocery store, but only after they had checked and discovered that Pop had a permit to keep a .38 handgun in the store. They leaned on him and he caved almost immediately.

"She was always nagging at me," he complained.

That was what Delaney meant when he worried about missing the obvious. He and Pierce should have checked immediately to see if the old man had a gun. It never hurt to get the simple, evident things out of the way first. It was a mistake to think all criminals were great brains; most of them were stupes.

He pondered all the known facts in the Ellerbee homicide and couldn't see anything simple and obvious that he had missed. He thought the case probably hinged on the character of the dead man and his relationship with his patients.

He reflected awhile and admitted he had an irrational contempt for people who sought aid for emotional problems. He would never do it; he was convinced of that. The death of Barbara, his first wife, had left him numb for a long time. But he had bulled his way out of that funk—by himself.

Still, he had no hesitation in seeking help for physical ills. A virus, a twinge of the liver, a skin lesion that wouldn't heal—and off he went to consult a physician. So why this disdain for people who took their inner torments to a trained practitioner?

Because, Delaney supposed, there was an element of fear in his prejudice. Psychologists and psychiatrists were dealing with something you couldn't see. There was a mystery there, and dread. It was like taking your brain to a witch doctor. Still, Delaney knew that if he was going to get anywhere on the Ellerbee case he'd have to cultivate and evince sympathy for those who fled to the witch doctor.

He left the house early, deciding to walk to the Ellerbees' townhouse to meet Abner Boone. It was a dull day with a cloud cover as rough as an elephant hide. The air smelled of snow, and a hard northwest wind made him grab for his homburg more than once.

On impulse, he stopped in at a First Avenue hardware store. All the clerks were busy, for which he was thankful. He found a display of hammers and picked up a ball peen. He hefted it in his hand, swinging it gently in a downward chop. So many useful tools made lethal weapons. He wondered which came first. If he had to guess, he'd say weapons evolved into tools.

That shiny round knob could puncture a man's skull if swung with sufficient force—no doubt about that. A man could do it easily, but then so could a woman if she were strong and determined. He replaced the hammer in the display, having learned absolutely nothing.

Boone was waiting for him across the street from the townhouse. He was huddling in his parka, hands in his pockets, shoulders hunched.

"That wind's a bitch," he observed. "My ears feel like tin."

"I feel the cold in my feet," Delaney said. "An old cop's complaint. The feet are the first to go. Did you talk to Suarez?"

"Yes, sir, I did. On the phone. He was tied up with a million other things."

"I imagine."

"He sounds like a patient man. Very polite. Said to thank you for keeping in touch, and he's grateful for what we've done so far."

"What about Parnell?"

"He'll get him going on the financial reports immediately. I think he was a little embarrassed that he hadn't thought of it himself."

"He's got enough to think about," Delaney said absently, staring across the street. "That's the place—the gray stone building?"

"That's the one, sir."

"Smaller than I thought it would be. Let's wander around a little first."

They walked over to East End Avenue, inspecting buildings on both sides of 84th Street. The block contained a mix of apartment houses with marbled lobbies, crumbling brownstones, a school, smart townhouses, dilapidated tenements, and a few commercial establishments on the avenue corners.

They looked at the East River, turned, and walked back to York.

"Plenty of areaways," Boone observed. "Open lobbies and vestibules with the outer door unlocked. The perp could have gone into any of them to get out of the rain."

"Could have," Delaney agreed. "But then how did he get into the Ellerbees' building? No signs of forced entry. What I'm wondering about is what the killer did afterward. Walk away in the rain, leaving the front door open? Or did the killer have a car parked nearby? Or maybe stroll over to York or East End and take a cab? Both avenues are two-way."

"My God, sir," the Sergeant said, "you're not thinking of checking taxi trip-sheets for that night, are you? What a job!"

"We won't do it right now, but it may become necessary. Besides, there couldn't have been so many cabs working that Friday night. It wasn't just raining; it was a flood. Well, this street isn't going to tell us anything; let's go talk to the widow; it's almost six."

The outer door of the Ellerbee townhouse was unlocked, leading to a lighted vestibule with mailboxes and a bell plate of polished brass. Boone tried the inner door.

"Locked," he reported. "This is the inner door Doctor Samuelson found open when he arrived."

"Fine door," Delaney said. "Bleached oak with beveled glass. You can ring now, Sergeant."

Boone pressed the button alongside the neatly printed nameplate: DR. DIANE ELLERBEE. The female voice that answered was unexpectedly loud:

"Who is it?"

"Sergeant Abner Boone, New York Police Department. I spoke to you earlier today."

The buzzer sounded and they pushed in. They stood a brief moment in the entranceway. Delaney tried the door of the Piedmont Gallery. It was locked.

They looked about curiously. The hall and stairway were heavily carpeted. Illumination came from a small crystal chandelier hung from a high ceiling.

"Very nice," Delaney said. "And look at that banister. Someone did a great restoration job. Well, let's go up. Sergeant, you do the talking."

"Don't let me miss anything," Boone said anxiously.

Delaney grunted.

The woman who greeted them at an opened door on the second floor was tall, stiff. Braided flaxen hair, coiled atop her head, made her appear even taller.

A Valkyrie, was Delaney's initial reaction.

"May I see your identification, please?" she said crisply.

"Of course," Boone said, and handed over his case with shield and ID card.

She inspected both closely, returned the folder, then turned to Delaney.

"And who are you?" she demanded.

He was not put off by her loud, assertive voice. In fact, he admired her caution; most people would have accepted Boone's credentials and not questioned anyone accompanying him.

"Edward X. Delaney, ma'am," he said in a quiet voice. "I am a civilian consultant assisting the New York Police Department in the investigation of your husband's death. If you have any questions about my presence here—any doubts at all—I suggest you telephone First Deputy Commissioner Ivar Thorsen or Acting Chief of Detectives Michael Ramon Suarez. Both will vouch for me. Sergeant Boone and I can wait out here in the hall while you make the call."

She stared at him fixedly. Then: "No," she said, "that won't be necessary; I believe you. It's just that since—since it happened, I've been extra careful."

"Very wise," Delaney said.

They stepped into the receptionist's office, and both men noted that Dr. Diane Ellerbee double-locked and chained the door behind them.

"Ma'am," Boone said, "is the floor plan of this office the same as—uh, the one upstairs?"

"You haven't seen it?" she asked, surprised. "Yes, my husband's and my office are identical. Not in decorations or furnishings, of course, but the layout of the rooms is the same."

She ushered them into her private office, leaving open the connecting door to the receptionist's office. She got them seated in two cretonne-covered armchairs with low backs.

"Not too comfortable, are they?" she said—the first time she had smiled: a shadow of a smile. "Deliberately so. I don't want my young patients nodding off. Those chairs keep them twisting and shifting. I think it's productive."

"Doctor Ellerbee," Boone said solemnly, leaning forward, "I'd like to express the condolences of Mr. Delaney and myself on the tragic death of your husband. From all accounts he was a remarkable man. We sympathize with you on your loss."

"Thank you," she said, sitting behind her desk like a queen. "I appreciate your sympathy. I would appreciate even more your finding the person who killed my husband."

During this exchange, Delaney had been examining the office, trying not to make his inspection too obvious.

The room seemed to him excessively neat, almost to the point of sterility. Walls were painted a cream color, the carpet a light beige. There was one ficus tree (which looked artificial) in a rattan basket. The only wall decorations were two framed enlargements of Rorschach blots that looked as abstract as Japanese calligraphy.

"Both of us," Boone continued, "have read your statement to the investigating officers several times. We don't want to ask you to go over it again. But I would like to say that occasionally, after a shocking event like this, witnesses recall additional details days or even months later. If you are able to add anything to your statement, it would help if you'd contact us immediately."

"I certainly hope it's not going to take months to find my husband's killer," she said sharply.

They looked at her expressionlessly, and she gave a short cough of laughter without mirth.

"I know I've been a pain in the ass to the police," she said. "And so has Henry—my father-in-law, Henry Ellerbee. But I have not been able to restrain my anger. All my professional life I have been counseling patients on how to cope with the injustices of this world. But now that they have struck me, I find it difficult to endure. Perhaps this experience will make me a better therapist. But I must tell you in all honesty that at the moment I feel nothing but rage and a desire for vengeance—emotions I have never felt before and which I seem unable to control."

"That's very understandable, ma'am," Boone said. "Believe me, we're just as anxious as you to identify the killer. That's why we asked for this meeting, hoping we might learn something from you that will aid our investigation. First of all, would it hurt too much to talk about your husband?"

"No," she said decisively. "I'll be thinking about Simon and talking about Simon for the rest of my life."

"What kind of a man was he?"

"A very superior human being. Kind, gentle, with a marvelous sympathy for other people's unhappiness. I think everyone in the profession who knew him or met him recognized how gifted he was. In addition to that, he had a first-class mind. He could get to the cause of a psychiatric problem so fast that many of his associates called it instinct."

As she spoke, Delaney, while listening, observed her closely. Ivar Thorsen and Monica had been right: Diane Ellerbee was a regal beauty.

A softly sharp profile suitable for a coin. Sky-blue eyes that seemed to change hue with her temper. A direct, challenging gaze. A porcelain complexion. A generous mouth that promised smiles and kisses.

She was wearing a severely tailored suit of pin-striped flannel, but a tent couldn't have concealed her figure. She didn't move; she flowed.

What was so disconcerting, almost frightening, was the woman's completeness. She wasn't a Valkyrie, he decided; she was a Brancusi sculpture—something serene that wooed the eye with its form and soothed with its surface. "Marvelous" was the word that came to his mind—meaning something of wonder. Supernatural.

"Don't get me wrong," she said, fiddling with a ballpoint pen on her desk and looking down at it. "I don't want to make Simon sound like a perfect man. He wasn't, of course. He had his moods. Fits of silence. Rare but occasional outbursts of anger. Most of the time he was a sunny, placable man. When he was depressed, it was usually because he felt he was failing a patient. He set for himself very high goals indeed, and when he felt he was falling short of his potential, it bothered him."

"Did you notice any change in him in, say, the last six months or a year?" Boone asked.

"Change?"

"In his manner, his personality. Did he act like a man with worries or, maybe, like a man who had received serious threats against his life?"

She pondered that for a moment. "No," she said finally, "I noticed no change."

"Doctor Ellerbee," Boone said earnestly, "we are currently investigating your husband's patients, under the terms of an agreement negotiated between Doctor Samuelson and the NYPD. Are you familiar with that compromise?"

"Oh, yes," she said. "Julie told me about it."

"Do you think it possible that one of the patients may have been the assailant?"

"Yes, it's possible."

"Have you yourself ever been attacked by one of *your* patients?"

"Occasionally."

"And how do you handle that?"

"You must realize," she said with a wry smile, "that most of my patients are children. Still, my first reaction is to protect myself. And I am a strong woman. I refuse to let myself be bullied or suffer injury."

"You fight back?"

"Exactly. You'd be surprised at how effective that technique can be."

"Did you and your husband talk business when you were alone together?"

"Business?" she said, and the smile became broader and more charming. "Yes, we talked business—if you mean discussing our cases. We did it constantly. He sought my reactions and advice and I sought his. Sergeant, this is not a profession that ends when you lock your office door for the night."

"The reason I asked, ma'am, is this: Your husband had a great number of patients, particularly if you include all he'd discharged. It's going to take a lot of time and a lot of work to investigate them all. We were hoping you might be able to help us speed up the process. If your husband discussed his cases with you—as you say he did—would you be willing to pick out those patients you feel might be violent?"

She was silent, staring at them both, while her long, tapered fingers played with the pen on the desk top.

"I don't know," she said worriedly. "It's a troublesome question, involving medical ethics. I'm not sure how far I should go on this. Sergeant, I'm not going to say yes or no at this moment. I think I better get some other opinions. Julie Samuelson's, for one. If I acted on impulse, I'd say, hell, yes, I'll do anything I can to help. But I don't want to do the wrong thing. Can I get back to you? It shouldn't take more than a day or so."

"The sooner the better," Boone said, then glanced swiftly at Delaney, signaling that he was finished.

Delaney, who was pleased with the way the Sergeant had conducted the interrogation, hunched forward in his chair, hands clasped between spread knees, and stared at Diane Ellerbee.

"Doctor," he said, "I have a question—a very personal question you may find offensive. But it's got to be asked. Was your husband faithful to you?"

She threw the ballpoint pen across the desk. It fell to the floor, and she didn't bother to retrieve it. They saw her spine stiffen, jaw tighten. Those sky-blue eyes seemed to darken. She glared at Edward X. Delaney.

"My husband was faithful," she said loudly. "Faithful from the day we were married. I realize people say that the wife is always the last to know, but I swear to you I *know* my husband was faithful. We worked at our marriage, and it was a happy one. I was faithful to Simon, and he was faithful to me."

"No children?" Delaney said.

She gave a slight grimace—pain, distaste?

"You go for the jugular, don't you?" she said harshly. "No, no children. I'm incapable. Is that going to help you find my husband's killer?"

Delaney rose to his feet, and a second later, Sergeant Boone jumped up.

"Doctor Ellerbee," Delaney said, "I want to thank you for your cooperation. I can't promise that what you've told us will aid our investigation—

but you never know. It would help a great deal if you'd be willing to name those of your husband's patients you feel might be capable of homicidal violence."

"I'll talk to Julie," she said, nodding. "If he approves, I'll do it. Either way, I'll be in touch as soon as I can."

Boone handed over his card. "I can be reached at this number, Doctor Ellerbee, or you can leave a message. Thank you for your help, ma'am."

Outside, they walked west to York Avenue, fists jammed into their pockets, shoulders hunched against the cutting wind.

"Nice job," Delaney said. "You handled that just right."

"A beautiful, beautiful woman," Boone said. "But what did we get? Zilch."

"I'm not so sure. It was interesting. And yes, she's a beautiful woman."

"You think she was telling the truth, sir? About her husband being faithful?"

"Why not? You're faithful to Rebecca, aren't you? And I know I'm faithful to Monica. Not all husbands sleep around. Sergeant, I think you better make an appointment for us with Doctor Samuelson as soon as possible. Maybe we can convince him to tell her to pick out the crazies from her husband's patient list."

"She sure seems to rely a hell of a lot on his opinion."

"Oh, you noticed that too, did you?"

They parted on York. Boone headed uptown to his apartment; Delaney walked down to his brownstone.

He had left a note for Monica, telling her that he might be late and to go ahead and have dinner if she was hungry. But she had waited for him, keeping a casserole of veal and onions warm in the oven.

While they ate, he told her about the interview with Dr. Diane Ellerbee. He wanted to get her reaction.

"She sounds like a woman under very heavy pressure," Monica said when Delaney finished describing the interview.

"Oh, hell, yes. The death of her husband has gotten to her—no doubt of that. That's why she's been leaning on the Department; at least it gives her the feeling that she's doing something. Both Abner and I thought she put unusual reliance on Doctor Samuelson. Granted that he's the president of an important professional association, still it sounded like she doesn't want to make a move without consulting him. A curious relationship. Abner is going to set up a meet with Samuelson. Maybe we'll learn more."

"Do you believe her about her husband being faithful?"

"I have no reason not to believe," he said cautiously.

"I've never heard even a whisper of gossip about them," Monica said. "Things like that usually get out—one way or another."

"I suppose so. But I think Diane Ellerbee is a very complex woman. She's going to take a lot of study."

"You don't suspect her, do you, Edward?"

He sighed. "Oh, hell—I suspect everyone. You know I go by percentages, and most homicides are committed by relatives or close friends. So, sure—the widow has got to be a suspect. But up to now, I admit, there isn't an iota of evidence to make me doubt her innocence. Well, we're just beginning."

He helped Monica clean up and put the dishes in the washer. Then he went into the study, poured himself a small Rémy, and put on his reading glasses. He wrote out a complete report of the interrogation of Dr. Diane Ellerbee and slid it into the file folder neatly labeled with her name.

He was interrupted twice. The first phone call came from Boone, who said that he had made an appointment with Samuelson for 7:00 A.M. the following morning.

"Seven o'clock! I'm just dragging myself out of bed at that hour."

"Me, too," Boone said mournfully. "But these psychiatrists apparently start the day early—to take patients before they go off to work."

"Well, all right, we'll make it at seven. What's the address?"

The second call was from Jason, who had just returned to the city from Brewster.

"No ball peen hammer, sir," he reported. "The handyman says he doesn't own one and never has. I think he's telling the truth."

"Probably," Delaney agreed. "It was just a gamble and had to be checked out."

"And the victim wasn't very mechanical," Jason went on. "He owned maybe a tack hammer and a screwdriver—five-and-ten tools like that. Whenever any repairs had to be done, even like changing a washer, the caretaker was called in."

"You got to see the house?"

"Oh, yes, sir. Not as big as I thought it would be, but really beautiful. Even with all the trees bare, you can imagine what that place must look like in spring and summer. Plenty of land with a sweet little brook running through. Patio, garden, swimming pool—the whole bit."

"It sure sounds great," Delaney said. "I've got to get up there and take a look. Jason, we've got Parnell working on the financial backgrounds of the two Ellerbees and Doctor Samuelson. What I'd like you to do is dig into their personal backgrounds. Ages, where born, living relatives, education, professional careers, and so forth. You can get most of that stuff from *Who's Who,* records of colleges, universities and hospitals, yearbooks of professional societies, and any other sources you can think of. Dig as deep as you think necessary."

"Well . . . sure," Jason said hesitantly. "But I've never done anything like that before, sir."

"Then it's time you learned. Don't lean on anyone too hard, but don't let them fluff you off either. It'll be a good chance to make contacts. You never know when you might be needing them again."

"Get started on it in the morning. When do you want this stuff, sir?"

"Yesterday," Delaney said. "Get a good night's sleep."

A little after midnight, in the upstairs bedroom, he went in to shower first, leaving Monica brushing her hair at the dressing table. She came into the open bathroom after he finished, catching him sucking in his gut and examining his body in the full-length mirror.

"Now I know you met Diane Ellerbee today," she said.

He gave her a sour grin. "You really know how to hurt a guy, don't you?"

She laughed and patted his bare shoulder. "You'll do for me, pops."

"Pops?" he said in mock outrage. "I'll pop you!"

They giggled, wrestled a moment, kissed.

Later, when they were in their beds, he said, "Well, she is a beautiful woman. Incredible. Correct me if I'm wrong, but can't great physical beauty be a curse?"

"How so?"

"It seems to me that a young woman who starts out tremendously lovely would have no incentive to develop her mind or talents or skills. I mean people worship her automatically. Some rich guy grabs her off and buys her everything she wants—so where's her ambition to be anything? She thinks she deserves her good fortune, and her looks will last forever."

"Well, that obviously didn't happen to Diane Ellerbee. She's a respected professional and she's got brains to spare. Maybe some beautiful women go the route you said, but not her. She's made her own good fortune. I told you I heard her speak, and the woman is brilliant."

"You don't think there's something cold and detached about her?"

"Cold and detached? No, I didn't get that impression at all."

"Maybe it was a poor choice of words. Forceful and self-assured. Will you agree to that?"

"Yes," Monica said slowly, "I think that's fair. But of course a psychotherapist has to be self-assured—or at least give that impression. You're not going to get many patients if you seem as neurotic as they are."

"You're probably right," he admitted. "But something about her disturbs me. It's the same feeling I get when I see a great painting or sculpture at the Met. It's pleasing visually, but there's something mysterious there. I've never been able to figure it out. I can look at a painting and really admire it, but sometimes it saddens me, too. It makes me think of death."

"Great beauty makes you think of death?"

"Sometimes."

"Did you ever consider seeking professional help?"

"Never," he said, laughing. "You're my therapist."

"Do you think Diane Ellerbee is more beautiful than I am?"

"Absolutely not," he said immediately. "To me, you're the most beautiful woman in the world."

"You really know what's good for you, don't you, buster?"

"You better believe it," he said, reaching out for her.

8

•

DR. SAMUELSON'S APARTMENT WAS ON THE 18TH FLOOR OF THE co-op at 79th Street and Madison Avenue. His office was on the ground floor of the same building. It was not unusual for him to descend to work in the automatic elevator, wearing a holey wool cardigan and worn carpet slippers.

Delaney and Boone huddled under the marquee of the building for a moment, trying to keep out of a sleety rain that had been falling all night.

"Just for the fun of it," Delaney said, "let's both of us go after this guy. Short, punchy questions with no logical sequence. Biff, bang, pow! We'll come at him from all angles."

"So he won't be able to get set?" Boone asked.

"Partly that. But mostly because he got me up so early on a miserable morning."

Dr. Samuelson opened the door to his office himself; there was no visible evidence that he employed a receptionist. He took their wet coats and hats and hung them away. He ushered them into a cluttered inner office in which all the furnishings seemed accumulated rather than selected. The place had a fusty air, and the few good antiques were in need of restoration. A stuffed barn owl moldered atop a bookcase.

In addition to an old horsehair patient's couch, covered with an Indian blanket, there were two creaky Morris chairs in the office. These Samuelson pulled up facing his massive desk. He sat behind it in a wing chair upholstered in worn maroon leather.

Sergeant Boone displayed his ID, introduced Delaney, and explained his role in the investigation.

"Oh, yes," Samuelson said in a high-pitched voice, "after you called last night I thought it best to make some inquiries. You both are highly recommended. I am willing to cooperate, of course, but I have already told the police everything I know."

"About the events of that Friday night," Delaney said, "when Ellerbee was killed. But there are things we need that are not included in your statement."

"For instance," Boone said, "how well did you know the victim?"

"Very well. Ever since he was my student in Boston."

Delaney: "Did you know his wife as well?"

"Of course. We visited frequently here in New York, and I was often their houseguest up in Brewster."

Boone: "Do you think a patient could have killed Ellerbee?"

"It's possible. Unfortunately, assaults on psychiatrists are not all that uncommon."

Delaney: "Was it a happy marriage?"

"The Ellerbees'? Yes, a very happy, successful marriage. They loved each other and, of course, had an additional link in their work."

Boone: "What kind of patient would attack Ellerbee?"

"A psychopath, obviously. Or someone temporarily deranged by the trauma of his analysis. It is sometimes an extremely painful process."

Delaney: "You said *his* analysis. You believe the killer was a man?"

"The nature of the crime would seem to indicate it. But it could have been a woman."

Boone: "Was Diane Ellerbee also your student?"

"No, she was Simon's student. That's how they met—when he was teaching."

Delaney: "Did he convince her to start her own practice?"

"He persuaded her, yes. We often joked about their Pygmalion-Galatea relationship."

Boone: "You mean he created her?"

"Of course not. But he recognized her gifts, her talents as a therapist. Before she met him, I understand, she was somewhat of a dilettante. But he saw something in her he thought should be encouraged. He was right. She has done—is doing—fine work."

Delaney: "How do you account for those two hammer blows to the victim's eyes?"

Samuelson exhibited the first signs of unease at this fusillade of rapid questions. He fiddled with some papers and they noted his hand trembled slightly.

He was a wisp of a man with narrow shoulders and a disproportionately large head balanced on a stalky neck. His complexion was grayish, and he wore wire-rimmed spectacles set with thick, curved lenses that magnified his eyes. Surprisingly, he had wavy russet hair that appeared to have been carefully blown dry.

He sipped his coffee and seemed to regain his poise.

"What was your question?" he asked.

Boone: "Those two hammer blows to the victim's eyes—could they have been a symbolic attempt to blind the dead man?"

"It is a possibility."

Delaney: "Do you think Simon Ellerbee was faithful to his wife?"

"Of course he was faithful! And she to him. I told you it was a happy, successful marriage. There are such things. I really don't see how all this is going to help you find the person who committed this despicable act."

Boone: "Diane Ellerbee was younger than her husband?"

"By about eight years. Not such a great gap."

Delaney: "She's a very beautiful woman. But you're certain she was faithful?"

"Of course I'm certain. There was never any gossip about them, never a rumor. And I was their closest friend. I would have heard or noticed something."

Boone: "Did you notice any change in Simon Ellerbee in the last six months or a year?"

"No, no change."

Delaney: "Nervousness? Fear? Sudden fits of silence or outbursts of anger? Anything like that?"

"No, nothing."

Boone: "Did he ever say he had been threatened by any of his patients?"

"No. He was an extremely competent man. I'm sure he would have known how to handle such threats—if any had been made."

Delaney: "Have you ever been married?"

"Once. My wife died of cancer twenty years ago. I never remarried."

Boone: "Children?"

"One son killed in an automobile accident."

Delaney: "So the Ellerbees were the only family you had?"

"I have brothers and sisters. But the Ellerbees were very close friends. Two beautiful people. I loved them both."

Boone: "They never fought?"

"Of course they fought occasionally. What married couple doesn't? But always with good humor."

Delaney: "When you went over to the Ellerbees' townhouse that Friday night and went upstairs, did you hear anything? Like someone might still be in the house, moving around?"

"No, I heard nothing."

Boone: "Did you smell anything unusual? Perfume, incense, a strong body odor—anything like that?"

"No. Just the damp. It was a very wet night."

Delaney: "There were no signs of forced entry, so we assume the victim buzzed the door open for someone he was expecting or knew. Now we're back to the possibility of one of Ellerbee's patients putting him down. We want Doctor Diane to go through her husband's caseload and select those she thinks might be capable of murder."

"Yes, she told me that. Last night."

Boone: "She relies on your opinion. Will you advise her to cooperate?"

"I have already so advised her. The law prevents her from giving you her husband's files, but I think that here the public good demands she at least name those parties she thinks might be capable of violence. You have the complete list and I assume will run a basic check on them all."

Delaney: "Checking that many alibis is almost impossible, so I'm glad you've encouraged Mrs. Ellerbee to cooperate. She obviously respects your opinions. Are you a father figure?"

Dr. Samuelson, confidence regained, relaxed. His enlarged eyes glittered behind the heavy glasses.

"Oh, I doubt that," he said softly. "Diane is a very independent woman. Her beauty warms the heart. But she is very intelligent and capable. Simon was a lucky man. I told him that often, and he agreed."

"Thank you for your help," Delaney said, rising abruptly. "I hope we may consult you again if we need more information."

"Of course. Anytime. You think you will find the person who did this thing?"

"If we're lucky," Delaney said.

Outside, they dashed across Madison to a luncheonette that had not yet filled up with the breakfast crowd. They ordered black coffee and jelly doughnuts and took them to a small, Formica-topped table alongside the tiled wall.

"I'm proud of you," Delaney said.

"How so?"

"You knew about Pygmalion and Galatea."

Boone laughed. "Blame it on crossword puzzles. You pick up a lot of useless information."

"Funny thing," Delaney said, "but just last night I was talking to Monica about the fact that so many beautiful women make a career out of just being beautiful. But from what Samuelson said, Simon was the one who convinced Diane she had a brain in addition to looks."

"I think the good doctor is in love with her."

"That wouldn't be hard. But what chance would he have? Did you see the photos of Ellerbee in the file? A big, handsome guy. Samuelson looks like a gnome compared to him."

"Maybe that's why he snuffed him," Boone said.

"You really think that?"

"No. Do you?"

"I can't see it," Delaney said. "But there's a hell of a lot I can't see about this thing. For instance, I asked Samuelson if Simon had fits of silence or outbursts of anger. Now that was an almost word-for-word quote from Diane. She said her husband was a lovely man, but occasionally had fits of silence and outbursts of anger. Samuelson, supposedly a close friend, says he never noticed anything like that."

"Maybe he thought it was of no consequence, or maybe he was trying to protect the memory of a dead friend."

"Right now, I'd say we can scratch Diane and Samuelson," Delaney said, "unless Parnell or Jason can come up with something. That leaves the victim's patients as our best bet. Will you call the widow and set up a meet to get the list of possibles from her?"

"Sure. I also better check in with Suarez's crew and find out how many of the patients they've already tossed."

"Right. You know, so far this whole thing is smoke—you realize that, don't you?"

"No doubt about that."

"Nothing hard," Delaney said fretfully, "nothing definite. It's really the worst part of a case—the opening, when everything is mush."

"No great hurry to clear it," the Sergeant said. "Is there?"

Delaney didn't want to tell him there was—that it had to be closed by the end of the year if Deputy Thorsen wanted that third star for Michael Suarez, but the Sergeant was a sharp man and probably aware of the Departmental politics involved.

"I'd just like to tidy it up fast," he said casually, "or admit failure and get back to my routine. Can you drop me?"

"Of course," Boone said, "if I can get that clunker started."

The Sergeant was driving his personal car, an old, spavined Buick he had bought at a city auction of towed-away cars. But the wheels turned, and he delivered Delaney to his brownstone.

"Give you a call, sir," he said, "as soon as I set up something with Doctor Diane."

"Good enough," Delaney said. "And brief Suarez on our talk with Samuelson. I promised to keep him in the picture."

Monica was in the living room, watching a women's talk show on television.

"What's the topic this morning?" Delaney inquired pleasantly. "Premature ejaculation?"

"Very funny," Monica said. "How did you make out with Samuelson?"

He was tempted to tell her about the doctor's comments about the Ellerbees' Pygmalion-Galatea relationship, but he didn't mention it, fearing it would sound like gloating.

"We got nothing you can hang your hat on," he said. "Just general background stuff. I'll tell you about it tonight."

He went into his study, sat at his desk, and wrote out a full report on the interrogation of Dr. Julius K. Samuelson, doing his best to recall the psychiatrist's exact words.

There was something in that interview that disturbed him, but he could not for the life of him think of what it was. He read over his report of the questioning, and still could not pinpoint it. But he was convinced something was there.

His vague disquiet was characteristic of the entire case, he decided. So far, the investigation of the murder of Dr. Simon Ellerbee was all obscure over-tones and subtle shadings. The damned case was a watercolor.

Most homicides were oils—great, bold slashings of pigment laid on with a wide brush or palette knife. Killings were generally stark, brutal affairs, the result of outsize passions or capital sins.

But this killing had the whiff of the library about it, something literary and genteel, as if plotted by Henry James.

Perhaps, Delaney admitted, he felt that way because the scene of the crime was an elegant townhouse rather than a roach-infested tenement. Or maybe because the people involved were obviously educated, intelligent, and with the wit to lie smoothly if it would serve their purpose.

But murder was murder. And maybe a delicate, polite case like this needed a lumbering, mulish old cop to strip away all the la-di-dah pretense and pin an artful, perceptive, refined killer to the goddamned wall.

9

•

"WE OUGHT TO START THINKING ABOUT THANKSGIVING," MON-ica said at breakfast. "It'll be here before you know it. A turkey, I sup-pose . . ."

"Oh . . . I don't know," Delaney said slowly.

"How about a goose?"

"A roast goose," he said dreamily. "Maybe with wild rice and brandied apples. Sounds good. You do the goose and I'll do the apples. Okay?"

"It's a deal."

"Are the girls coming down?"

"No, they're going to a friend's home. But they'll be here for Christmas."

"Good. Would you like to invite Rebecca and Abner for Thanksgiving dinner? We can't eat a whole goose by ourselves."

"That would be fun. I think they'd like it. How about Jason and his family?"

"That guy could demolish a roast goose by himself. But if I ask Boone, I'll have to ask Jason. I suspect he'll want to have Thanksgiving dinner at home with his family, but I'll check and let you know."

"What are your plans for today, Edward?"

"I want to stick around in case Abner calls to tell me when we're going to meet with Doctor Diane. Where are you off to?"

"More Christmas shopping. I want to get it all done and out of the way so I can relax and enjoy the holiday season."

"Until the bills come in," he said. "Have fun."

He went into the study to read the morning *Times* and smoke his breakfast cigar. He was halfway through both when the phone rang. He expected it to be Boone, but it was not.

"Edward X. Delaney here," he said.

"Good morning. This is Detective Charles Parnell."

"Oh, yes. How are you?"

"Fine, sir. And you?"

"Surviving," Delaney said. "You probably don't remember, but you and I have met. It was at a retirement party for Sergeant Schlossman."

"Sure," Parnell said, laughing. "I remember. I tried to chug-a-lug a quart bottle of Schaefer and upchucked all over Captain Rogers's new uniform. I haven't had a promotion since! Listen, Abner Boone said you wanted these financial reports on the people in the Ellerbee case as soon as possible."

"Don't tell me you've got them already?"

"Well, I may not be good, but I'm fast. I've got a single typed page on each of them. It's not Dun & Bradstreet, but it should give you what you want. I was wondering if I could bring them by and go over them with you. Then, if there's anything else you need, you can steer me in the right direction."

"Of course," Delaney said promptly. "I'll be in all morning. You have my address?"

"Yep. Be there in half an hour."

Delaney relighted his cigar and finished the *Times*. It was perfect timing; he had put the newspaper together neatly and was taking it into the living room to leave for Monica when the front doorbell chimed.

The detective they called Daddy Warbucks was wearing a black bowler with a rolled brim, and a double-breasted topcoat of taupe gabardine. He carried an attaché case of polished calfskin.

Seeing Delaney blink, Parnell grinned. "It's my uniform," he explained. "I work with bankers and stockbrokers. It helps if I look like I belong to the club. Off duty, I wear cord jeans and a ratty sweatshirt."

"Haven't seen a derby in years," Delaney said admiringly. "On you it looks good."

After his hat and coat had been hung away in the hall closet, the detective was revealed in all his conservative elegance: a three-piece suit of navy flannel with muted pinstripe, light blue shirt with starched white collar and cuffs, a richly tapestried cravat, and black shoes with a dull gloss—wing tips, of course.

"Sometimes I feel like a clown in this getup," he said, following Delaney back to the study, "but it seems to impress the people I deal with. Beautiful home you've got here."

"Thank you."

"You own the whole house?"

"That's right."

"If you ever want to rent out a floor, let me know. The wife and I and two kids are jammed into a West Side walk-up."

But his comments were without bitterness, and Delaney pegged him for a cheerful, good-natured man.

"Tell me something," he asked Parnell, "that suit fits so snugly, where do you carry your piece?"

"Here," Daddy Warbucks said. He turned, lifted the tail of his jacket, and revealed a snub-nosed revolver in a belt holster at the small of his back. "Not so great for a quick draw, but it's a security blanket. Do you carry?"

"Only on special occasions," Delaney said. "Listen, can I get you any-thing—coffee, a cola?"

"No, but thanks. I'm up to my eyeballs in coffee this morning."

"Well, then," Delaney said, "why don't you sit in that armchair and make yourself comfortable."

"I smell cigar smoke," Parnell said, "so I guess it's okay if I light a ciga-rette."

"Of course."

While the detective lit up, Delaney studied the man.

Crew-cut pepper-and-salt hair. A horsey face with deep furrows and laugh crinkles at the corners of the eyes. A good set of strong choppers. A blandly innocent expression. A rugged ugliness there, but not without charm. He looked like a good man to invite to a party.

"Well . . ." Parnell said, leaning over to snap open his attaché case, "how do you want to do this? Want to read the stuff first or should I give you the gist of it?"

"Suppose you summarize first," Delaney said. "Then I'll ask questions if I've got any."

"Okay," Parnell said. "We'll start with Doctor Julius K. Samuelson. His net worth is about one mil, give or take. Moneywise, he's a very cautious gentleman. CDs, Treasury bonds, and tax-free municipals. He owns his co-op apartment and office. Keeps too much in his checking account, but like I said, he's a mossback financewise. No stocks, no tax shelters, no high-fliers. He's made three irrevocable charitable trusts—all to hospitals with major psychiatric research departments. Nothing unusual. Nothing exciting. Any questions?"

"I guess not," Delaney said. "I don't suppose you got a look at his will?"

"No, I can't do that. I was lucky to learn about those charitable trusts. I really don't think there's anything in Samuelson for you, sir—lootwise. I mean, he's not rich-rich, but he's not hurting either."

"You're probably right," Delaney said, sighing. "What about the Eller-bees?"

"Ah," Charles Parnell said, "now it gets mildly interesting. If you were thinking maybe the wife knocked off the husband for his assets, it just doesn't work. He was doing okay, but she's got megabucks of her own."

"No kidding?" Delaney said, surprised. "How did she do that?"

"Her father died, leaving a modest pile to her mother. Two years later, her mother died. She had some money of her own as well. Diane Ellerbee inherited the whole bundle. Then, a year after that, a spinster aunt conked, and Diane *really* hit the jackpot—almost three mil from the aunt alone."

"Diane was an only child?"

"She had a younger brother who got scragged in Vietnam. He had no family of his own—no wife or kids, I mean—so she picked up all the marbles."

"How many marbles?" Delaney asked.

"Her husband's will hasn't been filed for probate yet, but even without her take from him, I estimate the lady tips the scales at close to five mil."

"Wow!" Delaney said. "Beautiful *and* rich."

"Yeah," Parnell said, "and she handles it all herself. No business manager or investment counselor for her. She's been doing great, too. She's smart enough to diversify, so she's into everything: stocks, bonds, real estate, tax shelters, mutual funds, municipals, commercial paper—you name it."

Delaney shook his head in wonder. "Beautiful *and* rich *and* shrewd."

"You better believe it. And she's got nerve. Some of her investments are chancy stuff, but I've got to admit she's had more winners than losers."

"What about the victim?" Delaney asked. "How was he fixed?"

"Like Samuelson, he wasn't hurting. But nothing like his wife. I'd guess his estate at maybe a half-mil, after taxes. Here's something interesting: She handled his investments for him."

"Really?" Delaney said thoughtfully. "Yes, that *is* interesting."

"Maybe he didn't have the time, or just had no great desire to pile it up buckwise. Anyway, she did as well for him as she did for herself. They have no joint accounts. Everything is separate. They don't even file a joint return."

"What about his father?" Delaney asked. "Was he giving Simon anything?"

Daddy Warbucks smiled. "Henry Ellerbee, the great real estate tycoon? That's a laugh. I had to do a money profile on the guy about six months ago. He's a real cowboy. Got a million deals working and he hasn't got two nickels to rub together. He lost control of Ellerbee Towers and he's mortgaged to the hilt. If everyone calls in his paper at once, the only place he'll be sleeping will be in bankruptcy court. I'll bet you and I have more hard cash than he does. Help out Simon? No way! More likely he was leaning on his son. Well, that's about all I've got. Do you have any more questions?"

Delaney pondered a moment. "I don't think so. Not right now. If you'll leave me your typed reports, I'll go over them. Then I may need your help on some details."

"Sure," Parnell said. "Anytime. When Simon Ellerbee's will is filed for probate, I'll be able to get the details for you."

"Good," Delaney said. "I'd appreciate that." He looked at the detective narrowly. "You like this kind of work?" he asked.

"Love it," the other man said immediately. "You know what I drag down per year. Snooping into other people's private money affairs is a kind of fantasy life for me. I'm fascinated by their wealth, and I imagine how I'd handle it—if I had it!"

"You working on anything interesting right now?"

"Oh, yeah," Daddy Warbucks said. "It's lovely—a computerized check-kiting scam. This guy worked in the computer section of a big Manhattan bank. He knows banking and he knows computers—right? So he starts out kiting checks, opening accounts at three or four New York City banks under phony names with fake ID he bought on the street. He started out small with a ten-G investment. Within six months, taking advantage of the float, he's shuffling deposits and transfers up to a quarter of a mil."

"Good God!" Delaney said. "I thought there were safeguards against that."

"It's the float!" Parnell cried. "That wonderful, marvelous, goddamned float! You can't safeguard against that. Anyway, like most check-kiters, this guy couldn't stop. He could have cashed in, grabbed his profits, and taken off for Brazil. But the scam was working so well, he decided to go for broke. He starts opening accounts in New Jersey, Connecticut, and so forth. Longer float, more profits. Then he realizes that if he had accounts in California, he'll have maybe a ten-day or two-week float. So, on his vacation, he flies out to the West Coast and opens a dozen accounts, using the same phony names as in New York and giving the New York banks as references! How do you like that?"

"As you said, it's lovely."

"The kicker is this," the detective said. "By this time the nut has got so many accounts and so many names, with checks flying all over the country, that he can't keep track of it all. So he writes his own program and fits it into one of the computers at the bank where he works. His personal program that can only be tapped by a code word, and he's the only one who knows that. So now his bank's computer is running this guy's check-kiting con. Can you believe that he had run his total up to more than two mil before the roof fell in?"

"How did they catch up with him?"

"It was an accident. Some smart lady in an Arizona bank was supposed to monitor heavy out-of-state deposits and transfers. She was out sick for a week, and when she got back to work, she found her desk piled high. She began to wade through the stuff, dividing it up by account numbers. She spotted all these deposits and transfers made by the same person, gradually increasing in size. She knew what that probably meant, and blew the whistle. It'll take at least a year to straighten out the mess. Meanwhile the guy is languishing in durance vile because he can't make bail. And a few months ago he could have cashed in and skipped with two mil. I figure it wasn't just greed that kept him going. I think he was absolutely mesmerized by the game. He just wanted to see how far he could go."

"A fascinating case," Delaney agreed.

"Yeah, but right now it's a mess. I mean, every state where he operated wants a piece of this guy, plus the Feds, plus the banks, and God knows who else. The funniest thing is that nobody lost any money. In fact, practically everyone *made* money because they were putting his fake deposits to work until he transferred the funds. The only one who lost was the perp. And all he lost was his original ten grand. There's a moral there somewhere, but I don't know what it is."

Delaney offered Parnell a beer, but the detective reluctantly declined, saying he had to get down to Wall Street for lunch with two hotshot arbitragers.

He handed over three typewritten reports and his card in case more information was needed. They went out into the hallway and Delaney helped Daddy Warbucks on with his natty coat.

"Really a great home," Parnell said, looking around. "I'd like one exactly like it. Well, maybe someday."

"Just don't start kiting checks," Delaney warned.

"Not me," the detective said, laughing. "I haven't got the chutzpah. Besides, I can't work a computer."

They shook hands and Delaney thanked the other man for his help. Parnell departed, bowler cocked at a jaunty angle, attaché case swinging.

Delaney went back to the kitchen, smiling. He had enjoyed the company of Daddy Warbucks. He was always interested in other dicks' cases—especially new scams and innovative criminal techniques.

He made a "wet" sandwich, leaning over the sink to eat it. Slices of canned Argentine corned beef with a layer of sauerkraut and a few potato chips for crunch. And Dijon mustard. All on thick slabs of sour rye. Washed down with dark Heineken.

Finished, he cleaned up the kitchen and returned to the study. He put on his reading glasses and went over the three financial statements Parnell had given him. He saw nothing of importance that Daddy Warbucks hadn't covered in his oral report.

The detective was right: The idea that Diane Ellerbee might have chilled her husband for his gelt just didn't wash; she had ten times his wealth and Delaney couldn't see her as an inordinately avaricious woman.

So that, he supposed, was that. Unless Jason T. Jason came up with something in the biographies, the only way to go was investigation of Simon Ellerbee's patients.

And right on cue, the telephone rang. This time it *was* Abner Boone. He said Dr. Diane Ellerbee would see them that evening at nine o'clock.

"Suppose I pick you up about fifteen minutes early," Boone suggested.

"Make it a half hour early," Delaney said. "Charlie Parnell stopped by, and I want to bring you up to date on what he found out."

10

•

DELANEY TURNED SIDEWAYS ON THE FRONT PASSENGER SEAT, looking at Abner Boone as he filled him in on Charlie Parnell's report. They were parked near the East 84th Street townhouse.

Boone was a tall, gawky man who walked with a shambling lope, wrists and ankles protruding a little too far from his cuffs. He had short, gingery hair, lightly freckled complexion, big, horsey teeth. There was a lot of "country boy" in his appearance and manner, but Delaney knew that masked a sharp mind and occasionally painful sensitivity.

"Well, sir," the Sergeant said when Delaney had finished, "the lady sure sounds like a powerhouse. All that money to manage, two houses, and a successful career. But you know who interests me most in this thing?"

"The victim?" Delaney guessed.

"That's right. I can't get a handle on him. Everyone says how brilliant he was. Maybe that's so, but I can't get a mental picture of him—how he dressed, talked, what he did on his time off. From what Doctor Diane and Samuelson told us, he seems almost too good to be true."

"Well, you can't expect his widow and best friend to put him down. I'm hoping his patients will open up and tell us a little more about him. I guess it's about time; we don't want to keep the doctor waiting."

On the lobby intercom, Dr. Diane Ellerbee told them to come up to the third floor, then buzzed them in. They tramped up the stairway, carrying their hats. She met them in the hallway and shook hands firmly with both of them.

"This may take a little time," she said briskly, "so I thought we'd be more comfortable in the sitting room."

She was wearing a long-sleeved jumpsuit of black silk, zipped from high collar to shirred waist. Her wheaten hair was down, splaying about her shoulders in a silken skein. As she led the way toward the rear of the house, Delaney admired again her erect carriage and the flowing grace of her movements.

She ushered them into a brightly lighted chamber, comfortably cluttered with bibelots, framed photos, bric-a-brac. One wall was a ceiling-high bookcase jammed with leather-bound sets, paperbacks, magazines.

"The rooms downstairs are more formal than this," she said with a half-smile. "And neater. But Simon and I spent most of our evenings here. It's a good place to unwind. Let me have your coats, gentlemen. May I bring you something—coffee, a drink?"

They both politely declined.

She seated them in soft armchairs, then pulled up a ladder-back chair with a cane seat to face them. She sat primly, spine straight, chin lifted, head held high.

"Julie—" she started, then: "Doctor Samuelson approves of my cooperating with you, but I must say I am not absolutely certain I am doing the right thing. The conflict is between my desire to see my husband's murderer caught and at the same time protect the confidentiality of his patients."

"Doctor Ellerbee," Delaney said, "I assure you that anything you tell us will be top secret as far as we're concerned."

"Well . . ." she said, "I suppose that's as much as I can hope for. One other thing: The patients I have selected as potential assailants are only six out of a great many more."

"We've got to start somewhere, ma'am," Boone said. "It's impossible for us to run alibi checks on them all."

"I realize that," she said sharply. "I'm just warning you that my judgment may be faulty. After all, they were my *husband's* patients, not mine. So I'm going by his files and what he told me. It's quite possible—probable, in fact—that the six people I've selected are completely innocent, and the guilty person is the one I've passed over."

"Believe me," Delaney said, "we're not immediately and automatically going to consider your selections to be suspects. They'll be thoroughly investigated, and if we believe them to be innocent, we'll move on to others in your husband's caseload. Don't feel you are condemning these people simply by giving us their names. There's more to a homicide investigation than that."

"Well, that makes me feel a little better. Remember, psychotherapy is not an exact science—it is an uncertain art. Two skilled, experienced therapists examining the same patient could very likely come up with two opposing diagnoses. You have only to read the opinions of psychiatrists testifying in court cases to realize that."

"We used to call them alienists," Delaney said. "Usually they confused a trial more than they helped."

"I'm afraid you're right," she said with a wan smile. "Objective criteria are hard to recognize in this field. Well, having said all that, let me show you what I've done."

She rose, went over to a small Sheraton-styled desk, came back with two pages of typescript.

"Six patients," she told them. "Four men, two women. I've given you their names, ages, addresses. I've written a short paragraph on each, using my husband's notes and what he told me about them. Although I've listed their major problems, I haven't given you definitive labels—schizoid, psychotic, manic-depressive, or whatever. They were not my patients, and I refuse to attempt a diagnosis. Now let me get started."

She donned a pair of wire-rimmed reading glasses. Curiously, these old-fashioned spectacles softened her chiseled features, gave her face a whimsical charm.

"I should warn you," she said, "I have listed these people in no particular order. That is, the first mentioned is not, in my opinion, necessarily the most dangerous. All six, I believe, have the potential for violence. I won't read everything I've written—just give you a very brief synopsis. . . .

"Number One: Ronald J. Bellsey, forty-three. He saw my husband three times a week. Apparently a violent man with a history of uncontrollable outbursts of anger. Ronald first consulted my husband after injuring his wife in a brutal attack. At least he had sense enough to realize he was ill and needed help.

"Number Two: Isaac Kane, twenty-eight. He was one of my husband's charity patients, treated once a week at a free clinic. Isaac is what they call an idiot savant, although I hate that term. He is far from being an idiot, but he is retarded. Isaac does absolutely wonderful landscapes in pastel chalk. Very professional work. But he has, on occasion, attacked workers and other patients at the clinic.

"Number Three: Sylvia Mae Otherton, forty-six. She saw my husband twice a week, but frequently made panic calls. Sylvia suffers from heavy anxieties, ranging from agoraphobia to a hatred of bearded men. On the few occasions when she ventured out in public, she made vicious and unprovoked attacks against men with beards."

"Was your husband bearded, ma'am?" Boone asked.

"No, he was not. Number Four: L. Vincent Symington, fifty-one. Apparently his problem is a very deep and pervasive paranoia. Vince frequently struck back at people he believed were persecuting him, including his aged mother and father. He saw my husband three times a week.

"Number Five: Joan Yesell, thirty-five. She is a very withdrawn, depressed young woman who lives with her widowed mother. Joan has a history of three suicide attempts, which is one of the reasons I have included her. Suicide, when tried unsuccessfully so often, often develops into homicidal mania.

"And finally, Harold Gerber, thirty-seven. He served in Vietnam and won several medals for exceptional valor. Harold apparently suffers intensely from guilt—not only for those he killed in the war, but because he came back alive when so many of his friends died. His guilt is manifested in barroom brawls and physical attacks on strangers he thinks have insulted him.

"And that's all I have. You'll find more details in this typed report. Do you have any questions?"

Delaney and Boone looked at each other.

"Just one thing, doctor," Delaney said. "Could you tell us if any of the six was being treated with drugs."

"No," she said immediately. "None of them. My husband did not believe in psychotropic drugs. He said they only masked symptoms but did nothing to reveal or treat the cause of the illness. Incidentally, I hold the same opinion, but I am not a fanatic on the subject as my husband was. I occasionally use drugs in my practice—but only when the physical health of the patient warrants it."

"Are you licensed to prescribe drugs?" Delaney asked.

She gave him a hard stare. "No," she said, "but my husband was."

"But of course," Boone said hastily, "it's possible that any of the six could be using drugs on their own."

"It's possible," Dr. Ellerbee said in her loud, assertive voice. "It's possible of anyone. Which of you gets this report?"

"Ma'am," Delaney said softly, "you have just the one copy?"

"That's correct. I made no carbon."

"You wouldn't happen to have a copying machine in your office, would you? It would help a great deal if both Sergeant Boone and I had copies. Speed things up."

"There's a copier in my husband's outer office," she said, rising. "It'll just take a minute."

"We'll come along if you don't mind," Delaney said, and both men stood up.

She looked at them. "If you're thinking about my safety, I thank you—but there's no need, I assure you. I have lived in this house since Simon died. There are people here during the day, but I'm alone at night. It doesn't frighten me. I won't let it frighten me. This is my *home*."

"If you'll allow us," Delaney said stubbornly, "we'll still come along. It'll give us a chance to see the scene—to see where it happened."

"If you wish," she said tonelessly.

She took a ring of keys from the desk drawer, then led the way along the hall. She unlocked the door of her husband's office and turned on the light. The floor of the receptionist's room was bare boards.

"I had the carpeting taken up and thrown out," she said. "It was stained, and I didn't wish to have it cleaned."

"Have you decided what to do with this space, ma'am?" Boone asked.

"No," she said shortly. "I haven't thought about it."

She went over to the copier in the corner and switched it on. While she was making a duplicate of her report, they looked about.

There was little to see. The outer office was identical in size and shape to the one on the second floor. It was aseptically furnished with steel desk, chairs, filing cabinet. There was no indication it had been the scene of murderous frenzy.

Dr. Ellerbee turned off the copier, handed each of them her two-page report.

"I wouldn't care to have this circulated," she said sternly.

"It won't be," Delaney assured her. "Doctor, would you mind if we took a quick look into your husband's office?"

"What for?"

"Standard operating procedure," he said. "To try to learn more about your husband. Sometimes seeing where a victim lived and where he worked gives a good indication of the kind of man he was."

She shrugged, obviously not believing him, but not caring.

"Help yourself," she said gesturing toward the inner door.

She sat at the receptionist's desk while they went into Dr. Simon Ellerbee's private office. Boone switched on the overhead light.

A severe, rigorous room, almost austere. No pictures on the white walls. No decorations. No objets d'art, memorabilia, or personal touches. The room was defined by its lacks. Even the black leather patient's couch was as sterile as a hospital gurney.

"Cold," Boone said in a low voice.

"You wanted a handle on the guy," Delaney said. "Here's a piece of it: He was organized, logical, emotionless. Notice how all the straight edges are parallel or at right angles? A very precise, disciplined man. Can you imagine spending maybe twelve hours a day in a cell like this? Let's go; it gives me the willies."

They reclaimed their coats and hats from the sitting room, thanked Dr. Diane Ellerbee for her assistance, and said they'd keep her informed of the progress of the investigation.

"I warn you," Delaney said, smiling, "we may call on you for more help."

"Of course," she said. "Anytime." She seemed tired.

Out on the street, walking slowly to the car, Boone said, "Ballsy lady. Most women would have gone somewhere else to live or asked a friend to stay awhile after something like that happened."

"Mmm," Delaney said. "She claims she's not frightened and I believe her. By the way, did you notice how she referred to those patients by their first names? I wonder if all shrinks do that. It reminds me of the way cops talk to suspects to bring them down."

"I thought it was just to—you know—to show how sympathetic you are."

"Maybe. But using a suspect's first name diminishes him, robs him of his dignity. It proves that you're in a position of authority. You call a Mafia chief Tony when he's used to being called Mr. Anthony Gelesco and it makes him feel like a two-bit punk or a pushcart peddler. Well, all that's smoke and getting us nowhere. Tomorrow morning check to see if Chief Suarez's men have talked to any of those six patients. We better start with their whereabouts at the time of the homicide."

"Even if Suarez's guys have talked to them, you'll still want them double-checked, won't you, sir?"

"Of course. As far as I'm concerned, this investigation is just starting. And get hold of Jason Two; see how he's coming along on the biographies. I'd like him to finish up as soon as possible; we're going to need his help knocking on doors."

Sergeant Boone drove Delaney home. Outside the brownstone, before Delaney got out of the car, Boone said, "What did you think of Doctor Diane's selections, sir? They all seem like possibles to me."

"Could be. You know, when I talked to Doc Walden, he tried to convince me that most people who go to psychotherapists aren't nuts or crazies or weirdos; they're just poor unfortunates with king-size emotional hang-ups. But all these people on Doctor Diane's list sound like half-decks. Good night, Sergeant."

Monica was in the living room, working the *Times* crossword puzzle. She looked up as Delaney came in, peering at him over the top of her Ben Franklin glasses.

"How did it go?" she asked.

"I need something," he said. "Maybe a tall scotch with a lot of ice and a lot of soda."

He mixed the drinks in the kitchen and brought them back to the living room. Monica held her glass up to the light.

"You have a heavy hand with that scotch bottle, kiddo," she said. She tried a sip. "But I forgive you. Now tell me—how did it go?"

Delaney slumped in his high wing chair covered with bottle-green leather worn glassy smooth. He loosened his tie, unbuttoned his collar, and sighed.

"It went all right. She gave us a list of six possibles."

"Then what are you so grumpy about?"

"Who says I'm grumpy?"

"I do. You've got that squinchy look around the eyes, and you're gritting your teeth."

"I am? Well, it's not going to work."

"What's not going to work?"

"The investigation. *My* investigation. Now we've got six people to check out, and I have only Boone and Jason. I can't do any legwork myself without a tin to flash. So, in effect, there are two men to investigate six suspects. Oh, it could be done if we had all the time in the world, but Thorsen wants this thing cleared up by the end of the year."

"Only one answer to that, isn't there? Ask Ivar for more help."

"I don't know how Chief Suarez would take that. He said he'd cooperate in any way he could, but I have a hunch he still sees me as competition."

"Then instead of asking Ivar for more men, ask Suarez. That makes him part of the team, doesn't it? Gives him a chance to share the success if you find out who killed Simon Ellerbee."

He stared at her reflectively. "I knew I married a great beauty," he said. "Now I realize I also married a great brain."

She sniffed. "You're just finding that out? Why don't you call Suarez right now."

"Too late," Delaney said. "I'll wake up that family of his. I'll get hold of him first thing in the morning. Meanwhile I've got a little work to do. Don't wait up for me; go to bed whenever you like."

He rose, lumbered over to her, swooped to kiss her cheek. Then he took his drink into the study. He closed the connecting door to the living room in case Monica wanted to watch the Johnny Carson show.

He sat at his desk, put on his heavy black-rimmed glasses, and slowly read through Dr. Diane's two-page report. Then he read it again.

There was more there than she had given them in her oral summary. The six paragraphs described very disturbed people who showed every evidence of being out of control. Any one of them seemed to have the potential for ungovernable violence.

Delaney sat back and gently tinked the rim of his highball glass against his teeth. He thought about Simon Ellerbee. What was it like, he wondered, to spend your life working with people whose thought processes were so chaotic?

It was, he supposed, like being in a foreign country where all the natives were hostile, spoke a strange language, and even the geography of their world was terra incognita.

He imagined that any man who deliberately ventured into the alien land might suffer from bewilderment and disorientation. He'd have to clamp a tight hold on his own feelings to keep from being swept away by disorder.

Delaney remembered that cold, disciplined office of Dr. Simon Ellerbee. Now he could understand why a psychiatrist would want to work in rigidly geometric surroundings where parallel lines never met and hard edges reminded that arrangement and sequence did exist, and logic was not dead.

11

•

ISAAC KANE HAD BEEN GOING TO THE CLINIC EVERY WEDNESDAY. He was given endless tests. Sometimes, with the permission of his mother, he was handed pills or liquids to swallow. They made him do things with wooden blocks and photographed him on videotape. Then he would spend an hour with Dr. Simon.

Kane didn't mind talking to the doctor. He was a nice, quiet man and really seemed interested in what Isaac had to say. In fact, Dr. Simon was about the only one who listened to Isaac; his mother wouldn't listen, and other people made fun of the way he talked. There was so much Kane wanted to say, and sometimes he couldn't get it out fast enough. Then he went, "Bub-bub-bub," and people laughed.

But Dr. Simon stopped coming to the clinic, so Kane stopped, too. They tried to get him to continue coming in every Wednesday, but he just wouldn't do it. They kept at him, and finally he had to hit some of them. That did the trick, all right, and they didn't bother him anymore.

So now he could spend all his days at the Harriet J. Raskob Community Center on West 79th Street. The clinic had been painted all white—Isaac didn't like that—but the Center was pink and green and blue and yellow. It was warm in there, and they let him work on his pastel landscapes.

The head of the Center, Mrs. Freylinghausen, sold some of Kane's landscapes and gave the money to his mother. But she kept enough to buy him a wonderful box of at least a hundred pastel crayons in all colors and hues, an easel, paper, and panels. When he ran out of supplies, Mrs. Freylinghausen bought him more—Isaac wasn't very good at shopping—and locked up all his property when the Center closed at 9:00 P.M.

Most of the people who came to the Center were very old, some in wheelchairs or on walkers. They were as nice to Isaac Kane as Mrs. Freylinghausen. But there were younger people, too, and some of them weren't so nice. They mimicked Isaac's "Bub-bub-bub" and they tripped him or pushed his elbow when he was working or tried to steal his chalks. One girl liked to touch him all over.

Sometimes they got him so mad that he had to hit them. He was strong, and he could really hurt someone if he wanted to.

One afternoon—Kane didn't know what day it was—Mrs. Freylinghausen

came out of her office with two men and headed for the corner where Isaac
had set up his easel under a skylight. Both the men were big. The older wore
a black overcoat and the other a dark green parka. Both carried their hats.

"Isaac," Mrs. Freylinghausen said, "I'd like you to meet two friends of
mine who are interested in your work. This gentleman is Mr. Delaney, and
here is Mr. Boone."

Isaac shook hands with both of them, leaving their palms smeared with
colored chalk. They both smiled and looked nice. Mrs. Freylinghausen
moved away.

"Mr. Kane," Delaney said, "we just saw some of your landscapes, and we
think they're beautiful."

"They're okay, I guess," Isaac said modestly. "Sometimes they're not, you
know, what I want. I can't always get the colors just right."

"Have you ever seen Turner's paintings?" Delaney asked.

"Turner? No. Who is he?"

"An English painter. He worked in oil and watercolor. He did a lot of
landscapes. The way you handle light reminds me of Turner."

"Light!" Isaac Kane cried. "That's very hard to do." And then, because
he wanted to say so much about light, he began to go "Bub-bub-bub . . ."

They waited patiently, not laughing at him, and when he got out what he
wanted to say, they nodded understandingly.

"Mr. Kane," Boone said, "I think we may have a mutual friend. Did you
know Doctor Ellerbee?"

"No, I don't know him."

"Doctor Simon Ellerbee?"

"Oh, Doctor Simon! Sure, I know him. He stopped coming to the clinic.
What happened to him?"

Boone glanced at Delaney.

"I'm afraid I have bad news for you, Mr. Kane," Delaney said. "Doctor
Simon is dead. Someone killed him."

"Gee, that's too bad," Isaac said. "He was a nice man. I liked to talk to
him."

He turned back to his easel, where a sheet of grainy paper had been pinned
to a square of cardboard. He was working on an idyllic farm scene with a
windmill, thatched cottage, a running brook. There were plump white clouds
in the foreground and, beyond, dark menacing rain clouds. The rendition of
shadows and the changing light saved the work from mawkishness.

"What did you talk to Doctor Simon about?" Delaney asked.

"Oh . . . everything," Isaac said, working with a white chalk to get a little
more glitter on the water's surface. "He asked me a lot of questions."

"Mr. Kane," Boone said, "can you think of anyone who might have
wanted to hurt Doctor Simon?"

He turned to face them. They saw a rudely handsome young man clad in
stained denim overalls, a red plaid shirt, tattered running shoes. His brown

hair was cut short enough to show pink scalp. Dark eyes revealed nothing, but there was a sweet innocence in his expression.

"That's the way some people are," he said sadly. "They want to hurt you."

"Do people hurt you, Mr. Kane?" Delaney asked.

"Sometimes they try, but I don't let them. I hit them and then they stop. I don't like mean people."

"But Doctor Simon never hurt you, did he?"

"Oh, no—he was a nice man! I never—he would—we talked and—" But then there was so much he wanted to say about Dr. Simon that he began to stutter again. They waited, but he had nothing intelligible to add.

"Well, we've got to get going," Delaney said. "Thank you for giving us so much time." He looked down at Kane's ragged running shoes. "I hope you have boots or galoshes," he said, smiling. "It's snowing outside."

"I don't care," Isaac said. "I just live around the corner. I don't need boots."

They all shook hands. Delaney and Boone headed for the doorway. A young girl with disheveled hair was propped up against the wall of the vestibule. She looked at them with glazed eyes and said, "Oink, oink."

Out on the sidewalk, Boone said, "She had us pegged."

"Stoned out of her skull," Delaney said grimly.

They were double-parked on 80th Street. Boone had propped a POLICE OFFICER ON DUTY card inside the windshield, and for once it had worked: He still had his hubcaps. They got in, started the engine, turned on the wheezy heater, sat a few moments, shivering, and watched the wet snow drift down.

"Poor guy," Boone observed. "Not much there."

"No," Delaney agreed. "But you never know. He seems to be quick with his fists when he thinks someone is out to hurt him."

"How could Simon Ellerbee hurt him?"

"Maybe he asked one question too many. It's possible."

"What was the business about the boots and galoshes?" Boone said.

"Those two sets of unidentified tracks on the Ellerbees' carpet."

"Jesus!" the Sergeant said disgustedly. "I forgot all about them."

"Well, we still don't know if Kane owns boots. All he said was that he wasn't wearing them today. I think we better get back to my place, Sergeant. Chief Suarez said he'd call at noon, and I have a feeling he's a very prompt man."

"You think he's checking with Thorsen, sir?"

"Of course. If I was in Suarez's place I'd say something like this: 'Deputy, Delaney wants six more detectives. That's okay with me, but I don't want to give him any of the people working the case for me. It would hobble what we're doing. So I'd like to assign six new bodies to Delaney.' "

"You think Thorsen will go for that?"

"Sure he will. He's got no choice."

With the holiday traffic getting heavier and the snow beginning to pile up, it took them almost a half hour to get over to the East Side. Boone parked in front of the 251st Precinct house, leaving his ON DUTY card on display. Then they trudged next door to Delaney's brownstone.

"How about a sandwich?" Delaney suggested. "We've got some cold roast beef, sweet pickle relish, sliced onions. Maybe a little pink horseradish. How does that sound?"

"Just right," Boone said. "A hot coffee wouldn't go bad either."

Delaney spread old newspapers on the kitchen table and they ate their lunch hunched over that.

"Now let's see . . ." Delaney said. "You told me that Suarez's men have checked out four of the names on our list?"

"That's right, sir. Just their whereabouts at the time of the homicide. As of this morning, they hadn't gotten around to Otherton or Gerber."

"We'll have to double-check them all anyway. If we get the six new people, I want to assign one to each possible. But I want to question each of the patients personally. That means you or Jason Two will have to come with me to show your ID."

"I talked to Jason. He says he'll be finished with the biogs by tonight. He'll call you."

"Good. I want you there when he makes his report. We'll hit Otherton this afternoon. We won't call her first; just barge in. The other four we'll have to brace in the evening or over the weekend. Sergeant, can you think of anything we should be doing that we're not?"

Boone had finished his sandwich. He sat back, lighted a cigarette.

"I'd like to get a lead on that ball peen hammer," he said. "We didn't ask Isaac Kane if he had one."

"Don't worry," Delaney said. "We'll be getting back to that lad again. I can't see the two women owning a hammer like that—but you never know. We'll have to lean on the four men. Maybe one of them is a do-it-yourself nut or does his own car repairs or something like that."

"How do you get rid of a hammer?" Boone said. "You can't burn it. The handle maybe, but not the head. And the first crew on the scene checked every sewer, catch basin, and garbage can in a ten-block area."

"If I was the killer," Delaney said, "I'd throw it in the river. Chances are good it'd never be found."

"Still," Boone said, "the perp might have—"

But just then the phone rang, and Delaney rose to answer it. "I hope that's Suarez," he said.

"Edward X. Delaney here . . . Yes, Chief . . . Uh-huh. That's fine . . . Monday will be just right . . . Of course. Maybe you and I can get together next week . . . Whenever you say . . . Thank you for your help, Chief."

He hung up and turned to Boone. "He didn't sound too happy about it, but six warm bodies are coming in Monday morning. I'll want you there; maybe you know some of those guys. More coffee?"

"Please. I'm just getting thawed."

"Well, drink up. Then we'll descend on Sylvia Mae Otherton. Sure as hell no woman with agoraphobia is going out on a day like this."

She lived in an old battleship of an apartment house on East 72nd Street between Park and Lexington avenues. Boone drove around the block twice, trying to find a parking space, then gave up. He parked in front of the marquee, and when an indignant doorman rushed out, the Sergeant flashed his shield and quieted him down.

The cavernous lobby was lined with brownish marble that needed cleaning, and the steel Art Deco elevator doors obviously hadn't been polished in years. The carpeting was fretted, and the whole place had a musty odor.

"A mausoleum," Delaney muttered.

There was a marble-topped counter manned by an ancient wearing an old-fashioned hearing aid with a black wire that disappeared into the front of his alpaca jacket. Boone asked for Miss Sylvia Mae Otherton.

"And who shall I say is calling?" the gaffer asked in sepulchral tones.

The Sergeant showed his ID again, and the white eyebrows slowly rose.

The lobby attendant picked up the house phone and punched a three-digit number with a trembling forefinger. He turned his back to them; all they could hear was murmurs. Then he turned back to them.

"Miss Otherton would like to know the purpose of your visit."

"Tell her we want to ask a few questions," Boone said. "It won't take long."

More murmurs.

"Miss Otherton says she is not feeling well and wonders if you can come back another time."

"No, we cannot come back another time," Boone said, beginning to steam. "Ask her if she prefers to see us in her home or should we take her down to the station house and ask the questions there."

The white eyebrows rose even farther. More murmurs. Then he hung up the phone.

"Miss Otherton will see you now," he said. "Apartment twelve-C." Then, his bleary eyes glistening, he leaned over the counter. "Is it about that doctor who got killed?" he asked in a conspiratorial whisper.

They turned away.

"She was devastated," he called after them. "Just devastated."

"Damned old gossip," the Sergeant said angrily in the elevator. "By tonight everyone in the building will know Otherton had a call from the cops."

"Calm down," Delaney said. "Everyone loves a gruesome murder—especially an unsolved one. They'd like to think the perp will get away with it."

Boone looked at him curiously. "You really believe that, sir?"

"Sure," Delaney said cheerfully. "It feeds their fantasies. They can dream of knocking off wife, husband, boss, lover, or that pain in the ass next door—and walking away from it scot-free."

Boone pushed the buzzer at the door of apartment 12-C. They waited. And waited. Finally they heard sounds of bolts being withdrawn, and the door opened a few inches, held by a chain still in place.

A muffled voice said, "Let me see your identification."

Obediently, the Sergeant passed his ID wallet through the chink. They waited. Then the door closed, the chain came off, and the door was opened wide.

"Wipe your feet on the mat," the woman said, "before you come in." They obeyed.

The apartment was so dimly lighted—heavy drapes drawn across all the windows—that it was difficult to make out much of anything. Heavy furniture loomed along the walls, and they had a muddled impression of an enormous overstuffed couch and two armchairs placed about a round cocktail table.

Delaney smelled sandalwood incense, and, as his eyes became accustomed to the gloom, he saw vaguely Oriental wall hangings, a torn shoji used as a room divider.

The woman who faced them, head bowed, wadded tissue clutched in one hand, seemed as outlandish as her overheated apartment. She wore a loose garment of black lace over a lining of deep purple satin. The pointed hem came to her ankles, and her small feet were shod in glittery evening slippers.

She wore a torrent of necklaces: pearls and rhinestones and shells and wooden beads. Some were chokers and some hung to her shapeless waist. Her plump fingers were equally adorned: rings on every finger, and some with two and three rings. And as if that weren't enough, stacks of bracelets climbed both arms from wrists to elbows.

"Miss Sylvia Mae Otherton?" Sergeant Boone asked.

The bowed head bobbed.

"I wonder if we might take off our coats, ma'am. We won't stay long, but it is warm in here."

"Do what you like," she said dully.

They took off their coats, and, holding them folded, hats on top, took seats on the couch. It was down-filled, and unexpectedly they sank until they were almost swaddled.

The only illumination in the room came from a weak, blue-tinted bulb in an ornate floor lamp of cast bronze shaped like a striking cobra. In this watery light they strained to see the features of Sylvia Mae Otherton when she folded herself slowly into one of the armchairs opposite them. They could smell her perfume; it was stronger than the incense.

"Miss Otherton," Boone said gently, "as I suppose you've guessed, this

concerns the murder of Doctor Simon Ellerbee. We're talking to all his patients as part of our investigation. I know you'll want to help us find the
person responsible for Doctor Ellerbee's death."

"He was a saint," she cried. "A saint!"

She raised her head at this last, and they got a clear look at her for the first
time.

A fleshy face, now riddled with grief. Chalky makeup, round patches of
rouge, and lips so caked with lipstick that they were cracked. Her black hair
hung limply, uncombed, and long glass pendants dangled from her ears. Under brows plucked into thin carets her eyes were swollen and brimming.

"Miss Otherton," Boone continued, "it's necessary that we establish the
whereabouts of Ellerbee's patients on the night of the crime. Where were
you that Friday evening?"

"I was right here," she said. "I very, very rarely go out."

"Did you have any visitors that night?"

"No."

"Did you see any neighbors—in the lobby or the hallways?"

"No."

"Did you receive any phone calls?"

"No."

Boone gave up; Delaney took over.

"How did you spend that evening, Miss Otherton?" he asked. "Read?
Watch television?"

"I worked on my autobiography," she said. "Doctor Simon got me started.
He said it would help if I tried to recall everything and write it down."

"And did you then show what you had written to Ellerbee?"

"Yes. And we'd discuss it. He was so sympathetic, so understanding. Oh,
what a beautiful man!"

"You saw him twice a week?"

"Usually. Sometimes more when I—when I had to."

"How long had you been seeing Doctor Ellerbee?"

"Four years. Four years and three months."

"Did you feel he was helping you?"

"Oh, yes! My panic attacks are much less frequent now. And I don't do
those—those things as often. I don't know what's going to happen to me
with Doctor Simon gone. His wife—his widow—is trying to find another
therapist for me, but it won't be the same."

"What things?" Boone said sharply. "You said you don't do those things
as often. What were you referring to?"

She raised her soft chin. "Sometimes when I go out, I hit people."

"Have they done anything to you?"

"No."

"Just anyone?" Delaney said. "Someone on the street or in a restaurant?"

"Men with beards," she said in a husky voice, her head slowly bowing again. "Only men with beards. When I was eleven years old, I was raped by my uncle."

"And he had a beard?"

She raised her head and stared at him defiantly. "No, but it happened in his office, and he had an old engraving of Ulysses Grant on the wall."

It's Looney Tunes time, Delaney thought, and was vaguely ashamed they had dragged that confession from this hapless woman.

"But your assaults on bearded men became less frequent after you started seeing Doctor Ellerbee?"

"Oh, yes! He was the one who made the connection between bearded men and the rape."

"When was the last time you made an attack on a stranger?"

"Oh . . . months ago."

"How many months?"

"One or two."

"It must have been very painful for you—when Doctor Ellerbee told you the reason for your hostility toward bearded men."

"He didn't *tell* me. He never did that. He just let me discover it for myself."

"But that was painful?"

"Yes," she said in a whisper. "Very. I hated him then, for making me remember."

"Was this a recent discovery?"

"Months ago."

"How many months?"

"One or two," she said again.

"But earlier you called Doctor Simon a saint. So your hatred of him didn't last."

"No. I knew he was trying to help me."

Delaney glanced at the Sergeant.

"Miss Otherton," Boone said, "did you know any of Doctor Simon's other patients?"

"No. I rarely saw them, and we never spoke."

"Do you know Doctor Diane Ellerbee?"

"I met her twice and spoke to her once on the phone."

"What do you think of her?" Boone asked.

"She's all right, I guess. Awfully skinny. And cold. She doesn't have Doctor Simon's personality. He was a very warm man."

"Do you know of anyone who might have wanted to harm him? Anyone who threatened him?"

"No. Who would want to kill a *doctor?* He was trying to help everyone."

"Did you ever attack Doctor Simon?"

"Once," she said and sobbed. "I slapped him."

"Why did you do that?"

"I don't remember."

"How did he react?"

"He slapped me back, not hard. Then we hugged each other, laughing, and it was all right."

She seemed willing enough to continue talking—eager in fact. But the sandalwood incense, her perfume, and the steamy heat were getting to them.

"Thank you, Miss Otherton," Delaney said, struggling out of the depths of the couch. "You've been very cooperative. Please try to recall anything about Doctor Simon that might help us. Perhaps a name he mentioned, or an incident. For instance, do you think his manner or personality changed in, say, the last six months or year?"

"Strange you should ask that," she said. "I thought he was becoming a little quieter, more thoughtful. Not depressed, you understand, but a little subdued. I asked him if anything was worrying him, and he said no."

"You've been very helpful," Boone said. "We may find it necessary to come back and ask you more questions. I hope you won't mind."

"I won't mind," she said forlornly. "I don't have many visitors."

"I'll leave my card," the Sergeant said, "in case you remember something you think might help us."

In the elevator, going down, Delaney said, "Odd. She says he was such a warm guy. That's not the feeling I got from that private office of his."

"I wonder what was bothering him," Boone said. "If anything was."

"The question is," Delaney said, "did she hate him enough to dust him? She says she hated him after he made her recall the rape. Maybe he dredged up something else out of her past that really set her off."

"You think she's strong enough to bash in his skull?"

"When the adrenaline is flowing, a flyweight could do that, and she's a hefty woman."

"Yeah. That's why I'm going home and shave. I don't want to take any chances!"

• • •

THAT NIGHT, AFTER dinner, Delaney told Monica about his day. She listened intently, fascinated.

"Those poor people," she mourned when he had finished.

"Yes. They're not exactly demented, but neither Isaac Kane nor Sylvia Mae has both oars in the water. And there are four more patients I want to meet."

"It depresses you, Edward?"

"It's not exactly a million laughs."

He had started a small fire in the grate and turned off the living room lamps. They sat on the couch, close together, staring into the flames. Suddenly he put his arm about her shoulders.

"You okay?" she asked.

"Yes," he said. "But it's cold out there, and dark."

12

•

"IT'S GOING TO BE A MIXED-UP WEEKEND," HE WARNED MONICA on Saturday morning. "I want to brace the other four patients before the new boys report in on Monday morning. And Jason called; he's coming by this afternoon."

"Don't forget to ask Boone and Jason about Thanksgiving dinner."

"I'll remember," he promised.

He went into the study to scribble a rough schedule, consulting the patients' addresses on Dr. Diane Ellerbee's list. He decided to hit Ronald J. Bellsey and L. Vincent Symington on Saturday and Joan Yesell and Harold Gerber on Sunday.

He and Boone would have to return to the brownstone to hear Jason's report, and it was possible some of the patients wouldn't be home. But if all went well, Delaney could spend Sunday evening bringing his files up to date in preparation for briefing the six new detectives.

By the time Boone arrived, Delaney had the weekend organized. Everything but the weather. It was a miserable day, with lowering clouds, sharp gusts of rain, and a mean wind that came out of the northwest, whipping coattails and snatching at hats.

Bellsey lived on East 28th Street. They drove south on Second Avenue, windshield wipers working in fits and starts, and the ancient heater fighting a losing battle against the windchill factor.

"I keep hoping someone will steal this heap," the Sergeant said. "But I guess even the chop shops don't want it. One of these days I'll hit the lottery and get a decent set of wheels. By the way, I talked to the dick who checked out Bellsey. The subject claims he was home on the night Ellerbee got snuffed. His wife confirms. Not much of an alibi."

"Not much," Delaney agreed. "Did you find out what Bellsey does for a living?"

"Yeah. He's manager of a big wholesale butcher on West Eighteenth Street. They handle high-class meats and poultry, and sell only to restaurants and hotels."

"That reminds me," Delaney said. "Would you and Rebecca like to come over for Thanksgiving Day dinner? We're having roast goose."

"Sounds good to me," Boone said. "Thank you, sir. But I'll have to check with Rebecca first in case she's made other plans."

"Sure. Either way, why don't you ask her to give Monica a call."

Ronald J. Bellsey lived in a new high-rise on the corner of Third Avenue. They found a parking space on 29th Street and walked back through the windswept rain, holding on to their hats. They were then told by the lobby attendant that Mr. and Mrs. Bellsey were not at home, having gone shopping no more than fifteen minutes earlier.

"Shit," the Sergeant said as they plodded back to the car. "Well, I guess we can't expect to win them all."

"We'll try him again this afternoon," Delaney said. "No one's going to spend all day shopping in this weather. Let's give L. Vincent Symington a go. He lives in Murray Hill; Thirty-eighth Street east of Park. Did you get any skinny on him?"

"He's a bachelor. Works for an investment counseling outfit on Wall Street. On the night of the murder, he says he was at a big dinner-dance at the Hilton. Some of the other guests remember seeing him there, but it was such a mob scene, he could easily have ducked out, murdered Ellerbee, and gotten back to the Hilton without anyone noticing he was gone. It's never neat and tidy—is it, sir?"

"Never," Delaney said. "Always loose ends. You know what they call them in the navy? Irish pennants. That's what this case is—all Irish pennants."

Symington lived in an elegant townhouse with bay windows on the first two floors, fanlights over the upper windows, and a mansard roof of greened copper. A lantern of what appeared to be Tiffany glass hung suspended over the front door.

"Money," Delaney pronounced, surveying the building. "Probably all floor-throughs."

He was right; there were only five names listed on the gleaming brass bell plate. L. VINCENT SYMINGTON, printed in a chaste script, was opposite the numeral 3. Boone pressed the button and leaned down to the intercom grille.

"Who is it?" a fluty voice asked.

"Sergeant Abner Boone, New York Police Department. Is this Mr. Symington?"

"Yes."

"Could we speak to you for a few minutes, sir?"

"What precinct are you from?"

"Manhattan North."

"Just a minute, please."

"Cautious bastard," Boone whispered to Delaney. "He's calling the precinct to see if I exist."

Delaney shrugged. "He's entitled."

They waited almost three minutes before the buzzer sounded. They pushed inside and climbed the carpeted stairs. The man waiting for them on the third-floor landing might have been wary enough to check with Manhattan North, but he nullified that prudence by failing to ask for their ID.

"I suppose this is about Dr. Ellerbee," he said nervously, retreating to his doorway. "I've already talked to the police about that."

"Yes, sir, we know," the Sergeant said. "But there are some additional questions we wanted to ask."

Symington sighed. "Oh, very well," he said petulantly. "I hope this will be the end of it."

"That," Boone said, "I can't guarantee."

The apartment was meticulously decorated and looked, Delaney thought, about as warm and lived-in as a model room in a department store. Everything was just so: color-coordinated, dusted, polished, shining with newness. No butts in the porcelain ashtrays. No stains on the velvet upholstery. No signs of human habitation anywhere.

"Beautiful room," he said to Symington.

"Do you *really* think so? Thank you so much. You know, everyone thinks I had a decorator, but I did it myself. I can't tell you how *long* it took. I knew exactly what I wanted, but it was *ages* before it all came together."

"You did a great job," Boone assured him. "By the way, I'm Sergeant Boone, and this is Edward Delaney."

"Pleased, I'm sure," Symington said. "Forgive me for not shaking hands. I'm afraid I've got a thing about that."

He took their damp hats and coats, handling them with fingertips as if they might be infected. He motioned them to director's chairs: blond cowhide on stainless-steel frames. He stood lounging against an antique brick fireplace with a mantel of distressed oak.

He was wearing a jumpsuit of cherry velour that did nothing to conceal his paunch. A gold medallion hung on his chest, and a loose bracelet of chunky gold links flopped on his wrist when he gestured. His feet were bare.

"Well," he said with a trill of empty laughter, "I suppose you know *all* about me."

"Beg pardon, sir?" Boone said, puzzled.

"I mean, I suppose you've been digging into Doctor Simon's files, and you know all my dirty little secrets."

"Oh, no, Mr. Symington," Delaney said. "Nothing like that. We have the names and addresses of patients—and that's about it."

"That's hard to believe. I'm sure you have ways . . . Well, I have nothing to hide, I assure you. I've been seeing Doctor Simon for six years, three times a week. If it hadn't been for him, I'm sure I would have been a *raving* maniac by now. When I heard of his death, I was devastated. Just devastated."

And, Delaney recalled, the lobby attendant at Sylvia Mae Otherton's apartment house said she was devastated. Perhaps all of Ellerbee's patients were devastated. But not as much as the doctor . . .

"Mr. Symington," Boone said, "were your relations with Doctor Simon friendly?"

"Friendly?" he said with a theatrical grimace. "My God, no! How can you be friendly with your shrink? He hurt me. Continually. He made me uncover things I had kept hidden all my life. It was *very* painful."

"Let me try to understand," Delaney said. "Your relations with him were kind of a duel?"

"Something like that," Symington said hesitantly. "I mean, it's not all fun and games. Yes, I guess you could say it was a kind of duel."

"Did you ever attack Doctor Simon?" Boone asked suddenly. "Physically attack him?"

The gold chain clinked as Symington threw out his arm in a gesture of bravura. *"Never!* I never touched him, though God knows I was tempted more than once. You must understand that most people under analysis have a love-hate relationship with their therapist. I mean, intellectually you realize the psychiatrist is trying to help you. But emotionally you feel he's trying to hurt you, and you resent it. You begin to suspect him. You think he may have an ulterior motive for making you confess. Perhaps he's going to black-mail you."

"Did you really believe that Doctor Simon might blackmail you?" Delaney asked.

"I thought about it sometimes," Symington said, stirring restlessly. "It wouldn't have surprised me. People are such shits, you know. You trust them, you even love them, and then they turn on you. I could tell you stories . . ."

"But you stuck with him for six years," Boone said.

"Of course I did. I *needed* the man. I was really dependent on him. And, of course, that made me resent him even more. But kill him? Is that what you're thinking? I'd never do that. I loved Doctor Simon. We were very close. He knew so much about me."

"Did you know any of his other patients?"

"I knew a few other people who were going to him. Not friends, just acquaintances or people I'd meet at parties, and it would turn out that they were his patients or former patients."

"To your knowledge," Boone said, "was he ever threatened by a patient?"

"No. And if he was, he'd never mention it to another patient."

"Did you notice any changes in his manner?" Delaney asked. "In the past year or six months."

L. Vincent Symington didn't answer at once. He came over to the long sectional couch opposite their chairs and stretched out. He stuffed a raw silk cushion under his head and stared at them.

He had a doughy face, set with raisin eyes. His lips were unexpectedly full and rosy. He was balding, and the naked scalp was sprinkled with brown freckles. Delaney thought he looked like an aged Kewpie doll, and imagined his arms and legs would be sausages, plump and boneless.

"I loved him," Symington said dully. "Really loved him. He was almost Christlike. Nothing shocked him. He could forgive you anything. Once, years ago, I went off the deep end and punished my parents. Really hurt them. Doctor Simon got me to face that. But he didn't condemn. He never condemned. Oh, Jesus, what's going to happen to me?"

"You haven't answered my question," Delaney said sternly. "Did you notice any change in him recently?"

"No. No change."

Suddenly, without warning, Symington began weeping. Tears ran down his fat cheeks, dripped off, stained the cushion. He cried silently for several minutes.

Delaney looked at Boone and the two rose simultaneously.

"Thank you for your help, Mr. Symington," Delaney said.

"Thank you, sir," Boone said.

They left him there, lying on his velvet couch in his cherry jumpsuit, wet face now turned to the ceiling.

Outside, they ran for the car, splashing through puddles. They sat for a moment while Boone lighted a cigarette.

"A butterfly?" he said. "Do you think?"

"Who the hell knows?" Delaney said roughly. "But he's a real squirrel. Listen, I'm hungry. There's a Jewish deli on Lex, not too far from here. Great corned beef and pastrami. Plenty of pickles. Want to try it?"

"Hell, yes," the Sergeant said. "With about a quart of hot coffee."

The delicatessen was a steamy, bustling place, fragrant with spicy odors. The decibel level was high, and they shouted their orders to one of the rushing waiters.

"Good scoff," Boone said to Delaney when their sandwiches came. "How did you happen to find this place?"

"Not one of my happier moments. I was a dick two, and I was tailing a guy who was a close pal of a bent-nose we wanted for homicide in a liquor store holdup. The guy I was hoping would lead us to the perp came in here for lunch, so I came in, too. The guy ordered his meal, and when it was served, he got up and headed for the rear of the place. The john is back there, so I figured he was going to take a leak, then come back and eat his lunch. But when he didn't return in five minutes, I thought, Oh-oh, and went looking. That's when I found out there's a back door, and he was long gone. I guess he spotted me and took off. So I came back and finished my lunch. The food was so good, I kept coming here every time I was in the neighborhood."

"Did you get the perp?"

"Eventually. He made the mistake of belting his wife once too often, and she sang. He plea-bargained it down to second degree. That was years ago; he's probably out of the clink by now."

"Robbing more liquor stores."

"Wouldn't doubt it for a minute," Delaney said with heavy good humor. "It was the only trade he knew."

"You know," said Boone, "that Symington didn't strike me as the kind of guy who'd own a ball peen hammer."

"Or galoshes either. But it wouldn't surprise me if he owned a pair of cowboy boots. These people we're dealing with are something. They hold down good jobs and make enough loot to see a therapist three times a week. I mean they *function*. But then they get talking, and you realize their gears don't quite mesh. They think that if A equals B, and B equals C, then X equals Y. We've got to start thinking like that, Sergeant, if we expect to get anywhere on this thing. No use looking for logic."

They were silent awhile, looking idly at the action in the deli as customers arrived and departed, the sweating waiters screamed orders, and the guys behind the hot-meat counter wielded their long carving knives like demented samurai.

"I think," Boone said, "that maybe Symington really was in love with Ellerbee. Sexually, I mean."

"It's possible," Delaney said. "It's even possible that Ellerbee responded. Maybe the good doctor was iced because of a lover's quarrel. But that just shows how this warped world is getting to me. Finished? I think we better get back; Jason said he'd be there at one o'clock."

"I hope he's found something heavy."

"Don't hold your breath," Delaney advised.

Monica had been out doing volunteer work at a local hospital. When she returned home, she had found Jason T. Jason sitting outside the brownstone in the unmarked police car. She brought him into the kitchen and they were having a coffee when Delaney and Boone walked in. The three men went into the study, Jason carrying a manila envelope.

"So," Delaney said to Jason, "how did you make out?"

The black cop was a boulder of a man: six-four, 250—and very little of that suet. His skin was a ruddy cordovan that always seemed polished to a high gloss. He wore his hair clipped short, like a knitted helmet, but his sharply trimmed mustache stretched from cheek to cheek. His hands were hams and his feet bigger than Delaney's.

Jason Two lived with his wife, Juanita, and two young sons in Hicksville, Long Island. He had been six years in the Department and had two citations, a number of solid busts and some good assists. He was hoping for a detective's shield—but so were twenty thousand other cops.

"I don't know how I did," he confessed, opening the manila envelope. "First time I looked for a perp in a *library*. I got three reports here, on the two Ellerbees and Doc Samuelson. I did them up on my older boy's typewriter. I'm a two-fingered typist, both thumbs, so there's a lot of marking out and corrections, but I think you'll be able to read them. Anyway, they're mostly cut-and-dried stuff: dates, ages, education, family background, their college degrees, and so forth. To be honest, sir, I don't think it all amounts to diddly-squat. I mean, I can't see any of it helping us find Ellerbee's killer."

"Nothing unusual?" Delaney asked. "Nothing that struck you as being out of the ordinary or worth taking a second look at?"

"Not really," Jason said slowly. "About the most unusual thing was that Samuelson had a breakdown some years ago. That seemed odd to me: a psychiatrist cracking up. They said it was exhaustion from overwork. He was out of action for about six months. But then he went back to his office and took up his caseload again."

Delaney turned to Boone. "He said his wife died of cancer, didn't he, and his son was killed in an automobile accident? That would be enough to knock anyone for a loop. Anything else, Jason?"

"Well, sir, I collected all the facts and figures I could in the time I had. All that's in my reports. Most of it came from books, newspapers, and professional journals. But I talked to a lot of people, too. Friends and associates of all three doctors. And after I got the factual stuff I wanted, I'd bullshit awhile with them. Funny how people run off at the mouth when they hear it's a murder investigation. Anyway, I heard some stuff that may or may not mean anything. I didn't put it in my reports because it was just hearsay. I mean, none of it is hard evidence."

"You did just right, Jase," Sergeant Boone said. "We need every scrap we can get. What did you hear?"

"First of all, practically every guy I talked to mentioned how beautiful Diane is. They all sounded like they were in love with her. I've never seen her, but she must be some foxy lady."

"She is," Delaney and Boone said simultaneously, and they all laughed.

"Well, everyone said how lucky Doc Simon was to hook on to someone like her: a looker with plenty of the green. But one guy swears Ellerbee wasn't all that anxious to marry, but she had her mind set on it. I told you I heard a lot of rumors. Some of the guys admitted they made a play for her, even after she was married, but it was no dice; she was straight."

"Any gossip about Doctor Simon playing around?" Delaney asked.

"Nada," Jason said. "Apparently he was a cold, controlled kind of guy. I mean, he was pleasant enough, good company and all that, but a secret man; he didn't reveal much. At least that's what most people said. But I talked to one woman—she's the secretary of that association he belonged to—and she said she saw Ellerbee at a dinner about a month before he was iced. She said she was surprised at how he had changed since she saw him last. She said he was smiling, and a lot more outgoing than he had been. Seemed really happy, she said."

Delaney and Boone stared at each other.

"Crazy," the Sergeant said, shaking his head.

Delaney explained to Jason why they were puzzled. He told him that Sylvia

Mae Otherton had claimed Ellerbee had become quieter, more thoughtful, not depressed but subdued.

"It doesn't jibe," Jason said. "One of those ladies must be wrong."

"Not necessarily," Delaney said. "Maybe they just caught him in different moods. But what's interesting is that they both noticed a recent change in his disposition. I'd like to know what brought that on. It's probably nothing, but still . . . Sergeant, why don't you tell Jason about the patients we've seen."

When Boone finished, Jason said, "Whoo-ee! Those people—doesn't sound like their elevators go to the top floor."

"They're a little meshuggah," Delaney admitted. "Sometimes they make sense and sometimes they're way out in left field. Our problem is going to be separating what's real from what's part of their never-never world. I don't see how we can do anything but let them blabber and then try to figure the meaning later. I'll have to warn the new people about that when they come in Monday morning."

"Sir," Boone said, "how are you going to handle those guys—assign one to each of the patients?"

"That was my first plan, and maybe it would work if we were covering punks and small-time hoods. But these subjects are mostly educated and intelligent, even if their brains rattle a little. I think we'll get better results if each detective has a chance to talk to three or four of the patients. And then select the one he feels he can work with best. You know how sometimes a witness will clam up with one dick and then spill his guts to another because he feels the second guy is more simpatico. We'll try to pair detective and subject so it'll do us the most good."

They talked for another hour, discussing how they would organize the investigation so detectives wouldn't be duplicating each other's work unless a double-check was deemed necessary.

Delaney decided that Boone and Jason would each be responsible for scheduling and supervising three detectives. The two of them would then submit daily reports to Delaney on the activities of their squads.

"I expect a certain amount of confusion at first," he told them, "but I want the two of you to coordinate your planning as much as possible. I'll keep the files, which will be open to all of you. Just tell your guys to put *everything* in their reports, no matter how stupid or meaningless they might think it. And the first thing I want done is to have these six patients run through Records. If they're as violent as Doctor Diane seems to think, some of them should have sheets."

They traded ideas a while longer, then Delaney glanced up at the walnut-cased regulator on the wall, a relic from a demolished railroad station.

"Getting late," he said. "Why don't the three of us try Ronald J. Bellsey again—just walk in on him without warning. He should be home by now. Jason, we'll take your car and you can drop us back here."

On the drive south, Delaney remembered to ask Jason Two if he and his family would like to come for Thanksgiving Day dinner.

"Thank you, sir," the officer said, "but we've already signed on with Juanita's parents. They're making a big deal out of it, and the kids and the old folks would kill me if I canceled."

"Don't even consider it," Delaney said. "We'll make it another time. Your boys should see their grandparents as often as possible. I wish I could see more of my grandchildren."

They double-parked in front of Bellsey's high-rise. Boone flashed his ID and asked the doorman to keep an eye on their car. There was no house phone; the lobby attendant explained they'd have to use the intercom. In addition, they were told to stand in front of a small, ceiling-mounted television camera that would relay their picture via closed circuit to a monitor in Bellsey's foyer.

"Cute gimmick," Delaney said.

"First time I've been on TV," Jason said, grinning. "Should I do a buck-and-wing or something?"

Boone spoke softly to Bellsey on the intercom, then held up his shield before the camera's eye.

"Apartment 2407," he reported to the others. "He said to come up, but he didn't sound too happy about it."

In the elevator, Delaney said to Jason, "Don't be bashful about chiming in when we question this guy. Let's overwhelm him with muscle."

The door of Apartment 2407 was jerked open by a stocky, red-faced man wearing a rugged sport jacket and whipcord slacks. Behind him, a smallish, graying woman stood in the foyer archway, hands clasped, peering at them timidly.

"I suppose this is about Ellerbee," Bellsey burst out angrily. "I already talked to the cops about that."

"We know you did, Mr. Bellsey," Boone said. "That was just a preliminary questioning. Unfortunately, you're involved in a murder investigation, and we—"

"What do you mean I'm involved?" Bellsey demanded, his voice rising. "Jesus Christ, I was just one of his patients! I don't know a damned thing about how he got killed."

"Mr. Bellsey," Delaney said stonily, "are you going to keep us standing out here in the hallway while you shout at us and the neighbors get an earful?"

"Screw the neighbors! I don't see why I have to be harassed like this."

Jason T. Jason shoved his big bulk forward. "No one's harassing you," he said quietly. "Just a few questions and we'll be out of your hair."

Bellsey looked up at the big cop. "Shit!" he said disgustedly. "Well, come on in then. I want you to know you're interrupting our dinner." He turned to the woman.

"Lorna, you get back to the kitchen; this has nothing to do with you."

The woman scurried away.

"Your wife?" Delaney asked as the three men entered the apartment.

"Yeah," Bellsey said. "Leave her out of this."

He didn't offer to take their coats and made no effort to get them seated. So they all remained standing in a tight little group.

"I'm Sergeant Boone and these men are Delaney and Jason. Your full name is Ronald J. Bellsey?"

"That's right. The J. is for James in case you're interested."

"When was the last time you saw Doctor Ellerbee?"

"On Thursday afternoon, the day before he was killed. Don't tell me you didn't get that from his appointment book. Or is that expecting too much brains from cops?"

"Be nice, Mr. Bellsey," Delaney said softly. "You get snotty with us and you'll be answering our questions at the precinct house and waiting a long, long time for your dinner. Is that what you want?"

He glowered at them.

Bellsey was heavy through the shoulders and chest. His neck was short and thick, supporting a squarish head topped with an ill-fitting toupee. He stood leaning belligerently forward, pugnacious jaw thrust out, hands balled into fists.

"Mr. Bellsey," Boone said, "you claim you were home on the night Ellerbee was killed."

"That's right."

"All night?"

"Yeah. I got home around seven and didn't go out of the house until Saturday. Ask my wife; she'll tell you."

"Did you have any visitors Friday evening? See any neighbors? Make or receive any phone calls?"

"No."

"Do you have a police record, Mr. Bellsey?" Delaney asked. "We'll check, of course, but it would be smart if you told us first."

Bellsey opened his mouth to speak, then shut it with a click of teeth. He hesitated, then tried again.

"I was never really arrested," he said grudgingly. "Not formally, I mean. But I got into trouble a few times. I don't know what's on my record."

"What kind of trouble?" Jason asked.

"Fights. I was defending myself."

"How many times?"

"Once. Or twice."

"Or maybe more?"

"Maybe. I don't remember."

"Ever get in a fight with Doctor Ellerbee?" Boone asked. "Ever attack him?"

"Shit, no! He was my doctor. A decent guy. I liked him."

"How long had you been seeing him?"

"About two years."

"You own a car?" Delaney asked suddenly.

Bellsey looked at him, puzzled. "Sure."

"What kind?"

"Last year's Cadillac."

"Where do you keep it?"

"In the basement. We have an underground garage."

"You ever do any repairs on it yourself?"

"Sometimes. Minor stuff."

"You own tools?"

"Some."

"Where do you keep those?"

"In the trunk of the car."

Delaney glanced at Boone.

"Mr. Bellsey," the Sergeant said, "did Ellerbee ever mention to you that he had been attacked or threatened by a patient?"

"No."

"Did you know any of his other patients?"

"No."

"Did you notice any change recently in his manner or personality?"

"No, he was just the same."

"What's 'the same'?" Jason asked. "What kind of a man was he?"

"Calm, cool, and collected. Never blew his stack. Never raised his voice. A real put-together guy. I cursed him out once, and he never held it against me."

"Why did you curse him out?"

"I don't remember."

"When you went out shopping today," Boone said, "what did you wear?"

"What did I wear?" Bellsey said, bewildered. "I wore a rain hat and a lined trench coat."

"Galoshes? Boots?"

"No. A pair of rubbers."

"You work for a wholesale butcher?" Delaney said.

"That's right."

"What do you do—slice salami?"

"Christ, no! I'm the manager. Production manager."

"You oversee the butchers, loaders, drivers—is that it?"

"Yes."

"You must deal with some rough guys."

"They think they are," Bellsey said grimly. "But they shape up or ship out."

"You ever do any boxing?" Jason Two asked.

"Some. When I was in the navy. Middleweight."

"Never professionally?"

"No."

"You keep in shape?"

"I sure do," Bellsey boasted. "Jog five miles twice a week. Lift iron. Go to a health club once a week for a three-hour workout on the machines. What the hell has all this got to do with Ellerbee's murder?"

"Just asking," Jason said equably.

"You're wasting my time," Bellsey said. "Anything else?"

"I think that's all," Delaney said. "For now. Have a nice dinner, Mr. Bellsey."

There were other people in the elevator; they didn't talk. But when they got into Jason's car, Sergeant Boone said, "A real sweetheart. How did you pick up on the boxing, Jase?"

"He looks like a pug. The way he stands and moves."

"We'll have to get into the trunk of that Cadillac," Delaney said. "The ball peen. And let's try to talk to the wife when he's not around."

"You think he could be it?" Boone asked.

"Our best bet yet," Delaney said. "A guy with a sheet, a short fuse, and he's a brawler. I think we better take a very close look at Mr. Bellsey."

• • •

THAT NIGHT, AFTER dinner, he wanted to write out reports of the questioning of L. Vincent Symington and Ronald J. Bellsey. But Monica said firmly that she had to make a start on addressing Christmas cards, so he deferred to her wishes.

She sat in his swivel chair behind his desk in the study. As she worked, adding a short personal note to each card, he slumped in one of the worn club chairs, nursing a small Rémy. He told her about Symington and Bellsey.

When he finished, she said definitely, "It was Bellsey. He's the one who did it."

Delaney laughed softly. "Why do you say that?"

"He sounds like a dreadful man."

"Oh, he is a dreadful man—but that doesn't make him a killer."

She went back to her Christmas cards. A soft cone of light shone down from a green student lamp on the desk. Delaney sat in dimness, staring with love and gratitude at the woman who brightened his life.

He saw her pursed lips as she wrote out her holiday greetings, dark eyes gleaming. Her glossy black hair was gathered in back with a gold barrette. Strong face, strong woman. He thought of what his life would be like, sitting alone in that shadowed room, without her warm presence, and a small groan escaped him.

"What are you thinking?" she asked, without looking up.

He didn't tell her. Instead, he said, "Did you ever work a jigsaw puzzle?"

"When I was a kid."

"Me, too. Remember how you spilled all the pieces out of the box onto a tabletop, hoping none of them was missing. Then you turned all the pieces picture-side up and looked for the four pieces with two straight edges. Those were the corners of the picture. After you had those, you put together all the pieces with one straight edge to form the frame. Then you gradually filled in the picture."

She looked up at him. "The Ellerbee case is a jigsaw puzzle?"

"Sort of."

"And you know what the picture is going to be?"

"No," he said with a tight smile, "but I see some straight edges."

13

•

SUNDAY WAS THE BEST DAY OF THE WEEK FOR HAROLD GERBER. He didn't have to see anyone; he didn't have to talk to anyone. He bought his Sunday *Times* on Saturday night, along with a couple of six-packs. The paper, the beer, and two pro football games on TV filled up his Sundays. He never left the house.

Gerber had lost a lot of weight in Vietnam and never put it back on. He had lost a lot of things there, including his appetite. So on Sunday morning he usually had some juice, a piece of toast, and two cups of coffee with sugar and cream. That carried him through to evening, when he might heat up a frozen dinner that came in a cardboard box and tasted like the container.

For some reason, on Sundays he never got out the photographs and looked at them again. All those guys—grinning, scowling, laughing, mugging it up for the camera. Some of the photos were autographed, just like Gerber had autographed some of the shots they took of him. A family album . . . It fed his fury.

Since he couldn't comprehend it himself, Gerber could appreciate why other people were unable to understand the way he felt and why he did the things he did. Gerber couldn't figure it out, and no one else could either.

Doc Simon was coming close, really beginning to pin it down, but now Ellerbee was dead, and Gerber wasn't about to start all over again with another therapist. He had tried two before he found Ellerbee, but they had turned out to be bullshit artists, and Gerber knew after a few sessions that they weren't going to do him a damned bit of good.

Dr. Simon Ellerbee was different. No bullshit there. He went right in with a sharp scalpel, and all that blood didn't daunt him. He was tearing Harold Gerber apart and putting him back together again. But then Doc Simon got himself scragged and Gerber was alone again, with no one but ghosts for company.

The checks from his parents came regularly, every month, and he was on partial disability, so he wasn't hurting for money. Harold Gerber was just hurting for life, wondering if he was fated to drag his corpse through the world for maybe another fifty years, acting like a goddamn maniac and really wanting the whole fucking globe to blow up—the sooner the better.

That Sunday morning, driving down to Gerber's place in Greenwich Village, Delaney said to Boone, "I feel guilty about making you work this weekend. Rebecca probably thinks I'm a slave driver."

"Nah," Boone said. "She's used to my working crazy hours. I guess every detective's wife is."

"Jason volunteered to come along, but weekends are the only chance he gets to spend some time with his sons. That's important, so I told him to stay home today. When the new guys come in, we should all be able to keep reasonable hours. Did you find out anything about this Gerber?"

"Nothing. Suarez's men hadn't gotten around to him yet. So all we have is what Doctor Diane put in her report: He's thirty-seven, a Vietnam veteran with a lot of medals and a lot of problems. Gets into fights."

"Another Ronald Bellsey?"

"Not exactly," Boone said. "This Gerber sometimes attacks strangers for no apparent reason. And once he put his fist through a plate-glass window and ended up in St. Vincent's Emergency where they stitched him up."

"That's nice," Delaney said. "An angry young man."

"Something like that," Boone agreed.

Harold Gerber lived in a run-down tenement on Seventh Avenue South, around the corner from Carmine Street. The windows of the first two floors were covered with tin, and the stoop was clotted with garbage. The façade of the six-story building was chipped, stained with rust, defaced with graffiti.

Inspecting this dump, Delaney and Boone had the same reaction: How could anyone living there afford an uptown shrink?

"Maybe he doesn't pay rent," Delaney suggested. "See that empty lot next door? Some developer's assembling a parcel. Once he gets the remaining tenants out, he'll demolish that wreck and have enough spare feet to put up a luxury high-rise."

"Could be," Boone said. "Right now it looks like a Roach Motel."

In the littered vestibule they discovered all the mailboxes had been jimmied open. The intercom had been wrenched from the wall to dangle suspended from its wires. The front door had been pried open so often that now it couldn't be closed. The odor of rot and urine was gagging.

"Jesus!" Boone said. "Let's get in and out of here fast."

"Have we got an apartment number for him?"

"No. We'll have to bang on doors."

They cautiously climbed a tilted wooden stairway, the loose banister carved and hacked. More graffiti on the damp plaster walls. The doors on the first two floors were nailed shut. They began knocking on third-floor doors. No answers. No sounds of habitation.

They got an answer on the fourth floor.

"Go away," a woman screamed, "or I'll call the cops."

"Lady, we *are* the cops," Boone shouted back. "We're looking for Harold Gerber. What apartment?"

"Never heard of him."

They went up to the fifth, stepping over piles of broken laths and crumbling plaster. They found two more occupied apartments, but no doors were unlocked, and no one knew Harold Gerber—they said.

Finally, on the sixth floor, they banged on the chipped door of the rear apartment.

"Who is it?" a man yelled.

"New York Police Department. We're looking for Harold Gerber."

"What for?"

Delaney and Boone looked at each other.

"It's about Doctor Simon Ellerbee," Boone said. "A few questions."

They heard the sounds of bolts sliding back. The door was opened on a thick chain. They saw a slice of a man clad in a turtleneck sweater and plaid mackinaw.

"ID?" he said in a hoarse voice.

The Sergeant held up his shield. The chain was slipped, the door was opened.

"Welcome to the Taj Mahal," the man said. "Keep your coats on if you don't want to freeze your ass off."

They stepped in and looked around.

It was a slough, and obviously the occupant had done nothing to make it even marginally livable. Clothing and possessions were piled helter-skelter on the cot, a single rickety bureau, on the floor. The scummy sink was piled with unwashed dishes, the two-burner stove thick with grease. It was so cold that the inside of the window was coated with a skim of ice.

"The toilet's in the hall," the man said, grinning. "But I wouldn't recommend it."

"Harold Gerber?" Boone asked.

"Yeah."

"May we sit down, please?" Delaney asked. "I'm worn out from that climb. My name is Delaney and this is Sergeant Abner Boone."

"Sergeant . . ." Gerber said in his gravelly voice. "I was a sergeant once. Then I got busted."

He threw clothing off the cot, removed a six-pack from one spindly chair, and lifted a small black-and-white TV set from another.

"We still got electricity and water," he said, "but no heat. The fucking landlord is freezing us out. Take it easy when you sit down; the legs are loose."

They gingerly eased onto the chairs. Gerber sat on the cot.

"You think I did it?" he said with a cracked grin.

"Did what?" Boone said.

"Fragged Doc Ellerbee."

"Did you?" Delaney asked.

"Shit, no. But I could have."

"Why?" Boone said. "Why would you want to kill him?"

"Who needs a reason? You like my home?"

"It's a shithouse," Delaney told him.

Gerber laughed. "Yeah, just the way I want it. When they tear this joint down, I'm going to look for another place just like it. A buddy of mine—he lives in Idaho—came back from Nam and tried to pick up his life. He gave it six months and couldn't hack it. So he took off all his clothes, every stitch, and walked bare-ass naked into the woods without a thing—no weapons, no watch, no matches—absolutely nothing. Well, Manhattan is my woods. I like living like this."

"What happened to him?" Delaney said. "Your buddy."

"A ranger came across him a couple of years later. He was wearing clothes and moccasins made out of animal skins. His hair and beard were long and matted. He had built himself a lean-to and planted some wild stuff he found growing in the woods that he could eat. Made a bow and arrows. Set traps. Had plenty of meat. He was doing great. Never saw anyone, never talked to anyone. I wish I had the balls to do something like that."

They stared at him, seeing a lean, hollowed faced shadowed by a three-day beard. The skin was pasty white, nose bony, eyes brightly wild. Uncombed hair spiked out from under a black beret. Gerber moved jerkily, gestures short and broken.

The sweater and mackinaw hung loosely on his lank frame. Even his fingers seemed skeletal, the nails gnawed away. And on his feet, heavy boots.

"You wear those boots all the time?" Boone said.

"These? Sure. They're fleece-lined. I even sleep in them. I'd lose toes if I didn't."

"How long did you know Doctor Ellerbee?" Delaney asked.

"I don't want to talk about that," Gerber said.

"You don't want to help us find his killer?" Boone said.

"So he's dead," Gerber said, shrugging. "Half the guys I've known in my life are dead."

"He didn't die of old age," Delaney said grimly. "And he didn't die in an accident or in a war. Someone deliberately bashed in his skull."

"Big deal," Gerber said.

Delaney looked at him steadily. "You goddamned cocksucking son of a bitch," he said tonelessly. "You motherfucking piece of shit. You wallow in your pigsty here, feeling sorry for yourself and, gosh, life is unfair, and gee, you got a raw deal, and no one knows how sensitive you are and how it all hurts, you lousy scumbag. And meanwhile, a good and decent man—worth ten of the likes of you—gets burned, and you won't lift a finger to help find his murderer because you want the whole world to be as miserable as you are. Ellerbee's biggest mistake was trying to help a turd like you. Come on, Sergeant, let's go; we don't need any help from this asshole."

There was cold silence as they began to rise warily from their chairs. But then Harold Gerber held out a hand to stop them.

"You—what's your name? Delehanty?"

"Delaney."

"I like you, Delaney; you're a no-bullshit guy. Doc Simon was like that, but he didn't have your gift of gab. All right, I'll play your little game. What do you want to know?"

They eased back onto the fragile chairs.

"When was the last time you saw Ellerbee?" Boone asked.

"The papers said he was killed around nine o'clock. Right? I saw him five hours earlier, at four o'clock that Friday afternoon. My usual time. It'll be in the appointment book."

"Was he acting normally?"

"Sure."

"Notice any change in him in the last six months or a year?"

"What kind of change?"

"In his manner, the way he acted."

"No," Gerber said, "I didn't notice anything."

"Do you know any of his other patients?" Delaney asked.

"No."

"Did Ellerbee ever mention that he had been attacked or threatened by anyone?"

"No."

"Did you ever attack him?" Boone said. "Or threaten him?"

"Now why would I want to do anything like that? The guy was trying to help me."

"Analysis is supposed to be painful," Delaney said. "Weren't there times when you hated him?"

"Sure there were. But those were temporary things. I never hated him enough to off him. He was my only lifeline."

"What are you going to do now? Find another lifeline?"

"No," Gerber said, then grinned: a death's-head. "I'll just go on wallowing in my pigsty."

"Do you own a ball peen hammer?" Boone asked abruptly.

"No, I do not own a ball peen hammer. Okay? I'm going to have a beer. Anyone want one?"

They both declined. Gerber popped the tab on a can of Pabst and settled back on the cot, leaning against the clammy wall.

"How often did you see Ellerbee?" Delaney said.

"Twice a week. I'd have gone more often if I could have afforded it. He was helping me."

"When was the last time you got in trouble?"

"Ah-ha," Gerber said, showing his teeth. "You know about that, do you? Well, I haven't acted up in the last six months or so. Doc Simon told me if I got the urge—felt real out, you know—I could call him any hour of the day or night. I never did, but just knowing he was there was a big help."

"Where were you the Friday night he got killed?"

"Bar-hopping around the Village."

"In the rain?"

"That's right. I didn't get home until after midnight. I was in the bag."

"Do you remember where you went?"

"I have some favorite hangouts. I guess I went there."

"See anyone you know? Talk to anyone?"

"The bartenders. They'll probably remember me; I'm the world's smallest tipper—if I tip at all. Usually I stiff them. Bartenders and waiters tend to remember things like that."

"Can you recall where you were from, say, eight o'clock to ten?"

"No, I can't."

"You better try," Boone advised. "Make out a list of your hangouts—the ones you hit that Friday night. There'll be another cop coming around asking questions."

"Shit," Gerber said, "I've told you guys all I know."

"I don't think so," Delaney said coldly. "I think you're holding out on us."

"Sure I am," Gerber said in his hoarse voice. "My deep, dark secret is that I once met Doc Simon's wife and I wanted to jump her. She's some sweet piece. Now are you satisfied?"

"You think this is all a big, fat joke, don't you?" Delaney said. "Let me tell you what we're going to do about you, Mr. Gerber. We're going to check you out from the day you were popped to this minute. We're going to talk to your family, relatives, friends. We'll go into your military record from A to Z. We'll even find out why you got busted from sergeant. Then we'll talk to people in this building, your women, the bartenders, anyone you deal with. We'll question the strangers you assaulted and the doctors at St. Vincent's who stitched you up. By the time we're through, we'll know more about you than you know about yourself. So don't play cute with us, Mr. Gerber; you haven't got a secret in the world. Come on, Boone, let's go; I need some fresh air."

While they were picking their way carefully down the filthy staircase,

Boone said in a low voice, "Are we really going to do all that, sir? What you told him?"

"Hell, no," Delaney said grumpily. "We haven't got the time."

They sat in the car a few moments, the heater coughing away, while Boone lighted a cigarette.

"You really think he's holding out?" Boone asked.

"I don't know," Delaney said, troubled. "That session was nutsville. His moods shifted around so often and so quickly. One minute he's cooperating, and the next he's a wiseass cracking jokes. But remember, the man was in a dirty war and probably did his share of killing. For some guys—not all, but some—once they've killed, the others come easier until it doesn't mean a goddamn thing to them. The first is the hard one. Then it's just as mechanical as a habit. A life? What's that?"

"I feel sorry for him," Boone said.

"Sure. I do, too. But I feel sorrier for Simon Ellerbee. We've got to ration our sympathy in this world, Sergeant; we only have so much. Listen, it's still early; why don't we skip lunch and drive up to Chelsea. Maybe we can catch Joan Yesell at home. Then we'll be finished and can take the rest of the day off."

"Sounds good to me. Let's go."

Joan Yesell lived on West 24th Street, in a staid block of almost identical brownstones. It was a pleasingly clean street, garbage tucked away in lidded cans, the gutters swept. Windows were washed, façades free of graffiti, and a line of naked ginkgo trees waited for spring.

"Now this is something like," Delaney said approvingly, "Little Old New York. O. Henry lived somewhere around here, didn't he?"

"East of here, sir," Boone said. "In the Gramercy Park area. The bar where he drank is still in business."

"In your drinking days, Sergeant, did you ever fall into McSorley's Old Ale House?"

"I fell into every bar in the city."

"Miss it?" Delaney asked curiously.

"Oh, God, yes! Every day of my life. You remember the highs; you don't remember wetting the bed."

"How long have you been dry now—four years?"

"About. But dipsos don't count years; you take it day by day."

"I guess," Delaney said, sighing. "My old man owned a saloon on Third Avenue—did you know that?"

"No, I didn't," Boone said, interested. "When was this?"

"Oh, hell, a long time ago. I worked behind the stick on afternoons when I was going to night school. I saw my share of boozers. Maybe that's why I never went off the deep end—although I do my share, as you well know. Enough of this. What have you got on Joan Yesell?"

"One of Suarez's boys checked her out. Lives with her widowed mother.

Works as a legal secretary in a big law firm up on Park. Takes home a nice buck. Never been married. Those three suicide attempts Doctor Diane mentioned proved out in emergency room records. She claims that on the evening Ellerbee was killed she was home all night. Got back from work around six o'clock and never went out. Her mother confirms."

"All right," Delaney said, "let's go through the drill again. The last time— I hope."

The ornate wood molding in the vestibule had been painted a hellish orange.

"Look at this," Delaney said, rapping it with a knuckle. "Probably eighteen coats of paint on there. You strip it down and there's beautiful walnut or cherry underneath. You can't buy molding like that anymore. Someone did a lousy restoration job."

There were two names opposite the bell for apartment 3-C: Mrs. Blanche Yesell and J. Yesell.

"The mother gets the title and full first name," Delaney noted. "The daughter rates an initial."

Boone identified himself on the intercom. A moment later the door lock buzzed and they entered. The interior was clean, smelling faintly of disinfectant, but the colors of the walls and carpeting were garish. The only decorative touch was a plastic dwarf in a rattan planter.

The ponderous woman waiting outside the closed door of apartment 3-C eyed them suspiciously.

"I am Mrs. Blanche Yesell," she announced in a hard voice, "and you don't look like policemen to me."

Sergeant Boone silently proffered his ID. She had wire-rimmed pince-nez hanging from her thick neck on a black silk cord. She clamped the spectacles onto her heavy nose and inspected the shield and identification card carefully while they inspected her.

The blue-rinsed hair was pyramided like a beehive. Her features were coarse and masculine. (Later, Boone was to say, "She looks like a truck driver in drag.") She had wide shoulders, a deep bosom, and awesome hips. All in all, a formidable woman with meaty hands and big feet shod in no-nonsense shoes.

"Is this about Doctor Ellerbee?" she demanded, handing Boone's ID back to him.

"Yes, ma'am. This gentleman is Edward Delaney, and we'd like to—".

"I don't want my Joan bothered," Mrs. Yesell interrupted. "Hasn't the poor girl been through enough? She's already told you everything she knows. More questions will just upset her. I won't stand for it."

"Mrs. Yesell," Delaney said mildly, "I assure you we have no desire to upset your daughter. But we are investigating a brutal murder, and I know that you and your daughter want to do everything you can to help bring the vile perpetrator to justice."

Bemused by this flossy language, the Sergeant shot Delaney an amazed glance, but the plushy rhetoric seemed to mollify Mrs. Yesell.

"Well, of course," she said, sniffing, "I and my Joan want to do everything we can to aid the forces of law and order."

"Splendid," Delaney said, beaming. "Just a few questions then, and we'll be finished and gone before you can say Jack Robinson."

"I used to know a man named Jack Robinson," she said with a girlish titter.

A certified nut, Sergeant Boone thought.

She opened the door and led the way into the apartment. As overstuffed as she was: velvets and chintz and tassels and lace and ormolu, and whatnots, all in stunning profusion. Plus two sleepy black cats as plump as hassocks.

"Perky and Yum-Yum," Mrs. Yesell said, gesturing proudly. "Aren't they cunning? Let me have your coats, gentlemen, and you make yourselves comfortable."

They perched gingerly on the edge of an ornate, pseudo-Victorian love seat and waited until Mrs. Yesell had seated herself opposite them in a heavily brocaded tub chair complete with antimacassar.

"Now, then," she said, leaning forward, "how may I help you?"

They looked at each other, then back at her.

"Ma'am," Sergeant Boone said softly, "it's your daughter we came to talk to. She's home?"

"Well, she's home, but she's lying down right now, resting, and I wouldn't care to disturb her. Besides, I'm sure I can answer all your questions."

"I'm afraid not," Delaney said brusquely. "Your daughter is the one we came to see. If we can't question her today, we'll have to return again until we can."

She glared at him, but he would not be cowed.

"Oh, very well," she said. "But it's really quite unnecessary. Oh, Joan!" she caroled. "Visitors!"

Right on cue, and much too promptly for one who had been lying down, resting, Joan Yesell entered from the bedroom with a timid smile. The men stood to be introduced. Then the daughter took a straight-back chair and sat with hands clasped in her lap, ankles demurely crossed.

"Miss Yesell," Boone started, "we know how the murder of Doctor Simon Ellerbee must have shocked you."

"My Joan was devastated," Mrs. Yesell said. "Just devastated."

Another one! Delaney thought.

Boone continued: "But I'm sure you appreciate our need to talk to all his patients in the investigation of his death. Could you tell us the last time you saw Doctor Simon?"

"On Wednesday afternoon," the mother said promptly. "The Wednesday before he died. At one o'clock."

The Sergeant sighed. "Mrs. Yesell, these questions are addressed to your daughter. It would be best if she answered."

"On Wednesday afternoon," Joan Yesell said. "The Wednesday before he died. At one o'clock."

Her voice was so low, tentative, that they strained to hear. She kept her head down, staring at her clasped hands.

"That was the usual time for your appointment?"

"Yes."

"How often did you see Doctor Simon?"

"Twice a week."

"And how long had you been consulting him?"

"Four years."

"Three," Mrs. Yesell said firmly. "It's been three years, dear."

"Three years," the daughter said faintly. "About."

"Did Doctor Ellerbee ever mention to you that he had been attacked or threatened by any of his patients?"

"No." Then she raised her head to look at them with faraway eyes. "Once he was mugged while he was walking to his garage late at night, but that happened years ago."

"Miss Yesell," Delaney said, "I have a question you may feel is too personal to answer. If you prefer not to reply, we'll understand completely. Why were you going to Doctor Ellerbee?"

She didn't answer at once. The clasped hands began to twist.

"I don't see—" Mrs. Yesell began, but then her daughter spoke.

"I was depressed," she said slowly. "Very depressed. I attempted suicide. You probably know about that."

"And you feel Doctor Simon was helping you?"

She came briefly alive. "Oh, yes! So much!"

She could not, in all kindness, be called an attractive young woman. Not ugly, but grayly plain. Mousy hair and a pinched face devoid of makeup. She lacked her mother's bold presence and seemed daunted by the older woman's assertiveness.

Her clothing was monochromatic: sweater, skirt, hose, shoes—all of a dull beige. Her complexion had the same cast. She looked, if not unwell, sluggish and beaten. Even her movements had an invalid's languor; her thin body was without shape or vigor.

"Miss Yesell," Boone said, "did you notice any change in Doctor Simon recently? In his manner toward you or in his personality?"

"No," Mrs. Blanche Yesell said. "No change."

"Madam," Delaney thundered, "will you allow your daughter to answer our questions—*please*."

Joan Yesell hesitated. "Perhaps," she said finally. "The last year or so. He seemed—oh, I don't know exactly. Happier, I think. Yes, he seemed happier. More—more lighthearted. He joked."

"And he had never joked before?"

"No."

"You have stated," Boone said, "that on the night Ellerbee was killed, you returned home directly from work and never went out again until the following day. Is that correct?"

"Yes."

Delaney turned to Mrs. Yesell with a bleak smile. "Now is your chance, ma'am," he said. "Can you confirm your daughter's presence here that night?"

"Of course."

"Did you have any visitors, see any neighbors, make or receive any phone calls that night?"

"No, we did not," she said decisively. "Just the two of us were here."

"Read? Watched television?"

"We played two-handed bridge."

"Oh?" Delaney said, rising to his feet. "And who won?"

"Mama," Joan Yesell said in her wispy voice. "Mama always wins."

They thanked the ladies politely for their help, reclaimed coats and hats, and left. They didn't speak until they were back in the car.

"I can understand why the daughter's depressed," Delaney remarked.

"Yeah," Boone said. "The old lady's a dragon."

"She is that," Delaney agreed. "The only time the daughter contradicted her was about Ellerbee's manner changing. The mother said no."

"How the hell would she know?" Boone said. "She wasn't seeing him twice a week."

"Exactly," Delaney said. "Could you drop me uptown, Sergeant? Let's call it a day."

Just before Delaney got out of the car in front of his brownstone, Boone said, "If you had to make a wild guess, sir, which of the six would you pick as the perp?"

"Oh, I don't know," Delaney said thoughtfully. "Maybe Ronald Bellsey. But only because I don't like the guy. Who's your choice?"

"Harold Gerber—for the same reason. We're probably both wrong."

Delaney grunted. "Probably. Too bad there's not a butler involved. See you tomorrow morning, Sergeant. Give my best to Rebecca."

Monica was in the kitchen, cutting up chicken wings. She had four prepared bowls before her: Dijon mustard, Worcestershire sauce, chicken broth, flavored bread crumbs. She looked up when he came in, and he bent to kiss her cheek.

"Just one sandwich," he pleaded. "I haven't had a thing all day, and we're not eating for hours. One sandwich won't spoil my appetite."

"All right, Edward. Just one."

He rummaged through the refrigerator, saying, "I really deserve this. I've had a hard day. Did you know that psychiatrists have a very high suicide rate? The highest of all doctors except ophthalmologists."

He was standing at the sink, but turned to face her, sandwich clamped in one big hand, a glass of beer in the other.

"Don't tell me you think Doctor Ellerbee crushed in his own skull with a hammer?"

"No, I just mentioned it because I'm beginning to understand what shrinks go through. No wonder they need a month a year to recharge their batteries. These patients of Ellerbee's are wild ones. It's hard to get a handle on them. They don't live in my world."

Monica nodded.

"Do you think women are more sensitive than men?" he asked her.

"Sensitive?" Monica said. "Physically, you mean? Like ticklish?"

"No, not that. Sensitive to emotions, feelings, the way people behave. We've been asking everyone if they noticed any change recently in Doctor Ellerbee's manner. The reason is to find out if he was being threatened or blackmailed or anything like that. All the men we asked said they saw no change. But so far, three women have said yes, they noticed a change. They don't agree on *how* he changed, but all three said there was a difference in his manner in the last six months. That's why I asked you if women are more sensitive to that sort of thing than men."

"Yes," Monica said, "we are."

Five hours later, when Delaney had finished bringing his files up to the minute and Monica had long since cleaned up the dinner dishes, he came out of his study and asked, "Do you know anyone who's under analysis?"

She looked up at him. "Yes, Edward, I know two or three women who are in therapy."

"Well, will you ask them how they pay? I mean, do they fork over cash or a check after every session or does the doctor bill them by the month? I'm just curious about how the shrink's money comes in."

"You think that has something to do with Ellerbee's murder?"

"I don't know. There's so much I don't know about this case. Like how does a psychiatrist get patients? Referrals from other doctors? Or do patients walk in off the street or use the Yellow Pages? I just don't know."

"I'll ask around," Monica promised. "I suspect every case is different."

"I suspect the same thing," he grumbled. "Makes it hard to figure percentages."

And, four hours later, when they were in their upstairs bedroom preparing for sleep, he said, "I haven't even looked at the Sunday *Times*. Was there anything on the Ellerbee case?"

"I didn't notice anything. But there's an interesting article in the magazine section about new colors for women's hair. Would you like me to get pink streaks, Edward?"

"I'd prefer kelly green," he said. "But suit yourself."

"Monster," she said affably and crawled into her bed.

"You know what I think?" he said. "I think absolute craziness and absolute normality are extremes, and very few people fit into either category. Most of us suffer varying degrees of abnormality that can range from mild eccentricity to outright psychosis. Look at that article on hair coloring. I'll bet a lot of women are going to dye their hair pink or orange or purple. That doesn't make them all whackos."

"What's your point, Edward?"

"This afternoon I said those patients we've been questioning don't live in my world. But that's not true; they do live in my world. They're just a little farther along toward craziness than I am, so I find it difficult to understand them."

"What you're saying is that we're all loonies, some more, some less."

"Yes," he said gratefully. "That's what I mean. I've got to keep in mind that I share the patients' queerness, but to a milder degree."

She turned her head to stare at him.

"Don't be so sure of that, buster," she said, and he gave a great hoot of laughter and climbed into her bed.

14

•

"I STOPPED AT THE PRECINCT ON MY WAY OVER," BOONE SAID ON Monday morning. "Talked to the Sergeant handling paperwork for Suarez's investigation. He says the new people will be here by nine o'clock. Gave me a copy of the roster. He wasn't happy about losing them."

"No," Delaney said, "I don't imagine he would be."

"You don't think Chief Suarez will send us six dummies, do you, sir?" Jason T. Jason asked.

"Sabotage?" Delaney said, smiling. "No, I don't think he'll do that. Not with Deputy Thorsen looking over his shoulder. But if any of these men don't work out, we'll ask for replacements."

"They're not all men, sir," Boone said. "Five men and a woman. And one of the guys is a black—Robert Keisman. You know him, Jase?"

"Oh, sure. He's a sharp cat; you won't need a replacement for him. They call him the Spoiler because for a time there he was assigned to busting bunco artists and three-card-monte games in the Times Square area. One of the guys he grabbed screamed, 'You're spoiling all our fun!' and the name stuck. You know any of the others, Sergeant?"

"I've worked with two of them. Not much flash, but they're solid enough. Benny Calazo has been around a hundred years. He's slowing down some, but he still makes all the right moves. The other guy I know is Ross Konigsbacher. He's a dick two. They call him Kraut. He's built like a Dumpster, and maybe he likes to use his hands too much. But he's thorough; I'll say that for him. The other people I don't know."

"All right," Delaney said. "Let's get set up for this. We're going to need more chairs in here—five more should do it."

They carried in chairs from the living room and kitchen and arranged them in a rough semicircle facing the desk in the study. They also brought in extra ashtrays.

"I was going to let them read my reports on the six patients," Delaney said, "but I decided not to. I don't want them prejudiced by my reactions to those people. We'll just give them a brief introduction, hand them their assignments, and turn them loose. I'm hoping we can get them out on the street by noon. You two decide who you want to partner first, then switch around from day to day."

The new recruits began arriving a little before 9:00 A.M. Sergeant Boone served as doorman, showing them where to hang their coats and bringing them back to the study to introduce them to Delaney and Jason Two.

By 9:15, everyone was present and Boone closed the doors. Delaney had hidden his glasses away, firmly believing that wearing spectacles while issuing orders was counterproductive, being a sign of physical infirmity in a commanding officer.

"My name is Edward X. Delaney," he said in a loud, forceful voice. "Former Captain, Commander of the Two-Five-One Precinct, and former Chief of Detectives prior to my retirement several years ago. As you probably know, I am assisting Chief Suarez in his investigation of the Ellerbee homicide. Are you all familiar with that case?"

They nodded.

"Good," he said. "Then I won't have to repeat the details. By the way, you can smoke if you like."

He waited while a few of them lighted cigarettes. Detective Brian Estrella, a string bean of a man, took pipe and pouch from his jacket pockets and started slowly packing the tobacco.

Delaney told them that the first job of this "task force," as he called it, was to investigate six of the victim's patients who had a history of violence. He emphasized that these people were not yet considered suspects, just subjects worth checking out in depth. Later they might have to investigate other of Ellerbee's patients.

"The first thing you'll want to do," he said, "is to run them through Records and see if any of them have sheets."

He said that eventually each detective would be assigned to one patient. But for the first few days, they'd be moved around, meeting the patients, questioning them, digging into their backgrounds and personal lives.

"We're hoping," he continued, "you will each find one subject who will think you simpatico and talk a little more freely. Now let me give you a rundown on the people we're dealing with."

He was gratified to see all the detectives take out their notebooks and ballpoints.

He delivered brief summaries of the six patients.

When he finished, he turned to Boone. "Anything to add, Sergeant?"

"Not about the people, sir; I think you've covered what we know. But the hammer . . ."

"I was getting to that."

Delaney told them that the murder weapon was apparently a ball peen hammer. It had not been found, and none of the six subjects had admitted owning such a tool. He urged them to make a search for the hammer an important part of their investigation.

He also reminded them of the two sets of footprints and suggested they query the subjects as to ownership of rubbers, galoshes, boots, or any other type of foul-weather footwear.

"If you can get their shoe size," he told them, "so much the better. We have photos of the footprints. Anything else, Boone?"

"No, sir."

"Anything you want to add, Jason?"

"No, sir."

"All right," Delaney said to the others. "Any questions?"

The female detective, Helen K. Venable, raised her hand. "Sir," she said, "are these people all crackpots?"

There was some amused laughter, but Delaney didn't smile. "This job is going to take patience and understanding. Your first impression might be of a bunch of whackos, but don't underestimate them because of that. Remember, quite possibly one of them had the intelligence, resolve, and cunning to zap Doctor Ellerbee and, so far, get away with it."

Benjamin Calazo, the old gumshoe, raised a meaty hand. "I'd like to take Isaac Kane. My brother's kid is retarded. A sweet boy, no harm in him, but like you said, he needs patience and understanding. I've learned to deal with him, so if it's okay with you, I'd like to take on Isaac Kane."

"Fine with me," Delaney said. "Anyone else got a preference?"

Robert Keisman, the Spoiler, spoke up: "If no one else wants him, I'll start with the Vietnam vet—what's his name? Gerber? I can jive with those guys."

"He's all yours," Delaney said. "Just watch your back; I think the kid can be dangerous. Any other preferences?"

There were none, so they set to work making assignments, arranging schedules, exchanging phone numbers so any of them could be reached at any hour, either directly or by leaving a message.

Boone selected Detectives Konigsbacher, Calazo, and Venable for his squad. Jason had Estrella, the pipe smoker; Keisman; and Timothy (Big Tim) Hogan, a short, blunt man as bald as a peeled egg.

Delaney impressed on all of them the need for daily reports, as complete as they could make them.

"Include everything," he told them. "Even if it seems silly or insignificant. If you think it's important, contact Boone or Jason immediately. If you can't get hold of them, call me any hour of the day or night. Now let's get moving. The trail is getting colder by the day, and the Department wants to close out this file as soon as possible. If you need cars, backup, special equipment, or the cooperation of technical squads, just let me know."

They all shook his hand and tramped out, along with Boone and Jason. Delaney returned the extra chairs to their proper places and emptied the ashtrays. Then he called Suarez, but the Chief was in a meeting and not available. Delaney left his name and asked that Suarez call him back.

He sat at his desk, put on his reading glasses, lighted a cigar. Working from the duty roster, from what Boone and Jason had told him, and from his own observations, he made a list of the newly assigned detectives on a pad of yellow legal paper. It went like this:

Boone's squad—
1. Ross (Kraut) Konigsbacher. Heavy. Muscular. Blond mustache. Likes to use fists. Faint scar over left eyebrow.
2. Benjamin Calazo. Old flatfoot. White hair. Heavy hands, keratosis on backs. Picked Isaac Kane.
3. Helen K. Venable. Short. Chubby. Reddish brown hair. Very intense. Deep voice.

Jason's squad—
1. Brian Estrella. Tall. Stringy. Smokes pipe. Left-handed. Prominent Adam's apple.
2. Robert (Spoiler) Keisman. Black. Slender. Elegant. Packs shoulder holster. Picked Harold Gerber.
3. Timothy (Big Tim) Hogan. Stubby. Bald. Big ears. Nicotine-stained fingers. Whiny voice.

Finished, Delaney read over the list and could visualize the new people, recognize them as individuals. He put his notes in the back of the top drawer of his desk. Comments on their performance would be added later. Some of them might earn citations out of this.

Pushing aside the yellow pad, he searched through his file cabinet and dug out a wide worksheet pad designed for accountants. It had fourteen ruled columns and provided enough horizontal lines for what he proposed to devise: a time schedule for the night Dr. Simon Ellerbee was murdered.

He listed the names of individuals at the top of columns. Down the left margin of the page he noted times from 4:00 P.M. on the fatal day to 1:54 A.M., when the body was discovered.

This was donkeywork, he knew, but it had to be done. It would require constant reference to the reports, statements, and Dr. Ellerbee's records in his file cabinet. And all the times would be approximate. Even the time of death, estimated at nine o'clock by the ME, could be off by an hour or more. Still, you had to start somewhere.

He started with the first column:

Dr. Simon Ellerbee:
  4:00 P.M.—Appointment with Harold Gerber.
  5:00—Appointment with Mrs. Lola Brizio. Who is she?
Check.
  6:00—Tells wife he expects late patient, but doesn't tell her who or when. Appointment not listed in book. Receptionist doesn't know who or when. Tells wife he will leave N.Y. for Brewster at 9:00. That suggests late patient at 7:00 or 8:00.
  9:00—Dead.
Dr. Diane Ellerbee:
  6:00—Leaves office after speaking to husband.
  6:30—Departs Manhattan, driving.
  8:00—Arrives Brewster home.
  11:30—Calls Manhattan office. No answer. Calls twice more, times not stated.
  12:00—Calls Brewster police. No report of highway accident.
  Calls Manhattan garage, time not stated, learns Simon's car is still in slot.
  1:15—Calls Dr. Samuelson.
Dr. Julius K. Samuelson:
  7:00 P.M.-?—Dinner with friends at Russian Tea Room.
  8:30–11:30—Concert at Carnegie Hall.
  11:30–12:30(?)—Nightcap at St. Moritz.
  1:15 A.M.—Receives Diane's call.
  1:45—Arrives 84th Street townhouse.
  1:54—Finds body, calls 911.

When the phone rang, Delaney was startled and jagged his pen across the page.

"Chief Suarez is calling," a voice announced.

"How are you doing, Chief?" Delaney asked.

"Surviving," Suarez said with a sigh. "I hope you have some good news for me."

"I'm afraid not, Chief, but I would like to get together with you—just to keep you informed of what we're doing."

"Yes," Suarez said, "I would appreciate that."

"Would you care to drop by here, Chief? I'll be in all day and it shouldn't take long."

A hesitation. "A bad day. So much to do. I do not expect to get uptown until this evening. Will eight or nine o'clock be too late for you?"

"Not at all. I'll be here."

"Suppose I stop at your place on my way home. I will call you first to tell you when I am leaving. Will that be satisfactory?"

"That's fine," Delaney said. "See you tonight."

He put down the receiver and went back to the time schedule.

Henry Ellerbee:
   9:00—Charity dinner at Plaza. Presence confirmed.
Receptionist:
   5:00 or 6:00?—When did she leave. Check.
Isaac Kane:
   9:00—Leaves Community Center when it closes. Goes home?
Sylvia Mae Otherton:
   9:00—At home alone. No confirmation.
L. Vincent Symington:
   9:00—Dinner-dance at Hilton. Could have left, gone back.
Ronald J. Bellsey:
   9:00—Home all night. Wife confirms.
Harold Gerber:
   9:00—Bar-hopping, no recollection of where. No confirmation.
Joan Yesell:
   9:00—Home all night. Mother confirms.

Delaney had just started reading over what he had written when the phone rang again. It was Boone.

"I'm in Ronald Bellsey's garage with the Kraut," he reported. "Bellsey's Cadillac is here. I called his meat market, and he's at work all right. There's no one around. I can get into that Cadillac trunk. I've got my picks."

He paused. Delaney thought it over.

"Where are you calling from, Sergeant?"

"A public phone in the garage."

"All right, go into the trunk. Just look it over, then call me back. If there's any trouble, I authorized you to make the break-in, and Chief Suarez and Deputy Thorsen authorized me. Don't put *your* ass on the line."

"There won't be any trouble," Boone assured him. "Right now the place is deserted, and the Kraut will stand lookout."

"Call me back," Delaney repeated, and hung up.

He tried to concentrate on the time schedule, but couldn't. When the phone rang again, he grabbed it.

"Boone again," the Sergeant said in an excited voice. "I got in! There's a ball peen hammer in there, an old one, all greasy."

"Glom on to it," Delaney said at once. "Get it to the techs as soon as possible. Can you relock the trunk?"

"No strain."

"Good. Bellsey will never miss his hammer for a day or two."

He hung up, smiling, and went back to the schedule, satisfied that things were beginning to happen. They were *making* them happen.

He read over the timetable twice, paying attention to every word. Then he pushed the pad away, leaned back in his swivel chair, lighted a cigar.

What interested him even more than those half-confirmed and unconfirmed alibis was what Dr. Simon Ellerbee did the last three hours of his life.

Did the mystery patient show up and stay longer than usual? Not likely; every patient got the forty-five-minute hour. Did Ellerbee work at his caseload while waiting for the patient to arrive? Did he read, listen to music, watch television?

Delaney looked at his watch and thought of a sandwich. *Eat!* When did the bastard eat? He told his wife he'd be leaving New York about nine o'clock. Even if he were planning on a late supper in Brewster at 10:30, that was a long time to go without food. Delaney didn't think it was humanly possible.

He retrieved the autopsy report from the file and flipped through the pages until he found what he sought. The victim had eaten about an hour before his death. Stomach contents included boiled ham, Swiss cheese, rye bread, mustard. Ellerbee had been a man after his own heart.

So part of those three hours had been spent consuming a sandwich. Did Ellerbee go out for it? In that weather? Doubtful. He probably went down one floor to the kitchen and made himself a snack. But that wouldn't use up many minutes of that three-hour period.

The gap in the victim's time schedule bothered Delaney. It was not neat, ordered, logical—the way he liked things. Too many unanswered questions:

1. Why didn't Ellerbee tell his wife the name of the late patient and when he or she was expected?

2. Why didn't he tell his receptionist?

3. If the late patient was expected at, say, seven o'clock, then Ellerbee could have left for Brewster at eight. But he told his wife he'd be leaving at nine. Ergo, the patient was expected at eight o'clock. But if that was so, how come the autopsy showed he had eaten an hour before death? It was ridiculous to suppose he munched on a sandwich while listening to a troubled patient.

4. How did Ellerbee spend the time from six to eight o'clock, assuming the late patient *was* scheduled for eight?

5. Those two sets of tracks—did the doctor expect *two* late patients that night?

It was, Delaney acknowledged, probably much ado about nothing. But it gnawed at him, and he suddenly decided he'd take on this puzzle himself. He couldn't sit in his study all day, waiting for phone calls and reports from his task force. He'd hit the street and do a little personal sleuthing.

He started by searching through the records for the name and address of Doctor Simon's receptionist. He finally found them: Carol Judd, living on East 73rd Street. Clipped to her card was Boone's report on her alibi for the night of the murder: She said she had been shacked up with her boyfriend in his apartment. He confirmed.

Delaney looked up her phone number in the Manhattan directory. He called, mentally keeping his fingers crossed. It rang seven times and he was about to hang up when suddenly the receiver was lifted.

"Hello?" A breathless voice.

"Miss Carol Judd?"

"Yes. Who is this?"

"My name is Edward X. Delaney," he said, speaking slowly and distinctly. "I am a civilian consultant with the New York Police Department, assisting in the investigation of the death of Doctor Simon Ellerbee. I was hoping you—"

"Hey," she said, "wait a minute, let me put these groceries down. I just walked through the door."

He waited patiently until she came on the line again.

"Now," she said, "who are you?"

He went through it again. "I was hoping you might give me a few minutes of your time. Some questions have come up that only you can answer."

"Gee, I don't know," she said hesitantly. "Ever since my name was in the papers, I've been getting crazy calls. Real weirdos—you know?"

"I can imagine. Miss Judd, may I suggest you call Doctor Diane Ellerbee and tell her that you have received a call from me and that I'd like to ask you a few questions. I'm sure she'll tell you that I am not a weirdo. I'll give you my number and you can call me back. Will you do that, please?"

"Well . . . I guess so. It may take some time getting through to her if she has a patient."

"I'll wait," Delaney said and gave her his phone number.

He cleared the clutter from his desk, replacing all the records back in their proper file folders. He kept out the time schedule and read it over again. That three-hour gap in Ellerbee's activities still intrigued him, and he hoped Carol Judd could supply some answers.

It was almost twenty minutes before she called back.

"Doctor Diane says you're okay," she reported.

"Fine," he said. "I wonder if I could come over now; I'm not too far from where you live."

"Right this minute? Gee, you better give me some time to straighten up this place; it's a mess. How about half an hour?"

"I'll be there. Thank you."

That gave him time for a Michelob and a "wet" sandwich, eaten while leaning over the kitchen sink. It consisted of meat scraped off the bones of leftover chicken wings, with sliced tomatoes and onions and Russian dressing—all jammed into an onion roll as big as a Frisbee.

Then, donning his hard black homburg and heavy overcoat, he set out to walk down to East 73rd Street.

It was the kind of day that made pedestrians step out: cold, clear, brilliant, with sharp light dazzling the eyes and a wind that stung. The city seemed renewed and glowing.

He strode down Third Avenue, mourning the passing of all those familiar Irish bars, including his father's saloon. There was now a health food store where that had been. It was change all right, but whether it was progress, Delaney was not prepared to say.

Carol Judd lived in a fourteen-story apartment house that had glass doors, marble walls in vestibule and lobby, and a pervasive odor of boiled cabbage. Delaney identified himself on the intercom and was buzzed in immediately. He rode up to apartment 9-H in an automatic elevator that squeaked alarmingly.

If she had spent the last half-hour tidying up, Delaney hated to think of what her tiny studio apartment had been before she started. It looked like a twister had just blown through, leaving a higgledy-piggledy jumble of clothing, books, records, cassettes, and what appeared to be a collection of Japanese windup toys: dancing bears, rabbits clashing cymbals, and somersaulting clowns.

"Pardon the stew," she said, smiling brightly.

"Not at all," he said. "It looks lived-in."

"Yeah," she said, laughing, "it is that. Would you believe I've had a party for twenty people in here?"

"I'd believe it," he assured her, and thought, The poor neighbors!

She lifted a stack of fashion magazines out of a canvas sling chair, and he lowered himself cautiously into it, still wearing his overcoat, his homburg on his lap. Unexpectedly, she crossed her ankles and scissored down onto the floor without a bump, an athletic feat he admired.

In fact, he admired her. She was tall, lanky, and in tight denim jeans seemed to be 90 percent legs. She was not beautiful, but her perky features were vivacious, and her mop of blond curls—an Orphan Annie hairdo—had an outlandish charm. She wore a T-shirt that had a portrait of Beethoven printed on the front.

"Miss Judd," he started, "I'll try to make this as brief as possible; I don't want to take up too much of your time."

"I've got plenty," she told him. "I've been looking for a job, but no luck yet. When I spoke to Doctor Diane before, she said she's looking for me, too, and thinks she may be able to get me something with a shrink she knows who's opening a clinic for rich alcoholics."

"How long did you work for Doctor Simon Ellerbee?"

"Almost five years. Gee, that was a dreamy job. Good hours and very little work. No pressure—you know?"

"I assume you handled his appointments, took care of the billing, and things of that nature?"

"That's right. And I could use their kitchen for lunch. They even invited me and Edith Crawley—she's Doctor Diane's receptionist—up to their Brewster home for a weekend every summer. That's a dreamy place. And, of course, I got the whole month of August off every year."

"Did you like Doctor Simon?"

"A wonderful, wonderful man. Swell to work for. I really had eyes for him, but I knew that would get me nowhere. You've seen Doctor Diane? Too much competition!" She laughed merrily, clasping her knees with her arms and rocking back and forth on the floor.

"What hours did you work?"

"Nine to five. Usually. Sometimes he would ask me to come in a little earlier or stay a little later if a hysterical woman was scheduled. You know, some of those crazy ladies could scream rape—it's possible."

"Did it ever happen—that a woman patient screamed rape?"

"It never happened to Doctor Simon, but it happened to a friend of his, so he was very careful."

"Let's talk about the Friday he was killed. Did anything unusual happen that day?"

She thought a moment. "Noo," she said finally, "it was ordinary. Lousy weather; it poured all day. But nothing unusual happened in the office."

"What time did you leave?"

"A few minutes after five. Right after Mrs. Brizio arrived."

"Ah," he said, "Mrs. Lola Brizio . . . She was the last patient listed in his appointment book."

"That's right. She came in once a week, every Friday, five to six."

"Tell me about her."

"Mrs. Brizio? Gee, she must be sixty—at least. And very, very rich. That dreamy chinchilla coat she wears—I could live five years on what she paid for that. But a very nice lady. I mean, not stuck-up or anything like that. Real friendly. She was always telling me the cute things her grandchildren said."

"What was her problem?"

"Kleptomania. Can you believe it? With all her loot. She'd go in these stores, like Henri Bendel, and stuff silk scarves and costume jewelry in her handbag. Been doing it for years. The stores knew about it, of course, and kept an eye on her. They never arrested her or anything because she was such a good customer. I mean, she bought a lot of stuff in addition to what she stole. So they'd let her swipe what she wanted and just add it to her bill. She always paid. She came to Doctor Simon about three years ago." Carol Judd burst out laughing. "The first session she had, she stole a crystal ashtray off Doctor Simon's desk, and he didn't even notice until she was gone. Can you imagine?"

"Sixty years old, you say?"

"At least. Probably more."

"A big woman?"

"Oh, no! A little bitty thing. Not even five feet tall. And fat. A roly-poly."

"All right," Delaney said, tentatively eliminating Mrs. Lola Brizio as a possible suspect, "after she arrived at five o'clock, you left a few minutes later. Is that correct?"

"Right."

"Did Doctor Simon tell you he was expecting a late patient?"

"No, he didn't."

"Wasn't that unusual?"

"Oh, no, it happened all the time. Like maybe in the evening he'd get a panic call from some patient who had to see him right away. The next morning he'd just leave a note on my desk telling me to bill so-and-so for a session."

"Did Doctor Diane ever have late patients?"

"Oh, sure. They both did, all the time."

"Apparently, after six o'clock, when Mrs. Lola Brizio was gone, Doctor Simon told his wife that he was expecting a late patient, but didn't tell her who or when. Isn't that a little surprising?"

"Not really. Like I said, it happened frequently. They'd tell each other so it wouldn't interfere with their plans for the night—dinner or the theater, you know—but I don't think they'd mention who it was that was coming in. There was just no need for it."

Delaney sat silently, brooding, and somewhat depressed. As explained by Carol Judd, the mystery patient now seemed no mystery at all. It was just routine.

"And you have no idea who the late patient was on that Friday night?" he asked her.

"No, I don't."

"Well, whoever had the appointment," he said, trying to salvage something from his inquiries, "was probably the last person to see Doctor Simon alive. And may have been the killer. But let's suppose the late patient arrived at seven and left at eight. Would it—"

"Fifteen minutes to eight. Patients got forty-five minutes."

"What did the doctor do in those fifteen minutes between patients?"

"Relax. Return phone calls. Look over the files of the next patient. Maybe have a cup of coffee."

"All right," he said, "let's suppose the late patient arrived at seven and left at fifteen minutes to eight. Do you think it's possible that sometime during the evening Doctor Simon got a phone call from *another* patient who wanted to see him? A second late patient?"

"Of course it's possible," she said. "Things like that happened all the time."

Which left him, he thought, nowhere.

"Thank you very much, Miss Judd," he said, heaving himself out of the silly canvas sling and putting on his hat. "You've been very cooperative and very helpful."

She rose from her folded position on the floor without using her hands— just unflexed her limber body and floated up.

"I hope you catch the person who did it," she said, suddenly solemn and vengeful. "I wish we had the death penalty. Doctor Simon was a dear, sweet man, and no one deserves to die like that. I cried for forty-eight hours after it happened. I still can't believe he's gone."

Delaney nodded and started for the door. Then he stopped and turned.

"One more thing," he said. "Did Doctor Simon ever mention to you that he had been attacked or threatened by a patient?"

"No, he never did."

"In the past year or six months, did you notice any change in him? Did he act differently?"

She stared at him. "Funny you should ask that. Yes, he changed. In the last year or so. I even mentioned it to my boyfriend. Doctor Simon became, uh, moodier. He used to be so steady. The same every day: pleasant and kind to everyone. Then, in the last year or so, he became moodier. Some days he'd really be up, laughing and joking. And other days he'd be down, like he had the weight of the world on his shoulders."

"I see."

"About a month ago," she added, "he wore a little flower in his lapel. He had never done that before. He really was a dreamy man."

"Thank you, Miss Judd," Delaney said, tipping his homburg.

When he came outside, he found the day transformed. A thick cloud cover was churning over Manhattan, the wind had taken on a raw edge, the light seemed sourish and menacing. The gloom fitting his mood exactly.

He was disgusted with himself, for he had been trying to bend the facts to fit a theory instead of devising a theory that fit all the facts. That kind of thinking had been the downfall of a lot of wild-assed detectives.

It was those two sets of footprints soaked into the Ellerbees' carpet that

had seduced him. That and the gap in the victim's time schedule. It seemed
to add up to *two* late patients on the murder night. But though Carol Judd
said it was possible, there wasn't a shred of evidence to substantiate it.

Still, he told himself stubbornly, it was crucial to identify Ellerbee's late
visitor or visitors. One of them had been the last person to see the victim
alive and was a prime suspect.

Plodding uptown, he remembered what he had said to Monica about
assembling a jigsaw puzzle. He had told her that he had found some straight-
edged pieces and was putting together the frame. Then all he needed to do
was fill in the interior pieces of the picture.

Now he recalled that some puzzles were not pictures at all. They were
rectangles of solid color: yellow, blue, or blood red. There was no pattern,
no clues of shape or form. And they were devilishly hard to complete.

When he entered the brownstone, he heard the phone ringing and rushed
down the hallway to the kitchen. But Monica was there and had already
picked up.

"Who?" she said. "Just a minute, please." She covered the mouthpiece
with her palm and turned to her husband. "Timothy Hogan," she reported.
"Do you know him?"

"Hogan? Yes, he's one of the new men. I'll talk to him."

She handed him the phone.

"I couldn't get ahold of Jason or Boone," Hogan whined, "so that's why
I'm calling. I'm at St. Vincent's Hospital."

"What happened?"

"I started checking out that Joan Yesell. She didn't report to work today.
Okay? So I go down to her place in Chelsea. She ain't home, and her mother
ain't home. So I start talking to the neighbors. Okay? This Joan Yesell, she
tried to do the Dutch yesterday afternoon, but blew it. Just nicked her left
wrist with a kitchen knife. A lot of blood, but she's okay. They kept her here
overnight, under observation. Her mother is signing her out right now. You
want I should question them?"

"No," Delaney said promptly, "don't do that. Let them go home. You
can catch up with them tomorrow. Do you know what time yesterday she
cut herself?"

"They brought her into St. Vincent's Emergency about four-thirty, so I
guess she sliced herself around four o'clock. Okay?"

"Thank you, Hogan. You did exactly right to call me. Pack it in for the
day."

He hung up and turned to Monica. He told her what had happened.

"The poor woman," she said somberly.

"If she tried suicide yesterday at four o'clock, it couldn't have been more
than an hour after Boone and I had questioned her. I hope to God we didn't
trigger it."

"How did she seem when you left?"

"Well, she's a mousy little thing and suffers from depression. She was very quiet and withdrawn. Dominated by her mother. But she sure didn't seem suicidal. I wonder if it was anything we said."

"I doubt that. Don't worry about it, Edward."

"This morning I was happy that things were beginning to happen, that we were *making* them happen. But I didn't figure on anything like this."

"It's not your fault," she assured him. "She's tried before, hasn't she?"

"Three times."

"Well, there you are. Don't blame yourself."

"Son of a bitch," he said bitterly. "I just don't get it. We talk to her, very politely, no arguments, we leave, and she tries to kill herself."

"Edward, maybe it was just talking about the murder that pushed her over the edge. If she's depressed to start with, reminding her of the death of someone who was trying to help her might have made her decide life wasn't worth living."

"Yes," he said gratefully, "it could have been that. I'm going to have a slug of rye. Would you like one?"

"I'll have a white wine. We're having linguine with clam sauce tonight. I added a can of minced clams and a dozen fresh cherrystones."

"Very good," he said approvingly. "In that case, I'll have a white wine, too. By the way, Chief Suarez is stopping by later. I don't know what time, but he'll call first. I'd like you to meet him; I think you'll like him."

After dinner, Delaney went into the study to write out a report on Carol Judd. Suarez called around eight o'clock and said he was on his way uptown. But it was almost nine before he arrived. Delaney took him into the living room and introduced him to Monica.

"What can I get you, Chief?" he asked. "You look like you could use a transfusion."

Suarez smiled wanly. "Yes, it has been that kind of a day. Would a very, very dry gin martini on the rocks be possible?"

"Of course. Monica, would you like anything?"

"A small Cointreau would be nice."

Delaney went into the kitchen and made the drinks. He put them on a tray along with a brandy for himself.

"Delightful," Chief Suarez said when he tasted his. "Best martini I've ever had."

"As I told you," Delaney said, shrugging away the compliment, "I have no good news for you, but I wanted you to know what we've been doing."

Rapidly, concisely, he summarized the progress of his investigation to date. He omitted nothing he thought important, except the lifting of the ball peen hammer from Ronald Bellsey's Cadillac. He expressed no great optimism, but pointed out there was still a lot of work to be done, particularly on those vague alibis of the six patients.

Monica and the Chief listened intently, fascinated by his recital. When he finished, Suarez said, "I do not believe things are as gloomy as you seem to suggest, Mr. Delaney. You have uncovered several promising leads—more, certainly, than we have found. I commend you for persuading Doctor Diane Ellerbee to furnish a list of violence-prone patients. But you should know, that lady and the victim's father continue to bring pressure on the Department, demanding a quick solution."

"That's Thorsen's problem," Delaney said shortly.

"True," Suarez said, "and he handles it by making it *my* problem." He glanced around the living room. "Mrs. Delaney, you have a lovely home. So warm and cheerful."

"Thank you," she said. "I hope you and your wife will visit us. A social visit—no talk of murder."

"Rosa would like that," he said. "Thank you very much."

He sat a moment in silence, staring into his glass. His long face seemed drawn, olive skin sallow with fatigue, the tic at the left of his mouth more pronounced.

"You know," he said with his shy, rueful smile, "since the death of Doctor Ellerbee, there have been perhaps fifty homicides in the city. Many of those, of course, were solved immediately. But our solution rate on the others is not what it should be; I am aware of that and it troubles me. I will not speak to you of our manpower needs, Mr. Delaney; I know you had the same problem when you were in the Department. I mentioned all this merely to tell you how grateful I am for your assistance. I wish I could devote more time to the Ellerbee murder, but I cannot. So I am depending on you."

"I warned you from the start," Delaney said. "No guarantees."

"Naturally. I realize that. But your participation lifts part of my burden and gives me confidence that, during this difficult time, I badly need. Mrs. Delaney, do you have faith in your husband?"

"Absolutely," she said.

"And do you think he will find Ellerbee's killer?"

"Of course he will. Once Edward sets his mind on something, it's practically done. He's a very tenacious man."

"Hey," Delaney said, laughing, "what's this—the two of you ganging up on me?"

"Tenacious," Chief Suarez repeated, staring at the other man. "Yes, I think you are right. I am not a betting man, but if I was, I would bet on you, Mr. Delaney. I have a good feeling that you will succeed. Now I have a favor I would like to ask of you."

"What's that?"

"I would like it if we could call each other by our Christian names."

"Of course, Michael."

"Thank you, Edward."

"And I'm Monica," she said loudly.

They all laughed, and Delaney went into the kitchen for another round of drinks.

After the Chief had left, Delaney came back into the living room and sprawled into his chair.

"What do you think of him?" he asked.

"A very nice man," Monica said. "Very polite and soft-spoken. But he looks headed for a burnout. Do you think he's tough enough for the job?"

"It'll make him or break him," Delaney said roughly. "Headquarters is a bullring. Turn your back for a second and you get gored. Monica, when I was telling him what we're doing in the Ellerbee case, was there anything special that caught your attention? Something that sounded false? Or something we should have done that we haven't?"

"No," she said slowly, "nothing in particular. It sounded awfully complicated, Edward. All those people . . ."

"It *is* complicated," he said, rubbing his forehead wearily. "In the first stages of any investigation, you expect to be overwhelmed by all the bits and pieces that come flooding in. Facts and rumors and guesses. Then, after a while, if you're lucky, they all fall into a pattern, and you know more or less what happened. But I admit this case has me all bollixed up. I've been trying to keep on top of it with reports and files and time schedules, but it keeps spreading out in more directions. It's so complex that I'm afraid I may be missing something that's right under my nose. Maybe I'm getting too old for this business."

"You're not getting older," she said loyally, "you're getting better."

"Keep telling me that," he said.

15

•

DURING THE NEXT TWO DAYS, THE DISORDER IN THE ELLERBEE case that had troubled Edward X. Delaney showed signs of lessening.

"It's still confusion," he told Sergeant Boone, "but it's becoming *organized* confusion."

Driving his little task force with stern directives, he was able to move them around so each had the chance to eyeball several patients. By Wednesday night, Delaney, Boone, and Jason were able to achieve optimum pairings of detective and subject. They went like this:

Benjamin Calazo—Isaac Kane.
Robert Keisman—Harold Gerber.
Ross Konigsbacher—L. Vincent Symington.
Helen K. Venable—Joan Yesell.
Timothy Hogan—Ronald J. Bellsey.
Brian Estrella—Sylvia Mae Otherton.

"If it doesn't work out," Delaney told his people, "we'll switch you around until we start getting results."

Brian Estrella, the pipe smoker, hoped he wouldn't be switched from Sylvia Mae Otherton. The woman fascinated him, and he thought he could do some good there.

On the morning he started out to meet her for the first time, his horoscope in the *Daily News* read: "Expect a profitable surprise." And as if that wasn't encouraging enough, his wife, Meg, called from the nursing home to report she was feeling better, her hair was beginning to grow back in, and she would be home soon.

Which was, Estrella knew, a lie—but a brave, happy lie all the same.

Sergeant Boone had warned him what to expect, but still it was something of a shock to walk into that dim, overheated apartment and confront someone who looked like all she'd need would be a broomstick to soar over the rooftops.

She was wearing a voluminous white garment which could have been a bedsheet except that it was inset with triangles of white lace. It hung quite low, almost to the floor, but not low enough to hide Otherton's bare feet. They were short and puffy, the toenails painted black.

Boone had mentioned the woman's jewelry and perfume, the wildly decorated room and burning incense. It was all there, but what surprised Detective Estrella was Otherton's patience. After all, this was the third time she had been braced by the cops on the Ellerbee kill, and he expected her to be hostile and indignant.

But she led him into her apartment without demur and answered his questions freely without once reminding him that she had replied to the same queries twice before. He appreciated that, and decided to try an absolutely honest approach to see if that might tempt her into additional disclosures.

"You see, ma'am," he said, "we're most concerned about your whereabouts the night of the crime. You've told us you were here alone. That may be true, but we'd feel a lot better if we could confirm it. Did you go out at all that night?"

"Oh, no," she said in a low voice. "I very rarely go out. That's part of my problem."

"And you say you had no visitors, saw no one, made and received no phone calls?"

She shrugged helplessly. "No, I'm afraid not."

"I wish you'd think hard and carefully about that night, Miss Otherton, and see if you can remember anything that will help confirm what you've told us."

"I'll try," she said. "Really I will."

Estrella looked at that face marred with clown's makeup and suddenly realized that with the chalky mask removed, and the long, unkempt hair brushed, she would be reasonably comely—maybe not pretty but pleasant enough.

To his horror, he found himself blurting all that out, and more, telling this strange woman how she might improve her appearance, her dress, not so much to impress others but for the sake of her own self-esteem.

"You mustn't stay locked up in here," he said earnestly. "You must try to get out into the world."

She stared at him, and her eyes slowly filled, tears began to drip down her fleshy cheeks. He was distressed, thinking he had insulted her. But . . .

"Thank you," she said in a choky voice. "It's kind of you to be concerned. To show an interest. Most people laugh at me. Doctor Simon never did. That's why I loved him so much. I know I am not living a normal life, but with Doctor Simon's help I was trying to come out of it. Now, with him gone, I don't know what I'm going to do."

Then she told Detective Estrella about her childhood rape and her aversion to bearded men—things he already knew. She said her life was a sad tangle, and she was close to giving up hope of "ever getting my head together."

Estrella told her how important it was to think positively, and then told her of his wife's terminal illness and how courageously she was dealing with that.

"Your mental attitude," he said, "is even more important than the way you look. But I think in your case, those things are connected. And if you start by improving your appearance, your state of mind will improve too, and the way you live."

She brought them little glasses of dry sherry, and they began to converse in an animated fashion, discovering they had a common interest in astrology, lecithin, numerology, and UFOs. He asked if he might smoke a pipe, and she said yes, she had always admired men who smoked pipes.

After a while, Estrella was enjoying their conversation so much—he hadn't had a long talk with a woman in months; his visits to Meg were severely limited—that he felt guilty because he had forgotten the reason he was there.

"I hope, Miss Otherton—" he started, but she interrupted.

"Sylvia," she said.

"Sylvia," he repeated. "That's a lovely name. It means 'forest maiden.' Did you know that? My first name is Brian, which means 'strong and powerful,' and you can see how silly that is! But what I was going to say, Sylvia, is that I hope if you can think of anything you feel might help us find Doctor Ellerbee's killer, you'll give me a call. I'll leave you my card."

She stared at him a long moment. "I know how to find out who did it," she said intensely.

He felt a surge of excitement. "How?" he said hoarsely.

She rose, went into the bedroom, came back carrying a Ouija board and planchette.

"Do you believe?" she asked him.

"It can't do any harm," he said, shrugging.

"You *must* believe," she said, "if the spiritualistic messages are to come through."

"I believe," he said hastily. "I really do."

She put the board on the round cocktail table, and they pulled their armchairs close, leaning forward. She put her fingertips lightly on the planchette and closed her eyes.

"Now ask the question," she said in a hollow voice.

"Who killed Doctor Ellerbee?" Detective Estrella said.

"No, no," she said. "The questions must be directed to those who have passed over."

"Doctor Ellerbee," Estrella said, happy that Edward X. Delaney wasn't there to see what he was doing, "who killed you?"

They waited in silence. The planchette did not move.

"Who crushed your skull, Doctor Ellerbee?" the detective asked in a quiet voice.

He watched, fascinated, as the planchette under Sylvia Mae Otherton's fingertips began to move slowly. Not smoothly, but in little jerks. It took a long time, but the pointer moved from letter to letter and spelled out B-L-I-N-D: blind. Then it stopped.

Otherton opened her eyes. "What did it say?" she asked eagerly.

"Blind," Estrella said. "It spelled out 'blind.' "

"What do you suppose that means?"

"I don't know."

"It couldn't have been a blind man who did it, could it?"

"I doubt that very much."

"We could try again," she said hopefully.

"I've got to go," he told her. "Maybe next time."

"You'll come back?"

"Of course. But there are some things I have to check out first."

Before he left he got from her the names of the few friends who called her occasionally, and the list of neighborhood stores that delivered her groceries and drugs.

"Thank you for your help, Sylvia," he said.

She went up on her toes to kiss his cheek. "Thank you, Brian," she said breathlessly.

Going down in the elevator, he debated with himself whether or not to include the Ouija board episode in his report. He finally decided to put it in. Hadn't Delaney said he wanted *everything?*

And *everything* was exactly what Delaney was getting in the daily reports. He was satisfied; better too much than not enough. Most of the stuff was boilerplate, but there were some significant revelations:

—Benjamin Calazo reported that Isaac Kane said he had left the Community Center at 9:00 P.M. on the night of the crime, but Kane admitted he hadn't returned home right away. He was unable or unwilling to account for the intervening time.

—L. Vincent Symington, according to Ross Konigsbacher, had a sheet. A few years previously he had been arrested in a raid on a gay after-hours joint on 18th Street. There was no record of the disposition of the case.

—Timothy Hogan spent some time schmoozing with workers at Ronald J. Bellsey's wholesale meat market, and had learned that six months ago Bellsey and a butcher had a bloody fight with meat hooks that resulted in serious injuries to the butcher. He had sued, but the case was settled out of court.

—Joan Yesell, Helen K. Venable wrote, had injured herself more seriously in her suicide attempt than first thought. Tendons in her wrist had been cut, and Yesell was not expected to return to work for at least a month.

—Detective Robert Keisman reported that Harold Gerber's sheet listed several arrests for assaults, refusing to obey the lawful order of a police officer, and committing a public nuisance. Because of Gerber's war record, all charges were eventually dropped. But, Keisman noted, Gerber had received a less than honorable discharge from the army due to several offenses, including slugging an officer.

—Finally, Brian Estrella wrote about his meeting with Sylvia Mae Otherton, briefly mentioning the incident involving the Ouija board. Edward X. Delaney told Monica about that, thinking she'd be amused. But that most rational of women didn't laugh.

All in all, Delaney was gratified. He had the feeling that the investigation was beginning to lurch forward. It was not unlike an archaeological dig, with each layer scraped away bringing him closer to the truth.

Detective Ross (Kraut) Konigsbacher thought he already knew the truth about L. Vincent Symington: The guy was a screaming faggot. It wasn't only that arrest on his record, it was the way he dressed, the way he walked, even the way he handled a cigarette.

Every dick had a different way of working, and Konigsbacher liked to circle his prey, learn all he could about him, study his lifestyle. Then, when he felt he knew his target from A to Z, he'd go for the face-to-face and shatter the guy with what he had learned about him.

The Kraut talked to Symington's neighbors, the super of his townhouse, owners of stores where he shopped. Konigsbacher even got in to interview the personnel manager of the investment counseling firm where Symington worked.

Using a phony business card, Konigsbacher said he was running a credit check on Symington in connection with a loan application for a cooperative apartment. The manager gave Symington a glowing reference, but the Kraut discounted that because he thought the personnel guy was a fruitcake, too.

Outside of business hours, L. Vincent Symington liked to prowl. He dined at a different restaurant almost every night, sometimes alone, sometimes with another man, never with a broad.

After dinner, he'd go bar-hopping. But invariably, around midnight, he'd end up in a place on Lexington Avenue near 40th Street, the Dorian Gray. From the outside it didn't have much flash; the façade was distressed pine paneling with one small window that revealed a dim interior with lighted candles on the tables and a piano at the rear. It was usually crowded.

On the third night Konigsbacher tailed Symington to the Dorian Gray, waited about five minutes, then went inside. It turned out to be the most elegant gay bar the Kraut had ever seen—and he had seen a lot of them, from the Village to Harlem.

This joint was as hushed as a church, with everyone speaking in whispers and even the laughter muted. The black woman at the piano played low-keyed Cole Porter, and the bartender—who looked like a young Tyrone Power—seemed never to clink a bottle or glass.

The Kraut stood a moment at the entrance until his eyes became accustomed to the dimness. There were maybe two or three women in the place, but all the other patrons were men in their thirties and forties. Practically all of them wore conservative, vested suits. They looked like bankers or stock-brokers, maybe even morticians.

Most of the guys at the small tables were in pairs; the singles were at the bar. Konigsbacher spotted his victim sitting alone near the far end. There was an empty barstool next to him. The Kraut sauntered down and swung aboard. The bartender was there immediately.

"Good evening, sir," he said. "What may I bring you?"

The Kraut would have liked a belt of Jack Daniel's with a beer chaser, but when he looked around he saw all the other customers at the bar were having stemmed drinks or sipping little glasses of liqueur.

"Vodka martini straight up with a twist, please," he said, surprised to find himself whispering.

"Very good, sir."

While he waited for his drink, he glanced at the tinted mirror behind the bar and locked stares with L. Vincent Symington. They both looked away.

He drank half his martini, slowly, then pulled a pack of Kents and a disposable lighter from his jacket pocket. The beautiful bartender was there immediately with a small crystal ashtray. The Kraut lighted his cigarette, then left the pack and lighter on the bar in front of him.

A few moments later Symington took a silver case from his inside pocket, snapped it open, selected a long, cork-tipped cigarette.

"I beg your pardon," he said to Konigsbacher in a fluty voice. "I seem to have forgotten my lighter. May I borrow yours?"

It was like a dance, and the Kraut knew the steps.

"Of course," he said, flicked the lighter, and held it for the other man. Symington grasped his hand lightly as if to steady the flame. He took a deep drag of his cigarette and seemed to swallow the smoke.

"Thank you," he said. "Dreadful habit, isn't it?"

"Sex, you mean?" Konigsbacher said, and they both laughed.

Ten minutes later they were seated at a small table against the wall, talking earnestly. They leaned forward, their heads almost touching. Beneath the table, their knees pressed.

"I can tell, Ross," Symington said, "that you take *very* good care of yourself."

"I try to, Vince," the Kraut said. "I work out with weights every morning."

"I really should do that."

He hesitated, then asked, "Are you married, Ross?"

"My wife is; I'm not."

Symington leaned back and clasped his hands together. "Love it," he said. "Just *love* it! My wife is; I'm not. I'll have to remember that."

"How about you, Vince?"

"No. Not now. I was once. But she walked out on me. Taking, I might add, our joint bank account, our poodle, and my personal collection of ancient Roman coins."

"So you're divorced?"

"Not legally, as far as I know."

"You really should be, Vince. You might want to remarry someday."

"I doubt that," Symington said. "I doubt that very much."

"It's a sad, sad, sad, sad world," the Kraut said mournfully, "and we must grab every pleasure we can."

"Truer words were never spoken," the other man agreed, snapped his fingers at the pretty waiter, and ordered another round of drinks.

"Vince," Konigsbacher said, "I have a feeling we can be good friends. I hope so, because I don't have many."

"Oh, my God," Symington said, running his palm over his bald pate. "You, too? I can't *tell* you how lonely I am."

"But there's something you should know about me," the Kraut went on, figuring it was time to get down to business. "I'm under analysis."

"Well, for heaven's sake, *that's* no crime. I was in analysis for years."

"*Was?* You're not now?"

"No," Symington said sorrowfully. "My shrink was killed."

"Killed? That's dreadful. An accident?"

The other man leaned forward again and lowered his voice. "He was murdered."

"Murdered? My God!"

"Maybe you read about it. Doctor Simon Ellerbee, on the Upper East Side."

"Who did it—do they know?"

"No, but I keep getting visits from the police. They have to talk to all his patients, you know."

"What a drag. You don't know anything about it—do you?"

"Well, I have my ideas, but I'm not telling the cops, of course. Hear no evil, see no evil, speak no evil."

"That's smart, Vince. Just try to stay out of it."

"Oh, I will. I have my own problems."

"What kind of a man was he—your shrink?"

"Well, you know what they're like; they can be just *nasty* at times."

"How true. Do you think he was killed by one of his patients?"

Symington swiveled his head to look carefully over both shoulders, as if suspecting someone might be listening. Then he leaned even closer and spoke in a conspiratorial whisper.

"About six months ago—it was on a Friday night—I was crossing First Avenue. I had just had dinner at Lucky Pierre's. That's a marvelous restaurant—really the yummiest escargots in New York. Anyway, it was about nine o'clock, and I was crossing First Avenue, and there, stopped for a light, was Doctor Ellerbee. I saw him plain as day, but he didn't see me. He was driving his new green Jaguar. Then the light changed and he headed uptown. Now I ask you, what does that suggest?"

Konigsbacher was bewildered. "That he had been somewhere?"

"Somewhere with *someone*. And obviously not his wife; she was nowhere to be seen; he was alone in the car."

"I don't know, Vince," the Kraut said doubtfully. "He could have been anywhere. Seeing a patient, for instance, or at a hospital. Anything."

"Well," Symington said, sitting back and smirking with satisfaction, "that's not the *only* thing. I could tell the cops but won't. Let them do their own dirty work."

"Very wise. You keep out of it."

"Oh, I intend to. I don't want to get involved."

Konigsbacher peered at his watch. "Oh dear," he said, "it's later than I thought. I'll have to split."

"Must you, Ross?"

"I'm afraid so, Vince," the Kraut said, having decided to play this fish slowly. "Thank you for a lovely evening. I really enjoyed it."

"It *was* fun, wasn't it? Do you think you might drop in here again?"

"I think I might. Like tomorrow night."

They both laughed, beamed at each other, shook hands lingeringly. Konigsbacher departed, leaving the other man to pick up the tab. Fuck him.

Driving home to Riverdale, the Kraut went over the night's conversation. Not much, but a hint of goodies to come. He'd put it all in his report and let Delaney sort it out.

Edward X. Delaney read the report with something less than admiration. He knew what the Kraut was doing and didn't like it. But after thinking it over, he decided to let the detective run and see what he turned up. Delaney wasn't about to indulge in a soggy philosophical debate over whether or not the end justified the means. He had more immediate concerns.

The techs reported on the ball peen hammer lifted from the trunk of Ronald Bellsey's Cadillac. Negative. Not only no bloodstains, but no indications, even, that the damned thing had been recently used. Sergeant Boone did another lock-picking job and slipped it back into the trunk.

The problem of the late patient continued to nag Delaney. He kept thinking he had solved it, only to find he had uncovered a bigger mystery.

Going through Simon Ellerbee's appointment book for the umpteenth time, he noted that occasionally late patients were scheduled—6:00, 7:00, 8:00, and even 9:00 P.M. He attempted to see if there was any pattern, if certain patients habitually made late appointments.

He then reasoned that late patients who were *not* scheduled in the appointment book—the ones who made panicky phone calls—would certainly be noted in Dr. Ellerbee's billing ledger. Hadn't Carol Judd said that the doctor would leave a note on her desk the next morning, telling her to bill so-and-so for an evening session?

It made sense, but he could find no billing ledger, or anything that resembled it, among the records sent over by Suarez's investigative team. He and Boone spent a frustrating afternoon on the phone, trying to locate it.

Dr. Diane Ellerbee said yes, her husband had kept such a financial journal, with each session noted: name of patient, date, and time. She assumed the police had taken it when they gathered up the rest of Simon's records.

Carol Judd also said yes, there had been such a billing ledger. She kept it in the top drawer of her desk in the outer office, and used it to send out invoices and statements to patients.

Dr. Diane, when he called back, agreed to make a search for the journal, and then phoned to say she could not find it in the receptionist's desk, her husband's office, or anywhere else.

Boone talked to the Crime Scene Unit men and the detective who had taken all the files from the victim's office. None of them could recall seeing anything resembling a billing ledger.

"All right," Delaney said, "so it is missing. Did the killer grab it? Probably. Why? Because it would show how often he or she had been a late patient."

"I don't get it," Boone said.

"Sure you do. We add up the number of sessions for one particular patient in one month, as noted in the appointment book. Then we compare that to the patient's total billing for the month. If the bill is higher than it should be by, say, a hundred bucks, we can figure that the patient had one unscheduled session."

"Now I get it," Boone said. "But it's all smoke if we can't find the damned ledger."

Delaney learned more about the business practices of psychiatrists from Monica, who, as promised, had talked to her friends who were in analysis.

"They said their doctors generally sent monthly bills," she reported. "Sometimes it gets complicated when the patient has medical insurance that includes psychotherapy. And some companies have health plans for their employees that pay all or part of psychological counseling fees."

"What does the shrink do if the patient can't or won't pay?"

"Gets rid of them," Monica said. "The theory is that if you pay for therapy, it'll seem more valuable to you. If you get it for nothing, that's what you'll think it's worth. Some shrinks will carry patients for a while if they're having temporary money problems. And some shrinks will adjust their fees or accept stretched-out payments. But no psychiatrist is going to work for free, except for charity. Which reminds me, buster—how much are you getting for all the hours you're putting in on the Ellerbee case?"

"Bupkes is what I'm getting," Delaney said.

• • •

THANKSGIVING DAY ARRIVED at just the right time to provide a much needed respite from records, reports, and unanswered questions.

The roast goose, with wild rice and brandied apples, was pronounced a success. Rebecca Boone had brought a rum cake for dessert, soaked with liquor. She had even prepared a little one, without rum, for her husband.

They carried dessert and coffee into the living room, and lounged in soft chairs with plates of cake on their laps and didn't even mention the Ellerbee case—for at least three minutes.

"You'll laugh at me," Rebecca said, "but I think a total stranger did it."

"Brilliant," her husband said. "The doctor wouldn't buzz the downstairs door for a stranger, and there were no signs of forced entry. So how did the stranger get in?"

"That's easy. He waited in the shadows, maybe behind a parked car, and when the late patient arrived, the killer rushed right in after him, threatening him with the hammer or a gun or knife. And that's why," she finished triumphantly, "there were two sets of footprints on the carpeting."

"It's possible," Delaney admitted. "Anything's possible. But why would a stranger want to kill Doctor Ellerbee? There were no drugs on the premises, and nothing was missing—except that damned billing ledger. I can't believe Ellerbee was murdered for that."

"The killer was in love with Diane Ellerbee." Monica said flatly, "and wanted the husband out of the way so he could marry the widow."

"That's sufficient motive," Delaney acknowledged, "if we could find the tiniest scrap of evidence that Doctor Diane had been playing around—which we can't."

"Maybe she wasn't playing around," Monica said. "Maybe the killer had a crazy passion for her that she wasn't even aware of."

"Why *do* people murder?" Rebecca asked.

Delaney shrugged. "A lot of reasons. Greed, fear, anger, jealousy—the list goes on and on. Sometimes the motive is so trivial that you can't believe anyone would kill because of it."

"I had a case once," Sergeant Boone said, "where a guy stabbed his neighbor to death because the man's dog barked too much. And another where a guy shot his wife because she burned a steak while she was broiling it."

"Did you ever have a case," Monica asked, "where a wife killed her husband because he ate sandwiches while leaning over the kitchen sink?"

The Boones laughed. Even Delaney managed a weak grin.

"What do you think the motive was in the Ellerbee case?" Rebecca asked.

"Nothing trivial," Delaney said, "that's for sure. Something deep and complex. What do you think it was, Sergeant?"

"I don't know," Boone said. "But I doubt if it was money."

"Then it must have been love," his wife said promptly. "I'm sure it had something to do with love."

She was a short, plump, jolly woman with a fine complexion and long black hair falling loosely about her shoulders. Her eyes were soft, and there was a cherub's innocence in her expression. She was wearing a tailored flannel suit, but nothing could conceal her robust grace.

Delaney was aware that she treated him with a deferential awe, and it embarrassed him. Monica addressed Boone familiarly as Abner or Ab, but Rebecca wouldn't dare address Delaney as Edward. And since Mr. Delaney was absurdly formal, she simply used no name or title at all.

"Why do you think love was the motive, Rebecca?" he asked her.

"I just feel it."

The Sergeant burst out laughing. "There's hard evidence for you, sir," he said. "Let's take that to the DA tomorrow."

Later that night, when they were preparing for bed, he said to Monica, "Do you agree with Rebecca—that love was the motive for Ellerbee's murder?"

"I certainly think it was involved," she said. "If it wasn't money, it had to be love."

"I wish I could be as sure of anything," he said grouchily, "as you are of everything."

"You asked me, so I told you."

"If you women are right," he said, "maybe we should forget about checking out violence-prone patients and concentrate on love-prone patients."

"Are there such animals?" she asked. "Love-prone people?"

"Of course there are. Men who go from woman to woman, needing love to give their life meaning. And women who fall in love at the drop of a hat— or a pair of pants."

"You're a very vulgar man," she said.

"That's true," he agreed. "Has Rebecca put on weight?"

"Maybe a pound or two."

"She's not pregnant, is she?"

"Of course not. Why do you ask that?"

"I don't know . . . there was a kind of glow about her tonight. I just thought . . ."

"If she were pregnant, she'd have told me."

"I guess. If they are going to have children, they better get cracking—if you'll excuse another vulgarism. Neither of them is getting any younger."

He was sitting on the edge of his bed, dangling one of his shoes. Monica came over, plumped down on his lap, put a warm arm about his neck.

"I wish you and I had children, Edward."

"We do. I think of your girls as mine. And I know you think of my kids as yours."

"It's not the same," she said. "You know that. I mean a child who's truly ours."

"It's a little late for that," he said. "Isn't it?"

"I suppose so," she said sadly. "I'm just dreaming."

"Besides," he added, "would you want the father of your child to be a man who eats sandwiches leaning over the kitchen sink?"

"I apologize," she said, laughing. "I shouldn't have mentioned that in front of company, but I couldn't resist it."

Before she released him, she put her face close to his, stared into his eyes, said, "Do you love me, Edward?"

"I love you. I don't want to think how empty and useless my life would be without you."

She kissed the tip of his nose, and he asked, "What brought that on?"

"All the talk tonight about love and murder," she said. "It bothered me. I just wanted to make sure the two don't necessarily go together."

"They don't," he said slowly. "Not necessarily."

16

•

NO ONE KNEW HOW OR WHERE THE EXPRESSION STARTED, BUT that year everyone in the Department was using "rappaport." Street cops would say, "I get good rappaport on my beat." Detectives would say of a particular snitch, "I got a good rappaport with that guy."

Actually, when you analyzed it, it was a useful portmanteau word. Not only did you have rapport with someone, but you could rap with them. It fit the bill.

Detective Robert Keisman figured to establish a rappaport with Harold Gerber, the Vietnam vet. The black cop, skinny as a pencil and graceful as a fencer, knew what it was like to feel anger eating at your gut like an ulcer; he thought he and Gerber would have a lot in common . . .

. . . Until he met Gerber, and saw how he lived.

"This guy is a real bonzo," he told Jason.

But still, intent on establishing a rappaport, Keisman costumed himself in a manner he thought wouldn't offend the misanthropic vet: worn jeans, old combat boots, a scruffy leather jacket with greasy buckskin fringe, and a crazy cap with limp earflaps.

He didn't mislead Gerber; he told him he was an NYPD dick assigned to the Ellerbee case. And in their first face-to-face, he asked the vet the same questions Delaney and Boone had asked, and got the same answers. But the Spoiler acted like he didn't give a shit whether Gerber was telling the truth or not.

"I'm just putting in my time, man," he told the vet. "They're never going to find out who offed Ellerbee, so why should I bust my hump?"

Still, every day or so Keisman would put away his elegant Giorgio Armani blazer and Ferragamo slacks. Then, dressed like a Greenwich Village floater, he'd go visit Gerber.

"Come on, man," he'd say, "let's get out of this latrine and get us a couple of brews."

The two of them would slouch off to some saloon where they'd drink and talk the day away. Keisman never brought up the subject of Ellerbee's murder, but if Gerber wanted to talk about it, the Spoiler listened sympathetically and kept it going with casual questions.

"I'm nowhere yet," he reported to Jason Two, "but the guy is beginning to open up. I may get something if my liver holds out."

One afternoon he and Gerber were in a real dump on Hudson Street when suddenly the vet said to Keisman, "You're a cop—you ever ice a guy?"

"Once," the Spoiler said. "This junkie was coming at me with a shiv, and I put two in his lungs. I got a commendation for that."

Which was a lie, of course. Keisman had been on the Force for ten years and had never fired his service revolver off the range.

"Once?" Harold Gerber jeered. "Amateur night. I wasted so many in Nam I lost count. After a while it didn't mean a thing."

"Bullshit," the Spoiler said. "I don't care how many you kill, it still gets to you."

"Now that *is* bullshit," the vet said. "I'm telling you, man, you never give it a second thought. See that guy over there—the fat slob at the bar trying to make out with the old whore? I never saw him in my life. But if I was carrying a piece and felt like it, I could walk up to him, plink his eyes out, and never lose a night's sleep."

"You're crapping me."

"I swear," Gerber said, holding up a palm. "That's the way I feel—or don't feel."

"Shit, man, you're a walking time bomb."

"That's right. Doc Ellerbee was trying to grow me a conscience again, but it was heavy going."

"Too bad he was dusted," Keisman said. "Maybe he could have helped you."

"Maybe," Gerber said. "Maybe not."

He went over to the bar and brought back another pitcher of beer. "You pack a gun?"

"Sure," Keisman said. "Regulations."

"Lend it to me for a minute," Harold Gerber said. "I'll put that shithead out of his misery."

"You crazy, man?" the Spoiler said, definitely nervous. "I don't give a fuck what you do, but I lend you my iron and it's my ass."

"Slob," Gerber muttered, glaring at the man at the bar. "If you won't lend me, maybe I'll just go over and kick the shit out of him."

"Come on," Keisman said. "I'm on duty; I'm not even supposed to be drinking, especially with a pistol like you."

"Well . . ." the vet said grudgingly, "if it wasn't for that, I'd put the bastard away. It wouldn't mean a thing to me. If I was alone, I'd just ace him, come back to the table, work on my beer, and wait for the blues to come get me."

"I believe you would."

"You bet your ass I would. It wouldn't be the first time. What if I told you I put Doc Ellerbee down—would you believe me?"

"Did you?"

"If I told you I did, would you believe me?"

"Sure, I'd believe you. Did you do it?"

"I did it," Harold Gerber said. "He was a nosy fucker."

Detective Robert Keisman reported this conversation to Jason, and the two of them decided they better bring it to Delaney in person.

It hadn't been a good day for Delaney. Too many phone calls; too many people leaning on him.

It started right after breakfast when he went into the study to read the morning *Times*. There was a front-page article, with runover, about the declining solution rate for homicides in the New York area. It wasn't cheerful reading.

The lead-in was about the murder of Dr. Simon Ellerbee, and how, after weeks of intensive investigation, the police were no closer to a solution than they had been the day the body was found. Delaney was halfway through the article when the phone rang. "Thorsen," he said aloud and picked up.

"Edward X. Delaney here," he said.

"Edward, this is Ivar. Did you see that thing in the *Times?*"

"Reading it now."

"Son of a bitch!" the Deputy said bitterly. "That's all we need. Did you come to that paragraph about Suarez?"

"Not yet."

"Well, it said that he's Acting Chief of Detectives, and implied that the outcome of the Ellerbee case will probably have a crucial effect on his permanent appointment."

"That's true enough, isn't it? Ivar, what's all the foofaraw about the Ellerbee case? Suarez must have at least a dozen other recent unsolved homicides in his caseload."

"Come on, Edward, you know the answer to that: Ellerbee was *someone*. The moneyed East Side people couldn't care less if some hophead gets knocked off in the South Bronx. But Ellerbee was one of their own kind: an educated professional, wealthy, with a good address. So the powers that be figure if it could happen to him, it could happen to them, and they're running scared. I've already had four phone calls on that *Times* article this morning. That kind of publicity the Department doesn't need."

"Tell me about it."

"Any progress, Edward?"

"No," Delaney said shortly. "A lot of bits and pieces, but nothing earthshaking."

"I don't want to pressure you, but—"

"But you are."

"I just want to make certain you're aware of the time element involved. If this thing isn't cleared up by the first of the year, we might as well forget about it."

"Forget about trying to find Ellerbee's killer?"

"Now you really are acting like Iron Balls. You know what I mean. The Ellerbee file will remain open, of course, but we'll have to pull manpower. And Suarez goes back to his precincts—if he's lucky."

"I get the picture."

"Oh, by the way," the Admiral said breezily, "you may be getting calls from the Ellerbees—the widow and the father. To get them off my back, I suggested that you represent our best chance of solving the case."

"Thank you very much, Ivar. I really appreciate your kind cooperation."

"I thought you would," the Deputy said, laughing. "I'll keep in touch, Edward."

"Please," Delaney said, "don't bother."

The two Ellerbees called all right. Both were in a surly mood to start with, and even surlier when they hung up.

Delaney would give them no comfort whatsoever. He said several leads were being followed, but no one had been identified as a definite suspect, and a great deal of work remained to be done.

"When do you think you'll have some good news?" Henry Ellerbee demanded.

"I have no idea," Delaney said.

"When do you think you'll find the killer?" Dr. Diane Ellerbee said sharply.

"I have no idea," Delaney said.

The three phone calls irritated him so much that he was tempted to seek the solace of a good sandwich—but he resisted. Instead, he went to his files, driving himself to read through the records one more time.

The purpose here was to immerse himself in the minutiae of the case. At this stage he could not allow himself to judge some details significant and some meaningless. All had value: from the hammer blows to Ellerbee's eyes to Sylvia Mae Otherton's use of a Ouija board.

Now there was a curious coincidence, he suddenly realized. The victim had been deliberately blinded, and the Ouija planchette had spelled out "blind." What did that mean—if anything? He began to feel that he was sinking deeper into the irrational world of Ellerbee's patients.

Hundreds of facts, rumors, and guesses had been accumulated, with more coming in every day. What detection came down to, in a case of this nature, was a matter of choice. Selection: that was the detective's secret—and the poet's.

He was bleary-eyed when Jason and Keisman arrived, providing a welcome break.

Delaney listened carefully as the Spoiler gave a complete accounting of his most recent conversation with Harold Gerber.

When the black detective finished, Delaney stared at him thoughtfully.

"What's your take?" Delaney finally asked. "You think he was telling the truth or was it just drunken bragging?"

"Sir, I can't give you a definite answer, but I think it's a big possible. That guy is bonkers."

"So far we've had at least ten fake confessions on the Ellerbee homicide. Suarez's men have checked them all out. Zero, zip, zilch. Just crazies and people wanting publicity. But we've got to take this one seriously."

"Pull him in?" Jason suggested.

"No," Delaney said. "If he turns out to be clean, that will be the end of Keisman's contact with him. He'll know who spilled the confession."

"You can say that again," the Spoiler agreed. "And I really don't enjoy the idea of that whacko being sore at me."

"Then you'll have to check out his confession yourself. Find out what time he got there. Did he have an appointment? Was he the late patient? How did he get up to Ellerbee's office: subway, bus, taxi? He knows the victim was killed with a ball peen hammer because Boone and I asked him if he owned one and he said no. So ask him where he got the hammer, and check it out. Then ask him what he did with the hammer after he killed Ellerbee, and check *that* out. Ask him how many times he hit the victim and how Ellerbee fell. Facedown or -up? Finally, ask him if he did anything else to the corpse. That business of the two hammer blows to the eyes was never released to the media; only the killer would know about it. I could be wrong, but I think Gerber is just blowing smoke. He may have thought about chilling Ellerbee, maybe dreamed about it, but I don't think he did it. He's so fucked up that he'd admit kidnapping Judge Crater if it occurred to him."

"I feel sorry for the guy," Jason said.

"Sure," Delaney said, "but don't feel *too* sorry. Remember, he could be our pigeon. But what interests me even more than the confession was what he wanted to do to the fat guy at the bar. Keisman, you think he meant it?"

"Absolutely," the Spoiler said immediately. "I'm convinced of that. If I hadn't calmed him down and got him talking about other things, he'd have jumped the guy."

"Well, he's done it before," Delaney said. "The man is a walking disaster. Jason, I think you better work on this, too. Check out that confession both ways from the middle. Keisman, were you able to find out where Gerber was drinking the night of the murder?"

"Negative, sir. I talked to three or four bartenders who know him—they all say he's strictly bad news—but none of them can remember whether or not he came in that Friday night. After all, it was weeks ago."

Delaney nodded, looking down at his clasped hands. He was quiet a long moment, then he spoke in a low voice without raising his eyes.

"Do me a favor, Jason. There's got to be a counseling service for Vietnam veterans somewhere in town. A therapy clinic maybe, or just a place where he can go and talk with other vets. See if you can get some help for him, will you? I hate to see that guy go down the drain. Even if he didn't zap Ellerbee, he's heading for bad trouble."

"Yes, sir," Jason Two said. "I'll try."

After they left, Delaney went back to the study and added a report on Harold Gerber's confession to his file. Another fact or fantasy to be considered. He thought it was fantasy, not because Gerber wasn't capable of murder but because Delaney just couldn't believe the Ellerbee case would break that easily and that simply.

Maybe, he admitted ruefully, he didn't want it to. It would be as disappointing as a game called off because of rain. If he was absolutely honest, he'd concede he was enjoying the investigation. Which proved there was life in the old dog yet.

• • •

ANOTHER PERSON WHO was enjoying the search for Simon Ellerbee's killer was Detective Helen K. Venable. For the first time in her career she was on her own, not saddled with a male partner who insisted on giving her unwanted and unneeded advice or asked her raunchy questions about her sex life.

Also, she felt a strong affinity for Joan Yesell. Venable was younger than the Yesell woman, but she too had a bitch of a mother, lacked a special man in her life, and sometimes felt so lonely she could cry—but not try to slash her wrists; things never got that bad.

She had talked to Joan twice, and thought they hit it off well, even though that bulldog mother was present at both meetings and kept interrupting. Venable asked the same questions that Delaney and Boone had asked, and got the same answers. She also asked a few extras.

"Joan," she said, "did you ever meet Simon Ellerbee's wife, Diane?"

"I met her once," Yesell said nervously. "While I was waiting for my appointment."

"I hear she's stunning. Is she?"

"Oh, yes! She's beautiful."

"In a hard sort of way," Mrs. Blanche Yesell said.

"Oh?" the detective said, turning to the mother. "Then you've met her, too?"

"Well . . . no," Mrs. Yesell said, flustered. "But from what my Joan says . . ."

"I've never seen Diane," Venable said to the daughter. "Can you describe her?"

"Tall," Joan Yesell said, "slender and very elegant. A natural blonde. She was wearing her hair up when I met her. She looked like a queen—just lovely."

"Humph," Mrs. Yesell said. "She's not so much."

Following orders, Venable included this little byplay in her report to Boone, although she didn't think it meant a thing. Neither did the Sergeant, who initialed the report and forwarded it to Delaney, who made no judgment but filed the report away.

On the Friday night following Thanksgiving, restless in her Flatbush apartment and bored with her mother's chittering about the latest scandal in the *National Enquirer,* Helen decided to drive over to Chelsea and have another talk with Joan Yesell.

She phoned first, but the line was busy and she didn't bother calling again. She got into her little Honda and headed for New York—which was what most Brooklynites called Manhattan. She had nothing special in mind to ask Joan Yesell; it was just a fishing expedition. And also, she was lonely.

Helen was happy to find Mrs. Yesell out. Joan seemed delighted to see the detective. She made them a pot of tea and brought out a plate of powdered doughnuts. They were comfortable with each other and chatted easily about what they had eaten for Thanksgiving dinner. Then Helen asked, "How's the wrist coming along?"

"Better, thank you," Joan said. "I'm getting strength back in my fingers. I exercise by squeezing a rubber ball. The doctor said he'll take the bandage off next week, but he wants me to wear an elastic strap for a while."

"The next time you feel like doing something like that, will you call me first?"

"All right," Joan said faintly.

"Promise?"

"I promise."

Then the talk got around to tyrannical mothers, and they traded anecdotes, each trying to outdo the other with tales of outrageous maternal despotism.

"I've got to get my own place," Helen said, "or I'm going to go right up the wall. The only trouble is, I can't afford it. You know what rents are like today."

"I'd love to get out, too," Joan said forlornly. Then she suddenly brightened. "Listen, I make a good salary. Do you think we might take a place together?"

"That's an idea . . ." the detective said cautiously. She liked Joan and thought they would get along, but even if she were ruled out as a suspect it was possible her problems would be too severe for Helen to live with.

Still, they talked for a while about where they'd like to live (Manhattan), the kind of place they'd need (preferably a two-bedroom apartment), and how much rent they could afford.

"I'll need a desk," Venable said. "For my typewriter and reports."

"I'll want at least one cat," Joan said.

"I have some furniture. My bed is mine."

"I don't own any of these things," Joan said, looking around at the over-stuffed apartment. "And even if I did, I wouldn't want any of it for my own place. Our own place. I hate all this; it's so suffocating. You should see the Ellerbees' home; it's beautiful!"

"His office, too?"

"Well, that was very—you know, sort of empty. I mean, it was all right, but very white and efficient. Almost cold."

"Was he like that?"

"Oh, no. Doctor Simon was a very warm man. Very human."

"Which reminds me," Helen said, "if you and I ever do get an apartment together, what about men? Would you object if I brought a man home—for the night?"

Yesell hesitated. "Not if we had separate bedrooms. Do you do that often?"

"Bring a guy home to my place? Are you kidding? If I did that, my mother would have one of her famous nosebleeds. No, the only times I've been with men have been at their place, in cars, and once at a motel."

Joan said nothing, but lowered her eyes. She touched the bandage on her left wrist lightly. The two, like enough to pass as sisters, sat in silence awhile, the detective staring at the bowed head of the other woman.

"Joan," she said gently, "you're not a virgin, are you?"

"Oh, no," Yesell said quickly. "I've been with a man."

"A man? One man?"

"No. More than one."

"But it never lasted?"

Joan shook her head.

"No," Helen said, "it never does—the bastards!" Then, because she could see that Joan was depressed by this kind of talk, she changed the subject. "I wish I had your figure. But I've got a weight problem and these doughnuts aren't helping."

They talked about diets and aerobic dancing and jogging for a while and then got into clothes and how difficult it was to find anything nice at a decent price. After about an hour, the doughnut plate being empty, the detective rose to leave.

"Take care of yourself, kiddo," she said, leaning forward to kiss Joan's cheek. "I expect I'll be around again—it's my job—but don't be bashful about calling me if you're feeling blue. Maybe we could have a pizza together or take in a movie or something."

"I'd like that," Joan said gratefully. "Thank you for dropping by, Helen."

At the door, the detective, tugging her knitted cap down around her ears, said, "Where's Mama tonight—sowing some wild oats?"

"Oh, no," Joan said, laughing, "nothing like that. She's at her bridge club. They're neighborhood women, and they get together every Friday night without fail. It usually breaks up around eleven, eleven-thirty."

"I wish my old lady would get out of the house occasionally," Helen grumbled. "One night without her is like a weekend in the country."

She was halfway down the stairs when it hit her, and she started trembling. She didn't stop shaking until she got into the Honda, locked the doors, and took a deep breath. She sat there in the darkness, gripping the wheel, thinking of the implications of what she had just heard.

She knew Joan Yesell's alibi: She had come home from work at about

6:00 on the Friday night Simon Ellerbee was killed, and had never left the house. Her mother had said yes, that was true.

But now here was mommy dearest out to play bridge every Friday night and not returning until 11:00 or 11:30. That would give Joan plenty of time to get up to East 84th Street and get home again before her mother returned.

And why was Mrs. Blanche Yesell lying? Because she was trying to protect "my Joan."

Wait a minute, Detective Venable warned herself. If Mama's bridge club was like most of them, they'd rotate meeting places, with each player acting as hostess in turn. Maybe on the murder night they all met and played bridge in the Yesells' apartment.

But if that was so, why hadn't Joan or her mother mentioned it? It would have given them three more witnesses to Joan's presence that night.

No, Mrs. Blanche Yesell had gone elsewhere for her weekly bridge game.

But what if there was no game that night? It was raining so hard, maybe they decided to call it off, and Mrs. Yesell really was at home, playing two-handed bridge with her daughter.

Helen leaned forward, resting her forehead on the rim of the steering wheel, trying to figure out what to do next. First of all, she wasn't about to throw poor Joan to the wolves. Not yet. Second of all, she wasn't about to turn over a juicy lead like this to one of the men and let him grab the glory.

It had happened to her too many times in the past. She'd uncover something hot in an investigation and they'd take the follow-up away from her, saying in the kindliest way imaginable, "Helen, that's nice going, but we'll want a guy with more experience to handle it."

Bull*shit!* It was all hers, and this time she was going to track it down herself. Wasn't that what a detective was supposed to do?

She decided not to submit a report to Boone on the night's conversation with Joan Yesell or even mention the mother's Friday-night bridge club and how it was possible she was lying in confirming her daughter's alibi. When Detective Venable checked it all out, *then* she'd report it. Until that time, all those more experienced guys could go screw.

• • •

THAT SAME EVENING, one of those more experienced guys, Edward X. Delaney, was in a mellow mood. His irritation of the afternoon had disappeared with a dinner of pot roast, potato pancakes, and buttered carrots—all sluiced down his gullet with two bottles of dark Löwenbräu.

Monica leaned forward to pat his vested stomach. "You ate everything on your plate except the flowers," she said. "Feeling better?"

"A lot better," he affirmed. "Let's just leave everything for now and have our coffee in the living room."

"There's nothing to leave. We went through everything like a plague of locusts."

"I remember my mother used to say a good digestion is a blessing from heaven. Was she ever right."

In the living room, Monica said, "You don't talk much about your mother."

"Well, she died when I was five; I told you that. So my memories are rather dim. I have some old snaps of her in the attic. I'll dig them out one of these days. A lovely woman; you'll see."

"What did she die of, Edward?"

"In childbirth. So did the baby. My brother."

"Was he baptized?"

"Of course. Terence. Terry."

"What was your father's first name?"

"Marion—believe it or not. He never remarried. So you and I are both only children."

"But we have each other."

"Thank God for that."

"Edward, why don't you go to church anymore?"

"Monica, why don't you go to the synagogue anymore?"

They both smiled.

"A fine couple of heathens we are," he said.

"Not so," she said. "I believe in God—don't you?"

"Of course," he said. "Sometimes I think He'd like to be Deputy Commissioner Thorsen."

"You nut," she said, laughing. "Want to watch the news on TV?"

"No, thanks. I think I'll spend a nice relaxed evening for a change. I need a—"

The phone rang.

He got heavily to his feet. "There goes my nice relaxed evening," he said. "Bet on it. I'll take it in the study."

It was Dr. Diane Ellerbee.

"Mr. Delaney," she said, "I want to apologize for the way I spoke to you this morning. I realize you're volunteering your time, and I'm afraid I was rather hard on you."

"Not at all. I know how concerned you are. Sometimes it's tough to be patient in a situation like this."

"I'm driving up to Brewster tonight," she said. "To spend the weekend. There's something I'd like to tell you that may or may not help your investigation. Would it be possible for me to stop by your home for a few minutes?"

"Of course. We've finished dinner, so come whenever you like."

"Thank you," she said. "I'll be there shortly."

He went back into the living room and reported the conversation to Monica.

"Oh, lord," she said. "We've got to get the kitchen cleaned up. Are there fresh towels in the hall bathroom? Do I have time to change?"

"To what?" he said. "You look fine just the way you are. And yes, there are fresh towels in the bathroom. Take it easy, babe; this isn't a visit from the Queen of England."

But by the time Dr. Diane arrived, the kitchen was cleaned up, the living room straightened, and they were sitting stiffly, determined not to be awed by the visitor—and not quite succeeding.

Diane Ellerbee was graciousness personified. She complimented them on their charming home, unerringly selected the finest piece in the living room to admire—a small Duncan Phyfe desk—and assured Delaney that the vodka gimlet he mixed for her was the best she had ever tasted.

In fact, she played the grande dame so broadly that he made a cop's instant judgment: The woman was nervous and wanted something. Having concluded that, he relaxed and watched her with a faint smile as she chatted with Monica.

She was wearing a sweater and skirt of mushroom-colored wool, with high boots of buttery leather. No jewelry, other than a plain wedding band, and very little makeup. Her flaxen hair was down, and her classic features seemed softened, more vulnerable.

"Mr. Delaney," she said, turning to him, "was that list of patients I gave you any help?"

"A great deal. They are all being investigated."

"I hope you didn't tell them I gave you their names?"

"Of course not. We merely said we're questioning all your husband's patients—which is true—and they accepted that."

"I'm glad to hear it. I still don't feel right about picking out those six, but I wanted to help any way I could. Do you think one of them could have done it?"

"I think possibly they are all capable of murder. But then, a lot of so-called normal people are, too."

"I really don't know exactly how you go about investigating people," she said with a confused little laugh. "Question them, I suppose."

"Oh, yes. And their families, friends, neighbors, employers, and so forth. We go back to them several times, asking the same questions over and over, trying to spot discrepancies."

"Sounds like a boring job."

"No," he said, "it isn't."

"Edward has the patience of a saint," Monica said.

"And the luck of the devil," he added. "I hope."

The doctor laughed politely. "Does luck really have much to do with catching a criminal?"

"Sometimes," he said, nodding. "Usually it's a matter of knocking on enough doors. But sometimes chance and accident take a hand, and you get a break you didn't expect. The criminal can't control luck, can he?"

"But doesn't it work the other way, too? I mean, doesn't luck sometimes favor the criminal?"

"Occasionally," he agreed. "But it would be a very stupid criminal who depended on it. 'The best laid schemes . . .' and so on and so on." He turned to Monica. "Who said that?" he asked her, smiling.

"Shakespeare?" she ventured.

"Robert Burns," he said. "Shakespeare didn't say *everything*." He turned to Diane Ellerbee. "Now it's your chance. Who wrote, 'O what a tangled web we weave, when first we practice to deceive!'?"

"That *was* Shakespeare," she said.

"Sir Walter Scott," he said, still smiling. "Did you say you had something to tell me, doctor?"

"Oh, you'll probably think it's silly," she said, "but it's been bothering me, so I thought I'd tell you anyway. The first time you and Sergeant Boone came to see me, you asked a lot of questions, and I answered them to the best of my ability. After you left, I tried to remember everything I had said, to make sure I hadn't unintentionally led you astray."

She paused.

"And?" he said.

"Well, it probably means nothing, but you asked if I had noticed any change in Simon over the last six months or year, and I said no. But then after thinking it over, I realized there had been a change. Perhaps it was so gradual that I really wasn't aware of it."

"But now you feel there was a change?" Delaney asked.

"Yes, I do. Thinking over this past year, I realize Simon had become— well, distant and preoccupied is the only way I can describe it. He had been very concerned about his patients, and I suppose at the time I thought it was just overwork that was bothering him. But yes, there was a change in him. I don't imagine it means anything, but it disturbed me that I hadn't given you a strictly accurate answer, so I thought I better tell you."

"I'm glad you did," Delaney said gravely. "Like you, I don't know if it means anything or not, but every little bit helps."

"Well!" Diane Ellerbee said, smiling brightly. "Now I do feel better, getting that off my conscience."

She drained her gimlet, set the glass aside, and rose. They stood up. She offered her hand to Monica.

"Thank you so much for letting me barge in," she said. "You have a lovely, lovely home. I wish the two of you would come up to Brewster soon and see our place. It's not at its best in winter, but Simon and I worked so hard to make it something special, I'd like to have you see it. Could you do that?"

"We'd be delighted," Monica said promptly. "Thank you."

"Let's wait for a weekend when no blizzards are predicted," Diane Ellerbee said, laughing. "The first good Saturday—all right?"

"We don't have a car," Delaney said. "Would you object if Sergeant Boone and his wife drove us up?"

"Object? I'd love it! I have a marvelous cook, and Simon and I laid down some good wines. I enjoy having company, and frankly it's lonely up there now. So let's all plan on getting together."

"Whenever you say," Monica said. "I'm sorry you have to leave so soon. Drive carefully."

"I always do," Dr. Ellerbee said lightly. "Good night, all."

Delaney locked and bolted the front door behind her.

"What an intelligent woman!" Monica said when he came back to the living room. "Isn't she, Edward?"

"She is that."

"You'd like to see her Brewster home, wouldn't you?"

"Very much. The Boones will drive us up. We'll make a day of it."

"What she said about her husband changing—does that mean anything?"

"I have no idea."

"She really is beautiful, isn't she?"

"So beautiful," he said solemnly, "that she scares me."

"Thanks a lot, buster," she said. "I obviously don't scare you."

"Obviously," he said, and headed toward the study door.

"Hey," Monica said, "I thought you weren't going to work tonight."

"Just for a while," he said, frowning. "Some things I want to check."

17

•

DETECTIVE BENJAMIN CALAZO WAS A MONTH AWAY FROM RETIREMENT and dreading it. He came from a family of policemen. His father had been a cop, his younger brother was a cop, and two uncles had been cops. The NYPD wasn't just a job, it was a *life*.

Calazo didn't fish, play golf, or collect stamps. He had no hobbies at all, and no real interests outside the Department. What the hell was he going to do—move the wife to a mobile home in Lakeland, Florida, and play shuffleboard for the rest of his days?

The Ellerbee case seemed like a good way to cap his career. He had worked with Sergeant Boone before, and knew he was an okay guy. Also, Boone's

father had been a street cop killed in the line of duty. Calazo had gone to the
funeral, and you didn't forget things like that.

The detective had asked to be assigned to Isaac Kane for the reason he
stated: His nephew was retarded, and he thought he knew something about
handling handicapped kids. Calazo had three married daughters, and sometimes he wondered if they weren't retarded when he was forced to have
dinner with his sons-in-law—a trio of losers, Benny thought; not a cop in
the lot.

His first meeting with Isaac Kane went reasonably well. Calazo sat with
him for almost three hours at the Community Center, admiring the kid's
pastel landscapes and talking easily about this and that.

Every once in a while Calazo would spring a question about Dr. Simon
Ellerbee. Isaac showed no hesitation in answering, and the subject didn't seem
to upset him. He told the detective pretty much what he had told Delaney
and Boone—which didn't amount to a great deal.

The boy didn't display any confusion until Calazo asked him about his
activities on the night of the murder.

"It was a Friday, Isaac," Calazo said. "What did you do on that night?"

"I was here until the Center closed. Ask Mrs. Freylinghausen; she'll tell
you."

"Okay, I'll ask her. And after the Center closed, what did you do then?"

"I went home."

"Uh-huh. You live right around the corner, don't you, Isaac? So I guess
you got there around nine-five or so. Is that correct?"

Kane didn't look at the detective, but concentrated on adding foliage to a
tree in his landscape.

"Well, uh, it was probably later. I walked around awhile."

"That was a very rainy night, Isaac. A bad storm. You didn't walk about
in that, did you?"

"I don't remember!" Kane said, breaking one of his chalks and flinging it
away angrily. "I don't know why you're asking me all these questions, and
I'm not going to answer any more. You're just—" He began to stutter un-
intelligibly.

"All right," Benny said mildly, "you don't have to answer any more questions. I just thought you'd want to help us find out who killed Doctor
Simon."

Kane was silent.

"Hey," the detective said, "I'm getting hungry. How about you? There's
a fast-food joint on the corner. How's about I pick up a couple of burgers
and coffee for us and bring them back here?"

"Okay," Isaac Kane said.

Calazo brought the food and they had lunch together. An old lady wheeled
up her chair and stared at the detective with ravenous eyes. He gave her his

slice of dill pickle. He didn't mention Ellerbee again, but got Kane talking about his pastels and why he did only landscapes.

"They're pretty landscapes," Isaac explained. "Not like around here. Everything is clean and peaceful."

"Sure it is," the detective said. "But I notice you don't put in any people."

"No," Kane said, shaking his head. "No people. Those places belong to me."

Calazo checked with Mrs. Freylinghausen. She confirmed that Isaac Kane came in every day and stayed until the Community Center closed at nine o'clock. The detective thanked her and walked around the corner to Kane's home, timing himself. Even at a slow stroll it took less than two minutes.

Kane lived with his mother in the basement apartment of a dilapidated brownstone on West 78th Street. It was next to an ugly furniture warehouse with rusty steel doors for trucks and sooty windows on the upper floors. Both buildings were marred with graffiti and had black plastic bags of garbage stacked in front. Some of the bags had burst or had been slashed open.

Benjamin Calazo could understand why Isaac Kane wanted to draw only pretty places, clean and peaceful.

He walked cautiously down three crumbling steps to a littered doorway. The name over the bell was barely legible. He rang, and waited. Nothing. Rang again—a good long one this time. A tattered lace curtain was yanked aside from a streaky window; a gargoyle glared at him.

Calazo held his ID close to the window. The woman tried to focus, then she disappeared. He waited hopefully. In a moment he heard the sounds of locks opening, a chain lifted. The door opened.

"Mrs. Kane?" he asked.

"Yeah," she said in a whiskey-blurred voice. "What the hell do you want?"

A boozer, he thought immediately. That's all I need.

"Detective Benjamin Calazo, NYPD," he said, "I'd like to talk to you about your son."

"He ain't here."

"I know he's not here," Calazo said patiently. "I just left him at the Center. I want to talk to you *about* him."

"What's he done now?" she demanded.

"Nothing, as far as I know."

"He's not right in the head. He's not responsible for anything."

"Look," the detective said. "Be nice. Don't keep me standing out here in the cold. How's about letting me in for a few questions? It won't take long."

She stood aside grudgingly. He stepped in, closed the door, took off his hat. The place smelled like a subway urinal—only the piss was eighty proof. The half-empty whiskey bottle was on the floor, a stack of paper cups beside it.

She saw him looking. "I got a cold," she said. "I been sick."

"Yeah."

She tried a smile. Her face looked like a punched pillow. "Want a belt?" she asked.

"No, thanks. But you go ahead."

She sat on the lumpy couch, poured herself a drink, slugged it down. She crumpled the cup in her fist, threw it negligently toward a splintered wicker wastebasket. Bull's-eye.

"Nice shot," Calazo said.

"I've had a lot of practice," she said, showing a mouthful of tarnished teeth.

"Is Mr. Kane around?" the detective asked. "Your husband?"

"Yeah, he's around. Around the world. Probably in Hong Kong by now, the son of a bitch. Good riddance."

"Then you and your son live alone?"

"So what?"

"You on welfare?"

"Financial assistance," she said haughtily. "We're entitled. I'm disabled and Isaac can't hold a job. You an investigator?"

"Not for welfare," Calazo said. "Your son goes to the Community Center every day?"

"I guess so."

"Don't you know?"

"He's of age; he can go anywhere he likes."

"What time does he leave for the Center?"

"I don't know; I sleep late. When I wake up, he's gone. What the hell is all this about?"

"You're not asleep when he gets home from the Center, are you? What time does he get here?"

She peered at him through narrowed eyes, and he knew she was calculating what lies she could get away with. Not that there was any need to lie, but this woman would never tell the truth to anyone in authority if she could help it.

She stalled for time by taking another shot of the booze, crumpling the paper cup, tossing it toward the wastebasket. This time it fell short.

"No," she said finally, "I'm not asleep in the evening. He gets home at different times."

"Like what?"

"After nine o'clock."

"How much after nine?"

"Different times."

"Now I'll tell you what this is about," the old gumshoe said tonelessly. "This is about a murder, and if you keep jerking me around, I'm going to run your ass down to the drunk tank so fast your feet won't touch the ground.

You can dry out with all those swell people in there until you decide to answer my questions straight. Is that what you want?"

Her face twisted, and she began to cry. "You got no right to talk to me like that."

"I'll talk to you any goddamned way I please," Calazo said coldly. "You don't mean shit to me."

He swooped suddenly, grabbed her bottle of whiskey, headed for the stained sink in a kitchenette so malodorous he almost gagged.

She came to her feet with a howl. "What are you doing?" she screamed.

"I'm going to dump your booze," he said. "Then go through this swamp and break every fucking jug I can find."

"Please," she said, "don't do—I can't—the check isn't due for—I'm an old woman. What do you want to hurt an old woman for?"

"You're an old drunk," he said. "An old smelly drunk. No wonder your son gets out of the house every day." He held the whiskey bottle over the sink. "What time does he get home at night?"

"At nine. A few minutes after nine."

"Every night?"

"Yes, every night."

He tilted the bottle, spilled a few drops.

She wailed. "Except on Fridays," she said in a rush. "He's late on Fridays. Then he comes home at ten, ten-thirty—like that."

"Why is he late on Fridays? Where does he go?"

"I don't know. I swear to God I don't."

"Haven't you asked him?"

"I have, honest to God I have, but he won't tell me."

He stared at her a long time, then handed her the whiskey bottle. She took it with trembling claws, hugged it to her, cradling it like an infant.

"Thank you for your cooperation, Mrs. Kane," Detective Calazo said.

Outside, he walked over to Broadway, breathing deeply, trying to get rid of the stench of that shithouse. It wasn't the worst stink he had ever smelled in his years on the Force, but it was bad enough.

He found a sidewalk telephone kiosk that worked and called his wife.

"I'm coming home for dinner, hon," he reported, "but I'll have to go out again for a while. You want me to pick up anything?"

"We're having knockwurst," she said. "There's a little mustard left, but maybe you better get a new jar. The hot stuff you like."

"Okay," he said cheerfully. "See you soon."

That night, warmed by a good solid meal (knockwurst, baked beans, sauerkraut), Calazo was back at 79th Street and Broadway by 8:30. He drove around, looking for a parking space, and ended up pulling into the driveway of the warehouse next to the Kanes' brownstone, ignoring a big sign: NO PARKING OR STANDING AT ANY TIME.

He locked up carefully and walked back to the Community Center, taking up his station across the street. He trudged up and down to keep his feet from getting numb, but never took his eyes off the lighted windows of the Center for more than a few seconds.

The Medical Examiner had said that Simon Ellerbee had died at 9:00 P.M. But that was an estimate; it could be off by a half hour either way. Maybe more.

So if Isaac Kane had left the Community Center at nine o'clock on that Friday night, he could have made it across town to East 84th Street, bashed in Ellerbee's skull, and been home by 10:00, 10:30. Easily. Benny Calazo didn't think the boy did it, but he *could* have.

The lights in the Center began to darken. Calazo leaned against a mailbox, chewing on a cold cigar, and waited. A lot of people came out, one on crutches, two using walkers. Then Isaac appeared.

The detective crossed the street and tailed him. It didn't take long. Isaac went directly home. Calazo got into his parked car and watched. He sat there until 10:30, freezing his buns. Then he drove home.

That was on a Wednesday night. The detective spent Thursday morning and afternoon checking out Kane at the clinic where he had met with Dr. Ellerbee. They wouldn't show him Kane's file, but Calazo talked to several people who knew him.

They confirmed that Isaac was usually a quiet, peaceable kid, but had occasional fits of uncontrollable violence during which he physically attacked doctors and nurses. Once he had to be forcibly sedated.

On Thursday night, Calazo went through the same drill again: tailing Kane home from the Community Center, then waiting to see if he came out of the brownstone again. Nothing.

He took up his post a little earlier on Friday evening, figuring if anything was going to happen, it would be on that night.

Isaac Kane left the Center a few minutes before nine o'clock. Calazo got a good look at him from across the street. He was all dolled up, with a tweed cap, clean parka, denim jeans. He was carrying a package under his arm. It looked like one of his pastels wrapped in brown paper.

He turned in the opposite direction, away from his home, and Calazo went after him. He tailed Kane uptown on Broadway to 83rd Street, and west toward the river. Isaac crossed West End Avenue, then went into a neat brownstone halfway down the block.

The detective slowed his pace, then sauntered by the brownstone, noting the address. Kane was not in the vestibule or lobby. Calazo took up his patrol across the street, lighting a cigar, and walking heavily up and down to keep the circulation going. He wondered how many miles he had plodded like this in his lifetime as a cop. Well, in another month it would be all over.

Kane came out of the brownstone about 10:15. He was no longer carrying the package. Calazo tailed him back to his 78th Street home. When Isaac was inside, the detective went home, too.

He was out early the next morning and parked near the neat brownstone on West 83rd Street a few minutes before 8:00 A.M. He figured that most people would be home at that hour on a Saturday. He went into the vestibule and examined the bell plate. There were twelve apartments.

He began ringing, starting at the top and working his way down. Every time the squawk box clicked on and someone said, "Who is it?," Calazo would say, "I'd like to talk to you about Isaac Kane." He got answers like "Who?" "Never heard of him." "Get lost." "You have the wrong apartment." And a lot of disconnects.

Finally he pushed the 4-B bell. A woman's voice asked, "Who is it?," the detective said, "I'd like to talk to you about Isaac Kane," and the woman replied anxiously, "Has anything happened to him?" Bingo. The names opposite the bell were Mr. & Mrs. Judson Beele and Evelyn Packard.

"This is Detective Benjamin Calazo of the New York Police Department," he said slowly and distinctly. "It is important that I speak to you concerning Isaac Kane. Will you let me come up, please? I will show you my identification."

There was a long silence. Calazo waited patiently. He was good at that. Then the door lock buzzed, he pushed his way in, and clumped up the stairs to the fourth floor.

There was a man standing in the hallway outside apartment 4-B. He was wearing a flannel bathrobe and carpet slippers. A Caspar Milquetoast with rimless glasses, a fringe of fluff around his pale scalp, and some hair on his upper lip that yearned to be a mustache and didn't quite make it. Calazo thought a strong wind would blow the guy away.

He proffered his ID and the man examined the wallet carefully before he handed it back.

"I'm Judson Beele," he said nervously. "What's this all about? You mentioned Isaac Kane to my wife."

"Could I come in for a few minutes?" the detective asked pleasantly. "It shouldn't take long."

There were two women in the warm, comfortable living room. Both were in bathrobes and slippers. A hatchet-faced blonde, smoking a cigarette in a long holder, was standing. The other, younger, with softer features, was in a wheelchair. There was an afghan across her lap, concealing her legs.

Beele made the introductions. The blonde was his wife, Teresa. The girl in the wheelchair was his wife's sister, Evelyn Packard. Calazo bowed to both women, smiling. Like most veteran detectives, he knew when to play Mr. Nasty and when to play Mr. Nice. He reckoned niceness would do for this household. That wife looked like she had a spine.

"I want to apologize for disturbing you at this hour," he said smoothly. "But it's a matter of some importance concerning Isaac Kane."

"Is Isaac all right?" a jittery Evelyn Packard said. "He hasn't been in an accident, has he?"

"Oh, no," Calazo said, "nothing like that. He's fine, as far as I know. Could I sit down for a few minutes?"

"Of course," the wife said. "Let me have your hat and coat. We were just having coffee. Would you care for a cup?"

"That would be fine. Black, please."

"Judson," she said, "bring the coffee."

Calazo made a few comments about the weather and what an attractive home they had. Meanwhile he was taking them in, trying to figure the tensions there, and also eyeballing the apartment. The first things he noted were five of Isaac's pastels on the walls. Someone had done a nice job framing them.

"Good coffee," he said. "Thank you. Well, about Isaac Kane . . . I notice you have some of his drawings here. Pretty things, aren't they?"

"They're beautiful!" Evelyn burst out. "Isaac is a genius."

Her sister laughed lightly. "Picasso he ain't, dear," she advised. "They're really quite commercial. But remarkable, I admit, considering his—his background."

"I've been thinking of buying one of his things," the detective said. "Would you mind if I asked how much you paid for these? Without the frames."

"Oh, we didn't buy them," Teresa Beele said. "They were gifts to Evelyn. Isaac is madly in love with her."

"Teresa!" her sister said, blushing. "You know that's not so."

"It is so. I see how he looks at you."

"Isaac is a lonely boy," Judson Beele said in a troubled voice. "I don't think he has many friends. Evelyn is . . ." He didn't finish.

Calazo turned to the young woman in the wheelchair. "How did you meet him, Miss Packard?"

"At the Center. Teresa took me there once, and I never want to go again; it's so depressing. But I met Isaac, and he asked if he could come visit me."

"A perfect match," her sister murmured, fitting another cigarette into the long holder.

Bitch, Calazo thought. "And how long have you known him, Miss Packard?"

"Oh, it's been about six months now. Hasn't it, Judson?"

"About," her brother-in-law said, nodding. Then to Calazo: "Can you tell us what this is all about?"

"In a minute," the detective said. "Does he come to visit you every Friday night, Miss Packard?"

"He comes a-courting," Teresa said blithely, and Calazo realized he could learn to hate that woman with very little effort.

"Yes," the girl in the wheelchair said, lifting her chin. "He visits on Friday night."

"*Every* Friday night? Hasn't he ever missed? Come to see you some other night?"

She shook her head. "No. Always on Friday night." She looked at the other two. "Isn't that right?"

They agreed. Isaac Kane visited only on Friday nights. Every Friday night. For almost six months.

"You're always here when he comes?" Calazo asked the Beeles. "You're never out—to a movie or somewhere else?"

"We're here," the wife said grimly. "I wouldn't leave Evelyn alone with that person. Considering his mental condition, I think it best that we be present."

"Teresa!" her sister said angrily. "Isaac has always been perfectly well behaved."

"Still, you never know with people like that."

"Look," Calazo said. "There was a very minor robbery in the brownstone where Kane lives. It doesn't amount to much, but it's my job to check the whereabouts of everyone in the building at the time it happened. It was four weeks ago, at about nine-thirty on a Friday night."

"He was here," Evelyn said, promptly and firmly. "He couldn't have done it because he was here. Besides, Isaac wouldn't do anything like that."

"All of you would swear that he was here?" the detective said, looking from one to another.

They nodded.

It wasn't complete. It wasn't absolutely perfect. But it never was. There were always possibilities: forgetfulness, deliberate lying, unknown motives. But it would take a hundred years to track down everything, and even then there might be blanks, questions, doubts.

Calazo couldn't recall ever clearing a case where every goddamned thing was tied up neatly. You went so far and then decided on the preponderance of evidence and your own instinct. There came a time when more investigation and more and more was just gunning an engine with no forward motion: a waste of time.

"I think Isaac Kane is clean," he declared, standing up.

"Of course he is," Evelyn Packard said stoutly. "He's a dear, sweet boy. He'd never do anything bad."

"Sure," her sister said skeptically.

Her husband blinked behind his rimless glasses.

"How did you connect Isaac with us?" Teresa Beele asked.

"I followed him to this building last night," he told her. "Then, this morning, I rang every bell until I found someone who knew him."

"My," she said mockingly, "aren't you the smart one."

"Sometimes," he said, staring at her coldly.

"Judson," she said, "bring the policeman his hat and coat."

Calazo drove home and spent Saturday afternoon working on a report for Boone. He wrote that in his opinion Isaac Kane could be cleared, and further investigation was unwarranted.

When he had finished, he read over what he had written and reflected idly on the relationship between Teresa and Judson Beele, and between Evelyn Packard and Isaac Kane, and between Teresa and her sister, and between Evelyn and her brother-in-law.

"You know, hon," he said to his wife, "life really is a fucking soap opera."

"I wish you wouldn't use words like that," she said.

"Soap opera?" he asked innocently. "What's wrong with soap opera?"

"Oh, you," she said.

He laughed and goosed her. "What's for dinner?" he said.

• • •

CALAZO WASN'T THE only one thinking about Saturday night dinner. Detective Timothy (Big Tim) Hogan was beginning to wonder if he would ever eat again.

It had been a long day. Hogan was parked outside Ronald J. Bellsey's high-rise by 8:00 A.M., and sat there for almost an hour. Just when he thought it might be safe to make a quick run for a coffee and Danish, he saw Bellsey's white Cadillac come out of the underground garage.

The subject was alone in the car, and Hogan tailed him over to the wholesale meat market on West 18th Street. Bellsey parked and went inside. Hogan had no idea how long he'd be there, but figured this would be a good chance to brace Bellsey's wife without her husband being present.

Hogan was not a great brain and he knew it. So he always did his best to go by the book, thinking that would keep him out of trouble. It hadn't, but none of his stupidities had been serious enough to get him broken back to the ranks—so far.

It wasn't strictly true that Big Tim was stupid, but he was unimaginative and not strong at initiating new avenues of investigation. Another problem was that he didn't *look* like a detective, being short, dumpy, and bald, with a whiny voice. His third wife called him Dick Tracy, which Hogan didn't think was funny at all.

As soon as Bellsey was safely inside his place of business, the detective drove back to the high-rise to put the arm on the wife. As long as he was deserting the subject, he could have stopped for breakfast right then, but it didn't occur to him. Hogan found it difficult to keep two ideas in his head at the same time.

Mrs. Lorna Bellsey let him into her apartment without too much of a hassle. She was so flustered that she didn't even ask to see his ID. Hogan planned to lean on her hard. He didn't even take his hat off, fearing his nude pate wouldn't enhance the image of the hard-boiled detective.

She was a wisp of a woman with thinning gray hair and defeated eyes. She was wearing something shapeless with long sleeves and a high neck that effectively hid her body. Hogan wondered what she was like in bed, and guessed she'd be similar to his second wife who, during sex, would say things like, "The ceiling needs painting."

"Look, Mrs. Bellsey," he started, scowling at the timid woman, "you know why I'm here. Your husband is involved in the murder of Doctor Ellerbee, and we don't believe he was home that night like he says."

"He was," she said nervously, "he really was. I was here with him."

"From when to when?"

"All evening. All night."

"And he never went out?"

"No," she said, lowering her eyes. "Never. He was here all the time."

"Did he tell you to say that?"

"No, it's the truth."

"Did he say if you didn't back him up, he'd belt you around?"

"No," she said, finally showing a small flash of spirit, "it's not like that at all."

"You say. We're checking all your husband's hangouts—those bars he goes to where he beats up strangers. If we find out that he wasn't here that night, do you know what we'll do to you for lying?"

She was silent, clasping her hands tightly, knuckles whitening.

"Come on, Mrs. Bellsey," Hogan said in a loud, hectoring voice, "make it easy on yourself. He went out that night, didn't he?"

"I don't know," she said in a low, quavery voice.

"What do you mean you don't know?"

She didn't answer.

"Do I have to take you in?" he demanded. "Arrest you as an accessory? March you through the lobby in handcuffs? Put you in a filthy cell with whores and dope fiends? Come on, what do you mean you don't know if he went out?"

"I had a headache," she said faintly. "A migraine. I went to bed early."

"How early?"

"About eight-thirty I think it was."

"On the night Ellerbee was killed?"

"Yes."

"Your husband was here then?"

"Yes."

"You went into the bedroom?"

"Yes."

"Did you close the door?"

"Yes. He was watching television."

"Did you sleep?"

"Well, I took my medicine. It makes me very drowsy."

"So you slept?"

"Sort of."

"What time did you get up?"

"I got up around eleven to go to the bathroom." She wouldn't look at him when she said that.

"At eleven," Hogan repeated. "Was your husband here then?"

"Yes, he was," she said defiantly. "I saw him."

"But you didn't see him from eight-thirty to eleven?"

She began to cry, small tears sliding down her cheeks.

"Don't yell at me," she said, choking. "Please."

"Answer my question. Otherwise I'll take you downtown."

"No!" she screamed at him. "I didn't see him from eight-thirty to eleven."

Got him! Detective Timothy Hogan thought with savage satisfaction.

He drove back to 18th Street, delighted with his coup and hoping he hadn't lost Bellsey to mar the triumph. But the white Cadillac was still outside the meat market. Hogan parked nearby where he could watch the door. He urinated into an empty milk carton he always brought along on stakeouts for emergencies.

He sat there all day, getting hungrier and hungrier, and cursing his failure to buy a sandwich, candy bar, coffee—anything. He went through almost a pack of cigarettes, but the son of a bitch still didn't come out.

"What the hell is he *doing* in there?" the detective said aloud. And having said it, began to dream of what the market contained: steaks, chops, ground meat, chickens. It made him faint to think about it, he was so ravenous.

He dozed off a couple of times, but when he jerked awake, the Cadillac was still there. Hogan stuck it out, trying to keep himself alert by recalling the interrogation of Mrs. Lorna Bellsey and planning how he would word it in his report: play down the threats, play up the subtlety of his questions.

It was almost 8:45 P.M.—the streetlights on—when Bellsey came out of the meat market with two other guys. They stood joking, laughing, pushing each other. Hogan wondered if they had been boozing.

Finally they separated. Bellsey got in his car and took off. Hogan followed him up Eighth Avenue, sticking close in the heavy traffic, not wanting to lose him after sitting for so many hours and nearly dying of hunger.

Bellsey hung a left on 53rd Street and headed for the river through a darkened factory and warehouse district. Where the *hell* is he going? Hogan puzzled, and dropped back a half-block as traffic thinned. The Cadillac turned onto Eleventh Avenue and went two blocks, slowing. Then Bellsey found a parking slot and pulled in.

Beautiful, Hogan thought. It was a great neighborhood—if your life insurance was paid up.

He cruised along slowly and saw the subject go into a tavern. The street lighting wasn't the brightest, but Hogan could make out the name of the place: TAIL OF THE WHALE. Charming. Why didn't they call it Moby's Dick and be done with it?

He parked and walked back. The windows were steamed up, and he couldn't see inside, but it looked like a seaman's bar, a boilermaker joint, and if you asked for an extra-dry martini with two olives, they'd look at you with loathing and throw your ass out on the street.

He couldn't make up his mind whether to go in, wait in his car for Bellsey to come out, or just scratch the day and go home. What decided him was a big sign over the door: FRANKS, BURGERS, CHILI DOGS, HOT SANDWICHES. He went in.

It was about what he figured: a real bucket of blood. White tiled walls slick with grease. And old-fashioned mahogany bar on one side, tables and booths on the other. A TV set suspended from the tin ceiling on chains. Lighted jukebox and cigarette machine. In the back, a grill and steam table presided over by a fat black who was dripping sweat onto the sausages.

Hogan saw Bellsey at the bar, talking to two other guys. It looked like they were all working on doubles. The detective slid into an empty booth across the room and started on a new pack of cigarettes. He looked around.

A good crowd for so early in the evening; by midnight it would probably be jammed. Bellsey was the best-dressed man in the joint. Most of the others looked like cruds: construction workers in hard hats, seamen with stocking caps, a sprinkling of derelicts. There was one bum facedown on a table, sleeping off a drunk.

Hogan couldn't figure why a moneyed guy like Bellsey would patronize a grungy joint like this—until he saw that the wall behind the bar was covered with framed and autographed photos of boxers: dead ones, old ones, new ones—all in trunks, gloved, posed in attitudes of ferocious attack.

Big Tim remembered that Jason had said Bellsey was an ex-pug, so he probably dropped in here to gas about fights and fighters. The guys he was talking to, and the bartender, had all the stigmata: hunched shoulders, bent noses, cauliflower ears. They looked like they could chew up Timothy Hogan and spit him over the left-field fence.

"Yeah?"

He looked up, startled. A waitress was slouched by his booth. She was an old dame with lumpy legs encased in thick elastic stockings. There was a heavy wen on her chin with two wiry black hairs sticking out.

"What kind of bottled beer you got?" he asked her.

"Bud, Miller, Heineken."

"I'll have a Bud and a burger."

"Okay."

"Make the burger rare."

"Lotsa luck," she said dourly and shuffled away.

He had two hamburgers—so bad that he would have walked out after the first bite if he hadn't been so hungry. Even the dill pickle was lousy. How in hell could a cook spoil a pickle?

He saw that Bellsey was alone now, talking to the bartender. Hogan carried his second bottle of beer and glass over to the bar and took a nearby stool. The two men were arguing about who had the better right hook, Dempsey or Louis.

Hogan took a swallow of beer. "What about Marciano?" he said loudly.

Bellsey turned slowly to look at him. "Who the fuck asked you?" he demanded.

"I was just—" the detective started.

"Just butt out," the other man advised. "This is a private conversation."

If Timothy Hogan had had any sense, he'd have stopped right there, finished his beer, paid his bill, and left. He could see his first guess had been right: Bellsey *had* been boozing that afternoon, maybe all day, and was carrying a load.

He wasn't swaying or slurring his speech or anything like that, but his eyes were shrunken and bloodshot, and he was leaning forward with a truculent chin thrust out. He looked ready and eager to climb into a ring and go ten.

"What the hell you staring at?" Bellsey said to him. "You piece of shit."

Hogan reached casually inside his jacket to touch his holster. He knew it was there, but he wanted to make sure.

"Take it easy," he said to Bellsey. "I don't like talk like that."

"Well, fuck you, fatso," Bellsey said. "You don't like it, wheel your ass somewhere else."

"Hey, Ron," the bartender said in a raspy voice, "cool it. More trouble I don't need."

By this time the bar had quieted. Everyone seemed to have his head down, staring into his drink. But they were all listening.

"No trouble, Eddie," Bellsey said. "Not from this little shithead."

"Mister," the bartender said to Hogan, "do me a favor: Finish your beer, pay up, and try another joint. Please."

It gave the detective an out, and finally he had enough sense to take it. He finished his beer, put a bill on the bar.

"What kind of a place you running here?" he said aggrievedly and stalked toward the door.

"Asshole!" Bellsey yelled after him.

Hogan walked toward his car, thinking the subject was a real psycho and an odds-on favorite for having bashed Ellerbee's skull. He was so intent on planning what he was going to put in his report to Jason T. Jason that he didn't hear the soft footfalls behind him.

The first punch was to his kidneys and felt like someone had swung a sledgehammer. He went stumbling forward, mouth open, gasping for air. He tried to grab at a trash can for support, but a left hook crunched into his ribs just below the heart, and he went down into the gutter, fumbling at his holster.

Heavy shoes were thudding into his gut, his head, and he tried to cover his eyes with folded arms. It went on and on, and he vomited up the beer and burgers. Just before he lost consciousness he was certain he was gone, and wondered why he was dying in a street like this, his vital report unwritten.

A different report from Roosevelt Hospital went up and down the chain of police command, and eventually a blue working the case called Jason. He, in turn, alerted Boone. By midnight, the two of them were at Roosevelt, talking to doctors and guys from Midtown North, trying to collect as much information as they could before taking it to Edward X. Delaney.

They woke him up a little after 5:00 A.M. Sunday morning and related what had happened. He told them to come over as soon as possible. He said he'd have coffee for them.

"What is it, Edward?" Monica said drowsily from her bed.

"Tell you later," he said. "Boone and Jason are coming over for a few minutes. You go back to sleep."

When they arrived, he took them into the kitchen. He was wearing his old flannel bathrobe with the frayed cord. His short hair spiked up like a cactus.

He had used the six-cup percolator and put a tray of frozen blueberry muffins in the oven. They sat around the kitchen table, sipping the steamy black coffee and munching on muffins while Sergeant Boone reported what had happened.

A squad car on patrol had spotted Detective Timothy Hogan lying semi-conscious in the gutter and had called for an ambulance. It wasn't until they got him to Roosevelt Emergency that they found his ID and knew that one of New York's Finest had been assaulted.

"He had his ID?" Delaney said sharply.

"Yes, sir," Boone said. "And his gun."

"And his wallet," Jason added. "Nothing missing. It wasn't one of your ordinary, everyday muggings."

"But he's going to be all right?"

"Oh, hell, yes," Boone said. "Cracked ribs, bruised kidneys, a gorgeous shiner, and assorted cuts and abrasions. He looks like he's been through a meat grinder—stomped up something fierce."

"I think his pride was hurt more than anything else," Jason offered.

"It should be," Delaney said grumpily. "Letting himself be jumped like that. You talked to him?"

"For a while," Boone said. "They got him shot full of painkillers so he wasn't too coherent."

He told Delaney what they had been able to drag out of a groggy Timothy Hogan:

How he had made Mrs. Lorna Bellsey admit she was asleep and could not swear that her husband was home from eight-thirty to eleven o'clock on the murder night.

How he had followed Bellsey up to the Tail of the Whale on Eleventh Avenue and gotten into a hassle with him at the bar.

How he was unexpectedly attacked while he was returning to his car.

"He swears it was Ronald Bellsey," Boone said.

"He saw him?" Delaney demanded. "He can positively identify him?"

"Well . . . no," Boone said regretfully. "He didn't get a look at the perp, and apparently no words were spoken."

"Jesus Christ!" Delaney said disgustedly. "Can you think of any mistakes Hogan *didn't* make? Did the investigating officers go back to the bar—what's its name?"

"Tail of the Whale. Yes, sir, they covered that bar and four others in the area. No one saw anything, no one heard anything, no one knows Ronald J. Bellsey or anyone resembling him. And no one admits seeing Tim Hogan either. It's a blank."

"You want us to pull Bellsey in, sir?" Jason Two asked. "For questioning?"

"What the hell for?" Delaney said irritably. "He'll just deny, deny, deny. And even if we get the bartender and customers to admit there was a squabble in the Tail of the Whale, that's no evidence that Bellsey put the boots to Hogan. I'm going to call Suarez in a couple of hours and ask him to put a lid on this thing. We'll go at Bellsey from a different angle."

Sergeant Boone took folded papers from his inside jacket pocket and handed them to Delaney. "Benny Calazo stopped by my place last night and dropped off this report. He says that in his opinion, Isaac Kane is clean."

"You trust his opinion?" Delaney said sharply.

"Absolutely, sir. If Calazo says the kid is clean, then he is. Ben has been around a long time and doesn't goof. I was thinking . . . Hogan's going to be on sick leave for at least a month. How about putting Calazo onto Bellsey? If anyone can put the skids under that bastard, Ben will do it."

"Fine with me," Delaney said. "Brief him on Bellsey and tell him for God's sake not to turn his back on the guy. Jason, you're still working with Keisman on Harold Gerber's confession?"

"Yes, sir. Nothing new to report."

"Keep at it. There's one blueberry muffin left; who wants it?"

"I'll take it," Jason Two said promptly. "I could OD on those little beauties."

After they were gone, Delaney sat at the kitchen table and finished his lukewarm coffee, too keyed up to go back to bed. He reflected on the latest developments and decided he had very little sympathy for Detective Timothy Hogan. You paid for your stupidity in this world one way or another.

He rinsed out the cups and saucers, set them in the rack to dry, cleaned up the kitchen. He took Calazo's report on Isaac into the study and put on his glasses. He read slowly and with enjoyment. Calazo had a pungent style of writing that avoided the usual Department gibberish.

When he finished, Delaney put the report aside and lighted a cigar. He pondered not so much the facts Calazo had recounted but what he had implied.

The detective (covering his ass) had said there was a possibility he was wrong, but he believed Isaac Kane innocent of the murder of Dr. Simon Ellerbee. He was saying, in effect, that there were no perfect solutions, only judgments.

Edward X. Delaney knew that mind-set well; it was his own. In the detection of crime, nothing cohered. It was an open-ended pursuit with definite answers left to faith. There was a religious element to detection: Rational investigation went only so far. Then came the giant step to belief for which there was no proof.

Which meant, of course, that the detective had to live with doubt and anxiety. If you couldn't do that, Delaney thought—not for the first time— you really should be in another line of business.

18

•

DETECTIVE HELEN VENABLE WAS HAVING A PARTICULARLY SEVERE attack of doubt and anxiety. She was uncertain of her own ability to establish the truth or falsity of Joan Yesell's alleged alibi without seeking the advice of her more experienced male colleagues.

She was nervous about her failure to report Mrs. Blanche Yesell's possible absence from her apartment on the murder night. She was worried that there were inquiries she should be making that she was not. And she fretted that an entire week had to pass before she could confirm or deny the existence of the stupid bridge club.

But her strongest doubt was a growing disbelief in Joan's guilt. That soft, feeling, quiet woman, so overwhelmed by the hard, brutal, raucous world of Manhattan, was incapable of crushing the skull of a man she professed to admire. Or so Detective Venable thought.

She met with Joan every day, spoke to her frequently on the phone, went out with her Monday night for a spaghetti dinner and to a movie on Thursday afternoon. The closer their relationship became, the more Helen was convinced of the woman's innocence.

Joan was almost physically sickened by the filth and ugliness of city streets. She was horrified and depressed by violence in any form. She could not endure the thought of cruelty to animals. The sight of a dead sparrow made her weep. She never objected to Helen's squad room profanity, but the detective could see her wince.

"Kiddo," Venable told her, "you're too good for this world. Angels finish last."

"I don't think I'm an angel," Joan said slowly. "Far from it. I do awful, stupid things, like everyone else. Sometimes I get so furious with Mama that I could scream. You think I'm goody-goody, but I'm not."

"Compared to me," Helen said, "you're a saint."

Frequently, during that week, the detective brought the talk around to Dr. Simon Ellerbee. Joan seemed willing, almost eager, to speak of him.

"He meant so much to me," she said. "He was the only therapist I ever went to, and I knew right from the start that he would help me. I could see he'd never be shocked or offended by anything I'd tell him. He'd just listen in that nice, sympathetic way of his. I'd never hold back from him because I knew I could trust him. I think he was the first man—the first person—I really and truly trusted. We were so close. I had the feeling that things that hurt me hurt him, too. I suppose psychiatrists are like that to all their patients, but Doctor Simon made me feel like someone special."

"Sounds like quite a guy," Venable said.

"Oh, he was. I'm going to tell you something, but you must promise never to tell anyone. Promise?"

"Of course."

"Well, sometimes I used to daydream about Doctor Simon's wife dying. Like in a plane crash—you know? Quick and painless. Then he and I would get married. I imagined what it would be like seeing him every day, living with him, spending the rest of my life with him."

"Sounds to me like you were in love with him, honey."

"I suppose I was," Yesell said sorrowfully. "I guess all his patients were. You call me a saint; he was the real saint."

Another time she herself brought up the subject of the murder:

"Are the police getting anywhere?" she asked Venable. "On who killed Doctor Simon?"

"It's slow going," the detective admitted. "No good leads that I know of, but a lot of people are working on it. We'll get the perp."

"Perp?"

"Perpetrator. The one who did it."

"Oh. Well, I hope you do. It was an awful, awful thing."

They talked about the apartment they might one day share. They talked about their mothers, about clothes, and foods they liked or hated. They recalled incidents from their girlhood, giggled about boys they had known, traded opinions on TV stars and novelists.

It was not a rare occurrence, this closeness between detective and suspect. For did they not need each other? Even a murderer might find the obsession of his pursuer as important to himself as it was to the hunter. It gave meaning to their existence.

"Gotta work late on Friday night, dear," Venable told her target. "Reports and shit like that. I'll call you on Saturday and maybe we can have dinner or something."

"I'd like that," Joan said with her timid smile. "I really look forward to seeing you and talking to you on the phone."

"Me, too," Helen said, troubled because she was telling the truth.

On Friday night at seven o'clock, Helen was slouched down in her Honda, parked two doors away from the Yesells' brownstone. She could watch the entrance in her rearview mirror, and kept herself alert with a little transistor radio tuned to a hard-rock station.

She sat there for more than an hour, never taking her eyes from the doorway. It was almost 8:15 when Blanche Yesell came out, bundled up in a bulky fur coat that looked like a bearskin. There was no mistaking her; she was hatless and that beehive hairdo seemed to soar higher than ever.

Venable slid from the car and followed at a distance. It didn't last long; Mrs. Yesell scurried westward and darted into a brownstone one door from the corner. The detective quickened her pace, but by the time she got there, the subject had disappeared from vestibule and lobby, with no indication of which apartment she had entered.

Helen stood on the sidewalk, staring up, flummoxed. If Calazo had been faced with the problem, he probably would have rung every bell in the joint, demanding, "Is Mrs. Blanche Yesell there?" And within an hour, he'd have statements from the other bridge club members and know if Mrs. Yesell was or was not at home on the murder night and could or could not testify as to her daughter's presence.

But such direct action did not occur to Helen. She pondered how she might identify and question the bridge club members without alerting the Yesells that Joan's alibi was being investigated.

She went back to the Honda and sat there a long time, feeling angry and ineffective because she couldn't think of a clever scam. Finally, taking a deep breath, she decided she better write a complete report on Mrs. Yesell's Friday night bridge club and dump the whole thing in Sergeant Boone's lap.

It was a personal failure, she acknowledged, and it infuriated her. But the fear of committing a world-class boo-boo and being bounced down to uniformed duty again was enough to convince her to go by the book. It turned out to be a smart decision.

• • •

IF HELEN WAS suffering from doubts, Detective Ross Konigsbacher was inflated with confidence, convinced he was on a roll. On the same night Helen was brooding unhappily in her Honda, the Kraut was rubbing knees with L. Vincent Symington at a small table at the Dorian Gray.

Symington had insisted on ordering a bottle of Frascati, served in a silver ice bucket. The detective had made no objections, knowing that Symington would pick up the tab. That was one thing you could say for the creep: There were no moths in his wallet.

"A dreadful day," he told Konigsbacher. "Simply *dreadful*. This is a nice little wine, isn't it? One crisis after another. I'm on Wall Street, you know—I don't think I told you that—and today the market simply collapsed. What do you do, Ross?"

"Import-export," he said glibly, having prepared for the question. "Plastic and leather findings. Very dull."

"I can imagine. Are you in the market at all?"

"I'm afraid not."

"Well, if you ever decide to take a flier, talk to me first; I may be able to put you into something sweet."

"I'll do that. But my wife has been nagging me about a new fur coat, so I won't be able to take a flier in stocks or anything else for a while."

"What a shame," Symington said. "Women can be *such* bitches, can't they? Are you still working out, Ross?"

"Every morning with the weights."

"Oh, my!" the other man said, laughing brightly. "You're getting me all excited. And what does your *wife* do while you're exercising in the morning?"

"She snores."

"Now that *is* dull. Here, let me fill your glass. This goes down easily, doesn't it?"

"Like some people I know," the Kraut said, and they both shook with silent laughter.

"Vince, have you had any more visits from the cops—about the murder of your shrink?"

"Not a word. But I'm sure they're investigating me from A to Z. Let them; I have nothing to hide."

"I hope you have a good alibi for the time it happened."

"I certainly do," Symington said virtuously. "I was at a very posh affair at the Hilton. My company was giving a birthday dinner for the founder. A dozen people saw me there."

"Come on, Vince," Konigsbacher said, smiling. "Don't tell me you were there all night. I know how boring those things can be. Didn't you sneak out for a teensy-weensy drink somewhere else?"

"Oh, Ross," the other man said admiringly, "you *are* clever. Of course I split for a while. Simply couldn't endure all that business chitchat. I found the grungiest, most vulgar bar in the city over near Eighth Avenue. It's called Stallions. How does that grab you? Rough trade? You wouldn't believe! I just sat in a corner, sipped my Perrier, and took it all in. What a spectacle! You and I must drop by there some night just for laughs. I've never seen so much black leather in my *life!*"

"Meet anyone interesting?" the detective asked casually.

"Well, if you must know . . ." Symington said coyly, twirling his wineglass by the stem, "there was one boy . . . I bought him a drink—he was having banana brandy; can you imagine!—and we talked awhile. His name was Nick. He was one of those dese, dem, and dose boys, and said he wanted to be an actor. 'Hamlet?' I asked, but it went right over his head! I spent a fun hour there, and then I went back to the party at the Hilton. I'm sure not a soul noticed I had been gone."

"Oh, Vince," the Kraut said seriously, "I hope you weren't gone during the time your psychiatrist was killed. The cops aren't dummies, you know. They're liable to find out you left the party and come around to question you again."

"You think so?" the other man said, beginning to worry. "Well, as a matter of fact, I *was* away from the Hilton from about nine to ten o'clock or so, but I can't believe the cops could discover that."

"They might," Detective Konigsbacher said darkly. "They have their ways."

"Oh, God!" Symington said despairingly. "What do you think I should do? Maybe I'll look up those two cops who came to question me and tell them about it. That would prove I have nothing to hide, wouldn't it?"

"Don't do that," the Kraut said swiftly. "Don't volunteer anything. Just play it cool. And if they dump on you for not telling them about being away from the party, tell them you forgot. After all, that boy—what was his name?"

"Nick."

"Nick can back up your story."

"If they can ever find him," the other man said dolefully. "You know what those kids are like—here today, gone tomorrow."

"Well, don't worry about it," Konigsbacher advised. "As long as you're innocent, you have nothing to fear. You *are* innocent, aren't you, Vince?"

"Pure as the driven snow," Symington said solemnly, and both men laughed immoderately.

"Ross, have you had dinner yet?"

"As a matter of fact, I haven't. You?"

"No, and I'm famished. I know absolutely the *chicest* French bistro in town; their bouillabaisse is divine. Would you care to try it? My treat, of course."

"Sounds like fun," Konigsbacher said. "It's got to be better than my wife's cooking. She can't boil water without burning it."

"Ross, you're a scream!"

Symington paid the bill and they left for the chicest French bistro in town. The detective told himself he was living high off the hog and plotted how he might make this cushy duty last. Incomplete reports to Sergeant Boone and Delaney would help.

• • •

DELANEY HIMSELF WAS sinking in a swamp of incomplete data. He couldn't get a handle on the alibis of Otherton, Bellsey, Yesell, or Symington, and Harold Gerber's confession was still neither verified nor refuted. Other than eliminating Kane as a suspect, little hard progress had been made.

What Delaney found most bothersome about this puzzle wasn't the factual alibis but the enigmas that showed no signs of yielding to investigation. In his dogged, methodical way, he made a list of what he considered the key mysteries that seemed to defy solution:

Major riddles:
1. Who was the late patient Dr. Ellerbee was expecting on the night he was killed?
2. Why were there two sets of wet footprints on the townhouse carpeting?
3. What was the meaning of the hammer blows to the victim's eyes after he was dead?
4. Who stole the billing ledger—and for what reason?
5. What was the cause of Ellerbee's change of personality during the past year?

Minor riddles:
1. Did L. Vincent Symington's sighting of Dr. Ellerbee driving alone on a Friday night have any significance?
2. Why did Joan Yesell attempt suicide immediately after she was questioned about the case?
3. What was the real purpose of Dr. Diane Ellerbee's visit to the Delaneys' home—and her unexpected friendliness?

He hunched over his desk, studying the list with the feeling—a hope, really—that finding the answer to one riddle would serve as a key, and all the others would then give up their secrets in a natural progression, the entire case suddenly revealed as a rational and believable chain of events. It existed, he was convinced, and remained hidden only because he hadn't the wit to see it.

He was rereading his list of conundrums when the phone rang.

"Edward X. Delaney here."

"This is Detective Charles Parnell, Mr. Delaney. How are you, sir?"

"Fine, thank you. And you?"

"Having fun," Daddy Warbucks said, laughing. "I'm ass-deep in numbers, trying to put away a guy who was running a Ponzi scam in Brooklyn. Took his relatives, friends, and neighbors for about a hundred big ones. Interesting case. I'll have to tell you about it someday. But the reason I called . . . I promised you I'd follow up on Simon Ellerbee's will. It's been filed for probate, and I can give you the scoop."

"Excellent," Delaney said. "Wait a minute until I get pen and paper . . . Okay, what have you got?"

"Everything goes to his wife, Diane, except for some specific bequests. Twenty thousand to his alma mater, ten to his father, five to Doctor Samuelson, one thousand to his receptionist, Carol Judd, and small sums to the super of the townhouse, the Polish couple who work for the Ellerbees up in Brewster, and a few others. That's about it. Nothing that might be the motive for murder that I can see."

"Doesn't sound like it," Delaney said slowly. "The widow's got plenty of her own. I can't see her chilling him for a little more."

"I agree," Parnell said. "The only thing interesting in the will is that Ellerbee specifically cancels all debts owed to him by his patients. Apparently some of the screwballs were strictly slow-pay, if not deadbeats. Well, Ellerbee's will wipes the slate clean. That was decent of him."

"Yes," Delaney said thoughtfully, "decent. And a little unusual, wouldn't you say?"

"Oh, I don't know," Daddy Warbucks said. "Everyone says he was a great guy. Always helping people. This sounds right in character."

"Uh-huh," Delaney said. "Well, thank you very much. You've been a big help, and I'll make sure Chief Suarez knows about it."

"It couldn't hurt," Detective Parnell said.

After Delaney hung up, he stared at the notes he had jotted down. He pondered a long while. Then, sighing, he reached for his "agony list" of unsolved puzzles. He added a fourth item under *Minor riddles:* Why did Dr. Ellerbee cancel his patients' debts?

And, having done that, he tramped gloomily into the kitchen, hoping to find the makings of a prodigious sandwich that might relieve his depression.

• • •

DETECTIVE BRIAN ESTRELLA was also thinking of food. Since his wife, Meg, had been in the hospital and nursing home, he had been baching it and hating every minute. He was unused to solitude, and a real klutz when it came to cooking and household chores.

He had what he considered a brainstorm: He called Sylvia Mae Otherton on Friday night and suggested, with some diffidence, that they have dinner together. He would find a Chinese take-out joint and buy enough food for both of them. All Sylvia would have to supply would be hot tea. She thought it was a marvelous idea.

Estrella bought egg rolls, barbecued ribs, noodles, wonton soup, shrimp in lobster sauce, fried rice, sweet-and-sour pork, fortune cookies, and pistachio ice cream. Everything was packed in neat cardboard containers, and they even put in plastic forks and spoons, paper napkins.

It was like a picnic, with all the opened containers on the cocktail table along with cups of hot tea Sylvia provided. They agreed it was just the kind of spicy, aromatic food to have on a cold winter night with a hard wind rattling the windows and flurries of snow glistening in the streetlight.

The detective didn't neglect to compliment Sylvia on how attractive she looked, and indeed she had done much to improve her appearance. Her hair was washed and coiffed in a loose, fluffy cut. The excess makeup was gone, and the garish costume replaced by a simple shirtwaist.

More important, her manner had undergone a transformation. She seemed at once confident and relaxed. She smiled and laughed frequently, and told Estrella she had gone out that afternoon and spent two hours shopping, going from store to store—something she hadn't done since Dr. Ellerbee died.

"That's wonderful," the detective said. "See, you *can* do it. You should try to get out of the house every day, even if it's only for a few minutes."

"I intend to," Otherton said firmly. "I'm going to take charge of my life. And I owe it all to you."

"Me? What did I do?"

"You cared. You have no idea how important that was to me."

They finished everything and cleared away the empty containers. Then Sylvia asked about Estrella's wife, and he told her the doctors didn't hold out much hope, but Meg was in good spirits and spoke optimistically of coming home soon.

"I think she knows she's not going to do that," the detective said in a low voice, "but she tries to keep cheerful so *I* don't get depressed."

"She sounds like a wonderful woman, Brian."

"Yes. She is."

Then, before he knew it, he was telling Sylvia all about Meg, their life together, the child they had lost (leukemia), and how sometimes Estrella wondered how he was going to get through the rest of his life without his wife.

He poured it all out, realizing now how lonely he had been and how he had been hoping to tell someone how he felt. It was a kind of tribute to Meg: public acknowledgment of the happiness she had given him.

Sylvia listened intently, only asking sympathetic questions, until Estrella was done. They were sitting close together on the couch and, halfway through his recital, she took his hand and held it tightly.

She wasn't coming on to him; he knew that. Just offering the comfort of her physical presence, and he was grateful. When he had finished, he raised her hand and lightly kissed her fingertips.

"Well . . ." he said, "that's the sad story of my life. Forgive me for making you listen to all this. I know you have your own problems."

"I only wish I could help you," she said sorrowfully. "You've helped me so much. Now let's have an after-dinner drink."

She rose to bring the decanter from an ornate Korean cupboard.

"Oh," she said, "pardon me a moment; I have to make a short phone call."

The reproduction of a fin de siècle French phone was on a small, marble-topped Victorian stand. She dialed a three-digit number.

"Charles?" she said. "This is Sylvia Mae Otherton. How are you tonight? . . . Good . . . Fine, thank you . . . Anything for me today? . . . Thank you, Charles. Good night."

She came back to Estrella with the sherry.

"No mail today," she said lightly. "Not even a bill."

He stared at her. Then he glanced at his wristwatch. Fourteen minutes after nine. He put his pipe aside.

"Sylvia," he said in a strained voice, "was that the guy at the lobby desk you were talking to?"

"Yes, that was Charles. He works nights. I called to ask if there's any mail in my box. It saves me a trip downstairs. My agoraphobia again!"

"You call him every night to check on your mail?"

"Yes. Why do you ask?"

"You always call about this time?"

"Usually. But why—"

She stopped, her eyes widened, her mouth fell open. One hand flew to cover it.

"Oh, God!" she gasped.

"You told us you hadn't made any phone calls that night."

"I forgot!" she wailed. "It's a regular habit, a routine, and I forgot. Oh, Brian, I'm so sorry. But I'm sure I called Charles that night."

"I'll be right back," Estrella said. "Keep your fingers crossed."

He went down to the lobby, identified himself, and talked to Charles for almost five minutes. The clerk swore that Sylvia Otherton called about her mail between 9:00 and 9:30 every weekday evening.

"A lot of the tenants do that," he said. "Especially the older ones. Saves them a trip downstairs. And I don't mind. Things are slow around here at night, and it gives me someone to talk to, something to do."

"Does Otherton ever miss calling you?"

"Not that I remember. Every night during the week, like clockwork."

"Between, say, nine and nine-thirty?"

"That's right."

"Do you remember her calling on a Friday night four weeks ago—the night of that terrific rainstorm?"

"I can't remember that particular night. All I know is that she hasn't missed a night since I've been working here, and that's almost three years now."

"Thank you, Charles."

Upstairs again, Estrella said, "Sylvia, as far as I'm concerned, you're cleared—and that's what I'm going to put in my report."

He thought that would please her, but instead she looked like she was about to cry.

"Does that mean I won't be seeing you anymore?"

He touched her shoulder. "No," he said gently, "it doesn't mean that."

"Good," she said happily. "Brian, would you like to try the Ouija board again? Maybe it will help you find out who did it."

"Sure," he said, "let's try."

They sat as they had before, the board between them on the cocktail table. Sylvia put her fingers lightly on the planchette and closed her eyes.

"Doctor Ellerbee," Detective Brian Estrella said in a hollow voice, "was the person who killed you a stranger?"

The planchette did not move.

Estrella repeated his question.

The planchette jerked wildly. It spelled out KGXFTD, then stopped.

"Doctor Ellerbee," the detective tried once more, "was the person who killed you a stranger?"

The planchette moved slowly. It pointed to N and then to I. NI. Then it stopped.

"Sylvia," Brian said softly, "I don't think we're getting anywhere. It spelled out NI. That doesn't mean anything."

She opened her eyes. "Maybe he's just not getting through to me tonight. His spirit may be busy with another medium."

"That could be it," Estrella acknowledged.

"But we'll try again, won't we, Brian?" she asked anxiously.

"Absolutely," he said.

• • •

ON SATURDAY AFTERNOON, Delaney, Boone, and Jason held a council of war. They shuffled through all the reports that had come in during the week and discussed reassignments.

"Estrella says Otherton is clean," Delaney said. "You willing to accept that?"

"I am, sir," Jason said promptly. "He did a thorough job on her—checked all her friends and neighborhood stores. It was just by luck that he got onto the phone call to the lobby clerk. I think she's clean."

"Boone?"

"I'll go along with Jase, sir."

"What's this Ouija board nonsense in his report? It's the second time he's mentioned that. Is the man a flake?"

"No, sir," Jason Two said. "He's a steady, serious kind of guy. But his wife is very sick, and maybe he's got that on his mind."

"Oh," Delaney said. "I didn't know that and I'm sorry to hear it. Does he want a leave of absence?"

"No, he says he wants to keep on working."

"Probably the best thing," Delaney said. "All right, let's clear Otherton. She may be a nutcase, but I can't see her as a killer. Now about this report from Detective Venable . . . That *is* interesting. Sounds to me like Mrs. Yesell has been leading us up the garden path."

"Her story sure needs work," Sergeant Boone said. "If Otherton is cleared, how about switching Estrella to Joan Yesell? He can work with Helen on finding the members of Mrs. Yesell's bridge club."

"Yes," Delaney said, "let's do that. Boone, you're working with Calazo on Ronald J. Bellsey?"

"Every chance I get."

"And, Jason—you and Keisman are covering Harold Gerber?"

"That's right, sir. Nothing new to report."

"And Konigsbacher has nothing new to report on Symington. But I've got something new that may interest you."

He told them about Detective Parnell's report—that Dr. Simon Ellerbee's will had specifically canceled all his patients' outstanding bills.

"Now what the hell do you suppose that means?" he asked the two officers.

They both shook their heads.

"Beats me," Boone said.

"Probably nothing," Jason said.

"Probably," Delaney said, sighing. "We've sure got a lot of probabilities in this case and damned little we can sink our teeth in. Well, what can I tell you except to keep plugging and pray for a break."

After they left, he returned to the study to paw through the scattered reports again. He was in a sour, dispirited mood. "Keep plugging." That was stupid, unnecessary advice to give his aides. They were experienced police officers and knew that plugging was the name of the game.

What always bemused Delaney in cases like this was the contrast between the grand passion that incited the murder of a human being and the pedestrian efforts of the police to solve it.

In a crazy kind of way, it was like solving the mystery of a Rembrandt by analyzing pigments, brushstrokes, and the quality of the canvas, and then saying, "There! Your mystery's explained." It wasn't, of course. Mystery was mystery. It defied rational explication.

Even if the Ellerbee homicide was closed, Delaney suspected the solution would merely be a resolution of the facts. The enigma of human behavior would remain hidden.

19

•

TWO WEEKS BEFORE CHRISTMAS, AND THE CITY HAD NEVER BEEN more enchanting. The "city" being Manhattan, and more particularly midtown Manhattan, with streets glowing with lights and tinsel. Amplified carols rang out everywhere, along with the jingle of bells and cash registers. The annual shopping frenzy was in full swing, stores mobbed, the spending fever an epidemic. "Take my money, miss—*please!*"

But downtown, on Seventh Avenue South, there were no lights, no tinsel, no carols. Just some foul remains of the last snowfall, clotted with garbage and dog droppings. Harold Gerber's tenement showed no festive trappings. Paint peeled, plaster fell away, the bare, lathed walls oozed a glutinous slime that smelled of suppuration.

"O little town of Bethlehem," Detective Robert Keisman sang.

"How about 'Come, All Ye Faithful'?" Jason suggested.

The two detectives were lounging around Gerber's ruinous pad, working on a six-pack of Schaefer. The two black officers were wearing drifter duds, and all three men were bundled in down jackets, with caps and gloves. It was damp, and cold enough to see their breath.

"Let's go through it once more," Jason Two said.

"Ahh, Jesus," Gerber said, "do we have to?"

"Sure we have to," Keisman said lazily. "You're aching to get your ass locked up, aren't you? Spend a nice warm holiday in durance vile—right? You say you snuffed Doc Ellerbee. Well, yeah, that may be so, but on the other hand you may just be jerking us around."

"See, Harold," Jason said, "we run you in, and it turns out you're just a bullshit artist wasting everyone's time—well, that don't look so good on our records."

"Shit," Gerber said, "you write out any kind of a confession you like—put anything in it you want—and I'll sign it."

"Nah," the Spoiler said, "that's not how it's done, Harold. You got to tell us in your own words. You say you took a cab over to Ellerbee's townhouse on that night?"

Gerber: "That's right."

Jason: "What kind of cab? Yellow, Checker, gypsy?"

Gerber: "I don't remember."

Keisman: "How long did it take you to get there?"

Gerber: "Maybe twenty minutes."

Jason: "Where did the cabby drop you?"

Gerber: "Right in front of Ellerbee's office."

Keisman: "How did you get in?"

Gerber: "Rang the bell. When he answered, I told him I was in a bad way and had to see him. He let me in."

Jason: "You were carrying the hammer?"

Gerber: "Sure. I carried it with me for the express purpose of killing Ellerbee. It was a premeditated murder."

Keisman: "Uh-huh. Now tell us again where you got the hammer."

Gerber: "I boosted it from that hardware store near Sheridan Square."

Jason: "Just put it under your jacket and walked out?"

Gerber: "That's right."

Keisman: "We checked with them. They lose a lot to shoplifters, but no ball peen hammers."

Gerber: "They don't know their ass from their elbow."

Jason: "All right, now you're inside Ellerbee's townhouse, carrying a hammer. What did you do next?"

Gerber: "Walked upstairs."

Keisman: "You were wearing your boots?"

Gerber: "Sure, I was wearing boots. It was a fucking wet night."

Jason: "You see anyone else in the townhouse?"

Gerber: "No. Just Ellerbee. He let me into his office."

Keisman: "He was alone?"

Gerber: "Yeah, he was alone."

Jason: "Did you talk to him?"

Gerber: "I said hello. He started to say, 'What are you doing—' and then I hit him."

Keisman: "He was facing you when you hit him?"

Gerber: "That's right."

Jason: "How many times did you hit him?"

Gerber: "Two or three. I forget."

Keisman: "Where did you hit him? His brow, top of his head, temples—where?"

Gerber: "Like on the hairline. Not on top of his head. High up on the forehead."

Jason: "He went down?"

Gerber: "That's right."

Keisman: "On his back?"

Gerber: "Yeah, on his back."

Jason: "Then what did you do?"

Gerber: "I saw he was dead, so I—"

Keisman: "You didn't hit him again when he was down?"

Gerber: "What the hell for? The guy was fucking dead. I've seen enough stiffs to know that. So I got out of there, walked over to York, and got a cab going south."

Jason: "And what did you do with the hammer?"

Gerber: "Like I told you—I pushed it in a trash can on Eighth Street."

Keisman: "Why did you kill him, Harold?"

Gerber: "Jesus, how many times do I have to tell you? He was a nosy fucker. After a while he knew too much about me. Hey, let's have another brew; I'm thirsty."

The three sat there in silence, the two officers staring at the other man's wild, flaming eyes. As usual, Gerber needed a shave, and uncombed hair still spiked out from under his black beret.

"You going to take me in?" he asked finally.

"We'll think about it," Jason Two said.

"I did it. That's God's own truth. I'm guilty as hell."

They didn't reply.

"Hey, you guys?" Gerber said brightly, straightening up. "I'm moving. A city marshal showed up with an eviction notice. I've got to vacate the premises, as they say."

"Yeah?" the Spoiler said. "Where you moving to?"

"Who the hell knows? I've got to look around. I want another place as swell as this one."

"Need any help moving?" Jason offered.

"Moving *what?*" Harold Gerber said with a ferocious grin. "I can carry all my stuff in a shopping bag. I'm going to leave a lot of shit right here. You guys want any books? I've got a pile of paperbacks over there under the sink. Some hot stuff. You're welcome to any or all."

"Yeah?" Jason said. "Let's take a look. Maybe there's something my wife would like. She's always got her nose in a book."

He squatted down at the sink, began to inspect the jumble of books. He pulled out a thick one.

"What's this?" he said. "A Bible?"

"Oh, that . . ." Gerber said casually. "I fished it out of a garbage can. I flipped through it. A million laughs."

Jason inspected the book.

"Douay Version," he read aloud. "That's a Catholic Bible, isn't it? You a Catholic, Harold?"

"I was. Once. What are you?"

"Baptist. Mind if I take this along?" Jason Two asked, holding up the Bible.

"Be my guest," Gerber said. "Read the whole thing. I won't tell you how it comes out."

They sat around a while longer before the two officers left, promising Gerber they'd tell him the next day whether or not they would arrest him.

They sat in Jason's car, the heater on, trying to get warm.

"He's full of crap," Keisman said. "A complete whacko."

"Oh, yeah," Jason agreed. "Doesn't even know how Ellerbee died."

"Why do you figure he wants to get busted?"

"I don't know for sure. Something to do with guilt, I suppose. What happened in Vietnam . . . It's too deep for me."

"What's with the Bible?" the Spoiler asked, jerking a thumb at the book. "Why did you glom on to that?"

"Look at it," Jason Two said, ruffling the pages. "It's full of dog-ears. Someone's been doing some heavy reading. And I don't believe he found it in a garbage can. *Nobody* throws out a Bible."

"Jase, that's the Baptist in you talking."

"Maybe. But he says he used to be a Catholic, and this is a Catholic edition. Funny a backslid Catholic should find a Catholic Bible in a garbage can."

" 'God moves in a mysterious way His wonders to perform.' "

"Hey," Jason said admiringly, "there's more to you than Gucci after all, isn't there?"

"I was brought up right," Keisman said. "Didn't go bad until—oh, maybe the age of six or so."

"Well . . ." Jason T. Jason said, staring down at the book in his hands, "it may be nothing, but what say we give it the old college try?"

The Spoiler groaned. "You mean check every Catholic church in the city?"

"I don't think we'll have to do that. Just the ones in Greenwich Village. I'm hoping that poor son of a bitch was praying in some church on that Friday night."

"Man, you really dig the long shots, don't you?"

Because of previous arrests, there was a photo of Harold Gerber in his NYPD file, and Jason cajoled a police photographer into making two copies, one for himself, one for Keisman.

• • •

AT THE SAME time, Detective Calazo was having more serious photo problems. Apparently there was no shot of Ronald Bellsey in the files. Calazo could have requested that a police photographer take a telephoto of Bellsey without the subject's knowledge—but that meant making out a requisition and then waiting.

The old, white-haired gumshoe had been around a long time, and knew a lot of ways to skin a cat in what he sometimes called the "Dick Biz." He looked up the name and address of a trade magazine, *The Wholesale Butcher*, and visited their editorial offices on West 14th Street.

Sure enough, they had a photograph of Ronald J. Bellsey in their files. Calazo flashed his potsy and borrowed the shot, promising to return it. He didn't bother asking them not to tell Bellsey about his visit. Let them tell the fink; it would do him good to sweat a little.

Then Benny, with the aid of Sergeant Boone, when he could spare the time, tailed the subject for almost a week. He discovered that Bellsey had three bars he favored: the Tail of the Whale on Eleventh Avenue, a tavern on Seventh Avenue near Madison Square Garden, and another on 52nd Street, just east of Broadway.

He also discovered that Bellsey got his ashes hauled two afternoons a week by a Chinese hooker working out of a fleabag hotel on West 23rd Street. She had a sheet a yard long, all arrests for loitering, solicitation, and prostitution. She was getting a little frazzled around the edges now, and Calazo figured she'd be lucky to get twenty bucks a pop.

He didn't move on her—just made sure he put her name (Betty Lee), address, room, and phone number in his report to Boone. Then he turned his attention to those three hangouts Bellsey frequented.

All three were patronized by boxers, trainers, managers, agents, bookies, and hangers-on in the fight racket. And all three had walls covered with photos and paintings of dead and living pugs, along with such memorabilia as bloodied gloves, trunks, shoes, and robes.

Calazo then checked the records at Midtown North and Midtown South to see how many times the cops had been called to the three joints, and for what reasons. This would have been an endless task, but Benny had friends in every precinct in Manhattan, so, with a little help, the job took only two days.

After winnowing out incidents of public drunkenness, free-for-all donnybrooks, robberies, attempted rape, and one case of indecent exposure, Calazo was left with four unsolved cases of assault that pretty much followed the pattern of the attack on Detective Timothy Hogan.

In all four episodes, a badly beaten man had been found on the sidewalk, in an alley, or in the gutter near one of the three bars. None of the victims could positively identify his assailant, but all four had been drinking in one of Bellsey's favorite hangouts.

Showing the borrowed photo to owners, waiters, bartenders, and regular customers, Calazo learned a lot about Bellsey—none of it good. The detective was convinced the subject had been responsible for the four unsolved assaults, plus the attack on Tim Hogan. But he doubted if there would ever be enough evidence to arrest, let alone indict and convict.

His main problem, he knew, was to determine if Bellsey was really at home on the night Ellerbee was killed. Mrs. Lorna Bellsey had told Hogan that she hadn't actually seen her husband from eight-thirty to eleven o'clock. But that didn't necessarily mean he wasn't there.

In addition to solving that puzzle, Calazo was determined to do something about Hogan's beating. Big Tim was *estupido,* but still he was a cop, and that meant something to Benjamin Calazo.

Also, he hated guys like Ronald J. Bellsey who thought they could muscle their way through life and never pay any dues. So, in his direct way, Calazo began to plot how he might solve his problems and, at the same time, cut Bellsey off at the knees.

The fact that he would be retired, an ex-cop, in another three weeks, was also a factor. He would end his career gloriously by teaching a crud a lesson, avenging a fellow officer and, with luck, discovering who hammered in Dr. Ellerbee's skull.

That would be something to remember when he was playing shuffleboard in Florida.

• • •

IF EDWARD DELANEY had known what Calazo was planning, he'd have understood how the detective felt and sympathized. But that wouldn't have prevented him from yanking Calazo off the case. Personal hatreds had a way of fogging a man's judgment, and the downfall of Ronald Bellsey was small potatoes compared to finding Ellerbee's killer.

At the moment, Delaney had concerns of his own. Chief Suarez called and, in almost despairing tones, asked if there had been any progress. Delaney told him there had been a few minor developments, no break-throughs, and suggested the two of them get together and review the entire investigation. They agreed to meet at Delaney's home at nine o'clock on Wednesday night.

"I wish Mrs. Suarez could come with you," Delaney said. "I know my wife would like to meet her."

"That is most kind of you, sir," Suarez said. "I shall certainly ask her, and if we are able to arrange for the children, I am sure she will be delighted to visit your charming home."

Delaney repeated this conversation to Monica. "The guy talks like a grandee," he said. "He must drive those micks at headquarters right up the wall."

"Well, we got an invitation, too," Monica said. "Diane Ellerbee called and asked if we'd like to come up to her Brewster place with the Boones this Saturday. I told her I'd check with you first, then call her back. I spoke to Rebecca and she said she and Abner would love to go. Shall I tell Diane it's okay for Saturday?"

"Oh-ho," he said. "Now it's 'Diane,' is it? What happened to 'Doctor Ellerbee'?"

"I have a lot in common with her," Monica said loftily, "and it's silly not to be on a first-name basis."

"Oh? What do you have in common with her?"

"She's a very intelligent woman."

"You win," he said, laughing. "Sure, call and tell her we'll be there on Saturday. Is she going to feed us?"

"Of course. She said she's thinking about a buffet dinner for early evening."

"A buffet," he said grumpily. "That's as bad as a cafeteria."

• • •

PROMPTLY AT NINE o'clock on Wednesday evening, Michael and Rosa Suarez arrived at the brownstone, both wearing what Delaney later described as Sunday-go-to-meeting clothes. Introductions were made and the two couples settled down in the big living room, close to the fireplace, where a modest blaze warmed and mesmerized.

They talked of the current cold snap, of the problems of raising children, of the high cost of ground beef. Mrs. Suarez spoke little, at first, but Delaney had prepared hot rum toddies (with lemon and nutmeg), and after two small cups of that, Rosa's shyness thawed and she began to sparkle.

Monica brought out a plate of her special Christmas treats: pitted dates stuffed with almond paste, covered with a flaky pastry crust and then rolled in shredded coconut before baking. Rosa tried one, rolled her eyes ecstatically.

"Please," she begged, "the recipe!"

Monica laughed and held out her hand. "Come into the kitchen with me, Rosa. We'll trade secrets and let these two grouches talk business."

Delaney took Suarez into the study and provided cigars.

"First of all," the Chief said, "I must tell you that I have been forced to cut the number of men assigned to the Ellerbee homicide. We were getting no results, nada, and the murder was a month ago. More than a month. Since then there have been many, many things that demand attention. What I wish to say is that you and the people assigned to you are now our only hope. You understand why it was necessary to pull men off this case?"

"Sure," Delaney said genially. "What are you averaging—four or five homicides a day? I know you have a full plate and can't give any one case the coverage it needs. Believe me, Chief, it's always been that way. The problem comes with the territory."

"On the phone you spoke of some developments. But nothing important?"

"No," Delaney said, "not yet."

He then told Suarez how Isaac Kane and Sylvia Mae Otherton had been eliminated as suspects.

"That leaves us with four possibly violent patients, one of whom has confessed. I don't think that confession is worth a tinker's dam—but still, it's got to be checked out. The alibis of the other three are being investigated. At the moment, I'd say that Joan Yesell is the most interesting. It seems likely her mother lied when she told us Joan was home at the time of the killing. I've got two people working on that."

"So you are making progress."

"I don't know if you can call it progress," Delaney said cautiously. "But we are eliminating the possibles and getting down to the probables. Yes, I guess that's progress."

Suarez was silent, puffing on a cigar. Then he said, "But what if—"

Delaney held up a palm to stop him. "What if! Chief, the what-ifs can kill you if you let them. I think we've cleared Kane and Otherton. I believe it on the basis of good detective work and a little bit of luck. But what if Kane offed Ellerbee, and then cabbed back to the Beeles' apartment on West Eighty-third Street? They might remember him being there on the murder night, but couldn't swear to the time he arrived. And what if Otherton called the lobby clerk from *outside* on the night of the murder? What if she clubbed Ellerbee and then used his office phone to call the clerk just to set up an alibi? All I'm saying is that you can drown yourself in what-ifs. A detective has got to be imaginative, but if you let yourself get *too* imaginative, you're lost."

Michael Ramon Suarez gave him a wan smile. "That is very true—and a lesson I am still learning. It is a danger to assume that all criminals are possessed of super intelligence. Most of them are quite stupid."

"Exactly," Delaney agreed. "But some of them are also quite shrewd. After all, it's their ass that's on the line. What I believe is that all detectives have to walk a very thin line between the cold, hard facts and the what-ifs. Sometimes you have to go on a wing and a prayer."

"But in spite of all this, Edward, you are still confident the Ellerbee case can be cleared?"

"If I didn't believe that, I'd have told you and Thorsen and cleared out. I have a sense the pace is quickening. We've already eliminated two possible suspects. I think we're going to eliminate more."

Suarez sighed. "And what if you eliminate all six suspects? Where do you go from there?"

Delaney smiled grimly. "There you go with a what-if again. If all six are cleared, I can't tell you what I'll do next. *Someone* killed Ellerbee; we know that. If all six patients are eliminated, then we'll look around for other directions to take."

The other man looked at him curiously. "You do not give up easily, do you?"

"No, I do not. From all accounts, Doctor Ellerbee was a decent man living a good, worthwhile life. I don't like the idea of someone chilling him and walking away scot-free."

"Time," the Chief said, groaning. "How much time can we give this thing?"

"As long as it takes," Delaney said stonily. "I worked a murder-rape for almost two years and finally got the perp. I know your career depends on this being cleared up as soon as possible. But I've got to tell you now that if it isn't, and the detectives you've given me are withdrawn, I'll keep working it myself."

"Forever?"

"No, not forever. I may be an obstinate son of a bitch, but I'm not a romantic. At least I don't think I am. The time may come when I'll have to admit defeat. I've done that before; it won't kill me. Shall we see what the ladies are up to?"

The ladies were back in the living room, sitting close together on the couch and obviously enjoying each other's company.

"We must do this again," Monica said. "Our children will be home for Christmas, but perhaps after the holidays . . ."

"Then you must visit our home," Chief Suarez said. "For dinner. Rosa makes a paella that is a hint of what heaven must be like."

"I have a feeling," Delaney said, "that this friendship is going to prove fattening. Tell me, how did you two meet?"

"Rosa's parents owned a bodega in East Harlem," Suarez said. "It was ripped off, and I was a detective third at the time and sent to investigate. The first thing I said to her was, 'I shall marry you.' Is that not so, Rosa?"

She nodded happily. "And you?" she asked Monica.

"My first husband was murdered. Edward had charge of the case, and that's how we met."

Rosa was shocked. "And did"—she faltered—"was the killer caught?"

"Oh, yes," Monica said. "Edward never gives up. He is a very stubborn man."

"That is what I believe also," Suarez said. "It is very encouraging."

"Chief," Delaney said, "if the Ellerbee killing isn't cleared, and you don't get permanent appointment, I suppose you'll be returned to precinct duty. Can you take that?"

Suarez shrugged, spreading his hands helplessly. "It would be a disappointment. I would not be honest if I said I did not care. I could endure it, but still it would be a defeat. I think I would be more sorry for Thorsen than for myself. He has worked very hard to bring minorities into appointive ranks. My failure would be his failure as well."

"Don't worry too much about Ivar," Delaney advised. "He'll land on his feet. He's learned how to survive in the political jungle. Something I never did. But you're a young man with your career ahead of you. Do you have any contacts with the Hispanic political structure in the city?"

"I know some of the people, of course," Suarez said cautiously. "But I am not close to them, no."

"Get close to them," Delaney urged. "They have a lot of clout now, and are going to have more as voting patterns change. Let them know you're around. Invite them to your home for dinner. All politicians like the personal touch. That's their business. If Rosa's paella is as good as you say, you may have a secret weapon there."

Her hands flew to her face to hide her blush, and she giggled.

"I'm serious about this," Delaney continued. "You're getting up in ranks where you'll have to pay as much attention to politics as you do to police work. Think of it as another part of your job. I wasn't able to hack it, but don't make my mistakes. This is a big, brawling, confused city, and politics is the glue that holds it together. I admit that sometimes the glue smells like something the cat dragged in—but can you think of a better, more human system? I can't. I'm willing to see us go blundering along, making horrendous mistakes. It can be discouraging, but it's a hell of a lot better than a storm trooper shouting, 'You *vill* obey orders!' So get into politics, Chief. Or at least touch bases with the heavies. It could do you a lot of good."

"Yes," Suarez said thoughtfully, "I think you are correct. I have been so busy with the nuts and bolts of my job that I have neglected the personal relations that might have made my job easier. Thank you for your advice, Edward."

"Don't just thank me—*do* it!"

• • •

LATER THAT NIGHT, preparing for bed, Delaney said, "Nice, nice people."

"Aren't they," Monica agreed. "That Rosa is a doll. Were you really serious about him cultivating the politicos?"

"Absolutely. If he wants to protect his ass. Thorsen can do just so much. But Suarez would be wise to build up some political muscle with the power brokers."

"Well, if he's going to do that, I better take Rosa in hand. She dresses like a frump. She's really a very attractive woman and could do a lot more with herself than she does."

"You mean," he said solemnly, "you want to convert her into a sex object?"

"And you can go to hell," his wife said, but Delaney was still pursuing Suarez's career.

"I don't know the man too well," Delaney said. "A couple of meetings, a couple of phone calls . . . But I have the feeling his strong suit is administration. I really don't think he's got the basic drive to be a good detective. He's a little too cool, too detached. There's no obsession there."

"Is that what a good detective needs—an obsession?"

"You better believe it. Abner Boone has it and I'm betting Jason has it, too."

"Do you have it?"

"I suppose," he said shortly. He turned to stare at her. "You're a beautiful woman. Did I ever tell you that?"

"Not recently."

"Well, I'm telling you now."

"And what, pray, is the reason for this sudden romantic frenzy?"

"I thought you might be properly appreciative," he said, winking at her.

"I am," she said, crooking a finger at him.

20

•

DETECTIVES HELEN VENABLE AND BRIAN ESTRELLA HAD NEVER worked together before, but they found to their pleased surprise that they made a good team. He thought her a bright, vigorous woman willing to take on her share of the donkeywork. She thought him a bit stodgy, but smart and understanding. Best of all, he didn't pull any of that macho bullshit she was used to from other cops.

She told him everything she had learned about Joan Yesell, and especially the business of Mrs. Blanche Yesell and her Friday night bridge club.

"The old bitch was lying to us," she said bitterly.

"Maybe and maybe not," Estrella said. "There was a bad storm that night; the bridge game could have been called off. In that case she was probably home like she says. What's your take on Joan?"

"I can't believe she's the perp. I swear to God, Brian, she wouldn't hurt a fly."

"But she'll hurt herself. She's suicidal, isn't she?"

"Suicidal, yes; homicidal, no."

He went through the slow routine of packing his pipe, tamping down the tobacco, lighting up, puffing. "Helen, sounds to me like you've already made up your mind about this woman. You like her?"

"Very much. We're even talking about sharing an apartment."

"Take it easy," he advised. "Wait'll we clear her first."

"Brian, she's such a little mouse. She hasn't got a mean bone in her body. I tell you she's just incapable of snuffing Ellerbee—or anyone else. She cries when she sees a stray dog."

"Uh-huh," he said. "The meanest killer I ever scragged raised gerbils."

"You want to talk to Joan and see for yourself?"

"Not yet," he said. "You keep up the buddy-buddy routine with her, but don't tell her I'm working with you."

Without making it obvious, he spent all week double-checking Venable's investigation—and couldn't fault it. He talked to doctors at St. Vincent's, with fellow employees at Yesell's law office, with neighbors, storekeepers, even the postman who delivered mail to the Yesells' brownstone.

Everything he heard substantiated what Helen had told him: Joan Yesell was a timid, withdrawn woman. The only gossip Estrella picked up was that

Blanche Yesell was a real battle-ax who treated her daughter like a cretin without the brains or will to make her own decisions.

On Friday night the two detectives were slouched in Venable's Honda parked a few doors down from the Yesells' home.

"With my luck," Helen said gloomily, "Mama Blanche will have the bridge club meeting at her apartment tonight."

"Doesn't make any difference," Estrella said. "If she does, you and I will tail two of the women after the game breaks up. Brace them, get their names and addresses, and we'll take it from there. But if Mrs. Yesell comes out—"

And, while he was talking, she did come out. She turned eastward and crossed the street.

"That's her," Venable said tensely.

"Okay," Estrella said, "you go after her and get the number of the building she goes into. I'm going to make a phone call. Meet you back here."

Helen took off after the scurrying Mrs. Yesell. Brian headed for Eighth Avenue and used a wall phone in an all-night deli. He called the Yesells' apartment.

A faint voice: "Hello?"

"Mrs. Blanche Yesell, please," Estrella said.

"She's not here right now. Who's calling?"

"This is Detective Brian Estrella of the New York Police Department. To whom am I speaking?"

"This is Joan Yesell, Mrs. Blanche Yesell's daughter."

"Miss Yesell, it is important that I contact your mother tonight. There's a document we'd like her to sign. It's just routine, but we do have to go by the rules and regulations, you know."

"A document? About Doctor Ellerbee's death?"

"Yes. Just her statement that she was home with you on that night. Could you tell me where I might reach her?"

"She's at her bridge club."

"Could you give me the phone number so I can contact her?"

"Well, she's at Mrs. Ferguson's tonight."

"Do you have the phone number?" he persisted.

She hesitated a moment, then gave him the number. Using a ballpoint pen, he jotted it down on the back of his hand.

"Thank you very much, Miss Yesell."

A few minutes later he was back at the Honda. Helen was waiting for him.

"I got the address," Venable said.

"And I got the name and phone number. We're in business."

• • •

THE NEXT MORNING Delaney felt equally optimistic as he and Monica set out with the Boones for Diane Ellerbee's country home. "Looks like a splendid day," Delaney gloated.

And so it was. A blue sky shimmered like a butterfly's wing. The sun was a hot plate and there, to the east, one could see a faint smudge of white moon. The sharp air bit like ether, and the whole world seemed scrubbed and polished.

Traffic was heavy, but they made surprisingly good time, stopping only once at a Brewster gas station to ask directions, use the rest rooms, and buy five gallons of gas in gratitude.

They drove slowly along a country road, commenting on the mailboxes: a windmill, a miniature house, a model plane.

"Very cutesy," Delaney said. "What's the Ellerbees' going to be—a little black leather couch with a red flag?"

But the mailbox marked ELLERBEE was the plain aluminum variety. It was at the entrance to a narrow side road that curved through a stand of skeleton trees up to the house and outbuildings. The gentle rise was not high enough to be called a hill, but sufficiently elevated to provide a pleasant view of the rolling countryside.

Boone drove onto the graveled apron outside the three-car garage. Parked outside was a dusty Volkswagen and the Ellerbees' Jeep station wagon. The garage door was up, and they could see Dr. Simon's bottle-green XJ6 Jaguar sedan and Dr. Diane's silver and black 1971 Mercedes-Benz.

"I've got to get a look at that Mercedes," Delaney said. "It's a beauty."

He and Boone went into the garage while their wives slowly strolled up to the main house along a curving pathway of slate flagstones.

Delaney and Boone spent a few minutes admiring the handsome cars in the garage.

"I'll take the Jag," Boone said, then laughed. "Can you imagine me driving up to Midtown North in that buggy? They'd know I was in the bag for sure."

"Mmm," Delaney said. "I wonder why she hasn't sold it. Who needs a Jaguar *and* a Mercedes?"

"Maybe she can't find a buyer," the Sergeant said. "About all I can afford is that old Beetle parked outside. Who do you suppose owns it?"

They walked up to the main house. The door was open, and on the small stoop, awaiting them, was Dr. Julius Samuelson.

"Now you know who owns the Beetle," Delaney said, sotto voce.

Inside, there was warmth, fragrance from scented pressed logs blazing in a fireplace, and redolent cooking odors.

"Ahh," Delaney said, sniffing appreciatively, "garlic. I love it."

"You better," Dr. Diane said, laughing. "That's Beef Bourguignon bubbling away, and my cook has a heavy hand with the garlic. But there's fresh parsley in the salad, and that should help. Now let's all have a drink before I give you the grand tour." She gestured toward a marble-topped sideboard laden with bottles and decanters.

The spacious living room had exposed oak ceiling beams and a fieldstone fireplace. Floors were random-width pine planking. French doors at the rear opened onto a tiled patio and the swimming pool, now emptied and covered.

The master bedroom on the ground floor and the guest bedrooms on the second had individual fireplaces and private baths. The modern kitchen was fitted with butcher-block counters and track lighting. There was a small attached greenhouse.

The dining room was dominated by an impressive ten-foot table topped with a single plank of teak that looked thick enough to stop a cannonball.

There was no disguising the loving care (and money) that had gone into that home. Later, Delaney remarked to Monica that there wasn't a single piece of furniture, painting, rug, or bibelot that he didn't covet for his own.

But finally, what impressed the guests the most was the informal comfort: warm colors, glowing wood, gleaming brass and copper. It was easy to understand how such a place could serve as sanctuary from the steel and concrete city.

Looking around, Delaney could appreciate Dr. Diane's fury at her husband's murder and her desire for vengeance. For he knew that possessions charm most when shared with others, and thought it possible that since Dr. Simon's death, all those lovely things had begun to pall. Now they were just *things* to Diane Ellerbee.

The women bundled up to stroll across the patio and inspect the design of the formal English garden. Dr. Samuelson stayed close to the living room fire, but Delaney and Boone took a turn around the grounds, admiring the view and imagining what a gem this place would be in spring and summer.

They wandered down behind the main house, beyond the swimming pool and garden. Hands in their pockets, shoulders hunched, they tramped to a copse of bony trees. And there they saw the stream, looking black and cold, with a lacework of ice building out from both banks.

"Fish?" Abner Boone said. "D'you suppose?"

"Could be," Delaney said. "Depends on where it comes from. And where it ends up. I wonder if they swim in it in the summer."

He pried a small stone loose from the hard earth and tossed it into the water. But they could not judge its depth.

Back in the house, everyone had another drink and clustered around the fireplace. It was early afternoon, but already the day had grayed, the sun had lost its brilliance.

"I'm going to put out some hors d'oeuvres," Diane said. "Marta and Jan worked all morning on the food, but I let them go home. We can serve ourselves, can't we?"

"Of course," Delaney said with heavy good humor. "We're all housebroken. What can I do to help?"

"Not a thing," she said. "Just eat. Julie, give me a hand in the kitchen."

He followed her obediently.

There was a feast of appetizers: boiled shrimp, chunks of kielbasa, olives stuffed with peppers, sweet gherkins, smoked salmon and sturgeon, thick slices of sharp cheddar and Stilton, four different kinds of crackers and biscuits, chicken livers in a wine sauce, paper-thin slices of prosciutto, and brisling sardines in olive oil.

"Here goes my diet," Rebecca Boone said, sighing.

"Just remember to leave room for dinner," Diane said, laughing.

"Edward will do his share," Monica Delaney said. "He could live on food like this."

"Live and thrive," her husband agreed happily, sampling everything. "This salmon makes me believe in God."

Finally they were surfeited and sat back with glazed eyes, holding up hands in surrender.

"Julie," Diane Ellerbee said crisply, "let's clean up."

But Delaney was on his feet before Samuelson could struggle out of his armchair.

"It's my turn," he said to Samuelson. "You just sit there and relax. I'm good at this; Monica trained me."

So he and Diane cleaned up the living room, Delaney demonstrating his proficiency as a waiter with four or five plates laid along a steady, outthrust arm.

In the kitchen, he admired her efficiency. All the leftovers went into separate airtight containers. Plates and cutlery were rinsed in a trice and stacked in the dishwasher. She worked with quick grace, not a wasted movement.

She was wearing black cashmere—sweater and skirt—and her flaxen hair was coiled high and held in place with an exotic tortoiseshell comb. He saw her in profile and once again marveled at the classic perfection of her beauty: something chiseled—the stone cut away to reveal the image.

"Well!" she said brightly, looking at her aseptic, organized kitchen. "I think that does it. Thank you for your help. Shall we join the others?"

"A moment," he said, holding out a hand to stop her. "I think you deserve a report on what we've been doing."

She stared, the hostess's mask dropping, features hardening: the vengeful widow once again.

"Yes," she said. "Thank you. I was hoping you'd volunteer."

They sat close together on high stools at the butcher-block counter. They could hear soft conversation and laughter from the living room. But the kitchen provided a sense of secret intimacy as he told her what they'd learned.

"In my judgment," he concluded, "Kane and Otherton are clean. That leaves four of the patients you gave us. Their alibis are still being checked. It's a long, laborious process, and we are still left with the mysterious second set of footprints."

"What do you mean?" Diane said.

"There were apparently two visitors to your husband's office that night.

At the same or different times? We don't know. Yet. Now I have a question for you: Were you surprised that your husband canceled all his patients' outstanding bills?''

She peered at him in the gloom, wide-eyed, her mouth open. "Oh," she said. "How did you find out about that?"

"Doctor Ellerbee," he said patiently, "this is a criminal investigation. Everything is important until proved otherwise. Naturally we were interested in the probate of your husband's will, hoping it might give us a lead. Were you surprised that he forgave his patients' debts?"

"No, I wasn't surprised. He was a very generous man. It was entirely in character for him to do something like that."

"Then you were aware of what was in his will before he died?"

"Of course. Just as he was aware of what was in my will. We had no secrets from each other."

"You and your late husband had the same attorney, did you?"

"No," she said, "as a matter of fact we didn't. Simon used an old college friend of his—a man I couldn't stand. I have my own attorney."

"Well, it isn't important," Delaney said, waving it away. "About those four patients we haven't yet cleared—did you ever meet them personally?"

"I met several of my husband's patients," she said. "Usually briefly, and by accident. Is there one in particular you want to know about?"

"Joan Yesell."

"The suicidal woman? Yes, I met her once. Why do you ask?"

"It's possible that she's given us a fake alibi. What was your take on her?"

"I only met her for a moment—hardly long enough to form an opinion. But I thought her a rather plain, unattractive woman. Not much spark to her. But as I say, it was just a brief meeting. My husband introduced her and that was that. And now I think we should join the others."

But before they went into the living room, she put a hand lightly on his arm.

"Thank you for keeping me informed, Mr. Delaney," she said huskily. "I know you're working very hard on this, and I appreciate it."

He nodded and held open the swinging kitchen door for her. She passed close to him and he caught her scent: something strong and musky that stirred him.

They came into the living room, where the other four sat logy with food and drink.

"Doctor Ellerbee," Delaney said, hoping to stir his friends. "Doctor Samuelson . . . did it ever occur to you that the roles of the detective and the psychiatrist are very similar? We both use the same investigative techniques: endless interrogation, the slow amassing of what may or may not be consequential clues, the piecing together of a puzzle until it forms a recognizable pattern. Psychiatrists are really detectives—are they not?"

Dr. Julius K. Samuelson straightened up, suddenly alert and interested.

"The techniques may be similar," he said in his high-pitched voice, "but the basic motives are antipodal. The detective is conducting a criminal investigation. He seeks to assign blame. But blame is not in the psychiatrist's lexicon. The patient cannot be punished for what he has become. He is usually a victim, not a criminal."

"You mean," Delaney said, deliberately provoking, "he is without guilt? What about a psychopath who kills? Is he totally guiltless?"

"I think," Diane said in assertive tones, "that what Julie is suggesting is that the act of murder is in itself prima facie evidence of mental or emotional instability."

"Oh-ho," Delaney said. "The poor lads and lasses who kill—all sick, are they? To be treated rather than punished. And what of the man who molests children? Just a little ill, but blameless?"

"And what about the guy who kills for profit?" Sergeant Boone said hotly. "We see it all the time: some innocent slugged down for a few bucks. Is the killer to go free because society hasn't provided him with a guaranteed income? You think a total welfare state will eliminate murder for profit? No way! People will continue to kill for money. Not because they're sick, but because they're greedy. Capital punishment is the best treatment."

"I don't believe in the death penalty," Rebecca Boone said stoutly.

"I agree," Diane said. "Execution is not the answer. Statistics prove it doesn't act as a deterrent."

"It sure as hell deters the guy who gets chopped," Delaney said. "He's not going to get paroled, go out, and kill again. The trouble with you psychiatrists is that you're as bad as priests: You think everyone can be redeemed. Tell them, Sergeant."

"Some people are born rotten and stay rotten the rest of their lives," Boone said. "Ask any cop. The cruds of this world are beyond redemption."

"Right!" Delaney said savagely. He turned to the two doctors. "What you won't admit is that some people are so morally corrupt that they cannot be helped. They accept evil as a way of life. They love it! They enjoy it! And the world is better off without them."

"What about someone who kills in passion?" Monica asked. "A sudden, uncontrollable passion."

"Temporary insanity?" Boone said. "Is that what you're pleading? It just won't wash. We're supposed to be *Homo sapiens*—wise, intelligent animals with a civilized rein on our primitive instincts. A crime of passion is a *crime*—period. And the reasons should have no effect on the verdict."

Then they all began to argue: blame, guilt, capital punishment, parole, the conflict between law and justice. Delaney sat back happily and listened to the brouhaha he had started. A good house party. Finally . . .

"Did you ever notice," he said, "that when a killer is nabbed bloody-handed, the defense attorney always goes for the insanity plea and hires a battery of 'friendly' psychiatrists?"

"And meanwhile," Boone added, "the accused announces to the world that he's become a born-again Christian and wants only to renounce his wicked ways and live a saintly life."

"You're too ready to find excuses for your patients," Delaney said to the two psychiatrists. "Won't you admit the existence of evil in the world? Would you say Hitler was evil or just mentally ill?"

"Both," Dr. Samuelson said. "His illness took the form of evil. But if it had been caught in time it could have been treated."

"Sure it could," Delaney said grimly. "A bullet to the brain would have been very effective."

The argument flared again and gradually centered on the problem of the "normal" person living a law-abiding existence who suddenly commits a totally inexplicable heinous crime.

"I had a case like that once," Delaney said. "A dentist in the Bronx . . . Apparently under no great emotional stress or business pressures. A quiet guy. A good citizen. But he started sniping at people from the roof of his apartment house. Killed two, wounded five. No one could explain why. I think he's still in the acorn academy. But I never thought he was insane. You'll laugh when I tell you what I think his motive was. I think he was just bored. His life was empty, lacked excitement. So he started popping people with his hunting rifle. It gave a kick to his existence."

"A very penetrating analysis," Samuelson said admiringly. "We call it anomie: a state of disorientation and isolation."

"But no excuse for killing," Delaney said. "There's never an excuse for that. He was an intelligent man; he knew what he was doing was wrong."

"Perhaps he couldn't help himself," Diane Ellerbee said. "That does happen, you know."

"No excuse," Delaney repeated stubbornly. "We all may have homicidal urges at some time in our lives, but we control them. If there is no self-discipline, then we're back in the jungle. Self-discipline is what civilization is all about."

Diane smiled faintly. "I'm afraid we're not all as strong as you."

"Strong? I'm a pussycat. Right, Monica?"

"I refuse to answer," she said, "on the grounds that I might incriminate myself."

Diane laughed and got up to prepare dinner. The women set out plates, glasses, thick pink napkins, and cutlery on linen place mats.

The Beef Bourguignon was in two cast-iron Dutch ovens that had to be handled with thick asbestos mitts. Delaney and Boone carried the pots into the dining room and set them on trivets. Samuelson handled the salad bowl and baskets of hot, crusty French bread. Then Diane Ellerbee put out a '78 California cabernet sauvignon.

"That's beautiful," Delaney said, examining the label.

"The last of the last case," their hostess said sadly. "Simon and I loved it so much. We kept it for special occasions. Mr. Delaney, would you uncork the bottles?"

"My pleasure," he said. "All of them?"

"All," she said firmly. "Once you taste it, you'll know why."

They had plenty of room at the long table. The hostess sat at the head and filled plates with the stew, and small wooden bowls with the salad.

"It's heaven," Monica said. "Diane, you'll never make me believe this is stew meat."

"As a matter of fact, it's sirloin. Please, when you're ready for seconds, help yourself; I'm too busy eating."

They were all busy eating, but not too busy to keep the talk flowing. Abner Boone was seated next to Monica, and Rebecca was paired with Dr. Samuelson. Delaney sat on the right of the hostess.

"I hope," he said, leaning toward her, "you weren't upset by the conversation before dinner. All that talk about crime and punishment."

"I wasn't upset at all," she assured him. "I found it fascinating. So many viewpoints . . ."

"I was a little hard on psychiatrists," he admitted. "I'm really not that hostile toward your profession. I was just—"

"I know what you were just," she interrupted. "You were trying to get an argument started to wake everyone up. You succeeded brilliantly, and I'm grateful for it."

"That's me," he said with a wry smile. "The life of the party. One thing you said surprised me."

"Oh? What was that?"

"Your objection to capital punishment. After what you've been through, I'd have thought you'd be in favor of the death penalty."

"No," she said shortly, "I'm not. I want Simon's murderer caught and punished. To the limit of the law. But I don't believe in an eye for an eye or a life for a life."

He was saved from replying by Dr. Samuelson, who raised a hand and called in a squeaky voice. "A question!" They all quieted and turned to him. "Will anyone object if I sop up my gravy with chunks of this marvelous bread?"

There were no objections.

As the hostess had predicted, the wine went swiftly, and the stew and salad were almost totally consumed. Later, when the table was cleared, the women went into the kitchen, shooing the men back to the living room. The room had become chilly, and Samuelson added two more pressed logs to the fireplace.

"There's central heating, of course," he told the others, "but Diane prefers to keep the thermostat low and use the fireplaces."

"Can't blame her for that," Abner Boone said. "Saves on fuel, and an open fire is something special. But shouldn't she have a screen?"

"I think there's one around," Samuelson said vaguely, "but she doesn't use it."

They sat staring into the rejuvenated blaze.

"I was afraid we might have upset Doctor Ellerbee," Delaney said to Samuelson, "with all our talk about murders. But she says no."

"Diane is a very strong woman," Samuelson said. "She has made a very swift recovery from the trauma of Simon's death. Only occasionally now do I see how it has affected her. Suddenly she is sad, or sits in silence, staring at nothing. It is to be expected. It was a terrible shock, but she is coping."

"I suppose her work helps," Boone said.

"Oh, yes. Dealing with other people's problems is excellent therapy for your own. I speak from personal experience. Not a total cure, you understand, but a help. Tell me, Mr. Delaney, you are making progress in the investigation?"

"Some," he said cautiously. "As Doctor Ellerbee probably told you, we're still working on the alibis. I haven't yet thanked you for getting her to cooperate."

Samuelson held up a hand. "I was happy to assist. And do you think any of the patients she named might have been capable of the murder?"

"Too early to tell. We've eliminated two of them. But there's one, a woman, who claims an alibi that doesn't seem to hold up."

"Oh? Did Diane give you any background on her?"

"Suffers from depression. And she has attempted suicide several times. Once since we started questioning her."

"Well . . ." the psychiatrist said doubtfully, "she may be the one you seek, but I find it hard to believe. I can't recall a case when a suicidal type turned to homicide. I am not saying it could not happen, you understand, but the potential suicide and the potential murderer have little in common. Still, human behavior is endlessly different, so do not let my comments influence your investigation."

"Oh, they won't," Delaney said cheerfully. "We'll keep plugging."

The women came in, and the men rose. They talked for a while, and then, catching Monica's look, Delaney suggested it might be time for them to depart, not knowing what traffic would be like on Saturday night. The hostess protested—but not too strongly.

They thanked Dr. Ellerbee for her hospitality, the wonderful food, and complimented her again on her beautiful home.

"Do plan to come back," she urged them. "In the spring or summer when the trees are out and the garden is planted. I think you'll like it."

"I know we shall," Monica said. She and Rebecca embraced their hostess and they were on their way.

On the drive back to Manhattan, Delaney said, "Do you suppose Samuelson is staying for the weekend?"

"You dirty old man," Monica said. "What if he does?"

"She's got three servants," Abner Boone said. "The Polack couple and him."

"Oh, you picked up on that, did you?" Delaney said. "You're right. 'Julie, mix the drinks. Julie, get the coffee.' He hops."

"I think he's in love with her," Rebecca said.

"Well, why not?" Monica said. "A widow and a widower. With so much in common. I think it's nice they have each other."

"He's too old for her," the Sergeant said.

"You think so?" Delaney said. "I think she's older than all of us. Good Lord, that's a grand home!"

"A little *too* beautiful," Rebecca said. "Like a stage set. Did you notice how she kept emptying the ashtrays?"

"If it's full ashtrays you want," Delaney said, "how about stopping at our place for a nightcap?"

21

•

DETECTIVE ROSS KONIGSBACHER HAD TO ADMIT HE WAS ENJOYING the best duty in fourteen years with the Department. This faggot he was assigned to, L. Vincent Symington, was turning out to be not such a bad guy after all.

He seemed to have all the money in the world, and wasn't shy about spreading it around. He picked up all the tabs for dinners and drinks, and insisted on taking cabs wherever they went—even if it was only a five-block trip. He was a manic tipper, and he had already started buying gifts for the Kraut.

It began with a bottle of Frangelico that Vince wanted him to taste. Then Ross got an identification bracelet of heavy silver links, a cashmere pullover, a Countess Mara tie, a lizard skin belt, a foulard ascot. Every time they met, Symington had a present for him.

Ross had been invited to Vincent's apartment twice, and thought it the greatest pad he had ever seen. On one of those visits, Symington had prepared dinner for them—filet mignon that had to be the best steak Konigsbacher ever tasted.

Meanwhile, the Kraut was submitting bullshit reports to Sergeant Boone, wanting this assignment to go on forever. But Boone couldn't be scammed that easily, and recently he had been pressuring Konigsbacher to show some results: Either confirm Symington's alibi or reject it. So, sighing, Ross did some work.

The first time he went into Stallions, he bellied up to the bar, ordered a beer, and looked around. Symington had been right: He had never seen so much black leather in his life. All the weirdos were trying to look like members of motorcycle gangs. Their costumes creaked when they moved, and they even had zippers on their cuffs.

"Nick been around?" he asked the hennaed bartender casually.

"Nick who, darling? I know three Nicks."

"The kid who wants to be an actor."

"Oh, *him*. He's in and out of here all the time."

"I'm casting for a commercial and might have a bit for him. If you see him, tell him, will you?"

"How can he get in touch with you, sweet?"

"My name is Ross," Konigsbacher said. "I'll be around."

The bartender nodded. No last names, no addresses, no phone numbers.

The Kraut spent more time at Stallions than he did at home. He slowly sipped beers in the late afternoons and early evenings before his dinner dates with Symington. He began to like the place. You could get high just by breathing deeply, and if the Kraut wanted to set a record for drug busts, he could have made a career out of this one joint.

It took him five days. He was sitting at a small corner table, working on a brew, when a kid came over from the bar and lounged in front of him. He had a 1950 duck's-ass haircut with enough grease to lubricate the *QE2*. He was wearing tight stonewashed jeans, a T-shirt with the sleeves cut off, and a wide leather bracelet with steel studs.

"You Ross?" he asked lazily, eyes half-closed, doing an early Marlon Brando.

"Yeah," the Kraut said, touching a knuckle to his blond mustache. "You Nick?"

"I could be. Sidney pointed you out. Something about a commercial bit."

"Pull up a chair. Want a beer? Or would you prefer a banana brandy?"

Then the kid's eyes opened wide. "How'd you know what I drink?"

"A fegela told me. You know what a fegela is? A little bird. Now sit down."

Nick hesitated a moment, then pulled up a chair.

"You don't look like a film producer to me," he said.

"I'm not," Konigsbacher said. "I'm a cop." Then, when Nick started to rise, the Kraut clamped onto his wrist and pulled him down again. "Be nice," he said. "You're carrying a switchblade on your hip. It shows. I could run you in on a concealed weapons charge. It probably wouldn't stick, but it would be a pain in the ass for you and maybe a night in the slammer where the boogies will ream you. Is that what you want?"

The kid had moxie; he didn't cave.

"Let's see your ID," he said coldly.

Konigsbacher showed it to him, down low, so no one else in the bar would notice.

"Okay," Nick said, "so you're a cop. What do you want?"

Symington was also right about the accent; it came out "waddya wan'?"

"Just the answers to a few questions. Won't take long. Do you remember a Friday night early in November? There was a hell of a rainstorm. You were in here that night."

"You asking me or telling me?"

"I'm asking. A rainy Friday night early in November. A guy came in, sat with you, bought you a few banana brandies. This was about nine, ten o'clock. Around there."

"Yeah? What'd he look like?"

Konigsbacher described L. Vincent Symington: balding, flabby face, little eyes. A guy running to suet, probably wearing a bracelet of chunky gold links.

"What's he done?" Nick asked.

"Do you remember a guy like that?" Ross asked patiently.

"I don't know," the kid said, shrugging. "I meet a lot of guys."

The Kraut leaned forward, smiling. "Now I tell you what, sonny," he said in a low, confidential voice, "you keep smart-assing me, I'm going to put the cuffs on you and frog-march you out of here. But I won't take you to the station house. I'll take you into the nearest alley and kick your balls so hard that you'll be singing soprano for the rest of your life. You don't believe it? Just try me."

"Yeah, I met a guy like that," Nick said sullenly. "A fat old fart. He bought me some drinks."

"What was his name?"

"I don't remember."

"Try," Ross urged. "Remember what I said about the alley, and try real hard."

"Victor," the kid said.

"Try again."

"Vince. Something like that."

Konigsbacher patted his cheek. "Good boy," he said.

As far as the Kraut was concerned, that was enough to clear L. Vincent Symington. He had never believed in the poof's guilt in the first place. Vince could never kill anyone with a hammer. A knife maybe—a woman's weapon. But not a hammer.

So, Konigsbacher thought sadly, that was the end of that. He'd submit a report to Boone and they'd shift him to some shit assignment. No more cashmere sweaters and free dinners and lazy evenings sitting around Symington's swell apartment, soaking up his booze and trading dirty jokes.

But maybe, the Kraut thought suddenly, just maybe there was a way he could juggle it. He would clear Symington—he owed the guy that—but it didn't mean the gravy train had to come to a screaming halt. Confident again, he headed for dinner at the Dorian Gray, wondering what Vince would bring him tonight.

• • •

ROBERT KEISMAN AND Jason thought Harold Gerber might be a whacko, but he was innocent of the murder of Dr. Simon Ellerbee. Gerber's confession was what Keisman called a "blivet"—four pounds of shit in a two-pound bag.

The Vietnam vet just didn't know enough of the unpublished details to fake a convincing confession. But Delaney wanted the guy's innocence proved out one way or another, and that's what the two cops set out to do.

The Catholic Bible was a flimsy lead. They had no gut reaction one way or the other. The only reason they worked at it was that they had nothing else. It was just something to do.

They started with the Manhattan Yellow Pages and found the section for Churches—Roman Catholic. There were 103 listings, some of them with odd names like Most Precious Blood Church and Our Lady of Perpetual Help. The thought of visiting 103 churches was daunting, but when they picked out the ones in the Greenwich Village area, the job didn't seem so enormous.

The Spoiler took the churches to the east of Sixth Avenue and Jason Two took those to the west. Carrying their photos of Harold Gerber, they set out to talk to priests, rectors, janitors, and anyone else who might have seen Gerber on the night Ellerbee was murdered.

It was the dullest of donkeywork: pounding the pavements, showing their ID, displaying Gerber's photograph, and asking the same questions over and over: "Do you know this man? Have you ever seen him? Has he been in your church? Does the name Harold Gerber mean anything to you?"

Sometimes the church would be locked, no one around, and Keisman and Jason would have to go back two or three times before they could find someone to question. They worked eight-hour days and met after five o'clock to have a couple of beers with Harold Gerber. They never told him what they were doing, and he always asked complainingly, "When are you guys going to arrest me?"

"Soon, Harold," they'd tell him. "Soon."

They kept at it for four days, and were beginning to think they were drilling a dry hole. But then the Spoiler got a break. He was talking to a man who worked in an elegant little church on 11th Street off Fifth Avenue. The old man seemed to be a kind of handyman who polished pews and made sure the electric candles were working—jobs like that.

He examined Keisman's ID, then stared at the photo of Harold Gerber.

"What's he wanted for?" he asked in a creaky voice.

"He's not wanted for anything," the Spoiler lied smoothly. "We're just trying to find him. He's in the Missing Persons file. His parents are anxious. You can understand that, can't you?"

"Oh, sure," the gaffer said, still staring at Gerber's photo. "I've got a son of my own; I know how they'd feel. What does this kid do?"

"Do?"

"His job. What does he work at?"

"I don't think he works at anything. He's on disability. A Vietnam vet. A little mixed up in the head."

"That I can understand. A Vietnam veteran, you say?"

"Uh-huh."

"And he's a Catlick?"

"That's right."

"Well," the handyman said, sighing. "I'll tell you. There's a priest—well, he's not really a priest. I don't mean he's unfrocked or anything like that. But he's kind of wild, and he's got no parish of his own. They more or less let him do his thing, if you catch my drift."

Keisman nodded, waiting patiently.

"Well, this priest," the janitor went on, enjoying his long story more than the Spoiler was, "Father Gautier, or Grollier, some name like that—he opened a home for Vietnam vets. Gives them a sandwich, a place to flop, or just come in out of the cold. I'm not knocking him, y'understand; he's doing good. But he's running a kind of scruffy joint. It's not a regular church."

"Where does he get the money?" the detective asked. "For the sandwiches, the beds, or whatever? The Church finance him?"

"You kidding? He does it all on his own. He gets donations from here, there, everywhere. Somehow he keeps going."

"That's interesting," Keisman said. "Where's his place located?"

"I don't know," the old guy said. "Somewhere south of Houston Street, I think. But I don't know the address."

"Thank you very much," the Spoiler said.

He told Jason about the priest, and they agreed it was the best lead—the *only* lead—they had uncovered so far. So they started making phone calls.

They phoned the Archdiocese of New York, the Catholic Press Association, Catholic Charities, the American Legion, asking if anyone knew the address of a Catholic priest who was running a shelter for Vietnam vets somewhere around Houston Street in Manhattan. No one could help them.

Then they called the Catholic War Veterans and got it: Father Frank Gautier, in a storefront church on Mott Street, a block south of Houston.

"Little Italy," Jason said. "I used to pound a beat down there."

"Wherever," Keisman said. "Let's go."

They found the place after asking four residents of the neighborhood. It looked like a Mafia social club, the plate-glass window painted an opaque green, and no name or signs showing. The door was unlocked and they pushed in. There was a big front room that looked like it might have been a butcher shop at one time: tiled walls, a stained plank floor, tin ceiling.

But it was warm enough. Almost too warm. There were about a dozen guys, maybe half of them blacks, sitting around on rickety chairs, reading paperbacks, playing cards, dozing, or just counting the walls. They all looked like derelicts, with unlaced boots, worn jeans, ragged jackets. One was in drag, with a blond wig and a feathered boa.

No one looked up when the two officers came in. Keisman stood close to a man holding a month-old copy of *The Wall Street Journal*.

"Father Gautier around?" he asked pleasantly.

The man looked up, slowly examined both of them, then turned to a back room.

"Hey, pop!" he roared. "Two new fish for you!"

The man who came waddling out of the back room was shaped like a ripe pear. He was wearing a long-sleeved black blouse with a white, somewhat soiled clerical collar. His blue Levi's were cinched with a cowboy belt and ornate silver buckle. He was bearded and had a thick mop of pepper-and-salt hair.

"Father Gautier?" Jason asked.

"Guilty," the priest said in a hoarse voice. "Who you?"

They showed him their IDs.

"Oh, God," he said, sighing, "now what? Who did what to whom?"

"No one we know of," Keisman said. He held out the photo of Harold Gerber. "You know this man?"

Gautier looked at the photograph, then raised his eyes to the officers. "You got any money?" he demanded.

They were startled.

"Money!" the priest repeated impatiently. "Dough. Bucks. You want information? No pay, no say. Believe me, it's for a good cause. You'll get your reward in heaven—or wherever."

Sheepishly Jason and Keisman pulled out their wallets. They each proffered a five. Gautier grabbed the bills eagerly.

"You, Izzy!" he yelled at one of the lounging blacks. "Take this to Vic's and get us a ham. Tell him it's for us, and if it has as much fat on it as the last one, we'll come over there and trash his place. Bone in."

"Yassa, massa," the black said, touching a finger to his forehead.

"You two come with me," the Father said, and led the way into the back room. He took them into a cluttered office hardly larger than a walk-in closet. He closed the door, turned to face them.

"Yeah, I know him," he said. "Harold Gerber. What's he done?"

"Nothing we know for sure," the Spoiler said. "We're just trying to establish his whereabouts on a certain Friday night."

"He was here," Gautier said promptly.

"Hey," Jason said, "wait a minute. We haven't told you *which* Friday night."

The priest shook his head. "Doesn't make any difference. Harold is here *every* Friday night. Has been for more than a year now."

The two officers looked at each other, then back to the priest.

"Why Friday nights?" Keisman asked.

Gautier stared at him fixedly. "Because I hear confessions on Friday nights."

"You trying to tell us," Jason said, "that Gerber has been confessing to you every Friday night for more than a year?"

"I'm not *trying* to tell you, I *am* telling you. Every Friday night. Take it or leave it. If you don't believe me, I'll put on a damned cassock, go into a court of law, and swear by Almighty God I'm telling the truth."

"I don't think that'll be necessary, Father," Keisman said. "What time does he usually get here?"

"Around nine o'clock. I hear confessions from eight to ten. Then he usually sits around awhile, bullshitting with the boys. If he can spare it, he leaves a couple of bucks."

"No disrespect to you, Father," Jason said, "but the guy was going to a psychiatrist."

"I know he was. I'm the one who convinced him to get professional help."

"So if he was going to a shrink, what did he need you for?"

"He was brought up a Catholic," Frank Gautier said. "You don't shake it easily."

"You think he was making progress?" the Spoiler asked.

The priest got angry. "Are you making progress? Am I making progress? What's this making progress shit? We're all just trying to survive, aren't we?"

"I guess we are at that," Jason said softly. "Thank you for your time, Father. I think we got what we came for."

At the door, Keisman turned back. "Who does the cooking around here?" he asked.

"I do," the priest said. "Why do you think I'm so fat? I sample."

Jason Two smiled and raised a pink palm. "Peace be unto you, brother," he said.

"And peace be unto you," Gautier said seriously. "Thanks for the ham. You saved us from another night of peanut butter sandwiches."

Outside, walking back to the car, Jason Two said, "Nice guy. You think he's lying? Protecting one of his boys?"

"I doubt he *can* lie," Keisman said. "I think that Gerber is doing exactly what Gautier said—confessing his sins every Friday night."

"Crazy world," Jason said.

"And getting crazier every day. Will you do the report for Delaney?"

"Sure. Tonight. What do you want to do right now?"

"Let's go back and have a beer or two with Gerber. That poor slob."

• • •

DETECTIVE BENJAMIN CALAZO sat lumpishly in the rancid lobby of the fleabag hotel on West 23rd Street, waiting for Betty Lee, the Chinese hooker, to return from her daily visit to her mother. Mama-san lived down on Pell Street and looked to be a hundred years old at least.

Calazo had been tailing Betty for four days and thought he had her time-habit pattern down pat. Left the hotel around 9:00 A.M., had coffee and a buttered bagel at a local deli, then cabbed down to Chinatown. Spent the morning with Mama, sometimes bringing her flowers or a Peking duck. A good daughter.

Then back to the hotel by noon. The first john would arrive soon after—probably a guy on his lunch hour. Then there would be a steady parade until three or four o'clock, when business would slack off and Betty would go out to dinner. Things picked up again after five o'clock and continued good until two in the morning.

Betty wasn't pounding the pavements as far as Calazo could tell. She had a regular clientele, mostly older guys with potbellies and cigars. There were also a few furtive young kids who rushed in and out, looking around nervously like they expected to get busted at any minute.

Betty Lee herself was far from what Benny Calazo envisioned as the ideal whore. She was dumpy and looked like she bought her clothes in a thrift shop. But she must have had something on the ball to attract all those johns. Maybe, Calazo mused idly, she did cute things with chopsticks—it was possible.

She came into the hotel lobby. Benny folded his *Post,* heaved himself to his feet, and followed her into the cage elevator. They started up. He knew her room was 8-D.

"Good morning," he said to her pleasantly.

She gave him a faint smile but said nothing.

When she got off on the eighth floor, he followed her down the hall to her door. She whirled and confronted him.

"Get lost," she said sharply.

He showed her his shield and ID.

"Oh, shit," she said wearily. "Again? Okay. How much?"

"I don't want any grease, Betty."

"A nice blow job?" she said hopefully.

He laughed. "Just a few minutes of your time."

"I got a client in fifteen minutes."

"Let him wait. We going to discuss your business in the hall or are you going to invite me in?"

Her little apartment was surprisingly neat, clean, tidy. Everything dusted, everything polished. There was a small refrigerator, waist-high, and a framed photograph of John F. Kennedy over the bed. Calazo couldn't figure that.

"You like a beer?" she asked him.

"That would be fine," he said gratefully. "Thank you."

She got him a cold Bud, one of the tall ones. He sat there in his overcoat and old fedora, so worn that there was a hole in the front at the triangular crease.

"Betty," he said, "you got a nice thing going here. You take care of the locals?"

"Of course," she said, astonished that he would ask such a question. "And the prick behind the lobby desk. And the alkie manager. How else could I operate?"

"Yeah," he said, "it figures. I've been checking you the last three or four days. Regulars mostly, aren't they?"

"Mostly. Some walk-in trade. Friends of friends."

"Sure, I understand. You got a regular named Ronald Bellsey?"

"I don't ask last names."

"All right, let's concentrate on Ronald. Comes in two afternoons a week. A chunky guy, an ex-pug."

"Maybe," she said cautiously.

"What kind of a guy is he?"

"He's a pig!" she burst out.

"Sure he is," Calazo said cheerfully. "Likes to hurt you, doesn't he?"

"How did you know that?"

"That's the kind of guy he is. I want to take him, Betty. With your help."

"Take him? You mean arrest him?"

"No."

"Kill him?"

"No. Just teach him to straighten up and fly right."

"You want to do that here?"

"That's right."

"He'll kill me," she said. "You take him here and you *don't* kill him, he'll come back and kill *me*."

"I don't think so," Detective Calazo said. "I think that after I get through with him, he'll stay as far away from you as he can get. So you'll lose one customer—big deal."

"I don't like it," she said.

"Betty, I don't see where you have any choice. I don't want to close you down, I really don't, though I could do it. All I want to do is punish this scumbag. If he does come back, you can always tell him the cops made you do it."

She thought about it a long time. She went to the small refrigerator and poured herself a glass of sweet wine. Calazo waited patiently.

"If he gets too heavy," Betty Lee said finally, "I could always go to Baltimore for a while. I got a sister down there. She's in the game, too."

"Sure you could," the detective said, "but believe me, he's not going to come on heavy. Not after I get through with him."

She took a deep breath. "How do you want to handle it?" she asked him. He told her. She listened carefully.

"It should work," she said. "Give it to him good."

• • •

DETECTIVES VENABLE AND Estrella walked in on Mrs. Gladys Ferguson without calling first. They didn't want her phoning Mrs. Yesell and saying something like: "Blanche, two police officers are coming to ask me about you and our bridge club. What on earth is going on?"

Mrs. Ferguson turned out to be a tall, dignified lady who had to be pushing eighty. She walked with a cane, and one of her shoes had a built-up sole, about three inches thick. She was polite enough to the two cops after they identified themselves, but cool and aloof.

"Ma'am," Estrella started, "we'd like to ask you a few questions in connection with a criminal investigation we're conducting. Your answers could be very important. I'm sure you'll want to cooperate."

"What kind of a criminal investigation?" she asked. "Into what? I've had nothing to do with any crime."

"I'm sure you haven't," Detective Estrella said. "This involves the whereabouts of witnesses on a night a crime was committed."

She stared at him. "And that's all you're going to tell me?"

"I'm afraid it is."

"Will I be called to testify?" she said sharply. "At a trial?"

"Oh, no," Detective Helen Venable said hastily. "It's really not a sworn statement we want from you or anything like that. Just information."

"Very well, then. What is it you wish to know?"

"Mrs. Ferguson," Estrella said, "are you a member of a bridge club that meets on Friday nights?"

Her composure was tried, but it held. "What on earth," she said in magisterial tones, "does my bridge club have to do with any criminal activity?"

"Ma'am," Helen said, beginning to get teed off, "if you keep asking *us* questions, we're going to be here all day. It'll be a lot easier for all of us if you just answer our questions. Are you a member of a bridge club that meets on Friday nights?"

"I am."

Estrella: "*Every* Friday night?"

"That is correct."

Venable: "How long has this club been meeting?"

"Almost five years now. We started with two tables. But members died or moved away. Now we're down to one."

Estrella: "And you've never missed a single Friday night in those five years?"

"Never. We're very proud of that."

Venable: "Have all the current members of the club been together for five years?"

"No. There have been several changes. But the four of us have been playing together for—oh, I'd say about two years."

Estrella: "I presume you rotate as hostesses. The game is held at a different home each Friday?"

"That is correct. I wish you would tell me exactly what you're trying to get at."

Estrella: "Do you recall a Friday night early in November this year? There was a tremendous rainstorm—one of the worst we've ever had."

"There's nothing wrong with my memory, young man. I remember that night very well."

Venable: "In spite of the dreadful weather, your bridge club met?"

"You're not listening to me, young lady. I *told* you we have not missed a single Friday night in almost five years."

Estrella: "And at whose home was the game that particular night?"

"Right here. That is one of the reasons I remember it so clearly. It was supposed to be held at the home of another member. But the weather was so miserable, I called the others and asked if they'd mind coming to me." She tapped her built-up shoe with her cane. "Because of this, I don't navigate too well in foul weather. The other members kindly agreed to come here. It wasn't a great imposition; they all live within two blocks."

Venable: "At whose home was the game originally scheduled?"

"Mrs. Blanche Yesell."

Venable: "But she came here instead?"

"Must I repeat everything twice?" Mrs. Gladys Ferguson said testily. "Yes, she came here instead, as did the others."

Estrella: "We just want to make certain we understand your answers completely, Mrs. Ferguson. What time do you ladies usually meet?"

"The game starts at eight-thirty, promptly. The members usually arrive a little before that. We end at ten-thirty, exactly. Then the hostess serves tea and coffee with cookies or a cake. Everyone usually departs around eleven o'clock."

Detective Venable took our her notebook. "We already know that you and Mrs. Blanche Yesell are two of the members. Could you give us the names and addresses of the other two?"

"Is that absolutely necessary?"

Estrella: "Yes, it is. You'll be assisting in the investigation of a violent crime."

"That's hard to believe—the Four Musketeers involved in a violent crime. That's what we call ourselves: the Four Musketeers."

Venable: "The names and addresses, please."

The detectives spent the next two days questioning the other two members of the club. They were both elderly widows of obvious probity. They corroborated everything that Mrs. Gladys Ferguson had stated.

"Well," Estrella said, staring at his opened notebook, "unless the Four Musketeers are the greatest criminal minds since the James Gang, it looks like Mrs. Yesell is lying in her teeth. She wasn't home that night, and her daughter is still on the hook."

"Son of a bitch!" Helen Venable said bitterly. "I still can't believe Joan was the murderer. Brian, she's just not the type."

"What type is that?" he asked mildly. "She's human, isn't she? So she's capable."

"But *why?* She keeps saying how much she admired the doctor."

"Who knows why?" he said, shrugging. "We'll let Delaney figure that out. Let's go up to Midtown North and borrow a typewriter. We'll work on the report together. I'd like to get it to Sergeant Boone tonight. I have a heavy date with a Ouija board."

"And I was going to share an apartment with her," Venable mourned.

"Count yourself lucky," Estrella advised. "You could have picked Jack the Ripper."

22

•

"I HOPE YOU HAVE SOME GOOD NEWS FOR ME," FIRST DEPUTY Commissioner Ivar Thorsen said. "I sure could use some."

The Admiral was slumped in a leather club chair in the study, gripping a beaker of Glenfiddich and water, staring into it as if it might contain the answers to all his questions.

"Ivar, you look like you've been through a meat grinder," Delaney said from behind his cluttered desk.

"Something like that," Thorsen said wearily. "A tough day. But they're all tough. If you can't stand the heat, get out of the kitchen. Isn't that what they say?"

"That's what they say," Delaney agreed. "Only you happen to like the kitchen."

"I suppose so," the Deputy said, sighing. "Otherwise why would I be doing it? When I leave here, I've got to get over to the Waldorf—a testimonial party for a retiring Assistant DA. Then back downtown for a meeting with the Commish and a couple of guys from the Mayor's office. We're getting a budget bump, thank God, and the problem is how to spend it."

"That's easy. More street cops."

"Sure, but who gets the jobs—and where? Every borough is screaming for more."

"You'll work it out."

"I suppose so—eventually. But to get back to my original question—any good news?"

"Well . . ." Delaney said, "there have been developments. Whether they're good or not, I don't know. So far we've eliminated four of the patients: Kane, Otherton, Gerber, and Symington. Some good detective work there and some luck. Anyway their alibis have been proved out—to my satisfaction at least."

"But you've still got two suspects?"

"Two *possible* suspects. One is Ronald Bellsey, a nasty brute of a man. Detective Calazo is working on him. In his last report, Calazo says he hoped to have definite word on Bellsey within a few days. Calazo is an old cop, very thorough, very experienced. I trust him.

"The other possible suspect, more interesting, is Joan Yesell, suicidal and suffering from depression. Her mother claims she was home at the time of the murder. Detectives Venable and Estrella have definitely proved the mother is lying. She was somewhere else and can't possibly alibi her daughter."

"You're going to pick them up?"

"Mother and daughter? No, not yet. I've switched everyone except Calazo to round-the-clock surveillance of the daughter. Meanwhile we're digging into her background and trying to trace her movements on the day of the murder."

"Why do you think the mother lied?"

"Obviously to protect the daughter. So she must have some guilty knowledge. But it doesn't necessarily have anything to do with Ellerbee's death. Joan Yesell could have been shacked up with a boyfriend, and the mother is lying to protect her reputation—or the boyfriend's."

Thorsen took a gulp of his drink and regarded the other man closely.

"Yes, that's possible. But you have that look about you, Edward—the end-of-the-trail look, a kind of suppressed excitement. You really think this Joan Yesell is involved, don't you?"

"I don't want to get your hopes up too high, but yes, there's something that's not kosher there. I've spent all afternoon digging through the files, pulling out every mention of the woman. Some of the stuff that seems innocent on first reading takes on a new meaning when you think of her as a killer. For instance, right after Boone and I questioned her for the first time, she attempted suicide. That could be interpreted as guilt."

"What would be her motive?"

"Ivar, we're dealing with emotionally disturbed people here, and ordinary motives don't necessarily hold. Maybe the doctor uncovered something in Yesell's past so painful that she couldn't face it and couldn't endure the thought of Ellerbee knowing it. So she offed him."

"That's possible, I suppose. Sooner or later you're going to have to confront her, aren't you?"

"No doubt about that," Delaney said grimly. "And the mother, too. But I want to do my homework first—learn all I can about Joan and her movements on the murder night. Maybe she really was with a boyfriend. If so, we'll find out."

"Meanwhile," Deputy Thorsen said, "the clock is running out. Ten days to the end of the year, Edward. That's when the PC selects his Chief of Detectives."

Delaney took a packet of cigars from his desk drawer, held it out to the Admiral. But the Deputy shook his head. Delaney lighted up, using a gold Dunhill cutter his first wife had given him as a birthday present twenty years ago.

"At least," he said, puffing, "this investigation has taken the heat off the Department. Right? You're not getting pressure from the victim's widow and father anymore, are you? And I haven't seen anything on the case in the papers for two weeks."

"I'd like to see something in the papers," Thorsen said. "A headline like: COPS SOLVE ELLERBEE MURDER. That would be a big help to Suarez."

"How's he doing? I haven't spoken to him for a while. Maybe I'll give him a call tonight."

"He's a better administrator than he is a detective. But I suppose you saw that, Edward."

"Well, we've still got ten days. For what it's worth, I believe we'll clear it before the end of the year, or the thing will just drag on and on with decreasing hopes for a solution."

"Don't say that," the Deputy said, groaning. "Don't even suggest it. Well, thank you for your hospitality; I've got to start running again."

"Before you go, Ivar, tell me something—how are your relations with the DA's office?"

"The Department's relations or mine, personally?"

"Yours, personally."

"Pretty good. They owe me some favors. Why do you ask?"

"I have a feeling that if we can pin the killing on Ronald Bellsey or Joan Yesell, there's not going to be much hard evidence. All circumstantial. Would the DA take the case, knowing the chances of a conviction would be iffy?"

"Now you're opening a whole new can of worms," Thorsen said cautiously. "Ordinarily I'd say no. But this homicide attracted so much attention that they might be willing to take a chance just for the publicity. They're as eager for good media coverage as we are."

Delaney nodded. "Well, you might sound them out. Just to get their reaction."

Thorsen stared at the other man fixedly. "Edward, you think this Joan Yesell could be it?"

"At the moment," Delaney said, "she and Ronald Bellsey are all we've got. Light a candle, Ivar."

"One candle? I'll set fire to the whole church."

After the Deputy departed, Delaney returned to his study and called Suarez. But the Chief wasn't home. Delaney chatted a few minutes with Rosa, wishing her a Merry Christmas, and asked her to tell her husband that he had called—nothing important.

Then he went back to the stack of reports on Ronald Bellsey. According to Calazo, the subject was a prime suspect in four brutal beatings in the vicinity of Bellsey's hangouts.

Add to that Delaney's personal reactions to the man, and you had a picture of a thug who got his jollies by pounding on weaker men, including Detective Timothy Hogan. There was little doubt that Bellsey was a sadistic psychopath. The question remained: Was he a homicidal psychopath?

Uncertainties gnawed. Would a loco who derived pleasure from punishing another human being with his fists and boots resort to hammer blows to kill? If Ellerbee had been beaten and kicked to death, Delaney would have been surer that Bellsey was the killer.

He groaned aloud, realizing what he was doing: applying logic to a guy who acted irrationally. You couldn't do that; you had to adopt the subject's own illogic. Once Delaney did that, he could admit that Bellsey might use a ball peen hammer, an icepick, or kill with a bulldozer if the madness was on him.

Joan Yesell might be suicidal and depressed, but she didn't seem to share Bellsey's mania for wild violence. But who knew what passions were cloaked by that timid, subdued persona she presented to the world? Outside: Mary Poppins; inside: Lizzie Borden.

Between the two of them, Delaney leaned toward Yesell as the more likely suspect, but only because her alibi had been broken.

He knew full well how thin all this was. If he wanted to be absolutely honest, he'd have to admit he was no closer to clearing the Ellerbee homicide than he had been on the evening of Thorsen's first visit.

He looked at his littered desk, at the open file cabinet overflowing with reports, notes, interrogations: all those muddled lives. All that confusion of wants, fears, frustrations, hates.

He thrust his hands deep into his pockets and went lumbering into the living room where Monica sat reading the latest Germaine Greer book.

"What's wrong, Edward?" she asked, peering over her glasses and catching his mood.

"We're all such shitheads!" he burst out. "Every one of us gouging our way through life fighting and scrambling. Not one single, solitary soul knowing what the fuck is going on."

"Edward, why are you so upset? Because life is disordered and chaotic?"

"I suppose so," he muttered.

"Well, that's your job, isn't it? Making sense of things. Finding the logic, the sequence, the connecting links?"

"I suppose so," he repeated. "To make sense out of the senseless. Up at Diane Ellerbee's place, I said detectives are a lot like psychiatrists—and so we are. But psychiatrists have dear old Doctor Freud and a lot of clinical research to help them. Detectives have percentages and experience—and that's about it. And detectives have to analyze a dozen people in a single case. Like this Ellerbee thing . . . I feel like giving up and telling Ivar I just can't hack it."

"No," she said, "I don't think you'll do that. You have too much pride. I can't believe you're going to give up."

"Nah," he said, kicking at the carpet. "I'm not going to do that. It's just that someone—the murderer—is playing with me, jerking me around, and I can't stand that. It infuriates me that I can't identify the killer. It offends my sense of decency."

"And of order," she added.

"That, too," he agreed. He laughed shortly. "Goddamn it, I don't know what to do next!"

"Why don't you have a sandwich," she suggested.

"Good idea," he said.

• • •

ON THAT SAME evening, Detective Ross Konigsbacher was lounging on Symington's long sectional couch. He was dragging on one of Vince's home-made cigarettes and sipping Asti Spumante.

"No one drinks champagne anymore," Symington had said. "Asti Spumante is *in*."

So the Kraut was feeling like a jet-setter, with his pot and *in* drink.

He was also feeling virtuous because he had filed a report clearing Vincent of any complicity in the murder of Dr. Simon Ellerbee. That had been his official duty. And, as he had anticipated, he had been rewarded by being shifted to a shit detail—spending eight hours that day sitting in a car outside the Yesells' home waiting for Joan to come out. She hadn't.

"A great meal, Vince," he said dreamily. "I really enjoyed it."

"I thought you'd like the place," Symington said. "Wasn't that smoked goose breast *divine?*"

When they had returned to the apartment after dinner, Vince had changed into a peach-colored velour jumpsuit with a wide zipper from gullet to crotch.

"And that silk underwear," Konigsbacher remembered. "Thank you *so* much. You've been so good to me, Vince. I want you to know I appreciate it."

Symington waved a hand. "That's what friends are for. We *are* friends, aren't we?"

"Sure we are," the Kraut said. And because he felt himself hazing from the grass and all the booze they'd had that night, he figured he better make his pitch while he was still conscious.

"Vince," he said, "I've got a confession to make to you. I know you're going to *hate* me for it, but I've got to do it."

"I won't hate you," Symington said, "no matter what it is."

"You better hear me first. Vince, I'm a cop, a detective assigned to check you out on the Ellerbee kill. Here—here's my ID."

He fished out his wallet. Symington looked at the shield and card.

"Oh, Ross," he said in a choked voice, "how *could* you?"

"It was my *job*," the Kraut said earnestly. "To get close to you and learn your movements the night of the murder. I admit that when I started, I really thought of you as a suspect. But as I got to know you, Vince, I realized that you're completely incapable of a vicious act of violence like that."

"Thank you, Ross," Symington said in a low voice.

"But," Konigsbacher said, taking a deep breath, "you stated you had left the party at the Hilton about the time Ellerbee was killed."

"Only for a little while," Symington said nervously. "Just to get a breath of air. I told you where I went, Ross."

"I know, I know," the detective said, patting one of Vince's pudgy hands. "But you can see how it complicates things."

Symington nodded dumbly.

"It was a serious problem for me, Vince. I knew you were innocent. My problem was whether or not to report that you had left the Hilton. I worried about it a long time, and you know what I finally decided? Not to mention it at all. I just don't think it's important. I just stated that you were at the Hilton all evening and couldn't possibly be involved. You're cleared, Vince, completely cleared."

"Thank you, Ross," Symington said in a strangled voice. "Thank you, thank you. How can I ever thank you enough?"

"We'll think of something, won't we?" the Kraut said.

• • •

TWO DAYS BEFORE Christmas, Edward Delaney, wearing hard homburg and lumpy overcoat, trudged through a mild fall of snow to buy a Scotch pine for the holidays. When he saw the prices, he almost settled for something skinnier and scrawnier.

But, what the hell, Christmas only comes once a year, so he bought the fat, bushy tree he wanted and lugged it home, dragged it into the living room, and got to work. He went up to the attic and brought down the old-fashioned cast-iron Christmas tree stand with four screw clamps, and boxes and boxes of ornaments, some of them of pre–World War II vintage. He also carried down strings of lights, shirt cardboards wound with tinsel, and packages of aluminum foil icicles, carefully saved from more Christmases than he cared to remember.

He was trying a string of lights when Monica came bustling in, wearing her sheared beaver, burdened with two big shopping bags of store-wrapped Christmas gifts. Her cheeks were aglow with the cold and the excitement of spending money. She stopped in the doorway and stared at the tree, wide-eyed.

"Happy Chanukah," he said, grinning.

"And a Merry Christmas to you, darling. Oh, Edward, it's a marvelous tree!"

"Isn't it," he said. "I'm not going to tell you how much it cost or it would spoil your pleasure."

"I don't care what it cost; I love it. Let me take off my coat and put these things away, and we'll decorate it together. What a tree! Edward, the fragrance fills the whole room."

Turning the radio to WQXR and listening to Vivaldi, they spent two hours decorating their wonderful tree. First the strings of lights, then the garlands of tinsel, then the individual ornaments, then the foil icicles. And finally Delaney cautiously climbed the rickety ladder to put the fragile glass star on the top.

He descended, turned on the lights, and they stood back to observe the effect.

"Oh, God," Monica said, "it's so beautiful I want to cry. Isn't it beautiful, Edward?"

"Gorgeous," he said, touching her cheek. "I hope the girls like it. When are they coming?"

• • •

DETECTIVE BENJAMIN CALAZO was not a cop who had just fallen off the turnip truck. He had been around a long time. He had been wounded twice, and had once booted a drug dealer into the East River and let the guy swallow some shit before hauling him out.

Benny knew that some of the younger men in the NYPD regarded him with amused contempt because of his white hair and shambling gait. But that was all right; when he was their age he treated his elders the same way. Until he learned how much the gaffers could teach him.

Calazo was a good cop, serious about his job. He had witnessed a lot of crap, on the streets and in the Department, but he had never lost his Academy enthusiasm. He still believed what he was doing was important. The Sanitation guys, for instance—a lousy job but absolutely essential if the public didn't want to drown in garbage. The same way with cops; it had to be done.

Most of the time Calazo went by the book. But like all experienced cops, he knew that sometimes you had to throw the book out the window. The bad guys didn't follow any rules, and if you went up against them with strict adherence to regulations, you were liable to get your ass chopped off.

This Ronald Bellsey was a case in point. The detective knew that Bellsey was guilty of the attacks near his hangouts, plus the stomping of Detective Tim Hogan. Calazo also knew there was no way Bellsey could be racked up legally for his crimes. Not enough evidence to make a case.

So the choice was between letting Bellsey waltz away free or becoming prosecutor, judge, and jury himself. The fact that Bellsey had been going to a shrink to cure his violent behavior didn't cut any ice with Calazo and he went about planning the destruction of Ronald Bellsey without a qualm. The fact that Calazo was completely fearless helped. If a guy like Bellsey could cow him, then his whole life had been a scam.

When headquarters had been in that old building on Centre Street, there had been a number of nearby shops catering to the special needs of cops: gunsmiths, tailors, guys who made shoulder holsters that didn't chafe, and such esoterica as ankle holsters, knife sheaths, brass knuckles, and the like.

There was one place that made the best saps in the world, any length and weight you wanted, rigid or pliable. Sixteen years ago Calazo had bought a beauty: eight inches long with a wrist thong. Made of supple calfskin and filled with birdshot, it was double-stitched, and in all the years he had used it, it had never popped a stitch. And it had done rough duty.

When he prepared to confront Ronald Bellsey, that beautiful sap was the first thing that went into Calazo's little gym bag. He also packed handcuffs, a steel come-along, and two thick rolls of wide electrician's tape. He had his .38 Special in a hip holster. He didn't think he'd need anything else.

It was a Thursday afternoon, and Bellsey always got it off at three. Calazo arrived at Betty Lee's fleabag hotel at 2:45 and called upstairs from the lobby to make sure the coast was clear. She gave him the okay.

"You got it straight?" he asked her, taking off his fedora and overcoat. "He knocks, you let him in, and I take over from there. Then you get lost. Don't come back for an hour at least. Two would be better. He'll be gone by then."

"You're sure this will go okay?" she said nervously.

"Like silk," Calazo said. "Not to worry. You're out of it."

Bellsey was a few minutes late, but the detective didn't sweat it. When the knock came, Calazo nodded at Betty Lee, then stepped to the side of the door.

"Who is it?" she called.

"Ronald."

She opened the door. He came in. Hatless, thank God. The detective took one step forward and laid the sap behind Bellsey's left ear. It was a practiced blow, not hard enough to break the skin, but strong enough to put Bellsey facedown on the carpet.

"Thank you, Betty," Calazo said. "Out you go."

She grabbed up her coat and scampered away. Ben locked and chained the door behind her. He patted Bellsey down but found no weapons. The only thing he took was Ronald's handkerchief, somewhat soiled—which was okay with Calazo.

It took a lot of lifting, pulling, hauling, but finally the detective pulled Bellsey up into a ratty armchair. He wound tape around his torso to keep him upright. He taped his ankles to the legs of the chair. Then he taped his forearms tightly to the arms. Bellsey would only be able to move his hands.

Finally, Calazo stuffed Bellsey's handkerchief into the man's mouth. He watched closely to make certain his color wasn't changing. Then, when he was satisfied Bellsey was breathing through his nose, he went into the bathroom, got a glass of water, brought it back, and threw it into Bellsey's face.

It took about three minutes and another glass of water before Ronald roused. He looked around him dazedly with glazed eyes.

"Good morning, glory," Detective Calazo said cheerily. "Got a little headache, have you?"

He felt around on Bellsey's scalp and found the welt behind the left ear. Bellsey winced when he touched it.

"No blood," Calazo said, displaying his fingertips. "See?"

Bellsey was choking on the handkerchief, trying to spit it out.

"We got some ground rules here," the detective said. "The gag comes out if you promise not to scream. One scream and the gag goes back in. No one's going to notice one scream in a joint like this. Got it? You want the gag out?"

Bellsey nodded. Calazo pulled out the handkerchief. Bellsey licked his gums and lips, then looked down at his taped arms. He flapped his hands a few times. He tested the tape around his chest, then his legs. He looked up at Calazo standing over him, softly smacking his sap into the palm of one hand.

"Who the fuck're you?" Bellsey demanded hoarsely.

"The Scarlet Pimpernel," Calazo said. "Didn't you recognize me?"

"How much you want?"

"Not much," the detective said. "Just a little information."

Bellsey strained against his bonds. Then, when he realized that was futile, he began to rock back and forth on the chair.

"Stop that," Calazo said.

"Fuck you," Bellsey said, gasping.

The detective brought the sap thudding down on the back of the man's right hand. Bellsey opened his mouth to shriek, and Calazo jammed the wadded handkerchief back in his mouth.

"No screams," he said coldly. "Remember our agreement? Gonna keep quiet?"

Bellsey sat a moment, breathing deeply. Finally he nodded. Calazo pulled out the gag.

"You better kill me," Bellsey said. "Because if you don't, when I get loose I'm going to kill you."

"Nah," Ben Calazo said, "I don't think so. Because I'm going to hurt you—I mean *really* hurt you, just like you've hurt so many other people. And you're never going to be the same again. After you get hurt bad, your whole life changes, believe me."

Something in Bellsey's eyes altered. Doubt, fear—whatever—shallowed their depths.

"Why do you want to hurt me?"

"That's easy. I don't like you."

"What'd I ever do to you?"

"What'd those four guys you stomped ever do to *you?*"

"What four guys?"

Calazo brought the sap down again on the back of Bellsey's left hand. The man's head jerked back, his eyes closed, his mouth opened wide. But he didn't scream.

"The hand . . ." Calazo said. "A lot of little chicken bones in there. Mess up your hands and you're in deep trouble. Even after lots of operations they never do work right again. Now tell me about the four guys."

"What four—" Bellsey started, but when he saw his captor raise the sap again, he said hastily, "All right, all right! I got into some hassles. Street fights—you know? They were fair fights."

"Sure they were," Calazo said. "Like that detective you took outside the Tail of the Whale. A kidney punch from behind. Then you gave him a boot. That was fair."

Bellsey stared at him. "Jesus Christ," he gasped, "you're a cop!"

Calazo brought the bludgeon down on the back of Bellsey's right hand: a swift, hard blow. They both heard something snap. Bellsey's eyes glazed over.

"You did it—right?" the detective said. "The four guys near your hang-outs and the cop outside the Tail of the Whale. All your work—correct?"

Ronald Bellsey nodded slowly, looking down at his reddened hands.

"Sure you did," Calazo said genially. "A tough guy like you, it had to be. It's fun slugging people, isn't it? I'm having fun."

"Let me go," Bellsey begged. "I admitted it, didn't I? Let me loose."

"Oh, we got a way to go yet, Ronald," Calazo said cheerfully. "You're not hurting enough."

"God a'mighty, what more do you want? I swear, I get out of here, I'm going to cut off your schlong and shove it down your throat."

Calazo brought the sap down again on the back of Bellsey's right hand. The man passed out, and the detective brought more water to throw in his face.

"Keep it up, sonny boy," he said when Bellsey was conscious again. "I'd just as soon pound your hands to mush. You're not going to do much fighting with broken hands, are you? Maybe they'll fit you with a couple of hooks."

"You're a cop," Bellsey said aggrievedly. "You can't do this."

"But I *am* doing it—right? Get a good look at me so you can pick me out of a lineup. The trouble with you tough guys is that you never figure to meet anyone tougher. Well, Ronald, you've just met one. Before I'm through with you, you're going to be crying and pissing your pants. Meanwhile, let's get to the sixty-four-dollar question: Where were you the night your shrink was killed?"

"Oh, my God, is that what this is all about? I was home all night. I already told the cops that. My wife was there. She says the same thing."

"What'd you do at home all night? Read the Bible, do crossword puzzles, count the walls?"

"I watched television."

"Yeah? What did you watch?"

"That's easy. We got cable, and I remember from nine to eleven there was a special on Home Box: *Fifty Years of Great Fights, 1930–1980.* It was films from all the big fights, mostly heavyweights. I watched that."

Calazo looked at him thoughtfully. "I saw that show that night. Good stuff. But you could have chilled your shrink and checked *TV Guide* just to give yourself an alibi."

"You fucker," Bellsey said in a croaky voice, "I really did—"

But Calazo snapped the sap down on the back of Bellsey's left hand, and the bound man writhed with pain. Tears came to his eyes.

"See," the detective said, "you're crying already. Don't call me names, Ronald; it's a nasty habit."

Calazo stood there, staring steadily down at his captive. Bellsey's hands had ballooned into puffs of raw meat. They lay limply on the arms of the chair, already beginning to show ruptured blood vessels and discolored skin.

"I wish I didn't believe you," Calazo said. "I really wish I thought you were lying so I could keep it up for a while. I hate to say it, but I think you're telling the truth."

"I am, I am! What reason would I have to kill Ellerbee? The guy was my *doctor,* for Christ's sake!"

"Uh-huh. But you hurt five other guys for no reason, didn't you? Well, before I walk off into the sunset, let me tell you a couple of things. Betty Lee had nothing to do with this. I told her if she didn't, she'd be in the clink. You understand that?"

Bellsey nodded frantically.

"If I find out you've been leaning on her," Calazo continued, "I'm going to come looking for you. And then it won't be only your hands; it'll be your thick skull. You got that?"

Bellsey nodded again, wearily this time.

"And if you want to come looking for *me,* I'll make it easy for you: The name is Detective Benjamin Calazo, and Midtown North will tell you where to find me. Just you and me, one on one. I'll blow your fucking head off and wait right there for them to come and take me away. Do you believe that?"

Ronald Bellsey looked up at him fearfully. "You're crazy," he said in a faltering voice.

"That's me," Calazo said. "Nutty as a fruitcake."

With two swift, crushing blows, he slammed the sap against Bellsey's hands with all his strength. There was a sound like a wooden strawberry box crumpling. Bellsey's eyes rolled up into his skull and he passed out again. The stench of urine filled the air. The front of Bellsey's pants stained dark.

Detective Calazo packed his little gym bag. He put in the sap, the rolls of remaining tape. Then he stripped the tape from Bellsey's unconscious body, wadded it up, and put that in the bag, too. He donned fedora and overcoat. He looked around, inspecting. He remembered the glass he had used to throw water in Bellsey's face, and took that.

He opened the hallway door, wiped off the knob with Bellsey's handkerchief, and threw it back onto the slack body. He rode down in the elevator, walked casually through the lobby. The guy behind the desk didn't even look up.

Calazo called the hotel from two blocks away.

"There's a sick man in room eight-D," he reported to the clerk. "I think he's passed out. Maybe you better call for an ambulance."

Then he drove home, thinking of how he would word his report to Sergeant Boone, stating that, in his opinion, Ronald J. Bellsey was innocent of the murder of Dr. Simon Ellerbee.

• • •

THE GIRLS ARRIVED at the Delaney brownstone on the afternoon of Christmas Eve: Mary and Sylvia, two bouncy young women showing promise of becoming as buxom as their mother. The first thing they did was to squeal with delight at the sight of the Christmas tree.

Sylvia: "Fan-tastic!"

Mary: "Incredibobble!"

The second thing they did was to announce they would not be home for Christmas Eve dinner. They had dates that evening with two great boys.

"What boys?" Monica demanded sternly. "Where did you meet them?"

Mother and daughters all began talking at once, gesturing wildly. Delaney looked on genially.

It became apparent that on the train down from Boston, Mary and Sylvia had met two *nice* boys, seniors at Brown. They both lived in Manhattan, and had invited the girls to the Plaza for dinner and then on to St. Patrick's Cathedral for Handel's *Messiah* and midnight mass.

"But you don't even know them," Monica wailed. "You pick up two strangers on the train, and now you're going out with them? Edward, tell them they can't go. Those men may be monsters."

"Oh, I don't know . . ." he said easily. "Any guys who want to go to St. Pat's for midnight mass can't be all bad. Are they supposed to pick you up here?"

"At eight o'clock," Sylvia said excitedly. "Peter—he's my date—said he thought he could borrow his father's car."

"And Jeffrey is mine," Mary said. "Really, Mother, they're absolutely respectable, very well behaved. Aren't they, Syl?"

"Perfect gentlemen," her sister vowed. "They hold doors open for you and everything."

"Tell you what," Delaney said, "when they arrive, ask them in for a drink. They're old enough to drink, aren't they?"

"Oh, Dad," Mary said. "They're *seniors*."

"All right, then ask them in when they come for you. Your mother and I will take a look. If we approve, off you go. If they turn out to be a couple of slavering beasts, the whole thing is off."

"They're not slavering beasts!" Sylvia objected. "As a matter of fact, they're rather shy. Mary and I had to do most of the talking—didn't we, Mare?"

"And they're going to wear dinner jackets," her sister said, giggling. "So we're going to get all dressed up. Come on, Syl, we've got to get unpacked and dressed."

"Oh, sure," Delaney said solemnly. "Go your selfish, carefree way. Your mother and I have been waiting months to see you, but that's all right. Go to the Plaza and have your partridge under glass and your Dom Perignon. Your mother and I will have our hot dogs and beans and beer; we don't mind. Don't even think about *us*."

The two girls looked at him, stricken. But when they realized he was teasing, flew at him, smothering him with kisses.

He helped them upstairs with their luggage, then came down to find Monica in the kitchen, sliding a veal casserole into the oven.

"What do you think?" she asked anxiously.

He shrugged. "We'll take a look at these 'perfect gentlemen' and see. At least they're picking up the girls at their home; that's a good sign."

Just then they heard chimes from the front door.

"Now who the hell can that be?" Delaney said. "Don't tell me Peter and Jeffrey have turned up three hours early."

But when he looked through the judas, he saw a uniformed deliveryman holding an enormous basket of flowers, the blooms lightly swathed in tissue paper. Delaney opened the door.

"Mr. and Mrs. Delaney?"

"Yes."

"Happy Holiday to you, sir."

"Thank you, and the same to you."

He signed for the flowers, handed over a dollar tip, and brought the basket back to the kitchen.

"Look at this," he said to Monica.

"My God, it's enormous! Is it for the girls?"

"No, the deliveryman said Mr. and Mrs. Delaney."

Monica pulled the tissue away carefully, revealing a splendid arrangement of carnations, white tea roses, lilacs, and mums, artfully interspersed with maidenhair fern.

"It's gorgeous!" Monica burst out.

"Very nice. Where the hell did they get lilac this time of year? Open the card."

Monica tore it open and read aloud: " 'Happy Holidays to Monica and Edward Delaney from Diane Ellerbee.' Oh, Edward, wasn't that sweet of her?"

"Thoughtful," he said. "She must have spent a fortune on that."

"Would you like a carnation for your buttonhole?" Monica asked mischievously.

He laughed. "Have you ever seen me wear a flower?"

"Never. Not even at our wedding."

"What would you think if I suddenly showed up with a rose in my lapel?"

"I'd suspect you had fallen in love with another woman!"

They had a leisurely dinner at the kitchen table: veal casserole, three-bean salad, and a small bottle of California chablis that wasn't quite as dry as the TV commercials claimed. They talked about how well the girls looked and what time they should be home from their date.

"Make it two o'clock," Delaney said. "I forget how long midnight mass lasts, but they'll want to stop off somewhere for a nightcap."

"Two in the morning?" Monica said dubiously. "When I was their age I had to be home by ten in the evening."

"And that was only a few years ago," he said innocently.

"You!" she said, slapping his shoulder lightly. "I better go upstairs and see how they're coming along."

"Go ahead," he said. "I'll clean up in here."

After he had set the kitchen to rights, he inspected his liquor supply, wondering what he might offer the girls' gentlemen callers.

They'd know about martinis, he suspected, and daiquiris, margaritas, and black russians. He thought of the cocktails that had been popular when he was their age: whiskey sours, manhattans, old-fashioneds, and fizzes, smashes, and flips.

He suddenly decided to give them a taste of the old days, and stirred up a big pitcher of bronx cocktails, taking little sips until he had the mixture of gin, sweet and dry vermouth, and orange juice just right. Then he put the pitcher in the fridge to chill.

He went into the living room and plugged in the Christmas lights. He sat solidly in his favorite chair, stared at the beautiful tree, and brooded about Calazo's report exonerating Ronald Bellsey. How could the detective be so *sure?*

He had the feeling that Calazo's judgment had resulted from more than a friendly dialogue between cop and subject. But whatever it was, the report had to be accepted. They had taken the investigation of Bellsey's alibi as far as it could go. Which left Joan Yesell . . .

When he heard the door chimes, he glanced at the mantel clock and saw it was a few minutes after eight. At least they were prompt. He lumbered into the hallway to let them in, shouting upstairs, "Your perfect gentlemen are here!"

God, they were so young! But street cops now seemed young to Delaney. And what was worse, the nation had elected presidents who were younger than he.

The boys certainly were presentable in their dinner jackets. He didn't particularly care for ruffled shirts and butterfly bow ties—but different times, different fashions. What worried him most was that he couldn't tell one from the other, they were so alike. He addressed both as "young man."

"A drink while we're waiting?" he suggested.

"Don't go to any trouble, sir," one of them said.

"We have a reservation at nine, sir," the other one said.

"Plenty of time," Delaney assured them. "It's already mixed."

He brought in the pitcher of bronx cocktails and poured.

"Merry Christmas," he said.

"Happy Holidays," they said in unison, tried their drinks, then looked at each other.

"A screwdriver," one of them said. "Sort of."

"But there's vermouth in it," the other one said. "Right, sir?"

"Right."

"Whatever it is, it's special. I'd just as soon forget about the Plaza and stay right here."

"A bronx cocktail," Delaney said. "Before your time. Gin, sweet and dry vermouth, and orange juice."

"I'm going to sell it in mason jars," one of them said. "My fortune is made."

Delaney liked them. He didn't think they were especially handsome—go try to figure out what women saw in men—but they were alert, witty, re-spectful. And they didn't scorn small talk, so the conversation went smoothly.

Monica came down first, and both youths rose to their feet: another plus. Delaney poured her a cocktail and listened, as, within five minutes, she learned their ages, where they lived in Manhattan, what their fathers did for a living, what their ambitions were, and at what hour they intended to return her treasures, safe, sound, and untouched by human hands.

When Mary and Sylvia entered, they seemed so lovely to Delaney that his eyes smarted. He poured them each a half-cocktail, and a few minutes later said, "I guess you better get going. You don't want to keep the Plaza waiting. And remember, two o'clock is curfew time. Five minutes after that and we call the FBI. Okay?"

The girls gave him a quick kiss and then they were gone.

"Please, God," Monica said, "let it be a wonderful night for them."

"It will be," Delaney said, closing, locking, and chaining the door. "Nice boys."

"Peter's going on to medical school," Monica reported as they returned to the living room, "and Jeffrey wants to be an architect."

"I heard," Delaney said, "and I was disappointed. No cops."

The cocktail pitcher was still half-full, and he got ice cubes from the kitchen and poured them each a bronx on the rocks.

"Should we put the presents under the tree tonight or wait for tomorrow morning?" he asked.

"Let's wait. Edward, you go to bed whenever you like. I'll wait up for them."

"I was sure you would," he said, smiling. "And I plan to keep you com-pany."

He sat relaxed in the high wing chair covered with bottle-green leather, worn to a gloss. Monica wandered over to Diane Ellerbee's basket of flowers placed on their Duncan Phyfe desk. She made small adjustments in the ar-rangement.

"It really is gorgeous, Edward."

"Yes—" he started, then stopped. He rose slowly to his feet. "What did you say?" he asked in a strangled voice.

Monica turned to stare at him. "I said it was gorgeous. Edward, what on earth is the matter?"

"No, no," he said impatiently. "I mean when the flowers first arrived and I brought them into the kitchen. What did you say then?"

"Edward, what *is* this?"

"What did you say then?" he shouted at her. *"Tell me!"*

"I said they were beautiful and wondered if they were for the girls. You said no, they were for us."

"And what else?"

"I asked if you wanted a buttonhole. You said you didn't."

"Right!" he said triumphantly. "I asked if you had ever seen me wear a flower. You said no, not even at our wedding. Then I asked what you'd think if I showed up wearing a rose in my lapel. And what did you say then?"

"I said I'd suspect you had fallen in love with another woman."

He smacked his forehead with an open palm. "Idiot!" he howled. "I've been a goddamned *idiot!*"

He went rushing into the study and slammed the door. Monica looked on in astonishment. After a few minutes she settled down to watch a Christmas Eve program on television.

She resisted the temptation to look in at him for almost an hour, then, maddened by curiosity, she opened the study door just a few inches and peeked inside. He was standing at the file cabinet, his back to her, flinging reports left and right. She decided not to interrupt.

An hour later, figuring this nonsense had gone on long enough, she marched resolutely into the study and confronted him. He was slumped wearily in his swivel chair behind the desk, wearing his horn-rimmed specs. He was holding a sheet of paper, staring at it.

"Edward," she said severely, "you've got to tell me what's going on."

"I've got it," he said, looking up at her wonderingly. "The man was in love."

23

•

IT WAS SUPPOSED TO BE A FESTIVE DAY. THEY ALL CAME DOWN-stairs in pajamas, bathrobes, and slippers and opened the tenderly wrapped packages stacked under the tree. "Oh, you shouldn't have done it!" . . . "Just what I wanted!"

Delaney had given Monica a handsome choker of cultured pearls which she immediately put on.

Then they all sat around the kitchen table for a big breakfast: juice, eggs, ham, hashed-brown potatoes, buttermilk biscuits, lots of coffee, glazed doughnuts, and more coffee.

Delaney moved through all this jollity with a glassy smile, his thoughts far away. At 10:00 A.M. he ducked into his study to call Carol Judd, Simon Ellerbee's receptionist. No answer. He called every hour on the hour. Still no answer. Where the devil *was* the woman? He sighed. Spending Christmas Day with the boyfriend, he supposed. She was entitled.

There were calls to the girls from Peter and Jeffrey. That took an hour—at least. And then all the Delaneys sallied forth for a stroll down Fifth Avenue. They admired Christmas decorations, the tree at Rockefeller Center, and ended up having lunch at Rumpelmayer's.

They walked home up Madison Avenue, the girls stopping every minute to Ooh and Aah at the windows of the new boutiques. Back in the brownstone, Delaney got on the phone again to Carol Judd. Still no answer.

They spent a pleasant afternoon hearing about the girls' lives at school, but although Delaney listened, he was in a fever of impatience and hoped it didn't show.

After dinner he dived back into his study and continued to call Carol Judd, without success. Trying to control his anger, he went to the files and pulled out certain notes that now had a significance he hadn't recognized before.

Finally, at 10:00 P.M., he reached her.

"Edward X. Delaney here. I spoke to you a few weeks ago in connection with the police investigation into the death of Doctor Simon Ellerbee."

"Oh, yes. Merry Christmas, Mr. Delaney."

"Thank you. And a Happy Holiday to you."

He was forcing himself to slow down, play it cool. He didn't want to alert this young woman.

"Miss Judd, a few questions have come up that I think only you can answer. I was wondering if you'd be kind enough to give me a few minutes of your time."

"Well, I can't right now."

That probably meant the boyfriend was there.

"At your convenience," Delaney said.

"Umm . . . well, I'm working now."

"Glad to hear it," he said. "With another psychiatrist?"

"No, I'm with a dentist on West Fifty-seventh Street."

"I'll bet I know the building," he said. "Corner of Sixth Avenue?"

"That's right," she said. "Don't tell me your dentist is there?"

"No," he said, "but my podiatrist is. I have great teeth but flat feet. Miss Judd, you've been so cooperative that I'd like to take you to lunch. Do you get an hour?"

"Early. At twelve o'clock."

"There's a fine restaurant on Seventh Avenue just south of Fifty-seventh. The English Pub. Do you know it?"

"I've seen it but I've never been in."

"Good food, generous drinks. Could you meet me there for lunch tomorrow at, say, twelve-fifteen?"

"Sure," she said cheerfully. "Sounds like fun."

He was at the English Pub promptly at noon on December 26th. He took a table for two, sitting where he could watch the door. Carol Judd came in at 12:20 and stood looking around. He rose, waved at her. She came over laughing. He held the chair for her.

"Hey," she said, looking around at the restaurant, "this is keen."

He hadn't heard anyone use the word "keen" in twenty years, and he smiled.

"Nice place," he said. "There's been a restaurant here as long as I can remember. It used to be called the Studio, I think. Would you like a drink?"

"What're you having?"

"Vodka gimlet."

"I think I'd like a strawberry daiquiri. Okay?"

She was wearing a denim smock that hid her limber body. But her blond curls were still frizzy, and her manner as perky as before. She chatted easily about her new job and the funny things that happen in a dentist's office.

"Maybe we better order," he suggested, handing her a menu. "We can talk while we eat."

"Sure," she said. "What're you having?"

"I'm going for the club sandwich," he said. "I'm a sandwich freak. You have whatever looks good to you."

"Cheeseburger," she said, "with a lot of fries. And another strawberry daiquiri. Hey, you know what happened? Doc Simon left me a thousand dollars in his will!"

"I heard that," Delaney said. "Very nice of him."

"He was a sweetheart," Carol Judd said. "Just a sweetheart. I don't have the check yet, but I got a letter from the lawyers. When the money comes, me and my boyfriend are going to take a great weekend in Bermuda or the Bahamas or someplace like that. I mean it's found money—right?"

"Right," Delaney said. "Enjoy it."

"How you coming on the investigation? You find the guy who did it yet?"

"Not yet. But I think we're making progress."

Their food was served. She doused her cheeseburger and French fries with ketchup. Delaney slathered his wedges of club sandwich with mayonnaise.

"Carol," he said casually, "you told me you did the billing for Doctor Ellerbee. Is that correct?"

"Sure. I mailed out all the bills."

"How did you keep track of who owed what?"

"In a ledger. I logged in every patient's visit. We billed monthly."

"Uh-huh. Did you know the billing ledger is missing?"

She had her mouth open to take a bite of cheeseburger, but stopped. "You're kidding," she said. "First I heard of it. Who would want that?"

"The killer," Delaney said. "Maybe. Where did you keep it?"

"In the top drawer of my desk."

"Everyone knew that? I mean patients and other people coming in and out of the office?"

"I suppose so. I didn't try to keep it hidden or anything like that. No point, was there?"

"I guess not. Carol, the last time I spoke to you, we talked about Doctor Simon's change of mood in the last year. You said he was up and down, happy one day, depressed the next."

"That's right. He became, you know, changeable."

"And also," Delaney said cheerfully, "you mentioned that he wore a flower in his buttonhole."

"Well, it really wasn't in his buttonhole because he didn't have one on his suit. But it was pinned to his lapel, yes."

"And it was the first time you had seen him wear a flower?"

"That's right. I kidded him about it, and we laughed. He was happy that day."

"Thank you," Delaney said gratefully. "Now let's get back to that billing ledger for a minute. Were there patients who didn't pay or were slow on their payments?"

"Oh, sure. I guess every doctor has his share of slow payers and out-and-out deadbeats."

"And how did Doctor Ellerbee handle them?"

"I'd mail out second and third notices. You know—very polite reminders. We had a form letter for it."

"And what if they didn't pay up, even after the notices? What happened then? Did he drop them?"

"He never did," she said, laughing and wiping ketchup from her lips with her napkin. "He was really such a sweet, easygoing guy. He'd say, 'Well, maybe they're a little strapped,' and he'd keep treating them. A soft touch."

"Sounds like it," Delaney said. He had finished his club sandwich and the little container of coleslaw. Now he sat back, took a deep breath, and said, "Do you remember the name of the patient who owed Doctor Ellerbee the most money?"

"Sure," Carol Judd said promptly, popping the last French fry into her mouth with her fingers. "Joan Yesell. She owed almost ten thousand dollars."

"Joan Yesell?" he repeated, not letting his exultation show. "Ten thousand dollars?"

"About."

"That was more than any other patient owed?"

"A *lot* more."

"Did you send her second and third notices?"

"At first I did, but then the doctor told me to stop dunning her. He said she probably couldn't afford it. So he just carried her."

"Thank you," Delaney said. "Thank you very much. Now, how about some dessert?"

"Well . . ." Carol Judd said. "Maybe."

He plodded home on a steely-gray afternoon, smoking a Cuesta-Rey 95 and thinking he owned the world. Well, he didn't have it *all*, but he had most of it. Enough that made sense. The problem was: Where did he go from here?

The brownstone was silent and empty. The women, he supposed, were out exchanging Christmas gifts. He went into the study and got on the horn. It took almost an hour to locate Boone and Jason and summon them to a meeting at nine o'clock that night. He was ruthless about it: *Be here.*

But when they arrived and he had them seated, the study door closed against the chatter of the women in the living room, he wondered how he might communicate his own certainty. He knew it might sound thin, but to him it was sturdy enough to run on.

"Listen," he began. "I'm convinced Simon Ellerbee was in love, or having an affair, or both, with Joan Yesell. Four women, including his wife, said that his personality changed recently. But they don't agree on *how* it changed. He was up, he was down, he was this, he was that: a good picture of a guy so mixed up he couldn't see straight. Also, Ellerbee was carrying Yesell on the books. She owed him about ten grand and he was making no effort to collect. I got that from Carol Judd, his receptionist, just this afternoon."

The two officers were leaning forward, listening intently. He saw he would have no problem convincing them; they *wanted* to believe.

"That would explain his will," Boone said slowly. "Canceling his patients' debts. He put that in for Yesell's benefit. Right, sir?"

"Right. She owed much more than any other patient. Also, I went through his appointment book again. She's down as a late patient eleven times this year, always on Friday nights. But the interesting thing is that notation of those Friday night visits stopped in April. Only I don't think the sessions stopped. I believe they went on, but he didn't write them down in his book."

"You think he was screwing her?" Jason asked.

"Had to be," Delaney said. "A healthy, good-looking guy like that. They weren't playing tiddledywinks up in his office."

"Doctor Diane and Samuelson swear he was faithful," Boone pointed out.

"Maybe they didn't know," Delaney said. "Or maybe they were lying to protect his reputation. At the moment it's not important. What is important is that Yesell was meeting him late in his office on Friday nights while his wife was heading up to Brewster. I'll bet my left nut that's what was happening. Also I dug out a report from Konigsbacher that states Symington saw Ellerbee driving uptown alone on First Avenue at about nine o'clock on a Friday night. I figure he had just dropped off Yesell at her brownstone and was heading up to Brewster."

"The Yesell dame has no car," Jason said, nodding. "So she probably took a cab or bus to Ellerbee's office. Then he drove her home. That listens."

"Another thing," Boone said. "Right after we questioned her the first time, she tried to slit her wrists. That could mean guilty knowledge."

"And how about Mama lying to give her an alibi," Jason added. "I think we got enough right there."

They looked at each other, smiling grimly as they realized they had no hard evidence at all.

"We're going to have to brace her," Delaney said. "Sooner or later. Her and her mother, too. Really lean on them. But there are a few things I'd like to learn first. If she killed Ellerbee, what was the motive? Maybe he had promised to divorce his wife and marry her and then reneged or kept stalling. That's one possibility. Another is that he knocked her up."

"Jesus Christ," the Sergeant said. *"Her?"*

"It's possible," Delaney argued. "That woman detective, Helen Venable, she's close to Yesell, isn't she? See if she can find out if Yesell is pregnant or if she had an abortion. And while Venable is doing that, Jason, you find out who her personal physician is, and see what he can tell you. Probably not a goddamned thing, but *try*. Meanwhile, Boone, you get a man to St. Vincent's Emergency and wherever else she was taken after those suicide attempts. Try to get a look at the records and talk to the doctors and nurses. See if anyone noted pregnancy on her chart."

"A long shot," Boone said dubiously.

"Sure it is, but it's got to be done. Also, cover all the hardware stores in her neighborhood and in the area where she works. See if any clerk remembers selling a ball peen hammer to a woman answering her description."

"You really think she chilled Ellerbee, sir?" Jason asked curiously.

"I really think she was there that night and knows more than she's telling us. Anyway, see what you can find out, and tomorrow night let's all three of us confront her. Maybe we'll take Detective Venable along so Yesell won't be so frightened. But I want to wring that young lady dry."

"We could take her in," Boone suggested.

"For what?" Delaney demanded. "Unless we can tie her to the purchase of a hammer, we've got zilch. Our only hope is to break her down. I don't like doing it—she seems like a mousy little thing—but we can't let that influence us. I busted a woman once who stood four-nine and weighed about ninety pounds, soaking wet. She bashed in her boyfriend's skull with a brick while he was sleeping. Sometimes the mousy little things can surprise you. Well, Sergeant," Delaney concluded, looking directly at Boone. "What do you think?"

"As Jason said, it listens," Boone said cautiously. "I mean it all comes together and makes sense. So Joan Yesell and Ellerbee were making nice-nice. The only thing that sticks me is *why?* The doc had the most beautiful wife in the world—wealthy and smart, too. Why in God's name would he risk all that for a fling with someone like Yesell? Compared to Diane, she's a shadow."

"Right," Delaney said, nodding. "I've been thinking about that. I don't want to get too heavy, but here's how I figure it. We know Diane was

Ellerbee's student. He sees this absolutely beautiful girl who doesn't want to be anything but beautiful . . . a princess. So he decides to convince her to use her brain. She follows his advice and goes on to make a great career. Sergeant, remember Samuelson talking about the Pygmalion-Galatea syndrome? That's what it was. Now, years later, Ellerbee meets Joan Yesell. He sees something there, too, and tries to bring it out. You know what his problem was? He had to *improve* his women. There are guys like that. They can't love a woman for what she is. They have to remake her to conform to some vision of their own. Does any of that make sense?"

"I've got a brother-in-law like that," Jason said. "Always nudging my sister to do this, do that, wear this, wear that. He just won't let her *be*. I give them another year or two. Then they'll split."

"That's it exactly," Delaney said gratefully. "And I think that was part of the attraction Ellerbee felt for Joan Yesell. He wanted to *create* her. Another thing—everyone kept telling Ellerbee how lucky he was. Remember? Man, are you ever lucky being married to a real goddess with all those bucks! Now I ask you: How long could *you* take that? Wouldn't it begin to wear after a while? Isn't it possible you'd prefer a plain little shadow who thinks you're God Almighty? Or maybe Ellerbee was just bored. Or Yesell was the greatest lay since Cleopatra—or at least better than Diane. In any case there are enough reasons to account for Ellerbee's infidelity. The poor guy," Delaney added, shaking his head. "He needed professional help."

24

•

THEY ALL WORKED AS FAST AS THEY COULD, BUT IT WAS NO GOOD. By the evening of December 27th, Delaney had learned little more.

Helen Venable said she'd swear on a stack of Bibles yea high that Joan Yesell was not pregnant and never had been—but she couldn't prove it one way or the other. Jason had no luck with Yesell's physician. The doctor wouldn't talk and ordered the cop out of his office. Boone's men got nothing from St. Vincent's or the other emergency room that had handled Yesell's suicide attempts.

The canvassing of hardware stores yielded no better results. No one remembered selling a ball peen hammer to anyone resembling Joan Yesell. The super at her brownstone was questioned, but he didn't even know what a ball peen was, let alone own one. So that was that.

"All right," Delaney said, sighing, "let's go talk to the lady. The funny thing is, about a week ago, I suggested to Deputy Thorsen that maybe Mama Yesell had lied to cover up her daughter's affair with a boyfriend. That was on the mark, but who the hell could have guessed the boyfriend was the victim?"

They drove downtown in Jason's car and met Venable in front of Joan's brownstone.

"You going to take her in?" Helen demanded.

"Let's wait and see," Delaney said. "We've got no warrant, and right now we can't show probable cause. If she confesses—that's something else again. She's home?"

"She and Blanche both."

"Fine. You buzz her on the intercom and talk. Then we'll all go up."

When they marched into that overstuffed apartment, the two plump cats looked up at them sleepily but didn't bother rising. Blanche Yesell's reaction was more electric.

"What is the meaning of this intrusion?" she said sharply, her beehive hairdo bobbing with fury. "Haven't we suffered enough? This is harassment, pure and simple, and I assure you the police department will be hearing from my lawyer."

Delaney decided to set the tone of the interrogation right then and there.

"Madam," he thundered, "you lied to us. Do you wish to be arrested for obstruction of justice? If not, just sit down and keep your mouth shut!"

It stunned her into silence. Mother and daughter sat down abruptly on the ornate settee. After a few seconds they clasped hands and looked fearfully up at the four cops.

"You," Delaney said harshly, addressing Mrs. Blanche Yesell. "You said you were here with your daughter on the night Doctor Ellerbee was killed. A deliberate falsehood. Do you wish to revise your statement now, madam?"

"Well, uh . . ." she said, "I might have stepped out for a few minutes."

"A few minutes," he repeated scornfully, then turned to the three officers. "Did you hear that? A few minutes! Isn't that beautiful?" He turned back to the mother. "More like three hours and probably four. And we have the statements of your bridge club members to prove it. Three respectable women testifying to your perjury. Do you dare deny it?"

He had her intimidated, but she wasn't willing to give up yet.

"My Joan is innocent!" she cried in an anguished voice.

"Is she?" Delaney said contemptuously. "Is she really? And that's why you found it necessary to lie to us, was it?" He moved to confront the daughter, whose face had become ashen. "And now you, Miss Yesell. Were you aware that in his will Doctor Ellerbee canceled his patients' outstanding bills?"

The unexpected question startled her. She shook her head dumbly.

"How much did you owe him?" he said sternly.

"I don't remember," she faltered, "exactly."

"Sergeant Boone," Delaney said, "how much did Joan Yesell owe Doctor Ellerbee?"

"About ten thousand dollars," Boone said promptly.

"Ten thousand dollars," Delaney repeated, glaring at the young woman. "Much, much more than any other patient. And Doctor Ellerbee was making no effort to collect this debt. Why do you suppose that was, Miss Yesell?"

"He was a very kind man," her mother said in a low voice. "And we didn't have—"

"You had enough," Delaney interrupted roughly. "Your daughter had a good-paying job. You had enough to pay him if you had wanted to or he had dunned you for it. Boone, how do you see it?"

"I figure their affair started about a year ago," the Sergeant said glibly. "Then, around April, it got really serious. That was when he stopped noting her late Friday night visits in his appointment book."

"Friday nights," Delaney said, nodding. "Every Friday night he could make it. His wife would take off for Brewster, and you," he said, staring at the mother, "you would take off for your bridge game. A sweet setup. Did he promise to divorce his wife and marry you?" he shouted at Joan Yesell.

She began weeping, burying her face in her palms. Detective Venable took one step toward her, then stopped. She knew better than to interfere.

"We know, Joan," Delaney said, suddenly gentle. "We know all about your affair with Doctor Simon. Did he tell you he loved you?"

Her bowed head moved up and down.

"Sure he did," Delaney said in a soft voice. "Said he was going to divorce his wife and marry you. But he kept stalling, didn't he? So you . . . Jason, where do you suppose she got the hammer?"

"That's easy," the officer said. "Buy one in any hardware store in town. Then throw it in a trash can when you're finished with it."

"*No, no, no!*" Joan Yesell screamed, raising a tear-streaked face. "It wasn't like that at all."

"You stop this!" Mrs. Blanche Yesell said indignantly. "You stop it this instant. You're upsetting my Joan."

"No, madam, I will not stop," Delaney said stonily. "Your Joan was having an affair with a married man who was found murdered. We're going to get the truth if it takes all night." He whirled on the daughter. "You were there, weren't you? The night he was killed?"

She nodded, tears starting up again.

"What time did you get there?"

"A little before nine o'clock."

"Why so late?"

"It was raining so hard I couldn't get a cab. They were all on radio call. So I had to take a bus."

"What bus?"

"Across town to First Avenue. Then up First."

"Did you call Ellerbee to tell him you'd be late?"

"Yes."

"What did he say?"

"He said he'd wait."

"You got up to East Eighty-fourth Street and got off the bus. You walked over to his office?"

"Yes."

"What were you wearing?"

"A raincoat."

"Boots?"

"Yes, I was wearing rubber boots. And I had an umbrella."

"All right, now you're at the townhouse. Then what?"

"The downstairs door was open."

"Which door? Outer? Inner?"

"Both. The outer door is always open. But this time the inner door was open, too."

"How far? Wide open? A few inches?"

"A few inches."

"Then what did you do?"

"Before I went in, I rang his bell. He always told his late patients to give three short rings. So that's what I did. But he didn't buzz back."

"And you went in anyway? Through the opened door?"

"Yes."

"Did you see tracks on the carpet? Wet footprints?"

"I didn't notice."

"Then what?"

"I went upstairs, calling his name. No one answered."

"And when you got to his office?"

Her head sank down again. She shuddered. Her mother slid an arm around her shoulders.

"Then what?" Delaney insisted. "When you got to his office?"

"I found him. He was dead."

"Where was he?"

"In the outer office. Where the receptionist sat."

"What was his position?"

"I beg your pardon?" she said.

"Was he in a chair, lying on the floor, or what?"

"Don't you *know*?" Blanche Yesell said.

"Shut up!" Delaney snarled at her.

"He was on the floor," Joan said, trembling. "Faceup. All bloody."

"What did you do then?"

"I screamed."

"And then?"

"I turned and ran."

"Did you touch anything in the room?"

"No."

"Did you bend over him, feel for his pulse?"

"No, no, no!"

"Then how did you know he was dead?"

"I just knew it. His eyes were all . . ."

"Why didn't you call the police?" Sergeant Boone asked.

"I don't know. I panicked. I wanted to get out of there."

"Where's the book?" Delaney said.

"What book?"

"The billing ledger. That you took from the top drawer of the reception-ist's desk."

"I didn't! I swear I didn't! I didn't touch a thing."

"What did you do then?"

"I ran out of the office, down the stairs, out of the building."

"Did you see anyone in the townhouse?"

"No."

"Hear anything—like someone might be in one of the other offices?"

"No."

"Smell anything—any unusual odors?"

"No."

"Then what?"

"I ran over to York Avenue. It was still raining. I finally got a cab and came home."

"What kind of a cab?" Jason asked. "What color?"

"One of the big ones with those fold-up seats."

"A Checker?"

"Yes, a Checker cab."

"What time did you get home?" Delaney asked.

"A little before ten o'clock. I think."

"And you, madam," Delaney said, turning to Mrs. Yesell. "When did you get home? Let's have the truth this time."

She lifted her wattled chin. "About eleven-fifteen."

"And your daughter told you what had happened?"

"Yes. My Joan was crying. Almost hysterical. I thought I'd have to call a doctor for her."

"Did you?"

"No. I gave her some aspirin and a nice cup of hot tea."

"And then you concocted the fake alibi to lead us astray."

"I didn't think we should get involved. Joan had nothing to do with the death of that man."

Delaney groaned and looked at the officers with a hopeless shrug. "She didn't think they should get involved. How do you like that?" He turned back to Joan Yesell. "All right," he said, "let's go through it again."

This time he was even more demanding, pressing her ferociously for details. Were there other passengers on the buses she took uptown on the murder night? Could she describe the drivers? Did she see anyone when she walked over to the townhouse from First Avenue? What time had she called Ellerbee to tell him she would be delayed? Could she describe the driver of the cab she took home?

Then: When, precisely, had her affair with Ellerbee started? (In March.) How often did they meet? (As often as they could—two or three times a month.) Did he say he wanted to divorce his wife and marry her? (Yes.) When did he first speak about getting a divorce? (About three months ago.) Did he give her money? (No, but he gave her gifts.) Like what? (Jewelry, occasionally. A silk scarf. Things like that.)

Did Mrs. Yesell know of her daughter's liaison? (Yes.) Did you object, madam? (Uh . . . not exactly.) Did Ellerbee say his wife was aware of his infidelity? (He didn't say.) But he did say he was going to ask her for a divorce? (Yes.) But you don't know if he ever did? (No.)

During the whole interrogation, Delaney was at his ruthless best, alternately threatening and conciliatory, roaring and then speaking in the gentlest of tones. He would bully both women to tears, then slack off to give them time to recover. When Joan came close to hysteria, he would switch to the mother, keeping them both off-balance with unexpected questions.

Finally, when it had gone on more than two hours, and neither Delaney nor the three officers had sat down or removed their coats, he said suddenly: "All right, that's enough for now. Keep yourself available, Miss Yesell. There will be more questions. Don't even think of leaving town; you'll be watched."

He began to lead the procession from the apartment.

Detective Venable said hesitantly, "May I stay awhile?"

Delaney looked at her thoughtfully for a moment. "Yes," he said, "you do that. Have a nice cup of tea."

• • •

JASON DROVE THEM uptown. Boone and Delaney sat in the backseat.

"That place smelled of cats," the Sergeant said. "I don't care how often you change the litter box; you got cats, your apartment is going to smell of cats."

They discussed how they were going to check the buses and cab Joan Yesell claimed to have taken on the murder night. Probably an impossible task, involving bus schedules, drivers' time cards, and taxi trip-sheets, but it had to be done.

"You men write up reports on tonight's questioning," Delaney ordered. "I'll do the same. Between the three of us, we should be able to recall everything."

They pulled up in front of Delaney's brownstone, but he made no movement to get out.

"All right," he said, "let's take a vote. Jason, was she telling the truth?"

"I think she's clean, sir," the officer said. "Mostly because I can't see her having the muscle or the guts to pound in the skull of a guy she loved."

"Sergeant?"

"I think she was telling the truth. The second go-around was a replay of the first. Either she's one hell of an actress or she's telling it like it was."

"Yes," Delaney said morosely, "I'm afraid both of you are right."

"And besides," Boone added, "when we were up in Brewster, Samuelson said he doubted if a suicidal type would go for a homicide."

Delaney slowly stiffened. He turned to stare at the Sergeant.

"Lordy, lordy," he said with a wobbly smile. "I do believe you just uttered the magic words."

He got out of the car without further comment and trudged up the steps to the front door. He put his homburg and overcoat in the hall closet, then went into the living room. The girls were at the theater with Peter and Jeffrey, but Monica was home, simultaneously watching television and meticulously checking her Christmas card list against those they had received in return. He stooped to kiss her cheek.

"How did it go?" she asked him.

"Okay," he said. "Tell you about it later. I've got a call to make and then some things to look up. I never get to see you anymore," he complained.

"And whose fault is that?" she demanded.

It took him almost thirty minutes to locate Dr. Murray Walden, including a call to Deputy Thorsen to get the police psychiatrist's unlisted number. He finally tracked down Walden at a big dinner-dance at the Americana. The doctor had to be paged.

"This better be important, Delaney," the psychiatrist said. "You dragged me away from the best tango New York has seen since Valentino."

"It is important. One question, but it's crucial. And I'd like a yes or no answer."

"That I can't guarantee. I told you, in my business nothing is definite."

"You guys are as bad as lawyers. All right. I'll try anyway. We've got a subject with a history of suicide attempts. Four, to be exact. Is such a person capable of homicide?"

Silence.

"Hello?" Delaney said. "Walden? Are you there?"

"Yes, but let me get this straight. Is a suicidal type capable of homicide? Is that your question? The answer is yes. Under certain circumstances, anyone is capable of murder. But if you're asking me if it's probable, the answer is no. In fact, I've never heard of a suicidal type turning to homicide. That's not to say it's not possible."

"Thank you very much, doctor," Delaney said. "Go back to your tango."

He spent another half hour pulling certain reports and notes from the file cabinet. He laid all the documents on his desk, edges aligned and touching. He stared down at them with grim satisfaction, noting how they resembled pieces of that jigsaw puzzle, finally coming together and fitting.

He opened the door to the living room.

"Monica," he called, "could you come in for a while?"

She looked up. "Oh-ho. Feeling guilty for neglecting me, are you?"

"Sure I am," he said, smiling. "Also, I want your take on something."

She came into the study and took the club chair facing his desk.

"My," she said, "you look solemn."

"Do I? Serious maybe, not solemn. Listen, this may take some time." He hunched forward, forearms on his desk, and told Monica of the night's events.

"What do you think?" he asked after he had related Joan Yesell's story.

"The poor girl," Monica said slowly. "Were you hard on her, Edward?"

"As hard as I had to be. Does it sound to you like she's telling the truth?"

"I can believe it. A vulnerable woman like that. Not getting any younger. A good-looking man telling her that he loves her. Edward, it was a *romance,* like she's watched on TV. Maybe her last chance to have a close relationship with a man. And sex. If he didn't offer to divorce his wife and marry her, I don't think she would have insisted or even objected. Just being with him was so important to her."

"That's the way I see it," he said, nodding. "And you've got to remember he was her *doctor,* giving her sympathy and understanding and confidence. A real father figure."

"Transference," Monica said. "That's what they call it."

"Whatever," Delaney said. "Anyway, I think she's innocent of the murder, and so do Boone and Jason. So that puts us back to square one—right? And we've still got the problem of the other set of footprints. But then, just before I got out of the car, Boone said something that triggered a memory. He reminded me that when we were up in Brewster, Samuelson had said that he didn't think a suicidal personality was capable of homicide."

"I don't remember him saying that."

"You were in the kitchen cleaning up when we were talking about it. Boone's mentioning it reminded me of something. That call I made was to Doctor Murray Walden, the Department's psychiatrist, a very brainy guy. He substantiated Samuelson's comment: that it was extremely unlikely a potential suicide would turn to homicide."

"Edward, why is that so important? It's added evidence that Joan Yesell is innocent, isn't it?"

"It's more than that. Because when the Sergeant mentioned it, I remembered the meeting I had with Diane Ellerbee when she gave me the names of six of her husband's patients—all presumably capable of murder. She said she was including Joan Yesell because suicide, when tried so often, often develops into homicidal mania. Just to check my memory, I dug out my notes on that conversation. And here it is." He held up a sheet of paper. "That's what she said. Now Diane is an experienced psychologist. Why should she say something like that when Samuelson and Walden say it's a crock of shit?"

He looked at Monica steadily, seeing how her face tightened as she began to understand the full import of what he had just told her.

"Edward, are you suggesting . . ."

"I'm not suggesting anything; I'm stating it flatly with no doubts whatsoever: Diane Ellerbee knocked off her husband."

"But you don't—"

"Wait a minute," he interrupted, holding up a palm. "Before you tell me I'm nuts, let me give you some background on this. Let's start with my own stupidity in not seeing it sooner. About seventy-five percent of all murders are committed by the spouse, relatives, or friends of the victim. I've known that since the day I got my gold shield. But I forgot the percentages in this case. Why? Probably because Diane Ellerbee was so beautiful, so intelligent. She overwhelmed me. And, like an idiot, it never occurred to me to think of her as a vicious, cold-blooded killer."

"But she couldn't—"

"Hold on," he interrupted again. "Let me finish. Neglecting the percentages wasn't the worst of my stupidities; I neglected the obvious. Which, in this case, was her statement that she left Manhattan that night about six-thirty and got up to Brewster around eight. Who says so? She says so. Where's the proof? There is no proof. And like the moron I am, I never even doubted her story, didn't try to prove it out one way or the other."

"That doesn't mean she's guilty."

"No? Here's the scenario as I see it:

"Simon Ellerbee really has a thing for this Joan Yesell. And he's straight; he's not scamming her. So he tells his wife he wants a divorce. I figure that happened maybe three weeks, a month before he was killed. Or maybe she found out about Yesell herself—who knows? But the idea of divorce really shakes her. He's dumping the golden goddess for a wimp? She starts plotting.

"So on the murder night, as usual, she tells him she'll drive up to Brewster early, and he can follow after he gets rid of his late patient who, Diane knows, is probably Yesell. Diane gets her car out of the garage, but she never leaves Manhattan. Maybe she drives around, but I have a feeling she parks somewhere on East Eighty-fourth, where she can see the door of the townhouse, and just sits and waits.

"Yesell is late that night and doesn't show. But I figure Diane is in such a state that it doesn't matter. I think she intended to kill the two of them—I really do. She wants to waltz in on them while they're in each other's arms. Then she'll bash in their skulls with her trusty little hammer. Where she got the ball peen, I don't know yet, but I'll find out.

"Anyway, she's got herself psyched up for murder, and when Yesell hasn't shown up by, say, eight-thirty, Diane says to herself, the hell with it, I'm going to kill the man who betrayed me. Gets out of the car, plods through the rain, goes up to her husband's office, and kills him. The fatal blows landed high on his head, but from the back. So he had turned away from her, not expecting death. Afterward she rolls him over, hammers out his eyes.

"Monica, let me get you a drink; you look a little pale."

He went into the kitchen, brought back a bottle of Frascati and two glasses. Then he sat down again, and poured the wine.

"Was I too graphic? I'm sorry. But do you see any holes in the story? It hangs together, doesn't it? Makes a crazy kind of logic?"

"I suppose," Monica said hesitantly. "But *why,* Edward? Was it just the woman scorned?"

"That was part of it, sure, but there was more to it than that. I completely misjudged that woman. I thought her cold, always in control, always thinking before she acted. But now I believe that behind that façade is a very passionate woman."

There were other things Delaney wanted to tell his wife. Why Diane Ellerbee had crushed her husband's eyes, for instance. But he thought Monica, now looking forlorn and shaken, had heard enough gore and violence for one night.

"Let's go watch some TV comedy," he suggested. "Or just sit and talk. We haven't had an evening together in a long time."

She smiled wanly. "No, we haven't. What are you going to do now, Edward? Arrest her?"

He shook his head. "I don't have enough for that yet. Everything I told you is just supposition. We'll have to try and come up with hard evidence. Maybe we will, maybe we won't. But I can tell you one thing: That bloody lady is not going to walk away from this whistling a merry tune."

25

•

EARLY ON THE MORNING OF DECEMBER 28TH, A SATURDAY, Delaney called Boone and Jason and asked both men to come to the brownstone at 11:00 A.M. By the time they had arrived, he had assembled more reports, notes, and data he felt clearly pointed to the guilt of Dr. Diane Ellerbee.

He sat them down and went through his presentation again, much as he had related it to Monica the night before.

"As I see it," he finished, "there's no way we're going to prove or disprove she went up to Brewster that night at the time she claimed. Unless an eyewitness comes forward—which is about as likely as a blizzard in July. But let's assume she had the opportunity to waste him. That leaves the motive and method."

"Seems to me you've got the motive, sir," Boone said. "A wife being dumped for another woman. I've handled a dozen homicides like that."

"Sure you have," Delaney said. "Happens all the time. But I think there was more to it than that. This gets a little heavy, but bear with me. Here we have a beautiful young woman who's enjoying all the perks that beautiful young women enjoy. Then she becomes Ellerbee's student. He sees her potential and tells her that if she doesn't use her brain, she's nothing but a statue. Get it? He's saying that her looks don't mean damn-all; it's just a lucky accident of birth. He's not impressed by her beauty, he tells her, but he's impressed by her brain and convinces her that she's got to use it if she wants a fulfilling life. Okay so far?"

"He's trying to improve her," Jason Two said. "Like we talked about before."

"Right! He's telling her that beauty is only skin deep. She goes along with that, makes a happy marriage and a successful career. Then, suddenly, she finds out he's got eyes for another woman. Get that—he's got *eyes* for another woman."

The Sergeant said, "So you think that's why she put his eyes out?"

"Had to be," Delaney said definitely. "Not only was he being unfaithful to her, but he was going back on everything he had told her. So, after he was dead, she blinded him. Now you'll never find anyone more beautiful than me, you son of a bitch—that's what she was saying."

"Hey," Jason said, "that's one crazy lady."

"Maybe she was when she did it," Delaney admitted, "but after it was done she covered up like an Einstein and diddled us with no trouble at all. I mean she was *thinking* every step of the way, acting like the outraged widow seeking justice and making a great show of cooperating with us any way she could. No dummy she."

"We're never going to hang it on her," Boone said. "What have we got?"

"It's all circumstantial," Delaney said. "And thin at that. But we've got to try to flesh it out. Here's what I want you men to do today . . . You can divide it up any way you like. First, check out that Manhattan garage where the Ellerbees kept their cars when they were in town. Find out if the garage does any servicing or repairs. If so, did they lose a ball peen hammer in the last three months? If that doesn't work, go up to Brewster. They keep that Jeep station wagon up there; they must have a local garage or gas station doing their servicing. Ask the same question: Are you missing a ball peen hammer? I've got a couple of things I want to check out. Let's all meet back here at, say, nine o'clock tonight and compare notes. Boone, you look doubtful. Aren't you convinced she did it?"

"Oh, I'm convinced," the Sergeant said mournfully. "After listening to Joan Yesell's story, Diane becomes the number one suspect. The only thing that bothers me is that I think she's going to walk."

"Jason?"

"Yeah, I think the lady killed her husband. But like the Sergeant says, pinning her is something else again."

"We'll see," Delaney said stolidly. "We'll see."

After they left, he went into the kitchen to fortify himself. The women had gone shopping and then planned to catch the Christmas show at Radio City Music Hall. So Delaney had the house to himself. More important, he had the refrigerator to himself.

There was a marvelous loaf of marbled rye: half-rye, half-pumpernickel baked in a twist. With thick slices of smoked turkey, chips of kosher dill pickle, and a dousing of Tiger sauce, a great condiment he had discovered. At first taste it was sweet-and-sour. A moment later, sweat broke out on your scalp and steam came out of your ears.

He took that sandwich and a frosty bottle of Tuborg into the study and ate while he worked.

What was bothering him was this: In the first interview with Diane Ellerbee, she stated that she had noticed no recent change in her husband's behavior. Then, days later, she had come over to Delaney's brownstone and said yes, on second thought, she realized his manner had altered.

Now what in hell caused her to change her mind?

It took him almost a half hour to find it, but find it he did. When he first phoned Carol Judd, he had suggested she call Diane Ellerbee to check him out. Carol had called, and met with him—at which time she had described the changes in Dr. Simon's personality; how he had started to wear a flower in his lapel.

Comparing the dates of his meeting with Judd and Diane's visit to the brownstone, Delaney guessed what had happened. But he had to confirm it. He dialed Carol Judd's number and, because he was a superstitious man, he told himself that if she was home, it would be a good omen and his theory would prove out.

She was home.

"Miss Judd?" he boomed. "Edward X. Delaney here."

"Oh, hi, Mr. Delaney. That was a nice lunch we had. When are we going to do it again?"

He laughed. "It looks like I owe you a lot of lunches. But meanwhile there's one little question you can answer for me. Remember when I first called you, I suggested you check with Diane Ellerbee to make sure I wasn't just a telephone freak."

"Sure, I remember that. I called and she said you were okay and I could talk to you."

"Uh-huh. Now for my question: Did she call you back later and ask you what questions I had asked?"

Silence for a second. Then: "Let's see . . . I think she called the next day. She was trying to find me a job, you know. We talked about that for a while and . . . Yes, you're right; she wanted to know what questions you had asked."

"And you told her," Delaney said, "that I had asked if you had noticed any change in her husband's personality. And you told her what you told me—right?"

"I really can't remember, but I suppose I did. Shouldn't I have?"

"Of course you should!" he said heartily. "Thank you for your help, Carol. And I was serious about having another lunch. May I call you?"

"Anytime," she said breezily.

He hung up, smiling coldly. That was some brainy lady. Not Carol Judd, but Diane Ellerbee. When she heard that he had asked if the victim's manner had changed, she realized he had probably asked the same question of Joan Yesell and Sylvia Mae Otherton and received similar answers.

But she, the wife, who should have been the most sensitive to her husband's moods, had said, oh, no, he hadn't changed. So, having lied and fearing that Delaney would pick up on it, she had hiked herself to the brownstone and confessed: Oops, I made a mistake; he had become moody in the past year.

Delaney could appreciate her thinking; she had made an error and was covering up. That was okay; her ass was on the line and she had to improvise to protect it. He could understand that. But as far as he was concerned, it was another indication of her guilt. Nothing that would condemn her in a court of law, but significant.

There was another question that had to be answered. He phoned Detective Charles (Daddy Warbucks) Parnell, and the wife said he was working at a Staten Island precinct and could probably be reached there. She gave Delaney the number, but when he called, they said Parnell had already left, heading for One Police Plaza.

Delaney finally tracked him down. After an exchange of pleasantries, he asked Parnell, "Do you know the attorney who wrote Simon Ellerbee's will and put it into probate?"

"Yeah, I know the guy. Not well, but I know him. What do you need?"

"Just the date when Ellerbee made out his will. That business of canceling his patients' outstanding bills—I'd like to find out when Ellerbee decided on that."

"I don't know if he'll tell me, but I'll try. On Saturdays he's usually playing squash at his club. I'll call him there and get back to you one way or another."

"Thank you," Delaney said gratefully. "I'll be here."

He went back to the kitchen for another Tuborg and brought it into the study, sipping thoughtfully out of the bottle. He returned to the matter of how Simon Ellerbee had changed in the last year of his life, after he had started his affair with Joan Yesell. He wondered why Simon's mentor, Dr. Samuelson, hadn't noticed any change in his closest friend's personality.

Delaney dug out the report on Samuelson and there it was:

Boone: "Did you notice any change in Simon Ellerbee in the last six months or a year?"

Samuelson: "No, no change."

Delaney stared at the written record of that exchange. Something wasn't kosher. For a brief moment he wondered if Samuelson had been an accessory to Diane Ellerbee's crime. He couldn't see it. Still . . .

He phoned Dr. Samuelson.

"Edward X. Delaney here," he said. "How are you today, sir?"

"Weary," Samuelson said. "Patients this morning. Saturday afternoons I reserve to get caught up on my reading. Professional journals. Very dull stuff."

"I can imagine," Delaney said. "Doctor, something important has come up concerning Simon Ellerbee's death, and I need your help. I was wondering if I could see you tomorrow morning. I know it'll be Sunday, but I hoped you'd still be willing to talk to me."

"Sure, why not?" Samuelson said. "What time?"

"Oh, say ten o'clock. All right?"

"In my office. I'll see you then."

Satisfied, Delaney hung up and swiveled back and forth in his chair, ruminating. He thought about the relationship between Samuelson and Diane Ellerbee, and remembered the way she had treated him when they were at Brewster. He also recalled Rebecca Boone's comment on the drive home.

"I think he's in love with her," Rebecca had said.

The anklebone was connected to the kneebone which was connected to the thighbone which was connected to the hipbone. Humming, Delaney went to his file cabinet and dug out the biographies.

He found what he was looking for in Jason's report on Samuelson. Some years ago, the doctor had a breakdown and was out of action for about six months. The dates were carefully noted. God bless Jason Two.

Next, Delaney looked up the date of Diane and Simon Ellerbee's marriage. Samuelson's crackup had occurred about two weeks later. Now that *was* interesting. Nothing you could take to the bank, but interesting. Another little piece falling into place.

He was still pondering the significance of the Ellerbee-Samuelson relationship when the phone rang. He picked it up, but before he had a chance to speak—

"Charles Parnell here," the detective said, laughing.

"Oh, yes. Thank you for calling back. How'd you make out?"

"Struck gold. The guy had won his squash match—against someone he's been trying to beat for years, so he was celebrating with dry martinis. Just high enough to talk more than he should have. Anyway, Ellerbee made out his will about five years ago. But the clause about his patients' outstanding bills was a codicil added three weeks before he died. Any help?"

"It's beautiful," Delaney said. "Thank you very much, and a Happy New Year to you and yours."

"Same to you, sir."

Another little piece of the puzzle: Ellerbee canceling Joan Yesell's bills just three weeks before he was wasted—about the time, Delaney figured, the victim told his wife he wanted a divorce. Was he just being generous to his new love or did he have a premonition of his death?

Simon: "Diane, I want a divorce."

Diane: "I'll kill you!"

Delaney could believe that imagined dialogue; the lady was capable of it. The lady was also capable of lying glibly when it was required. He had asked her if she was surprised by the clause in her husband's will about his patients' bills. No, she had said, she wasn't surprised, because she was aware of what was in his will. And that, Delaney figured, was world-class lying.

Thinking of what all this meant, he trundled into the kitchen and pulled a long white apron over his heavy, three-piece cheviot suit. The apron had KISS THE COOK printed on the front. Then he set to work preparing dinner for his family.

Since it was Saturday night, they would have hot dogs with toasted rolls, baked beans with a chunk of salt pork and an onion tossed in for flavor, and both hot and cold sauerkraut.

By nine o'clock the Delaneys' brownstone was jumping. Peter and Jeffrey had arrived, bringing along a new board game called "Love at First Sight," in which you threw dice to move from square one (Blind Date) to the winning square (Happy Marriage).

At about the same time the boys showed up, Boone and Jason arrived and were whisked into the study, the door firmly closed against the noisy gaiety in the living room.

" 'Tis the season to be jolly," Delaney said ruefully. "And they're doing it right here tonight. Before you tell me how you made out, let me fill you in on what I've been doing."

He told them why Diane had revised her statement about her husband's mood swings in the past year and the fact that Simon added the codicil to his will just three weeks before his death. He also discussed Dr. Samuelson's curious relationship with Diane.

"I called him," he said. "He agreed to see me tomorrow at ten. I think I'll lean on him."

"You want me to come along, sir?" Boone asked.

"No," Delaney said. "Thanks. But I think this better be a one-on-one. Also, he knows I have no official position; I'm just a friend of the family, so to speak. Maybe he'll be a little more open and spill. You've got to realize that everything I've told you won't make the DA lick his chops, but I think it's all evidence that we're heading in the right direction. Now let's hear what you dug up today. You both look like canary-eating cats, so I hope it's good news."

"The first thing we did," Boone said, "was to check the Manhattan garage where the Ellerbees kept their cars. It's just a parking garage, no servicing and no repairs. I don't think they even have a screwdriver in the place, let alone a ball peen hammer. So we drove up to Brewster. We went by the Ellerbee home. She had a crowd up there today, all women from what we could see. Maybe it's her garden club or something. Anyway, we stopped at a phone, and I called and got the houseman. I said I was from Al's Garage, soliciting business. He said, sorry, they dealt with May's Garage and Service Station, and were perfectly satisfied. I thanked him, and we went over to May's. It was that easy. Jase, you take it from there."

"We find the owner," Jason Two said, "a fat old tub named Ernest May. We flash our tin and ask him if he's lost a ball peen hammer in the last three months or so. His jaw dropped a mile, and he looks at us like we're from Mars or something. 'How the hell did you know that?' he says. Well, it comes out that, yeah, a ball peen hammer turned up missing about three months ago. It was the only ball peen in the joint, and he had to go out and buy a new one. He can't put an exact date on when he lost the hammer, but he figures it was early in October. Sergeant?"

"We asked him who had access to the tools in the garage," Boone said, "and he showed us around. Hell, *everyone* had access to the tools; they were laying all over the joint. It could have been one of his mechanics, a customer waiting to have a car serviced, or maybe just a sneak thief. I wish we could have brought you more, sir, but that's about it. At least we know there's a ball peen hammer missing from a Brewster garage."

Delaney pulled at his lower lip. "This Ernest May—he knows Diane El-lerbee?"

"Oh, hell, yes," the Sergeant said. "She's a good customer. Brings in all her cars to gas up. And for tune-ups. He put in new plugs in that Jeep station wagon not too long ago. The way he talked, she's at his place almost every weekend she's up there, for this or that."

Delaney nodded. "You know where the ball peen hammer is right now? Boone? One guess."

"At the bottom of that stream that runs through Ellerbee's property."

"Right," Delaney said decisively. "Under the ice. And getting silted over."

"A search warrant?" Jason suggested. "We could get some frogmen up there with grapples."

Delaney shook his head. "There's not a judge in the country who'd sign a warrant on the basis of what we've got. We can't tie her directly to boosting the hammer. We could scam it and send in frogmen claiming they were from some phony state environmental agency wanting to test the water or the streambed or some such shit. But even if they found the hammer, what good would it do us? Tainted evidence. And after being under running water for two months, would there be identifiable fingerprints or bloodstains? I doubt it."

"Goddamn it!" Boone burst out. "It's there, I know it is."

"You know it," Delaney said, "and I know it, and Jason knows it. So what? It's not going to put Diane in the slammer."

"What does that mean, sir?" Jason said anxiously. "We're not going to bust her?"

"No," Delaney said slowly, "it doesn't mean that. But right now we have nothing that would justify arrest, indictment, or conviction. There's got to be a way to destroy her, but at the moment I don't know what it is."

"You think if we brace her—" Boone said, "I mean really come on hard—she might crack?"

"And confess? Not that lady. You know what she'd say? 'I don't have to answer any of your questions.' And she'd be exactly right."

"Snookered," Jason Two said.

"No," Delaney said. "Not yet."

• • •

BY MIDNIGHT, THE brownstone had emptied out: Boone and Jason gone, Peter and Jeffrey departed. The girls were up in their bedroom, doing their hair and giggling. Delaney made his nightly rounds, checking locks on doors and windows. Then, wearily, he dragged himself to the master bedroom, slumped on the edge of his bed, and tried to get up enough energy to undress.

Monica was at the vanity, brushing her hair. He watched her a long time in silence, the pleasure of that sight restoring his strength.

"You want to tell me about it?" she asked without turning around.

"Sure," he said, and related everything that had happened since he had first decided on Diane Ellerbee's guilt.

"You can't arrest her?" Monica said.

"Not on the basis of what we've got so far."

"But you're certain? Certain she did it?"

"I am. Aren't you?"

"I guess," she said, sighing. "But it's hard to admit it. I admired that woman."

"I did, too. I still admire her—but for different reasons. She thought this whole thing out very, very carefully. The only mistakes she's made so far are little ones—nothing that could bring an indictment."

"I must have missed something in her," Monica said. "Something that you saw and I didn't."

"It goes back to that conversation we had about beautiful women and how they think."

She put her brush aside and came over to him. She stood in front of him in a peach-colored nightgown and matching peignoir.

"Turn around," she said.

"What?"

"Sit sideways on the bed," she ordered. "Take off your tie and open your shirt and vest."

He obeyed, and she began to massage the meaty muscles of his neck and shoulders. Her strong fingers dug in, kneading and pinching.

"Oh, God," he said, groaning, "don't stop. What do you charge by the hour?"

"On the house," she said, her clever hands working. "Tell me—how do beautiful women think?"

"They can't face reality. Or at least not *our* reality. They live in a shimmering crystal globe. You know—those paperweights: a Swiss chalet scene. You turn them upside down and snow falls. It's a never-never land. Beautiful women live in it. Admiration from all sides. The love of wealthy men. They don't have to lift a finger, and their future is assured. All wants granted."

"You think Diane was like that?"

"Had to be. Beauty is a kind of genius; you can't deny it. You got it or you don't. Then along comes Simon Ellerbee, her teacher. He convinces her she's got a good brain too. Not only is she beautiful, but she's brainy. That crystal ball she lives in is now shinier and lovelier than ever."

"Then he asks for a divorce?"

"Right! Oh, hon, that feels so good. Up higher around my neck. Yes, her husband asks for a divorce. I'll bet my bottom dollar it was the first failure in her life. A defeat. We all learn to cope with defeats and disappointments. But not beautiful women; they're insulated in their crystal globes. It must have devastated her. The man who convinced her that she had a brain not only doesn't want her brain anymore, but doesn't want *her*. Can you imagine what that did to her ego?"

"I can imagine," Monica said sadly.

"When someone hurts you, you hurt back: that's human nature. But this was a cataclysmic hurt. And she responded in a cataclysmic way: murder. I told you that her reality was different from ours. When Simon asked for a divorce, he wasn't only destroying her, he was demolishing her world. And all for a little, plain, no-talent woman? If such things could happen, then Diane's reality had no substance. You can see that, can't you?"

"I told you," Monica said, "you see more than I do."

She moved away from him and began to turn down the blankets and sheet on her bed.

"Open the window tonight?" he asked her.

"Just a crack," she said. "It's supposed to be below freezing by morning."

He went in for a shower. Scrubbed his teeth, brushed his hair, climbed into his old-fashioned pajamas. When he came back into the bedroom, Monica was sitting up in her bed, back against the headboard.

"You don't like me much tonight, do you?" he said.

"It's not a question of liking you, Edward. But sometimes you scare me."

"Scare you? How so?"

"You know so much about Diane. It all sounds so logical, the way you dissect her. What do you think about *me?*"

He put a palm softly to her cheek. "That you're an absolutely magnificent woman, and I hate to imagine what my life would be without you. I love you, Monica. You believe that, don't you?"

"Yes. But there's a part of you I'll never understand. You can be so—so *strict* sometimes. Like God."

He smiled. "I'm not God. Not even close. Do you think Diane Ellerbee should get off scot-free?"

"Of course not."

"Of course not," he repeated. "So the problem now is how she can be made to pay for what she did."

"How are you going to do that, Edward?"

"I'm going to turn over her crystal globe," he said coldly, "and watch the snow come down."

He turned off the light and found his way to Monica's bed. She pulled the blankets up to their chins.

"Please don't tell me that I scare you," he begged. "That scares *me.*"

"You don't really scare me," she said. "It's just the way you become obsessed with a case."

"Obsessed? I guess so. Maybe that's the way you've got to be to get anything done. I just don't like the idea of someone getting away with murder. It offends me. Is that so awful?"

"Of course not. But sometimes you can be vindictive, Edward."

"Oh, yes," he readily agreed. "I plead guilty to that."

"Don't you sympathize with Diane at all?"

"Sure I do. She's human."

"Don't you feel sorry for her?"

"Of course."

"But you're going to destroy her?"

"Completely," he vowed. "But that's enough about Doctor Diane Eller-bee. What about us?"

"What about us?"

"Still friends?"

"Come closer," Monica said. "I'll show you."

"Oh, yes," he said, moving. "Thank you, friend."

26

•

DELANEY PREPARED CAREFULLY FOR HIS MEETING WITH DR. JULIUS K. Samuelson: went over once again the biography Jason had submitted, reviewed his report on the first interrogation, read his notes on Samuelson's comments and behavior during that visit to Brewster.

He had told Boone and Jason that he intended to lean on Dr. Samuelson. But in cops' lexicon, there are varieties of leaning, from brutal hectoring to the pretense of sorrowful sympathy. In this case, Delaney decided, tough intimidation would be counterproductive; he might achieve more with sweet reasonableness—an approach Delaney characterized as the "I need your help" style of interrogation.

He lumbered over to Samuelson's office at 79th Street and Madison Avenue. It was a harshly cold morning, the air still but the temperature in the teens. Delaney was thankful for his flannel muffler, vested suit, and balbriggan underwear. He thrust his gloved hands into his overcoat pockets, but he felt the cold in his feet, a numbing chill from the frozen pavement.

The doctor greeted him at the office door with a tentative smile. The little man was wearing his holey wool cardigan and worn carpet slippers. He seemed staggered by the weight of Delaney's overcoat, but he hung it away manfully and offered a cup of black coffee from a desk thermos. Delaney accepted gratefully.

"Doctor Samuelson," Delaney began, keeping his voice low-pitched and conversational, "thank you for giving me your valuable time. I wouldn't have bothered you, but some things have come up in the investigation of Simon Ellerbee's death that puzzle us, and I hoped you might be able to help."

The doctor made a gesture. "Whatever I can do," he said.

"First of all, we have discovered that for the past year or so, Doctor Simon had been having an affair with Joan Yesell, one of his patients."

Samuelson stared at him through the thick curved lens of his wire-rimmed glasses. "You are certain of this?"

"Absolutely, sir. Not only from a statement by the lady concerned, but from the testimony of corroborating witnesses. You were probably the Ellerbees' best friend, doctor—saw them frequently in town, visited their Brewster home on weekends—yet in our first meeting you stated that Doctor Simon was faithful to his wife, and theirs was a happy marriage. You had no inkling of Simon's infidelity?"

"Well—ah—I might have had a suspicion. But you cannot condemn a man because of suspicion, can you? Besides, poor Simon is dead, and what good would it do to tarnish his reputation? Is this important to your investigation?"

"Very important."

"You mean the patient involved, this Joan Yesell, may have killed him?"

"She is being watched."

Samuelson shook his head dolefully. "What a dreadful thing. And what a fool he was to get involved with a patient. Not only a horrendous breach of professional ethics, but a despicable insult to his wife. Do you think she was aware of his philandering?"

"She says no. Do you think she was?"

"Mr. Delaney, how can I possibly answer a question like that? I don't know what Diane thinks."

"Don't you, doctor? I noticed some unusual facts in your personal history. First, you were acquainted with both Ellerbees for some time prior to their marriage. Second, you suffered a breakdown two weeks after their marriage. Third, you continue to maintain a close relationship with Diane. I don't wish to embarrass you or cause you pain, but whatever you tell me will be of tremendous help in convicting Simon's killer. And will, of course, be held in strictest confidence. Doctor Samuelson, are you in love with Diane Ellerbee?"

The diminutive man looked like he had been struck a blow. His narrow shoulders sagged. The large head on a stalky neck fell to one side as if he hadn't the strength to support it. His grayish complexion took on an even unhealthier pallor.

"Is it that obvious?" he asked with a failed smile.

Delaney nodded.

"Well, then—yes, I love her. Have since the first time I met her. She was studying with Simon then. My wife had died years before that. I suppose I was a lonely widower. Still am, for that matter. I thought Diane was the most beautiful woman I had ever met. Had ever seen. Her beauty simply took my breath away."

"Yes, she's lovely."

"Every man who has met her feels the same way. I have always felt there is something unearthly about her beauty. She seems to be of a different race than human. There! You see the extent of my hopeless passion?"

That line was spoken with wry self-mockery.

"Why hopeless?" Delaney asked.

"Look at me," Samuelson said. "A shrimp of a man. Twenty years older than Diane. And not much to look at. Besides, there was Simon: a big, handsome, brilliant fellow closer to her own age. I could see the way she looked at him, and knew I had no chance. Is all this making me a prime suspect in the murder?"

"No," Delaney said, smiling, "it's not doing that."

"Well, I didn't do it, of course. I could never do anything like that. I abhor violence. Besides, I loved Simon almost as much as I did Diane—in a different way."

"You've spent a lot of time with her, doctor. Especially since her husband's death. Would you say she's a proud woman?"

"Proud? Not particularly. Confident, certainly."

"Very sure of herself?"

"Oh, yes."

"Obstinate?"

"She can be stubborn on occasion."

"What you're saying is that she likes her own way?"

Samuelson thought that over for a few seconds. "Yes," he said finally. "I think that's a fair assessment: She likes her own way. That's hardly a fault, Mr. Delaney."

"You're right, sir, it isn't; we all like to get our own way. Prior to Simon's death, did Diane give any indication at all that she was aware of her husband's unfaithfulness? Please think carefully before you answer, doctor; it's very important."

Samuelson poured them both more coffee, emptying the desk thermos. Then he sat back, patting the waves of his heavy russet hair. Delaney wondered again if it might be a rug.

"I honestly cannot give you a definite answer," the psychiatrist said. "Certain things, the way people talk and act, can seem perfectly normal, innocuous. Then someone like you comes along and asks, can you interpret that talk and those actions in this manner—is the person in question suspicious, jealous, paranoid, depressive, or whatever? And almost invariably the speech and actions can be so interpreted. Do you understand what I am saying, Mr. Delaney? Human emotions are extremely difficult to analyze. They can mean almost anything you want them to mean: open and above board or devious and contrived."

"I do understand that, doctor, and agree with you. But even with that disclaimer, can you state definitely that Diane was *not* aware of her husband's infidelity?"

"No, I cannot say that."

"Then, from your observations of her during the past year, can you say she *may* have been aware?"

"Possibly," Dr. Samuelson said cautiously.

Delaney sighed, knowing he was not going to get any more than that.

"Doctor, Diane strikes me as being a very controlled woman, always in command of herself. Do you agree?"

"Oh, yes."

"Did you ever see her when she was not in control?"

"Only once," Samuelson said with a rueful smile. "And then it was over such a stupid thing. It happened last year. I was out at their Brewster home for the weekend. It was in the fall, and quite cool. Simon liked to have dinner on the patio, and planned to grill steaks on the barbecue. Diane insisted it was too cold to eat out-of-doors, and wanted us to stay inside. A furious argument erupted. I stayed out of it, of course. They really went at it, hammer and tongs, and said a lot of things I'm sure they were sorry for later. Finally Diane grabbed the package of steaks—they were beautiful sirloins—ran out of the house, and threw them in the stream. That was the end of our steak dinner. But at least it had the effect of clearing the air, and after a while we were laughing about it. We opened two cans of tuna and had a salad and baked potatoes."

"Indoors?" Delaney said.

"Indoors," Samuelson said. "That was the only time I ever saw Diane lose her temper. But I admit her anger was frightening."

"I recall," Delaney said, "that when I was speaking to her of the possibility of patients assaulting their psychiatrists, I asked her if she had ever been attacked. She said most of her patients were children, but when they struck her, she hit back. Is this the usual treatment in situations like that?"

Dr. Samuelson shrugged. "It is not a technique that I myself would use, but whatever works . . . Psychotherapy is not an exact science."

"So I have learned. One final question, doctor—a very personal one: Have you asked Diane Ellerbee to marry you?"

Samuelson looked at him strangely. "I think you are in the wrong business, Mr. Delaney. Perhaps you should be sitting behind this desk."

"You haven't answered my question."

"The answer is yes, I asked Diane to marry me. She said no."

"A very independent woman," Delaney remarked.

Samuelson nodded.

Schlepping home in the cold, Delaney pondered the interview and what it had yielded. Not a hell of a lot. He liked that story about Diane throwing the sirloins in the stream. Last year, steaks; this year, a ball peen hammer.

The one question he hadn't been able to ask still gnawed at him: *Doctor Samuelson, do you think Diane Ellerbee murdered her husband?* Samuelson would have been outraged, and, considering his infatuation, would have been on the phone, warning her, the moment Delaney left his office. Better that Diane should believe herself unsuspected and safe. The shock would be that much greater.

He suddenly acknowledged they had all they were going to get. It was time for him to make his move. Not because of Thorsen's end-of-the-year deadline, although that was a consideration, but because the investigation had come up against a blank wall.

There was not going to be a sudden, neat denouement, the killer nabbed and proven guilty. He would have to settle for a half-loaf. But it would not be the first time that had happened to him, he reflected grimly, and he could live with it. *All* was best, but something was better than nothing.

He worked out the way he was going to handle it, manipulating people by appealing to their self-interest. It wouldn't be perfect justice—but when had justice ever been perfect?

He stopped at a couple of shops on the way home, and when he entered his empty brownstone—the women out shopping again, he supposed—he headed directly for the kitchen. There he made himself two toasted bagel sandwiches layered with cream cheese, sliced red onion, and capers. One sandwich got a thick slab of lox, the other smoked sturgeon.

He spent almost an hour on the phone, tracking down Thorsen and Suarez. He finally got everything coordinated, and both men promised to be at the brownstone at 9:30 P.M. Then he tried calling Dr. Diane Ellerbee at her office and at her Brewster home, but got no answer.

He worked all afternoon putting his files in order, holding out only those documents he might need. He then made notes of the presentation he intended to deliver to Thorsen and Suarez. He was confident he would succeed; he couldn't see that they had any choice but to go along with him.

He leaned back in his swivel chair, realizing it was all winding down. End of the trail. There was a certain satisfaction in that, and a certain sadness, too. It had been a nice chase, an excitement, but now it was done.

He reviewed the way he had handled it and couldn't see how he might have worked it differently with better results. If he had made any error, it was in looking for complexities in a homicide that was essentially simple: The Case of the Betrayed Wife. A detective couldn't go far wrong if he stuck to the obvious.

• • •

THAT NIGHT DELANEY began by throwing them a curveball.

"Chief," he said to Suarez, "I want you to arrest Doctor Diane Ellerbee for the murder of her husband."

Thorsen was the first to recover. "My God, Edward," he said, "the last time we spoke, you said you thought it was the patient—what's her name?"

"Joan Yesell. No, she's clean. She was there on the night Ellerbee was killed, but she didn't do it."

"So it was the wife?" Suarez said wonderingly. "All the time it was the wife while we were chasing the patients?"

"That's right," Delaney said. "This is a long story, so bear with me."

He stood and began pacing back and forth behind his desk, occasionally glancing at the notes he had prepared.

He started with the affair between Simon and Joan Yesell, and how it had gone on for almost a year. Diane had probably been aware of it soon after it started, but it was only three weeks prior to his death that Simon had asked for a divorce.

"There's motive enough for you," Delaney said. "The scorned woman."

He analyzed the personality of Diane: a beautiful woman who had lived a fortunate and sheltered life and never suffered a disappointment. Then her husband says he wants to leave her for a Plain Jane and her whole world collapses.

He described Joan Yesell, a woman energized by love for the first time in her life. She would, Delaney said, have been willing to let the affair continue indefinitely, but he promised her marriage.

"So," Delaney said, "that's our triangle: three passionate and very flummoxed people."

Then Delaney reviewed the murder night, starting with the victim's announced intention of seeing a late patient: Diane's unproven statement that she had left Manhattan for Brewster; Joan Yesell's inability to get a cab, and her late arrival at the townhouse to find Dr. Simon dead.

"Diane had the motive," Delaney argued. "She had the opportunity, and here's how she got the means . . ."

He told them about the ball peen hammer stolen from the Brewster garage where the Ellerbees' cars were serviced. He described the stream running through the Ellerbees' property, and stated firmly that he believed the hammer had been thrown into the stream.

He began to pile on supporting evidence: the clause in Simon's will canceling his patients' outstanding bills, Joan Yesell's debt of nearly ten thousand dollars, Diane's erroneous statement that suicide-prone patients often become homicidal. . . .

"All right," Delaney said at last, "let's have your questions. I'm sure you've got them."

"In the absence of the billing ledger," Suarez said, "how do you know

Joan Yesell would benefit most from the doctor's canceling of patients' debts?"

Delaney explained that Simon's receptionist, Carol Judd, had provided that information.

Thorsen asked why Delaney was so certain of the intensity of the Ellerbee–Joan Yesell affair.

Delaney told them about the last interrogation of Yesell, her mother's attempt to alibi her, and Samuelson's acknowledgment that he had suspected for some time that Simon was involved with another woman. Delaney did not mention the flower that Simon wore in his lapel; he doubted they would consider that firm evidence of a romantic passion.

"Why would Ellerbee want to start an affair with such a dull woman," the Chief asked, "if his wife is as lovely as you say?"

Delaney repeated what he had told Boone and Jason—that Simon wanted to improve his women and had tired of being married to a paragon, with his friends constantly telling him how lucky he was.

"Maybe," Delaney added, "he wanted a relationship in which *he* was the paragon. It must be difficult being married to a work of art."

"Let's get back to that missing billing ledger," the Deputy said. "Who do you figure took it—Diane or Joan Yesell?"

"Diane," Delaney said promptly. "Look, Diane wants to implicate Yesell. That's why she gave us Joan's name in the first place. But at the same time, she doesn't want us to find out about Simon's affair. Diane is a very complex woman, torn between a need for vengeance and a need to protect her own self-esteem."

"Why did she put out his eyes?" Ivar asked—and with that question Delaney knew he had convinced them.

Again he repeated what he had told Boone and Jason—that Simon had persuaded Diane that her beauty meant little, but then had begun to look at another woman. She couldn't stand that.

There was silence.

"That's all?" Delaney said. "No more questions?"

Then, thinking it might be discreet to leave them alone for a few moments, he went into the kitchen and mixed himself a tall rye highball. He drank half of it off immediately, standing at the sink, then brought the remainder back into the study along with drinks for the others.

"All right," he said. "Did she or didn't she? Chief, what do you think?"

"I think she did it," Suarez said mournfully, his sad face sagging. "A beautiful woman like that—it is a true tragedy."

"Ivar?"

"Oh, she's guilty as hell," the Admiral said. "No doubt about it. But you know what you've got, Edward. Zero, zip, and zilch."

"Hard evidence, you mean?" Delaney said. "Of course I know that. And we're not going to get it. Continuing this investigation would be just spinning our wheels. But I want Diane Ellerbee charged for the murder of her husband."

"What good would that do?" Thorsen demanded, looking at him narrowly. "She'd be out in two hours, and that would be the end of that. And the DA will call us assholes for arresting her."

"I'll tell you what it'll do for *me*," Delaney said coldly. "It'll ruin her. The arrest will be headlined in every newspaper in town, and featured on every TV news program. She's going to walk anyway, isn't she? You know it and I know it. But we can drag her through the mud first. Even when she goes free, everyone will be saying, 'Where there's smoke, there's fire.' You think her reputation can take that? Or her career? I know we'll never get a conviction on what I've got—probably not even an indictment—but by God, we can make her suffer. That's what *I* want.

"As for you two, what you get out of this hyped-up circus is what *you* want: headlines of an important arrest, with statements by you, Chief, that you're convinced the Ellerbee homicide is cleared. Statements by you, Ivar, congratulating Suarez on his exceptional detective work in solving this extremely difficult case. Don't you think the PC is going to read the papers and watch TV?"

The two men turned and stared at each other.

"I do not know . . ." Suarez said hesitantly. "I am not sure . . . The law . . ."

Delaney whirled on him. "The law?" he said, snorting. "What the hell has the law got to do with this? We're talking about justice here. She's got to be made to pay. But this can't be decided on the basis of either law or justice. This is strictly a political decision."

"Welcome to the club," Thorsen said with a small smile. "But what if she sues for false arrest?"

"I wish she would," Delaney cried, "but she's too smart for that. Because that would bring her into a courtroom, and the carnival would continue. And the whole business of her late husband's affair would be dragged through the press. You think she'd enjoy that? Her lawyers won't let her sue the city after they look over what we've got. No way! They're going to tell her to forget it, lay low, and don't make waves."

"It's a gamble," the Deputy said thoughtfully. "Charging someone when we know we don't have an icicle's chance in hell of getting a conviction."

"I told you it was a political decision," Delaney said. "It's two days until the end of the year. You can still pull this out if you've got the balls for it."

"I do not like it," Suarez said. "It is somehow shameful. But still, the woman is guilty—no?"

"When would you want to do this?" Thorsen asked.

"Take her?" Delaney said. "Tomorrow night if I can set up a meet."

"Do you want the Chief and me there?"

"No, I don't think that would be wise. You keep your distance until it's done. But have your statements ready, and schedule a press conference. My God, Ivar, you know how to use the media; you've been doing it long enough. I'll take Boone and Jason. They've worked hard on this thing and should be in on the kill. And, by the way, Chief—I've got a list of people, including Boone and Jason, who deserve recognition for a hard job well done."

"Of course," Suarez said with a wave of his hand. "It is understood."

"Good. I'll hold you to that. Now let's get to the nitty-gritty and figure how this is going down."

27

•

HE FINALLY GOT THROUGH TO DIANE ELLERBEE LATE ON MONDAY morning, December 30th.

"Edward X. Delaney here," he said briskly. "Doctor, there's been a major development in the investigation of your husband's death—something I think you should know about."

"You've found the killer?"

"I'd rather not talk about it on the phone. Could we meet sometime this evening?"

They finally agreed on 8:30 P.M. at the East 84th Street townhouse. Delaney hung up, satisfied, then immediately called Boone, asking him to pick him up at the brownstone at eight o'clock.

"And bring Jason with you," he told the Sergeant. "I'd like both of you to be in uniform."

"My God, sir, my blues need cleaning and pressing!"

"Try to get it done this afternoon. If you can't, wear them the way they are. Full equipment for both of you."

A short pause, then: "We're busting her?"

"Tell you tonight at eight," Delaney said, enjoying the suspense game as much as anyone.

He had promised his ladies a fine lunch, and put the Ellerbee case from his mind for a few hours while he acted the expansive host. He took them to Prunelle's on East 54th Street, where the women were suitably impressed with the Art Deco decor and burled maple walls.

"On the first day of the new year," Delaney vowed as they finished, "I am going to start my six thousand four hundred and fifty-eighth diet."

"Another of your one-day diets?" Monica said cruelly.

"You like me massive," he told her. "More of me to love."

"Hah!" she said.

Their luncheon took almost two hours, and after, the women declared their intention of checking out the post-Christmas sales in Fifth Avenue stores. Delaney left them outside the restaurant determined to walk home and work off some of those calories.

The temperature hovered around the freezing mark, but it was a bright, pleasant day with a washed blue sky dotted with puffy clouds. He tramped north on Madison Avenue, marveling at the proliferation of art galleries, antique shops, and boutiques.

It was a long walk, almost thirty blocks, and he was happy to get in the warm brownstone, unlace his shoes, and treat himself to a cigar. He sat heavily in his swivel chair in the study and began plotting the confrontation with Diane Ellerbee.

He would dress somberly with white shirt and black tie. Something like a mortician, he thought, amused. The only prop he'd need, he decided, would be a clipboard holding a heavy sheaf of papers. It meant nothing, of course, but it would impress.

He was confident of his ability to wing it, adjusting his attitude and manner to counter her responses. Never for a moment did he expect her to admit anything; she would deny, deny, deny. But, being a civilian, he could badger her in ways a police officer on duty could not. He would not let her off the hook.

What he needed to do, he determined, was to rattle her from the start, knock her off balance, and keep her confused. She was an intelligent woman with an enormous ego. His best course would be to dent that self-esteem and then keep her disturbed and witless.

He wanted her to say to herself, "Can this be happening to *me?*"

So sure was he of her guilt that he designed her downfall coldly and without mercy. He never questioned his own motives. If Monica had said to him, "What right do you have to do this?" he would have looked at her in astonishment. For it wasn't *his* right; it was society's right—or perhaps God's.

Boone and Jason arrived promptly at eight o'clock, both in full uniform. He called them into the study for a few minutes to give them a quick rundown.

"We're going to take her tonight," he said. "Let me do the talking, but if you think I've missed something, don't be afraid to chime in. And don't be surprised to hear me state suppositions as facts; I want her to believe we've got a lot more than we actually have."

"One thing we haven't got is a warrant," Boone reminded him.

"True," Delaney said, "but we have probable cause. This is not a minor offense she's being charged with, and I think the courts will hold that a warrantless arrest was justified in this case by the gravity of the crime."

He didn't tell them that it was extremely unlikely the case would ever come to trial; they were smart cops and could figure that out for themselves.

"If this thing self-destructs," he told them, "neither of you will suffer. There will be no notations on your records that you participated. I have Deputy Thorsen's word on that. On the other hand, if it goes down as planned, Chief Suarez assures me you'll get something out of it. Any questions? No? Then let's get this show on the road."

They drove over to East 84th in Jason's car. When they stood in the lobby of the townhouse, Delaney was pleased with the way they looked: three big men with the physical presence to command respect. Or to intimidate.

He rang her bell. The intercom clicked on.

"Who is it?"

"Delaney," he said tensely.

"I'm in my office, Mr. Delaney. Please come up to the second floor."

The door lock buzzed. They pushed in and silently climbed the staircase. She was waiting in the hallway, and blinked when she saw the officers in uniform.

"Is this an official visit, Mr. Delaney?" she asked with a tight smile.

"You've already met Sergeant Boone," he said, ignoring her question. "This man is Officer Jason who, incidentally, was on the scene when the homicide was discovered. May we come in?"

She led the way into her office, and once again he admired her carriage: head held high, shoulders back, spine straight. But nothing was stiff; she moved with sinuous grace.

Her hair was up in a braided crown, her face free of makeup, that marvelous translucent complexion aglow. She was wearing an oversize block-check shirt in lavender and black, cinched at the waist with a man's necktie. And below, pants of purple suede, so snug that Delaney wondered if she had to grease her legs to get into them.

She sat regally behind her desk, hands held before her, fingertips touching to form a cage. Delaney pulled up an uncomfortable straight chair to face her directly. The two officers sat behind him in the cretonne-covered armchairs.

All three men had left their overcoats in the car, and Delaney's homburg as well. But he had instructed them to wear their caps and not to remove them indoors. Now they sat with peaks pulled low, as solid and motionless as stone monoliths.

"You say you have discovered something about my husband's death?" Dr. Ellerbee said, voice cool and formal.

With slow deliberation Delaney took a leather spectacle case from his inside jacket pocket, removed his reading glasses, donned the glasses, adjusting the bows carefully. He then looked down at the clipboard on his lap, made a show of flipping over a few pages.

He glanced sharply at the doctor. "Let's start from the beginning," he said in a hard, toneless voice. "For the past year your late husband was having an affair with one of his patients, Joan Yesell. Not only was this a violation of professional ethics, but it was also a betrayal of his marriage vows and a grievous insult to you personally."

He was watching her closely as he spoke, and saw no signs of surprise or horror. But those touching fingers clenched to form a ball of whitened knuckles, and the porcelain complexion blanched.

"You don't—" she began, her voice now dry and cracked.

"The evidence cannot be controverted," Delaney interrupted. He flipped through more pages on his clipboard. "We have the sworn statements of Miss Yesell, her mother, the testimony of an eyewitness who saw the doctor driving away after delivering Yesell to her home on a Friday night. And the clause canceling his patients' outstanding bills in your late husband's will was expressly designed to benefit Miss Yesell. Now do you wish to deny that Doctor Simon was carrying on an illicit relationship?"

"I was not aware of it," she said harshly.

"Ah, but you were. You are an intelligent, perceptive woman. We are certain you were aware of your husband's transgression."

Diane Ellerbee stood abruptly. "I think this meeting is at an end," she said. "Please leave before I—"

Delaney reached out to slap the top of her desk with an open palm. The sharp crack made her jump.

"Sit down, madam!" he thundered. "You are going nowhere without our permission."

She stared at him, blank-faced, and then slowly lowered herself back into her chair.

"Let's get on with it," Delaney said. "We don't want to waste too much time on a tawdry murder." That got to her, he could see, and he peered down at his clipboard, flipping pages with some satisfaction.

"Now, then," he said, looking up at her again, "the evidence we have uncovered indicates that you became aware of your husband's affair sometime last year, probably soon after it started. This is supposition on my part, but I would guess you let it continue because you hoped it was just a passing fancy and would soon end."

"I don't have to answer any of your questions," she said.

Delaney showed his big yellow teeth in something approximating a smile. "But I haven't asked any questions, have I? Let me continue. About three weeks prior to his death, your husband came to you, confessed his love for Joan Yesell, and asked for a divorce. There went your hope that his adulterous relationship was a temporary infatuation. Worse, it was a tremendous blow to your self-esteem."

"You're a dreadful man," she whispered.

"That's true," he said, almost happily, "I am. Let me psychoanalyze *you*, doctor, for a few minutes. Turn the tables, so to speak. You are a beautiful and wealthy woman, and all your life you've lived in a cocoon, protected and sheltered from reality. What do you know about a waitress's aching feet or how hard the wife of a poor man works? It's all been peaches and cream, hasn't it? All those relatives dying and leaving you money. A successful career. And best of all, being worshiped by men. You could see it in their eyes and the way they acted. Every man you ever met wanted to jump on your bones."

"Stop it," she said. "Please stop it."

"Never a defeat," he continued relentlessly. "Never even a disappointment. But then your husband comes to you, says Bye-bye, kiddo, I want to leave you to marry another woman. And a quiet, timid, plain, rather dowdy woman at that. It was the worst thing that could possibly happen to you. Because you couldn't handle defeat. Didn't know how—you had no experience. So all you could feel was anger. Your husband's declaration of love for Yesell not only destroyed you, but it destroyed your world."

He paused a moment, expecting a reply. But when she said nothing, he flipped more pages on his clipboard, then looked up at her again.

"All right," he said, "so much for the psychoanalysis, doctor. No charge. But I think it gives us a motive a jury would believe. Now let's talk about the weapon—the ball peen hammer that crushed your husband's skull and put out his eyes. We spent a lot of time on that hammer, Doctor Ellerbee, and, lo and behold, we discovered a ball peen hammer was stolen sometime in October from May's Garage and Service Station in Brewster, where you take your cars. You could have lifted it. It's possible, isn't it? And where do you think that hammer is now? At the bottom of the brook that runs through your land. Which is why we're getting a warrant to drag the stream. And if we find it—what then? Fingerprints and bloodstains, I suppose. You'd be amazed at what the laboratory men can do these days."

She stirred restlessly, moving her body in the chair and turning her head back and forth. She reminded Delaney of one of the great cats he had seen behind bars in the Central Park Zoo—a cheetah, he recalled—whipping its head from side to side, pacing, endlessly pacing, plotting how to get out.

"Not much more now," he said stonily. "You couldn't handle your anger, so you got hold of the hammer and started planning. It had to be on a Friday night, because that's when Joan Yesell came up here, and she and your husband made love on his black leather coach. Right? So, on that stormy night, you didn't drive up early to Brewster at all, did you?"

"I did!" she cried. "I did!"

"Don't jerk me around," he said, tapping his clipboard. "We've got evidence here that you didn't. That instead you stayed in Manhattan, watched the townhouse, waiting for Joan Yesell to arrive. But she was late that night. Your anger was building, building . . . Finally you came in here and murdered your husband. And then smashed his eyes because he had the effrontery to look at another woman."

She stared at him with horrified wonder.

"Why are you doing this to me?" she asked. *"Why?"*

He stood suddenly and slammed a hard fist down on her desk top, a heavy blow that made everyone in the room jump. He leaned far over the desk.

"Why?" he said in a strangled voice, glaring at her. "*Why*? Because you visited my home, you were sweet to my wife, you invited us to your home and fed us. You actually sat down at table with us and acted the bountiful hostess. Then you sent us flowers. The beginning of your downfall—if only you could have known. But throughout you've played me for a fool—a *fool*! And that I can't take. You want to know why? That's why!"

He subsided into his chair, his fury ebbing. She looked at him, bewildered, not understanding. Boone and Jason understood but remained silent.

The silence grew. He gave her time, watching her face working. He guessed what was going through her mind. He could almost see her confidence slowly returning as she reviewed everything he had said. She straightened in her chair, raised a hand to make certain her braids were in place.

"You don't know that I stole a hammer from May's," she said finally, "and you certainly can't prove it."

"That's true," Delaney said, nodding.

"And you can't prove that I stayed in Manhattan that night."

He nodded again.

"You can't even prove that I knew about my husband's sleazy little affair," she concluded triumphantly. "So you've got nothing."

He showed his teeth again. "We've got *you*, madam," he said.

She was shaken, expecting to hear a proven indictment. But this great, shaggy bear of a man sat silently, staring at her over his reading glasses.

"Stop calling me 'madam,'" she said petulantly. "If you don't wish to address me as 'Doctor,' then 'Mrs. Ellerbee' will do as well."

He leaned forward. "Why don't we cut out the shit," he said pleasantly, using the crude word deliberately to further unsettle her. "You're going to waltz away from this, smiling bravely. If you don't know it, your lawyers will."

"Well, then," she said, "this has all been an exercise in futility, hasn't it?"

"Not quite. If I had my druthers, you'd be behind bars for ten-to-twenty, eating off tin plates and afraid to pick up the soap in the shower. But if I can't have that, I'll settle for second best." He extended a big hand, fingers spread wide, then slowly clenched them into a rocky fist. "I'm going to crush you, *madam*—just like that."

She looked at him, then looked at the two uniformed officers sitting behind him. They returned her stare.

"Let me tell you what's going to happen to you," Delaney said, hunching forward to rest his clasped hands on the desk. "We're going to make what they call a media event out of this. We're going to arrest you, charging you with the premeditated murder of your husband, Simon Ellerbee. You'll be taken to the nearest precinct house, photographed, and fingerprinted. Then you'll be allowed a phone call to your attorney. While you're waiting for him, you'll be locked in a cage. Won't that be nice? Oh, you'll be out in a few hours, I'm sure—maybe a day at the most. Meanwhile we'll have alerted the newspapers and television stations. It's going to be a circus: *Wife accused in brutal slaying of husband.* The media will love it. Prominent East Side couple. Wealthy, well-known psychiatrists. And the other woman—a patient! Have you ever been photographed wearing a bikini? I'll bet the tabloids get hold of the photo and splash it all over their front pages."

"You wouldn't dare," she gasped, her face suddenly a death's-head.

"Oh, I'd dare a great deal more than that, *madam*. Leaks to the press about your husband's affair. Maybe Joan Yesell can sell her story and make a few bucks—she's entitled."

"I'll sue you!" she screamed. "I'll sue all of you!"

"Be my guest," he said with a frosty smile. "You sue, and you're going to be in the headlines a long time, lady. But meanwhile your career is down the drain. No more kiddie patients for you. And wherever you go, for the rest of your life, people will point a finger and whisper, 'That's the woman they said killed her husband.' You'll never outlive that."

"You're a brute," she shouted at him, quivering with anger. "A brute!"

"A brute, am I? And what do you call someone who hammers in the skull of another human being and then crushes his eyes? I'm a brute but you're not—is that the way your mind works? You didn't really think you were going to get off scot-free, did you? This is an imperfect, unfair world, I admit, but you sin and you pay the price, one way or another. It's payment time for you, doctor."

"I didn't do it!" she howled desperately. "I swear I didn't!"

"You did it," he said, looking at her steadily. "You know it, I know it, these officers know it, the Department knows it. And pretty soon the whole city will. You're going to be a nine-day wonder, Doctor Ellerbee. Maybe they'll even make up rhymes about you—like 'Lizzie Borden took an axe . . . ' Won't it be great to be a superstar?"

She moved so swiftly they didn't have time to react. Instead of circling the desk, she launched herself over the top, claws out, going for Delaney's face. He jerked back, his chair went over with a crash, and he dragged her down atop him, hoping his glasses wouldn't break.

Boone and Jason Two pulled her off. She fought them frantically and they slammed her back into the chair behind the desk. Jason stood next to her, a meaty hand clamped on her shoulder.

Delaney climbed awkwardly to his feet. He set the chair upright, examined his reading glasses to make sure they weren't broken, and touched the stinging marks on his cheek. His fingers came away bloody. He pressed his handkerchief to the gouges.

"Anger," he said to the others, nodding. "Uncontrollable. The way she was when she killed her husband. Sergeant Boone, take a look out the window, see if the press is here."

Abner Boone looked down from the window fronting on East 84th Street. "They're here," he reported. "A lot of guys with cameras and a TV crew."

"Right on schedule," Delaney said quietly. "I should tell you, Mrs. Ellerbee, that because this is a felony arrest, you will be handcuffed."

She sat, huddled and shrunken, head bowed, arms crossed over her breast, holding her elbows. She would not look at him.

"Do you understand what you did?" he asked gently, still pressing a handkerchief to his cheek. "You killed a human being. The man betrayed you, certainly. But was that sufficient reason to take a human life? Sergeant . . ."

Abner Boone stepped close to Diane.

"You have the right to remain silent . . ." he started.

Delaney sat while they took her away. He had no desire to watch from the window. But he saw the flash of photographer's lights and heard the uproar. Deputy Thorsen had delivered.

He waited until the noise and confusion had died away. He was out of it now; let Thorsen and Suarez carry the ball. His job was finished. He had done what they asked him to do, and if the result was less than perfect, they got what they wanted.

He gingerly touched the back of his head. It had smacked the floor when his chair went over, and he suspected he'd have a welt there. He was, he acknowledged, getting a bit long in the tooth for that kind of nonsense.

It wasn't so much that he was physically tired, but the evening had taken a lot out of him. He couldn't summon the energy to rise and tramp home to Monica and the girls. So he tucked his reading glasses away and just sat there, fingers laced across his vest, and brooded.

His first wife, Barbara, had once accused him of acting like God's surrogate on earth. He didn't think that was entirely fair. He had lost his hubris, he was convinced. What drove him now was more a sense of duty. But duty to *what* he could not have said.

Despite those things he had shouted about Diane Ellerbee playing him for a fool, he felt more pity for her than anger. He thought her life had been so structured, so neat and secure, that she had never learned to handle trouble.

But he could continue forever making up excuses. He was a cop, with a cop's bald way of thinking, and the naked fact was that she had killed and had to be punished for it.

He dragged himself to his feet, and, as if it were his own home, made the rounds of doors and windows in the deserted townhouse, making certain they were securely locked.

He stopped suddenly, wondering where the hell his overcoat and homburg were. Probably still in Jason's car, now parked outside the precinct house. But when he went down to the first floor, he found them waiting for him, neatly folded on a marble-topped lobby table. God bless . . .

He pounded home, head down, hands in pockets. He pondered how much to tell Monica of what had happened. Then he decided to tell her everything;

he had to explain the jagged scrapes on his face. If it made him seem like a vindictive beast, so be it. He wasn't about to start lying to her now. Besides, she'd *know*.

He looked up suddenly, and beyond the city's glow saw the stars whirling their ascending courses. So small, he thought. All the poor, scrabbling people on earth caught up in a life we never made, breaking ourselves trying to manage.

Philosophers said you could laugh or you could weep. Delaney preferred to think there was a middle ground, an amused struggle in which you recognized the odds and knew you'd never beat them. Which was no reason to stop trying. Las Vegas did all right.

When he came to his brownstone, the lights were on, the Christmas wreath still on the door. And inside was the companionship of a loving woman, a tot of brandy, a good cigar. And later, a warm bed and blessed sleep.

"Thank you, God," he said aloud, and started up the steps.

28

•

DELANEY DIDN'T WANT THE GIRLS TO GO OUT ON NEW YEAR'S EVE.

"It's amateur night," he told Monica. "People who haven't had a drink all year suddenly think they've got to get sloshed. Then they throw up on you or get in their cars and commit mayhem. The safest place for all of us is right here, with the door locked."

Wails and tears from Mary and Sylvia.

Finally a compromise was devised: They would have a New Year's Eve party at the brownstone, with Peter and Jeffrey invited. The rug would be rolled up and there would be dancing. Formal dress: The ladies would wear party gowns and the men dinner jackets.

"There I draw the line," Delaney protested. "My tux is in the attic, and probably mildewed. Even if I can find it, I probably won't be able to get into it; I've put on a few ounces, you know."

"No tux, no party," Monica said firmly. "And the girls go out."

So, grumbling, he trudged up to the attic and dug out his tuxedo from a grave of mothballs. It was rusty and wrinkled, but Monica sponged and brushed it. He could wear the jacket unbuttoned, and Monica assured him that with his black, pleated cummerbund in place, no one would know that the top button of his trousers was, by necessity, yawning.

Still grousing, he left the brownstone and marched out to purchase party supplies and food for a light midnight supper. He dragged along a wheeled shopping cart and thought he cut an undignified figure with his cart and black homburg. But he met no one he knew, so that was all right.

He returned home two hours later to find numerous messages waiting for him. He went into the study to return the calls. He phoned Abner Boone first.

"How did it go, Sergeant?" he asked.

"Just about the way you told her it would, sir. She's out now, back in her townhouse."

"A lot of reporters?"

"*And* photographers *and* television crews. She cracked up."

"Cracked up? How do you mean?"

"A crying fit. Close to hysteria."

"Sorry to hear that. I thought she had more spine."

"Well, she just dissolved, and we had our hands full. Fortunately, when her lawyer showed up, he brought along Doctor Samuelson, and the doc gave her something that quieted her down. She didn't look so beautiful when she left."

"No," Delaney said grimly, "and her husband didn't look so beautiful on the floor of his office. Thank you for all your help, Sergeant, and please convey my thanks to Jason and all the others."

"I'll do that, sir, and a Happy New Year."

"Thank you. And to you and Rebecca. Give her our love."

"Will do. I hope we get a chance to work together again."

"I wouldn't be a bit surprised," Delaney said.

His next call was to First Deputy Commissioner Ivar Thorsen, who sounded very ebullient and maybe a wee bit smashed.

"Everything's coming up roses, Edward," he reported exuberantly. "We didn't make the first editions this morning, but we'll be in the afternoon papers. Four TV news programs so far, and more to come. The phone is ringing off the hook with calls from out-of-town papers and newsmagazines. It looks like the press thinks we've solved the case."

"That's what you wanted, isn't it?"

"Oh, hell, yes! The Commish is grinning like a Cheshire cat, and even the Chief of Operations has congratulated Suarez. I think Riordan knows he's lost. It looks good for Suarez to get the permanent appointment."

"Glad to hear it; I like the man. Ivar, Happy New Year to you and yours."

"Same to you, Edward. Give Monica a kiss for me. You'll be getting your case of Glenfiddich, but that doesn't begin to express my gratitude."

"All right, then," Delaney said, "send two cases."

They hung up laughing.

On impulse, he phoned Dr. Samuelson. He was unable to reach him at his apartment or office. Thinking Samuelson might still be attending Diane Ellerbee, he called her number. He was prepared to hang up immediately if she answered, but he got a busy signal.

He phoned repeatedly for almost a half hour, but couldn't get through. He thought perhaps Diane had taken the phone off the hook, or perhaps she was being bedeviled by calls from the media. But finally his call was answered.

"Yes? Who is this?"

He recognized the high-pitched, squeaky voice.

"Doctor Samuelson? Edward X. Delaney here."

"Ah."

"How is Doctor Ellerbee?"

"At the moment she is sleeping. I prescribed something. She is destroyed by this."

"I can imagine. Doctor, I have one question for you. You can answer or tell me to go to hell. Did you know, or guess, what she did?"

"Go to hell," the little man said and hung up.

The four Delaneys had an early pickup dinner, mostly leftovers, and then finished decorating the living room, rolled up the rug, and swept and waxed the bare floor. They prepared the midnight supper. Then they all went upstairs to dress.

"Shaving is murder," Delaney said to Monica in their bathroom. "She got me good."

"Want me to put on bandages or tape?"

"No. I'll leave them open to the air. I've been dabbing on hydrogen peroxide. They'll heal okay. Did you tell the girls what happened?"

"I just said you had assisted in the arrest of a mugger and had been attacked. They seemed satisfied with that."

"Good. When are the boys arriving?"

"They promised to be here by nine."

"What are you going to wear?"

"What would you like me to wear?" she asked coquettishly.

"The short black silk with no back and all the fringe," he said immediately. "It makes you look like a flapper from the twenties."

"So shall it be," she said, touching his cheek softly. "My poor wounded hero."

While they were dressing, she said, not looking at him, "You're absolutely certain she did it, Edward?"

"Absolutely. But you're not?"

"It's so hard to believe—that lovely, intelligent, talented woman."

"Loeb and Leopold were geniuses. There's no contradiction between intelligence and an urge to kill."

"Well, if she's guilty, as you say, I still don't understand why she's not going to be tried for it."

"The law," he said shortly. "We just don't have enough that'll stand up in court. But she'll pay."

"You think that's enough?" Monica said doubtfully.

"It's a compromise," he admitted. "I agree with you; a long prison term would have been more fitting. But since that was impossible, I went for what I could get. We all settle, don't we? One way or another. Who gets what they dream? We all go stumbling along, hoping for the best but knowing we're going to have to live with confusion, sometimes winning, sometimes cutting a deal, occasionally just being defeated. It's a mess, no doubt about it, but it's the price we pay for being alive. I like to think the pluses outnumber the minuses. They do tonight. You look beautiful!"

Peter and Jeffrey arrived promptly at nine o'clock, bringing along a bottle of Dom Perignon, which everyone agreed would not be opened until the stroke of midnight. Meanwhile, there were six bottles of Delaney's Korbel brut, and the party got off to a noisy, laughing start.

It took three glasses of champagne before Delaney finally broke down and consented to dance with his wife and stepdaughters. He shuffled cautiously around the floor with all the grace of a gorilla on stilts, and after one dance with each of the ladies was allowed (Allowed? Urged!) to retire to the sidelines where he stood beaming, watching the festivities and making certain glasses were filled.

At 11:30, dancing was temporarily halted while supper was served. There was caviar with chopped onions, grated hard-boiled eggs, sour cream, capers, melba toast, quarters of fresh lemon—all on artfully contrived beds of Bibb lettuce.

Monica and Delaney balanced their plates on their laps, but the young people insisted on sprawling on the floor. The television set was turned on so they could watch the mob scene in Times Square.

At about ten minutes to twelve the phone rang. Monica and Delaney looked at each other.

"Now who the hell can that be?" he growled, set his plate aside, and rose heavily to his feet. He went into the study and closed the door.

"Mr. Delaney, this is Detective Brian Estrella. Sorry to bother you at this hour, sir, but something came up I thought you should know about as soon as possible."

"Oh?" Delaney said. "What's that?"

"Well, right now I'm in Sylvia Otherton's apartment and we've been working on the Ouija board. You read about that in my previous reports, didn't you, sir?"

"Oh, yes," Delaney said, rolling his eyes upward. "I read about the Ouija board."

"Well, the first question we asked, weeks ago, was who killed him. And the board spelled out 'Blind.' B-L-I-N-D. Then, the second time, we asked if it was a stranger who killed him, and the board spelled out 'Ni.' N-I."

"Yes, I recall," Delaney said patiently. "Very interesting. But what does it mean?"

"Well, get this, sir . . ." Estrella said. "Tonight we asked the spirit of Simon Ellerbee whether it was a man or a woman who killed him, and the Ouija board spelled out 'Wiman.' W-I-M-A-N. Now that didn't make much sense at first. But then I realized this board has a slight glitch and is pointing to 'I' when it means 'O.' If you follow that, you'll see that the killer was blond, not blind. And the board meant to say 'No' instead of 'Ni' when we asked if the murderer was a stranger. And the final answer should have been 'Woman' instead of 'Wiman.' So as I see it, sir, the person we're looking for is a blond woman who was not a stranger to the victim."

"Thank you very much," Delaney said gravely.

THE TENTH COMMANDMENT

•

1

•

I WAS AN ONLY CHILD—AND SO I BECAME AN ONLY MAN.

My name is Joshua Bigg: a joke life played on me, as I am quite small. Five feet, three and three-eighths inches, to be precise. In a world of giants, those eighths are precious to the midget.

That was the first of fortune's tricks. There were others. For instance, I was orphaned at the age of three months when my parents were killed in the sudden collapse of a bridge over the Skunk River near Oskaloosa, Iowa. As their pickup truck toppled, I was thrown clear and was found later lying in a clump of laurel, gurgling happily and sucking my toe.

People said it was a miracle. But of course they weren't the orphan. Years later, when Roscoe Dollworth was teaching me to be an investigator, he had something to say on the subject. He had just learned that he had a small gastric ulcer, after months of worrying about stomach cancer. Just an ulcer. Everyone told him how lucky he was.

"Luck," Roscoe said, "is something that happens to other people."

I was raised by my mother's brother and his wife: Philo and Velma Washabaugh. He had an Adam's apple and she smelled of muffins. But they were dear, sweet people and gave me compassion and love. I wish I could say the same for their three sons and two daughters, all older (and taller) than I. I suppose it was natural that I should be treated as an interloper; I was never allowed to forget my diminutive size and parentless status.

My uncle owned a hardware store in Ottuma, Iowa. Not a prosperous store, but there was always sufficient food, and if I was required to wear the outgrown clothing of my older and larger cousins, it seemed ungrateful to complain.

On the basis of my high school grades and financial need, I was able to obtain a scholarship to Grenfall. It was a very small scholarship to a very small liberal arts college. During term I held a variety of jobs: waiter, movie usher, gas station attendant, tutor of football players, etc. In the summers I worked in the hardware store.

It was my ambition to become a lawyer but by the time I was graduated,

Bachelor of Arts, with honors, I had realized that a law degree was beyond my means.

A short man in tall America has a choice: he may become dark, embittered, malevolent, or clever, sunny, and manic. I chose the latter, determined that neither lack of bulk nor lack of funds would prevent me from making my way in a world in which I was forced to buy my clothes in Boys' Departments.

So, packing my one good blue suit, I stood on tiptoe to kiss uncle, aunt, and cousins farewell, and took the bus to New York City to seek my fortune. I was resolutely cheerful.

My first few years in the metropolis I lived in the YMCA on 23rd Street and worked at a succession of depressing jobs: dishwasher, drugstore clerk, demonstrator of potato peelers, etc. I lived a solitary, almost desolate life. I had no friends. I spent my free hours at museums (they didn't charge admittance then) or in the public library. I have always been an omnivorous reader. Balzac, Hugo, Dumas, and Theodore Dreiser are my favorite authors. I also enjoy reading history, biography, and novels in which the law plays an important part, as in Dickens.

Now I must tell you about my sex life. It won't take long.

It is true that in our society small men are at a decided disadvantage in wooing and winning desirable women. I have read the results of research studies proving that, in America, success is equated with physical size. Most corporation executives are large, imposing men. Most successful politicians are six-footers. Even the best-known attorneys and jurists, doctors and surgeons, seem to be men of heft. And then, of course, there are salesmen, policemen, professional football players, and bartenders. Size and poundage do count.

So I think it only natural that most women should link a man of impressive height and weight with determination, aggressiveness, energy, and eventual success. A small man, particularly a small, *penniless* man, is too frequently an object of amusement, pity, scorn, and automatic rejection.

However, during my four years at Grenfall College (coeducational), I had learned a valuable truth. And this was that if I wished to make myself attractive to women, I could not attempt to imitate the speech, manner, or forceful behavior of large or even normal-sized men. Rather, I could only succeed by exaggerating my minuteness, physical weakness, and meekness.

Despite what some advocates of the women's liberation movement may claim, I say there is a very strong "mother instinct" in most women, and they respond viscerally and warmly to helplessness, particularly in the male. So, during my college days, this was the string I plucked. And when they took me onto their laps, murmuring comforting words, I knew I was home free and might expect to see my fondest fantasy come true.

Six years before the story I am about to tell commences, I had been working as a temporary clerk in Macy's during the holiday season. After Christmas I was again unemployed, but I had money in my pocket and was able to take a week off without worries. I had a few good meals, wandered Manhattan, went to museums, read in libraries, saw the ballet, and called a young lady I had met while serving at the men's underwear counter. We went to a Chinese restaurant, saw a movie, and later I climbed onto her lap.

But then, since my funds were rapidly approaching the panic level once again, I bought the Sunday *Times* and spent the afternoon circling Help Wanted ads with a red crayon. I started out Monday morning, working my way up the eastern half of Manhattan. The fourth Help Wanted ad on my list was for a mailroom boy at a law firm. I was 26 and wasn't certain I qualified as a "boy." If necessary, I thought, I could lie about my age. But I didn't think it would be necessary. In addition to my shortness, I am small-boned and slender. My hair is almost flaxen, my eyes are softly brown, my features are regular. I shave only every other day. I felt my appearance was sufficiently juvenile to pass the initial inspection, and I headed right over.

TORT—the law firm of Tabatchnick, Orsini, Reilly, and Teitelbaum— was located on East 38th Street, in the Murray Hill section of Manhattan. It occupied a five-story converted townhouse, and when I arrived late in the morning, there was already a long line of men leading from the doorway, down the steps, along the sidewalk, halfway down the block. All ages, wearing overcoats, pea jackets, windbreakers, sweaters, whatever. Thin men, fat men, tall men, heavy men. I was, of course, the smallest.

"The mailroom job?" I asked the last man on line.

He nodded dolefully, and I took my place behind him. In a few moments, there were a half-dozen applicants behind *me*.

Then I noted a puzzling phenomenon: the line was moving forward swiftly, and men were exiting the building as fast as they entered. The flow was constant: the hopefuls in, the rejected out.

The man ahead of me grabbed the arm of one of the rejects.

"What's going on in there?" he asked.

The rebuffed one shook his head bewilderedly.

"Beats me," he said. "No interviews. No applications. No questions even. This high-muck-a-muck takes a look at me and says, 'Sorry. You won't do.' Just like that. A nut!"

I was moving with the line up the block, along the sidewalk, up the stairs, through the door and finally into a large, imposing entrance hall with vaulted ceiling and walnut-paneled walls. The line stumbled up a wide carpeted staircase, so quickly that I scarcely had time to inspect the framed Currier and Ives lithographs on the walls.

I made it rapidly to the second-floor landing. The line now wavered down a long hallway and ended at a heavy closed door of carved oak. Placed alongside the door was a small desk, and seated behind the desk was a young woman, poised, expressionless. As each rejected applicant exited from the oak door, she called "Next!"

As the line moved forward, and I heard "Next! Next! Next!", I could not

take my eyes from that comely guardian of the sacred portal. My initial reaction on seeing beautiful women is usually despair. They seem so unattain-
able to me, so distant, almost so *foreign*.

The line was moving forward quickly and I soon found myself the next
specimen to be exhibited on the other side of that forbidding oak door.

It opened. The doleful one who'd been in front of me exited, head hanging. I heard "Next!" and I stepped into the chamber and closed the door
softly behind me. I had a confused impression of an enormous, shadowed
room, lined with law books in glass-enclosed cases. There were club chairs,
a globe, a heavy dictionary on a pedestal.

But dominating the room was a gigantic mahogany desk, all carved flour-
ishes and curlicues. The top was bare of papers, but set precisely with a
student's lamp, blotter, pen-holder, letter opener, scissors—all leather-bound
or leather-trimmed. There was a telephone-intercom with rows and rows of
buttons and lights. Even the telephone handset had a leather-covered grip.

The man seated behind the desk appeared to have been bound in the same
material: dark calfskin perhaps. He seemed ancient; the hands resting motionless on the desktop were empty gloves, and the face had the withered
look of a deflated balloon.

But the blue eyes were bright enough, and when he said, "Come forward,
please," his voice had vigor and resonance.

I moved to the desk. He was seated in a high-backed swivel chair. It was
difficult to estimate his height, but I could see the narrow shoulders, a thin
neck, slender arms.

"How tall are you?" he asked abruptly.

I lost all hope.

"Five feet, three and three-eighths inches, sir," I said.

He nodded. "How soon can you start?" he said.

I don't believe my jaw dropped. I don't believe I staggered, blinked, and
swallowed. But I can't be sure.

"Immediately, sir," I said.

He nodded again. He leaned forward, lifted one of those dead hands, and
with a forefinger that looked like it had been pickled in brine, depressed one
of the buttons on the telephone intercom.

"Miss Apatoff," he said loudly, "the position has been filled. Thank the
others and dismiss them."

Then he sat back in his swivel chair again and regarded me gravely.

"Name?" he said.

"Joshua Bigg, sir."

He didn't laugh, or even smile.

"From where?" he asked.

"Iowa, sir."

"Education?"

"BA degree, sir. With honors."

"Miss Apatoff, the lady in the hallway, will take you to our office manager, Hamish Hooter. He will complete the necessary paperwork and instruct you in your duties."

"Thank you, sir."

"Salary?" he said.

"Oh, well, yes, sir," I said confusedly. "What *is* the salary?"

"A hundred a week," he said, still staring at me. "Satisfactory?"

"Oh yes, sir."

He raised one finger from the desk blotter. I took this as a gesture of dismissal, and turned to go. I was at the door when he called . . .

"Mr. Bigg."

I turned.

He had risen. Now I could see his size.

"I," he said proudly, "am five feet, three and *seven*-eighths inches tall."

Only after I had left the office did it occur to me to ask the pulchritudinous receptionist to whom I had just been speaking. "Oh, that's Mr. Teitelbaum, senior partner, and I'm Yetta Apatoff," she added, bending forward enough so that I got a glimpse of cleavage I would never forget. "Welcome to TORT."

And that's how I came to work for Tabatchnick, Orsini, Reilly, and Teitelbaum.

I stayed in the mailroom about two years, during which my salary was increased four times to a gratifying $150 a week, and my hopeless passion for Miss Yetta Apatoff, our nubile receptionist, grew in even larger increments.

And, finally, my opportunity for advancement came, as I knew it would.

One of the more than 50 employees of TORT was Mr. Roscoe Dollworth, who bore the title of Chief Investigator. This was a kindness since he was our *only* investigator. Dollworth was an ex–New York City policeman who had resigned from the Department for "medical reasons." He was an enormously fat drunk, but neither his girth nor his awesome intake of vodka (from a thermos kept in plain view on his desk) interfered with the efficient performance of his duties.

A salaried investigator for a large firm of attorneys is assigned the same tasks smaller legal associations might delegate to private investigators, as needed. Tracking down witnesses, verifying clients' alibis and those of the opposition, escorting recalcitrant witnesses to the courtroom, locating technical experts whose testimony might be advantageous, and so forth.

In addition, there had been several instances in which Roscoe Dollworth had conducted original investigations into the culpability of clients accused of crimes, although criminal defense was only a small part of TORT's activities. In all such cases, Dollworth's past association with the New York Police Department proved of great value. This was probably why his employment was continued despite that desktop jug of vodka. Also, the Chief Investigator was 61 years old at the time I joined Tabatchnick, Orsini, Reilly, and Teitelbaum, and he had made it clear that he intended to retire to Florida at the age of 65, to play shuffleboard and watch the pelicans.

I believe Roscoe Dollworth liked me. I know I liked him. He never made any slurring references to my size, and treated me more as a friend than as the lowest man on the TORT totem pole. So I was happy to run his errands: dash out to buy him a fresh quart of vodka or hurry back from my own lunch to bring him the hot pepperoni pizza he ate at his desk each day (the *whole* pizza, plus pickles, peppers, and a frightening wedge of pineapple cheesecake).

In return, he told me stories of cases in which he had been involved while he was a uniformed patrolman and later as a detective, third-grade. He also taught me the techniques and tricks of a professional investigator, all of which I found fascinating. I hadn't realized police methods were that complex, or how few of them could be found in books. They could only be learned through personal experience, or the experience of other cops.

Occasionally, when I had time, and always with the permission of one of the three senior partners of TORT (Sean Reilly had died seven years previously; he had choked to death on a piece of rare London broil), Roscoe Dollworth would send me out on an investigative task. These began as simple assignments: find the apartment number of so-and-so, check where this man parks his car, see if you can discover when this woman divorced her first husband.

Gradually, over a period of months, Dollworth's requests became more involved and more intriguing.

"Doing anything tonight, Josh? No? Good. Follow this guy. He says he goes to a chess club every Wednesday night. I ain't so sure. Don't let him spot you. This is a divorce action."

Or . . . "Find out who really owns this nightclub, will you? You'll have to start out down at the Hall, checking records. You'll learn how it's done."

Or . . . "See if this dame has any regular visitors. She lives alone—but who knows? You may have to slip the doorman a fin. But no more than that, or he won't respect you. This involves the probate of a will."

And so on . . .

I completed all my assignments successfully, and began to wonder if I didn't have a natural talent for investigation. Part of my success, I thought, might be due to my physical appearance. It was impossible for me to come on strong, and my shy, hesitant, almost helpless manner seemed to arouse the kind of sympathy which urged, "Let's help the boy out." And so I succeeded with the same methods that had aided me in my conquests of women: the whole world wanted to take me onto its lap.

I had been with TORT for almost two years when Roscoe Dollworth called me into his office, commanded me to shut the door and sit down.

This time, it wasn't about an assignment, exactly. It was about much more than that.

I said nothing, just watched Mr. Dollworth pour himself a paper cup of vodka from his thermos. He sipped it slowly, staring at me thoughtfully across his desk.

He was a blobby man, with a belly that kept his swivel chair two feet from his desk. His scraggly, straw-colored hair was thinning; patches of freckled scalp showed through. Darkish eyebrows were so snarled that I had seen him comb them. His nose had evidently been broken several times; it just didn't know which way to turn. His lips were glutinous, teeth tobacco-stained. But the eyes were hard and squinchy. Looking at those eyes made me happy I was his friend and not an enemy.

"Look, kid," he said finally in a deep, burpy voice, "let me tell you what's been happening. You know, I figure to retire in a couple of years, if this miserable ulcer don't kill me first. That means they got to replace me—right? So I went to old man Teitelbaum. He likes you—you know? He hired you because you're the only guy in the joint smaller than he is. You knew that, didn't you?"

"Yes," I said, "I knew."

"Well . . ." he said, sipping vodka, "you turned out real good. I mean, you work hard, don't steal stamps, and you're polite. Always ready with a smile. Everyone here likes you. Except maybe Hamish Hooter, that prick. But he don't like *anyone*. Except maybe Yetta Apatoff. Hooter would *like* to like her—about six inches' worth."

I nodded dumbly.

"So I says to Teitelbaum, how about promoting Josh Bigg to investigator? Let him work with me my last two years, I says, and I guarantee to teach him the ropes. By the time I step down, you'll have a spry young man ready to fill my shoes, a guy who knows his way around. I told Teitelbaum how good you done on those little jobs I gave you. This kid, I says, has got a good nut on his shoulders. Give him a chance, and you'll have an A-Number One Investigator in your organization."

I was excited. I slid forward to the edge of my chair. I leaned eagerly toward Dollworth.

"And what did he say?"

"He said no," the Chief Investigator said regretfully. "He said you were too young. He said you didn't have the experience. He said he wanted another ex-cop to take my place."

I collapsed.

"Wait a minute," Dollworth said, holding up a hand like a smoked ham. "I never take a turndown without I put up a fight. I said you might *look* young, but by the time I retire, you'll be thirty—right?—and your brain is older than that. Also, I says, as far as experience goes, I can teach you most of what you'll have to know, and the rest you'll pick up as you go along. And as for hiring an ex-cop, I says, if he wants another rumdum like me, that's his business. But an investigator gets out a lot, meets the public, and he should make a good impression as a representative of the firm. And you dress

neat, wear a jacket and pants that match, and a tie and all. Then I throw in
the clincher. Also, I tell Teitelbaum, you hire an ex-cop to take my place,
you'll be lucky to get away paying him twenty G's a year. You could get
Bigg to do the same work for half of that."

"What did he say to that?" I asked breathlessly.

"They're having a meeting this afternoon," Roscoe Dollworth said. "The
three senior partners. I'll let you know how it comes out. Meanwhile, my
jug is getting low. How's about you rushing the growler for me?"

Late that afternoon I was informed that the senior partners of Tabatchnick,
Orsini, Reilly, and Teitelbaum, in solemn conclave assembled, had decreed
that I was to be replaced in the mailroom and, for a period of two years, be
apprenticed to Chief Investigator Dollworth. At the end of that period, the
senior partners would accept Dollworth's judgment on whether I was or was
not qualified to assume his office upon his retirement. During my apprenticeship, I would continue to earn $150 a week.

"Don't worry about a thing," Roscoe Dollworth assured me, winking.
"It's in the bag. I'm going to run your ass ragged. You'll learn."

He did, and I did. For the next two years I worked harder than I thought
possible, sometimes putting in an eighteen-hour day in my determination to
master my new craft.

There were so many things Dollworth taught me that it would be impossible to list them all. They included a basic education in such matters as
criminal and civil law, the right of privacy, and the rules of evidence, and
instruction on such practical matters as how to pick a lock, the best methods
of shadowing on a crowded street, and what equipment to take along on an
extended stakeout. (The first item was an empty milk carton in which one
might relieve oneself.)

In addition to Dollworth's lectures and the actual investigations assigned
to me with increasing frequency, I also did a great deal of studying at home.
My books were manuals of the New York Police Academy, which Dollworth
obtained for me, plus heavy volumes on the law, legal procedures, and crim-
inology which I purchased or borrowed from the public library.

At the end of my two-year apprenticeship, I felt, with my indefatigable
optimism, that I had mastered the arcane mysteries of my new profession,
and was well qualified to become Chief Investigator of TORT. I must have
conveyed some of this conceit to my mentor, for a few days prior to his
retirement, he called me into his office, slammed the door, and delivered
himself of the following:

"You think you know it all, do you? You make me sick, you do! You
know nothing. *Nothing!* A wise wrongo could have you running around in
circles, chasing your tail. Wait'll you come up against a liar, a *good* liar. You
won't know if you're coming or going. You're just on the ground floor,
kiddo. You got a helluva lot to learn. I seen the way you look at that Yetta
Apatoff. If she said jump out the window, out you'd go. But what if a twist

exactly like her was a suspect, and you had to get the goods on her? Shit, all you'd see would be B&B, boobs and behind, and she'd take a walk. Bye-bye, birdie. Josh, you've got to learn to doubt *everyone*. Suspect *everyone*. It's a hard, cruel world out there, filled with bad guys and millions of others who would be bad if they weren't scared of being caught. Never, *never* believe what people tell you until you check it out. Never, *never* let your personal feelings interfere with your job. And most of all, never believe that because a woman is beautiful or a man is handsome, successful, and contributes to his church, that they can't be the slimiest crooks in the world. Most of the people you meet will be out to con you. So you just smile and say, 'Uh-huh,' and start checking them out. Josh, you've got a lot going for you. You got a brain on you, you can get people to open up, and you got a good imagination. Maybe too good. But what worries me most about you is that you're so innocent, so fucking *innocent!*"

But my shortcomings had not deterred Roscoe Dollworth from recommending me as his successor. A week later he was off to Florida with a set of matching luggage from the employees of TORT, a $5,000 retirement bonus, and a pair of fine German binoculars I gave him.

"To watch the pelicans," I told him.

"Sure, kid," he said, hitting my arm. "Very nice. I'll send you my address. Keep in touch. If I can ever help you out with the Department, let me know."

"Thank you, Mr. Dollworth," I said. "For everything."

During the next twenty-six months I was made mournfully aware of the difference between on-the-job training under the tutelage of an experienced investigator and having full responsibility, without supervision, for all investigative activities of Tabatchnick, Orsini, Reilly, and Teitelbaum.

First of all, requests for investigations flowed into my office from the three senior partners, seven junior partners (including Tabatchnick II and Orsini II and III), twelve associates, law clerks, paralegal assistants, and the despicable office manager, Hamish Hooter. It took me a while to get a system of priorities organized and to learn to deal with all these strong-willed and redoubtable individuals. (The legal profession seems to have the effect of first enlarging egos and then setting them permanently in concrete.)

Everyone wanted his request for information dealt with *instanter,* and initially I was overwhelmed; but, after observing the snail's speed unraveling of most of the litigation handled by TORT, I came to realize that there are two kinds of time. One has sixty minutes to an hour, twenty-four hours to a day, moving along at a brisk clip. And then there is legal time, oozing so sluggishly that movement can scarcely be noted.

When a business executive says, "I'll get that letter off to you tomorrow," he usually means tomorrow, or in a few days, or a week at the most. When a lawyer says, "I'll get that letter off to you tomorrow," he usually means in six weeks, next November, or never. Always, in the practice of law, is the unspoken admonition: "What's the rush?" Shakespeare wrote of "the law's delay," everyone is aware of the lethargy of the courts, and even the youngest, brightest, most vigorous attorney, fresh from law school, soon adjusts to tardiness as a way of life. The law, sir, is a glacier. Attempting to hurry it usually proves counterproductive.

Once I had recognized that central truth, I was able to relax, realize that very few requests involved a crisis, and devote all my energy and wit to mastering the techniques of my new profession. In all modesty, I do not believe I functioned too badly. At least, my salary rose to $12,500 at the end of my first year as Chief Investigator, and to $15,000 at the completion of my second. Surely this was proof that TORT was well satisfied with my performance. The increase enabled me to move from the YMCA into my own apartment, replenish my wardrobe, and invite Miss Yetta Apatoff to a dinner that included a small bottle of French wine. She did not, however, invite me onto her lap in return.

Not everything was cotton candy. I made mistakes, of course. Not mistakes, perhaps, so much as failures to foresee a possible course of events. For instance, I was assigned to pick up a supposedly friendly witness in a personal liability case and ensure his presence in the courtroom at the required time. When I showed up at his Bronx apartment, he simply refused to accompany me.

He was a loutish, overbearing individual, wearing a stained undershirt and chomping a soggy cigar.

"But you've got to come," I said.

"*Got* to?" he said, snorting. "I got to do nuttin."

"But you promised," I pleaded desperately.

"I changed my mind," he said casually.

"I insist you come with me," I said. I'm afraid my voice became slightly shrill.

"You *insist?*" he said. He laughed heartily. "What are you going to do— drag me down there, you little shit?"

I had to report my failure to the TORT attorney handling the case. Fortunately, he accepted my inefficiency philosophically, the witness's testimony was not crucial, a subpoena was not warranted, and he soon forgot the incident. But I did not; it rankled.

The next time I did my homework and learned all I could about the potential witness, even to the extent of following him for a few days and making notes of his activities.

As I anticipated, he also said he had changed his mind and refused to testify.

"Please change it back," I said. "I don't wish to inform your wife where you spent three hours yesterday afternoon."

He put on his coat.

He, too, said, "You little shit!"

So I learned to cope with those rare instances in which lack of physical bulk made my job more difficult. I was not a licensed private investigator, of course, and I had no desire to attempt to obtain a permit to carry a firearm. I felt I could handle all the demands of my job without resorting to violence.

But generally, those first two years as Chief Investigator of Tabatchnick, Orsini, Reilly, and Teitelbaum went swimmingly. I learned the truth of many of those things Roscoe Dollworth had shouted at me just before his retirement. People *did* lie, frequently for no reason other than they felt the truth was valuable and should not be revealed to a stranger without recompense. People *did* try to con me, and I soon learned to recognize the signs: a frank, open, unblinking stare and a glib, too-rapid way of speaking.

I also learned not to get personally involved with the people with whom I dealt, while maintaining a polite, sympathetic, low-key manner. I also learned an investigator's job requires infinite patience, an almost finicky attention to detail, tenacity, and the ability to endure long periods of boredom.

If I had one regret it was that circumstances never arose requiring an original investigation to uncover the truth in a case of some importance. I felt I had proved my ability to handle routine assignments that were, for the most part, matters requiring only a few phone calls, correspondence, or simple inquiries that needed no particular deductive talent. Now I craved more daring challenges.

My chance to prove my mettle came in February of my seventh year at TORT.

2

•

EACH MORNING I ARRIVED AT MY OFFICE AT ABOUT 8:30 A.M., carrying a container of black coffee and a buttered, toasted bagel. I liked to arrive early to organize my work for the day before my phone started ringing. On Tuesday morning, February 6th, I found on my desk blotter a memo from Leopold Tabatchnick: "I will see you in my office at 10:00 A.M. this morning, Feb. 6. L.T."

I postponed an outside inquiry I had planned to make that morning, and at 9:50 went into the men's room to make certain my hair was properly combed, the knot in my tie centered, and my fingernails clean. I also buffed my shoes with a paper towel.

The private offices of the senior partners occupied the largest (rear) suites on the second, third, and fourth floors, one over the other. Teitelbaum was on two, Orsini on three, Tabatchnick on four. Mr. Tabatchnick's secretary was seated at her desk in the hallway. She was Thelma Potts, a spinster of about sixty years, with a young face and whipped-cream hair. She wore high-necked blouses with a cameo brooch at the collar. She dispensed advice, made small loans, and never forgot birthdays or anniversaries. The bottom drawer of her desk was full of headache remedies, stomach powders, tranquilizers, Band-Aids, cough syrups, cold capsules, etc., available to anyone when needed. She kept a small paper cup among the drugs, and you were supposed to drop in a few coins now and then to help keep the pharmacy going.

"Good morning, Miss Potts," I said.

"Good morning, Mr. Bigg," she said. She glanced at the watch pinned to her bodice. "You're three minutes early."

"I know," I said. "I wanted to spend them with you."

"Oh, *you!*" she said.

"I thought you were going to find me a wife, Miss Potts," I said sorrowfully.

"When did I ever say that?" she demanded, blushing. "I am sure you are quite capable of finding a nice girl yourself."

"No luck so far," I said. "May I go in now?"

She consulted her watch again.

"Thirty seconds," she said firmly.

I sighed. We waited in silence, Miss Potts staring at her watch.

"Now!" she said, like a track official starting a runner.

I knocked once on the heavy door, opened it, stepped inside, closed it behind me.

Instead of law books here, the room was lined with aquaria of tropical fish. There were tanks of all sizes and shapes, lighted from behind. Bubbles rose constantly from aerators. The atmosphere of the room was oppressively warm and humid. There were guppies, sea horses, angels, zebras, pink damsels, clowns, ghost eels, fire fish, purple queens, swordtails, and a piranha.

They all made a glittering display in the clear, backlighted tanks, darting about, blowing bubbles, kissing the glass, coming to the surface to spit.

The first time I'd met Mr. Tabatchnick, he'd asked me if I was interested in tropical fish. I'd confessed I was not.

"Hmph," he'd said. "Then you have no conception of the comfort to be derived from the silent companionship of our finny friends."

This was followed by a half-hour, tank-by-tank tour of the room, with Mr. Tabatchnick expounding on the Latin names, lifestyles, dispositions, feeding habits, sexual tendencies, and depravities of his finny friends. Most, apparently, ate their young. The lecture, I discovered later, had to be tolerated by every new employee. Thankfully, it was a one-shot, never repeated.

The man seated in the leather swivel chair behind the trestle table appeared to be in his middle seventies. He had a ponderous head set on a large, square, neckless frame, held so rigidly that you wondered if he had left a wooden coat hanger in the shoulders of his jacket.

His hands were wide, with spatulate fingers, the skin discolored with keratosis. His arms seemed disproportionately long, and since he tended to lumber as he walked, with hunched shoulders, heavy head thrust forward, and a fierce scowl on his fleshy features, he was referred to by the law clerks and paralegal assistants as "King Kong." In very small voices, of course.

But there was nothing simian about his face. If anything, his were the features of a weary bloodhound, all folds and wrinkles, wattles and jowls, with protruding, rubbery lips (always moist), and eyes so lachrymose that he always seemed on the point of sobbing. His normal expression was one of mournful distress, and it was said that he used it with great effect during his days as a trial lawyer to elicit the sympathy of the jury.

"Good morning, Mr. Tabatchnick," I said brightly.

He bestowed upon me the nod of sovereign to serf, and gestured to a club chair at the side of the table.

"Sol Kipper," he said. His voice was stentorian, rumbling. An organ of a voice. I wished I had been in the courtroom to hear his summations.

"I beg your pardon, sir?" I said.

"Sol Kipper," he repeated. "Solomon Kipper, to be precise. The name means nothing to you?"

I thought desperately. It was not a name you would easily forget. Then it came to me . . .

"I remember," I said. "Solomon Kipper. A suicide about two weeks ago. From the top floor of his East Side townhouse. A small story in the *Times*."

"Yes," he said, the folds of skin wagging sadly, "a small story in the *Times*. I wish you to know, young man, that Sol Kipper was a personal friend of mine for fifty-five years and an esteemed client of this law firm for forty."

There didn't seem any fitting reply to that.

"We shall be handling the probate," Mr. Tabatchnick continued. "Sol Kipper was a wealthy man. Not *very* wealthy, but wealthy. Cut and dried. I anticipated no problems."

He paused, leaned forward, punched a button on the intercom on the table.

"Miss Potts," he said, "will you come in, please? Bring your notes on the conversation I had late yesterday afternoon with that stranger."

He settled back. We waited. Thelma Potts entered softly, carrying a spiral-bound steno pad. Mr. Tabatchnick did not ask her to sit down.

"Occasionally," he said in a magisterial tone, "I deem it appropriate, during certain telephone communications, to ask Miss Potts to listen in on her extension and make notes. Very well, Miss Potts, you may begin . . ."

Thelma flipped over a few pages and began to translate her shorthand, peering through rimless spectacles and speaking rapidly in a flat, precisely enunciated voice:

"At 4:46 P.M., on the afternoon of Monday, February 5th, this year, a call was received at the main switchboard downstairs. A male voice asked to speak to the lawyer handling the Kipper estate. The call was switched to me. The man repeated his request. I asked him exactly what it was he wanted, but he said he would reveal that only to the attorney of record. As is usual in such cases, I suggested he write a letter requesting an interview and detailing his interest in the matter. This he said he would not do, and he stated that if the lawyer refused to talk to him, he would be sorry for it later. Those were his exact words: 'He will be sorry for it later.' I then asked if he would hold. He agreed. I put him on hold, and called Mr. Tabatchnick on the intercom, explaining what was happening. He agreed to speak to the caller, but requested that I stay on the extension and take notes.''

I interrupted.

"The male voice on the phone, Miss Potts," I said. "Young? Old?"

She stared at me for a few seconds.

"Middle," she said, then continued reading her notes.

"Mr. Tabatchnick asked the purpose of the call. The man asked if he was handling the Kipper estate. Mr. Tabatchnick said he was. The man asked his name. Mr. Tabatchnick stated it. The man then said he had valuable information in his possession that would affect the Kipper estate. Mr. Tabatchnick asked the nature of the information. The caller refused to reveal it. Mr. Tabatchnick said he assumed then that the information would be available at a price. The caller said that was correct. His exact words were: 'Right on the button, baby!' Mr. Tabatchnick then suggested the caller come to his office for a private discussion. This the man refused to do, indicating he had no desire to have his conversation secretly recorded. But he said he would meet with Mr. Tabatchnick or his representative in a place of his, the caller's, choosing. Mr. Tabatchnick asked his name. The caller said 'Marty' would be sufficient. Mr. Tabatchnick asked his address, which Marty would not reveal. Mr. Tabatchnick then said he would have to give the matter some thought but would contact Marty if he or his representative wished to meet with him. Marty gave a number but the call had to be made within twenty-four hours. If Marty did not hear from Mr. Tabatchnick by five o'clock, Tuesday afternoon, February 6th, he would assume Mr. Tabatchnick was not interested in his, quote, valuable information regarding the Kipper estate, unquote, and he would feel free to contact other potential buyers. The conversation was then terminated.''

Miss Potts closed her steno pad with a snap, and looked up.

"Will that be all, Mr. Tabatchnick?" she asked.

He raised his heavy head. "Yes, thank you."

She drifted from the room, closing the door quietly behind her.

He stared somberly at me.

"Well?" he demanded. "What do you think?"

I shrugged. "Impossible to say, sir. Not enough to go on. Could be attempted blackmail, or attempted extortion, or just a cheap chiseler trying to make a couple of bucks on a fast con.''

"You think I should communicate with this man and arrange to meet him?"

"No, sir," I said. "I think *I* should. He said you or your representative."

"I don't like it," Leopold Tabatchnick said fretfully.

"I don't like it either, sir," I said. "But I think it wise to meet with him and try to find out what this 'valuable information' is he thinks he has."

"Mmm . . . yes . . . well . . ." Tabatchnick said, drumming his thick fingers on the tabletop.

Then he was silent a long moment, and I had the oddest impression that he knew something or guessed something he hadn't told me, and was debating with himself whether or not to reveal it. He finally decided not to.

"All right," he said finally, bobbing that weighty head slowly, "you call him and arrange to meet. Try to find out exactly what it is he's selling. Refuse to buy a pig in a poke. And don't commit the firm for any amount, large or small."

"Of course not, sir."

"Inform him you will deliver his terms to me."

"Yes, sir."

"Inform him that only I can authorize payment under these circumstances."

"I understand, sir."

"And endeavor to ascertain his full name and address."

"Yes, sir," I said, suppressing a sigh. Sometimes they still treated me like a mailroom boy.

3

•

WHEN I CAME OUT OF MR. TABATCHNICK'S FISH-LINED SANCTUARY, I stopped at Thelma Potts's desk to get the telephone number of the mysterious Marty, then proceeded down the main staircase.

Mr. Romeo Orsini was holding court on the third-floor landing, surrounded by aides, most of them women. He was in his middle sixties, tall, erect, with thick, marvelously coiffed snow-white hair. He carried himself with the vigor and grace of a man one-third his age, and his pink complexion, dark, glittering eyes, hearty good health, meticulous grooming, and self-satisfaction produced the image of the perfect movie or TV lawyer.

Romeo Orsini specialized in divorce actions, and was enormously successful in obtaining alimony and child support payments far in excess of his clients' most exaggerated hopes. It was also said that he was frequently the first to console the new divorcée.

I was hoping to slip around his group on the landing without being noticed, but his hand shot out from the circle and clamped on my arm.

"Josh!" he cried gaily. "Just the man I wanted to see!"

He drew me close and, not for the first time, I became aware of his cologne.

"Heard a joke I think you'll appreciate," he said slyly, grinning at me.

My heart sank. All the jokes he told me involved small men.

"There was this midget," he began, looking around his circle of aides. They were preparing their faces to break into instant laughter, several of them smiling already.

"And he married the tallest woman in the circus," Orsini continued. He paused for effect. I knew what was coming.

"His friends put him up to it!" he concluded, followed by guffaws, giggles, roars, and thigh-slapping by his assistants. To my shame, I laughed as loudly as any, and finally broke free to continue my descent, cursing myself.

On the ground floor, I was confronted with the bristling presence of Hamish Hooter, the office manager.

"See here, Bigg," he said.

That's the way Hooter began all his conversations: "See here." It made me want to reach up and punch him in the snoot.

"What is it, Hooter?" I said resignedly.

"What's this business about a private secretary?" he demanded, waving a sheet of paper in my face. I recognized it as a memo I had forwarded the previous week.

"It's all spelled out in there," I said. "I've been typing all my own correspondence up to now, but the workload is getting too much. I can't ask the secretaries and typists to help me out; they all have their own jobs."

"Dollworth didn't need a secretary," he sneered.

"Dollworth was a notoriously poor record-keeper," I said. "He admitted it himself. As a result, we have incomplete histories of investigations he conducted, no copies of letters he may have written, no memos of phone calls and conversations. Such records could be vital if cases are overturned on appeal or reopened for any reason. I really have to set up a complete file and keep it current."

"I can't believe you're so busy that you can't handle it yourself," he said. Then he added nastily, "You seem to have plenty of time to gossip with Yetta Apatoff."

I stared at him. He really was a miserable character. What's more, he *looked* like a miserable character.

He was of average height, but with such poor posture (rounded shoulders, bent back, protruding potbelly) that he appeared shorter. He had an extremely pale complexion, with small, watery eyes set too far apart. His lips were prim, and his nose looked like a wedge of cheddar. He had jet-black, somewhat greasy hair, and he was, I was happy to note, going bald in back. He combed his slick locks sideways in an attempt to conceal the tonsure.

His voice was high-pitched and reedy, somewhere between a whine and a yawp. He also had the habit of sucking his teeth after every sentence, as if he had a little fiber of celery in there and couldn't get it out. Let's see, what else . . . Oh yes, he had eyes for Yetta Apatoff (hot, beady eyes), and that alone was enough to condemn him as far as I was concerned. I knew they lunched together occasionally, and I could only conclude that she accompanied him out of pure kindness, as one might toss a peanut to a particularly disgusting, purple-assed orangutan in the zoo.

"So I gather I'm not getting a secretary," I said.

"You gather correctly," he said, sucking his incisors noisily.

I looked at him with loathing. But if I couldn't outwit that beast, I'd turn in my Machiavelli badge. I spun away from him, marched down to my office, slammed the door.

The first thing I did was call Marty's number. I let it ring ten times, but there was no answer. So I gathered up my notebook, stopwatch, and coat, and started out on a routine investigation.

Yetta Apatoff was at her desk, but she was busy with an elderly couple who were trying to explain something to her in heavily German-accented English. Yetta waggled her delicious fingers at me as I went by. I waggled back.

I spent the morning establishing that a young client could not have robbed a camera store in the Port Authority Bus Terminal, on Eighth Avenue at 40th Street at 12:06 P.M. and travel nineteen blocks in time to be positively identified at an electronics trade show at the Coliseum on Columbus Circle at Eighth Avenue and 59th Street at 12:14.

Three times I traveled from the Bus Terminal to the Coliseum by taxi, three times by subway, three times by bus (making the return trips by cab in all cases). I used the stopwatch and timed each northbound run to the split second, keeping very careful notes.

I completed the time trials at about 2:30 in the afternoon. I had a hamburger and dialed Marty's number from a pay phone. Still no answer. I was getting a little antsy. Marty had said the deadline was 5:00 P.M.

Yetta Apatoff was on the phone when I entered the TORT building at approximately 3:20. She smiled up at me (a glory, that smile!) and, still speaking on the phone, handed me a small sheet of paper. Another memo. This one was from Mr. Teitelbaum's secretary. I was to call her as soon as I returned.

I went into my office, took off my coat, dialed Marty's number. Still no answer. I then called Ada Mondora, Teitelbaum's secretary. She said he wanted to see me as soon as possible, but was busy with a client at the moment; she'd buzz me as soon as he was free.

Then I took off my jacket, sat down at the typewriter, and began to bang out a report on the time trials.

My office, on the first floor, was not quite as small as a broom closet. There was room for one L-shaped desk, with the typewriter on the short wing. One steel swivel chair. One steel armchair for visitors. One steel file cabinet. A wastebasket, a coat tree, a small steel bookcase. And that was it. When Roscoe Dollworth, with his explosive girth, had occupied the premises, this cubbyhole seemed filled to overflowing. I provided a little more space, but the room was still cramped and depressing. No windows. If I succeeded in obtaining a secretary, my next project would be larger quarters to accommodate the secretary. My ambition knew no limits.

I had almost finished typing my report when Ada Mondora called and said I could come up now. I put on my jacket, went into the men's room to make myself presentable, then climbed the stairs to the second floor.

"Hi, Josh," Ada said in her bass rumble. She was pushing fifty and sounded as if she had smoked Coronas all her life. "He's been trying to reach you all day. You can go right in."

"Thank you, Ada."

I went through the approved drill: knocked once, opened the door, stepped in, closed the door gently behind me.

Ignatz Teitelbaum was six years older than the day he hired me, but you'd never know it. Apparently he had reached a plateau, a certain number of years (seventy? seventy-five?), and then just didn't age anymore. He would go to his grave looking exactly as he did at that moment, the skin leathery, the blue eyes bright, the voice vigorous.

"Sit down, young man," he said to me.

I chose the club chair closest to the desk. The light from the student's lamp fell on me, but his face was in shadow.

"A client," he said abruptly. "Yale Stonehouse. Professor Yale Stonehouse. A very litigious man. You are familiar with the term?"

I murmured wisely.

"Well," he said. "Professor Stonehouse would sue, at any time, for any reason—or none at all. He sued plumbers and electricians who did repair work in his apartment. He sued his landlord. He sued department stores. He sued cabdrivers and the companies that employed them. He sued newspapers, magazines, manufacturers, hotels, the bus company, the telephone company, Consolidated Edison, the City of New York, the Boy Scouts of America, the makers of Tootsie Rolls, and a poor fellow who had the misfortune to jostle him accidentally on the street. On one occasion, Professor Stonehouse sued the United States of America."

"Did he ever win, sir?" I asked.

"Rarely," Mr. Teitelbaum said with a wintry smile. "And when he did, the damages granted were never sufficient to cover the cost of bringing the suit. In one case I recall, the bench awarded him one cent. But Professor Stonehouse didn't care—or said he didn't. He insisted the principle involved was all that counted." Mr. Teitelbaum paused to sigh heavily. "I am not certain Professor Stonehouse was completely sane. He was eccentric, certainly."

"*Was?*" I repeated. "Is the gentleman no longer our client? Or is he deceased?"

Mr. Teitelbaum ignored my questions and continued:

"As I said, we attempted to dissuade him from this unwarranted litigation, but he insisted. His suits, ah, provided good experience for some of the younger, newer members of the firm. In addition to the suits, we also handled the legal end of several investments Professor Stonehouse made in real estate and certain other properties. He was, I would say, well-to-do. Exactly how prosperous he was I had no way of knowing, since this firm did not prepare his will nor play any part in his general investments and estate planning. On the one occasion when I asked him if he had executed a will, he replied in hostile tones that it had been taken care of. His reaction to my question was such that I never cared to pursue the matter further. I merely assumed he had a will prepared by another attorney, a not uncommon practice."

Then he was silent. And I was silent, wondering where all this was leading.

Ignatz Teitelbaum laced his crinkled little fingers on the desktop. He looked down at them, and wiggled one at a time. He seemed surprised that they could still move. Staring at his hands, he continued his story in a quiet, dreamy voice . . .

"Yesterday, Professor Stonehouse's wife came to see me. She informed me that her husband had, after dinner one evening, simply walked out of their apartment without saying where he was going and never returned. Not to this date, he hasn't."

"Did he leave a note, sir? Did he take any clothes with him? Had he withdrawn any large amounts from his bank accounts? Did he give any hint of his intention to leave?"

Mr. Teitelbaum raised his head slowly to stare at me.

"I asked Mrs. Stonehouse those same questions. Her answers to all were negative."

"Mrs. Stonehouse went to the police, I presume?"

"Of course. They checked hospitals and the morgue, accident reports, things of that nature. They spoke to the Professor's associates at New York University. Stonehouse was retired, but was sometimes invited as a guest lecturer. His specialty was British maritime history of the seventeenth century. No one at the University had seen him or heard from him for months. The New York Police Department has listed Professor Yale Stonehouse as a Missing Person. I have some, ah, contacts in the Department and was able to speak

484 • LAWRENCE SANDERS •

to the investigating officer. It is his opinion that the Professor disappeared of his own free will and will reappear eventually for reasons of his own."

"Does the investigating officer have any evidence for that belief, sir?"

"Not that I was able to determine. Apparently the officer was basing his judgment on his experience and percentages in the analysis of the behavior of missing persons."

"Do you know, sir, if the investigating officer checked airport, bus terminals, and railroad stations?"

"He did, yes. No record of reservations in the Professor's name. But that is hardly conclusive. Reservations could have been made under another name, and tickets can frequently be purchased for cash without any reservations at all, as I am sure you are well aware."

"Yes, sir."

"But the investigating officer also showed a photograph of Professor Stonehouse to employees at airports, bus terminals, and railroad stations. No results."

"Did the Professor own a car, sir?"

"He did. It was still garaged the day after his disappearance."

I took a deep breath. "Well, sir, that seems to cover it. Can Mrs. Stonehouse offer any reason at all for her husband's absence?"

Mr. Teitelbaum made a vague gesture.

"She believes the Professor went for a walk and perhaps stumbled and fell or met with an accident that resulted in amnesia, and that he is now wandering the city with no knowledge of his identity."

"Ummm," I said. "Possible, sir, but not likely."

"No," he said, "not likely."

"How old was—how old *is* Professor Stonehouse?"

"Seventy-two."

"And Mrs. Stonehouse?"

"I would estimate in her late fifties. Perhaps sixty. Their children, a young daughter and young son, are thirty-one and twenty-eight respectively. The Stonehouses were married relatively late in life."

"Are the children married, sir?"

"No, they are not."

Then we sat in silence again. I mulled over what I had just heard. I had no ideas about it at all. The Professor's disappearance was simply inexplicable.

"May I ask a question, sir?" I said finally.

Ignatz Teitelbaum nodded gravely.

"What is our interest in the Professor's disappearance, sir?"

"Mrs. Ula Stonehouse wishes to retain us as legal counsel," he said tonelessly. "Her problem is threefold. First, she would like us to employ a private investigator to look further into her husband's disappearance. I believe I persuaded her that this would be a useless expenditure. I cannot imagine what a private investigator could possibly accomplish that officers of the Missing Persons Bureau have not already done. Do you agree?"

"Yes, sir. Sounds to me like the police have done a thorough job."

"Precisely. However, I was not able to convince Mrs. Stonehouse completely of that, so I assured her that the disappearance of her husband would be examined fully by our own investigation department."

Four years ago I was a mailroom boy and now I was a department. Success!

Mr. Teitelbaum continued: "Mrs. Stonehouse's second problem is financial in nature. All her husband's assets, including his checking and savings accounts, are in his name alone. So Mrs. Stonehouse, with no assets of her own, is, ah, feeling the pinch."

"I should think so, sir—if he's been gone a month."

"Yes. I am having the whole matter of the status of the assets of a missing person researched at the present moment. I believe I will be able to petition the court to grant the family an allowance for living expenses prior to the time her missing husband is declared legally dead—if indeed he is ever so declared."

"If he is, sir," I said, "I mean, declared legally dead at some future time, who gets the money? How is the estate divided?"

"The third problem," Mr. Teitelbaum said somberly. "Mrs. Stonehouse cannot find her husband's will. It seems to be missing."

4

•

THE MOMENT I RETURNED TO MY OFFICE, I CALLED MARTY AGAIN. Still no answer. It was then 4:25 P.M. I finished my report on the time trials, read it over, put the original in my Out basket, and the carbon in my file cabinet. I then started two new folders, labeling them KIPPER and STONE-HOUSE. At the moment, I had nothing to put in the latter, and only Marty's phone number to file in the former.

I relaxed for a few moments, put my feet up on the desk, and reviewed my recent interview with Teitelbaum.

All Teitelbaum wanted me to do was to meet and interview the Stonehouse family and servants, to ask them any questions I thought might be germane to the disappearance of the Professor, and generally to nose about and try to make some educated guesses as to what had actually happened.

"You are a clever young man," Mr. Teitelbaum had said. "Perhaps you will think of an approach or an angle that the police had neglected."

When he or the assigned TORT attorney went into court to beg that an allowance be granted to the Stonehouse family from the missing man's assets, Teitelbaum wanted to be able to assure the bench that every possible effort had been made to locate the Professor.

"We can already present the unsuccessful efforts of the New York Police Department," he'd suggested. "In addition, I want to show that Mrs. Stonehouse made a personal effort, working through us, her legal representative, to find her husband. I want you to keep a careful record of the number of hours you spend on this inquiry. The more, the better—without neglecting your other responsibilities, of course. In addition to that, I plan to place advertisements in the local papers offering a reward for information on the fate and present whereabouts of Professor Stonehouse. We may even have fliers printed up and distributed in their neighborhood, making the same offer of reward. Personally, I do not feel anything will come of these efforts, but the purpose is to prove to the court that we have made a bona fide effort to locate the missing man prior to petitioning for the right to draw on his assets without his permission."

That made sense to me. It was no great blow to my self-esteem to know that my investigation was to be merely part of a legal ploy and that no great results were expected.

Back in my office at four minutes to five, I dialed Marty's number once again. This time it was picked up after the third ring. A man's voice answered:

"Yeah?"

"Marty?"

"Yeah. Who's this?"

"I'm calling for Mr. Leopold Tabatchnick."

"About time. You got in just under the wire."

"I've been calling all day."

"Yeah?" he said. "Well, I been in and out."

It was a thick, clotty voice with an uneducated New York accent. He was silent, waiting for me to speak.

"Mr. Tabatchnick wants me to meet with you," I said politely. "At your convenience. To discuss matters relevant to the estate of Solomon Kipper."

"That's what I'm here for," he said cheerily. "I'm selling, and you're buying—right?"

"Uhh, that's to be determined," I said hastily. "When and where can we meet?"

He paused a moment, then:

"There's a gin mill on West 46th Street between Eighth and Ninth. Closer to Ninth. Called the Purple Cow. Meet me there at 11:30 tomorrow morning. Got that?"

I had been scribbling quick notes.

"I have it," I said. "How will I know you?"

"I'll be sitting in the last booth on the left," he said. Then his voice turned guttural. "You coming alone?"

"Of course," I said.

"Good," he said. "No foolishness."

He clicked off.

I hung up slowly, staring down at my notes. I tried to analyze how he had sounded. Not menacing, I finally concluded, but very sure of himself.

I sighed, added that note to the Kipper file, and stored it away in my steel cabinet. Then I put on my coat and started home, exchanging "Good nights" with other departing employees. Yetta Apatoff's desk was bare; apparently she had already left.

It had been a gray day, raw, the light coarse and the air smelling damply of snow. But the temperature had moderated somewhat; the wind still nibbled, but it had freshened, and the evening sky showed patches of pale blue. Rather than try to jam my way aboard crowded buses, I decided to walk home to the West 20s.

I lived on a street in Chelsea that had once been lined with private homes. Most of the houses had cast-iron railings in front, sandstone steps leading up to ornate front doors. Those that hadn't been gutted still had marble fireplaces and high ceilings with plaster embellishments.

My building had adequate heat and hot water because the owner lived there. On the first floor was a firm of architects, Armentrout & Pook; and Hooshang Aboudi, Inc., importers of general merchandise.

The owner and her daughter, Hermione and Cleo Hufnagel, lived on the second floor in separate apartments. I shared the third floor with Bramwell Shank, an elderly ex–ferryboat captain who was confined to a wheelchair. On the top floor, the fourth, were the apartments of Madama Zora Kadinsky, who said she had once sung at the Met and still practiced scales during the day. The other fourth-floor apartment was occupied by Adolph Finkel, a retail shoe salesman.

The apartments were dark but the ceilings were high and the fireplaces worked. I paid $350 a month plus utilities.

On this particular evening Bramwell Shank was waiting for me in the third-floor hallway. His bottle of muscatel was in his lap, with a clean glass ready for me and a half-empty one he was sipping. He wheeled himself into my apartment as soon as I unlocked the door and launched into a recital of the day's TV activities before I could get my coat off.

In his prime he must have been a stalwart bruiser, with solid shoulders, corded arms, and fists that looked like geological specimens. Now, imprisoned in a wheelchair, puddled by drink, he still had a thrusting, assertive brawler's presence. His voice rattled the windows and all his gestures were outsize and violent.

Because he was bald, he wore a captain's cap all day; below the peak of
the cap was a pulpy face that ranged from pink to deep purple. He wore
black turtleneck sweaters and a brass-buttoned blue officer's jacket.

I let him thunder on about the shows he had seen and when he paused to
fill our glasses again, I asked him if he'd care to eat with me.

"I was planning to scramble some eggs with salami," I said. "Maybe a
salad. And a piece of pie. You're welcome to share, Captain."

"Nah," he said. "I already made my own slop and et it. Where'd you get
the pie—Powerful Katrinka give it to you?"

That was what he called our landlady, Mrs. Hufnagel. It was an apt nick-
name; she stood five eleven and was at least a welterweight.

"Yes, she did," I said. "It's Dutch apple, and very good. Homemade."

"Uh-huh," he said, looking at me and grinning. "She's real friendly to
you, ain't she?"

"Isn't she friendly to *you?*"

"She don't bake me no pies. You going to the party?"

"What party?"

"Saturday night. Katrinka invited all the tenants."

"I haven't been invited."

"You will be."

"What's the occasion?"

"Valentine's Day—she says. But I got my own ideas about that."

"You're talking in riddles tonight, Captain."

He watched me assemble paper and kindling in the fireplace.

"You ain't doing that right!" he roared. "Pile up your kindling crisscross."

"I do it like this. It always works."

The fire caught this time, too. We were watching it, wineglasses in hand,
when there came a rapid knocking on the door.

" 'allo, 'allo!" caroled Mme. Kadinsky. "Joshy? You are een there?"

"Don't let her in," growled the Captain.

"Madame Kadinsky," I said, smiling at her. "Nice to see you. Do come
in."

She tapped my cheek. "You promised to call me Zora, you naughty boy."
Then she was inside the room, moving with quick little steps. "But you
already have company. The Captain Shink."

"Shank," he growled.

"I am interrupting somesing?" She laughed gaily.

"Not at all," I told her. "We're just having a glass of wine. Let me get
you a glass."

"Joshy," she said, "you are going to the party Saturday night?"

"I haven't been invited."

Like Bramwell Shank, she said, "You will be." They both smiled.

"What's going on with you two?"

Zora put a hand to her cheek, rolled her eyes.

"He don't know," Shank said.

"Tell me!" I burst out.

"Powerful Katrinka has her eye on you for Cleo," the Captain said.

They departed soon after, and I went into the kitchen to make my omelette. I suppose I felt a kind of smirky pride; I am as vain as the next man. The whole thing was ridiculous, of course. Cleo Hufnagel seemed a pleasant, soft-spoken young woman. We smiled and exchanged greetings. But more was impossible. Cleo was at least five ten, and taller in heels.

But my thoughts kept returning to the Great Hufnagel Plot. When the knock came I knew at once who it was. It was Mrs. Hufnagel bearing a plate covered with a paper napkin.

"Mrs. Hufnagel! What a surprise! Won't you come in?"

"Well . . . just for a minute. I don't want to disturb you."

"Not at all," I said. "Would you like a cup of coffee?"

"No, nothing, thanks," she said. "We just finished dinner. My, that was a fine meal Cleo cooked. Swiss steak with mashed potatoes, fresh string beans, and the best gravy ever. Have you had your coffee yet?"

I said truthfully that I hadn't.

"Well, Cleo baked these chocolate chip cookies and we thought you might enjoy some with your coffee."

"Mrs. Hufnagel, you're too generous."

"Try one," she commanded.

Obediently I bit into a cookie.

"Delicious," I said.

"Yes," she said, sighing. "That Cleo—so talented in the kitchen. She'll make some man a wonderful wife."

"I'm sure she will," I murmured. "Would you like the plate back now? I can put the cookies in a tin."

"No rush," she said. "You can return it whenever you like. Actually, Mr. Bigg, the cookies were just one of the reasons I came up. I *also* wanted to invite you to a party Cleo and I are having Saturday night."

5

•

THE PURPLE COW SMELLED OF SPILLED BEER AND CHEAP CIGARS, even at 11:30 A.M. The men at the bar hunched glowering over their drinks, awaiting the end of the world. I found Marty in the last booth on the left. He sat facing the door, fingers laced around a stein of beer. In the dim light he appeared to be about forty-five, skinny, with a pitted complexion and a pale, small mustache.

He watched me approach without interest. I stopped alongside his booth.

"Marty?" I said.

"Yeah?"

"I'm from Mr. Leopold Tabatchnick."

He showed his teeth. "Who are you, the office boy?"

I slid into the booth opposite him.

"I am Mr. Tabatchnick's executive assistant, acting on his behalf."

"That's sweet," he said.

"Could you tell me what this is all about?" I asked. "You claim you—"

"Want a drink?" he interrupted.

"No," I said. "Thank you."

"For what?" he said. "I wasn't going to pay for it."

"You claim you have information affecting the estate of the late Solomon Kipper. Is that correct?"

"I don't claim it. I got it."

"Could you tell me the nature of this information?"

"You kidding? That's what I'm selling."

I sighed and sat back.

"Then I'm afraid we've reached an impasse," I said. "Surely you don't expect us to make an offer for something we know nothing about."

He leaned toward me across the table. He had very sour breath. His eyes seemed almost colorless, and I noticed the lobe of his left ear was missing. He was dressed in a tweed cap, green anorak, maroon shirt, and flowered pink tie. The parka was stained, there was a stubble of whitish beard, and his nails were rimmed with black. His voice was even more gluey than it had sounded on the phone.

"Listen, sonny," he said, "I ain't asking you to make an offer; I'm going to tell you how much I want. Second of all, I ain't telling you what I got because then I got nothing to sell. That makes sense, don't it? I'll tell you this much: what I got is going to upset the applecart. With what I got, the Kipper will ain't worth the paper it's printed on."

"And how much are you asking for this information?"

"Fifty thousand," he said promptly. "Take it or leave it."

I think I succeeded in hiding my shock.

"That's a great deal of money," I said slowly.

"Nah," he said, "it's peanuts. How much is that estate—four mil? Five mil? It's worth fifty grand to make sure it goes to the right people, ain't it?"

"Well . . ." I said, "I'll certainly bring this to Mr. Tabatchnick's attention the moment I get back to the office."

"Don't jerk me around, sonny," he said. "I got another hot customer for this property. I'm meeting with them later today. First come, first served."

"I'll contact you as soon as Mr. Tabatchnick comes to a decision," I said. "Would you mind giving me your full name? You can't expect us to make a payment of that size to someone we know only as Marty."

He thought that over, squinching his eyes and wrinkling his nose.

"I guess it won't do no harm," he said. "It's Reape. R-e-a-p-e. Marty Reape. As in 'Rook before you Reape'—right? You can reach me at that number I gave you. I'll be in late this afternoon."

I nodded and slid out of the booth. "Nice meeting you, Mr. Reape."

"Yeah." He showed no intention of leaving with me. That this was a ploy to avoid being followed was obvious, but he underrated my professionalism.

Outside I turned west, crossed Ninth, and immediately chose a doorway for the stakeout. Then I settled down to wait, hands in my pockets. I stamped my feet occasionally to keep them from becoming lumps. Now and then I took my hands from my pockets to hold my ears. He came out finally and stood at the curb, zipping up his parka and looking around. Then he turned and started walking east toward Times Square.

He was on the south side of West 46th Street. I stayed on the north side, well back of him. The sidewalk was filling up with people rushing to get a lunch table at one of the restaurants that lined the street, so Marty Reape moved slowly. Even in the crowd the cap and anorak were easy to spot. If he suspected he might be followed, he certainly gave no indication of it; never once looked over his shoulder or glanced in a store window to catch a reflection. I tailed him to a few doors east of Eighth on 49th, where he turned into a building next to a porn movie house that was showing "Teenage Honey Pot." When he'd had time to clear the lobby I trotted across the street and ducked in. There was a directory on the greasy marble wall.

MARTIN REAPE: PRIVATE INVESTIGATIONS.

I practically ran back to the office to give Mr. Tabatchnick my report, but Thelma Potts said he was at lunch and that she would buzz me when he returned.

I had a cheeseburger and a container of milk sent in and ate at my desk while I typed a report of my meeting with Martin Reape. I put it away in the Kipper file and then I called Mr. Teitelbaum's office. *He* never went out to lunch; he had a cup of tea and two graham crackers at his desk. I told him I'd like to meet and question the Stonehouse family and I thought it would go a lot easier if he called first and set up the appointment for a time when all the family and the servants would be present.

"Yes, yes," he said testily. "I'll call you back." He hung up abruptly.

Maybe his graham crackers had been stale.

I had no sooner hung up than Thelma Potts called. I took the elevator to the fourth floor with two clerks carrying stacks of law books up to their eyebrows.

"Twice in two days," Thelma Potts said. "My, what would this company do without you?"

"Stick with me, kid," I said, "and you'll be wearing diamonds."

I knocked once and went in. He was feeding his fish, crumbling some white stuff into the tanks and making little sounds with his tongue and teeth. It sounded like, "nk, nk, nk."

"Mr. Tabatchnick," I said, "I had a meeting with Marty about the Kipper estate."

He went on feeding fish. "Sit down and tell me," he said.

When I mentioned the $50,000, Mr. Tabatchnick's hand jerked and one of his finny friends got an unexpected banquet. I finished describing the meeting and he came back to his swivel chair behind the trestle table, dusting his hands.

"I like it less and less," he said. "If he had asked for five hundred, or a thousand, or even five thousand, I would have assumed he was merely a cheap chiseler. But he obviously believes his information is of considerable value. And if he is a private investigator, he may indeed have discovered something of consequence. Repeat exactly what he said regarding the nature of his information."

"He said, quote, What I got is going to upset the applecart. With what I got, the Kipper will ain't worth the paper it's printed on. Unquote."

"And he said he has another potential customer?"

"Yes, sir. He said he was meeting with them later today. That's his word: 'them.' "

We sat in silence for a long time. Finally he stirred and said, "I dislike this intensely. As an officer of the court I cannot become involved in shenanigans. At the same time, I have a responsibility to our deceased client and to the proper distribution of his estate as set forth in his last will and testament."

He stared at me without expression. I didn't catch on for a moment. Then I knew what he wanted.

"Sir," I said, "is there anything odd about that will?"

"No, no," he said. "It's a relatively short and simple document. But I have not been entirely forthcoming with you, Mr. Bigg. On the morning of the day he committed suicide, Sol Kipper called this office and said he wished to execute a new will."

"I see," I said softly.

"Do you?" he said. "I don't. Now we have this 'Marty' claiming to have information that may invalidate the existing will."

"Yes, sir," I said. "You want to pay him, Mr. Tabatchnick?"

"I told you," he thundered, "I cannot let myself become involved!"

"Of course not, sir. But I'm not an officer of the court; I have latitude to act in this matter."

That was what he wanted to hear. Mr. Tabatchnick settled back, entwined his fingers across his solid stomach, regarded me gravely.

"What do you propose, Mr. Bigg?"

"The funds can't come from this firm, sir. There can be no connection, nothing on our books. The money must be made available from an outside source."

He thought a moment. "That can be arranged," he said finally.

"And I must be the only contact Reape knows. No one else in the firm can speak to him or meet with him."

"I agree."

"The first thing for me to do is to call Reape and tell him we agree to his terms. Before he makes a deal with his other customers. I will then arrange a date for the transfer, postponing it as long as possible. Then I hand over the money and he hands over his information or delivers it orally."

"Why do you wish to postpone the transfer as long as possible?"

"To give me time to devise some plan for getting the information without paying."

"Splendid, young man!" he said. "If you can. But your primary objective must be acquiring the information. I hope you understand that."

"I do, sir."

"Good. Keep me informed. I'll need a day or two to provide the funds."

"Mr. Tabatchnick, it would help if you could tell me something about the existing Kipper will. Specifically, who stands to inherit the most? And if the will is for some reason declared invalid, who would stand to profit the most?"

He looked down at his big hands, now clasped on the tabletop.

"For the moment," he said in a low voice, "I would prefer to keep that information confidential. Should the time come when it is vital to the successful conclusion of your, ah, investigation, I will then make available to you a copy of the will."

It was time for me to go.

"Mr. Bigg," he said.

I turned back from the door.

"This conversation never took place," he said sternly.

"What conversation, sir?" I asked.

He almost smiled.

6

•

I CALLED MARTY REAPE WHEN I RETURNED TO MY OFFICE. NO answer. I wondered if he was meeting with his other customers.

I took off my jacket and started hacking away at inquiries that had been submitted by junior partners and associates. Most of these could be handled with a single phone call or a letter, or a look into Roscoe Dollworth's small library of dictionaries, atlases, almanacs, census reports, etc.

What was the Hispanic population of the Bronx in 1964?

How long does it take to repaint a car?

In what year was penicillin discovered?

Who was the last man to be electrocuted in New York State?

What are the ingredients of a Molotov cocktail?

I tried twice to call Marty Reape. Ada Mondora called to say I had an appointment with the Stonehouse family. I was to be at their apartment on Central Park West and 70th Street at 8:00 P.M.

It was then about 4:30. I decided that instead of going home I would do better to have my dinner midtown, then go to West 70th Street. I checked my wallet, then I called Yetta Apatoff.

"Oh, Josh," she said. "I wish you'd called sooner. I would have loved to, but just a half hour ago Hammy asked me to have dinner with him."

"Hammy?"

"Hamish. Hamish Hooter."

She called him Hammy.

"Yes, well, I'm sorry you can't make it, Yetta. I'll try another time."

"Promise?" she breathed.

"Promise."

So I worked in the office until 6:30. I called Marty Reape twice more. No reply. I tried him again before I left the restaurant, where I ate alone. Again there was no answer. I began to fear that he had concluded a deal with his other customers.

I had time to spare, so I walked to 42nd Street, boarded a Broadway bus, and rode up to West 70th Street. Then I walked over to Central Park West. The sky was murky; a light drizzle was beginning to fall. Wind blew in sighing gusts and smelled vaguely of ash. A fitting night to investigate a disappearance.

The Stonehouses' apartment house was an enormous, pyramidal pile of brick. Very old, very staid, very expensive. The lobby was all marble and mirrors. I waited while the uniformed deskman called to learn if I would be received.

"Mr. Bigg to see Mrs. Stonehouse," he announced. Then he hung up and turned to me. "Apartment 17-B."

The elevator had been converted to self-service, but the walls and ceiling were polished walnut with beveled oval mirrors; the Oriental carpet had been woven to fit.

Seventeen-B was on the Central Park side. I rang the bell and waited for a long time. Finally the door was opened by a striking young woman. She smiled.

"Mr. Bigg?" she said. "Good evening, I'm Glynis Stonehouse."

She hung my coat in a foyer closet. Then she led me down a long, dimly lighted corridor lined with antique maps and scenes of naval battles. I saw why it had taken so long to answer the door. It was a hike to the living room. The apartment was huge.

She preceded me into a living room larger than my apartment. I had a quick impression of a blaze in a tiled fireplace, chairs and sofas of crushed velvet, and floor-to-ceiling windows overlooking the park. Then Glynis Stonehouse was leading me toward a smallish lady curled in the corner of an overstuffed couch, holding a half-filled wineglass. There was a bottle of sherry on the glass-topped table before her.

"My mother," Glynis said. Her voice was low-pitched, husky, and almost toneless.

"Mrs. Stonehouse," I said, making a little bow. "I'm Joshua Bigg from Mr. Teitelbaum's office. I'm happy to meet you."

"My husband's dead, isn't he?" she said. "I know he's dead."

I was startled by her words, but even more shocked by her voice. It was trilly and flutelike.

"Mother," Glynis said, "there's absolutely no evidence of that."

"I know what I know," Mrs. Stonehouse said. "Do sit down, Mr. Bigg. Over there, where I can look at you."

"Thank you." I took the chair she had indicated. I was thankful that my feet touched the floor, though only just.

"Have you dined?" she asked.

"Yes, ma'am, I have."

"So have we," she said brightly, "and now I'm having a glass of sherry. Glynis isn't drinking. Glynis never drinks. Do you, dear?"

"No, Mother," the daughter said patiently. "Would you care for something, Mr. Bigg?"

"A glass of sherry would be welcome," I said. "Thank you."

Glynis got a glass from a bar cart and filled it from her mother's bottle. She handed it to me, then seated herself at the opposite end of the couch. She was graceful and controlled.

"Mr. Teitelbaum told Mother you will be investigating my father's disappearance."

"Yes," I said. "We believe the police have done everything they possibly can, but surely it will do no harm to go over it again."

"He's dead," Mrs. Ula Stonehouse said.

"Ma'am," I said, "according to Mr. Teitelbaum, you believed your husband had met with an accident and was suffering from amnesia."

"I did think that," she said, "but I don't anymore. He's dead. I had a vision."

Glynis Stonehouse was inspecting her fingernails. I took out a notebook and pen. "I hate to go over events which I'm sure are painful to you," I said. "But it would help if you could tell me exactly what happened the evening the Professor disappeared."

Mrs. Stonehouse did most of the talking, her daughter correcting her now and then or adding something in a quiet voice. I took notes as Mrs. Stonehouse spoke, but it was really for effect, to impress them how seriously Tabatchnick, Orsini, Reilly, and Teitelbaum regarded their plight.

I glanced up frequently from my scribbling to stare at Mrs. Stonehouse.

As she talked, sipping her sherry steadily and leaning forward twice to refill her glass, her eyes, as pale as milk glass, flickered like candle flames. She had a mop of frizzy blonde curls, a skin of chamois, and a habit, or nervous tic, of touching the tip of her retroussé nose with her left forefinger. Not pushing it, but just touching it as if to make certain it was still there.

She had fluttery gestures, and was given to quick expressions—frowns, smiles, pouts, moues—that followed one another so swiftly that her face seemed in constant motion. She was dressed girlishly in chiffon. In her tucked-up position she was showing a good deal of leg.

She spoke rapidly, as if anxious to get it all out and over with. That warbling voice rippled on and on, and after a while it took on a singsong quality like a child's part rehearsed for a school play.

On the 10th of January the Stonehouse family had dinner at 7:00 P.M. Present were Professor Yale Stonehouse, wife Ula, daughter Glynis, and son Powell. The meal was served by the live-in cook-housekeeper, Mrs. Effie Dark. The maid, Olga Eklund, was away on her day off.

Glynis Stonehouse left the dinner table early, at about 8:00, to get to a performance of *Man and Superman* at the Circle in the Square. After dinner the family moved into the living room. At about 8:30, Professor Stonehouse went into his study. He came back to the living room a few minutes later and announced he was going out. He walked down the long corridor to the foyer. Later it was determined he had taken his hat, scarf, and overcoat. Mrs. Stonehouse and her son heard the outer door slam. The deskman in the lobby remembered that the Professor left the building at approximately 8:45.

He was never seen again.

This recital finished, mother and daughter looked at me expectantly, as if waiting for an instant solution.

"Has Professor Stonehouse attempted to communicate with you since his disappearance?"

"No," Glynis said. "Nothing."

"Was this a common occurrence—the Professor going out at that hour? For a walk, say?"

"No," Mrs. Stonehouse said. "He never went out at night."

"Rarely," Glynis corrected her. "Once or twice a year he went to a professional meeting. But it usually included a dinner, and he left earlier."

"He didn't say where he was going when he left on the evening of January 10th?"

"No," Mrs. Stonehouse said.

"You didn't ask, ma'am?"

The mother looked to her daughter for help.

"My father was—" she began, then said, "My father is a difficult man. He didn't like to be questioned. He went his own way. He was secretive."

"Would you say there was anything unusual in his behavior at dinner that night?"

This time daughter looked to mother.

"Nooo," Mrs. Stonehouse said slowly. "He didn't say much at the table, but then he never said much."

"So you'd say this behavior that evening was entirely normal? For Professor Stonehouse," I added hastily.

They both nodded.

"All right," I said. "There are a few things I'd like to come back to, but first I'd like to hear what happened after the Professor left."

At my request Mrs. Stonehouse took up her story again.

She and her son, Powell, stayed in the living room, watched a Beckett play on Channel 13, had a few drinks. Mrs. Dark came in at about 10:30 to say goodnight and went to her room at the far end of the apartment.

They did not begin to become concerned about the Professor's whereabouts until 11:00 P.M. They called the deskman in the lobby, who could only report that Stonehouse had left the building at 8:45 and hadn't returned. They awoke Mrs. Dark to ask if the Professor had mentioned anything to her about where he was going. She said he hadn't, but she shared their concern and joined them in the living room, wearing a robe over her nightgown. They then called some of the Professor's professional associates, apologizing for the lateness of the hour. No one had seen him or heard from him. He had no friends other than professional associates.

By 11:30 they all were worried and uncertain what they should do. They were hesitant about calling the police. If they called and he walked in a few minutes later, he'd be furious.

"He had a violent temper," Glynis said.

Glynis returned from the theater a little after midnight and was told of her father's absence. She suggested they call the garage to see if Stonehouse had taken out his car. Powell called and was informed that the car was still parked there.

The four of them waited until 2:00 A.M. and then called the local precinct. The officer they spoke to told them that it would not be a matter for the Missing Persons Bureau until the Professor was absent for 24 hours, but meanwhile he would check accident reports and hospital emergency rooms. He said he'd call them back.

They waited, awake and drinking coffee, until 3:20 when the police officer called and told them there were no reports of accidents involving Professor Stonehouse or anyone answering his description.

There seemed to be nothing more they could do. The next day they made more phone calls, and Powell rang the bells of neighbors and even walked around neighborhood streets, asking at newsstands and all-night restaurants. No one had seen his father or anyone like him.

After twenty-four hours had passed, they reported the Professor as a missing person to the New York Police Department, and that was that.

I took a deep breath.

"I don't like to take so much of your time on this first meeting," I said. "I hope you'll allow me to come back again, or call as questions occur to me."

"Of course," Glynis Stonehouse said. "And take as much time as you like. We're anxious to do anything we can to help."

"Just a few questions, then," I said, looking at her. "Did your father have any enemies? Anyone who might harbor sufficient ill-will to . . ."

I let that trail off, but she didn't flinch. Then again, she didn't look like the flinching type.

Glynis Stonehouse was taller than her mother. A compact body, curved with brio. Tawny hair hung sleekly to her shoulders. She had a triangular face with dark eyes of denim blue. Wide, sculpted lips with a minimum of rouge. She was wearing a simple shift, thin stuff that touched breast, hip, thigh. No jewelry.

I had the impression of a lot of passion there, kept under disciplined control. The dark eyes gave nothing away, and she rarely smiled or frowned. She had the habit of pausing, very briefly, before answering a question. Just a half-beat, but enough to convince me she was giving her replies extra thought.

"No, Mr. Bigg," she said evenly. "I don't believe my father had enemies who hated him enough to do him harm."

"But he did have enemies?" I persisted.

"There are a lot of people who disliked him. He was not an easy man to like."

"Oh, Glynis," her mother said sorrowfully.

"Mr. Bigg might as well know the truth, Mother; it may help his investigation. My father was—*is* a tyrant, Mr. Bigg. Opinionated, stubborn, dictatorial, with a very low boiling point. Constantly suing people for the most ridiculous reasons. Of course he had enemies, at the University and everywhere else he went. But I know of no one who disliked him enough to—to do him injury."

I nodded and looked at my notes.

"Mrs. Stonehouse, you said that just before leaving the apartment, Professor Stonehouse went into his study?"

"Yes, that's right."

"Do you know what he did in there?"

"No. The study is his private room."

"Off-limits to all," Glynis said. "He rarely let us in."

"He let *you* in, Glynis," her mother said.

"He even cleaned the room himself," Glynis went on. "He was working on a book and didn't want his papers disturbed."

"A book? What kind of a book?"

"A history of the *Prince Royal,* a famous British battleship of the seventeenth century."

"Has your father published anything before?"

"A few monographs and articles in scholarly journals. He's also an habitual writer of letters to the newspapers. Would you care for more sherry, Mr. Bigg?"

"No, thank you. That was delicious. Mrs. Stonehouse, your son is not here tonight?"

"No," she said. "He's . . ."

She didn't finish that, but leaned forward to fill her glass.

"My brother doesn't live here," Glynis said evenly. "Powell has his own place in the village. He stayed over the night Father disappeared because we were all so upset."

"Your brother and father didn't get along?" I asked.

"Well enough," she said. "Powell comes to dinner two or three times a week. In any event, the relations between my father and brother have nothing to do with your investigation."

"Powell tried so hard," her mother mourned.

Glynis leaned far across the couch to put a hand on her mother's arm. Her body was stretched out, almost reclining. I saw the bold rhythm of thigh, hip, waist, bosom, shoulder . . .

"We all tried hard, Mother," she said softly.

I closed my notebook, put it away. "I think I've asked you ladies enough questions for one evening. But before I leave, if I may, I'd like to see Professor Stonehouse's study, and I'd like to talk to your housekeeper for a few minutes."

"Of course," Glynis said, rising. I followed her over to a door on the far side of the room. It opened into a dining room, cold and austere, lit dimly.

There were two doors in the opposite wall, one the swinging type used in kitchens.

"That one to the kitchen?" I asked.

"Yes."

"And the other one to your father's study?"

"That's correct."

"Your mother told me that your father went into his study before he went out. But they couldn't have seen where he went. He might have gone into the kitchen."

"You're very sharp, Mr. Bigg," she said. "Mrs. Dark was still cleaning up in here after dinner, and she saw him go into his study."

Glynis opened the study door, reached in to turn on the light, then stood aside. I stepped forward to look in. For a moment I was close to her. I was conscious of her scent. It wasn't cologne or perfume; it was *her*. Warm, womanly, stirring. I walked forward into the study.

"I won't disturb anything," I said.

"I'm afraid we already have," she said. "Looking for Father's will."

"You didn't find it?" I said.

She shook her head, shiny hair swinging. "We found his passbook and checkbook, but no will."

"Did your father have a safe deposit box?"

"Not at either of the banks where he has his savings and checking accounts."

"Miss Stonehouse, are you sure a will exists?"

"Oh, it exists," she said. "Or did. I saw it. I don't mean I read it. I just saw it on his desk one night. It was four or five pages and had a light blue backing. When Daddy saw me looking at it, he folded it up and put it in a long envelope. 'My will,' he said. So I know it did exist."

"Does your mother know what's in it?"

"No. Father never discussed money matters with her. He just gave her an allowance and that was that."

"Did your father give you an allowance, Miss Stonehouse?"

She looked at me levelly.

"Yes," she said, "he did."

"And your brother?"

"No," she said. "Not since he moved out." Then she added irritably, "What has all this to do with my father's disappearance?"

"I don't know," I said truthfully, and turned back to the study.

It was a squarish chamber with a high-beamed ceiling. There was another tiled fireplace, built-in bookcases, large cabinets for oversized books, magazines, journals, rolled-up maps.

There was a club chair upholstered in maroon leather, with a hassock to match. Alongside it was a drum table with a leather top chased with gold leaf. A silver tray was on the drum table bearing a new bottle of Rémy Martin cognac, sealed, and two brandy snifters. A green-shaded floor lamp stood in back of the chair.

In the center of the study was a big desk with leather top and brass fittings, littered with papers, charts, maps, books, pencils and pens in several colors. Also, a magnifying glass, a pair of dividers, and a device that looked like an antique compass.

But it was the far wall that caught my eye. It was covered, from chair rail to ceiling, with model hull forms. I don't know whether you've ever seen hull models. They're made of hardwood, the hull sliced longitudinally. The flat side is fixed to the plaque. Each plaque bore a brass plate with the ship's name and date of construction. I stepped closer to examine them. I had never seen so many in one place, and never any as lovely.

Glynis had noted my interest. "Father had them made by a man in Mystic, Connecticut. When he dies, there won't be anyone left in the country who can carve hull models from the plans of naval architects."

"They're handsome," I said.

"And expensive."

But if that room had something to tell me, I couldn't hear it. I turned toward the door.

"Your father didn't have a safe?" I asked.

"No," she said. "And the drawers of his desk were unlocked."

"Did he usually leave them unlocked?"

"I really don't know. Mrs. Dark might."

I was wondering if she'd want to be present while I questioned Mrs. Dark, but I needn't have worried. She led me into the brightly lighted kitchen and said to the woman there: "Effie, this is Mr. Bigg. He's looking into Father's disappearance for the lawyers. Please answer his questions and tell him whatever he wants to know. Mr. Bigg, this is Mrs. Effie Dark. When you're finished here, I'm sure you can find your way back to the living room." Then she turned and left.

Mrs. Dark was a tub of a woman with three chins and a bosom that encircled her like a pneumatic tube. She had sausage arms, and ankles that lopped over nurse's shoes. Stuck in that roly-poly face were bright little eyes, shiny as blueberries in a pie. Her hips were so wide, I knew she had to go through doors sideways.

"Mrs. Dark," I said, "I hope I'm not disturbing you?"

"Why no," she said. "I'm just waiting for the water to boil, and then I'm going to have a nice cup of tea. Would you like one?"

"I'd love a cup of tea," I lied.

She heaved herself to her feet and went to the counter. While the tea was steeping, she set out cups, saucers, and spoons for us. I held my saucer up to the light and admired its translucence.

"Beautiful," I said.

"Nothing but the best," she said. "When it came to his own comfort, he didn't stint."

"How long have you been with the Stonehouse family, Mrs. Dark?"

"Since the Year One," she said. "I was the Professor's cook and housekeeper whilst I was married and before he was. Then my mister got took, and the Professor got married, so I moved in with him and his family."

I watched her pour us cups of russet-colored tea. She held her cup in both hands and savored the aroma before she took a sip. I did the same.

"Mrs. Stonehouse and Glynis told me what happened the night the Professor disappeared," I started. "They said they noted nothing unusual in his behavior that night. Did you?"

She thought a moment.

"Nooo," she said, drawling it out. "He was about the same as usual. He was a devil." She tasted the word on her plump lips, seemed to like it, and repeated it forcefully: "A devil! But I wouldn't take any guff from him, and he knew it. He liked my cooking, and I kept the place nice for him. He knew his wife couldn't run this menagerie, and his daughter wasn't interested. That's why he was as nice as pie as far as I was concerned. And he paid a good dollar, I'll say that."

"All this on a professor's salary?"

"Oh no. No no no. He comes from old money. His grandfather and father were in shipping. He inherited a pile."

"What was he so sore about?" I asked her. "He seems to have hated the world."

She shrugged her thick shoulders.

"Who can tell a thing like that? I know he had some disappointments in his life, but who hasn't? I know he got passed over for promotion at the University—that's why he resigned—and once, when he was younger, he got jilted. But nothing important enough that I know of that would turn him into the kind of man he was. To tell you the truth, I think he just enjoyed being mean. More tea?"

"Please."

I watched her pour and dilute with hot water. "They've been looking for the Professor's will," I said. "It's missing. Did you know that?"

"Did I? They tore my kitchen apart looking for it. Even the flour bin. Took me hours to get it tidy again."

"Glynis told me her father cleaned his study himself. Wouldn't let anyone in there. Is that right?"

"Recently," she said. "In the month before he disappeared. Before that, he let me in to dust and straighten up. We have a cleaning crew that comes in once a week to give the place a good going-over, vacuum the rugs and wash down the bathrooms—things like that. He'd let them in his study if I was there. Then, about a month before he vanished, he wouldn't let anyone in. Said he'd clean the place himself."

"Did he give any reason for this change?"

"Said he was working on this book, had valuable papers in there and didn't want them disturbed."

"Uh-huh," I said. "Mrs. Stonehouse and her daughter told me that just before he walked out on the evening of January 10th, he went into his study for a few minutes. Did you see him?"

"I did. I was in the dining room. It was Olga's night off, so I was cleaning up after dinner. He came in from the living room, went into the study, and came out a few minutes later. That was the last time I saw him."

"Did he close the study door after he went in?"

"Yes."

"Did you hear anything in there?"

"Like what?" she asked.

"Anything. Anything that might give me an idea of what he was doing. Thumping around? Moving furniture?"

She was silent, trying to remember. I waited patiently.

"I don't know . . ." she said. "It was a month ago. Maybe I heard him slam a desk drawer. But I couldn't swear to it."

"That's another thing," I said. "The desk drawers. Did he keep them locked?"

"Yes," she said definitely. "He did keep them locked when he wasn't there. I remember because once he lost his keys and we had to have a locksmith come in and open the desk."

"No one else had a key to his desk?"

"Not that I know of."

"Effie, what happened between the Professor and his son?"

"The poor lamb," she mourned. "Powell got kicked out of the house."

"Why?"

"He wouldn't get a job, and he wouldn't go back to the University to get his degree, and he was running with a wild bunch in Greenwich Village. Then the Professor caught Powell smoking pot in his bedroom, and that did it."

"Does Powell have a job now?"

"Not that I know of."

"How does he live?"

"I think he has a little money of his own that his grandmother left him. Also, I think Mrs. Stonehouse and Glynis help him out now and then, unbeknownst to the Professor."

"When did this happen?"

"Powell getting kicked out? More than a year ago."

"But he still comes here for dinner?"

"Only in the last two or three months. Mrs. Stonehouse cried and carried on so and said Powell was starving, and Glynis worked on her father, too, and eventually he said it would be all right for Powell to have dinner here if he wanted to, but he couldn't move back in."

"All right," I said. "Now what about Glynis? Does she work?"

"Not anymore. She did for a year or two, but she quit."

"Where did she work?"

"I think she was a secretary in a medical laboratory. Something like that."

"But now she does nothing?"

"She's a volunteer three days a week in a clinic downtown. But no regular job."

"Have many friends?"

"Seems to. She goes out a lot. The theater and ballet and so forth. Some weeks she's out every night."

"One particular boyfriend?"

"Not that I know of."

"Does she ever have her friends here? Does she entertain?"

"No," Mrs. Effie Dark said sadly. "I never see any of her friends. And there hasn't been much in the way of entertaining in this house. Not for years."

She waved a plump hand around, gesturing toward overhead racks, the utensils, the bins and spice racks, stove, in-the-wall oven, refrigerator, freezer.

"See all this? I don't use half this stuff for months on end. But when the kids were growing up, things were different. The Professor was at the University most of the day, and this place was filled with the kids' friends. There were parties and dances right here. Even Mrs. Stonehouse had teas and bridge games and get-togethers for her friends. My, I was busy. But we had another maid then, a live-in, and I didn't mind. There was noise and everyone laughed. A real ruckus. Then the Professor resigned, and he was home all day. He put a stop to the parties and dances. Gradually, people stopped coming, he was such a meany. Then we began living like hermits, tiptoeing around so as not to disturb him. Not like the old days."

I nodded and stood up.

"Effie," I said, "I thank you for the refreshments and for the talk."

"I like to talk," she said, grinning, "as you have probably noticed. A body could climb the walls here for the want of someone to chat with."

"Well, I enjoyed it," I said, "and I learned a lot. I hope you'll let me come back and chat with you again."

"Anytime," she said. "I have my own telephone. Would you like the number?"

As she dictated, I wrote it down in my notebook.

"Effie," I said in closing, "what do you think happened to Professor Stonehouse?"

"I don't know," she said, troubled. "Do you?"

"No," I said, "I don't."

When I went back into the living room Mrs. Stonehouse was alone, still curled into a corner of the couch. The sherry bottle was empty.

"Hi there," she fluted. She tried to touch her nose and missed.

"Hi," I said.

"Glynis went beddy-bye," she giggled.

I glanced at my watch. It was a few minutes to ten. Early for beddy-bye.

I caught the subway on CPW, got off at 23rd Street, and walked the three blocks to my home. I kept to the curb and I didn't dawdle. When I was inside the building, I felt that sense of grim satisfaction that all New Yorkers feel on arriving home safely. Now, if a masked intruder was not awaiting me in my living room, drinking my brandy, all would be well.

It was not a would-be thief awaiting me, but Captain Bramwell Shank, and he was drinking his own muscatel. His door was open, and he wheeled himself out into the hallway when he heard me climb the stairs.

"Where the hell have you been?" he said querulously. "Come on in and have a glass of wine and watch the eleven o'clock news with me."

"I think I better take a raincheck, Captain," I said. "I've had a hard day and I want to get to bed early." But I went in anyway, moved laundry off a chair, and sat watching the 24-inch color set.

"You get your invite to the party?" Captain Shank demanded, pouring himself another glass of wine.

"Yes," I said, "I got it."

"Knew you would," he said, almost cackling. "Happened just like I said, didn't it?"

I took a sip of wine, put my head back, closed my eyes.

The local news came on, and we heard more dire predictions of New York's financial fate. We saw a tenement fire in the Bronx that killed three. We watched the Mayor hand a key to the city to a champion pizza twirler.

I was contemplating how soon I could decently leave when the news came on. The anchorman read a few small items of local interest to which I drifted off. Then he said:

"Service was halted for an hour on the Lexington Avenue IRT this evening while the body of a man was removed from the express tracks at the 14th Street station. He apparently fell or jumped to his death at the south end of the station just as the train was coming in. The victim has tentatively been identified as Martin Reape of Manhattan. No additional details are available at this time. And now, a message to all denture wearers . . ."

"What?" I said, waking up. "What did he say?"

7

•

I READ THE STORY IN THE *TIMES* ON THE 23RD STREET CROSSTOWN bus in the morning. It was only a paragraph in "The City" column:

"Police are seeking witnesses to the death of Martin Reape of Manhattan who fell or jumped at the 14th Street station of the Lexington Avenue IRT subway. The accident occurred during the evening rush hour and resulted in delays of more than an hour. The motorman of the train involved told police he had just entered the station and had applied his brakes when 'the body came flying out of nowhere.' "

Rook before you Reape.

I made it to the office a few minutes before 9:00, called Thelma Potts, and told her I had to see Mr. Tabatchnick as soon as possible.

"You're getting to be a regular visitor," she said.

"Just an excuse to see you," I said.

"Oh *you!*" she said.

I spent an hour typing up a report of my conversations with the Stonehouses and Mrs. Dark. I tried to leave nothing out, because at that time I had no conception of what was important and what was just sludge. After reading over the report, I could detect no pattern, not even a vague clue to the Professor's disappearance. Just then Thelma Potts called to say Mr. Tabatchnick would see me. When I entered his office, he was standing behind the trestle table, drinking from a mug that had "Grandpa" painted on it. He was in a testy mood.

"What is so urgent that it couldn't wait until I had a chance to inspect my fish?"

I laid the *Times* column on his desk. I had boxed the Reape item with a red grease pencil.

Mr. Tabatchnick removed a heavy pair of black horn-rimmed glasses from his breast pocket. He took out a clean, neatly pressed handkerchief and slowly polished the glasses, breathing on them first. He donned the spectacles and, still standing, began to read. He read it once, looked up and stared at me, then read it again. His expression didn't change, but he lowered himself slowly into his swivel chair.

"Sit down, Mr. Bigg," he said. The voice wasn't irritable anymore. In fact, it sounded a little shaky. "What do you think happened?"

"I think he was murdered, sir. Pushed onto the tracks by that other customer or customers he was going to see."

"You have a vivid imagination, Mr. Bigg."

"It fits, sir."

"Then wouldn't he have had the money on him if he had sold the information? The paper mentions nothing of that. Or if he hadn't made the deal, wouldn't he have had the information on his person?"

"Not necessarily, sir. First of all, we don't know that his information was physical evidence. It may have been just something he knew. And it's possible he went to see his other customers just to discuss the details of the deal, and no exchange took place prior to his death. But after talking to him, his customers feared the payment would be only the first of a series of demands, and so they decided his death was the only solution."

He exhaled heavily.

"Very fanciful," he said. "And totally without proof."

"Yes, sir," I said, "I admit that. But during my meeting with Reape, I said something to the effect that fifty thousand was a lot of money, and he said, quote, It's worth fifty grand to make sure it goes to the right people, ain't it? Unquote. He was speaking of the estate, sir. So perhaps his other customers were the wrong people. You follow, Mr. Tabatchnick?"

"Of course I follow," he said furiously. "You're saying that with Reape out of the picture, the wrong people will profit. That means that the beneficiaries named in the existing will may include the wrong people."

He didn't like that at all. He leaned forward to read the Reape story for the third time. Then he angrily shoved the paper away.

"I wish," he said, "that I could be certain that this Reape person actually did possess what he claimed. He may merely have read the news story of Sol Kipper's suicide and devised this scheme to profit from the poor man's death. It might have been just a confidence game, a swindle."

"Mr. Tabatchnick, did the news story of Sol Kipper's suicide mention the value of his estate?"

"Of course not!"

"During my meeting with Reape, he said, quote, How much is that estate—four mil? Five mil? Unquote. Was that a close estimate of the estate, Mr. Tabatchnick?"

"Close enough," he said in a low voice. "It's about four million six."

"Well, how would Reape have known that if he hadn't been intimately involved with the Kipper family in some way? Surely his knowledge of the size of the estate is a fairly solid indication that he had the information he claimed."

Leopold Tabatchnick sighed deeply. Then he sat brooding, head lowered. He pulled at his lower lip. I was tempted to slap his hand and tell him his lips protruded enough.

I don't know how long we sat there in silence. Finally, Tabatchnick sighed again and straightened up. He put his thick hands on the tabletop, palms down.

"All right," he said, "I realize what you are implying. You feel that if Martin Reape told the truth and had evidence to upset the will of Sol Kipper, then an investigation into Kipper's suicide would be justified."

"The alleged suicide," I said. "Yes, sir, that's the way I feel."

"Very well," he said. "You may conduct a discreet inquiry. I repeat, a *discreet* inquiry. To avoid prejudicing your investigation. I will not disclose to you at this time the principal beneficiaries of Sol Kipper's estate."

"As you wish, sir," I said. "But it would help a great deal if you would give me some background on the man and his family. You mentioned that he had been a personal friend of yours for fifty-five years."

"Yes," he said. "We were classmates at CCNY together. I went on to law school and Sol went into his father's textile business. But we kept in touch and saw each other frequently. He was best man at my wedding, and I at his. Our wives were good friends. That was Sol's first wife. She died six years ago and Sol remarried."

Did I detect a note of disapproval in his voice?

"Sol was an enormously successful businessman. After his father's death, he became president of Kipmar Textiles, and expanded to include knitting mills in New England, South Carolina, Spain, and Israel. They went public ten years ago, and Sol became a wealthy man. He had three sons and one daughter by his first wife. All his children are grown now, of course, and married. Sol had eleven grandchildren. Shortly after his second marriage, he semiretired and turned over the day-to-day operations of Kipmar Textiles to two of his sons. The third son is a doctor in Los Angeles. His daughter lives in Boca Raton, Florida. What else would you care to know?"

"The second wife, sir—what can you tell me about her?"

"She is younger than Sol was—considerably younger. I believe she was on the stage. Briefly. Her name is Tippi."

Now I was certain I heard that note of disapproval in his voice.

"Yes, sir. And now the man himself. What was he like?"

"Sol Kipper was one of the dearest, sweetest men it has ever been my good fortune to know. He was generous to a fault. A fine, loving husband and an understanding father and grandfather. His children worshiped him. They took his death very hard."

"Why did he commit suicide, sir—if he did? Was there any reason for it?"

Tabatchnick wagged his big head sadly. "Sol was the worst hypochondriac I've ever known or heard about. He was continually running to doctors with imaginary physical ailments. It was a joke to his family and friends, but we could never convince him that he was in excellent health, even when doctor after doctor told him the same thing. He had only to read a medical article on some obscure illness and he was certain he had the symptoms. He dosed himself with all kinds of nostrums and, to my personal knowledge, swallowed more than fifty vitamin pills and mineral capsules a day. He was like that when he was young, and it worsened as he grew older, sometimes resulting in extreme depression. I assume he committed suicide while in that condition."

"After making an appointment with you to execute a new will?"

"That's the way it happened," Mr. Tabatchnick said crossly.

"I think that's about all, sir," I said, standing. "I'll report to you if there is anything you should know."

"By all means," he said. "If there is anything I can do to help, please let me know. You may call me at home, should that become necessary. I am in the book. I am depending on you, Mr. Bigg, to conduct your investigation quietly and diplomatically."

"Yes, sir, I understand. I'd like to start by talking to that officer who investigated Mr. Kipper's death. Do you happen to recall his name?"

"Not offhand, but Miss Potts has his name and phone number. I'll instruct her to give them to you."

"Mr. Tabatchnick, the detective will probably want to know the reason for our interest. May I tell him about Martin Reape?"

He pondered that for a while.

"No," he said finally, "I'd prefer you didn't. If nothing comes of this, the role of Reape will be of no significance, and I don't wish anyone else to know of our willingness to deal with him. If the detective asks the reason for our interest, tell him merely that it concerns the estate and insurance. I am sure that will satisfy him. You might take him to lunch or dinner. I suspect he may be more forthcoming over a few drinks and a good meal. I will approve any expense vouchers. Any *reasonable* expense vouchers."

Detective second-grade Percy Stilton was the cop on the Kipper case. I got his number from Thelma Potts. I called him the moment I returned to my office, but the man who answered said Detective Stilton would not come on duty until 4:00 P.M. I said I'd call him then.

I started typing notes of my conversation with Mr. Tabatchnick, leaving out all mention of Marty Reape. When I had done that I phoned the Stonehouse apartment; a very throaty voice answered. I assumed that it was the maid, Olga Eklund. Mrs. Stonehouse came on in that trilly voice. I asked her questions about her husband's health. He had been well at the time of his disappearance but had recently been ill.

"It started late in the summer," she said. "But it got progressively worse. October and November were very bad. But then he just snapped out of it. He was a Scorpio, you know."

"October and November?" I repeated. Then he must have recovered about a month prior to his disappearance.

"What was the nature of his illness, Mrs. Stonehouse?"

"Oh, I don't really know," she said blithely. "My husband was so tight-lipped about things like that. The flu, I suppose, or a virus that just hung on.

He simply refused to go to a doctor, but then he got so weak and miserable he finally had to go. Went several times, as a matter of fact, and the doctor did all kinds of tests. He must have discovered what it was, because Yale recovered very quickly."

"Could you tell me the doctor's name, Mrs. Stonehouse?"

"His name?" she said. "Now what *is* his name? Morton, I think, or something like that."

I heard her call, "Olga!" and there was confused talking in the distance. Then Mrs. Stonehouse came back on the phone. "Stolowitz," she said. "Dr. Morris Stolowitz."

I looked up the phone number of Dr. Morris Stolowitz. He was on West 74th Street, within easy walking distance of the Stonehouse apartment. I called, and a woman's voice answered: "Doctor's office." Doctor was busy with a patient. I left my name and number and asked that he get back to me.

I had my doubts that Dr. Stolowitz would ever return my call. I was debating the wisdom of asking Mrs. Stonehouse to intercede for me, when Hamish Hooter came barging into my office and threw my pay envelope onto the desk.

"See here," he said.

"What is it now, Hooter?"

"I've been trying to tell you in a nice way," he said, sucking his teeth noisily. "But apparently you're not catching on. Yetta Apatoff and I are an item. I want you to stop bothering her."

"If I am *bothering* her," I said, "which I sincerely doubt, let the lady tell me herself."

He muttered something threatening and rushed from my office, banging the door.

So, of course, I had to call Yetta immediately.

"Hi, it's Josh," I said, wondering why my speech became so throaty and—well, *intimate,* when I spoke to her.

"Hi, Josh," she said in her breathy, little girl's voice. "Long time no see."

Now, did that sound like a woman I was bothering?

"How about lunch today?" I suggested. "Just to celebrate payday?"

"Ooh, marvy!" she said. "Let's go to the Chink place on Third."

When I went out to her reception desk at noon, she was waiting for me, her coat on her arm, a fluffy powder-blue beret perched enchantingly on her blonde ringlets. She was wearing a tightly fitted knitted suit of a slightly darker blue, and when I saw that divine topography, I felt the familiar constriction of my breathing and my knee joints seemed excessively oiled.

While we walked over to Third Avenue, she took my arm, chatting innocently, apparently unaware of what her soft grip was doing to my heartbeat and respiration. As always when I was with her, I was blind and deaf to our surroundings. All my senses were zeroed in on her, and once, when she shivered with cold, said, "Brrr!" and hugged my arm to her yielding breast, I almost sobbed with joy.

In the restaurant all I wanted was to look at her, watch those perfect white teeth bite into a dumpling, note how the soft column of her throat moved when she swallowed, and how she patted her mouth delicately with a paper napkin when a small burp rose to her lips.

"Oh, Josh," she said, between bites and swallows, "did I tell you about this absolutely marvy sweater I saw in this store on Madison? I'd love to get it, but it's *soo* expensive, and also it's cut *way* down. I mean it really is a plunging neckline, and I suppose I'd have to wear a scarf with it, something that would cover me a little if I wore it to work, or maybe a blouse under it, but that would spoil the lines because it's *sooo* clinging, and it's like a forest green. Do you like green, Josh?"

"Love green," I said hoarsely.

"It costs *sooo* much, but maybe just this once I'll spend more than I should because I believe that if you really want something, you should get it no matter what it costs. I have this saying, 'I don't want anything but the best,' and that's really the way I feel, and I suppose you think I'm just terrible."

"Of course not. You deserve the—"

"Oh well," she said, giggling, "maybe I'll buy it as a birthday present to me from myself."

"It's your birthday?" I cried.

"Oh not yet, Josh. Not until next week. But I certainly hope you don't think I'm, you know, telling you that for any, you know, ulterior motive like I was angling for a present or anything, because I'm certainly not that kind of a girl."

"I know that, Yetta."

She reached across the table to put a hand briefly on mine.

We got fortune cookies with our ice cream. Yetta's fortune was A NEW LIFE AWAITS YOU. Mine read: A NEW LIFE AWAITS YOU.

Yetta stared at me, suddenly solemn.

"Josh," she said, "isn't that the strangest thing that ever happened to you? I mean, we're *both* going to have a new life. I certainly think that's strange. You don't suppose—?"

She broke off, glanced at her watch.

"Goodness," she said, "look at the time! I've really got to get back. Duty calls!"

We strolled back to the office together. Just before we got there I said, "Yetta, that store where you saw the sweater you liked . . ."

"Between 36th and 37th," she said. "On the West Side. It's in the window."

I resolutely stayed in my office all afternoon and worked hard on routine inquiries from the junior partners and associates. A few minutes after four o'clock, I called the officer who had investigated Sol Kipper's suicide. He answered the phone formally.

"Detective Percy Stilton."

"Sir," I said, "my name is Joshua Bigg. I work for the legal firm of Tabatchnick, Orsini, Reilly, and Teitelbaum. Mr. Tabatchnick gave me your name and address. He said you investigated the suicide of Solomon Kipper."

"Kipper?" he said. "Oh yes, that's right. I caught that one."

"I was hoping I could talk to you about it," I said. "This concerns a matter of estate and insurance claims."

"I can't show you the file," he said.

"Oh no," I said hastily. "Nothing like that. I mean, this isn't official. Very informal. You won't be asked to testify. I just wanted to ask a few questions."

"You say this concerns insurance?"

"Yes, sir."

"Uh-huh," he said. He was silent a moment. Then: "Well, I guess it wouldn't do any harm. You want to come over here?"

"I was wondering if we might meet somewhere. Dinner perhaps?"

"Dinner?" he said. "You on an expense account?"

"Yes, sir," I said.

"Great," he said. "I'm getting tired of pizza. Want to make it tonight?"

"That would be fine."

"I have to do some work later at Midtown Precinct North. That's on West 54th Street. I should be finished about eight o'clock, and be able to break loose for a while. I'll meet you at eight or thereabouts at the Cheshire Cheese on West 51st Street between Eighth and Ninth. It's veddy British."

I was tidying up my desk, getting ready to leave, when my phone rang. That was a welcome change.

"Joshua Bigg," I answered.

"Just a moment, Mr. Bigg," a woman's voice said. "Dr. Morris Stolowitz calling." When he came on he was loud and irascible. "What's this about Professor Stonehouse?" he demanded.

I told him who I was and whom I worked for, and explained that I wanted to talk to him. He wanted to know where I got his name and snarled that the doctor-patient relationship was confidential. In the end he said he could see me for five minutes the next day. He slammed down the phone and I decided to call it a day.

Since my route home took me to Madison Avenue, I found the store Yetta Apatoff had mentioned. The green sweater was in the window, displayed on a mannequin. Yetta hadn't exaggerated; that neckline didn't plunge, it submerged. About as far down as my spirits when I saw the price: $59.95. Maybe she'd like a nice handkerchief instead. I decided to think about it for a while; after all, her birthday wasn't until next week. I continued down Madison to 23rd Street, took a crosstown bus to Ninth Avenue, then walked home from there. Captain Shank wasn't on the third-floor landing to greet me, but I could hear his TV set blaring behind his closed door. I sneaked into my own apartment and shut my door ever so softly. I liked the old man, I really did, but I was not partial to muscatel.

At 7:30 I took the Eighth Avenue bus uptown and arrived at 51st Street ahead of time. I found the Cheshire Cheese, a few steps down from the sidewalk. It was, as Stilton had said, an English-style restaurant with a long bar on the left as you entered, and small tables for two along the right wall. In the rear, I could see a larger dining room with tables for four.

It was a pleasantly dim place, redolent with appetizing cooking odors and decorated with horse brasses and coats of arms. The theater crowd had already departed, and there were few diners: two men together, two couples, and a foursome. No Detective Stilton.

I waited near the entrance until a slender man wearing a long white apron came from behind the bar and approached me. He was polishing a wine goblet with a cloth.

"Sir?" he said.

"I'm meeting a gentleman," I said. "Perhaps I'll take a table and have a drink while I'm waiting."

"Very good," he said, looking around. "How about the corner?"

So that's where I was seated after I had hung up my coat. My back was to the wall, and I could watch the entrance. A waiter came over and I ordered a Scotch and water.

I had taken only one sip when a tall black man came into the Cheshire Cheese and looked around. He took off his coat and hat, stowed them on the open rack, and came walking directly toward me with a light, bouncy stride. I struggled out of my chair to shake his hand.

"Mr. Bigg?" he said. "I'm Stilton." As he shifted the free chair from my right to sit opposite me, the waiter scurried over to move the pewter serving platter, napkin, utensils, and water goblet in front of the detective.

"Waiting long?" Stilton asked.

"Just got here," I told him. "I'm having a drink. Something for you?"

He ordered a dry martini straight up, no twist or olive. It arrived with lightning speed.

"All right?" I asked him.

"Just right," he said. "How long have you been a Chief Investigator?"

He smiled at my shock. I managed to regain composure.

"Two years. But I was an assistant for two years before that. To a man named Roscoe Dollworth. He was with the Department. Did you know him?"

"Dolly? Oh hell yes. He was some kind of a cop before the sauce got to him. He still alive?"

"He's retired and living in Florida."

"I think we better order," he said. "We can talk while we're eating. I've got maybe an hour before the loot starts getting antsy. I know exactly what

I want. Roast beef on the bone, very rare. Yorkshire pudding. Whatever vegetable they're pushing. And a salad. And a mug of ale.''

I had a steak-and-kidney pie, salad, and ale.

"About this Kipper thing," Stilton said abruptly. "You say your interest is in the insurance?"

"The claim," I said, nodding. "We have to justify the claim with the company that insured him."

"What company is that?"

"Uh, Metropolitan Life," I said.

"That's odd," he said. "About a week after Kipper died, I got a visit from a claim adjuster from Prudential. He said they had insured Kipper."

He looked at me steadily. I think I was blushing. I know I couldn't meet his stare. I may have hung my head.

"You don't mind if I call you Josh, do you?" Stilton asked gently.

"No, I don't mind."

"You can call me Perce," he offered. "You see, Josh, two years in this business, or even four years, aren't enough to learn how to be a really good liar. The first rule is only lie when you have to. And when you do lie, keep it as close to the truth as you can and keep it simple. Don't try to scam it up. If you do, you're sure to get in trouble. When I asked you if your interest was the insurance, you should have said yes and let it go at that. I probably would have swallowed it. It's logical that lawyers handling the estate would be interested in a dead man's insurance. But then you started fumbling around with justifying the claim, and I knew you were jiving me."

"And I didn't even know the name of the company," I said sadly.

He put his head back and laughed, so loudly that the other diners turned to look.

"Oh, Josh," he said. "I don't know what company insured Kipper either. No claim adjuster ever visited me. I just said Prudential to catch your reaction. When you collapsed, I knew you were running a game on me."

Our food was served, and we didn't speak until the waiter left the table.

"Then you won't tell me about the Kipper case?" I said.

"Why the hell not?" he said, astonished. "I'm willing to cooperate. It's all a matter of public record. That boss of yours, the guy with the fish, could probably even get a look at the file if he pushed hard enough. How's the steak-and-kidney pie?"

"Delicious," I said. "I'm really enjoying it. Is your roast beef rare enough?"

"If it was any rarer, it would still be breathing. All right, now let me tell you about the Kipper thing. I went over the file before I left the office, just to refresh my memory. Here's what happened . . ."

As he spoke, and ate steadily, I glanced up frequently from my own plate to look at him.

I guessed him to be in his early fifties. He was about six feet tall, with narrow shoulders and hips. Very willowy. He was dressed with great care and polish, in a double-breasted blue pinstripe that closed at the lower button with a graceful sweep of a wide lapel. His shirt was a snowy white broadcloth with a short, button-down collar. He wore a polka-dot bow tie with butterfly wings. He had a gold watch on one wrist and a gold chain identification bracelet on the other. If he was wearing a gun—and I presumed he was—it certainly didn't show.

His color was hard to distinguish in the dim light, but I judged it to be a dark brown with a reddish tinge, not quite cordovan but almost. His hair was jet black and lay flat on his skull in closely cropped waves. His hands were long, fingernails manicured.

His eyes were set deep and wide apart. His nose was somewhat splayed, and his thick lips turned outward. High cheekbones, like an Indian. He had a massive jaw, almost square, and a surprisingly thick, corded neck. Small ears were flat to his head.

I would not call him a handsome man, but his features were pleasant enough. He looked amused, assured, and competent. When he was pondering, or trying to find the right word or phrase, he had the habit of putting his tongue inside his cheek, bulging it.

I think I was most impressed by the cool elegance of the man, totally unlike what I envisioned a New York police detective would be. He really looked like a business executive or a confident salesman. I thought this might be an image he projected deliberately, as an aid in his work.

"Let's start with the time sequence," he began. "This happened on January 24, a Wednesday. The first call went to 911, and was logged in at 3:06. That's P.M., the afternoon. A squad car was dispatched from the One-Nine Precinct and arrived at the premises at 3:14. Not bad, huh? Two cops in the squad. They took a look at what had happened and called their precinct. This was at 3:21. Everyone was doing their jobs. We don't fuck up *all* the time, you know. The squeal came to the Homicide Zone where I work at 3:29. It didn't sound like a homicide, but these things have to be checked out. I arrived at the scene at 3:43. I was with my partner, Detective Lou Emandola. We no sooner got in the place when the loot called and pulled Lou away. Some nut was holding hostages in a supermarket over on First Avenue, and they were calling out the troops.

"So Lou took off and I was left alone. I mean I was the only homicide guy there. There were plenty of cops, the ambulance guys, the Medical Examiner, the lab truck technicians, a photographer, and so forth. A real mob scene. I questioned the witnesses then, but they were so spooked I didn't get much out of them, so I left. I went back again that evening, and I went twice more. Also, I talked to neighbors, the ME who did the PM, your Mr. Tabatchnick, Kipper's doctor, and Kipper's sons. After all this, it looked like an open-and-shut suicide, and that's how we closed it out. Any questions so far?"

"Who made the first call to 911?" I asked.

"I'm getting to that," Stilton said. "I've hardly started yet." He paused, drained his tankard of ale, and looked at me. I called the waiter and ordered two more. The detective continued:

"Here's the story . . . First of all, you've got to understand the scene of the crime, although there was no crime, unless you want to call suicide a crime. Anyway, that townhouse is a palace. Huge? You wouldn't believe. You could sleep half of East Harlem in there. It's six floors high and it's got a double-basement, plus an elevator. I never did get around to counting all the rooms. Thirty at least, I'd guess, and most of them empty. I mean they were furnished, but no one lived in them. A terrible waste of space. The top floor, the sixth, is one big room fronting on the street. It runs halfway back the depth of the building. The rear half is an open terrace. The room up front is used for parties. It has a big-screen TV, bar, hi-fi equipment, movie projector, and so forth. The rear terrace has plants, and trees, and outdoor furniture. Sol Kipper took his dive from that terrace. It has a wall around it thirty-eight inches high—I measured it—but that wouldn't be hard to climb over, even for an old guy like Kipper."

He paused again to take a swallow of his new ale. I used the interruption to dig into my dinner. I had been so engrossed in his story, not wanting to miss anything, that I had neglected to eat. He had finished most of his beef and was now whittling scraps off the rib, handling his knife with the dexterity of a surgeon.

"The nearer the bone," he said, "the sweeter the meat. All right, here's what I found out: At 2:30 P.M. on that Wednesday, there were five people in the townhouse. Sol Kipper, his wife, Tippi—she's a looker, that one—and the three servants. Sol and Tippi were in their bedroom, the master bedroom on the fifth floor. The servants were on the ground floor, in and around the kitchen. Tippi was expecting a guest, a Protestant minister named Knurr. He was a frequent visitor, and he was usually served a drink or two and some little sandwiches. The servants were setting up for him.

"Mrs. Kipper came downstairs about ten minutes to three to make sure everything was ready for the Reverend Knurr. Now we got four people downstairs, and only Sol Kipper upstairs—right? In the back of the town-house there's a patio. Most of it is paved with tiles, and there's aluminum furniture out there: a cocktail table, chairs, an umbrella table—stuff like that. Farther in the rear is a small garden: a tree, shrubs, flowers in the summer, and so on. But most of the patio is paved with tiles. There are two ways of getting out there: one door through the kitchen, and French doors from the dining room.

"A few minutes after three, the four people hear a tremendous crash and a big, heavy thump on the patio. They all hear it. They rush to the kitchen door and look out, and there's Sol Kipper. He was squashed on the tiles. That was the thump they heard. And one of his legs had hit the umbrella table, dented it, and overturned it. That was the crash they heard. They ran out, took one look, and knew Sol Kipper was as dead as a mackerel—no joke intended."

Stilton finished his dinner. He pushed back his chair, crossed his knees, and adjusted his trouser crease. He lighted a cigarette and sipped at what remained of his ale.

"Instant hysteria," he went on. "Mrs. Kipper fainted, the cook started bawling, and right about then the front doorbell rang."

"The guest?" I said.

"Right. Reverend Knurr. The butler went to the front door, let him in, and screamed out what had just happened. I gather this Knurr more or less took charge then. He's a put-together guy. He called 911, and he got Tippi Kipper revived, and the others quieted down. By the time I got there, they had found the suicide note. How about some coffee?"

"Sure," I said. "Dessert? A brandy?"

"A brandy would be fine," he said. "May I suggest Rémy Martin?"

So I ordered two of those and a pot of coffee.

"I've got a lot of questions," I said tentatively.

"Thought you might have," he said. "Shoot."

"Are you sure there were only four people in the house besides Sol Kipper?"

"Absolutely. We searched every room when we got there. No one. And the witnesses swear no one left."

"The time sequence you gave me of what happened—did you get that from Mrs. Kipper?"

"And the servants. And Reverend Knurr. All their stories matched within a minute or so. None of them sounded rehearsed. And if you're figuring maybe they were all in on it together, forget it. Why should they all gang up on the old guy? According to the servants, he treated them just right. A fast man with a buck. The wife says the marriage was happy. None of them showed any signs of a struggle. No scratches or bruises—nothing like that. And if one of them, or all of them wanted to get rid of Sol, it would have been a lot easier to slip something into one of his pill bottles. You should have seen his medicine chest. He had a drugstore up there. And, of course, there was the suicide note. In his writing."

"Do you remember what it said?" I asked. "Exactly?"

"It was addressed to his wife. It said: 'Dear Tippi. Please forgive me. I am sorry for all the trouble I've caused.' It was signed 'Sol.' "

I sighed. Our coffee and cognac arrived, and we sat a moment in silence, then sipped the Rémy Martin. Very different from the California brand I drank at home.

"Did you check the wall on the terrace?"

Stilton looked at me without expression.

"You're all right," he said. "Dolly did a good job on you. Yes, we checked the terrace wall. It's a roughly finished cement painted pink. There were scrape marks on the top where Kipper went over. And there were crumbs of pink cement on the toes of his shoes, stuck in the welt. Any more questions?"

"No," I said, depressed. "Maybe I'll think of some later, but I can't think of any now. So it was closed out as a suicide?"

"Did we have any choice?" Detective Percy Stilton said almost angrily. "We have a zillion unsolved homicides to work on. I mean, out-and-out, definite homicides. How much time can we spend on a case that looks like a suicide no matter how you slice it? So we closed the Kipper file."

I took a swallow of brandy, larger than I should have, and choked on it. Stilton looked at me amusedly.

"Go down the wrong way?" he said.

I nodded. "And this suicide," I said, still gasping, "it sticks in my throat, too. Perce, how do you feel about it? I mean personally? Are you absolutely satisfied in your own mind that Sol Kipper committed suicide?"

He stared at me, bulging his cheek with his tongue, as if trying to make up his mind. Then he poured himself more coffee.

"It's trade-off time," he said softly.

"What?" I said. "I don't understand."

"A trade-off," he said. "Between you and me. You tell me what your interest is in how Sol Kipper died and I'll tell you what I personally think."

I took a deep breath and wished I had never asked Mr. Tabatchnick if I could tell the detective about Marty Reape. Tabatchnick had definitely said no. If I hadn't asked, I could have traded with Stilton without a qualm. I pondered where my loyalty lay. I decided.

"It means my job," I said, "if any of this gets out."

"No one will hear it from me," Stilton said.

"All right," I said. "I trust you. I've got to trust you. Here it is . . ."

And I told him all about Marty Reape. Everything, beginning with his telephone call to Mr. Tabatchnick, then my call to him, my meeting with him, what he said and what I said, the decision to meet his price, and how he died Wednesday evening under the wheels of a subway train.

Stilton listened closely to this recital, not changing expression. But he never took his eyes off me, and I noticed he chain-smoked while I was speaking. He was about to light another when I finished. He broke the cigarette in two and threw it down.

"I smoke too damned much," he said disgustedly.

"What do you think?" I said, leaning forward eagerly, "about Marty Reape?"

"Your boss could be right," he said slowly. "Reape could have been a cheap chiseler trying to pull a con."

"But he was killed!" I said vehemently.

"Was he?" Stilton said. "You don't know that. And even if he was, that doesn't prove he had the information he claimed. Maybe he tried to pull his little scam on some other people who aren't as civilized as you and your boss, and they stepped on him."

"But he knew the size of the Kipper estate," I argued. "Doesn't that prove he knew the family or had some dealings with them?"

"Maybe," he said. "And maybe Sol Kipper told someone what's in his will, and maybe that someone told Marty Reape. Or maybe Reape just made a lucky guess about the size of the estate."

It was very important to me to convince this professional detective that my suspicions about the death of Sol Kipper had merit and justified further investigation. So, having come this far in betraying Mr. Tabatchnick's trust, I felt I might as well go all the way.

"There's another thing," I said. "On the morning of the day Sol Kipper died, he called Tabatchnick and set up an appointment. He said he wanted to change his will."

Stilton had been turning his cigarette lighter over and over in his long fingers, looking down at it. Now he stopped his fiddling and raised his eyes slowly until he was staring at me.

"Jesus," he breathed, "the plot thickens."

"All right," I said, sitting back. "That's my trade. Now let's have yours. Do you really think Sol Kipper committed suicide?"

He didn't hesitate.

"That's the official verdict," he said, "and the file is closed. But there were things about it that bugged me from the start. Little things. Not enough to justify calling it homicide, but things, three, to be exact, that just didn't set right with me. First of all, committing suicide by jumping from the sixth floor is far from a sure thing. You can jump from a higher place than that and still survive.

"That's why most leapers go higher up than six stories. They want to kill themselves, but they don't want to take the chance of being crippled for life. This Kipper owned a textile company. He was semiretired, his sons run the business, but Kipper went there for a few hours three or four days a week. The office is on the thirty-fourth floor of a building in the garment center. He could have gone out a window there and they'd have had to pick him up with a blotter."

"Perce, what actually killed him when he went off the sixth-floor terrace?"

"He landed on his head. Crushed his skull. All right, it could happen from six floors. He could also break both arms and legs, have internal injuries, and still live. That could happen, too. It couldn't happen from thirty-four floors. That's the first thing that bothered me: a suicide from the sixth floor. It's like trying to blow your brains out with a BB gun.

"The second thing was this: When jumpers go out, from a window, ledge, balcony, whatever, they usually drop straight down. I mean, they just take one giant step out into space. They don't really leap. Practically all the jumpers I've seen have landed within six feet of the side of the building. They usually squash on the sidewalk. When they go from a really high place, maybe their bodies start to windmill. But even then they hit the sidewalk or, at the most, crush in the top of a parked car. But I've never seen any who were more than, say, six or seven feet out from the side of the building. Kipper's body was almost ten feet away."

I puzzled that out.

"Perce, you mean someone threw him over?"

"Who? There were four other people in that house—remember? Kipper weighed about one-sixty. None of the women could have lifted him over that terrace wall and thrown him so he landed ten feet from the side of the building. And the only man, the butler, is so fat it's all he can do to stand up. Maybe Kipper just took a flying leap."

"An old man like that?"

"It's possible," he said stubbornly. "The third thing is even flimsier than the first two. It's that suicide note. It said: 'I am sorry for all the trouble I've caused.' Get it? *'Caused.'* Please forgive me for something I've done. That note sounds to me like he's referring to something he did in the past, not something he was planning to do in a few minutes. Also, the note is perfectly legible, written in straight lines with a steady hand. Not the kind of hand-writing you'd expect from a guy so mixed up in his skull that a few minutes later he was going to take a high dive from his terrace. But again, it's possible. I told you it's flimsy. All the things that bug me are flimsy."

"I don't think they are," I said hotly. "I think they're important."

He gave me a half-smile, looked at his watch, and began to stow away his cigarette case and lighter.

"Listen," I said desperately, "where do we go from here?"

"Beats me," he said.

"Can't you—" I began.

"Reopen the case?" he said. "No way can I do that on the evidence we've got. If I even suggested it, my loot would have me committed. You're the Chief Investigator—so investigate."

"But I don't know where to start," I burst out. "I know I should talk to the Kipper family and servants, but I don't know what excuse I can give them for asking questions."

"Tell them what you told me," he advised. "Say you're collecting infor-mation to justify the insurance claim. They'll buy it."

"You didn't," I pointed out.

"They're not as cynical as I am," he said, grinning. "They'll believe what you tell them. Just remember what I said about lying. Keep it simple; don't try to gussy it up. While you're nosing around, I'll see what I can find out about how Marty Reape died. From what you told me, it's probably been closed as an accident—but you never know. Keep in touch. If anything turns up, you can always reach me at that number you've got or leave a message and I'll call back. Can I call you at Tabatchnick and whatever?"

I thought about that.

"Better not, Perce," I said. "I'd rather keep our, uh, relationship confidential."

"Sure," he said. "I understand."

"I'll give you my home phone number. I'm in almost every night."

"That'll do fine."

He copied my number in a little notebook he carried. It was black pinseal with gold corners. Like all his possessions, it looked smart and expensive.

I paid the bill, left a tip, and we walked toward the door.

"I still don't think it was a suicide," I said.

"You may be right," he said mildly. "But thinking something and proving it are entirely different. As any cop can tell you."

We put on our coats and moved out onto the sidewalk. He was wearing a navy blue chesterfield and a black homburg. A dandy.

"Thanks for the dinner, Josh," he said. "Real good."

"My pleasure," I said.

"Which way you going?" he asked.

"Ninth Avenue. I'll catch a downtown bus. I live in Chelsea."

"I'll walk you over," he said, and we headed westward.

"Don't give up on this one, Josh," he said, suddenly earnest. "I can't do it; my plate is full. But I've got the feeling someone is jerking us around, and I don't like it."

"I'm not going to give up," I said.

"Good," he said. "And thanks for meeting with me and filling me in."

"Listen," he added hesitantly, "if what you think turns out to be right, and someone snuffed Sol Kipper and pushed Marty Reape under a train, then they're not nice people—you know? So be careful."

"Oh sure. I will be."

"You carry a piece?" he asked suddenly.

It was a few seconds before I understood what he meant.

"Oh no," I said. "I don't believe in violence."

He sighed deeply.

"And a little child shall lead them," he said. "Good night, Josh."

8

•

I AWOKE THE NEXT MORNING BRIGHT-EYED AND BUSHY-TAILED.
Although Detective Stilton had insisted that all we had were unsubstantiated
suspicions, what he had told me confirmed my belief that the death of Sol
Kipper was not a suicide. And I was convinced that Stilton, despite his cautious disclaimers, felt the same way.

It had snowed slightly overnight; there was a light, powdery dusting on
sidewalks and cars. But it was melting rapidly as the new sun warmed. The
sky was azure; the air sparkled. It suited my mood perfectly, and as I set out
for my appointment with the missing Yale Stonehouse's doctor, I took the
weather as an augury of a successful day.

Dr. Stolowitz had his offices on the street floor of a yellow brick apartment
house that towered over neighboring brownstones. I arrived at 8:15. His
receptionist was tall, lanky, with a mobcap of frizzy red curls. Her thin features
seemed set in a permanent expression of discontent. I noticed her extremely
long, carmined fingernails and a bracelet of a dozen charms on her bony wrist
that jangled when she moved. She greeted me with something less than
warmth.

"Joshua Bigg to see Dr. Stolowitz," I said, smiling hopefully.

"You're early," she snapped. "Sit down and wait."

So I sat down and waited, coat and hat on my lap.

At precisely 8:25, another nurse came out—a little one this time—and
beckoned to me.

"Doctor will see you now," she said.

The man standing behind the littered desk was of medium height, stocky,
with a heavy belly bulging in front of his short white jacket. He was wearing
rimless spectacles with thick lenses that gave him a popeyed look. He was
smoking a black cigar; the air was rancid with fumes.

"Good morning, Doctor," I said.

"Five minutes," he snapped. "No more."

"I understand that, sir."

"Just what is your connection with Yale Stonehouse?" he demanded.

"As I explained to you on the phone," I said patiently, "I'm investigating
the Professor's disappearance."

"Are you a private detective?" he said suspiciously.

"No, sir," I said. "I am employed by the Professor's attorneys. You may check with Mrs. Stonehouse if you wish."

He growled.

He hadn't asked me to be seated.

"All right," he said. "Ask your questions. I may answer and I may not."

"Could you tell me when Professor Stonehouse consulted you, sir?"

He picked up a file from his desk and flipped through it rapidly, the cigar still clenched between his teeth.

"Seven times during October and November of last year. Do you want the exact dates of those visits?"

"No, sir, that won't be necessary. But Mrs. Stonehouse told me his illness started late last summer."

"So?"

"But he did not consult you until October?"

"I just told you that," he said peevishly.

"Could you tell me if Professor Stonehouse consulted any other physician prior to coming to you?"

"Now how the hell would I know that?"

"He mentioned no prior treatment?"

"He did not."

"Doctor," I said, "I don't expect you to tell me the nature of the Professor's illness, but—"

"Damned right I won't," he interrupted.

"But could you tell me if the Professor's illness, if untreated, would have proved fatal?"

His eyes flickered. Then he ducked his head, looked down, began to grind out his cigar butt in an enormous crystal ashtray. When he spoke, his voice was surprisingly mild.

"An ingrown toenail can be fatal if untreated."

"But when Professor Stonehouse stopped coming to see you, was he cured?"

"He was recovering," he said, the ill-tempered note coming back into his voice.

"Was his illness contagious?"

"What's this?" he said angrily, "a game of Twenty Questions?"

"I am not asking you to tell me the specific illness, Doctor," I said. "Just whether or not it was contagious."

He looked at me shrewdly.

"No, it was not a venereal disease," he said. "That's what you're really asking, isn't it?"

"Yes, sir. What would you say was the Professor's general mental attitude?"

"A difficult, cantankerous patient." (Talk about the pot calling the kettle black!) "But if you mean did he exhibit any symptoms of mental disability not connected with his illness, the answer is no, he did not."

He didn't realize what he had just revealed: that there were symptoms of mental disorder connected to the Professor's ailment.

"Did he ever, in any way, give you a hint of indication that he intended to desert his wife and family?"

"He did not."

"Would you characterize your patient's illness as a disease, Doctor?"

He looked at the clock on the wall.

"Your five minutes are up," he said. "Goodbye, Mr. Bigg."

I put on my coat in the outer office. Three or four people were waiting to see the doctor.

"Thank you very much," I said to the receptionist, giving her my best little-boy smile. It doesn't always work, but this time it did; she thawed.

"He's a bear, isn't he?" she whispered.

"Worse," I whispered back. "Is he always like that?"

She rolled her eyes. "Always," she said. "Listen, may I ask you a personal question?"

"Five feet, three and three-eighths inches," I said, and waved goodbye.

I stopped at the first phone booth I came to and called the office. I left a message for Thelma Potts telling her that I was engaged in outside work and would call later to let her know when I'd be in.

I took the Broadway bus down to 49th Street and walked over to the decrepit building where Marty Reape had his office. His name was still listed on the lobby directory, but when I got to the ninth floor, the door to Room 910 was open and a bearded man in stained painter's overalls was busy scraping with a razor blade at the outside of the frosted glass panel. Half of the legend, MARTIN REAPE: PRIVATE INVESTIGATIONS, was already gone.

I stood behind the painter and peeked through the open door. The room was totally bare. No desk, chair, file cabinet, or anything else. Just stained walls, dust-encrusted window, cracked linoleum on the floor.

"Want something?" the painter demanded.

"Do you know what happened to the furniture in this office?"

"Ask the manager," he said.

"Is this office for rent?"

"Ask the manager."

"And where will I find the manager?"

"Downstairs."

"Could you tell me his name?"

He didn't answer.

In the rear of the lobby was a steel door with a square of cardboard taped to it: MANAGER'S OFFICE. I opened the door with some effort. A flight of steel steps led steeply downward. I descended cautiously, hanging on to the gritty banister. A gloomy, cement-lined corridor stretched away to the back of the building. The ceiling was a maze of pipes and ducts. At the end of this tunnel was a scarred wooden door. I pushed in.

It was like going into a prisoner's cell. The only thing lacking was bars. Cement ceiling, walls, floor. No windows. The furniture looked like tenants' discards. There were two people in that cubbyhole. A very attractive Oriental girl clattered away at an ancient Underwood, pausing occasionally to brush her long black hair away from her face. A small brown man sat behind the larger desk, talking rapidly on the telephone in a language I could not identify. There was a neat brass plate on his desk: CLARENCE NG, MANAGER.

Neither of the occupants had looked at me when I entered. I waited patiently. Mr. Ng rattled on in his incomprehensible language, then suddenly switched to English.

"The same to you, schmuck!" he screamed, and banged down the phone. Then he looked at me.

"Ah, may I be of service, sir?" he asked softly.

"Perhaps you can help me," I said. "I'm looking for Martin Reape, Room 910. But his office is completely empty."

"Ah," he said. "Mr. Reape is no longer with us."

"Oh?" I said. "Well, could you tell me where he moved?"

"Ah," Mr. Ng said. "Mr. Reape did not move. Mr. Reape is dead."

"Dead?" I cried. "Good heavens! When did this happen?"

"Two days ago. Mr. Reape fell under a subway train. You were, ah, a friend of his?"

"A client," I said. "This is terrible. He had some very important papers belonging to me. Do you know what happened to his files?"

"His, ah, widow," Mr. Ng said. "She arrived yesterday and removed everything."

"And you let her?" I exclaimed.

The manager turned his palms upward and shrugged. "A man's widow is entitled to his possessions."

"But are you certain it *was* the widow?"

"Ah, Mr. Reape owed two months' back rent," Mr. Ng said smoothly. "The woman paid."

"That doesn't prove she was actually his widow," I said angrily.

The Oriental girl stopped typing, but didn't turn to look at me.

"It was her all right," she said. "I saw them together in the lobby once, and he introduced us."

"You see?" Mr. Ng said triumphantly. "The widow."

"Do you happen to have her phone number?"

"Ah, regrettably no."

"The home address, then?"

"Also, no."

"Surely it was on his lease?" I said.

"No lease," Mr. Ng said. "We rent by the month."

"Well, I'll look it up in the phone book, then," I said.

Mr. Ng paused for just a second. "Ah, no," he said sadly. "Mr. Reape had an unlisted number."

I thanked Mr. Ng and left. I walked through that dank tunnel and was almost at the stairway when I heard a shouted "Hey, you!" I turned. The Oriental girl was running toward me.

"Ten bucks," she said.

"What?" I said.

"Ten bucks," she repeated. "For the Reapes' address."

She plucked the bill from my fingers and was already flying back down the tunnel.

"It's in the phone book," she called.

I had little doubt but that Mr. Ng would get his share of the money.

I had to walk two blocks before I could find a Manhattan telephone directory. I opened it with some trepidation, fearing that I had been twice gulled. But it was there: the 49th Street office and another on 93rd Street.

I took an uptown bus on Eighth Avenue, still smarting at the ease with which I and my money had been parted.

The Reapes lived on Sorry Street, between Somber and Gaunt. The tallest building on the block appeared to be a welfare hotel; most of the brownstones had been converted to rooming houses, with drawn shades at the windows instead of curtains; and the basement stores all had front windows tangled with dusty ivy, drooping ferns, and scrawny philodendrons. Graffiti was everywhere, much of it in Spanish. I wondered what *puta* meant.

The Reapes' house was one of the better buildings, a three-story structure of gray stone, now greasy and chipped. There were few remnants of its former elegance: a fancily carved lintel, beveled glass in the door panels, an ornate brass escutcheon around the knob.

I pushed the bell alongside M. REAPE and waited. Nothing. I tried again. Still no answer. I tried once more, with no result. When I went back down to the sidewalk, an elderly lady with blue hair was just starting up the steps. She was laden down with two heavy bags of groceries.

"May I help you, ma'am?" I asked.

She looked at me, frightened and suspicious.

"Just up to the front door," I said. "Then I'll go away."

"Thank you, young man," she said faintly.

I carried her bags up and left them beside the inner door. When I came out again, she had negotiated only three steps, pausing on each to catch her breath.

"Asthma," she said, clutching her chest. "It's bad today."

"Yes, ma'am," I said sympathetically. "I wonder if you—"

"Sometime it's like a knife," she said, wheezing. "Cuts right through me."

"I'm sure it's painful," I said. "I'm looking for—"

"Didn't get a wink of sleep last night," she said. "Cough, cough, cough."

"Mrs. Reape," I said desperately. "Mrs. Martin Reape. She lives here. I'm trying to find her."

The suspicion returned.

"What do you want with her?" she demanded. "You're too sawed off to be a cop."

"I'm not a cop," I assured her. "It's about her husband's insurance."

That hooked her.

"Did he leave much?" she whispered.

"I'm sorry, but I can't tell you that. I'm sure you understand. But I think Mrs. Reape will be happy to see me."

"Well . . ." the old lady said, sniffing, "she ain't exactly hurting from what I hear. Unless I miss my guess, young man, you'll find her at The Dirty Shame. That's a saloon on the next block toward Broadway."

The Dirty Shame was one long, reasonably clean room, with a few tables and booths in the rear. But most of the action was at the bar. When I entered there was no doubt that a party was in progress. There must have been at least forty men and women in attendance.

The air was clotted with smoke and the din was continuous—shouts, laughter, snatches of song—competing with a jukebox playing a loud Irish jig. Two bartenders were hustling and the bartop was awash. A beefy, red-faced celebrant clamped an arm about my shoulders.

"Friend of Marty's?" he bawled.

"Well, actually, I'm—"

"Step right up," he shouted, thrusting me toward the bar. "Blanche is picking up the tab."

A glass of beer was handed to me over the heads of the mob. My new friend slapped me heartily on the back; half my beer splashed out. Then he turned away to welcome another newcomer.

It was a raffish crew that filled The Dirty Shame. They all seemed to know each other. I moved slowly through the throng, looking for the widow.

I finally found her, surrounded by a circle of mourners who were trying to remember the words of "When Irish Eyes Are Smiling." She was a suety woman with a mass of carroty hair, heavily made up. She wore a white mustache of beer foam. Her widow's weeds were of some thin, shiny material, straining at the seams and cut low enough in front to reveal the exuberant swell of a freckled bosom which had been heavily powdered.

"Mrs. Reape," I said, when she paused for breath, "I'd like to express my—"

"What?" she yelled, leaning down to me from her stool. "I can't hear you with all this fucking noise."

"I want to tell you how sorry I—"

"Sure, sure," she said, patting my shoulder. "Very nice. Hey, your glass is empty! Tim, let's have a biggie over here! You a friend of Marty's?"

"Well, actually," I said, "I was a client."

Perhaps I imagined it, but I thought her smile froze and became a grimace, wet lips stretched to reveal teeth too perfect to be her own.

"A client?" she repeated. "Well, he didn't have many of those."

She started to turn away, and I went on with a rush, fearing to lose her.

"Mrs. Reape," I said hurriedly, "I went up to your husband's office, but everything's been—"

"Yeah," she said casually, "I cleaned the place out. He had a bunch of junk there, but I got a couple of bucks from the ragpicker."

"What about his records?" I asked. "The files? He had some important paper of mine."

"No kidding?" she said, her eyes widening. "Jeez, I'm real sorry about that. I threw all that stuff out in the gobbidge last night."

"Then it might be in the garbage cans in front of your house?" I said helpfully.

"Nah," she said, not looking at me. "They collected early this morning. All that paper's in the city insinuator by now."

"Do you remember if—"

But then I was shouldered out of the way.

I left my stein on a table and slipped away from The Dirty Shame as inconspicuously as I could.

I put in a call to the office. Yetta Apatoff said no one had been looking for me.

"Josh, did you see that sweater I happened to mention to you?" she inquired.

I told her I had seen it and thought it lovely.

"It's so revealing," she said, giggling. "I mean, it doesn't leave *anything* to the imagination."

"Oh, I wouldn't say that," I said. "Exactly. Listen. Yetta, I won't be in until after lunch in case anyone wants me. Okay?"

"Sure, Josh," she said. "And green's really my color—don't you think?"

I finally got off the phone.

I arrived on West 74th Street with time to spare. I took up my station across the street from the office of Dr. Morris Stolowitz and down the block toward Columbus Avenue. The redheaded receptionist came out a few minutes after noon. I scurried across the street and walked directly toward her.

I lifted my head with a start of surprise. Then I stopped. I tipped my hat.

"We meet again," I said, smiling.

She stopped, too, and looked down at me.

"Why, it's Mr. Bigg," she said. "Listen, I hope you weren't insulted this morning. You know, when I asked you a personal question?"

"I wasn't insulted," I assured her. "People are always commenting on my size. In a way, it's an advantage; they never forget my name."

"Mine neither," she said. "Not that my name is so great. People are always making jokes about it."

"What is your name?"

"Peacock, Ardis Peacock."

"Ardis Peacock? Why, that's a lovely name. The peacock is a beautiful bird."

"Yeah," she said, "with a big tail. You live around here?"

"No, just taking care of business. I'm getting hungry and thought I'd grab something to eat. Any good places in the neighborhood?"

"Lots of them," she said. "There's a McDonald's on 71st Street and Amsterdam, and a Bagel Nosh on the east side of Broadway. But I usually go around the corner to Columbus Avenue. There's all kinds of restaurants there—Mexican, Indian, Chinese, whatever."

"Sounds good," I said. "Mind if I walk along with you?"

"Be my guest," she said.

We started back toward Columbus.

"Ever think of getting elevator shoes?" she asked me.

"Oh, I've thought of it, but they'd only give me another inch or so. Not enough to make a real difference. What I need is stilts."

"Yeah," she said, "it's a shame. I mean, here I am a long drink of water, and I think it's a drag. You should be taller and I should be shorter. But what the hell."

"You carry it well," I told her. "You've got good posture, and you're slender. Like a model."

"Yeah?" she said, pleased. "No kidding?"

We ate at the Cherry Restaurant on Columbus Avenue between 75th and 76th streets. Ardis ordered shrimp with lobster sauce. I had ham and scrambled eggs with home fries.

"That boss of yours gave me a hard time this morning," I said casually.

"Don't let it get you down," she advised. "He gives everyone a hard time. Me, especially. Sometimes I think he's got the hots for me."

"Shows he's got more sense than I thought," I said.

"Hey, *hey!*" she said. She turned and pushed me playfully. Almost off the stool.

"What was it all about?" she asked. "That Stonehouse guy you mentioned on the phone?"

"That's the one," I said. "He was seeing Dr. Stolowitz in October and November of last year. Remember him?"

"Do I ever!" she said. "What a crab. Always complaining about something. He had to wait, or the office was too cold, or the Doc's cigars were stinking up the place. He was a real pain in the you know where."

"Stolowitz should be happy he wasn't sued," I said. "This Stonehouse is always suing someone."

"Is he suing you?"

"Not me personally," I said, "but maybe the outfit I work for." Then I launched into the scenario I had contrived. "I'm an investigator with the claims division of a health insurance company. Isley Insurance. Ever hear of us?"

"No," she said, "can't say that I have."

"It's a small outfit," I admitted. "We specialize in health coverage for the faculties of educational institutions. You know: schools, colleges, universities—like that. Group policies. Well, this Stonehouse used to teach at New York University. He's retired now, but he's still covered because he pays the premiums personally. You follow?"

"Oh sure," she said. "I make out all the Medicare forms for Stolowitz. It's a pain in the you know what."

"I agree," I said. "Well, you know when you fill out those forms, you have to state the nature of the illness—right?"

"Of course," she said. "Always."

"Well, this Stonehouse refuses to state what was wrong with him. He says it's his own business, and asking him to reveal it is an invasion of his privacy."

"He's whacko!" she burst out.

"Absolutely," I said. "No doubt about it. He refused to tell Medicare and they rejected his claim. Now he's suing them."

"Suing Medicare?" she said, aghast. "That's the U.S. Government!"

"Correct," I said. "And that's who he's suing. Can you believe it?"

"Unreal," she said.

"Anyway, he also made a claim against my company, Isley Insurance. But he won't tell us what his illness was either. So naturally his claim was rejected, and now he's suing us. We'll fight it, of course, but it'll drag out and cost a lot of money. For lawyers and all. So we'd rather settle with him. How about some dessert?"

"Chocolate sundae," she said promptly.

I had another cup of coffee, and after she demolished her sundae, I lighted her cigarette. I always carry matches for other people's cigarettes.

"So I went to Stolowitz," I continued, "figuring maybe he'd tell me what Stonehouse was suffering from. But no soap."

"That's right," she said. "It's confidential between him and the patients. Me and the nurses, we got very strict orders not to talk about the patients' records. As if anyone *wanted* to. That place gives me the creeps. It's no fun working around sick people all the time, I can tell you."

The waiter dropped separate checks in front of us. I grabbed up both.

"Here," Ardis Peacock said halfheartedly, "let's go Dutch."

"No way," I said indignantly. "I asked you to lunch."

We walked slowly back toward her office.

"This Stonehouse thing has me stumped," I said, shaking my head. "All we need is the nature of the illness he had. Then we can process his claim. Now I guess we'll have to defend ourselves against his lawsuit."

I glanced sideways at her, but she hadn't picked up on it.

"I wish there was some way of getting a look at his file," I said fretfully. "That's all it would take. We don't need the file; just a look to see what his ailment was."

That did it. She took hold of my arm.

"It would save your company a lot of money?" she said in a low voice. "Just to find out why Stonehouse was sick?"

"That's right," I said. "That's all we need."

"Would it be like, you know, confidential?"

"I'd be the only one who would know where it came from," I said. "My company doesn't care where or how I get the information, just as long as I get it."

We walked a few more steps in silence.

"Would you pay for it?" she asked hesitantly. "I mean, I'm into those files all the time. It's part of my job."

She wanted $500. I told her my company just wouldn't go above $100, ignoring inflation and how people must live somehow.

"All you want to know is what his sickness was—right?"

"Right," I said.

"Okay," she said. "A hundred. Now?"

"Fifty now and fifty when you get me the information."

"All right." She smiled, as I discreetly slipped her the first payment. "You'll be hearing from me." With a cheery wave, Ardis strode off to work, and I hailed a cab for the East Side.

9

•

I STOOD ON THE SIDEWALK IN FRONT OF THE KIPPER TOWNHOUSE on East 82nd Street, between Fifth and Madison. To the west I could see the Metropolitan Museum. To the east the street stretched away in an imposing façade of townhouses, embassies, consulates, and prestigious foundations. No garbage collection problems on this block. No litter. No graffiti.

The Kipper home was an impressive structure of gray stone with an entrance framed in wrought iron. There were large bow windows on the third and fourth floors, the glass curved. I wondered what it cost to replace a pane. Above the sixth floor was a heavily ornamented cornice, and above that was a mansard roof of tarnished copper.

A narrow alleyway separated the Kipper building from the next building east. It had an iron gate and bore a small polished brass sign: DELIVERIES. I wondered if I would be sent around to the tradespeople's entrance.

Despite Detective Stilton's advice, I had decided not to attempt to claim that my visit was concerned with Sol Kipper's insurance. That would surely be handled by investigators from the insurance company involved, and I had neither the documentation nor expertise to carry off the impersonation successfully.

I rang the bell outside the iron grille door. The man who opened the carved oaken inner door almost filled the frame. He was immense, one of the fattest men I have ever seen. He was neither white nor black, but a shade of beige. He looked like the Michelin tire man, or one of those inflated rubber dolls which, when pushed over, bobs upright again. But I didn't think he'd bob upright from a knockdown. It would require a derrick.

"Yes, sah?" he inquired. His voice was soft, liquid, with the lilt of the West Indies.

"My name is Joshua Bigg," I said. "I am employed by Tabatchnick, Orsini, Reilly, and Teitelbaum, who are Mrs. Kipper's attorneys. I would appreciate a few minutes of Mrs. Kipper's time, if she is at home."

He stared at me with metallic eyes that bulged like the bowls of demitasse spoons. Apparently he decided I was not a potential assassin or terrorist, for . . .

"Please to wait, sah," he said. "A moment . . ."

He closed the door and I waited outside in the cold. True to his word, he was back in a moment and stepped down the short stairway to unlatch the iron door. He had unexpectedly dainty hands and feet, and moved in a slow, fastidious way as if he found physical action vulgar.

He led me into a tiled entrance hall that rose two floors and was large enough to accommodate a circus troupe. A wide floating staircase curved up to the left. There were double doors on both sides and a corridor that led to the rear of the house. The hall was decorated with live trees in pots and an oversized marble Cupid, his arrow aimed at me.

The butler took my hat and coat; I hung on to my briefcase. He then led me to the left, knocked once, opened the doors, and ushered me in.

This was obviously not the formal living room; more like a family room or sitting room. It was impossible to make a chamber of that size cozy or intimate, but the decorator had tried by placing chairs and tables in groups. He only succeeded in making the place look like the cardroom of a popular club. But it was cheerful enough, with bright colors, flower prints on the walls, and what to my untrained eye appeared to be an original Cézanne over the mantel.

There were two people in this cavern. As I walked toward them, the man rose to his feet, the woman remained seated, fitting a cigarette into a gold holder.

I repeated my name and those of my employers. The man shook my hand, a firm, dry grip.

"Mr. Bigg," he said. "A pleasure. I am Godfrey Knurr. This lady is Mrs. Kipper."

I set the briefcase I had been lugging all day on the floor and moved forward to light her cigarette.

"Ma'am," I murmured, "I'm happy to meet you."

"Thank you," she said, holding out a slender white hand. "Won't you sit down, Mr. Bigg? No, not there. That's Godfrey's chair."

"Oh, Tippi," he said in a bright, laughing voice. "Any chair will do. I think there are enough of them."

But I didn't take his chair. I selected one closer to the small fire in the grate and so positioned that I could look at both of them without turning.

"What a beautiful home you have, Mrs. Kipper," I said. "Breathtaking."

"More like Grand Central Station," Knurr said in his ironic way. Then he said exactly what Perce Stilton had said: "A terrible waste of space."

Mrs. Kipper made a sound, a short laugh that was almost a bark.

"You see, Mr. Bigg," she said, "Mr. Knurr is a minister, the Reverend Godfrey Knurr. He does a great deal of work with the poor, and he's hinted several times that it would be an act of Christian charity if I allowed a mob of his ragamuffins to live in my lovely home."

"Beginning with me," Knurr said solemnly, and they both laughed. I smiled politely.

"Ma'am," I said, "I hope you'll pardon me for not phoning in advance, but I was in the neighborhood on other company business and took the chance of calling on you. If you wish to confirm that I am who I claim to be, I suggest you phone Mr. Tabatchnick."

"Oh, I don't think that will be necessary," she said lazily. "How is dear Leonard?"

"Leopold, ma'am. In good health. Busy as ever."

"With that odd hobby of his? What is it—postage stamps or breeding Yorkies or something?"

"Tropical fish, ma'am," I said, passing her tests.

"Of course," she said. "Tropical fish. What a strange hobby for an attorney. You'd think he would prefer more energetic pets."

"Some of them are quite aggressive, Mrs. Kipper. Belligerent, in fact."

I was conscious of the Reverend Knurr regarding me narrowly, as if he were wondering if my words implied more than they meant. I hadn't intended them to, of course. I am not that devious.

"Well," Mrs. Kipper said, "I'm sure you didn't call to discuss Mr. Tabatchnick's fish. Just why *are* you here, Mr. Bigg?"

"It concerns your late husband's estate, ma'am," I said, and glanced toward Godfrey Knurr.

"Tippi, would you prefer I not be present?" he asked. "If it's something confidential—family matters—I can adjourn to the kitchen and gossip with Chester and Perdita for a while."

"Nonsense," she said. "I'm sure it's nothing you shouldn't hear. Mr. Bigg, Godfrey has been a close friend for many years, and has been a great help since my husband's death. You may speak freely in front of him."

"Yes, ma'am," I said submissively. "There is nothing confidential about it. At present, your attorneys are engaged in striking a tentative total value for your late husband's estate. This includes stocks, bonds, miscellaneous investments, personal property, and so forth. The purpose of this is for filing with the proper Federal and State authorities for computation of the estate tax."

"Godfrey?" she asked, looking to him.

"Yes," he said, "that's correct. Render unto Caesar what is Caesar's. In this case, Tippi, I'm afraid you're going to be unpleasantly surprised by what Caesar demands."

"Well, we'd like our computation of assets to be as accurate as possible," I continued. "It sometimes happens that the IRS and State Tax Bureau make estimates of the value of an estate that are, uh, in variance with those of the attorneys submitting the will to probate."

"You mean they're higher," Pastor Knurr said with his rueful laugh.

"Frequently," I agreed. "Naturally, as the attorneys of record, we hope to keep estate taxes to their legal minimum. I have been assigned the task of determining the value of this home, its furnishings, and your late husband's personal possessions."

Knurr settled back in his armchair. He took a pipe and tobacco pouch from the side pocket of his jacket. He began to pack the pipe bowl, poking the tobacco down with a blunt forefinger.

"This is interesting," he said. "How do you determine the value of a house like this, Mr. Bigg?"

That one was easy.

"Current market value," I said promptly. "How much you could expect to receive if it was put up for sale. Other factors would be the current property tax assessment and comparison with the value of other houses in the neighborhood. When it comes to furnishings, things get a little more complicated. We would like to base our evaluation on the original purchase cost minus depreciation—to keep the total value as low as possible, you understand—but the IRS usually insists on replacement value. And that, in these inflationary times, can sometimes be much more than the original cost."

"I should think so," Mrs. Kipper said sharply. "Why, some of my beautiful things couldn't be bought for double what I paid for them. And some simply can't be replaced at any price."

"Tippi," Knurr said, lighting his pipe with deep drags, "don't tell the tax people *that!*"

I paused, looking at him, while he got his pipe evenly lighted to his satisfaction. He used three matches in the process. His tobacco smoke smelled of fruit and wine.

The Reverend Godfrey Knurr was a few inches short of six feet. He was a stalwart man, bulging the shoulders and sleeves of his hairy tweed jacket. He wore gray flannel slacks and oxblood moccasins. A checked gingham shirt was worn without a tie, but buttoned all the way up. Still, it revealed a strong, corded neck. He had square hands with short fingers.

His hair and beard were slate-colored. The beard was not full; it was mustache and chin covering, cut straight across at the bottom. It was trimmed carefully around full, almost rosy lips. He had steady, brown, no-nonsense eyes, and a nose that was slightly bent. It was not a conventionally handsome face, but attractive in a craggy, masculine way. A lived-in face. His age, I estimated, was in the early forties, which would make him about ten years younger than Mrs. Kipper. He moved well, almost athletically, and had an erect carriage and forceful gestures.

I turned my attention back to the widow.

"My assignment," I said, "will necessitate my taking a complete inventory of the furnishings, I'm afraid. I don't expect to do that today, of course. It may take several days. I'll do my best not to inconvenience you, ma'am, and I'll try to be as unobtrusive as possible while I'm here. Today. I hope merely to make a preliminary survey, count the number of rooms, and plan how best to proceed with the inventory. Is that acceptable to you, Mrs. Kipper?"

"Damn!" she said fretfully. "I wish this was all over with."

She took another cigarette from a porcelain box on the table beside her. I sprang to my feet and rushed to light it.

"Thank you," she said, looking at me amusedly. "You're very polite. You don't smoke?"

"No, ma'am."

"Drink?"

"Occasionally," I said. "Wine mostly."

"For thy stomach's sake," Knurr rumbled.

"Would you care for a glass of wine now, Mr. Bigg?"

"Oh no, thank you, Mrs. Kipper. I'd really like to get started on my preliminary inspection."

"In a minute or two," she said. "How long have you been with Mr. Tabatchnick?"

"About six years."

"Married?"

"No, ma'am."

"No?" she said, widening her eyes theatrically. "Well, we'll have to do something about that!"

"Now, Tippi," Godfrey Knurr said, groaning, "don't start playing matchmaker again."

"What's so wrong with that?" she flashed out at him. "Sol and I were so happy together, I want everyone to be that happy."

Godfrey Knurr winked at me.

"Watch out for us, Mr. Bigg," he said with his brisk laugh. "Tippi brings them together and I marry them. It's a partnership."

"Oh, Godfrey," she murmured, "you make it all sound so—so cold-blooded."

"Cold blood—hot marriage," he said. "An ancient Greek proverb."

"Which you just made up," she said.

"That's right," he allowed equably, and now they both laughed.

"I wonder if I might—" I started.

"Well, if you won't have a drink, Mr. Bigg," the widow said, "I think the Reverend and I shall. The usual, Godfrey?"

"Please," he said.

I looked at him and I thought he shrugged a bit in resignation.

I did not believe Mrs. Kipper was being deliberately obstructive. She would let me inspect her home—in her own good time. She wanted to make it perfectly clear to me that she was mistress of this house, and her wish was law, no matter how foolish or whimsical others might think her. So I waited patiently while drinks were served.

Mrs. Kipper pushed a button at the end of a long extension cord. We waited in silence for a moment before the obese butler came stepping quietly into the room.

"Mom?" he asked.

"Drinks, Chester," she said. "The usual for the Reverend and me. Mr. Bigg isn't indulging."

"Yes, mom," he said gravely and moved out silently. For his size, he was remarkably light on his feet. His movements were almost delicate.

While he was gone, Mrs. Kipper began talking about the preview of an art exhibit at a Madison Avenue gallery she had attended the previous evening. Although she looked at me occasionally, ostensibly including me in the conversation, most of her remarks were directed to Knurr. In other words, she did not ignore me, but made little effort to treat me as other than a paid employee to whom one could be polite without being cordial. That was all right; it gave me a chance to observe the lady.

She was silver blonde, pretty in a flashy way, with her hair up and meticulously coiffed. Not a loose end or straggle. She had a really excellent, youthful figure: slender arms and smashing legs, artfully displayed by her short, sleeveless shift of buttery brown velvet. She had a small, perfect nose, and cat's eyes with a greenish tinge. Her thin lips had been cleverly made up with two shades of rouge to appear fuller.

It was a crisp face, unlined, with tight skin over prominent cheekbones. I wondered if that seamless face and perfect nose owed anything to a plastic surgeon's skill. She kept her sharp chin slightly elevated, and even when laughing she seemed to take care lest something shatter.

I thought she would make a brutal and vindictive enemy.

Chester came in with the drinks. They appeared to be a Scotch and soda for Knurr and a dry martini straight up for Mrs. Kipper. She spoke before the butler left the room.

"Chester," she said, "Mr. Bigg wishes to inspect the house, top to bottom. Will you escort him about, please? Show him anything he wishes to see?"

"Yes, mom," the butler said.

I rose hastily to my feet, gripping my briefcase.

"Mrs. Kipper," I said, "thank you for your kindness and hospitality. I appreciate your cooperation. Mr. Knurr, it's been a pleasure meeting you."

He stood up to shake my hand.

"Hope to see you again, Mr. Bigg," he said. "Good luck on your inventory."

"Thank you, sir."

I followed the mountainous bulk of Chester out of the room. He closed the doors behind us, but not before I heard the laughter, quickly hushed, of Mrs. Tippi Kipper and the Reverend Godfrey Knurr.

The butler paused in the entrance hall and turned to face me.

"You wish to see all the rooms, sah?"

"Please. I'm going to be taking an inventory of the furnishings. Not today, but during several visits. So you'll be seeing a lot of me. I'll try not to be too much of a nuisance."

He looked at me, puzzled.

"To figure the value of the estate," I explained. "For taxes."

"Ah, yes," the big man said, nodding. "Many beautiful, expensive things. You shall see. This way, sah."

He led the way along the corridor at the rear of the hall. He stopped before a conventional door and swung it open. Within was a sliding steel gate, and beyond that a small elevator. Chester opened the gate, allowed me to enter, then followed me in. He slid the gate closed; the outer door closed automatically, and I immediately became conscious of his sweet cologne. The butler pressed a button, a light came on in the elevator, and we began to ascend, slowly.

"How long have you been with the Kippers?" I asked curiously.

"Seventeen years, sah."

"Then you knew the first Mrs. Kipper?"

"I did indeed, sah. A lovely lady. Things have—"

But then he stopped and said nothing more, staring straight ahead at the steel gate.

The elevator halted abruptly. Chester pushed the gate aside and opened the outer door. He stepped out and held the door open for me.

"The sixth floor, sah."

I looked around.

"The main staircase doesn't come up this high?"

"It does not, sah. The main staircase stops on the fifth floor. But there is a back staircase, smaller, that comes all the way up. Also the elevator, of course."

I opened my briefcase, took out my notebook, and prepared to make what I hoped would appear to be official jottings.

This was the party room Detective Stilton had described to me, a single chamber that occupied the front half of the building. I noted bistro tables and chairs, a giant TV set, hi-fi equipment, a clear central area obviously used for dancing, a movie projector, etc.

"This room is used for entertaining?" I asked.

"Quite so, sah."

"And those two doors?"

"That one to the rear staircase, and that one to a lavatory," he said, pronouncing it la*vo*ratree.

"Mrs. Kipper does a lot of entertaining?"

"Not since Mr. Kipper's passing, sah. But she has said she will now begin again. A buffet dinner is planned for next week."

I wondered if I detected a note of disapproval in his voice, but when I glanced at him, he was staring into space with those opaque eyes, expressionless as a blind man's.

I walked toward the rear of the room. Two sets of French doors opened onto the terrace. I could see the potted plants, trees, and outdoor furniture Stilton had mentioned. I tried the knob of one of the doors. It was locked.

"Mrs. Kipper has ordered these doors to be kept locked, sah," Chester said in sepulchral tones. "Since the accident."

"Could I take a quick look outside, please? Just for a moment?"

He hesitated, then said, "As you wish, sah."

He had a heavy ring of keys attached to a thin chain fastened to his belt. He selected a brass key with no fumbling about and unlocked the door. He followed me out onto the terrace. I wandered around, making quick notes: *4 otdr tbls, 8 mtl chrs, cktl tbl, 2 chse lngs, 2 endtbls, plnts, trees, etc.*

I walked to the rear of the terrace. The cement wall had recently been repainted.

"This is where the accident happened?" I asked.

He nodded dumbly. I thought he had paled, but it may have been the hard outdoor sunlight on his face.

I leaned over cautiously and looked down. I didn't care what Perce had said, it seemed to me I was a long way up, and no one could survive a fall from that height.

Directly below was the ground-floor patio, with more outdoor furniture, and in the rear a small garden now browned and desolate. The patio was paved with tiles, as described. I could see where Sol Kipper had landed, because bright new tiles had replaced those broken when he hit.

I think that was the first time I really comprehended what I was doing. I was not merely trying to solve an abstract puzzle; I was trying to determine how a human being had met his death. That withered garden, those smashed tiles, the drop through empty space—now it all seemed real to me: the dark figure pinwheeling down, arms and legs outspread, wind whipping his clothing, ground rushing up, sickening impact . . .

"Did he cry out?" I asked in a low voice.

"No, sah," Chester said in a voice as quiet as mine. "We heard nothing until the poor mon hit."

I shivered.

"Cold out here," I said. "Let's go in."

Apparently Chester didn't enjoy using stairs, up or down, for we rode the elevator to the fifth floor.

"On this floor," Chester said, "we have the master bedroom, with two bathrooms, and Mrs. Kipper's dressing room. Also, the maid has her apartment on this floor, the better to be able to assist Mrs. Kipper. In addition, Mr. Kipper had a small private office on this floor. As you can see, sah, the main staircase stops here."

We went through all the rooms, or at least looked in at them, with me busily making notes. I was particularly interested in the master bedroom, an enormous chamber with furniture in cream-colored French provincial decorated with painted vines and flowers. Two bathrooms were connected to the bedroom, and another door led to Mrs. Kipper's dressing room.

This was a squarish area with a full-length, three-way mirror; a chaise longue covered in pink satin; a littered dresser, the mirror surrounded by electric bulbs; an antique phone on an ormolu-mounted table; and a brass serving cart with a small selection of bottles, glasses, and bar accessories. Two walls of the room were louvered folding doors.

"Mrs. Kipper's wardrobe, sah," Chester said. "Do you wish to see?"

"Oh no," I said hastily. "That won't be necessary."

"A hundred pairs of shoes," he remarked dryly.

There were two unused rooms on the fifth floor. One, Chester explained, had originally been the nursery, and the other had been the children's playroom.

"Before your time, I imagine," I said.

"Yes, sah," Chester said gravely. "My father was in service with the Kipper family at that time."

I looked at him with new interest.

"What is your last name, Chester?" I asked.

"Heavens," he said.

I thought at first that was an exclamation of surprise, but then he said, "Chester Heavens, sah," and I knew that we had something else in common.

"The maid is Perdita Schug," he continued, "and Mrs. Bertha Neckin is our cook and housekeeper. That is our permanent staff, sah. We three have our apartments here. In addition, the house is serviced by a twice-a-week cleaning crew and a janitor who comes in for a few hours each morning for garbage removal, maintenance chores, and jobs of that nature. Temporary staff are employed as needed for special occasions: large dinners, parties, dances, and so forth."

"Thank you, Chester," I said. Then, to convince him I was not interested in information or gossip extraneous to my assignment, I said, "The furnishings in the apartments of the permanent staff—are they owned by Mrs. Kipper?"

"Oh yes, sah. The furniture is, yes. We have a few personal possessions. Pictures, radios, bric-a-brac—things of that sort."

"I understand," I said, making quick notes.

We descended via elevator to the fourth floor. This level, Chester told me, was totally uninhabited. But all the rooms were furnished, all the doors unlocked. There were four bedrooms (each with its own bathroom) that had been used by the Kipper children. In addition, there were two large guest bedrooms, also with baths. There was also a sewing room, a completely equipped darkroom that had been used by one of the Kipper sons with an interest in photography, and one room that seemed designed and furnished with no particular activity in mind.

"What is this room?" I asked.

"Just a room, sah," Chester said casually, and I found myself repeating silently what Detective Stilton and Godfrey Knurr had already said: "A terrible waste of space."

The third floor appeared to be a little more lived-in. It included a comfortable, wood-paneled library-den which, Chester said, had frequently been used by the late Sol Kipper to entertain old friends at pinochle or gin rummy games, or just to have a brandy and cigar after dinner.

Also on this floor was the apartment of the cook-housekeeper, Mrs. Bertha Neckin. It was a snug suite with bright Indian rugs on polished parquet floors and a lot of chintz. Framed photographs were everywhere, mostly of children.

There were two more guest bedrooms on the third floor and one long chamber across the front of the house illuminated by two bow windows. This was called the "summer room" and was furnished with white wicker, circus and travel posters on the walls and, at one end, a little stage for the production of puppet shows, an enthusiasm, Chester told me, of all the Kipper children when they were young. I liked that room.

The second floor consisted of a large, mirrored ballroom, with a raised platform at one end for a band or entertainment. Straight chairs lined the walls, and there were connecting bathrooms and a small dressing room for the ladies.

Chester Heavens had his apartment on this floor. It consisted of a bedroom, small study, and bathroom. The furnishings revealed no more than the man himself. Everything was clean, neat, squared away. Almost precise. No photographs. Few books. A radio and a small, portable TV set. The paintings on the walls were empty landscapes.

"Very nice," I said politely.

Then I asked the butler if the house was ever filled, if all those bedrooms were ever used. He said they had been, when the first Mrs. Kipper was alive, during the holiday season. Then all the Kipper children and *their* children and sometimes cousins, aunts, and uncles came to spend a week or longer. There were big dinners, dances, parties. There was confusion, noise, and laughter.

"But not after Mr. Kipper remarried?" I asked.

"No, sah," he said, his face expressionless. "The family no longer gathers."

On the ground floor, in addition to the entrance hall and sitting room which I had already seen, were the formal living room, dining room, kitchen and pantry. I took a quick look through the French doors of the dining room at the patio. It looked even more forlorn that it had from six floors up.

Then Chester Heavens led me back along the corridor to the kitchen and pantry area. I had thought the kitchen in the Stonehouse apartment was large; this one was tremendous, with a floor area that must have measured 15 × 25 feet. It looked like a hotel or restaurant kitchen, with stainless steel fixtures and appliances, and utensils of copper and cast iron hanging from overhead racks.

There were four doors leading from the kitchen. One was the entrance from the corridor which we used. A swinging door led to the dining room. A rear door, glass paneled, allowed access to the patio. The fourth door was heavily bolted and chained, and had a peephole. Chester told me it opened onto the alleyway and was used for deliveries.

"Mrs. Neckin is off today," the butler said in his soft voice, "but perhaps you would care to meet the other member of our staff."

He led the way into the pantry. It was large enough to accommodate a square oak table and four high-backed oak chairs. Seated in one of the chairs, leafing idly through the afternoon *Post,* was a vibrant young lady who looked up pertly as we entered.

"Mr. Bigg," Chester said formally, "may I present our maid, Miss Perdita Schug. Perdita, this gentleman is Mr. Joshua Bigg. Stand up, girl, when you're meeting a guest of this house."

She rose lazily to her feet, smiling at me.

"How do you do, Miss Schug," I said.

"I do all right," she said saucily. "And you can call me Perdita. Everyone else does. Except Chester here, and I won't tell you what *he* calls me!"

He looked at her with the first emotion I had seen him exhibit—disgust.

"Watch your tongue, girl," he said wrathfully, and in reply she stuck out her tongue at him.

He turned away. I nodded at Perdita, smiling, and started to follow the butler. Then a buzzer sounded and I heard a sharp click. Chester looked up at the monitor mounted on the wall. It had two rows of indicators in a glass case. When a servant was summoned from anywhere in the house, the monitor buzzed and an indicator clicked up to show a white square. A label was pasted on the glass above each square showing in which room the button had been pushed. I counted the labels. Thirty-two.

"They'll want their tea now, I expect," Chester said. "Excuse me a moment, Mr. Bigg. Get the tray ready, Perdita."

I was standing in the pantry entrance. There was plenty of room, but Perdita brushed closely by.

"Pardon me," she said blithely, "but duty calls."

She took a plate from the refrigerator and whisked away the damp cloth covering it. The sandwiches were crustless and about the size of postage stamps. She put the plate on a doily on a large silver serving tray, then added a silver teapot, china cups and saucers, spoons, silver creamer and sugar bowl. She turned the light up under a teakettle on the range and, while the water was coming to a boil, dumped four teaspoons of tea into the pot, making no effort to measure it exactly. All her movements were deft and sure.

Chester returned and examined the tray.

"Napkins," he snapped.

Perdita opened the cupboard and added two small, pink linen napkins to the tray.

"Mr. Bigg," the butler said to me, "Mrs. Kipper asked if you were still in the house, and when I said you were, she requested that I inquire if you would care for a cup of tea or coffee."

"That's very kind of her," I said. "Coffee would be fine. If it isn't too much trouble."

"No trouble, sah," he assured me. "Perdita, make enough for all of us. I'll be back as soon as I've served."

The copper kettle was steaming now, and the butler filled the teapot. Then he lifted the tray up before him with both hands. He had to carry it extended at some distance; his stomach intruded. He moved down the corridor at a stately pace.

Perdita was no more than an inch or two taller than I. A dark, flashing button of a woman. Shiny black hair cut as short and impudently as a flapper's. Sparkling eyes. Her long tongue kept darting between small white teeth and wet lips. I watched her as she assembled our belowstairs treat.

She was formed like a miniature Venus. Almost as plump as that marble Cupid in the entrance hall. Creamy skin. In a steamy fantasy, I saw her wearing an abbreviated satin skirt, tiny lace apron and cap, pumps, a shocking décolletage—the classic French maid from the pages of *La Vie Parisiènne*. She frightened me with her animal energy, but I was attracted to her.

She came into the pantry bringing a plate of macaroons. She fell into the chair across the table from me. She put an elbow on the tabletop, cupped her chin in a palm. She stared at me, eyes glittering.

"You're cute," she said.

"Thank you, Perdita," I said, trying to laugh. "You're very kind."

"I am not kind," she protested. "I'm just telling you the truth. I always say what I feel—straight out. Don't you?"

"Well . . . not always," I said judiciously. "Sometimes that's difficult to do without hurting people."

"What do you think of me—straight out?"

I was rescued by the return of Chester Heavens. He sat down heavily at the oak table. He ate three macaroons swiftly: one, two, three.

"The coffee is ready," he said. "Perdita, will you do the honors?"

She rose, passed behind his chair. She stroked the back of his sleekly combed hair. He reached up to knock her hand away, but she was already in the kitchen.

"Please excuse the girl, sah," he said to me. "She has a certain wildness of spirit."

Perdita returned with the percolator and we sat having our coffee and macaroons. I wondered how to bring them around to a discussion of Sol Kipper's plunge.

"Sad times, sah," Chester said, wagging his big head dolefully. "Mr. Kipper was the best of marsters."

"A doll," Perdita said.

"It was a tragedy," I said. "I don't know the details, but it must have been very distressing to all of you."

Then they started reliving those horror-filled moments beginning when they heard the crash and thump on the patio. What they told I had already learned from Percy Stilton. Like him, I was convinced they were telling as much of the truth as they knew.

"And there were only the four of you in the house when it happened?" I asked.

"Five, sah," Chester said. "Counting poor Mr. Kipper."

"The janitor wasn't here then?"

"Oh no, sah. It was in the afternoon. He comes only in the morning."

"Terrible," I said. "What an awful experience. And Mrs. Kipper fainted, you say?"

"Just fell away," Perdita said, nodding. "Just crumpled right up. And Mrs. Neckin started screeching."

"Weeping, girl," the butler said reprovingly.

"Whatever," the maid said. "She was making enough noise."

"You all must have been terribly upset," I said, "when you heard the noise, rushed out, and saw him."

The butler sighed.

"A bad few moments, sah," he said. "Girl, are there more macaroons? If not, there is a pecan ring. Bring that. Yes, sah, it was a bad few moments.

The marster was dead, Mrs. Kipper had fainted, Mrs. Neckin was wailing—it was a trouble to know what to do."

"But then the Reverend Knurr rang the bell?" I prompted.

"Exactly, sah. That gentleman waiting outside was our salvation. He took charge, Mr. Bigg. Called the police department, revived Mrs. Kipper, moved us all into the sitting room and served us brandy. I don't know what we would have done without him."

"He seems very capable," I said, my attention wandering because Perdita had brought the pecan ring to the table. She was standing next to me, cutting it into wedges. Her soft hip was pressed against my arm.

"He is that, sah," Chester said, selecting the wedge with the most pecans on top and shoving it into his mouth. "A fine gentleman."

"Oh fine," Perdita said, giggling. "Just fine!"

"Watch your tongue, girl," he said warningly again, and again she stuck out her tongue at him. It seemed to be a ritual.

"I gather the Reverend is a frequent visitor," I said musingly, pouring myself another half-cup of coffee. "Where is his church?"

"He does not have a regular parish, sah," the butler said. "He provides personal counseling and works with the poor young in Greenwich Village. Street gangs and such."

"But he *is* a frequent visitor?" I repeated.

"Oh yes. For several years." Here the butler leaned close to me and whispered, "I do believe Mrs. Kipper is now taking religious instruction, sah. From Reverend Knurr. Since the death of her husband."

"The shock," I said.

"The shock," he agreed, nodding. "For then it was brought home to her the shortness of life on this earth, and the eternity of life everlasting. And only those who seek the love of the Great God Jehovah shall earn the blessing thereof. Yea, it is written that only from suffering and turmoil of the spirit shall we earn true redemption and forgiveness for our sins."

Then I knew what *his* passion was.

The monitor buzzer sounded again and I welcomed it. I stood up.

"I really must be going," I said. "Chester, I appreciate your invaluable assistance. As I told you, I shall be back again. I will call first. If it is inconvenient for you or Mrs. Kipper, please tell me and I'll schedule another time."

Perdita preceded me along the corridor to the entrance hall. I watched her move. She helped me on with my coat.

"Bundle up," she said, pulling my collar tight. "Keep warm."

"Yes," I said. "Thank you."

"Thursday is my day off," she said.

"Oh?"

"We all have our private phones," she said. "I'm in the book. Schug. S-c-h-u-g."

Back home that evening in my favorite chair, eating a spaghetti

Mug-o-Lunch, I scribbled notes to add to the Kipper file and jotted a rough report of my conversations with Dr. Stolowitz and Ardis Peacock.

I was interrupted in my work by a phone call. I was delighted to hear the voice of Detective Percy Stilton. His calling proved he was sincere in his promise to cooperate. I was almost effusive in my greetings.

"Whoa," he said. "Slow down. I got nothing great to tell you. I checked on Marty Reape. Like I figured, they closed it out as an accident. No witnesses came forward to say otherwise. What did they expect? In this town, no one wants to get involved. One interesting thing though: he had a sheet. Nothing heavy or they would have pulled his PI license. But he was charged at various and sundry times. Simple assault; charges dropped. Attempted extortion; charges dropped. Trespassing; no record of disposal. That tell you anything?"

"No," I said.

"Well, I asked around," Perce said. "This Reape apparently was a cruddy character. But they didn't find any great sums of money on the corpse. And they didn't find anything that looked like legal evidence of any kind. And that's about it. You got anything?"

I told him how I had gone to Reape's office looking for the evidence, left out how I had been conned by Mr. Ng; I described the mourners at The Dirty Shame. He laughed.

I told him I thought that someone had got to Blanche Reape before me, because she had money to pay the office rent and pick up the bill for the funeral party.

"Well . . . yes," Stilton said cautiously. "That listens. I can buy that. If the case was still open, I'd go over and lean on the lady and see if I could find out where those greenies came from. But I can't, Josh. She sounds like a wise bimbo, and if I throw my weight around, she might squeal. Then it gets back to the brass, and my loot wants to know what I'm doing working on a closed case. Then my ass is out on a branch, just hanging there. You understand?"

"Of course I understand," I said, and told him I didn't think there was anything we could do about Mrs. Reape other than rifling her apartment in hopes that she still had the evidence that got her husband killed. And burglary was out of the question.

Then I told Stilton all about my afternoon visit to the Kipper townhouse. He listened carefully, never interrupting until I mentioned that I had asked Chester Heavens if Sol Kipper had cried out while he was falling, and the butler said they hadn't heard a thing until the awful sounds of the body thumping to earth.

"Son of a bitch," Percy said again.

"What's wrong?" I asked.

"Nothing," he said, "except that I should have asked that question and didn't. You're okay, Josh."

I was pleased. I finished my report and we agreed I had discovered nothing that shed any additional light.

"Except that religious angle," Perce said. "Knurr being a minister and that fat butler sounding like a religious fanatic."

"What does that mean?" I asked.

"Haven't the slightest," he admitted cheerfully. "But it's interesting. You're going to keep on with it, Josh?"

"Oh sure," I said. "I'm going back there as often as I can. I want to talk to the cook-housekeeper, and I'd like to look around a little more. How do you like my cover story?"

"Fantastic," he said. "You're becoming a hell of a liar."

"Thank you," I said faintly.

10

•

I SLEPT LATE ON SATURDAY MORNING AND WOKE TO FIND IT WAS snowing: big fat flakes that were piling up rapidly. But the radio reported it would taper off by noon, and temperatures were expected to rise to the upper 30s.

I had a large breakfast and spent the day in the apartment, housecleaning and thinking about the cases.

In the early evening I showered and, in honor of the occasion, shaved. I dressed in a white oxford cloth shirt with a maroon rep tie, a navy blue blazer, gray flannel slacks, and polished black moccasins. Now I looked like a prep school student—but I was used to that.

I was tucking a white handkerchief into my breast pocket when someone knocked on my front door.

"Who is it?" I called before unlocking.

"Finkel," came the reply.

I opened the door, smiling, and motioned Adolph Finkel inside. He was the fourth-floor tenant who lived across the hall from Madame Zora Kadinsky.

"Uh, good evening, Bigg," he said. "I guess we're supposed to help Shank get downstairs."

I glanced at my watch.

"We have a few minutes," I said. "How about a drink to give us strength?"

"Well . . . don't go to any bother." But he let me press some Scotch on him.

"Happy days," I said.

"You're all dressed up," he said sadly. "I worked today and didn't have time to change."

"You look fine," I assured him.

He looked down at himself.

"The manager told me I shouldn't wear brown shoes with a blue suit," he said. "The manager said it doesn't look right for a shoe salesman to wear brown shoes with a blue suit. Of course, it's a ladies' shoestore where I work . . . but still. What do you think, Bigg?"

"Maybe black shoes would look better."

"I could go up and change," he said earnestly. "I have a pair of black shoes."

"Oh, don't bother," I said. "I doubt if anyone will notice."

He was tall, six-one at least, and exceedingly thin, with rounded shoulders, bent neck, head pecked forward like a hungry bird. He had a wild mass of kinky, mouse-colored hair hanging over a low brow. His complexion was palely blotched, washed-out. He had hurt eyes.

Apology was in his voice and in his manner. There is an ancient story of two men condemned to be shot to death. One spits in the face of his executioner. His companion reproves him, saying, "Don't make trouble." That was Adolph Finkel.

"Uh, do you think the party will be in Mrs. Hufnagel's apartment," he asked me, "or in Cleo's?"

"I really don't know. Probably Mrs. Hufnagel's."

"Uh, I suppose you go out with a lot of women?"

I laughed. "What gave you that idea, Finkel? No, I don't go out with a lot of women." Madame Kadinsky had been right. He was trying to discover if I had any interest in Cleo Hufnagel. "There is one," I said. "A girl at my office. She's lovely."

He beamed—or tried to. It was a mistake; it revealed his teeth.

Finkel and I took Captain Shank downstairs in his wheelchair. It wasn't as difficult as I feared it would be; we just tilted the chair back onto its big wheels and let it roll down, a step at a time. Finkel gripped the handles in back and I went ahead, trying to lift the footrest sufficiently to cushion the jars as the chair bumped down. It would have been a lot easier without Shank's roared commands. He carried wine I had bought.

When we arrived at the second-floor hallway, the three women, having heard our pounding descent, were waiting for us. I had been in error; the door to Cleo Hufnagel's apartment was open, and it was obvious the party would be held there.

"You said—" Finkel started to whisper.

"Forget it," I said, determined to stay as far away from him as I could.

I handed the wine to Mrs. Hufnagel and told her the bottles were contributions from Shank and myself.

"Isn't that nice!" she said. "Just look at this, Cleo. Look at what Mr. Bigg brought!"

"And the Captain," I reminded her.

" 'allo, 'allo, Joshy and Captain Shink!" Madame Zora Kadinsky caroled.

"Shank," he said.

Cleo's apartment, obviously furnished to her mother's taste, was dull, overstuffed, suffocating. The great Hufnagel Plot was being forwarded.

The party was a punch-and-cookies affair. I was glad I'd had a ham sandwich late in the afternoon. The punch tasted like fruit juice.

"What the hell is this?" asked Captain Shank. "No kick. Dump about half the muscatel into it."

I did so, and in a while I stole upstairs and got vodka and brandy to add to it. The guests had been stiffish, and forcing themselves to try to match the abundant party styles of Mrs. Hufnagel and Mme. Kadinsky. But less than an hour after our arrival things were brightening up.

Mme. Kadinsky sang "Ah, Sweet Mystery of Life" and other suboperatic selections. The Captain bellowed and pounded the arm of his wheelchair. Urged by Madame Kadinsky and her mother, Cleo and I sedately danced to "Stardust" rendered on an upright piano by Madame K. Finkel showed signs of cutting in, but Mrs. Hufnagel grappled him away to dance with her.

In time things progressed to a jig by Mrs. Hufnagel, skirts held high to reveal thick support hose, and a final maudlin rendering of "Auld Lang Syne." A very morose Finkel and I had great trouble getting Bramwell Shank back upstairs.

I was too keyed up to attempt to sleep immediately, so I sat in the darkness of the living room, dressed for bed, staring into the cold fireplace. It was, perhaps, almost 1:30 A.M., and I was dozing happily, trying to summon the strength to rise and go to bed, when I heard a light knocking at my door, a timid tapping.

"Who is it?" I whispered hoarsely.

A moment of silence, then: "Cleo. Cleo Hufnagel."

I unlocked and unchained the door. She was still wearing her party clothes.

"I was just going to bed," I said in a voice that sounded to me unnecessarily shrill.

"I just wanted to talk to you for a minute," she said.

"Uh, sure," I said, and ushered her in. She sat in my favorite armchair. I sat opposite her. I sat primly upright, my pajamaed knees together, my robe drawn tightly.

"First of all," she said in a low voice, "I want to thank you for what you did. The party was my mother's idea. I thought it would be horrible. And it was, until you helped. Then it turned out to be fun."

I made a gesture.

"Don't thank me," I said. "It was the punch."

She smiled wanly. "Whatever," she said, "I really enjoyed it."

"I did, too," I said. "It *was* fun. I'm glad you invited me."

"It was Mother's idea," she repeated, then drew a deep breath. "You see, I'm almost thirty years old, and she's afraid that I . . ."

Her voice faded away.

"Yes," I said gently, "I understand."

She looked up at me hopefully.

"Do you?" she said. Then: "Of course you do. You're intelligent. You know what she's doing. Trying to do. I wanted you to know that it was none of my doing. I'm sure it must be very embarrassing to you and I wanted to apologize. For my mother."

"Oh, Cleo," I said. "Listen, is it all right if I call you Cleo and you call me Josh?"

She nodded silently.

"Well, Cleo . . . sure, I know what your mother's doing. Trying to do. But is it so awful? I don't blame you and I don't blame her."

"It's just so—so vulgar!" she burst out. "And I wanted you to know that it wasn't my idea, that I'd never do anything like that."

"I know," I said consolingly. "It must be very distressing for you. But don't condemn your mother, Cleo. She only wants what she thinks is best for you."

"I know that."

"She loves you and wants you to be happy."

"I know that, too."

"So, would it be so terrible if we just let her do her thing? I mean, now that you and I know, it wouldn't be so awful to let her think she's helping you—would it?"

"I guess not."

We sat in silence awhile, not looking at each other.

"What about Adolph Finkel?" I asked finally.

"Oh no," she said instantly. "No. Did you see that he was wearing one brown shoe and one black shoe tonight?"

"No," I said, "I didn't notice."

"But it's not only that," she said. "It's everything."

"Is there anyone else you're interested in?" I asked. "I don't mean to pry, but we're being so frank . . ."

"No," she said. "No one else."

This was said in tones so empty, so devoid of hope, that my breath caught. I looked at her. She really was a tall, slender beauty, almost Spanish in her reserve and mystery. It was criminal that she should be unwanted.

"Listen, Cleo," I said desperately, "this doesn't mean that we can't be friends. Does it?"

She raised luminous eyes to look at me steadily. I couldn't see any implication there. Just deep, deep eyes, unfathomable.

"I'd like that," she said, smiling at last. "To be friends."

The whole thing lightened.

"We can learn some new dance steps. The Peabody."

"The Maxixe," she said and laughed a little.

Just before she slipped out into the hallway, she bent down to kiss my cheek. A little peck.

"Thank you," she said softly.

By the time I had rechained and relocked the door, I was wiped out, tottering. I didn't want to think, or even feel. I just wanted sleep, to repair my punished body and dull a surfeit of impressions, memories, conjectures.

I fell into bed. I was halfway into a deep, dreamless slumber when my phone rang.

"Lo?"

"Josh?"

"Yes. Who is this?"

"Ardis. Ardis Peacock. Remember?"

I came suddenly awake.

"Of course I remember," I said heartily. "How are you, Ardis?"

"Where have you been?" she demanded. "I been calling all night."

"Uh, I had a late date."

"You scamp, you!" she said. "Listen, I got what you wanted on Stonehouse."

"Wonderful!" I said. "What was his illness?"

"Do I get the other fifty bucks?"

"Of course you do. What was it?"

"You'll never guess," she said.

"What *was* it?" I implored.

"Arsenic poisoning," she said.

PART TWO

1

•

I WAS WAITING TO SEE MR. IGNATZ TEITELBAUM ON MONDAY morning, loitering outside his office and gossiping with Ada Mondora. She stared at me calculatingly.

"I don't know what to do," she said.

"About what?" I asked innocently.

"About you," she said. "And Yetta Apatoff. And Hamish Hooter."

"Oh," I said. "That." With a shamed, sinking feeling to learn that my intimate affairs were a matter of public knowledge.

"There's an office pool," she said. "Didn't you know?"

I shook my head.

"You put up a dollar," she explained, "on who marries Yetta—you or Hooter. Right now the betting is about evenly divided, so all you can win is another dollar."

"Who are you betting on?" I asked her.

She looked at me narrowly.

"I don't know," she said. "I haven't made up my mind. Are you serious about her, Josh?"

"Sure," I said.

"Uh-huh," she said. "We shall see what we shall see."

The door of Mr. Teitelbaum's office opened and Hamish Hooter exited, carrying a heavy ledger.

He looked at me, then looked at Ada Mondora, then strode away. Wordless.

"Mr. Personality," Ada said. "You can go in now, Josh."

He looked smaller than ever. He looked like a deflated football, the leather grained and wrinkled. He sat motionless behind that big desk, sharp eyes following me as I entered and approached. He jerked his chin toward an armchair. I sat down.

"Report?" he said, half-question and half-command.

"Mr. Teitelbaum," I started, "about this Stonehouse business . . . I hope you'll approve an expenditure of a hundred dollars. For confidential information."

"What information?"

"For a period of about six months, ending a month prior to his disappearance, Professor Stonehouse was suffering from arsenic poisoning."

If I was expecting a reaction, I was disappointed; there was none.

"Sir, the information was obtained in such a manner that the firm's name will not be connected with it. I believe it is valid. The Professor was a victim of arsenic poisoning beginning in late summer of last year. Finally the symptoms became so extreme that he consulted a physician. After a series of tests, the correct diagnosis was made."

"You know all this?" he asked. "For a fact?"

"I'm extrapolating," I admitted. "From information received from several sources. After the Professor became aware of what was going on, he apparently took steps to end the poisoning. In any event, he recovered. He was in reasonably good health at the time of his disappearance."

He began to swing slowly back and forth in his swivel chair, turning his head slightly each time he swung to keep me in view.

"You think he was being deliberately poisoned, Mr. Bigg?"

"Yes, sir."

"By a member of his family?"

"Or his household, sir. There are two servants. I don't see how else it could have been done. It's my impression that he rarely dined out. If he was ingesting arsenic, he had to get it in his own home."

"No one else in the household became ill?"

"No, sir, not to my knowledge. It's something I'll have to check out."

He thought about this a long time.

"Ugly," he said finally. There was no disgust in his voice, no note of disappointment in the conduct of the human race. It was just a judicial opinion: "Ugly."

"Yes, sir."

"What would be the motive?" he asked. "Presuming what you believe is true, why would anyone in the Stonehouse family wish to poison him?"

"That I don't know, sir. Perhaps it had something to do with the will. The missing will. Mr. Teitelbaum, can a person draw up his own will?"

He stared at me.

"A holographic will?" he said. "In the handwriting of the testator? Properly drawn and properly witnessed? Yes, it would be valid. With several caveats. A husband, for instance, could not totally disinherit his wife. A testator could not make bequests contrary to public policy. To finance the assassination of a president, for example. And so forth. There are other requirements best left to the expertise of an attorney. But a simple will composed by the testator could be legal."

"With what you know about Professor Stonehouse, sir, do you think he was capable of drawing up such a document?"

He didn't hesitate.

"Yes," he said. "He would be capable. In fact, it would be likely, considering the kind of man he was. You think that's what he did?"

"I just don't know," I admitted. "It's certainly possible. Did you ask Mrs. Stonehouse if her husband had dealings with any other attorneys?"

"I asked," he said, nodding. "She said she knew of none. That doesn't necessarily mean he didn't, of course. He was a very secretive man. Mr. Bigg, I find this whole matter increasingly disturbing. I told you I feared Professor Stonehouse was dead. I had nothing to base that belief on other than a feeling, instinct, a lifetime of dealing with the weaknesses of very fallible human beings. Your news that Professor Stonehouse was the victim of poisoning only confirms that belief." He paused. "We have both used the term 'victim.' You do not suppose, do you, that the poisoning could have been accidental?"

"I don't think so, sir." We sat awhile in silence. "Mr. Teitelbaum," I said, "do you want me to continue the investigation?"

"Yes," he said, in such a low voice that it came out a faint "Ssss."

"You don't feel the matter of the arsenic poisoning should be reported to the police?"

He roused, a little, and sat up straighter in his chair.

"No, not as yet. Continue with your inquiries."

I walked down to the main floor, hoping to have a moment to chat with Yetta Apatoff. But Mr. Orsini was just coming through the main entrance, the door held ajar for him by a worshipful aide, and two more bobbing along in his wake.

"Josh," he cried, grabbing my arm. "I've got a new one you'll love!"

He pulled me close. His aides clustered around, twittering with eagerness.

"This very short man is sitting in a bar," Orsini said, "and down at the other end he sees this great big gorgeous blonde by herself. Get the picture?"

When it was over I stumbled back to my office, called Ardis, and asked her to meet me on 74th and Amsterdam in twenty minutes, about 1:45. Next I rang up the Stonehouse residence and asked if I could come by at 2:00 P.M., to talk to the maid, Olga Eklund, and to pick up a photograph of Professor Stonehouse to be used on reward posters. This was a ruse to get into the house again. I spoke to Glynis Stonehouse; she told me that she and her mother would be happy to see me.

I grabbed a gyro and a Coke on my way to meet Ardis. She was on the northwest corner, waiting for me.

"Thank God! You're on time! I had one of the nurses cover for me, but if Stolowitz calls in and I'm not at my desk, he'll go crazy."

"Thank you, Ardis," I said in a low voice, handing her an envelope. "A big help."

"Anytime," she said, whisking the envelope out of sight. "You're in the neighborhood, give me a call. We'll have lunch—or whatever."

"I'll do that," I said.

I walked south on Central Park West to the Stonehouse apartment house and went through the business of identifying myself to the man behind the desk.

The door to 17-B was opened by a Valkyrie. She lacked only a horned helmet. This was undoubtedly Olga Eklund. She was almost a foot taller than I, broad in the shoulders and hips, with long, sinewy arms and legs. Her head seemed no wider than her strong neck, and beneath her black uniform I imagined a hard torso, muscle on muscle, and tight skin flushed with health.

I had fantasized flaxen tresses. They existed, but had been woven into a single braid, thick as a hawser, and this plait had been wound around and around atop her head, giving her a gleaming crown that added another six inches to her impressive height. The eyes, as I had fancied, were a deep-sea blue, the whites as chalky as milk. She wore no makeup, but the full lips were blooming, the complexion a porcelainized cream.

She gave such an impression of bursting good health, of strength and vitality, that it made me shrink just to look at her. She seemed of a different species, someone visiting from Planet 4X-5-6-Gb, to demonstrate to us earthlings our sad insufficiencies.

"Mr. Bigg," she asked in the sultry, throbbing voice that had conjured up all those exciting images when I had heard it on the phone.

"Yes," I said. "You must be Miss Eklund."

"Yah," she said. "Hat? Coat?"

She hung my things away in the hall closet. I followed her down the long corridor. She moved with a powerful, measured tramp. Beneath the skirt, rounded calves bunched and smoothed. She had the musculature of a trapeze artist, marble under suede. I was happy she hadn't offered to shake hands.

Mrs. Ula Stonehouse and Glynis were waiting for me in the living room. There was a tea service on one of the small cocktail tables, and at their urging I accepted a cup of tea from the efficient Olga Eklund.

"I'm sorry I have no news to report," I told mother and daughter. "I have discovered nothing new bearing on the Professor's disappearance."

"Mother said you asked about Father's health," Glynis said. "His illness last year. Did you speak to his doctor?"

She was curled into one corner of the long couch, her splendid legs tucked up under her.

"Yes, I spoke to Dr. Stolowitz," I said, addressing both of them. "He wouldn't reveal the exact nature of the illness, but I gathered it was some kind of flu or virus. Tell me, was anyone else in the family ill at the same time the Professor was sick?"

"Let me think," Mrs. Stonehouse said, cocking her head. "That was last year. Oh yes. I had a cold that lasted and lasted. And poor Effie was sniffling for at least a week. Glynis, were you sick?"

"Probably," the daughter said in her husky voice. "I don't really remember, but I usually get at least one cold when winter comes. Does this have anything to do with my father's disappearance, Mr. Bigg?"

"Oh no," I said hastily. "I just wanted to make certain he was in good health on January 10th. And from what you and Dr. Stolowitz have told me, he apparently was."

Glynis Stonehouse looked at me a moment. I thought she was puzzled, but then her face cleared.

"You're trying to determine if he might have had amnesia?" she asked. "Or be suffering some kind of temporary mental breakdown?"

"Yes," I said, "something like that. But obviously we can rule that out. Mrs. Stonehouse, I wonder if you'd mind if I talked to your maid for a few moments. Just to see if she might recall something that could help."

"Not at all," Glynis Stonehouse said before her mother could answer. "She's probably in the kitchen or dining room. You know the way; go right ahead. I've already instructed Olga to tell you whatever you want to know."

"Thank you," I said, rising. "You're very kind. It shouldn't take long. And then there are a few more things I'd like to discuss with you ladies, if I may."

I found the maid in the dining room, seated at one end of the long table. She was reading *Prevention*.

"Hi," I said brightly. "Miss Stonehouse said it was all right if I talked to you in private. May I call you Olga?"

"Yah," she said.

She sat erect, her straight spine not touching the back of the chair; seated, she still towered over me.

"Olga," I said, "I work for the family's attorneys and I'm investigating the disappearance of Professor Stonehouse. I was hoping you might be able to help me."

She focused those turquoise eyes on mine. It was like a dentist's drill going into my pupils. I mean I was *pierced*.

"How?" she said.

"Do you have any idea what happened to him?"

"No."

"I realize you weren't here the night he disappeared, but had you noticed anything strange about him? I mean, had he been acting differently?"

"No."

"At the time he disappeared, he was in good health?"

She shrugged.

"But he had been sick last year? Right? Last year he was very ill?"

"Yah."

"But then he got better."

"Yah."

I sighed. I was doing just great. Yah, no, and one shrug.

"Olga," I said, "you work here from one o'clock to nine, six days a week—correct?"

"Yah."

"You serve the afternoon lunch and dinner?"

"Yah."

"Did he eat anything special no one else ate?"

"No."

I gave up. The Silent Swede. Garbo was a chatterbox compared to this one.

"All right, Olga," I said, beginning to rise. "You've been very kind, and I want to—"

Her hand shot out and clamped on my arm, instantly cutting off the circulation. She drew me to her. I instinctively resisted the force. Like trying to resist a Moran tugboat. She pulled me right up to her. Then her lips were at my ear. I mean I could *feel* her lips on my ear, she clutched me so tightly.

"He was being poisoned," she whispered.

The warm breath went tickling into my ear, but I was too stunned to react. Was this the breakthrough I needed?

"By whom?" I asked.

"I could have saved him," she said.

I stared.

For answer to my unspoken question she solemnly raised the health and diet magazine and pointed to it.

She meant Stonehouse was sick of commercial-food processing, like everyone else.

In the living room Glynis and her mother were as I left them. Mrs. Stonehouse was licking the rim of a filled glass.

"Nothing," I said, sighing. "It's very frustrating. Well . . . I'll keep trying. The only member of the family I haven't spoken to, Mrs. Stonehouse, is your son. He was here the night his father disappeared. Perhaps he can recall something . . ."

They gave me his address and unlisted phone number. Then I asked to see any family photos they might have, and presently I was sitting nervously on the couch between the two women, and we went through the stack of photos slowly. It was an odd experience. I felt sure I was looking at pictures of a dead man. Yale Stonehouse was, or had been, a thin-faced, sour man, with sucked-in cheeks and lips like edges of cardboard. The eyes accused and the nose was a knife. In the full-length photos, he appeared to be a skeleton in tweed, all sharp angles and gangling. He was tall, with stooped shoulders, carrying his head thrust forward aggressively.

"Height?" I asked.

"Six feet one," Mrs. Stonehouse said.

"A little shorter than that, Mother," Glynis said quietly. "Not quite six feet."

"Color of hair?"

"Brownish," Ula said.

"Mostly gray," Glynis said.

We finally selected a glossy 8 × 10 publicity photo. I thanked Ula and Glynis Stonehouse and assured them I'd keep them informed of the progress of my investigation.

Downstairs, I asked the man behind the desk if he had been on duty the night Yale Stonehouse had walked out the apartment house, never to be seen again. He said No, that would be Bert Lord, who was on duty from 4:00 P.M. to midnight. Bert usually showed up around 3:30 to change into his uniform in the basement, and if I came back in fifteen or twenty minutes, I'd probably be able to talk to him.

So I walked around the neighborhood for a while, trying to determine Professor Stonehouse's possible routes after he left his apartment house.

There was an IND subway station on Central Park West and 72nd Street. He could have gone uptown or downtown.

He could have taken a crosstown bus on 72nd Street that would have carried him down to 57th Street, across to Madison Avenue, then uptown to East 72nd Street.

He could have walked over to Columbus Avenue and taken a downtown bus.

He could have taken an uptown bus on Amsterdam.

A Broadway bus would have taken him down to 42nd Street and eastward.

A Fifth Avenue bus, boarded at Broadway and 72nd Street, would have taken him downtown via Fifth to Greenwich Village.

The Seventh Avenue IRT could have carried him to the Bronx or Brooklyn.

Or a car could have been waiting to take him anywhere.

When I returned to the apartment house precisely seventeen minutes later, there was a different uniformed attendant behind the desk.

"Mr. Lord?" I asked.

"That's me," he said.

I explained who I was and that I was investigating the disappearance of Professor Stonehouse on behalf of the family's attorneys.

"I already told the cops," he said. "Everything I know."

"I realize that," I said. "He left the building about 8:45 on the night of January 10th—right?"

"That's right," he said.

"Wearing hat, overcoat, scarf?"

"Yup."

"Didn't say anything to you?"

"Not a word."

"But that wasn't unusual," I said. "Was it? I mean, he wasn't exactly what you'd call a sociable man, was he?"

"You can say that again."

I didn't. I said, "Mr. Lord, do you remember what the weather was like that night?"

He looked at me. He had big, blue, innocent eyes.

"I can't recall," he said. "It was a month ago."

I took a five-dollar bill from my wallet, slid it across the marble-topped desk. A chapped paw appeared and flicked it away.

"Now I remember," Mr. Bert Lord said. "A bitch of a night. Cold. A freezing rain turning to sleet. I remember thinking he was some kind of an idiot to go out on a night like that."

"Cold," I repeated. "A freezing rain. But he didn't ask you to call a cab?"

"Him?" he said. He laughed scornfully. "No way. He was afraid I'd expect two bits for turning on the light over the canopy."

"So he just walked out?"

"Yup."

"You didn't see which way he headed?"

"Nope. I couldn't care less."

"Thank you, Mr. Lord."

"My pleasure."

I went directly home, arrived a little after 5:00 P.M., changed into chino slacks and an old sports jacket, and headed out to eat. And there was Captain Bramwell Shank in his wheelchair in the hallway, facing the staircase. He whirled his chair expertly when he heard my door open.

"What the hell?" he said. "I been waiting for you to come home, and you been inside all the time!"

"I got home early," I explained. "Not so long ago."

"I been waiting," he repeated.

"Captain," I said, "I'm hungry and I'm going out for something to eat. Can I knock on your door when I come back? In an hour or so?"

"After seven," he said. "There's a rerun of *Ironsides* I've got to watch. After seven o'clock is okay. Nothing good on till nine."

Woody's on West 23rd was owned and managed by Louella Nitch, a widowed lady whose late husband had left her the restaurant and not much else. She was childless, and I think she sometimes thought of her clientele as her family. Most of the customers were from the neighborhood and knew each other. It was almost a club. Everyone called her Nitchy.

When I arrived on the blowy Monday night, there were only a dozen drinkers in the front room and six diners in back. But the place was warm, the little lamps on the tables gleamed redly, the jukebox was playing an old and rare Bing Crosby record ("Just a Gigolo"), and the place seemed a welcoming haven to me.

Louella Nitch was about forty and the skinniest woman I had ever seen. She was olive-skinned and she wore her hair cut short, hugging her scalp like a black helmet. Her makeup was liberally applied, with dark eyeshadow and precisely painted lips. She wore hoop earrings, Victorian rings, necklaces of baroque medallions and amulets.

She was seated at the front of the bar when I entered, peering at a sheaf of bills through half-glasses that made her small face seem even smaller: a child's face.

"Josh!" she said. "Where have you been? You know, I dreamed about you the other night."

"Thank you," I said.

I took the stool next to her and ordered a beer. She told me about her dream: she was attending a wedding and I stood waiting for the bride to come down the aisle; I was the groom.

"What about the bride?" I asked. "Did you get a look at her?"

She shook her head regretfully. "I woke up before she came in. But I distinctly saw you, Josh. You're not thinking of getting married, are you?"

"Not likely," I said. "Who'd have a runt like me?"

She put a hand on my arm. "You think too much about that, Josh. You're a good-looking man; you've got a steady job. Lots of girls would jump at the chance."

"Name one," I said.

"Are you serious?" she said, looking at me closely. "If you are, I could fix you up right now. I don't mean a one-night stand. I mean a nice, healthy, goodhearted neighborhood girl who wants to settle down and have kids. How about it? Should I make a call?"

"Well, uh, not right now, Nitchy," I said. "I'm just not ready yet."

"How old are you—twenty-eight?"

"Thirty-two," I confessed.

"My God," she said, "you've only got two years to go. Statistics prove that if a man isn't married by the time he's thirty-four, chances are he'll never get hitched. You want to turn into one of those old, crotchety bachelors I see mumbling in their beer?"

"Oh, I suppose I'll get married one of these days."

I think she sensed my discomfort, because she abruptly changed the subject.

"You here for a drink, Josh, or do you want to eat? I'm not pushing, but the chef made a nice beef stew, and if you're going to eat, I'll have some put aside for you before the mob comes in and finishes it."

"Beef stew sounds great," I said. "I'll have it right now. Can I have it here at the bar?"

"Why not?" she said. "I'll have Hettie set you up. There's a girl for you, Josh—Hettie."

"Except she outweighs me by fifty pounds."

"That's right," she said, laughing raucously. "They'd be peeling you off the ceiling!"

The stew was great.

I was putting on my parka when Louella Nitch came hurrying over.

"So soon?" she asked.

"Work to do," I lied, smiling.

"Listen, Josh," she said, "I wasn't just talking; if you want to meet a nice girl, let me know. I mean it."

"I know you mean it, Nitchy," I said. "You're very kind. But I'll find my own."

"I hope so," she said sadly. Then she brightened. "Sure you will. Remember my dream? Every time you've come in here you've been alone. But one of these days you're going to waltz through that door with a princess on your arm. A princess!"

"That's right," I said.

2

•

MR. TABATCHNICK, DUSTING FISH FEED FROM HIS FINGERS, looked at me as if he expected the worst.

"And exactly how, Mr. Bigg," he asked in that trumpeting voice, "were you able to gain entrance to the Kipper household?"

I wished he hadn't asked that question. But I couldn't lie to him, in case Mrs. Tippi Kipper called to check on my cover story. So I admitted I had claimed to be engaged in making an inventory of the Kipper estate. I had feared he would be angered to learn of my subterfuge. Instead, he seemed diverted. At least all those folds and jowls of his bloodhound face seemed to lift slightly in a grimace that might have been amusement.

But when he spoke, his voice was stern.

"Mr. Bigg," he said, "when a complete inventory of the estate is submitted to competent authorities, it must be signed by the attorney of record and, in this case, by the co-executor. Who just happens to be me. Failure to disclose assets, either deliberately or by inadvertence, may constitute a felony. Are you aware of that?"

"I am now, sir," I said miserably. "But I didn't intend to make the final, *legal* inventory. All I wanted to do was—"

"I am quite aware of what you wanted to do," he said impatiently. "Get inside the house. It wasn't a bad ploy. But I suggest that if Mrs. Kipper or anyone else questions your activities in the future, you state that you are engaged in a preliminary inventory. The final statement, to which I must sign my name, will be compiled by attorneys and appraisers experienced in this kind of work. Is that clear?"

"Yes, sir," I said. "Just one thing, sir. In addition to this Kipper matter, I am also looking into something for Mr. Teitelbaum. The disappearance of a client. Professor Yale Stonehouse."

"I am aware of that," he said magisterially.

"In addition to my regular duties," I reminded him. "So far, I have been able to keep up with my routine assignments. But the Kipper and Stonehouse cases are taking more and more of my time. It would help a great deal if I had the services of a secretary. Someone to handle the typing and filing."

He stared at me.

"Not necessarily full time," I added hastily. "Perhaps a temporary or part-time assistant who could come in a few days a week or a few hours each day. Not a permanent employee. Nothing like that, sir."

He sighed heavily. "Mr. Bigg," he said, "you would be astounded at the inevitability with which part-time or temporary assistants become permanent employees. However, I think your request has some merit. I shall discuss the matter with the other senior partners."

I was about to ask for a larger office as well, but then thought better of it. I would build my empire slowly.

"Thank you, Mr. Tabatchnick," I said, gathering up my file. "One final question: I'd like your permission to speak to the two Kipper sons, the ones who are managing the textile company."

"Why not?" he said.

"And what story do you suggest I give them, sir? As an excuse for talking to them about the death of their father?"

"Oh . . ." he said, almost dreamily, "I'll leave that to you, Mr. Bigg. You seem to be doing quite well—so far."

I called Powell Stonehouse. It was the second time I had tried to reach him that morning. A woman had answered the first call and told me that he was meditating and could not be disturbed. This time I got through to him. I identified myself, explained my interest in the disappearance of his father, and asked when I could see him.

"I don't know what good that would do," he said in a stony voice. "I've already told the cops everything I know."

"Yes, Mr. Stonehouse," I said, "I'm aware of that. But there's some background information only you can supply. It won't take long."

"Can't we do it on the phone?" he asked.

"I'd rather not," I said. "It concerns some, uh, rather confidential matters."

"Like what?" he said suspiciously.

He wasn't making it easy for me.

"Well . . . family relationships that might have a bearing on your father's disappearance. I'd really appreciate talking to you in person, Mr. Stonehouse."

"Oh . . . all right," he said grudgingly. "But I don't want to spend too much time on this."

The bereaved son.

"It won't take long," I assured him again. "Any time at your convenience."

"Tonight," he said abruptly. "I meditate from eight to nine. I'll see you for an hour after nine. Don't arrive before that; it would have a destructive effect."

"I'll be there after nine," I promised. "I have your address. Thank you, Mr. Stonehouse."

"Peace," he said.

That caught me by surprise. Peace. I thought that had disappeared with the Flower Children of the 1960s.

My next call was to butler Chester Heavens at the Kipper townhouse. I told him I'd like to come by at 2:00 P.M. to continue my inventory, if that was satisfactory. He said he was certain it would be, that "mom" had left orders that I was to be admitted whenever I asked.

I went out to lunch at 1:00 P.M., had a hot dog and a mug of root beer at a fast-food joint on Third Avenue. Then I walked back to Madison and took another look in the window of that dress shop. The green sweater was still there.

I arrived at the Kipper home ahead of time and walked around the block until it was 2:00 P.M. Then I rang the bell at the iron gate. I was carrying my briefcase, with pens, notebook, and rough plans I had drawn from memory of the six townhouse floors.

Chester Heavens let me in, looking like an extremely well-fed mortician. He informed me that Mrs. Kipper was in the sitting room with the Reverend Godfrey Knurr and a few other close friends. Mrs. Bertha Neckin and Perdita Schug were in the kitchen, preparing tea for this small party.

"You are most welcome to join us there, sah, if you desire a cup of coffee or tea," the butler said.

I thanked him but said I'd prefer to get my inventory work finished first. Then I'd be happy to join the staff in the kitchen. He bowed gravely and told me to go right ahead. If I needed any assistance, I could ring him from almost any room in the house.

I had something on my mind. On the afternoon Sol Kipper had plunged to his death, his wife said she had been with him in the fifth-floor master bedroom. Then she had descended to the ground floor. The servants testified to that. Minutes later, Kipper's body had thudded onto the tiled patio.

What I was interested in was how Mrs. Kipper had gone downstairs. By elevator, I presumed. She was not the type of woman who would walk down five long flights of stairs.

If she descended by elevator, then it should have been on the ground floor at the time of her husband's death. Unless, of course, Kipper rang the bell, waited for the lift to come up from the ground level, then used it to go up to the sixth-floor terrace.

But that didn't seem likely. I stood inside the master bedroom. I glanced at my watch. I then walked at a steady pace out into the hallway, east to the rear staircase, up the stairs to the sixth floor, into the party room, over to the locked French doors leading to the terrace. I glanced at my watch again. Not quite a minute. That didn't necessarily mean a man determined to kill himself *wouldn't* wait for a slow elevator. It just proved it was a short walk from the master bedroom, where the suicide note had been found, to the death leap.

I spent the next hour walking about the upper stories of the townhouse, refining my floor plans and making notes on furniture, rugs, paintings, etc., but mostly trying to familiarize myself with the layout of the building.

I examined the elevator door on each floor. This was not just morbid curiosity on my part; I really felt the operation of the elevator played an important part in the events of that fatal afternoon.

The elevator doors were identical: conventional portals of heavy oak with inset panels. All the panels were solid except for one of glass at eye level that allowed one to see when the elevator arrived. Each door was locked. It could only be opened when the elevator was stopped at that level. You then opened the door, swung aside the steel gate, and stepped into the cage.

Fixed to the jamb on the outside of each elevator door was a dial not much bigger than a large wristwatch. The dials were under small domes of glass, and they revolved forward or backward as the elevator ascended or descended. In other words, by consulting the dial on any floor, you could determine the exact location of the elevator and tell whether or not it was in motion.

I didn't know at the time what significance that might have, but I decided to note it for possible future reference.

As I was coming down to the ground floor, I heard the sounds of conversation and laughter coming from the open doors of the sitting room. Perdita Schug rushed by, carrying a tray of those tiny sandwiches. She hardly had time to wink at me. Chester Heavens followed her at a more stately pace, with a small salver holding a single glass of what appeared to be brandy.

I walked toward the kitchen and pantry. I turned at the kitchen door and looked back. From that point I could see the length of the corridor, the elevator door, the doors to the sitting room, and a small section of the entrance hall. I could not see the front door.

I went into the disordered kitchen, then back to the pantry. A lank, angular woman was seated in one of the high-backed chairs, sipping a cup of tea. She was wearing a denim apron over a black uniform with white collar and cuffs.

"Mrs. Neckin?" I asked.

She looked up at me with an expression of some distaste.

"Yus?" she said, her voice a piece of chalk held at the wrong angle on a blackboard.

"I'm Joshua Bigg," I said with my most ingratiating smile. I explained who I was, and what I was doing in the Kipper home. I told her Chester Heavens had invited me to stop in the kitchen before I left.

"He's busy," she snapped.

"For a cup of tea," I continued pointedly, staring at her. "For a nice, friendly cup of tea."

I could almost see her debating how far she could push her peevishness.

"Sit down, then," she said finally. "There's a cup, there's the pot."

"Thank you," I said. "You're very kind."

Irony had no effect. She was too twisted by ill temper.

"A busy afternoon for you?" I asked pleasantly, sitting down and pouring myself a cup.

"Them!" she said with great disgust.

"It's probably good for Mrs. Kipper to entertain again," I remarked. "After the tragedy."

"Oh yus," she said bitterly. "Him not cold, and her having parties. And I don't care who you tell I said it."

"I have no intention of telling anyone," I assured her. "I am not a gossip."

"Oh yus?" she said, looking at me suspiciously.

"You've been with the Kippers a long time, Mrs. Neckin?" I asked, sipping my tea. It was good, but not as good as Mrs. Dark's at the Stonehouses'.

"I was with Mr. Sol all my working days," she said angrily. "Long before *she* came along." The housekeeper accompanied this last with a jerk of a thumb over her shoulder, in the general direction of the sitting room.

"I understand she was formerly in the theater," I mentioned casually.

"The theater!" she said, pronouncing it thee-*ay*-ter. "A cootch dancer was what she was!"

Then, as if she were grateful to me for giving her an opportunity to vent her malice, she rose, went into the kitchen, and brought back a small plate of petit-fours. And she replenished my cup of tea without my asking.

Mrs. Neckin was a rawboned farm woman, all hard lines and sharp angles. The flat-chested figure under the apron and uniform moved in sudden jerks, pulls, twists, and pushes. When she poured the tea, I had the uneasy feeling that she'd much rather be wringing the neck of a chicken.

"He was a saint," she said, seating herself again. In a chair closer to mine, I noted. "A better man never lived. He's in Heaven now, I vow."

I made a sympathetic noise.

"I'm getting out," she said in a harsh whisper. "I won't work for that woman with Mr. Sol gone."

"It's hard to believe," I said, "that a man like that would take his own life."

"Oh yus!" she said scornfully. "Take his own life! That's what *they* say."

I looked at her in bewilderment.

"But he jumped from the terrace," I said. "Didn't he?"

"He may have jumped," she said, pushing herself back from the table. "I ain't saying he didn't. But what drove him to it? Answer me that: what drove him to it?"

"Her?" I said in a low voice. "Mrs. Kipper?"

"Her?" she said disgustedly. "Nah. She's got milk in her veins. She's too nicey-nice. It was *him*."

"Him?"

"Chester Heavens," she said, nodding.

"*He* drove Mr. Kipper to suicide?" I said. I heard my own voice falter.

"Sure he did," Mrs. Bertha Neckin said with great satisfaction. "Put the juju on him. That church of his. They drink human blood there, you know. I figure Chester called up a spell. That's what made Mr. Sol jump. He was drove to it."

I gulped the remainder of my tea. It scalded.

"Why would Chester do a thing like that?" I asked.

She leaned closer, so near that I could smell her anise-scented breath.

"That's easy to see," she said. "I know what's going on. I live here. I see." She made a circle of her left forefinger and thumb, then moved her right forefinger in and out of the ring in a gesture so obscene it sickened me. "That's what he wants. He's a nig, you know. I don't care how light he is, he's still a nig. And she's a white lady, dirt-cheap though she may be. That's why he put the juju on Mr. Sol. Oh yus."

I pushed back my chair.

"Mrs. Neckin," I said, "I thank you very much for the refreshment. You've been very kind. And I assure you I won't repeat what you've told me to a living soul."

In the corridor I stood aside as Perdita Schug came toward the kitchen with a tray of empty highball and wineglasses. She paused, smiling at me.

"Thursday," she said. "I'm off on Thursday. I'm in the book. I told you."

"Yes," I said, "so you did."

"Try it," she said. "You'll like it."

I was still stammering when she moved on to the kitchen.

I had advanced to the entrance hall when Chester Heavens came from the sitting room. He preceded Mrs. Tippi Kipper and the Reverend Godfrey Knurr. Through the open doors I could see several ladies sitting in a circle, chattering as they drank tea and nibbled on little things.

"Well, Mr. Bigg," Mrs. Kipper said in her cool, amused voice, "finished for the day?"

"I think so, ma'am," I said. "There's still a great deal to be done, but I believe I'm making progress."

"Did Chester offer you anything?" she asked.

"He did indeed, ma'am. I had a nice cup of tea, for which I am grateful."

"I wish that was all I had," Godfrey Knurr said, patting his stomach. "Tippi, you keep serving those pastries and I'll have to stop coming here."

"You must keep up your strength," she murmured, and he laughed.

They were standing side by side as the butler took Knurr's hat and coat, and mine, from the closet. He held a soiled trench coat for Knurr, then handed him an Irish tweed hat, one of those bashed models with the brim turned down all the way around.

"Can I give you a lift, Mr. Bigg?" Knurr said. "I've got my car outside."

His car was an old Volkswagen bug. It had been painted many times.

"Busted heater," he said as we got in. "Sorry about that. But it's not too cold, is it? Maybe we'll go down Fifth and then cut over on 38th. All right?"

"Fine," I said. Then I was silent awhile as he worked his way into traffic and got over to Fifth Avenue. "Mrs. Kipper seems to be handling it well," I remarked. "The death of her husband, I mean."

"She's making a good recovery," he said, beating the light and making a left onto Fifth. "The first few days were hard. Very hard. I thought for a while she might have to be hospitalized. Good Lord, she was practically an eyewitness. She heard him hit, you know."

"It was fortunate you were there," I said.

"Well. I wasn't *there*. I showed up a few minutes later. What a scene that was! Screaming, shouting, everyone running around. It was a mess. I did what I could. Called the police and so forth."

"Did you know him, Pastor?"

"Sol Kipper? Knew him well. A beautiful man. Generous. So generous. So interested in the work I'm doing."

"Uh, do you mind if I ask about that? The work you're doing, I mean. I'm curious."

"Do I mind?" he said, with that brisk laugh of his. "I'm delighted to talk about it. Well . . . Listen, may I call you Joshua?"

"Josh," I said, "if you like."

"I prefer Joshua," he said. "It has a nice Old Testament ring. Well, Joshua, about my work . . . Did you ever hear of the term 'tentmakers'?"

"Tentmakers? Like Omar?"

"Not exactly. More like St. Paul. Anyway, the problem is basically a financial one. There are thousands and thousands of Protestant clergymen and not enough churches to go around. So more and more churchmen are turning to secular activities. There's an honorable precedent for it. St. Paul supported his preaching by making tents. That's why we call ourselves tentmakers. You'll find the clergy in business, the arts, working as fund-raisers, writing books, even getting into politics. I'm a tentmaker. I don't have a regular church, although I sometimes fill in for full-time pastors who are on vacation, sick, hungover, or on retreat. Whatever. But mostly I support myself by begging." He glanced sideways at me, briefly. "Does that shock you?"

"No," I said. "Not really. I seem to recall there's an honorable precedent for that also."

"Right," he said approvingly. "There is. Oh hell, I don't mean I walk the streets like a mendicant, cup in hand. But it amounts to the same thing. You saw me at work today. I meet a lot of wealthy people, usually women, and some not so wealthy. I put the bite on them. In return I offer counseling or just a sympathetic ear. In nine cases out of ten, all they want is a listener. If they ask for advice, I give it. Sometimes it's spiritual. More often than not it's practical. Just good common sense. People with problems are usually too upset to think clearly."

"That's true, I think."

"So that's part of my tentmaking activities; spiritual adviser to the wealthy. I assure you they're just as much in need of it as the poor."

"I believe you," I said.

"But when they offer a contribution, I accept. Oh boy, do I accept! Not only to keep me in beans, but to finance the other half of my work. It's not a storefront church exactly. Nothing half so fancy as Chester Heavens' Society of the Holy Lamb up in Harlem. It's not a social club either. A combination of both, I guess. It's in Greenwich Village, on Carmine Street. I live in the back. I work with boys from eight to eighteen. The ones in trouble, the ones who have been in trouble, the ones who are going to get in trouble. I give them personal counseling, or a kind of group therapy, and plenty of hard physical exercise in a little gym I've set up in the front of the place. To work off some of their excess energy and violence."

By this time we were down at 59th Street where the traffic was truly horrendous. Knurr swung the Bug in and out, cutting off other drivers, jamming his way through gaps so narrow that I closed my eyes.

"Where are you from, Joshua?" The sudden question startled me.

"Uh—Iowa," I said. "Originally."

"Really? I was born right next door in Illinois. Peoria. But I spent most of my life in Indiana, near Chicago, before I came to New York. It's a great city, isn't it?"

"Chicago?" I said.

"New York," he said. "It's the only place to be. The center. You make it here or you never really make it. The contrasts! The wealth and the poverty. The ugliness and the beauty. Don't you feel that?"

"Oh yes," I said, "I do."

"The opportunity," he said. "I think that's what impresses me most about New York: the opportunity. A man can go to the stars here."

"Or to the pits," I said.

"Oh yes," he said. "That, too. Listen, there's something I'd like you to do. Say no, and I'll understand. But I wish you'd visit my place down in Greenwich Village. Look around, see what I'm doing. Trying to do. Would you do that?"

"Of course," I said instantly. "I'd like to. Thank you very much."

"I suspect I'm looking for approval," he said, glancing at me quickly again with a grin. "But I'd like you to see what's going on. And, to be absolutely truthful, there are a few little legal problems I hope you might be able to help me with. My lease is for a residential property and I'm running this church or club there, whatever you want to call it. Some good neighbors have filed a complaint."

I was horrified.

"Mr. Knurr," I said, "I'm not a lawyer."

"You're not?" he said, puzzled. "I thought you worked for Mrs. Kipper's attorneys?"

"I do," I said. "In a paralegal job. But I'm not an attorney myself. I don't have a law degree."

"But you're taking the estate inventory?"

"A preliminary inventory," I said. "It will have to be verified and authenticated by the attorney of record before the final inventory of assets is submitted."

"Oh," he said. "Sure. Well, the invitation still stands. I'll tell you my problems and maybe you can ask one of the attorneys in your firm and get me some free legal advice."

"That I'd be glad to do," I said. "When's the best time to come?"

"Anytime," he said. "No, wait, you better give me a call first. I'm in the book. Mornings would be best. Afternoons I usually spend with my rich friends uptown. Listening to their troubles and drinking their booze."

Then he pulled up outside the TORT offices. He leaned over to examine the building through the car window.

"Beautiful," he said. "Converted townhouse. It's hard to believe places like that were once private homes. The wealth! Unreal."

"But it still exists," I said. "The wealth, I mean. Like the Kipper place."

"Oh yes," he said, "it still exists." He slapped my knee. "I don't object to it," he said genially. "I just want to get in on it."

"Yes," I said mournfully. "Me, too."

"Listen, Joshua, I was serious about that invitation. The hell with the free legal advice. I like you, I'd like to see more of you. Give me a call and come down and visit me."

Acknowledging his invitation with a vague promise to contact him, I took my leave and headed to my office.

I was adding somewhat fretfully to my files of reports, wondering if I was getting anywhere, when my phone rang. It was Percy Stilton; he sounded terse, almost angry.

He asked me if I had come up with anything new, and I told him of my most recent visit to the Kipper townhouse. He laughed grimly when I related what Mrs. Neckin had said about Chester Heavens putting a curse on Sol Kipper.

"I should have warned you about her," Stilton said. "A whacko. We get a lot of those. They make sense up to a point, and then they're off into the wild blue yonder. What was your take on Godfrey Knurr?"

"I like him," I said promptly. "For a clergyman, he swears like a trooper, but he's very frank and open. He invited me down to Greenwich Village to see what he's doing with juvenile delinquents. He certainly doesn't impress me as a man with anything to hide."

"That's the feeling I got," Perce said. "And that's it? Nothing else?"

"A silly thing," I said. "About the elevator."

"What about the elevator?"

I explained that if Mrs. Kipper had come downstairs on that elevator, it should have been on the ground floor at the time her husband plunged to his death. Unless he had brought the elevator up again to take it from the master bedroom on the fifth floor to the sixth-floor terrace.

"He could have," Stilton said.

"Sure," I agreed. "But I timed the trip from bedroom to terrace. Walking along the hall and up the rear staircase. Less than a minute."

I didn't have to spell it out for him.

"I get it," he said. "You want me to talk to the first cops on the scene and see if any of them remember where the elevator was when they arrived?"

"Right," I said gracefully.

"And if it was on the ground floor, that shows that Mrs. Kipper brought it down, which proves absolutely nothing. And if it was on the sixth floor, it only indicates that *maybe* Sol Kipper took it up to his big jump from the terrace. Which proves absolutely nothing. Zero plus zero equals zero."

I sighed.

"You're right, Perce. I'm just grabbing at little things. Anything."

"I'll ask the cops," he said. "It's interesting."

"I suppose so."

"Josh, you sound down."

"Not down, exactly, but bewildered."

"Beginning to think Sol Kipper really was a suicide?"

"I don't know . . ." I said slowly. "Beginning to have some doubts about my fine theories, I guess."

"Don't," he said.

"What?"

"Don't have any doubts. I told you I thought someone was jerking us around. Remember? Now I'm sure of it. Early this morning the harbor cops pulled a floater out of the North River. Around 34th Street. A female Caucasian, about fifty years old or so. She hadn't been in the water long. Twelve hours at most."

"Perce," I said, "not . . . ?"

"Oh yeah," he said tonelessly. "Mrs. Blanche Reape. Positive ID from her prints. She had a sheet. Boosting and an old prostitution rap. No doubt about it. Marty's widow."

I was silent, remembering the brash, earthy woman in The Dirty Shame saloon, buying drinks for everyone.

"Josh?" Detective Stilton demanded. "You there?"

"I'm here."

"Official verdict is death by drowning. But a very high alcoholic content in the blood. Fell in the river while drunk. That's how it's going on the books. You believe it?"

"No," I said.

"I don't either," he said. "Sol Kipper falls from a sixth-floor terrace. Marty Reape falls in front of a subway train. His widow falls in the river. This sucks."

"Yes," I said faintly.

"What?" he said. "I can't hear you."

"Yes," I said, louder, "I agree."

"You bet your damp white fanetta!" he said furiously. Then suddenly he was shouting, almost gargling on his bile. "I don't like to be messed with," he yelled. "Some sharp, bright son of a bitch is messing me up. I don't like that. No way do I like that!"

"Perce," I said, "please. Calm down."

"Yeah," he said. "Yes, I mean. Yes. I'm calm now. All cool."

"You think the three of them . . . ?"

"Oh yes," he said. "Why not? Kipper was the first. Then Marty, because he had the proof. Then the widow lady. It fits. Someone paid her for the files. The evidence Marty had on the Kipper estate. Then she got greedy and put the bite on for more. Goodbye, Blanche."

"Someone would do that? Kill three people?"

"Sure," he said. "It's easy. The first goes down so slick, and so smooth, and so nice. Then they can do no wrong. They own the world. Why I'm telling you all this, Josh, is to let you know you're not wasting your time on this Kipper thing. I can't open it up again with what we've got; you'll have to carry the ball. I just wanted you to know I'm here, and ready, willing, and able."

"Thank you, Perce."

"Keep in touch, old buddy," he said. "I'll check on that elevator thing for you. That cocksucker!" he cried vindictively. "We'll fry his ass!"

Powell Stonehouse lived on Jones Street, just off Bleecker. It was not a prepossessing building: a three-story loft structure of worn red brick with a crumbling cornice and a bent and rusted iron railing around the areaway. I arrived a few minutes after 9:00 P.M., rang a bell marked Chard-Stonehouse, and was buzzed in almost immediately. I climbed to the top floor.

I was greeted at the door of the loft by a young woman, very dark, slender, of medium height. I stated my name. She introduced herself as Wanda Chard, in a whisper so low that I wasn't certain I had heard right, and I asked her to repeat it.

She ushered me into the one enormous room that was apparently the entire apartment, save for a small bathroom and smaller kitchenette. There was a platform bed: a slab of foam rubber on a wide plywood door raised from the floor on cinder blocks. There were pillows scattered everywhere: cushions of all sizes, shapes, and colors. But no chairs, couches, tables. I assumed the residents ate off the floor and, I supposed, reclined on cushions or the bed to relax.

The room was open, spare, and empty. A choice had obviously been made to abjure things. No radio. No TV set. No books. One dim lamp. There were no decorations or bric-a-brac. There was one chest of drawers, painted white, and one doorless closet hung with a few garments, male and female. There was almost nothing to look at other than Ms. Chard.

She took my coat and hat, laid them on the bed, then gestured toward a clutch of pillows. Obediently I folded my legs and sank into a semireclining position. Wanda Chard crossed her legs and sat on the bare floor, facing me.

"Powell will be out in a minute," she said.

"Thank you," I said.

"He's in the bathroom," she said.

There seemed nothing to reply to that, so I remained silent. I watched as she fitted a long crimson cigarette to a yellowed ivory holder. I began to struggle to my feet, fumbling for a match, but she waved me back.

"I'm not going to smoke it," she said. "Not right now. Would you like one?"

"Thank you, no."

She stared at me.

"Does it bother you that you're very small?" she asked in a deep, husky voice that seemed all murmur.

Perhaps I should have bridled at the impertinence of the question; after all, we had just met. But I had the feeling that she was genuinely interested.

"Yes, it bothers me," I said. "Frequently."

She nodded.

"I'm hard of hearing, you know," she said. "Practically deaf. I'm reading your lips."

I looked at her in astonishment.

"You're not!" I said.

"Oh yes. Say a sentence without making a sound. Just mouth the words."

I made my mouth say, "How are you tonight?" without actually speaking; just moving my lips.

"How are you tonight?" she said.

"But that's marvelous!" I said. "How long did it take you to learn?"

"All my life," she said. "It's easy when people face me directly, as you are.

When they face away, or even to the side, I am lost. In a crowded, noisy restaurant, I can understand conversations taking place across the room."

"That must be amusing."

"Sometimes," she said. "Sometimes it is terrible. Frightening. The things people say when they think no one can overhear. Most people I meet aren't even aware that I'm deaf. The reason I'm telling you is because I thought you might be bothered by your size."

"Yes," I said, "I understand. Thank you."

"We are all one," she said somberly, "in our weakness."

Her hair was jet black, glossy, and fell to her waist in back. It was parted in the middle and draped about her face in curved wings that formed a dark Gothic arch. The waves almost obscured her pale features. From the shadows, two luminous eyes glowed forth. I had an impression of no makeup, pointy chin, and thin, bloodless lips.

She was wearing a kimono of garishly printed silk, all poppies and parrots. When she folded down onto the bare floor, I had noted her feline movements, the softness. I did not know if she was naked beneath the robe, but I was conscious of something lubricious in the way her body turned. There was a faint whisper there: silk on flesh. Her feet were bare, toenails painted a frosted silver. She wore a slave bracelet about her left ankle: a chain of surprisingly heavy links. There was a tattoo on her right instep: a small blue butterfly.

"What do you do, Miss Chard?" I asked her.

"Do?"

"I mean, do you work?"

"Yes," she said. "In a medical laboratory. I'm a research assistant."

"That's very interesting," I said, wondering what on earth Powell Stonehouse could be doing in the bathroom for such a long time.

As if I had asked the question aloud, the bathroom door opened and he came toward us in a rapid, shambling walk. Once again I tried to struggle to my feet from my cocoon of pillows, but he held a palm out, waving me down. It was almost like a benediction.

"Would you like an orange?" he asked me.

"An orange? Oh no. Thank you."

"Wanda?"

She shook her head, long hair swinging across her face. But she held up the crimson cigarette in the ivory holder. He found a packet of matches on the dresser, bent over, lighted her cigarette. I smelled the odor: more incense than smoke. Then he went to the kitchenette and came back with a small Mandarin orange. He sat on the bare floor next to her, facing me. He folded down with no apparent physical effort. He began to peel his orange, looking at me, blinking.

"What's all this about?" he said.

Once again I explained that I had been assigned by his family's attorneys to investigate the disappearance of his father. I realized, I said, that I was going over ground already covered by police officers, but I hoped he would be patient and tell me in his own words exactly what had happened the night of January 10th.

I thought then that he glanced swiftly at Wanda Chard. If a signal passed between them, I didn't catch it. But he began relating the events of the evening his father had disappeared, pausing only to pop a segment of orange into his mouth, chomp it to a pulp, and swallow it down.

His account differed in no significant detail from what I had already learned from his mother and sister. I made a pretense of jotting notes, but there was really nothing to jot.

"Mr. Stonehouse," I said, when he had finished, "do you think your father's mood and conduct that night were normal?"

"Normal for him."

"Nothing in what he did or said that gave you any hint he might be worried or under unusual pressure? That he might be contemplating deserting his family of his own free will?"

"No. Nothing like that."

"Do you know of anyone who might have, uh, harbored resentment against your father? Disliked him? Even hated him?"

Again I caught that rapid shifting of his eyes sideways to Wanda Chard, as if consulting her.

"I can think of a dozen people," he said. "A hundred people. Who resented him or disliked him or hated him." Then, with a small laugh that was half-cough, he added, "Including me."

"What exactly was your relationship with your father, Mr. Stonehouse?"

"Now look here," he said, bristling. "You said on the phone that you wanted to discuss 'family relationships.' What has that got to do with his disappearance?"

I leaned forward from the waist, as far as I was able in my semirecumbent position. I think I appeared earnest, sincere, concerned.

"Mr. Stonehouse," I said, "I never knew your father. I have seen photographs of him and I have a physical description from your mother and sister. But I am trying to understand the man himself. Who and what he was. His feelings for those closest to him. In hopes that by learning the man, knowing him better, I may be able to get some lead on what happened to him. I have absolutely no suspicions about anyone, let alone accusing anyone of anything. I'm just trying to learn. Anything you can tell me may be of value."

This time the consultation with Wanda Chard was obvious, with no attempt at concealment. He turned to look at her. Their eyes locked. She nodded once.

"Tell him," she said.

He began to speak. I didn't take notes. I knew I would not forget what he said.

He tried very hard to keep his voice controlled. Unsuccessfully. He alternated between blatant hostility and a shy diffidence, punctuated with those small, half-cough laughs. Sometimes his voice broke into a squeak of fury. His gestures were jerky. He glanced frequently sideways at his companion, then glared fiercely at me again. He was not wild, exactly, but there was an incoherence in him. He didn't come together.

He had his father's thin face and angular frame, the harsh angles softened by youth. It was more a face of clean slants, with a wispy blond mustache and a hopeful beard scant enough so that a mild chin showed. He was totally bald, completely, the skull shaved. Perhaps that was what he had been doing in the bathroom. In any event, that smooth pate caught the dim light and gave it back palely. Big ears, floppy as slices of veal, hung from his naked skull.

He had tortoise shell eyes, a hawkish nose, a girl's tender lips. A vulnerable look. Everything in his face seemed a-tremble, as if expecting a hurt. As he spoke, his grimy fingers were everywhere: smoothing the mustache, tugging the poor beard, pulling at his meaty ears, caressing his nude dome frantically. He was wearing a belted robe of unbleached muslin. The belt was a rope. And there was a cowl hanging down his back. A monk's robe. His feet were bare and soiled. Those busy fingers plucked at his toes, and after a while I couldn't watch his eyes but could only follow those fluttering hands, thinking they might be enchained birds that would eventually free themselves from his wrists and go whirling off.

The story he told was not an original, but no less affecting for that . . .

He had never been able to satisfy his father. Never. All he remembered of his boyhood was mean and sour criticism. His mother and sister tried to act as buffers, but he took most of his father's spleen. His school marks were unacceptable; he was not active enough in sports; his table manners were slovenly.

"Even the way I stood!" Powell Stonehouse shouted at me. "He didn't even like the way I walked!"

It never diminished, this constant litany of complaint. In fact, as Powell grew older, it increased. His father simply hated him. There was no other explanation for his spite; his father hated him and wished him gone. He was convinced of that.

At this point in his recital, I feared he might be close to tears, and I was relieved to see Wanda Chard reach out to imprison one of those wildly fluttering hands and grasp it tightly.

His sister, Glynis, had always been his father's favorite, Powell continued. He understood that in most normal families the father dotes on the daughter, the mother on the son. But the Stonehouses were no normal family. The father's ill temper drove friends from their house, made a half-mad alcoholic of his wife, forced his daughter to a solitary life away from home.

"I would have gone nuts," Powell Stonehouse said furiously. "I was *going* nuts. Until I found Wanda."

"And Zen," she murmured.

"Yes," he said, "and Zen. Now, slowly, through instinct and meditation, I am becoming one. Mr. Bigg, I must speak the truth: what I feel. I don't care if you never find my father. I think I'm better off without him. And my sister is, too. And my mother. And the world. You must see, you must understand, that I have this enormous hate. I'm trying to rid myself of it."

"Hate is a poison," Wanda Chard said.

"Yes," he said, nodding violently, "hate is a poison and I'm trying hard to flush it from my mind and from my soul. But all those years, those cold, brutal scenes, those screaming arguments . . . it's going to take time. I know that: it's going to take a long, long time. But I'm better now. Better than I was."

"Oh, forgive him," Wanda Chard said softly.

"No, no, no," he said, still fuming. "Never. I can never forgive him for what he did to me. But maybe, someday, with luck, I can forget him. That's all I want."

I was silent, giving his venom a chance to cool. And also giving me a chance to ponder what I had just heard. He had made no effort to conceal his hostility toward his father. Was that an honest expression of the way he felt—or was it calculated? That is, did he think to throw me off by indignation openly displayed?

"Doubt *everyone*," Roscoe Dollworth had said. "Suspect *everyone*."

He had also told me something else. He said the only thing harder than getting the truth was asking the right questions. "No one's going to volunteer *nothing!*" Dollworth said that sometimes the investigator had to flounder all over the place, striking out in all directions, asking all kinds of extraneous questions in hopes that one of them might uncover an angle never before considered. "Catching flies," he called it.

I felt it was time to "catch flies."

"Your sister was your father's favorite?" I asked.

He nodded.

"How did he feel toward your mother?"

"Tolerated her."

"How often did you dine at your father's home? I mean after you moved out?"

"Twice a week maybe, on an average."

"Do you know what your father's illness was? Last year when he was sick?"

"The flu, Mother said. Or a virus."

"Do you know any of your sister's friends?"

"Not really. Not recently. She goes her own way."

"But she goes out a lot?"

"Yes. Frequently."

"Where?"

"To the theater, I guess. Movies. Ballet. Ask her."

"She's a beautiful woman. Why hasn't she married?"

"No one was ever good enough for Father."

"She's of age. She can do as she likes."

"Yes," Wanda Chard said, "I've wondered about that."

"She wouldn't leave my mother," Powell said. "She's devoted to my mother."

"But not to your father?"

He shrugged.

"Anything you can tell me about the servants?"

"What about them?"

"You trust them?"

"Of course."

"What did you and your father quarrel about? The final quarrel?"

"He caught me smoking a joint. We both said things we shouldn't have. So I moved out."

"You have an independent income?"

"Enough," Wanda Chard said quickly.

"Your sister doesn't have one particular friend? A man, I mean. Someone she sees a lot of?"

"I don't know. Ask her."

"Was your father on a special diet?"

"What?"

"Did he eat any special foods or drink anything no one else in the house ate or drank?"

"Not that I know of. Why?"

"In the last month or two before your father disappeared, did you notice any gradual change in his behavior?"

He thought about that for a few seconds.

"Maybe he became more withdrawn."

"Withdrawn?"

"Surlier. Meaner. He talked even less than usual. He ate his dinner, then went into his study."

"His will is missing. Did you know that?"

"Glynis told me. I don't care. I don't want a cent from him. Not a cent! If he left me anything, I'd give it away."

"Why did your mother stay with such a man as you describe?"

"What could she do? Where could she go? She has no family of her own. She couldn't function alone."

"Your mother and sister could have left together. Just as you left."

"Why should they? It's their home, too."

"You never saw your father's will?"

"No."

"Did you see the book he was working on? A history of the *Prince Royal*, a British battleship?"

"No, I never saw that. I never went into his study."

"Did your father drink? I mean alcohol?"

"Maybe a highball before dinner. Some wine. A brandy before he went to bed. Nothing heavy."

"Are you on any drugs now?"

"A joint now and then. That's all. No hard stuff."

"Your mother or sister?"

"My mother's on sherry. You probably noticed."

"Your sister?"

"Nothing as far as I know."

"Your father?"

"You've got to be kidding."

"Either of the servants?"

"Ridiculous."

"Do you love your mother?"

"I have a very deep affection for her. And pity. He ruined her life."

"Do you love your sister?"

"Very much. She's an angel."

Wanda Chard made a sound.

"Miss Chard," I said, "did you say something? I didn't catch it."

"Nothing," she said.

That's what I had—nothing. I continued "catching flies."

"Did your father ever come down here?" I asked. "To this apartment?"

"Once," he said. "I wasn't here. But Wanda met him."

"What did you think of him, Miss Chard?"

"So unhappy," she murmured. "So bitter. Eating himself up."

"When did he come here? I mean, how long was it before he disappeared?"

They looked at each other.

"Perhaps two weeks," she said. "Maybe less."

"He just showed up? Without calling first?"

"Yes."

"Did he give any reason for his visit?"

"He said he wanted to talk to Powell. But Powell was in Brooklyn, studying with his master. So Professor Stonehouse left."

"How long did he stay?"

"Not long. Ten minutes perhaps."

"He didn't say what he wanted to talk to Powell about?"

"No."

"And he never came back?"

"No," Powell Stonehouse said, "he never came back."

"And when you saw him later, in his home, did he ever mention the visit or say what he wanted to talk to you about?"

"No, he never mentioned it. And I didn't either."

I thought a moment.

"It couldn't have been a reconciliation, could it?" I suggested. "He came down here to ask your forgiveness?"

He stared at me. His face slowly congealed. The blow he had been expecting had landed.

"I don't know," he said in a low voice.

"Maybe," Wanda Chard murmured.

3

•

OLGA EKLUND AGREED TO MEET ME IN A HEALTH-FOOD CAFETERIA on Irving Place. The salad, full of sprouted seeds, was really pretty good. I washed it down with some completely natural juice.

I listened to her lecture on health and diet as patiently as I could. When she paused I said, "So when you told me Professor Stonehouse was being poisoned, you were referring to the daily food served in his house?"

"Yah. Bad foods. I tell them all the time. They don't listen. That Mrs. Dark, the cook—everything with her is butter and cream. Too much oil. Too rich."

"But everyone in the house eats the same thing?"

"Not me. I eat raw carrots, green salads with maybe a little lemon juice. Fresh fruit. I don't poison myself."

"Olga," I said, "you serve the evening meal every night?"

"Except my day off."

"Can you recall Professor Stonehouse eating or drinking anything the others didn't eat or drink?"

She thought a moment.

"No," she said. Then: "Except at night maybe. After I left."

"Oh? What was that?"

"Every night he worked in his study. Late, he would have a cup of cocoa and a brandy before he went to bed."

I was alive again.

"Where did the cocoa come from?"

"Come from?" she asked, puzzled. "From Holland."

"I mean, who made the cocoa every night for Professor Stonehouse?"

"Oh. Mrs. Dark made it before she went to bed and before I went home. Then, when the Professor wanted it late, Glynis would heat it up, skim it, and bring it to his study."

"Every night?"

"I think so."

"No one else in the house drank the cocoa?"

"I don't know."

It was sounding better and better.

"Let me get this sequence right," I said. "Every night Mrs. Dark made a pot of cocoa. This was before you went home and before she went to bed. Then, later, when the Professor wanted it, Glynis would heat it up and bring it to him in his study. Correct?"

"Yah," she said placidly, not at all interested in why I was so concerned about the cocoa.

"Thank you, Olga," I said. "You've been very helpful."

"Yah?" she said, surprised.

"Does Glynis go out very often? In the evening, I mean."

"Oh, yah."

"Does she have a boyfriend?"

She pondered that.

"I think so," she said, nodding. "Before, she was very sad, quiet. Now she smiles. Sometimes she laughs. She dresses different. Yah, I think she has a man who makes her happy."

"How long has this been going on? I mean, when did she start to be happy?"

"Maybe a year ago. Maybe more. Also, one night she said she was going to the theater. But I saw her that night in a restaurant on 21st Street. She did not see me and I said nothing to her."

"Was she with anyone?"

"No. But I thought she was waiting for someone."

"What time of night was this?"

"Perhaps nine, nine-thirty. If she had gone to the theatre, as she said, she would not be in the restaurant at that time."

"Did you ever mention that incident to her?"

"No," she said, shrugging. "Is no business of mine."

"What do you think of Powell Stonehouse, Olga?"

"He poisons himself with marijuana cigarettes." (She pronounced it "mary-jew-anna.") "Too bad. I feel sorry for him. His father was very mean to him."

I drained the remainder of all that natural goodness in my glass and rose to my feet.

"Thank you again, Olga," I said, "for your time and trouble. The food here is delicious. You may have made a convert of me."

What a liar I was getting to be.

When I got back to TORT I was confronted by Hamish Hooter, that tooth-sucking villain. "See here," Hooter said indignantly, glaring at me from sticky eyes, "what's this about a secretary?"

"I need one," I said. "I spoke of it to Mr. Tabatchnick."

"*I* am the office manager," he said hotly. "Why didn't you speak to *me?*"

"Because you would have turned me down again," I said in what I thought was a reasonable tone. "All I want is a temporary assistant. Someone to help with typing and filing until I complete a number of important and complex investigations."

I had always thought the description "He gnashed his teeth" was a literary exaggeration. But Hamish Hooter *did* gnash his teeth. It was a fascinating and awful thing to witness.

"We'll see about that," he grated, and whirled away from me.

As soon as I reached my desk I phoned Yetta Apatoff and made a lunch date for Friday, then got back to business.

Headquarters for Kipmar Textiles were located in a building on Seventh Avenue and 35th Street. When I phoned, a dulcet voice answered, "Thank you for calling Kipmar Textiles," and I wondered what the reaction would be if I screamed that I was suing Kipmar for six zillion dollars. After being shunted to two more extensions, I finally got through to a lady who stated she was Miss Gregg, secretary to Mr. Herschel Kipper.

I forbore commenting on the aptness of her name and occupation, but merely identified myself and my employer and asked if it might be possible for me to see Mr. Herschel Kipper and/or Mr. Bernard Kipper at some hour that afternoon, at their convenience. She asked me the purpose of my request, and I replied that it concerned an inventory of their late father's estate that had to be made for tax purposes.

She put me on hold—for almost five minutes. But I was not bored; they had one of those attachments that switches a held caller to a local radio station, so I heard the tag end of the news, a weather report, and the beginning of a country singer's rendition of "I Want to Destroy You, Baby," before Miss Gregg came on the line again. She informed me that the Kipper brothers could see me "for a very brief period" at 3:00 P.M. I was to come directly to the executive offices on the 34th floor and ask for her. I thanked her for her kindness. She thanked me, again, for calling Kipmar Textiles. It was a very civilized encounter.

I walked over from the TORT building, starting out at 2:30, heading due west on 38th. I strolled down Fifth Avenue to 35th, where I made a right into the garment district and continued over to Seventh. The garment center in Manhattan is quintessentially New York. From early in the morning till late at night it is thronged, jammed, packed. The rhythm is frantic. Hand-trucks and pedestrians share the sidewalks. Hand trucks, pedestrians, taxis, buses, private cars, and semitrailers share the streets. There is a cacophony that numbs the mind: shouts, curses, the bleat of horns, squeal of brakes, sirens, bells, whistles, the blast of punk rock from the open doors of music shops, the demanding cries of street vendors and beggars.

I suppose there were streets in ancient Rome similar to these, and maybe in Medieval European towns on market day. It is a hurly-burly, a wild tumult that simply sweeps you up and carries you along, so you find yourself trotting, dashing through traffic against the lights, shouldering your way through the press, rushing, rushing. Senseless and invigorating.

Kipmar's executive offices were decorated in neutral tones of oyster white and dove gray, the better to accent the spindles of gaily colored yarns and bolts of fabrics displayed in lighted wall niches. There were spools of cotton, synthetics, wools, silks, rayon, and folds of woven solids, plaids, stripes, checks, herringbones, satins, metallics, and one incredible bolt of a gossamer fine as a spider's web and studded with tiny rhinestones. This fabric was labeled with a chaste card that read: STAR WONDER. Special Order. See Mr. Snodgrass.

At the end of the lobby a young lady was seated behind a desk that bore a small sign: RECEPTIONIST. She was on the phone, giggling, as I approached, and I heard her say, "Oh, Herbie, you're just *awful!*" She covered the mouthpiece as I halted in front of her desk.

"Yes, sir?" she said brightly. "How may I help you?"

"Joshua Bigg," I said, "to see Mr. Kipper. I was told to ask for Miss Gregg."

"Which Mr. Kipper, sir?"

"Both Mr. Kippers."

"Just a moment, sir," she said. Then, *sotto voce,* "Don't go away, Herbie." She pushed some buttons and said primly, "Mr. Joshua Bigg to see Mr. Kipper. Both Mr. Kippers." She listened a moment, then turned to me with a divine smile. "Please take a seat, sir. Miss Gregg will be with you in a moment."

I sat in one of the low leather sling chairs. True to her word, Miss Gregg came to claim me in a moment. She was tall, scrawny, and efficient. I knew she was efficient because the bows of her eyeglasses were attached to a black ribbon that went around her neck.

"Mr. Bigg?" she said with a glassy smile. "Follow me, please."

She preceded me through a labyrinth of corridors to a door that bore a small brass plate: H. KIPPER, PRES.

"Thank you," I said to her.

"Thank *you,* sir," she said, ushered me in, then closed the door gently behind me.

It was a corner office. Two walls were picture windows affording a marvelous view of upper Manhattan. The floor was carpeted deeply, almost indecently. The desk was a slab of black marble on a chrome base—more table than desk. Two men stood behind the desk.

I had an initial impression that I was seeing double or seeing identical twins. They were in fact merely brothers, but Herschel and Bernard Kipper looked alike, dressed alike, shared the same speech patterns, mannerisms, and gestures; during the interview that followed I was continually confused, and finally looked between them when I asked my questions and let him answer who would.

Both were men of medium height, and portly. Both had long strands of thinning hair combed sideways over pink scalp. Their long cigars were identical.

Both were clad in high garment district fashion in steel-gray, raw silk suits. Only their ties were not identical. When they spoke their voices were harsh, phlegmy, with a smoker's rasp, their speech rapid, assertive. They asked me to be seated, although they remained standing, firmly planted, smoking their cigars and staring at me with hard, wary eyes.

Once again I explained that I was engaged in a preliminary inventory of their father's estate, and had come to ascertain if he had left any personal belongings in the offices.

"I understand he maintained a private office here," I added softly. "Even after his retirement."

"Well . . . sure," one of them said. "Pop had an office here."

"But no personal belongings," the other said. "I mean, Pop's desk and chairs and all, the furnishings, they belong to the company."

"No personal possessions?" I persisted. "Jewelry? A set of cuff links he might have kept in his desk? Photographs? Silver frames?"

"Sure," one of them said. "Pop had photographs."

"We took them," the other one said. "They were of our mother, and Pop's mother and father."

"And all us kids," the other said. "And his grandchildren. In plain frames. No silver or anything like that. And one photograph of *her*. She can have it."

"The bitch!" the other Kipper son said wrathfully.

I had pondered how I might introduce the subjects of Tippi and the will without seeming to pry. I needn't have fretted.

"I assume you're referring to the widow?" I said.

"I said bitch," one of them said, "and I mean bitch!"

"Listen," the other said, "we're not complaining."

"We're not hurting," his brother agreed. "But that gold-digger getting a piece of the company is what hurts."

"Who knows what that birdbrain might do?"

"She might dump her shares."

"Upset the market."

"Or waltz in here and start poking around."

"She knows zilch about the business."

"She could make plenty of trouble, that fake."

"I understand," I said carefully, "that she was formerly in the theater?"

"The theater!" one of them cried.

"That's a laugh!" the other cried.

"She was a nightclub dancer."

"A chorus girl."

"All she did was shake her ass."

"And she wasn't very good at that."

"Probably hustling on the side."

"What else? Strictly a horizontal talent."

"She played him like a fish."

"She knew a good thing when she saw one, and she landed him."

"And made his life miserable."

"Once the contract was signed, no more nice-nice."

"Unless she got what she wanted."

"The house, which they didn't need, and clothes, cars, cruises, jewelry—the works. She took him good."

"It hurt us to see what was going on."

"But he wouldn't listen. He just wouldn't listen."

"Uh," I said, "I understand she also persuaded your father to make contributions to charity. A certain Reverend Godfrey Knurr . . . ?"

"Him!"

"That gonniff!"

"Hundreds!"

"Thousands!"

"To his cockamamie club for street bums."

"Pop wasn't thinking straight."

"Couldn't see how they were taking him."

"Even after he's dead and gone."

"But you probably know that."

I didn't know it. Didn't know to what he was referring. But I didn't want to reveal my ignorance by asking questions.

"Well . . ." I said judiciously, "it's not the first time it's happened. An elderly widower. A younger woman. Does she have family?"

"Who the hell knows?" one of them said.

"She came out of nowhere," the other said. "A drifter. Chicago, I think. Somewhere near there."

"She doesn't talk about it."

"He met her in Vegas."

"Went out there on one of those gambling junkets and came back with a bride. Some bride! Some junket!"

"He lost!"

"We all lost."

"A chippie."

"A whore."

"Everyone could see it but him. Pussy-whipped."

"An old man like that. Our father. Pussy-whipped."

"It hurt."

They glowered at me accusingly. I ducked my head and made meaningless jottings in my notebook, pretending their anger was worth recording. Though I had learned more than I had hoped, there were questions I wanted desperately to ask, but I didn't dare arouse their suspicions.

"Well," I said, "I think that covers the matter of your father's personal belongings. There is one additional thing you may be able to help me with. A claim for a thousand dollars has been filed against the estate by an individual named Martin Reape. We have been unable to contact Mr. Reape, and we wondered if either of you is acquainted with him or knows the reason for the claim."

Again they looked at each other. Then shook their heads.

"Martin Reape?"

"Never heard of him."

"We thought it might possibly be a business expense. Is there any way . . . ?"

"Sure. It can be checked out."

"We got everything on film."

"We can tell you if he was a supplier, a customer, or whatever. Heshie, give Al Baum a call."

Heshie picked up a silver-colored phone.

"Get me Al Baum," he snapped. Then, in a moment, "Al? Herschel. I'm sending you down a lawyer. He wants to check into a certain individual. To see if he's on our books. You understand? Right. Al, you give him every possible cooperation."

He hung up.

"That's Al Baum, our comptroller," he said to me. "He's on the 31st floor. If we've got this guy—what's his name?"

"Martin Reape."

"If we've got this Martin Reape on our books Al will put him on the screen and see if we owe him. Okay?"

I stood up.

"Gentlemen," I said, "you've been very kind, and I appreciate it."

"You filed for probate yet?"

"Well, uh, I think you better talk to Mr. Tabatchnick about that. He's handling it personally."

"Sure . . . what else? Uncle Leo and Pop were old friends. They go way back together."

"Give Uncle Leo our best."

"I'll do that," I said. "Thank you again for your time and trouble."

I got out of there. They were still standing shoulder to shoulder behind the desk, still furious. Their cigars were much shorter now. The marble top was littered with white ash.

The 31st floor was different from the executive enclave on the 34th. Wood floors were carpeted with worn runners, walls were tenement green, chipped and peeling. There was no receptionist; directly in front of the elevators began a maze of flimsy metal cubicles. There was constant noise here; banging and clattering, shouted questions and screamed answers, and a great scurrying to and fro. Large office machines, some with keyboards, some with hidden keys clacking, some quiescent, burping forth a sheet or two of paper at odd moments.

I approached a desk where a young black man was shuffling through an enormous pile of computer printout. He wore wire-rimmed glasses, and a steel comb pushed into his Afro.

"I beg your pardon," I said timidly.

He continued his rapid riffling of the folded stack of paper before him.

"I beg your pardon," I said, louder.

He looked up.

"Say what?" he said.

"I'm looking for Mr. Baum. I wonder if—"

"Al!" he bawled at me. "Oh you, Al! Someone here!"

I drew back, startled. Before I knew what was happening, my elbow was gripped. A little butterball of a man had me imprisoned.

"Yes, yes, yes?" he spluttered. "Al Baum. What, what, what?"

"Joshua Bigg, Mr. Baum," I said. "I'm the—"

"Who, who, who?" he said. "From Lupowitz?"

"No, no, no," I said. It was catching. "From Tabatchnick, Orsini, Reilly, and Teitelbaum. Mr. Herschel Kipper just called and asked—"

"Right, right, right," he said. "Follow me. This way. Just follow me. Don't trip over the cables."

He darted away and I went darting after him. We rushed into an enormous room where tall gray modules were lined up against the walls, all with tape reels whirling or starting and stopping.

"Computers," I said foolishly.

"No, no, no," Baum said rapidly. "Data processing and retrieval. Payrolls, taxes, et cetera, but mostly inventory. Hundreds of yarns, hundreds of fabrics: all coded. What's this gink's name?"

"Reape," I said. "Martin Reape. R-e-a-p-e."

I scurried after him into a cramped corner office where a young lady sat before a keyboard and what appeared to be a large television screen.

"Josie," Baum said, "look up a Martin Reape. R-e-a-p-e." He turned to me. "What is he?" he asked. "A supplier? Buyer? What, what, what?"

"I don't know," I said, feeling like an idiot. "You may have paid him for something. A supplier. Call him a supplier."

Josie's fingers sped over the keyboard. Mr. Baum and I leaned over her shoulder, watching the screen. Suddenly printing began to appear, letter by letter, word by word, left to right, then down to the next line, with a loud chatter. Finally the machine stopped. The screen showed seven payments of five hundred dollars each. The payee was Martin Reape, the address was his 49th Street office. The first payment was made in August of the previous year. The last payment was made one week prior to the death of Sol Kipper.

"There he is," Al Baum said. "That what you wanted?"

"Yes," I said, feeling a fierce exaltation. "Would it be possible to see the canceled checks?"

"Why not?" he said. "We got everything on film. Josie?"

She pushed more buttons. The screen cleared, then was filled with a picture of the Kipmar Textile checks made out to Martin Reape. I leaned closer to peer. All the checks had been signed by Albert Baum, Comptroller.

I turned to him.

"You signed the checks?" I said.

I must have sounded accusing. He looked at me pityingly.

"Sure I signed. So, so, so?"

"Do you remember what it was for? I mean, why was Martin Reape paid that money?"

He shrugged. "I sign a thousand checks a week. At least. Who can remember? Josie, let's see the bills."

She pushed more buttons. Now the bills appeared on the screen. They had no printed heading, just the typewritten name and address of Martin Reape. Each was for $500. Each merely said: "For services rendered."

"See, see, see?" Al Baum demanded. "Down there in the corner of every bill? 'OK/SK.' That's Sol Kipper's initials and handwriting. He OK'd the bills, so I paid."

"You have no idea of the services Martin Reape rendered?"

"Nope, nope, nope."

"Is there any way I can get a copy of the bills and canceled checks?"

"Why not?" he said. "Mr. Heshie said to give you full cooperation. Right, right, right? Josie, run a printout on everything—totals, bills, checks: the works."

"Thank you," I said. "You've been very—"

"Happy, happy, happy," he rattled, and then he was gone.

I waited while Josie pushed more buttons, and printout came stuttering out of an auxiliary machine. I watched, fascinated, as it printed black-and-white reproductions of the bills from Martin Reape, the checks paid by Kipmar Textiles, and a neat summation of dates billed, dates paid, and totals. Josie tore off the sheet of paper and handed it to me. I folded it carefully and tucked it into my inside jacket pocket.

"Thank you very much," I said.

"Sure, bubi," she chirped.

I found a phone booth in the street-floor lobby, and looked up a number in my book. She answered on the first ring.

"Yes?" she said.

"Perdita?" I asked, "Perdita Schug?"

"Yes. Who's this?"

"Joshua Bigg. You probably don't—"

"Josh!" she said. "How cute! I was hoping you'd call."

"Yes . . . well . . . how are you?"

"Bored, bored, bored," she said. I wondered if she knew Al Baum. "What I need is a little excitement. A new love."

"Uh . . . yes. Well, why I called . . . I remembered you said Thursday was your day off. Am I correct?"

"Right on," she said. "I get off at noon tomorrow and I don't have to be back until Friday noon. Isn't that cute?"

"It certainly is," I said bravely. "What do you usually do on your day off?"

"Oh," she said, "this and that. I should go out to visit my dear old mother in Weehawken. You got any cuter ideas?"

"Well, I was wondering if you might care to have dinner with me to-morrow night?"

"I accept," she said promptly.

"We can make it early," I suggested, "so you'll have plenty of time to get over to New Jersey."

She laughed merrily.

"You're so funny, Josh," she said. "You're really a scream."

"Thank you," I said. "Is there any place you'd like to go? For dinner, I mean. Some place where we can meet?"

"Mother Tucker's," she said. "Second Avenue near Sixty-ninth Street. You'll like it. I hang out there all the time. Seven or eight o'clock, like that, OK?"

As I walked homeward west on my street, I saw Cleo Hufnagel coming east, arms laden with shopping. I hurried to help her.

"Thank you, Josh," she said. "I had no idea they'd be so heavy."

She was wearing a red plaid coat with a stocking hat pulled down to her eyes. The wind and fast walking had rosied her cheeks. Her eyes sparkled. She looked very fetching and I told her so. She smiled shyly.

"Home from work so soon?" I asked as we climbed the steps.

"I had the day off," she said, "but I'll have to work Saturday. You're home early."

"Playing hooky," I said. I took the other bag of groceries while she hunted for her keys. She unlocked the doors and held them open for me.

"Can I carry these into your kitchen for you?" I asked.

"Oh no," she said hastily. "Thank you, but most of these things are for Mother."

So I set the bag down in the hallway outside Mrs. Hufnagel's apartment after huffing my way up to the second floor.

"Thank you so much, Josh," Cleo said. "You were very kind."

I waved my hand. "No tip necessary," I said, and we both laughed. Then we just stood there, looking at each other. It didn't bother me that I had to look up to meet her eyes. I blurted out, "Cleo, would you like to come up to my place for a glass of wine after dinner?"

"Thank you," she said in a low voice. "I'd like that. What time?"

"About eight. Is that all right?"

"Eight is fine. See you then."

I trudged up to my apartment, meditating on what I had done.

Checking my wine cellar, I found I was in short supply, so after I showered and got into my Chelsea clothes I headed out on a run to the liquor store. Bramwell Shank was there on the landing, waiting for me with the wine in his lap.

"Goddamn!" he shouted. "I've been waiting here for you and all the time you've been in there!"

This was obviously my fault. I explained how I had come home early, and explained why, and offered to pick up anything he needed from the stores, and got away with a promise to have a drink with him when I came back in. This seemed a good idea or he might barge in later on my tête-à-tête with Cleo.

She arrived promptly at 8:00 P.M., knocking softly on my door. I leaped to my feet and upset what was left in a glass of wine on my chair arm. Fortunately, the glass fell to the rug without breaking, and none of the wine splashed on me.

"Coming!" I shouted. Hastily, I retrieved the glass and moved the armchair to cover the stain on the rug. Then I had to move the endtable to bring it alongside, and when I did that, the lamp tipped over. I caught it before it could crash, set it upright again, then rushed to the door.

"Come in, come in!" I said heartily and ushered her to the armchair. "Sit here," I said. "It's the most comfortable."

"Well . . ." Cleo Hufnagel said doubtfully, "isn't it a little close to the fire? Could you move it back a bit?"

I stared at her, then started laughing. I told her what had happened just before she entered. She laughed, too, and assured me a stained rug wouldn't offend her. So we moved everything back in place.

"Much better," she said, seating herself. "I do that all the time. Spilling things, I mean. You shouldn't have bothered covering it."

We settled down with drinks. Happily I asked her if she had noticed signs of rapprochment between Captain Shank and Madame Kadinsky. There had been signs of romance. That did it. In a moment she had kicked off her shoes and we were gossiping like mad.

Presently I heard myself saying, "But if they married, they might tear each other to tatters. Argue, fight. You know."

"Even that's better than what they had before, isn't it?"

The conversation was making me uneasy. I went into the kitchen to fetch fresh drinks.

"Cleo," I said when I came back, "I really know very little about what you do. I know you work in a library. Correct?"

"Yes," she said, lifting her chin. "I'm a librarian."

I spent five minutes assuring her that I admired librarians, that some of the happiest hours of my life had been spent in libraries, that they were a poor man's theater, a portal to a world of wonder, and she was in a noble and honored profession, etc., etc. I really laid it on, but the strange thing was that I believed every word of it.

"You're very kind," she said doubtfully. "But what it comes down to is some bored housewife looking for the new Jackie Onassis book or a Gothic. You're with a legal firm, Josh?"

"Yes," I said, "but I'm not a lawyer. I'm just an investigator."

I explained to her what I did. I found myself talking and talking. She seemed genuinely interested, and asked very cogent questions. She wanted to know my research sources and how I handled abstruse inquiries. I told her some stories that amused her: how I spent one Sunday morning trying to buy beer in stores on Second Avenue (illegal), how I manipulated recalcitrant witnesses, how people lied to me and how, to my shame, I was becoming an accomplished liar.

"But you've got to," she said. "To do your job."

"I know that," I said, "but I'm afraid I'll find myself lying in my personal life. I wouldn't like that."

"I wouldn't either," she said. "Could I have another drink?"

I came back from the kitchen with fresh drinks. She reached up with a languid hand to take her glass. She was practically reclining in the armchair, stretched out, her head far back, her stockinged feet toward the dying fire.

She was wearing a snug, caramel-colored wool skirt, cinched with a narrow belt, and a tight black sweater that left her neck bare. All so different from the loose, flowing costumes she usually wore. The last flickering flames cast rosy highlights on throat, chin, brow. She had lifted her long, chestnut hair free. It hung down in back of the chair. I wanted to stroke it.

I was shocked at how beautiful she looked, that willowy figure stretched out in the dim light. Her features seemed softened. The hazel eyes were closed, the lips slightly parted. She seemed utterly relaxed.

"Cleo," I said softly.

Her eyes opened.

"I just thought of something. I have a favor to ask."

"Of course," she said, straightening up in her chair.

I explained that one of my investigations involved a man who had been a victim of arsenic poisoning. I needed to know more about arsenic: what it was, how it affected the human body, how it could be obtained, how administered, and so forth. Could Cleo find out the titles of books or suggest other places where I might obtain that information?

"I can do that," she said eagerly. "I'm not all that busy. When do you need it?"

"Well . . . as soon as possible. I just don't know where to start. I thought if you could give me the sources, I'd take it from there."

"I'll be happy to," she said. "Did he die?"

"No, but he's disappeared. I think the poisoning had something to do with it."

"You mean whoever was poisoning him decided to, uh, take more direct measures?"

I looked at her admiringly. "You're very perceptive."

"I have a good brain, I know," she said. It was not bragging; she was just stating a fact. "Too bad I never get a chance to use it."

"Were you born in New York, Cleo?" I asked her.

"No," she said, "Rhode Island." She told me the story of her family. Her father had disappeared from Newport one day and Mrs. Hufnagel had brought tiny Cleo to Chelsea to live in the house, which had been bought with their last money as an investment.

I told her my little history—little in at least two ways. I told her how I was raised by my uncle and aunt and what I had to endure from my cousins.

"But I'm not complaining," I said. "They were good people."

"Of course they were, to take you in. But still . . ."

"Yes," I said. "Still . . ."

We sat awhile in silence, a close, glowing silence.

"Another drink?" I asked finally.

"I don't think so," she said. "Well, maybe a very small one. Just a sip."

"A nightcap?" I said.

"Right," she said approvingly.

"I'm going to have a little brandy."

"That sounds good," she said. "I'll have a little brandy, too."

So we each had a little brandy. I thought about her father, a shy man who flew kites before he vanished. It seemed to go with the quiet and winking embers of the fire.

"I've never flown a kite," I confessed. "Not even as a kid."

"I think you'd like it."

"I think I would, too. Listen, Cleo, if I bought a kite, could we go up to Central Park someday, a Sunday, and fly it? Would you show me how?"

"Of course—I'd love to. But we don't have to go up to Central Park. We can go over to those old wharves on the river and fly it from there."

"What kind of a kite should I buy?"

"The cheapest one you can get. Just a plain diamond shape. And you'll need a ball of string. I'll tear up some rags for a tail."

"What color would you like?" I said, laughing.

"Red," she said at once "It's easier to see against the sky, and it's prettier."

A green sweater for Yetta and a red kite for Cleo.

We sat in silence, sipping our brandies. After a while her free hand floated up and grasped my free hand. Hers was warm and soft. We remained like that, holding hands. It was perfect.

4

•

I AWOKE TO A SMUTTY DAY, A THICK SKY FILLED WITH WHIRLING gusts of sleet and rain. A taut wind from the west whipped the pedestrians hunched as they scurried, heads down. The TORT building didn't exhibit its usual morning hustle-bustle. Many of the employees lived in the suburbs, and roads were flooded or blocked by toppled trees, and commuter trains were running late.

I had brought in a container of black coffee and an apple strudel. I made phone calls over my second breakfast. The Reverend Godfrey Knurr agreed to show me his club that day, and Glynis Stonehouse said she would see me. She said her mother was indisposed, in bed with a virus. (A sherry virus, I thought—but didn't say it.)

Despite the wretched weather I got up to the West 70s in half an hour. Glynis Stonehouse answered the door. We went down that long corridor again, into the living room. I noticed that several of the framed maps and naval battle scenes had disappeared from the walls, to be replaced by bright posters and cheery graphics. Someone did not expect Professor Stonehouse to return.

We sat at opposite ends of the lengthy couch, half-turned so we could look at each other. Glynis said Mrs. Stonehouse was resting comfortably. I declined a cup of coffee. I took out my notebook.

"Miss Stonehouse," I started, "I spoke to your brother at some length."

"I hope he was—cooperative?"

"Oh yes. Completely. I gather there had been a great deal of, uh, enmity between Powell and his father?"

"He made my brother's life miserable," she said. "Powell is such a *good* boy. Father destroyed him!"

I was surprised by the virulence in her husky voice, and looked at her sharply.

The triangular face with cat's eyes of denim blue was expressionless, the sculpted lips firmly pressed. Her tawny hair was drawn sleekly back. A remarkably beautiful woman, with her own secrets. She made me feel like a blundering amateur; I despaired of ever penetrating that self-possession and discovering—what?

"Miss Stonehouse, can you tell me anything about Powell's ah, companion? Wanda Chard?"

"I don't know her very well. I met her only once."

"What is your impression?"

"A very quiet woman. Deep. Withdrawn. Powell says she is very religious. Zen."

"Your father met her two weeks before he disappeared."

That moved her. She was astonished.

"Father did?" she said. "Met Wanda Chard?"

"So she says. He went down to your brother's apartment. Powell wasn't at home. He stayed about ten minutes talking to Miss Chard. Your father never mentioned the visit?"

"No. Never."

"You have no idea why he might have visited your brother—or tried to?"

"None whatsoever. It's so out of character for my father."

"It couldn't have been an attempted reconciliation with your brother, could it?"

She pondered a moment.

"I'd like to think so," she said slowly.

"Miss Stonehouse," I said, "I'd like to ask a question that I hope won't offend you. Do you believe your brother is capable of physical violence against your father?"

Those blue eyes turned to mine. It was more than a half-beat before she answered. But she never blinked.

"He might have been," she said, no timbre in her voice. "Before he left home. But since he's had his own place, my brother has made a marvelous adjustment. Would he have been capable of physical violence the night my father disappeared? No. Besides, he was here when my father walked out."

"Yes," I said. "Do you think Wanda Chard could have been capable of physical violence?"

"I don't know," she said. "I just don't know. It's possible, I suppose. Perfectly normal, average people are capable of the most incredible acts."

"Under pressure," I agreed. "Or passion. Or hate. Or any strong emotion that results in loss of self-control. Love, for instance."

"Perhaps," she said.

Noncommittal.

"Miss Stonehouse," I said, sighing, "is Mrs. Dark at home?"

"Why, yes. She's in the kitchen."

A definite answer. What a relief.

"May I speak to her for a moment?"

"Of course. You know the way, don't you?"

When I entered the kitchen, Effie was seated at the center table, smoking a cigarette and leafing through the morning *Daily News*. She looked up as I came in, and her bright little eyes crinkled up with pleasure.

"Why, Mr. Bigg," she said, her loose dentures clacking away. "This *is* nice."

"Good to see you again, Effie. How have you been?"

"Oh, I've got no complaints," she said cheerily. "What are you doing out on such a nasty morning? Here . . . sit down."

"Thank you," I said. "Well, Effie, I wanted to ask you a few more questions. Silly things that probably have nothing to do with the Professor's disappearance. But I've got to ask them just to satisfy my own curiosity."

"Sure," she said, shrugging her fat shoulders, "I can understand that. I'm as curious as the next one. Curiouser."

"Effie, what time of night do you usually go to bed?"

"Well, I usually go to my room about nine-thirty, ten. Around then. After I've cleaned up here. Then I read a little, maybe watch a little television. Write a letter or two. I'm usually in bed by eleven."

I laughed. "Lucky woman. Do you leave anything here in the kitchen for the family? In case they want a late snack?"

"Oh, they can help themselves," she said casually. "They know where everything is." Then, when I was wondering how to lead into it, she added: "Of course, when the Professor was here, I always left him a saucepan of cocoa."

"Cocoa?" I said. "I didn't think people drank cocoa anymore."

"Of course they do. It's delicious."

"And you served the Professor a cup of cocoa before you went to bed?"

"Oh no. I just made it. Then I left it to cool. Around midnight, Miss Glynis would come in and just heat it up. Even if she was out at the theater or wherever, she'd come home, heat up the cocoa, and bring a cup to her father in his study."

"So I understand. Glynis brought the Professor his cup of cocoa every night?"

"That's right."

"And no one else in the house drank it?"

"No one," she said, and my heart leaped—until she said, "except me. I finished it in the morning."

"Finished it?"

"What was left in the pan. I like a cup of hot cocoa before I start breakfast."

That seemed to demolish the Great Cocoa Plot. But did it?

"Effie, who washed out the Professor's cocoa cup in the morning?"

"I did. He always left it on the kitchen sink."

"Why on earth did he drink cocoa so late at night?"

"He claimed it helped him sleep better." She snickered. "Just between you, me, and the lamppost, I suspect it was the brandy he had along with it."

"Uh-huh," I said. "Well, Effie, I think that covers it. There's just one other favor I'd like to ask. I want to take another look in the Professor's study."

"Help yourself," she said. "The door's unlocked."

"I don't want to go in alone."

"Oh?" She looked at me shrewdly. "So you'll have a witness that you didn't take anything?"

"Right," I said gratefully.

The study looked exactly as it had before. I stood near the center of the room, my eyes half-closed. I turned slowly, inspecting.

The drum table. Brandy bottle and two small balloon glasses on an Edwardian silver tray. The Rémy Martin bottle was new, sealed.

Where did he hide the will? Not up the chimney. Not in the littered desk. Not behind a secret panel. Ula and Glynis would have probed up the chimney, searched the desk, tapped the walls, combed every book and map.

But I thought I knew where the will was hidden.

Glynis seemed not to have moved since I left. Still reclined easily in a corner of the couch. She was not fussing with her scarf, stroking her sleeked-back hair, inspecting her nails. She had the gift of complete repose.

"Miss Stonehouse," I said, "could you spare me a few more minutes?"

"Of course."

"I have some very distressing information," I told her. "Something I think you should be aware of. I hoped to inform your mother, but since she is indisposed—temporarily, I trust—I must tell you."

She cocked her head to one side, looking puzzled.

"When your father was ill last year, for a period of months, he was suffering from arsenic poisoning."

Something happened to her face. It shrank. The flesh seemed to become less and the skin tightened onto bone, whitened and taut. Genuine surprise or the shock of being discovered?

"What?" she said.

"Your father. He was being poisoned. By arsenic. Finally, in time, he consulted a physician. He recovered. That means he must have discovered how he was being fed the arsenic. And by whom."

"Impossible," she said. Her voice was so husky it was almost a rasp.

"I'm afraid it's true," I said. "No doubt about it. And since your father rarely dined out, he must have been ingesting arsenic here, in his own home, in some food or drink that no one else in the house ate or drank, because no one else suffered the same effects. I have an apology to make to you, Miss Stonehouse. For a brief period, I thought the arsenic might have been given to him in that nightly cup of cocoa which you served him. Something I thought no one else in the household drank. But Mrs. Dark has just told me that she finished the cocoa every morning and was none the worse for it. So I apologize to you for my suspicions. And now I must try to find some other way that your father was being poisoned."

That jolted her. The repose was gone; she began to unbutton and button her black gabardine jacket. She was wearing a brassiere, but I caught quick glimpses of the smooth, tender skin of her midriff.

"You thought that I . . ." she faltered.

"Please," I said, "I do apologize. I know now it wasn't the cocoa. I'm telling you this because I want you to think very carefully and try to remember if your father ate or drank anything that no one else in the household ate or drank."

"You're quite sure he was being poisoned?" she said faintly.

"Oh yes. No doubt about it."

"And you think that had something to do with his disappearance?"

"It seems logical, doesn't it?"

Her face began to fill out again. Her color returned to normal. She looked at me squarely. She stopped fussing with her buttons and settled back into her original position. She took a deep breath.

"Yes," she said softly, "I think you're right. If someone was trying to kill him . . ."

"Someone obviously was."

"But why?"

"Miss Stonehouse," I said, "I just don't know. My investigation hasn't progressed that far. As yet."

"But you are making progress?"

It was my turn to be noncommittal.

"I have discovered several things," I said, "that may or may not be significant. But to get back to my original question, can you think of any way your father may have been poisoned? Other than the cocoa?"

She stared at me a long moment, but she wasn't seeing me.

"No," she said, "I can't. We all ate the same things, drank the same things. Father bought bottled water, but everyone drank that."

"He wasn't on a special diet of any kind?"

"No."

"Well . . ." I said, "if you recall anything, please let me know."

"Mr. Bigg," she said slowly, "you said you suspected me of poisoning my father's cocoa."

"Not exactly," I said. "For a time I did think the cocoa you served him might have been poisoned. But anyone in the household could have done that. But I realized I was mistaken after Mrs. Dark told me she finished the leftover cocoa every morning."

"She *told* you," Glynis Stonehouse said steadily. "I've never seen Mrs. Dark have a cup of cocoa in the morning, and I don't believe anyone else has either."

Again our eyes locked, but this time she was really looking at me, her gaze challenging, unblinking.

• • •

THE SLEET HAD lessened, but the sky was still drooling. I ducked into a curbside phone kiosk on Columbus Avenue and called the office, and chatted with Yetta Apatoff. I reminded her of our lunch date on Friday. She hadn't forgotten. Yetta said the office manager had left me a message. He had hired a temporary assistant for me. She would appear at my office at three o'clock, which still gave me time to run downtown to visit the good Reverend Knurr.

I took the Seventh Avenue IRT local down to Houston Street and walked up to Carmine Street. I stopped at a bodega along the way and bought a six-pack. I had the address, but was a few minutes early, so I walked by across the street, inspecting the premises. It was no smaller or larger than any of the other storefronts on the street. But the glass window and door had been painted a dark green. An amateur sign across the front read: TENTMAKERS CLUB. I crossed the street and went in. The door rang a bell as it opened.

"Halloo?" Knurr's voice shouted from the rear.

"Joshua Bigg," I yelled back.

"Be with you in a minute, Joshua. Make yourself at home."

There was a small open space as one entered. Apparently it was used as an office, for there was a battered wooden desk, an old, dented file cabinet, three chairs (none of which matched), a coat tree, and several cartons stacked on the floor. They all seemed to be filled with used and tattered paperback novels.

Beyond the makeshift office was a doorway curtained with a few yards of sleazy calico nailed to the top of the frame. I pushed my way through and found myself in a large bare chamber with fluorescent lights overhead. On the discolored walls were charts showing positions and blows in judo, jiujitsu, and karate. There were also a few posters advertising unarmed combat tournaments.

In one corner was a tangle of martial arts jackets, kendo staves and masks, dumbbells. There was a rolled-up wrestling mat against one wall.

I was inspecting an illustrated directory of kung fu positions and moves taped to the wall when the Reverend Godfrey Knurr entered from a curtained rear doorway.

"Joshua," he said, "good to see you. Thanks for coming."

"Here," I said, thrusting the damp brown bag at him. "I brought along a cold six-pack. For lunch."

He peeked into the bag.

"Wonderful," he said. "Come on back. I'll put the beer in the fridge and you can hang your things away."

There was a short corridor that debouched into kitchen and bedroom. The kitchen was just large enough to contain a wooden table and four chairs, refrigerator, sink, cabinets, and a tiny stove. The walls were pebbled with umpteen coats of paint. There was a small rear window looking out onto a sad little courtyard, squalid in the rain. The same view was available from the window in the bedroom. This was a monk's cell: bed, closet, chest of drawers, straight-back chair, bedside table with lamp and telephone, a bookcase.

"Not *quite* the Kipper townhouse, is it?" Knurr said. He was putting the beer in the refrigerator when we heard the jangle of the front doorbell.

"They'll be coming in now," he said. "Let's go up front."

I followed him to the gym. He was wearing a gray sweatsuit, out at elbow and knee. His sneakers were stained and torn; the laces broken and knotted.

Three boys were taking off wet things in the office. They tossed their outer apparel onto the desk, then came back to the larger room where they divested themselves of shoes, sweaters, shirts, and trousers, kicking these into a corner.

Knurr introduced me casually: "Joshua, these brutes are Rafe, Tony, Walt. This is Josh."

We all nodded. They appeared to me to be about 13 to 15, bodies skinny and white, all joints. Their faces and necks were pitted with acne.

The bell jangled again; more boys entered. Finally Knurr had a dozen boys milling around the gym in their drawers and socks.

"Cut the shit!" the Reverend yelled. "Line up and let's get started."

They arranged themselves in two files, facing him. At his command they began to go through a series of what I presumed were warm-up exercises, following Knurr. He stood with left foot advanced, left arm extended, hand clenched, knuckles down. The right foot was back, right arm cocked, right fist clenched. Then, at a shouted "Hah!" everyone took a step forward onto the right foot, striking an imaginary opponent with the right fist while bending the left arm and retracting the left fist to the shoulder. At the second "Hah!" they all took a step backward to their original position.

I revised my guess at their age group upward to 12 to 17. Some of them were quite large, including a six-foot black. There were four blacks, one Oriental, and two I thought were Hispanic. All were remarkably thin, some painfully so, and most had the poor skin tone of slum kids. There were scars and bruises in abundance, and one shambling youth had a black patch over one eye.

Knurr led them through a series of increasingly violent exercises, culminating with a series of high front and back kicks.

After the exercise period was finished, Godfrey Knurr assigned partners and the boys paired off. They went through what appeared to me to be mock combat. No actual blows were struck, no kicks landed, but it was obvious that all the youths were in dead earnest, punching and counterpunching, kicking out and turning swiftly to avoid their opponents' kicks. As they fought, Knurr moved from pair to pair, watched them closely, stopped them to demonstrate a punch or correct the position of their feet. He had a few words to say to each boy in the room.

"All right," he shouted finally. "That's enough. Unroll the mat. We'll finish with a throw."

The wrestling mat was spread in the center of the bare wood floor. They gathered around and I moved closer. Knurr strode out onto the mat and beckoned one of the lads.

"Come on, Lou," he said. "Be my first victim."

There was laughter, some calls and rude comments as the six-foot black stepped forward on the mat to face Knurr.

"All right," Knurr said, "lead at me with a hard right. And don't tighten up. Stay loose. Ready?"

Lou fell into the classic karate stance, then punched at Knurr's throat with his right knuckles. The pastor executed a movement so fast and flowing that I could scarcely follow it. He plucked the black's wrist out of the air, lifted it as he turned, bent, put a shoulder into the boy's armpit, pulled down on the arm, levered up, and Lou's feet went flying high in the air, cartwheeling over Knurr's head. He would have crashed onto the mat if Knurr hadn't caught him about the waist and let him down gently.

There was more laughter, shouts, exclamations of delighted surprise. The Reverend helped Lou to his feet and then they went through the throw very slowly, Knurr pausing frequently to explain exactly what he was doing, calling his students' attention to the position of his feet, how his weight shifted, how he used the attacker's momentum to help disable him.

"Okay," he said, "that was just a demonstration. Tomorrow you're all going to work on that throw. And you'll work on it and work on it until everyone can do it right. Then I'll show you the defense against it. Now . . . who's going to show up for the bullshit session tonight?" He looked around the room. But heads were hanging; no one volunteered. "Come on, come on," Knurr said impatiently, "you've got to pay for your fun. Who's coming for the talk?"

A few hands went up hesitantly, then a few more. Finally about half the boys had hands in the air.

"How about you, Willie?" Knurr demanded, addressing the shambling youth with the black eyepatch. "You haven't been around for weeks. You must have a wagonload of sins to confess. I especially want you."

This was greeted with laughter and shouts from the others.

"Right on!"

"Get him, Faddeh!"

"Make him spill everything!"

"He's been a *baaaad* boy!"

"Aw right," Willie said with a tiny grin, "I'll be here."

"Good," Knurr said. "Now dry off, all of you, then get the hell out of here. The gym will be open from five to eight tonight if any of you want to work out. See you all tomorrow."

They began to pick up their garments from the floor, with the noise and horseplay you'd expect. Knurr rolled up the mat and flung it against the wall. His sweatshirt was soaked dark under the arms, across the back and chest. While he showered I sat at the kitchen table, sipping beer from the can, listening to shouts and laughter of departing boys. I looked up through the window. In the apartment house across the courtyard an old woman fed a parakeet seeds from her lips, bird perched on finger.

Godfrey Knurr came into the kitchen wearing a terry-cloth robe, toweling head and beard. He put the towel around his neck, took a beer from the refrigerator. He sat across from me.

"Well?" he demanded. "What do you think?"

"Very impressive," I said. "You speak to them in their own language. They seem to respect you. They obey you. The only thing that bothers me is—"

"I know what bothers you," he interrupted. "You're wondering if I'm not teaching those monsters how to be expert muggers."

"Yes," I said. "Something like that."

"It's a risk," he admitted. "I know it exists. I keep pounding at them that they're learning the martial arts only for self-defense. And God knows they need it, considering what their lives are like. And they do need physical exercise."

"Does it have to be karate?" I asked. "Couldn't it be basketball?"

"Or tiddledywinks?" he said sourly. "Or I could read them Pindar's odes. Look, Joshua, most of those kids have records. Violence attracts them. All I'm trying to do is capitalize on that. Listen, every time they punch the air and shout 'Hah!' they're punching out the Establishment. I'm trying to turn that revolt to a more peaceable and constructive channel."

"You can kill with karate, can't you?" I asked him.

"I don't teach them killing blows," he said shortly. "Also, what you just saw is only half of my program. The other half is group therapy and personal counseling. I try to become a father figure. Most of their natural fathers are drunks, on drugs, or have disappeared. Vamoosed. So I'm really the only father they've got, and I do my damnedest to straighten out their tiny brains. Some of those brutes are so screwed up—you wouldn't believe! *Mens sana in corpore sano*. That's really what I'm hoping for these kids. What I'm working toward. Let's eat."

He had made a salad of cut-up iceberg lettuce topped with gobs of mayonnaise. The roast beef sandwiches had obviously been purchased in a deli; they were rounded with the meat filling, also slathered with mayonnaise. He opened two more beers for us and we ate and drank. And he talked.

He was a very intelligent, articulate man, and he talked well. What impressed me most about him was his animal energy. He attacked his sandwich wolfishly, forked the salad into his mouth in great, gulping mouthfuls, swilled the beer in throat-wrenching swallows.

"But it all costs money," he was saying. "Money, money, money: the name of the game. There's no church available for me—for any of the tent-makers. So we have to make our own way. Earn enough to do the work we want to do."

"Maybe that's an advantage," I said.

He looked at me, startled. "You're very perceptive, Joshua," he said. "If you mean what I think you mean, and I think you do. Yes, it's an advantage in that it keeps us in closer touch with the secular life, gives us a better understanding of the everyday problems and frustrations of the ordinary working stiff—and stiffess! A pastor who's in the same church for years and years grows moss. Sees the same people day in and day out until he's bored out of his skull. There's a great big, cruel, wonderful, striving world out there, but the average preacher is stuck in his little backwater with weekly sermons, organ music, and the terrible problem of how to pay for a new altar cloth. No wonder so many of them crawl in a bottle or run off with the soprano in the choir."

"How did you meet Tippi Kipper?" I asked.

Something fleeting through his eyes. He became a little less voluble.

"A friend of a friend of a friend," he said. "Joshua, the rich of New York are a city within a city. They all know each other. Go to the same parties. I was lucky enough to break into the magic circle. They pass me along, one to another. A friend of a friend of a friend. That's how I met Tippi."

"Was she in the theater?" I asked.

He grinned. "That's what she says. But no matter. If she wants to play Lady Bountiful, I'm the bucko who'll show her how. Don't get me wrong, Joshua. I'm grateful to Tippi Kipper and I'll be eternally grateful to her kind, generous husband and remember him in my prayers for the rest of my life. But I'm a realist, Joshua. It was an ego thing with the Kippers, I suppose. As it is for all my patrons. And patronesses."

"Sol Kipper contributed to your, uh, activities?" I asked.

"Oh sure. Regularly. What the hell—he took it off his taxes. I'm registered in the State of New York. Strictly nonprofit. Not by choice!" he added with a harsh bark of laughter.

"When you counsel your patrons," I said slowly, trying to frame the question, "the rich patrons, like Tippi Kipper, what are their problems mostly? I mean, it seems unreal to me that people of such wealth should have problems."

"Very real problems," he said soberly. "First of all, guilt for their wealth when they see poverty and suffering all around them. And then they have the same problems we all have: loneliness, the need for love, a sense of our own worthlessness."

He was staring at me steadily, openly. It was very difficult to meet those hard, challenging eyes.

"He left a suicide note," I said. "Did you know that?"

"Yes. Tippi told me."

"In the note, he apologized to her. For something he had done. I wonder what it was?"

"Oh, who the hell knows? I never asked Tippi and she never volunteered the information. It could have been anything. It could have been something ridiculous. I know they had been having, ah, sexual problems. It could have been that, it could have been a dozen other things. Sol was the worst hypochondriac I've ever met. I'm sure others have told you that."

"When did you see him last?" I asked casually.

"The day before he died," he said promptly. "On a Tuesday. We had a grand talk in his office and he gave me a very generous check. Then he had to go somewhere for a meeting."

We sat a few moments in silence. We finished our second beers. Then I glanced at my watch.

"Good heavens!" I said. "I had no idea it was so late. I've got to get back to my office while I still have a job. Pastor, thank you for a very delightful and instructive lunch. I've enjoyed every minute of it."

"Come again," he said. "And often. You're a good listener; did anyone ever tell you that? And bring your friends. And tell them to bring their checkbooks!"

I returned to the TORT building at about 2:50, scurrying out of a drizzly rain that threatened to turn to snow. Yetta Apatoff greeted me with a giggle.

"She's waiting for you," she whispered.

"Who?"

She indicated with a nod of her head, then covered her mouth with her palm. There was a woman waiting in the corridor outside my office.

She was at least 78 inches tall, and wearing a fake monkey fur coat that made her look like an erect gorilla. As I approached her, I thought this was Hamish Hooter's particularly tasteless joke, and wondered how many applicants he had interviewed before he found this one.

But as I drew closer, I saw she was no gorgon. She was, in fact, quite pleasant looking, with a quiet smile and that resigned placidity I recognized. All very short, very tall, and very fat people have it.

"Hello," I said. "I'm Joshua Bigg. Waiting for me?"

"Yes, Mr. Bigg," she said, not even blinking at my diminutive size. Perhaps she had been forewarned. She handed me an employment slip from Hooter's office. "My name is Gertrude Kletz."

"Come in," I said. "Let me take your coat."

I sat behind the desk and she sat in my visitor's chair. We chatted for almost half an hour, and as we talked, my enthusiasm for her grew. Hooter had seen only her huge size, but I found her sensible, calm, apparently qualified, and with a wry sense of humor.

She was married to a sanitation worker and, since their three children were grown and able to take care of themselves, she had decided to become a temporary clerk-typist-secretary: work she had done before her marriage. If possible, she didn't want to work later than 3:00 P.M., so she could be back in Brooklyn in time to cook dinner. We agreed on four hours a day, 11:00 A.M. to 3:00 P.M., with no lunch period, on Monday, Wednesday, and Friday.

She was a ruddy woman with horsey features and a maiden's innocent eyes. Her hair was iron-gray and wispy. For a woman her size, her voice was surprisingly light. She was dressed awkwardly, although I could not conceive how a woman of her heft could possibly be garbed elegantly. She wore a full gray flannel skirt that would have provided enough material for a suit for me. With vest. A no-nonsense white blouse was closed at the neck with a narrow black ribbon, and she wore a tweed jacket in a hellish plaid that would have looked better on Man-o-War. Opaque hose and sensible brogues completed her ensemble. She wore only a thin gold wedding band on her capable hands.

I explained to her as best I could the nature of my work at Tabatchnick, Orsini, Reilly, and Teitelbaum. Then I told her what I expected from her: filing, typing finished letters from my rough drafts, answering my phone, taking messages, doing simple, basic research from sources that I would provide.

"Think you can handle that, Mrs. Kletz?" I asked.

"Oh yes," she said confidently. "You must expect me to make mistakes, but I won't make the same mistake twice."

She sounded better and better.

"There is one other thing," I said. "Much of my work—and thus your work, too—will involve matters in litigation. It is all strictly confidential. You cannot take the job home with you. You cannot discuss what you learn here with anyone else, including husband, family, friends. I must be able to depend upon your discretion."

"You can depend on it," she said almost grimly. "I don't blab."

"Good," I said, rising. "Would you like to start tomorrow or would you prefer to begin on Monday?"

"Tomorrow will be fine," she said, heaving herself upright. "Will you be here then?"

"Probably," I said, thinking about my Friday schedule. "If not, I'll leave instructions for you on my desk. Will that be satisfactory?"

"Sure," she said equably.

I stood on tiptoe to help her on with that ridiculous coat. Then we shook hands, smiling, and she was gone. I thought her a very serene, reassuring woman, and I was grateful to Hamish Hooter. I'd never tell him that, of course.

The moment Mrs. Kletz had departed, I called Hooter's office. Fortunately he was out, but I explained to his assistant what was needed: a desk, chair, typewriter, wastebasket, stationery and supplies, phone, etc., all to be installed in the corridor directly outside my office door. By eleven o'clock the following morning.

"Mr. Bigg!" the assistant gasped in horror. I knew her: a frightened, rabbity woman, thoroughly tyrannized by her boss. "We cannot possibly provide all that by tomorrow morning."

"As soon as possible, then," I said crisply. "My assistant was hired with the approval of the senior partners. Obviously she needs a place to work."

"Yes, Mr. Bigg," she said submissively.

I hung up, satisfied. Today, a temporary assistant. Soon, a full-time secretary. A larger office. Then the *vvorrld!*

I spent the remainder of the afternoon at my desk. Outside, the snow had thickened; TORT employees with radios in their offices reported that three to five inches of snow were predicted before the storm slackened around midnight. Word came down from upstairs that because of the snowfall anyone who wished to leave early could do so. Gradually the building emptied until, by 5:00 P.M., it was practically deserted, the noise stilled, corridors vacant. I stayed on. It seemed foolish to go home to Chelsea and then journey uptown to meet Perdita Schug at Mother Tucker's at 7:00. So I decided to remain in the office until it was time for my dinner date.

I got up and looked out into the main hallway. The lights had already been dimmed and the night security guard was seated at Yetta Apatoff's desk. Beyond him, through the glass entrance doors, I saw a curtain of snow, torn occasionally by heavy gusts.

I went back into my office, wishing that Roscoe Dollworth had left a bottle of vodka hidden in the desk or file cabinet. A hopeless wish, I knew. Besides, on a night like that, a nip of brandy would be more to my liking. Now if only I had—

I sank slowly into my chair, suddenly realizing what it was that had puzzled me about Professor Yale Stonehouse's study: the bottle of Rémy Martin on the silver salver was new, uncorked, still sealed. That meant, apparently, that it had been there since the night he disappeared.

There was a perfectly innocent explanation, of course: he had finished his previous bottle the night before and had set out a fresh bottle, intending to return when he left the Stonehouse apartment on the night of January 10th.

There was another explanation, not so innocent. And that was that Professor Stonehouse had been poisoned not by doctored cocoa, but by arsenic added to his brandy. He had both cocoa and brandy every night before retiring. The lethal doses could have been added in either. And if he had discovered the source, it might account for the sealed bottle in his study.

I glanced at my watch. It was a few minutes past 5:30—a bad time to call. But I had to know. I dialed the Stonehouse apartment.

"Yah?" Olga Eklund said.

"Hi, Olga," I said. "This is Joshua Bigg."

"Yah."

"How are you?"

"Is not nice," she said. "The weather."

"No, it looks like a bad storm. Olga, I wonder if I could talk to Mrs. Dark for a moment—if it isn't too much trouble."

"I get her," she said stolidly.

I waited impatiently for almost three minutes before Mrs. Dark came on the line.

"Hello, dearie," she said brightly.

"Effie," I said, "I'm sorry to bother you at this hour. I know you must be busy with the evening meal."

"No bother. Everything's cooking. Now it's just a matter of waiting."

"I have a few more little questions. I know you'll think they're crazy, but they really are important, and you could be a big help in discovering what happened to the Professor."

"Really?" she said, pleasantly surprised. "Well, I'll do what I can."

"Effie, who buys the liquor for the family—the whiskey, wine, beer, and so forth?"

"I do. I call down to the liquor store on Columbus Avenue and they deliver it."

"And after they deliver it, where is it kept?"

"Well, I always make certain the bar in the living room is kept stocked with everything that might be needed. Plenty of sherry for you-know-who. The reserve I keep right here in the kitchen. In the bottom cupboard."

"And the Professor's brandy? That he drank every night?"

"I always kept an extra bottle or two on hand. God forbid we should ever run out when he wanted it!"

"How long did a bottle last him, Effie? The bottle in his study, I mean?"

"Oh, maybe ten days."

"So he finished about three bottles of cognac a month?"

"About."

"And those bottles were kept in the kitchen cupboard?"

"That's right."

"Who put a fresh bottle in the Professor's study?"

"He'd come in here and fetch it himself. Or I'd take it to him if he had a dead soldier. Or like as not, Glynis would bring him a new bottle."

"And there was usually a bottle of Rémy Martin in the living room bar as well?"

"Oh no," she said, laughing. "The brandy in there is Eyetalian. The Professor kept the good stuff for himself."

He would, I thought, gleeful at what I had learned.

"One more question, Effie," I said. "Very important. Please think carefully and try to recall before you answer. In the month or so before the Professor disappeared, do you remember bringing a fresh bottle of brandy to his study?"

She was silent.

"No," she said finally, "I didn't bring him any. Maybe Glynis did, or maybe he came into the kitchen and got it himself. Wait a minute. I'm on the kitchen extension; it'll just take me a minute to check."

She was gone a short while.

"That's odd," she said. "I was checking the cupboard. I remember having two bottles in there. There's one there now and one unopened bottle in the Professor's study."

"Do you recall buying any new bottles of Rémy Martin in the month or six weeks before the Professor disappeared?"

Silence again for a moment.

"That's odd," she repeated. "I don't remember buying any, but I should have, him going through three bottles a month. But I can't recall ordering a single bottle. I'll have to go through my bills to make sure."

"Could you do that, Effie?"

"Be glad to," she said briskly. "Now I've got to ring off; something's beginning to scorch."

"You've been very kind," I said hurriedly. "A big help."

"Really?" she said. "That's nice."

We hung up.

If I had been Professor Stonehouse, learning I was a victim of arsenic poisoning, I would have set out to discover how it was being done and who was doing it. And, I was certain, he had discovered who had been doing the fiddling.

It was then getting on to 6:00 P.M. I had no idea how long it would take me to get uptown in the storm, so I donned rubbers, turned up the collar of my overcoat, pulled my hat down snugly, and started out. I said goodnight to the security guard and stepped outside.

I was almost blown away. This was not one of your soft, gentle snowfalls with big flakes drifting down slowly in silence and sparkling in the light of streetlamps and neon signs. This was a maelstrom, the whole world in turmoil. Snow came whirling straight down, was blown sideways, even rose up in gusty puffs from drifts beginning to pile up on street corners.

There were at least twenty people waiting for the Third Avenue bus. After a wait that seemed endless but was probably no more than a quarter-hour, not one but four buses appeared out of the swirling white. I wedged myself aboard the last one. The ride seemed to take an eternity. At 69th, five other passengers alighted and I was popped out along with them. I fought my way eastward against the wind, bent almost double to keep snow out of my face.

And there, right around the corner on Second Avenue, was a neon sign glowing redly through the snow: MOTHER TUCKER'S.

"Bless you, Mother," I said aloud.

Perdita was there, in the front corner of the bar, perched on a stool, wearing a black dress cut precariously low. Her head was back, gleaming throat exposed, and she was laughing heartily at something the man standing next to her had just said. The place was jammed in spite of the weather, but Perdita was easy to find.

She saw me almost the instant I saw her. She slid off the barstool with a very provocative movement and rushed to embrace me with a squeal of pleasure, burying me in her *embonpoint.*

"Josh!" she cried, and then made that deep, growling sound in her throat to signify pleasure. "I never, never, never thought you'd show up. I just can't believe you came out in all this shit to see little me." Her button eyes sparkled, her tongue darted in and out between wet lips. "You poor dear, we must get you thawed out. Col, see if you can get a round from Harry."

"What's your pleasure, sir?" her companion asked politely.

"Scotch, please, with water."

We introduced ourselves. He was Clyde Manila—Colonel Clyde Manila. Perdita called him Col, which could have meant in his case either Colonel or Colonial.

A bearded bartender, working frantically, heard the call, paused, and cupped his ear toward Colonel Manila.

"More of the same, Harry, plus Scotch and water."

Harry nodded and in a few moments set the drinks before us. I reached for my wallet but Harry swiftly extracted the required amount from the pile of bills and change on the bar in front of the Colonel.

"Thank you, sir," I said. "The next one's on me."

"Forget it," Perdita advised. "The Col's loaded. Aren't you, sweetheart?"

"I mean to be," he said, swallowing half his drink in one enormous gulp. "No use trying to get home on a night like this—what?" His tiny eyes closed in glee.

He was genially messy in effect—white walrus mustache, swollen boozy nose, hairy tweed hacking jacket, all crowned with an ill-fitting ginger toupee.

"I'm awfully hungry," I said. "Perdita, do you think there's any chance of our getting a table?"

"Sure," she said. "Col, talk to Max."

Obediently he moved away, pushing his way through the mob.

"A pleasant place," I said to Perdita, who was winking at someone farther down the bar.

"This joint?" she said. "A home away from home. You can always score here, Josh. Remember that: you can always score at Mother Tucker's. Here comes Col."

I turned to see Colonel Manila waving wildly at us.

"He's got a table," Perdita said. "Let's go."

"Is he going to eat with us?" I asked.

"Col? No way. He never eats."

I wanted to thank him for obtaining a table for us, but missed him in the crush.

At the table she said, "I want another drink, and then I want a Caesar salad, spaghetti with oil and garlic, scampi, and a parfait for dessert."

I cringed from fear that I might not have enough to pay for all that. I do not believe in credit cards.

"What are you drinking?" I asked.

"Who knows?" she said. "I've been here since one o'clock this afternoon."

A waitress appeared in a T-shirt that said "Flat is Beautiful." We settled on a drink for Perdita and the waitress left.

"Don't worry about the check," Perdita said breezily. "Colonel Manila will pay."

"Absolutely not," I said indignantly. "I invited you. He doesn't have to pay for our dinner."

"Don't be silly," she said. "He likes to buy me things. I told you—he's loaded. Light my cigarette."

Talking to her was no problem; it was only necessary to listen. She babbled through our second round of drinks, through her gargantuan meal and a bottle of Chianti. I tried, several times, to bring the conversation around to the Kipper household, saying such things as: "I imagine this is better food than Mrs. Neckin's." But Perdita picked up on none of these leads; her monologue would not be interrupted. I gave up and asked for a check, but the waitress assured me, "It's been taken care of."

"I told you," Perdita said, laughing. "The Colonel's always doing things like that for me. He thinks it buys him something."

"And does it?" I asked her.

"Sure," she said cheerfully. "What do you think? Let's go back to the bar."

This was not really necessary as she was quite drunk already. We rejoined the Colonel, and the idea of going to Hoboken for clams was raised. I said I wouldn't. Two young men came and whispered in Perdita's ear and she told them to bug off. They disappeared quickly. The noise was incredible.

Colonel Clyde Manila was seated, lopsided, on Perdita's barstool. The moment he saw us, he slid off and bowed to Perdita.

"Keeping it warm f'you, dear lady," he said, in a strangled voice.

"Colonel," I shouted, "I want to thank you for your kindness. The dinner was excellent."

Those pale little eyes seemed to have become glassy. "Good show," he said.

"May I buy you a drink, sir?" I asked.

"Good show," he said.

"Oh, don't be such a pooper, Josh," Perdita said. "Come dance with me."

She clasped me in her arms, closed her eyes, began to shuffle me about. "I just love Viennese waltzes," Perdita Schug said dreamily.

"I think that's 'Beautiful Ohio,' " I said.

"Nasty brutes," Colonel Manila said. He was at my shoulder, staggering after us around the minuscule dance floor. "They smell, y'know. Did you ever sheep a shear?" I had suspected that he was Australian.

"The last time I saw Paris," Perdita crooned in my ear. "Let's you and me make yum-yum."

"Perdita," I said, "I really—"

"Can we go to your place?" she whispered.

"Oh no. No, no, no. Really. I'm afraid that wouldn't—"

"Where is your place?"

"Miles from here. Way downtown. West side."

"Where is your place?" she said. "Yum-yum."

"Way downtown," I started again.

"Col!" she screamed. "We're going."

"Good show," he said.

We came out of Mother Tucker's and turned our backs to a vindictive wind that stung with driven snow. Manila motioned and we went plodding after him around the corner onto 69th Street. He halted at a car and began to fumble in his coat pockets for his keys. We all piled into the front, Perdita sitting in the middle.

"A joint," the Colonel said.

"Oh no, sir," I said. "I thought it was a very pleasant restaurant."

Perdita, already fishing in her purse, got out a fat, hand-rolled cigarette, both ends twisted.

She lighted it, took a deep drag, and held it out to the Col. He took a tremendous drag and half the cigarette seemed to disappear in a shower of sparks.

"Now, then," the Colonel said. He handed the joint back to Perdita, then busied himself with switches and buttons. In a few moments he had the headlights on, engine purring, the heater going. The snow on the windows began to melt away.

"Whiskey," the Colonel said, like a drillmaster rapping out commands.

Perdita twisted around, got onto her knees on the front seat, and leaned far over into the rear compartment. Her rump jutted into the air. Colonel Manila slapped it lightly.

"There's a gel," he said affectionately.

She flopped back to her original position with a full decanter and three tumblers, all in cut crystal. She poured us all drinks, big drinks, then set the decanter on the floor between her feet.

I *knew* we would be stopped. I knew the police would arrest us. I could imagine the charges. Perhaps, I thought hopefully, I might get off with three years because of my youthful appearance and exemplary record.

Nothing of the sort happened. The Colonel drove expertly. Even after he turned on the radio to a rock-and-roll station and kept banging the steering wheel with one palm in time to the music, still he smoked, drank, stopped for traffic lights, negotiated turns skillfully, and pulled up right in front of my door, scrunching the limousine into a snowbank. I laughed shrilly.

"Well, this has certainly been a memorable evening," I said, listening to the quaver in my voice. "I do want to thank—"

"Out," Perdita Schug growled, nudging me. "Let's go."

I stumbled out hastily into the snow. She came scrambling after me. I looked back in at Colonel Clyde Manila. He waggled fingers at me. I waggled back. Perdita slammed the car door, then took my arm in a firm, proprietary grip.

"Up we go," she said gaily.

It was then around midnight. I think. Or it could have been ten. Or it might have been two. Whatever it was, I hoped Mrs. Hermione Hufnagel, Cleo, Captain Bramwell Shank, Adolph Finkel, and Madame Zora Kadinsky were all behind locked doors and sleeping innocently in their warm beds.

"Shh," I said to Perdita Schug, leading her upstairs. I giggled nervously.

"What's with this *shh* shit?" she demanded.

I got her inside my apartment. She was moving now with deliberate and exaggerated caution.

I switched on the overhead light. I draped our coats and hats over a chair back. She looked around the living room. I awaited her reaction. There was none. She flopped into my armchair.

"Come sit on my lap," she said with a vulpine grin.

I began to stammer, but she grabbed my wrist, drew me to her with surprising strength, and plunked me down onto her soft thighs.

She kissed me. My toes curled. Inside shoes and the rubbers I had neglected to remove.

"Mmm," she said. "That's better. Much better."

She wriggled around, pulled me tighter onto her lap. She had a muscled arm around my neck. She pressed our cheeks together. "The last time I saw Paris," she sang.

"Perdita," I said, giving it one last try, "I can't understand how you can endure doing the work you do. I mean, you've got so much personality and, uh, talent and experience. Why do you stay on as a maid for Tippi Kipper?"

"It's a breeze," she said promptly. "The pay is good. And I get meals and my own apartment. My own telephone. What should I be doing—selling gloves in Macy's?"

"But still, it must be boring."

"Sometimes yes," she said. "Sometimes no. Like any other job."

"Is Mrs. Kipper, ah, you know, understanding?"

"Oh sure," she said, laughing. "I get away with murder. That Chester Heavens would like to bounce my ass right out of there, and Mrs. Neckin called me 'the spawn of the devil.' They'd both like me out of there, but Tippi will never can me. Never."

"Why not?"

"Give us another kissy," she said.

I gave her another kissy.

"You're learning," she said. "Listen, Tippi plays around as much as I do. And she knows I know it."

"Plays around now or before? I mean, when her husband was alive?"

"Oh shit, Josh, she's *always* played around. As long as I've been there. That'll be four years come April."

"How do you know?"

"How do I know? Oh, you poor, sweet, innocent lamb. You think I don't smell the grass on her and see her underwear and notice her hair is done a different way when she comes home from what she said was a bridge party? Listen, a woman *knows* these things. A maid especially. Scratches on her back. Fingerprints on her ass. Oh, she's making it; no doubt about *that*. Listen, Josh, I'm out of joints. You got any Scotch?"

"Well . . . uh, sure," I said. "But are you certain you want—"

"Get me a Scotch," she commanded.

I got her a drink.

"Where's yours?" she asked.

"We'll share this one," I said.

"A loving cup," she said. "And then the yum-yum. Where's the bed?"

"In the bedroom."

"Not yet," she said, shaking a reproving finger at me. "Don't be in such a rush, tiger."

"I'm really not," I assured her. "I mean, it's not what you—"

She grabbed my arm and pulled me down onto her lap again. I went to my fate willingly.

"So cute," she said drowsily. "You really are cute."

"Tippi isn't making it with Knurr, is she?"

"Ho-ho-ho," Perdita Schug said. "Is she ever. Two, three times a week, at least. He's very big in her life right now. Even in the house—can you beat that? I mean it. And while Sol was alive, too. The two of them in the elevator. How does that grab you? Did you ever make it in an elevator, Josh?"

"No, I never have."

"Me, neither," she said sorrowfully. "But once in a closet," she said, brightening. "The funny thing is . . ." Her voice trailed away.

"What's the funny thing?" I asked.

"I could have him like that," she said, trying to snap her fingers. But they just slid over each other. "Knurr, I mean. He's warm for my form. Always coming on strong. Copping a feel when she isn't looking. The guy's a cocksman. A religious cocksman. Now I'm ready for yum-yum."

She found the bedroom. I didn't turn on the bedside lamp; there was enough illumination coming from the hallway. She looked around dazedly, put a hand against the wall to support herself. She turned her back to me.

"Unzip," she said.

Obediently, I drew the long zipper down to her waist. She shrugged the dress off her shoulders, let it fall to the floor, stepped out of it. She was wearing bra, panties, sheer black panty hose. She shook her head suddenly, flinging her short flapper-cut about in a twirl.

"I'm zonked," she announced.

She plumped down suddenly on the bed, fell back, raised her legs high in the air.

"Peel me," she said.

There were a lot of other questions I wanted to ask her about Tippi Kipper and the Reverend Godfrey Knurr, but somehow this didn't seem the right time. I peeled off her panty hose.

She rolled around and wiggled beneath the bedclothes, pulled sheet and blanket up to her chin. In a moment, a slim white arm popped out and she tossed brassiere and panties onto the floor.

"Okay, tiger," she said sleepily. "The time is now. The moment of truth."

I stooped to pick up her dress. I shook out the wrinkles and hung it away in the closet. I picked up her lingerie and draped it neatly over the dresser.

When I turned back to the bed, she was asleep, breathing steadily, her head turned sideways on the pillow.

I brought her shoes from the living room, set them neatly beside the bed.

I awoke the next morning with cricks in my neck, shoulders, hips, thighs, and ankles, from a rude bed I had made of two chairs. Sometimes small stature is advantageous. I staggered to my feet and, in my underwear, began to waggle, flapping my arms, shaking my legs, rotating my head on my neck, and so forth. Such is the resilience of youth that I was soon able to walk upright with just the merest hint of a limp.

Perdita still slept tranquilly, head sideways on the pillow, covers drawn up to her chin, knees bent, as I had left her. Only the slow rise and fall of the blanket proved she was not deceased.

I went into the bathroom as noisily as I could, slammed the door, sang in the shower. I brushed my teeth, decided it was unnecessary to shave, and came bouncing out, a towel wrapped demurely about my loins.

"Hello, hello, hello," I caroled, then peeked into the bedroom. She was still sleeping.

I dressed in fresh linen and clothing, trying to make as much noise as possible. Finally dressed, I went back into the kitchen and banged around, boiling water for instant coffee. I brought two filled cups into the bedroom and set them on the bedside table. It was almost 8:30.

I sat on the bed and shook her shoulder gently. Then with more vigor. Then, I am ashamed to say, violently. Her eyes suddenly opened. She stared at the opposite wall.

"Wha'?" she said.

"Perdita," I said gently, "it is I, Joshua Bigg, and you are in my apartment in Chelsea. Colonel Clyde Manila drove us here. Do you remember?"

"Sure," she said brightly. She sat up suddenly in bed, the covers falling to her waist, and reached to embrace me. I hugged her gingerly.

"Feel all right?" I asked.

"Marvy," she said. "Just marvy."

"There's coffee here. Would you like a cup?"

"Why not?" she said. "Got any brandy?"

"I do," I said.

"Slug me," she said.

I went into the living room for the brandy bottle. By the time I returned, she was out of bed and in her lingerie. She drank off a little of her coffee and I topped it off with brandy. She stuck in a forefinger, stirred it around, then licked her finger.

She sat on the edge of the bed, sipping her coffee royal. I sat next to her. She turned to look at me.

"Josh," she said tenderly, "was I good for you?"

"You were wonderful for me."

"I didn't make too much noise, did I?"

"Not at all," I assured her. "It was perfect."

"For me, too," she said, sighing. "Perfect. I feel so loose and relaxed. We must get together again."

"Absolutely," I said.

"I'm always at Mother Tucker's on Thursday. Just drop by."

"I will."

"Promise?"

"I promise," I said, kissing the tip of her nose.

She finished her coffee, took her purse, and scampered into the bathroom for a short while. She came out looking radiant, eyes sparkling, lips wet. She dressed swiftly. We put on our coats and hats.

"Kissy," she said, turning her face up to me.

I unlocked my door, we went out into the hallway, and there was Adolph Finkel. He stared at us. He coughed once, a short, explosive blast.

"Good morning, Finkel," I said.

"Good morning, Bigg," he said.

He goggled at Perdita Schug.

"Hi," she said brightly.

"Uh, hi," he said. He nodded insanely, his head bobbing up and down on his thin neck. Then he turned and fled down the steps ahead of us.

"A neighbor," I explained.

"Unreal," Perdita murmured.

I had planned to get a cab, but when we came out onto the street, there was a chocolate-colored Rolls-Royce, and Colonel Clyde Manila behind the wheel, his furred collar turned up to his ears, his black leather cap set squarely atop his gingery toupee. He was sipping from a cut-glass tumbler of Scotch.

It hadn't registered with me that it was a Rolls. I turned to Perdita in disbelief.

"He's still here?" I said. "Waiting for you?"

"Sure," she said. "What do you think?"

5

•

YETTA APATOFF WAS ON THE PHONE, BUT GAVE ME A WARM SMILE and a flutter of fingers as I passed. I fluttered in return. Workmen were busy in the corridor outside my office, moving a desk, swivel chair, lamp, and other accessories into position. A telephone installer was on his knees at the baseboard, running a wire to connect with my office phone.

I sat at my desk and went over the latest additions to my file of pending requests for investigation. I divided the stack into two piles: those I felt could be answered by Mrs. Kletz, and those it would be necessary to handle myself. I then went through those I had delegated to my new assistant and scrawled in the margins the sources where she could obtain the information required.

I had started going through the Manhattan Yellow Pages, but was dismayed by the number of chemical laboratories listed and decided to entrust my new assistant with a sensitive assignment. I left a typed note, asking her to call each of the labs listed and say that she represented the attorneys handling the estate of the late Professor Yale Stonehouse. A question had arisen concerning a check the Professor had written to the lab without any accompanying voucher. She was to ask each laboratory to consult their files to establish the date of billing and the purpose for which the money was paid.

On my way out I stopped at Yetta Apatoff's desk to tell her that my assistant would be in at eleven. She giggled.

"Oh, Josh," she said, "she's so big and you're so small. It's so *funny* seeing the two of you together."

"Yes, yes," I said impatiently. "But I'm sure you and everyone else in the office will get used to it."

"So *funny!*" she repeated, squinching up her face in mirth. I wished she hadn't done that; it gave her the look of a convulsed porker.

I told her I'd return in plenty of time to take her to lunch at one o'clock. She nodded, still giggling as I left. It seemed to me she was exhibiting a notable lack of sensitivity.

I took a cab up to the Kipper townhouse, pondering what I might say to Tippi if I got the opportunity and how I might draw her out on matters not pertaining to my alleged inventory of her late husband's estate. I could devise no devilishly clever ploy, and decided my best approach was to appear the wide-eyed innocent.

Chester Heavens answered my ring at the outside iron gate. "Good morning, sah," he said, friendly enough.

"Good morning, Chester. I trust I am not causing any inconvenience by dropping by without calling first?"

"Not at all, sah," he said, ushering me into the looming entrance hall and holding out his hands for my hat and coat. "Mom is breakfasting in the dining room. If you'll just wait a moment, sah, perhaps I should inform her of your arrival."

I waited, standing, until he returned. "Mom asks if you would care to join her for a cup of coffee, sah?"

"I'd like that very much."

Mrs. Kipper was seated at the head of a long table. In the center was a silver bowl of camelias and lilies. She held a hand out to me as I entered.

"Good morning, Mr. Bigg," she said, smiling. "You're out early this morning."

"Yes, ma'am," I said, moving forward quickly to take her hand. "I'm anxious to finish up. Almost as anxious, I imagine, as you are to see the last of me."

"Not at all," she murmured. "You've had breakfast?"

"Oh yes, ma'am."

"But surely you'll join me for a cup of coffee?"

"Thank you. I'd like that."

"Chester, will you clear these things away, please, and bring Mr. Bigg a cup. And more hot coffee."

"Yes, mom," he said.

"Now you sit next to me, Mr. Bigg," Tippi said, gesturing toward the chair on her right. "I've always enjoyed a late, leisurely breakfast. It's really the best meal of the day—is it not?" Her manner seemed patterned after Loretta Young or Greer Garson.

I must admit she made a handsome picture, sitting erect at the head of that long, polished table: Portrait of a Lady. In pastels. She was wearing a two-layer nightgown peignoir, gauzy and flowing, printed with pale gardenias.

She seemed born to that splendid setting. If the Kipper sons had been telling the truth, if she had the background they claimed, she had effected a marvelous transformation. The silver-blonde hair was up, and as artfully coiffed as ever. No wrinkles in that half-century-old face; its masklike crispness hinted of a plastic surgeon's "tucks." The brown eyes with greenish flecks showed clear whites, the nose was perfectly patrician, the tight chin carried high.

I felt a shameful desire to dent that assured exterior by risking her ire.

"Mrs. Kipper," I said, "a small matter has come up concerning your late husband's estate, and we hoped you might be able to help us with it. During an inventory of your husband's office effects, a bill was found in the amount of five hundred dollars, submitted by a certain Martin Reape. It is marked simply: 'For services rendered.' We haven't been able to contact this Mr. Reape or determine the nature of the services he rendered. We hoped you might be able to assist us."

I was watching her closely. At my first mention of Martin Reape, her eyes lowered suddenly. She stretched out a hand for her coffee cup and raised it steadily to her lips. She did not look at me while I concluded my question, but set the cup slowly and carefully back into the center of the saucer with nary a clatter.

It was a remarkable performance, but a calculated one. She should not have taken a sip of coffee in the midst of my question, and she should have, at least, glanced at me as I spoke. Roscoe Dillworth had told me: "They'll take a drink, light a cigarette, bend over to retie their shoelace—anything to stall, to give themselves time to think, time to lie believably."

"Reape?" Mrs. Kipper said finally, meeting my eyes directly. "Martin Reape? How do you spell that?"

"R-e-a-p-e."

She thought a moment.

"Nooo," she said. "The name means nothing to me. Have you found it anywhere else in his records?"

"No, ma'am."

Did I see relief in her eyes or did I just want to see it there as evidence of guilt?

"I'm afraid I can't help you," she said, shaking her head. "My husband was involved in so many things and knew so many people with whom I was not acquainted."

I loved that ". . . people with whom I was not acquainted." So much more aristocratic than ". . . people I didn't know." I was horribly tempted to ask her how Las Vegas was the last time she saw it. Instead, I said . . .

"I understand your husband was very active in charitable work, Mrs. Kipper."

"Oh yes," she said sadly. "He gave generously."

"So Mr. Knurr told me," I said.

There was no doubt at all that this was news to her, and came as something of a shock. She took another sip of coffee. This time the cup clattered back into the saucer.

"Oh?" she said tonelessly. "I didn't know that you and Godfrey had discussed my husband's charities."

"Oh my yes," I said cheerfully. "The Reverend was kind enough to invite me down to Greenwich Village to witness his activities there. He's a remarkable man."

"He certainly is," she said grimly. She took up her cigarette case, extracted and tapped a cigarette with short, angry movements. I was ready with a match. She smacked the cigarette into her mouth, took quick, sharp puffs. Now she was Bette Davis.

"What else did you and Godfrey talk about?" she asked.

"Mostly about the boys he was working with and how he was trying to turn their physical energy and violence into socially acceptable channels."

"Did he say anything about me?" she demanded. The mask had dropped away. I saw the woman clearly.

I hesitated sufficiently long so that she would know I was lying.

"Why no, ma'am," I said mildly, my eyes as wide as I could make them. "The Reverend Knurr said nothing about you other than that you and your husband had made generous contributions to his program."

Something very thin, mean, and vitriolic came into that wrinkle-free face. It became harder and somehow menacing. All I could think of was the face of Glynis Stonehouse when I told her I knew of her father's poisoning.

"Oh yes," she said stonily. "We contributed. Take a look at Sol's canceled checks. You'll see."

I could not account for her anger. It did not seem justified simply by the fact that I had had a private conversation with the Reverend Knurr. I decided to flick again that raw nerve ending.

"He did say how difficult it had been for you," I said earnestly. "I mean your husband's death."

"So you did talk about me," she accused.

"Briefly," I said. "Only in passing. I hope someday, Mrs. Kipper, you'll tell me about your experiences in the theater. I'm sure they must have been fascinating."

She hissed.

"He told you that?" she said. "That I was in the theater?"

"Oh no," I said. "But surely it's a matter of common knowledge?"

"Well . . . maybe," she said grudgingly.

"As a matter of fact," I said innocently, "I think I heard it first from Herschel and Bernard Kipper."

"You've been talking to *them?*" she said, aghast.

"Only in the line of duty," I said hastily. "To make a preliminary inventory of your late husband's personal effects in his office. Mrs. Kipper, I'm sorry if I've offended you. But the fact of your having been in the theater doesn't seem to me to be degrading at all. Quite the contrary."

"Yes," she said tightly. "You're right."

"Also," I said, "as an employee of a legal firm representing your interest, you can depend upon my rectitude."

"Your *what?*"

"I don't gossip, Mrs. Kipper. Whatever I hear in connection with a client goes no farther than me."

She looked at me, eyes narrowing to cracks.

"Yeah," she said, and I wondered what had happened to "Yes." Then she asked: "What a client tells a lawyer, that's confidential, right?"

"Correct, Mrs. Kipper. It's called privileged information. The attorney cannot be forced to divulge it."

Those eyes widened, stared at the ceiling.

"Privileged information," she repeated softly. "That's what I thought."

Knowing she believed me to be an attorney, I awaited some startling confession. But she was finished with me. Perhaps Knurr had told her I was not a member of the bar. In any event, she stood suddenly and I hastened to rise and move her chair back.

"Well, I'm sure you want to get on with your work, Mr. Bigg," she said, extending her hand, the lady again.

"Yes, thank you," I said, shaking her hand warmly. "And for the coffee. I've enjoyed our talk."

She sailed from the room without answering, her filmy robes floating out behind her.

"Have a good day," I called after her, but I don't think she heard me.

I felt I had to spend *some* time in the townhouse to give credence to my cover story, so I took the elevator up to the sixth floor. I went into the empty, echoing party room and wandered about, heels clacking on the bare floor. I was drawn to those locked French doors. I stood there, looking out onto the terrace from which Sol Kipper had made his fatal plunge.

Small, soiled drifts of snow still lurked in the shadows. There were melting patches of snow on tables and chairs. The outdoor plants were brown and twisted. It was a mournful scene, a dead, winter scene.

He came up here, or was brought up here, and he leaped, or was thrown, into space. Limbs flailing. A boneless dummy flopping down. Suicide or murder, no man deserved that death. It sent a bitter, shocking charge through my mouth, as when you bite down on a bit of tinfoil.

I felt, I *knew,* it had been done to him, but I could not see how. Four people in the house, all on the ground floor. Four apparently honest people. And even if they were all lying, which of them was strong enough and resolute enough? And how was it done? Then, too, there was that suicide note . . .

Depressed, I descended to the first floor. I stuck my head into the kitchen and saw Chester Heavens and Mrs. Bertha Neckin seated at the pantry table. They were drinking coffee from the same silver service that had just graced the dining room table.

Chester noticed me, rose immediately, and followed me out into the entrance hall where I reclaimed my hat and coat.

"Thank you, Chester," I said. "I hope I won't be bothering you much longer."

"No bother, sah," he said. He looked at me gravely. "You are coming to the end of your work?"

His look was so inscrutable that for a moment I wondered if he knew, or guessed, what I was up to.

"Soon," I said. "It's going well. I should be finished with another visit or two."

He nodded without speaking and showed me out, carefully trying the lock on the outer gate after I left.

I hailed a cab on Fifth and told the driver to drop me at the corner of Madison Avenue and 34th Street. From there I walked the couple of blocks to the ladies' wear shop to buy the green sweater for Yetta Apatoff. I described Yetta's physique as best I could, without gestures, and the kind saleslady selected the size she thought best, assuring me that with a sweater of that type, too small was better than too large, and if the fit wasn't acceptable, it could be exchanged. I had it gift-wrapped and then put into a shopping bag that effectively concealed the contents.

When I got back to my office, Mrs. Gertrude Kletz was seated at her new desk in the corridor. She was on the phone, making notes. I thought, gratified, that she looked very efficient indeed. I went to my own desk, sat down in my coat and hat, and made rapid, scribbled notes of my conversation with Mrs. Tippi Kipper. My jottings could not convey the *flavor* of our exchange, but I wanted to make certain I had a record of her denial of knowing Martin Reape, her admission of heavy contributions to the Reverend Godfrey Knurr, and the anger she had exhibited when she learned of my meeting with Knurr.

I was just finishing up when my new assistant came into the office, carrying a spiral-bound stenographer's pad.

"Good morning, Mrs. Kletz," I said.

"Good morning, Mr. Bigg."

We beamed at each other. She was wearing a tentlike flannel jumper over a man-tailored shirt. I asked her if her desk, chair, telephone, and supplies were satisfactory, and she said they were.

"Did you get all my notes?" I asked her. "Did they make sense to you?"

"Oh yes," she said. "No problems. I found the lab that did business with Professor Stonehouse."

"You didn't?" I said, surprised and delighted. "How many calls did it take?"

"Fourteen," she said casually, as if it was a trifle. A treasure, that woman! "They did two chemical analyses for Professor Stonehouse." She handed me a note. "Here's all the information: date and cost and so forth. They didn't tell me what the analyses were."

"That's all right," I said. "I know what they were. I think. Thank you, Mrs. Kletz."

"On the other research requests—I'm working on those now."

"Good," I said. "Stick with it. If you have any questions, don't be afraid to ask me."

"Oh, I won't be afraid," she said.

I didn't think she would be—of anything. I made a sudden decision. From instinct, not reason.

"Mrs. Kletz," I said, "I'm going out to lunch at one and will probably be back in an hour or so. If you get some time, take a look at the Kipper and Stonehouse files. They're in the top drawer of the cabinet. I'd like your reaction."

"All right," she said placidly. "This is interesting work, isn't it?"

"Oh yes," I agreed enthusiastically. "Interesting."

I took off my coat and hat long enough to wash up in the men's room. Then I put them on again, took up my shopping bag, and sallied forth to take Yetta Apatoff to lunch.

Fifteen minutes later we were seated at a table for two in the Chinese restaurant on Third Avenue. I ordered egg rolls, wonton soup, shrimp with lobster sauce, and fried rice. After all, it *was* a birthday celebration. Before the egg rolls were served, I withdrew the gift-wrapped package from the shopping bag and presented it to Yetta.

"Many happy returns," I said.

"Oh, Josh," she said, her eyes moons, "you *shouldn't* have. I had no idea . . . !" She tore at the gift-wrapped package with frantic fingers. When she saw the contents, her mouth made an O of delighted surprise.

"Josh," she breathed, "how did you *know?*" Understandably triumphant due to the lead I'd just taken over Hooter in the Apatoff Stakes, I nonetheless managed to smile modestly and flirt sheepishly for the rest of the meal. The warmth of Yetta's grasp as we parted definitely promised an escalation of our relationship in the very near future.

As I approached my office, I noticed Mrs. Kletz was poring over a file on her corridor desk. She was so engrossed that she didn't look up until I was standing next to her.

"Which one is that?" I asked, gesturing toward the folder.

"The Kipper case. I'm almost finished with it. People," she intoned with a sweetly sad half-smile. She wasn't saying, "The horror of them," she was saying, "The wonder of them."

"Yes," I said. "Come into my office, please, when you're finished with it."

I hung away my coat and hat and called Ada Mondora and asked for a meeting with Mr. Teitelbaum. She said she'd get back to me.

Mrs. Kletz had left on my desk the research inquiries she had answered, using the sources I had supplied. She'd done a thorough job and I was satisfied. I typed up first-draft memos to the junior partners and associates who had requested the information and left them for Mrs. Kletz to do the final copies. She came into my office as I was finishing, carrying the Kipper file.

"Sit down, Mrs. Kletz," I said, motioning toward my visitor's chair. "I have just one more rough to do and I'll be through. You did a good job on these, by the way."

"Thank you, sir," she said.

It was one of the few times in my life I had been called "Sir." I found it an agreeable experience.

I finished the final draft and pushed the stack across the desk to my assistant.

"I'll need two finished copies on these," I said. "Do what you can today and the rest can go over to Monday." I drew the Kipper file toward me and rapped it with my knuckles. "Strictly confidential," I said, staring at her.

"Oh yes. I understand."

"What do you think of it all?"

"Mr. Bigg," she said, "is it always the one you least suspect?"

I laughed. "Don't try to convince the New York Police Department of that. They believe it's always the one you *most* suspect. And they're usually right. Who do you suspect?"

"I think the widow and the preacher are in cahoots," she said seriously. "I think they were playing around before the husband died. He suspected and hired that private detective to make sure. When he had the evidence, he decided to change his will. So they killed him."

I looked at her admiringly.

"Yes," I said, nodding, "that's my theory, and it's a—it's an elegant theory that explains most of the known facts. After Sol Kipper died, Marty Reape tried blackmail. But he underestimated their determination, or their desperation. So he was killed. His widow inherited his files, including his copies of the Kipper evidence. She sold the evidence, or part of it, or perhaps she made copies, realizing what a gold mine she had. She got greedy, so she had to be eliminated, too. Does that make sense?"

"Oh yes. Tippi and Knurr, they were only interested in Mr. Kipper's money. But with the evidence he had, he could get a divorce, and her settlement would have been a lot less than she'll inherit now. So they murdered the poor man."

"It's an elegant theory," I repeated. "There's just one thing wrong with it: they couldn't have done it."

"I've been puzzling that out," she said, frowning. "Is it positive there was no one else in the house?"

"A hired killer? The servants say that no one came in and they saw no one leave. The police were there soon after Sol died, and they searched the house thoroughly and found no one."

"Could they be lying? The servants? For money?"

"I don't believe they're lying, and the detective who did the police investigation doesn't think they are either. If they were in on it, they would all have to be in on it. That means five people engaged in a murder conspiracy. I can't see it. The more people involved, the weaker the chain. Too many opportunities for continuing blackmail. Tippi and Knurr are too smart for that. I think it happened the way they told it: four people on the ground floor when Sol Kipper went to his death."

She sighed. "Leaving a suicide note," she said.

"Yes, there's that, too."

"What will you do now?"

"Well, I—" I stopped suddenly. What would I do now? "I don't know," I confessed to Mrs. Kletz. "I don't know what more I can do. I can follow Tippi or the Reverend Knurr. I can definitely establish that they are having an affair. But what good will that do? It won't bring me any closer to learning how the murder of Sol Kipper was engineered. And I'm just as convinced as you are that it *was* murder."

"Chicago," she said.

"What?"

"In your notes, Mr. Bigg. The Reverend told you he was from the Chicago area. Then the Kipper sons told you that they thought Tippi came from Chicago."

I took a deep breath. "Thank you, Mrs. Kletz," I said fervently. "That's exactly the sort of thing I hoped you might spot. I've been too close to this thing, but you came to it fresh. All right, maybe they're both from the Chicago area. What does that prove? Probably nothing. Unless they knew each other before they ended up in New York. Even that might not mean anything unless . . ."

"Unless," she said, "they had been involved together in something similar."

"Back in Chicago?"

"Yes."

"Yes," I agreed. "It's not much, but it might be sufficient to convince the NYPD to reopen their investigation. They've got resources and techniques to unravel this thing a lot faster than I could hope to. Meanwhile, I'll try to dig up what I can on the Chicago background of Tippi and Knurr. It may prove to be nothing, but I've got to—"

The phone rang. Mr. Teitelbaum was free now.

Ada Mondora clinked her gypsy jewelry at me and smiled pertly as I stood before her desk.

"I hear someone had a nice lunch today," she said archly.

"News does get around, doesn't it?" I said.

"What should we talk about?" she demanded. "Torts? Yetta just loves her sweater."

I groaned.

"I think my bet is safe," Ada said complacently. "I'm betting on you. Thelma will just die when she hears about the sweater."

"Thelma Potts? She's betting on Hooter?"

"Didn't you know?" Ada asked innocently, widening those flashing eyes and showing her brilliant white teeth. "As a matter of fact, Thelma and I have a private bet. Lunch at the Four Seasons. I know exactly what I'm going to order."

When I entered Mr. Teitelbaum's office, he was seated, as usual, behind his enormous desk, his pickled hands clasped on top. He motioned me to an armchair, asked for a report on the Stonehouse investigation.

Consulting my notes, I capsuled the results of my inquiries as briefly and succinctly as I could. I told him that I first suspected the nightly cup of cocoa was the means by which Professor Stonehouse was poisoned, but I now realized it was the brandy in the Professor's study. I reported that Stonehouse had submitted two substances for analysis at a chemical laboratory.

"I will try to obtain copies of those analyses, sir," I said. "I'd be willing to bet the arsenic was put into the Professor's cognac."

"By whom?"

I told him about my interviews with Powell Stonehouse and Wanda Chard, and my last meeting with Glynis Stonehouse. I said that Powell seemed to have easiest access to the poison, via Wanda Chard, but since he was banished from his father's home during the period of the poisoning, it seemed unlikely that he was the culprit, unless he was working in collusion with one or more of the other members of the household.

"You think that likely?" Mr. Teitelbaum asked in his surprisingly vigorous voice.

"No, sir."

"Surely not the wife, then? On her own?"

"No, sir."

"The servants?"

"No, sir," I said, sighing. "The daughter. But I must tell you, I have absolutely no proof to support that suspicion. I don't know where she could have obtained the arsenic. I don't know what her motive might possibly have been."

"Do you think her mentally unbalanced?"

"No, sir, I do not. Mr. Teitelbaum, it might help if you could explain to me what happens legally in this case. I mean, what happens to the assets of the missing man?"

It was his turn to sigh. He entwined his leathery fingers, looked down on his clasped hands on the desktop as if they were a ten-legged animal, a kind of lizard perhaps, that had nothing to do with him.

"Mr. Bumble said that the law is an ass," he said. "I might amend that to say that the law is usually half-ass."

A lawyer's joke. I laughed dutifully.

"The laws concerning the estate of a missing person are somewhat involved," he continued sharply. "Common law, as approved by the Supreme Court in 1878 in the case of Davie versus Briggs, establishes a presumption of death after seven years. However, the Stonehouse case must be adjudicated under the statutes of New York State, of which there are two applying to this particular situation."

I stifled a groan and settled a little deeper into my armchair. I was in for a lecture, when all I had wanted was a one-sentence answer.

"The Estates, Powers and Trusts Law allows a presumption of death after five years of continuous absence, providing—and this is one of the reasons I requested you make a thorough investigation—providing that the missing person was exposed to a specific peril of death and that a diligent search was made prior to application that a declaration of presumed death be issued by the court. At that point, after five years, assuming the two conditions I have just stated have been observed, the missing person may be presumed dead and his will submitted to probate. But if, subsequent to those five years, he suddenly appears, he may legally claim his estate. Thus, 'diligent search' is of paramount importance in the presumption of his death. Are you following me, Mr. Bigg?"

"Yes, sir," I said. "I think so."

"On the other hand," Mr. Teitelbaum said with great satisfaction, and I realized that, to a lawyer, "On the other hand" contains as much emotional impact as "I love you" would to a layman.

"On the other hand," he continued, "the Surrogate's Court Procedure Act, dealing with the administration of the estates of missing persons, provides that not until ten years after the date of disappearance does the missing person lose all interest in his property. The estate is then distributed to his heirs by will or the laws of intestacy. This is simply a statute of limitations on the time in which a missing person may claim his estate. After those ten years, he is, to all intents and purposes, legally dead, although he may still be alive. If he shows up in person after those ten years, he owns nothing."

"And during those ten years, sir? Can his dependents draw on his assets?"

"A temporary administrator, appointed by the court, preserves the assets of the estate, pays the required taxes, supports the missing person's family, and so forth. But once again, a diligent search must be made to locate the missing person."

"Now I am confused, sir," I said. "Apparently, under the first law you mentioned, a missing person can be declared dead after five years. Under the second law, it requires ten years before the estate can be divided amongst his heirs."

"A nice point," Mr. Teitelbaum said. "And one that has occasioned some heated debate amongst our younger attorneys and clerks to whom I assigned the problem. My personal opinion is that the two statutes are not necessarily contradictory. For instance, in the second case, under the Surrogate's Court Procedure Act, during the ten-year administration of the estate, the administrator or any interested person may petition for probate of the will by presenting sufficient proof of death. I would judge," he added dryly, "that the finding of the body would constitute sufficient proof."

"Uh, well, sir," I said, trying to digest all this, "what is going to happen to the Stonehouse family, exactly?"

"I would say," he intoned in his most judicial tones, "after reviewing the options available, that they would be wise to file for relief under the SCPA and accept in good spirit the appointment of a temporary administrator of Professor Stonehouse's estate. That is the course I intend to urge upon Mrs. Stonehouse. However, in all honesty, Mr. Bigg, I must confess that I have not been moving expeditiously in this matter. Mrs. Stonehouse and the children, while hardly individually wealthy, have sufficient assets of their own to carry them awhile without fear of serious privation. Their apartment, for instance, is a cooperative, fully paid for, with a relatively modest maintenance charge. I have, in a sense, been dragging my feet on an application for appointment of a temporary administrator until we can prove to the court that a diligent search for Professor Stonehouse has indeed been made. Also, I am quite disturbed by what you have told me of the attempted poisoning. I would like to see that matter cleared up before a court application is made. I would not care to see an allowance paid to a family member who might have been, ah, criminally involved in the Professor's disappearance."

"No, sir," I said. "I wouldn't either. Another point: supposing that an administrator is appointed for a period of ten years and nothing is heard from Professor Stonehouse during that time. Then his will goes to probate?"

"That is correct."

"And if no will can be found?"

"Then the division of his estate would be governed by the laws of intestacy."

"Could he disinherit his wife? If he left a will, I mean?"

"Doubtful. Disinheriting one's spouse is not considered in the public interest. However, he might disinherit his wife with a clear reason provable in a court of law."

"Like trying to poison him?"

"That might be sufficient reason for disinheritance," he acknowledged cautiously. "Providing incontrovertible proof was furnished."

"The same holds true for his son and daughter, I presume?"

Mr. Ignatz Teitelbaum took a deep breath.

"Mr. Bigg," he said, "the laws of inheritance are not inviolable. Even an expertly drawn will is not a sacred document. Anyone can sue, and usually does. Ask any attorney. These matters are usually settled by compromise, give-and-take. Litigation frequently results. When it does, out-of-court settlements are common."

"May I pose a hypothetical question, sir?"

"You may," he said magisterially.

"Suppose a spouse or child attempts to inflict grievous bodily harm upon the head of the family. The head of the family has proof of the attempt and disinherits the spouse or child in a holographic will that includes proof of the attempt upon his life. The head of the family disappears. But the will is never found. At the end of ten years, or earlier if the body is discovered, the estate is then divided under the laws of intestacy. The guilty person would then inherit his or her share?"

"Of course," he said promptly. "If the will was never found, and proof of the wrongdoing was never found."

"If the body was discovered tomorrow, sir, how long would it take to probate the will?"

"Perhaps a year," he said. "Perhaps longer if no will existed."

Then he was silent. He unlatched his fingers, spread his brown hands out on the desktop. His head was lowered, but his bright eyes looked up at me sharply.

"You think the body will be discovered tomorrow, Mr. Bigg?" he asked.

"I think it will be discovered soon, sir," I said. "I don't believe whoever did this has the patience to wait ten years."

"You're assuming a second will was drawn," he said. "Perhaps the head of the family never got around to it. Perhaps his original will is in existence and still valid."

I hadn't considered that possibility. It stunned me. But after pondering it a moment, it seemed unlikely to me. After getting the results of those chemical analyses, Professor Yale Stonehouse would surely write a new will or amend the original. It was in character for him to do that. He was an ill-natured, vindictive man; he would not take lightly an attempt to poison him.

"One final request, Mr. Teitelbaum," I said. "I am convinced that when Professor Stonehouse left his home on the night of January 10th, he went somewhere by cab or in a car that was waiting for him. It was a raw, sleety night; I don't think he'd wait for a bus or walk over to the subway. I can't do anything about a car waiting for him, but I can attempt to locate the cab he might have taken. All taxi drivers are required to keep trip sheets, but it would be an enormous task checking all the trip sheets for that night, even if the taxi fleet owners allowed me to, which they probably wouldn't. What I'd like to do is have posters printed up, bearing the photograph of Professor Stonehouse and offering a modest reward for any cabdriver who remembers picking him up at or near his home on the night of January 10th. I admit it's a very long shot. The posters could only go in the garages of fleet owners, and there are many independent cab owners who'd never see them. Still, there is a chance we might come up with a driver who remembers taking the Professor somewhere on that particular night."

"Do it," he said immediately. "I approve. It will be part of that 'diligent search' the law requires."

He started to say more, then stopped. He brought two wrinkled forefingers to his thin lips and pressed them, thinking.

"Mr. Bigg," he said finally, "I think you have conducted this investigation in a professional manner, and I wish to compliment you."

"Thank you, sir."

"However," he said sonorously, "it cannot be open-ended. The responsibility of this office is, of course, first and foremost to our clients. In this case we are representing the missing Professor Stonehouse and his family. I cannot hold off indefinitely the filing of an application for the appointment of a temporary administrator of the Professor's estate. It would not be fair to the family. Can you estimate how much more time you will require to complete your investigation?"

"No, sir," I said miserably. "I can't even guarantee that I will ever complete it."

He nodded regretfully.

"I understand," he said. "But I cannot shirk our basic responsibility. Another week, Mr. Bigg. I'm afraid that's all I can allow you. Then I must ask you to drop your inquiries into this, uh, puzzling and rather distasteful affair."

I wanted to argue. I wanted to tell him to go ahead with his legal procedures, but to let me continue digging. But in all honesty I didn't know what more I could do in the Stonehouse case after I placed those reward posters in taxi garages. Where did I go from there? I didn't know.

Mrs. Gertrude Kletz had left a memo in the roller of my typewriter. It read:

Mr. Bigg, your notes on the Kipper case question why Tippi was so upset when you told her you had a private meeting with Rev. Knurr. Well, if the two of them are in on this together, as you and I think, it would be natural for her to be upset because they are both guilty, and so must depend on each other. But they would be suspicious as neither of them are dumb, as you said, and so would be very suspicious of each other, fearing the other might reveal something or even connive to turn in the other, like when thieves fall out. I should think that if two people are partners in a horrible crime, they would begin to look at each other with new eyes and wonder. Because they both depend on each other so much, and they begin to doubt and wonder. I hope you know what I mean as I do not express myself very well. G.K.

I knew what she meant, and I thought she might be right. If Tippi and Knurr were beginning to look at each other with "new eyes," it might be the chink I could widen, an opportunity I could exploit.

I called Percy Stilton. The officer who answered said formally, "Detective Stilton is not available." I gave my name and requested that he ask Detective Stilton to call me as soon as possible.

My second call was to Mrs. Effie Dark. I chatted awhile with that pleasant, comfortable lady, and she volunteered the information I sought.

"Mr. Bigg," she said, "I checked my liquor store bills, and Professor Stonehouse didn't order any Rémy Martin for almost two months before he disappeared. I don't know why, but he didn't."

"Thank you, Effie," I said gratefully. "Just another brick in the wall, but an important one."

We exchanged farewells and hung up. It was then late Friday afternoon, the business world slowing, running down. There is a late Friday afternoon mood in winter in New York. Early twilight. Early quiet. Everything fades. Melancholy sweeps in. One remembers lost chances.

I sat there in my broom-closet office, the files of the Kipper and Stonehouse cases on my desk, and stared at them with sad, glazed eyes. So much passion and turbulence. I could not encompass it. Worse, I seemed to have been leached dry of inspiration and vigor. All those people involved in those desperate plots. What were they to me, or I to them? It was a nonesuch with which I could not cope, something foreign to my nature.

Me, a small, quiet, indwelling, nonviolent man. Suddenly, by the luck and accident that govern life, plunged into this foreign land, this *terra incognita*. What troubled me most, I think, was that I had no compass for this terrain. I was blundering about, lurching, and more than discovering the truth, I wanted most to know what drove me and would not let me put all this nastiness aside.

Finally, forcing myself up from the despair toward which I was fast plummeting, I packed the Kipper and Stonehouse folders into my briefcase, dressed in coat, scarf, hat, turned off the lights, and plodded away from the TORT building, the darkness outside seeming not half as black as that inside, not as forbidding, foreboding.

I did arrive home safely. I changed to casual clothes, then built a small blaze in the fireplace. After that luncheon, I was not hungry, but I had a cup of coffee and a wedge of pecan coffee ring. I sat there, staring into the flames. The file folders on the Kipper and Stonehouse cases were piled on the floor at my feet. My depression was again beginning to overwhelm me. I was nowhere with my first big investigation. I was a mild, out-of-place midget in a world of pushers and shovers. And I was alone.

I was alone, late on a Friday evening, wondering, as we all must, who I was and what I was, when there came a hesitant tapping at my door. I rose, still frowning with my melancholic reverie, and opened the door to find Cleo Hufnagel, her features as sorrowful as mine. I think it would not, at that moment, have taken much for us to fall into each other's arms, weeping.

"Here," she said stiffly, and thrust into my hands a sealed manila envelope.

"What is this?" I said bewilderedly.

"The information you wanted on arsenic."

I felt the thickness of the envelope.

"Oh, Cleo," I said, "I didn't want *you* to do the research. I just wanted the sources: where to look."

"Well, I did it," she said, lifting her chin. "I thought it might—might help you. Good night."

She turned to go. I reached out hastily, put a hand on her arm. She stopped, but she wouldn't look at me.

"Cleo, what is it?" I asked her. "You seem to be angry with me."

"Disappointed," she said in a low voice.

"All right—disappointed. Have I offended you in any way? If I have, I apologize most sincerely. But I am not aware of—"

I stopped suddenly. Adolph Finkel!

"Cleo," I started again, "we said we wanted to be friends. I know I meant it and I think you did, too. There must be honesty and openness between friends. Please, come inside, sit down, and let me tell you what happened. Give me that chance. If, after I have explained, you still wish to leave and never speak to me again, that will be your decision. But at least it will be based on facts."

I concluded that lawyer's argument and drew her gently into my apartment, closing and locking the door behind us. I got her into the armchair where she sat upright, spine straight, hands clasped in her lap. She stared pensively into the dying flames.

"Could we have a drink?" I asked. "Please? I think it might help."

She gave the barest nod and I hastened to pour us two small glasses of brandy. I pulled a straight-back chair up close to her and leaned forward earnestly, drink clasped at my knees.

"Now," I said, "I presume you are disappointed in me because of something Adolph Finkel may have alleged about my, uh, visitor this morning. Is that correct?"

Again, that brief, cold nod.

"Cleo, that young woman is an important witness in a case I am currently investigating, and I needed information from her. Here is exactly what happened . . ."

I think I may say, without fear of self-glorification, that I was at my most convincing best. I spoke slowly in a grave, intense voice, and I told Cleo nothing but the truth. I described my bus ride uptown in the storm, the atmosphere at Mother Tucker's, my meeting with Perdita Schug and Colonel Clyde Manila.

"It sounds like a fun place," Cleo said faintly, almost enviously.

"Oh yes," I said, encouraged, "we must go there sometime."

Then I went on to explain my failure to elicit any meaningful intelligence from Perdita during dinner, and how I had decided the evening was wasted and that I should return home alone by any means possible. I described how Perdita and the Colonel insisted on driving me in the chocolate-colored Rolls-Royce, and how we all drank, and they smoked joints en route. I held nothing back.

"I've never tried it," Cleo Hufnagel said reflectively. "I'd like to."

I tried to conceal my amazement at *that*. I described how Perdita Schug had forced her way into my apartment and how, after a drink, she had revealed information of inestimable value in the case under investigation.

"And then . . ." I said.

"And then?" Cleo asked sharply.

As delicately as I could, I explained what happened then.

During this part of my confession, Cleo had begun to smile, and when I described my makeshift bed and how I awoke a mass of aches and pains, she threw back her head and laughed outright. And my telling of the tender conversation in the morning, just prior to Perdita's departure, sent her into a prolonged fit of hearty guffaws and she bent over, shaking her head and wiping her streaming eyes with a knuckle.

"Then we came out into the hallway," I said, "and there was Adolph Finkel. I swear to you, Cleo, on our friendship, that's exactly what happened."

"I believe you, Josh," she said, still wiping her eyes. "No one could have made up a story like that. How did you get her home?"

I told her how we had discovered Colonel Manila still waiting in the snowdrift, and how they had driven me to work and then gone off together.

"Will you see her again?" she asked, suddenly serious.

I thought about that.

"Cleo, I cannot promise you I will not. Things may develop in the investigation that will necessitate additional conversations with her. But I assure you, my only motive in seeking her company will be in the line of business. I have no personal interest in Perdita whatsoever. Would you like another brandy?"

"Please," she said, and I went gratefully to replenish our glasses, fearing she might detect guilt in my face. I had told her the truth—but not the whole truth.

I came back with our drinks, pulled my chair closer, took her free hand in mine.

"Am I forgiven?" I asked.

She was looking uncommonly handsome that night. But each time I saw her I discerned new beauty. The long hair I had once thought of as only gleaming chestnut now seemed to me to have the tossing fascination of flame. The smile I had defined as pleasant but distant now appeared to me mysterious and full of promise. The thin nose was now aristocratic, the high, clear, brow bespoke intelligence, and the wide mouth, instead of being merely curvy, was now sensuous and madly desirable.

As for her figure, I could not believe I once thought her skinny. I saw now that she was elegant, supple as a willow wand, and her long arms and legs, slender hands and feet, were all of a piece, pliant and flowing. There was a fluency to her body, and I no longer thought of her as being a head taller than I. We were equals: that's what I thought.

"Of course I forgive you," she said in that marvelously low and gentle voice. "But there is nothing to forgive. The fault was mine. I have no claims on you. You can live as you please. I was just being stupid."

"No, no," I said hotly. "You were not stupid. Are not stupid."

"It was just that . . ." she said hesitantly. "Well, I was—I was hurt. I don't know why, but I was."

"I would never do anything to hurt you," I vowed. "Never! And I haven't forgotten about the kite either. I really am going to buy a red kite for us. With string."

She laughed. "I'm glad you haven't forgotten, Josh," she said, gently taking her hand from mine. "Now do you want to talk about what I found out? About the arsenic?"

I nodded, even though at that moment I most wanted to talk about us.

She took the envelope from the floor at my feet and opened the flap. I moved the table lamp closer.

"I'll leave all of this for you to read," she said. "Most of it is photocopies, and photostats from medical journals and drug company manuals. Josh, it's awfully technical. Maybe I better go over the main points, and that will be enough for you, and you won't have to read it all. That man you said was poisoned by arsenic—was he killed? I mean, was he fed a large quantity of arsenic at one time and died? Or small amounts over a period of time?"

"Small amounts," I said. "I think. And I don't believe he died. At least not from the arsenic."

"Well, arsenic comes in a lot of different chemical compounds. Powders, crystals, and liquids. There's even one type that fumes in air. Pope Clement the Seventh and Leopold the First of Austria were supposed to have been assassinated by arsenic mixed in wax candles. The fumes from the candles were poisonous, and whoever breathed them died."

"That's incredible," I murmured, and before I could help myself I had flopped to my knees alongside her chair and taken up one of her long, slender hands again. She let me.

"I think what you're looking for, Josh, is arsenic trioxide. It's the common form and the primary material of all the arsenic compounds."

"Yes," I said, putting my lips to the tips of her fingers. "Arsenic trioxide."

"It is white or transparent glassy lumps or a crystalline powder. It is soluble if mixed slowly and used extremely sparingly. It is odorless and tasteless. A poisonous dose would be only a small pinch. There might be a very slight aftertaste."

"Aftertaste," I repeated, kissing her knuckles, the back of her hand, then turning it over to kiss that pearly wrist with the blue veins pulsing faintly.

"Only two- or three-tenths of a gram of arsenic trioxide can kill an adult within forty-eight hours, so you can see how a tiny amount could cause illness." She obviously intended to finish her lecture despite the distractions. "Arsenic affects the red blood cells and kidneys, if I read these medical papers correctly. The symptoms vary greatly, but a victim of fatal arsenic poisoning might have headaches, vertigo, muscle spasm, delirium, and stupor. Death comes from circulatory collapse. In smaller doses, over a period of time, there would probably be a low-grade fever, loss of appetite, pallor, weakness, inflammation of the nose and throat. You notice that those symptoms are quite similar to the flu or a virus, and that's why arsenic poisoning is sometimes misdiagnosed. In tiny doses over a long period of time, there is usually no delirium or stupor."

"Stupor," I said, touching the tip of my tongue to the palm of her hand. Her entire arm quivered, but her voice was steady as she continued.

"After repeated poisonings, loss of hair and nails may result, accompanied by hoarseness and a hacking cough. Arsenic collects in the hair, nails, and skin. There is some evidence that Napoleon may have been poisoned with arsenic on St. Helena. It was found in a lock of his hair years later."

"Poor Napoleon," I whispered. I craned upward to sniff the perfume of her hair, to bury my face in the sweet juncture where neck met shoulder, to breathe her in. She, who would not brook diversion.

"An alert physician may sometimes spot a garlicky odor of breath and feces." She showed no evidence of slowing down. "Also, urine analysis and gastric washings usually reveal the presence of arsenic. But the symptoms are sometimes so similar to stomach flu that a lot of doctors don't suspect arsenic poisoning until it's too late."

"Too late," I groaned, pushing her hair aside gently to kiss her divine ear tenderly. She trembled a bit, but continued to read from her notes.

"Arsenic is no longer generally used in medicine, having been replaced by more efficient compounds. It was formerly used in the treatment of infections, joint disease, skin lesions, including syphilis, chronic bronchitis, anemia, psoriasis, and so forth. It's still used by veterinarians, but much less frequently than it once was. Most uses of arsenic today are in manufacturing. It is used for hardening copper, lead, and alloys, to make paint and glass, in tanning hides, in printing and dyeing fabrics. It's also used as a pigment in painting, in weed control, for killing rodents and insects, and in fireworks."

"Fireworks," I breathed, touching the fine silkiness of her hair. It was as soft and evanescent as cobwebs.

"Now, as to the availability . . . It's prohibited in food and drugs, and is being phased out as a weed killer. You might find it in rat poison and wood preservatives, but they'd be poisonous for their other ingredients, too. Arsenic is available commercially in large wholesale quantities. It is used in manufacturing parts of car batteries, for instance. But for uses like that, it's bought by the ton, and the government requires disclosure of the end-use. So what is a poor poisoner to do? It would be difficult to purchase an arsenic-containing product in a garden nursery or hardware store or pharmacy. It would probably be impossible."

"Impossible," I moaned. I was kneeling, an arm about her shoulders. The fingers of that hand touched her neck, ear, the loose strands of hair cascading down her back. My other hand stroked the arm closest to me, touched her timorously. I felt her shiver, but too soon she recovered her self-control.

"Still, arsenic trioxide is frequently used in medical and chemical laboratories for research. It is obtained from chemical supply houses by written order, and they must know with whom they are dealing. I mean, a stranger can't just write in and order a pound of arsenic. The usual order from a lab will be for 100 to 500 grams at a time. In its crudest form, it costs about ten dollars for 250 grams. High-purity arsenic trioxide costs about a dollar a gram. It seems to me that the easiest thing for a poisoner to do would be to steal a small amount of arsenic trioxide from the stock room of a research laboratory or a chemical lab at a university. Such a tiny bit is needed to kill someone that the amount stolen would probably never be noticed and— Oh, Josh!" she cried.

She dropped her research papers to the floor, slipped from the chair, fell onto her knees, twisted and flung herself into my arms. In that position, both of us kneeling, we were nearly of a height, and embraced eagerly. We kissed. Our teeth clinked. We kissed. We murmured such things as "I never"—and "I didn't—" and "I can't—" and "I wouldn't—" All of which soon became "I wanted—" and "I hoped—" and "I wished—" and, finally, "I love—"

Not a sentence was finished, nor was there need for it. After a while, weak with our osculatory explorations, we simply toppled over, fell to the floor with a thump, and lay close together, nose to nose in fact, staring into each other's eyes and smiling, smiling, smiling.

"I don't care," Cleo Hufnagel said in her low, hesitant voice. "I just don't care."

"I don't either," I said. "About anything but us."

"Us," she said, wonder in her voice.

"Us," I repeated. I smoothed the hair away from her temples, touched the smooth skin of her brow. When I pressed her yielding back, she moved closer to me, and we clove. I began to scratch her spine gently through the flannel of her jumper. She closed her eyes and purred with contentment.

"Don't stop," she said. "Please."

"I do not intend to," I said, and scratched away assiduously, widening the base of my operations to include shoulder blades and ribs.

"Oh," she sighed. "Oh, oh, oh. Are you a virgin, Josh?"

"No."

"I am."

"Ah?"

"But I don't want to be," she said. Then her eyes flicked open and she looked at me with alarm. "But not tonight," she added hastily.

"I understand," I assured her gravely. "This is grand. Just being with you."

"And having you scratch my back is grand," she sighed. "That's beautiful. Thank you."

"Thank *you*," I said. "Another brandy?"

"I don't think so," she said thoughtfully. "I feel just right. How old are you, Josh?"

"Thirty-two."

"I'm thirty-four," she said sadly.

"So?"

"I'm older than you are."

"But I'm shorter than you are."

She wriggled around so she could hold my face between her palms. She stared intently into my eyes.

"But that doesn't make any difference," she said. "Does it? My being older or your being shorter? That's not important, is it?"

"No," I said, astonished, "it's not."

"I've got to tell you something awful," she said.

"What?"

"I must get up and use your bathroom."

When we kissed goodnight I had to lift onto my toes as she bent down. But I didn't mind that, and neither of us laughed.

"Thank you for a lovely evening," I said.

She didn't answer, but drew her fingertips gently down my cheek. Then she was gone.

6

•

I REMEMBER THE NEXT DAY VERY WELL, SINCE IT HAD SUCH AN impress on what was to follow. It was the first Saturday of March, a gruff, blustery day with steely light coming from a phlegmy sky. The air had the sharp smell of snow, and I hurried through my round of weekend chores, laying in enough food so that I could enjoy a quiet, relaxed couple of days at home even if the city was snowed in.

I took care of laundry, dry cleaning, and shopping. I bought wine and liquor. I cleaned the apartment. Then I showered and shaved, dressed in slacks, sweater, sports jacket, and carpet slippers. A little after noon, I settled down with the morning *Times* and my third cup of coffee of the day.

I think I was annoyed when the phone rang. I was enjoying my warm solitude, and the jangle of the bell was an unwelcome reminder of the raw world outside my windows.

"Hello?" I said cautiously.

"Josh!" Detective Percy Stilton cried. "My main man! I'm sitting here in my drawers, my old lady's in the kitchen doing something to a chicken, and I'm puffing away on a joint big as a see-gar and meanwhile investigating this fine jug of Almaden Mountain White Chablis, vintage of last Tuesday, and God's in His Heaven, all's right with the world, and what can I do for you, m'man? I got a message you called."

"You sound in fine fettle, Perce," I said.

"Fine fettle?" he said. "I got a fettle on me you wouldn't believe—a tough fettle, a boss fettle. I got me a sweet forty-eighter, and nothing and nobody is going to pry me loose from hearth and home until Monday morning. You want to know about that crazy elevator—right? Okay, it was on the sixth floor when the first blues got to the Kipper townhouse. They both swear to it. So? What does that prove? Sol could have taken it up to his big jump."

"Could have," I said. "Yes. It's hard to believe an emotionally disturbed man intent on suicide would wait for an elevator to take him up one floor when he could have walked it in less than a minute. But I agree, yes, he could have done it."

"Let's figure he did," Stilton said. "Let's not try jamming facts into a theory. I've known a lot of good men who messed themselves up doing that.

The trick is to fit the theory to the facts. How you doing? Any great detecting to report?"

"Two things," I said.

I told him about those bills from Martin Reape I had found at Kipmar Textiles. The bills that had been approved for payment by Sol Kipper. And the canceled checks endorsed by Reape.

I awaited his reaction. But there was only silence.

"Perce?" I said. "You there?"

He started speaking again, and suddenly he was sober . . .

"Josh," he said, "do you realize what you've got?"

"Well, yes, certainly. I've established a definite connection between Sol Kipper and Marty Reape."

"You goddamned Boy Scout!" he screamed at me. "You've got hard evidence. You've got paper. Something we can take to court. Up to now it's all been smoke. But now we've got *paper*. God, that's wonderful!"

It didn't seem so wonderful to me, but I supposed police officers had legal priorities of which I was not aware. I went ahead and told Detective Stilton what I had learned about Tippi Kipper and the Reverend Godfrey Knurr, that they were having an affair and it had existed prior to Sol Kipper's death.

"Where did you get that?" he asked curiously.

I hesitated a moment.

"From the maid," I said finally.

He laughed. "Miss Horizontal herself?" he said. "I'm not going to ask you how you got her to talk; I can imagine. Well, it could be true."

"It would explain the Kipper-Reape connection," I argued. "Sol got suspicious and hired Marty to find out the truth. Reape got evidence that Knurr and Tippi were, ah, intimate. That's when Sol called Mr. Tabatchnick and wanted to change his will."

"Uh-huh. I follow. Sol gets dumped before he can change the will. Maybe the lovers find and destroy the evidence. Photographs? Could be. Tape recordings. Whatever. But street-smart Reape has made copies and tries blackmail. Goom-bye, Marty."

"And then after he gets bumped, his grieving widow tries the same thing."

"It listens," Stilton admitted. "I'd be more excited if we could figure out how they managed to waste Sol. And come up with the suicide note. But at least we've got more than we had before. When I get in on Monday, I'll run a trace on Knurr."

"And on Tippi," I said. "Please."

"Why her?"

I told him what the Kipper sons had said about her Las Vegas background and how she had originally come from Chicago, which had also been Knurr's home.

"May be nothing," Stilton said, "may be something. All right, I'll run

Tippi through the grinder, too, and we shall see what we shall see. Hang in there, Josh; you're doing okay."

"I am?" I said, surprised. "I thought I was doing badly. As a matter of fact, one of the reasons I called you was to ask if you could suggest a new approach. Something I haven't tried yet."

There was silence for a brief moment.

"It's your baby," he said at last. "But if I was on the case, I'd tail Tippi Kipper and the Reverend Knurr for a while."

"What for?" I asked.

"Just for the fun of it," he said. "Josh, my old lady is yelling and I better hang up. I think she wants to put me to work. Keep in touch. I'll let you know what the machine says about Knurr and Tippi."

"Thank you for calling," I said.

"You're perfectly welcome," he responded with mock formality, then laughed. "So long, Josh," he said as he rang off. "Have a good weekend."

I finished the *Times* and my cold coffee about the same time, then mixed a weak Scotch-and-water, turned the radio down low, and started rereading my notes on the Stonehouse case. I went back to the very beginning, to my first meeting with Mr. Teitelbaum. Then I read the record of my initial interviews with Mrs. Ula Stonehouse, Glynis, and Mrs. Effie Dark. I found something interesting. I had been in the kitchen with Mrs. Dark, and the interrogation went something like this:

Q: What about Glynis? Does she work?

A: Not anymore. She did for a year or two but she quit.

Q: Where did she work?

A: I think she was a secretary in a medical laboratory.

Q: But now she does nothing?

A: She does volunteer work three days a week in a free clinic down on the Lower East Side.

I closed the file folder softly and stared into the cold fireplace. Secretary in a medical laboratory. Now working in a clinic.

It was possible.

But Mr. Teitelbaum had given me only another week.

I put in some additional hours reading over the files and planning moves. After a solitary dinner I went out to get early editions of the *Times* and *News*. It was around 8:30, not snowing, sleeting, or raining, but the air was so damp, I could feel icy moisture on my face. I walked rapidly, head down. The streets were deserted. Very little traffic. I saw no pedestrians until I rounded the corner onto Tenth Avenue.

The Sunday *News* was in and I bought a copy of that. But the Sunday *Times* hadn't yet been delivered. There were a dozen people warming themselves in the store, waiting for the truck. I decided not to wait, but to pick up the *Times* in the morning. I started back to my apartment.

My brownstone was almost in the middle of the block. There was a street-lamp on the opposite side of the street. It was shedding a ghastly orange glow. The lamp itself was haloed with a wavering nimbus.

I was about halfway home when two men stepped out of an areaway a few houses beyond my brownstone and started walking toward me. They were widely separated on the sidewalk. They appeared to be carrying baseball bats.

I remember thinking, as my steps slowed, that what was going to happen was going to happen to me. Almost at the same time I thought it was an odd sort of mugging; attackers usually come up on a victim from behind. I halted and glanced back. There was a third assailant behind me, advancing as steadily and purposefully as the two in front.

I looked about wildly. The street was empty. Perhaps I should have started screaming and continued screaming until windows opened, heads popped out, and someone had the compassion to call the police. But I didn't think of screaming. While it was happening, I thought only of escape.

The two men to my front were now close enough for me to see they were wearing knitted ski masks with holes at the eyes and mouth. Now they were swinging their weapons menacingly, and I knew, knew, this was not to be a conventional mugging and robbery. Their intent was to inflict grievous bodily injury, if not death.

I took another quick look back. The single attacker was still approaching, but at a slower pace than the two ahead. His function appeared to be as a blocker, to prevent me from retreating from a frontal assault. He was waving the baseball bat in both hands, like a player at the plate awaiting the first pitch. He, too, was wearing a ski mask, but though I saw him only briefly, I did note that one of the eyeholes in the mask appeared opaque. He was wearing a black eyepatch beneath the mask.

Parked cars, bumper to bumper, prevented my fleeing into the street. I didn't dare dash up the nearest steps and frantically ring strange bells, hoping for succor before those assassins fell upon me. I did what I thought best; I turned and ran back, directly at the single ruffian. I thought my chances would be better against one than two. And each accelerating stride I took toward him brought me closer to the brightly lighted and crowded safety of Tenth Avenue. I think he was startled by my abrupt turn and the speed of my approach. He stopped, shifted uneasily on his feet, gripped the bat horizontally, a hand on each end.

I think he expected me to try to duck or dodge around him, and he was wary and off-balance when I simply ran into him full tilt. There was nothing clever or skilled in my attack; I just ran into him as hard as I could, feeling the hard bat strike across my chest, but keeping my legs moving, knees pumping.

He bounced away, staggered back, and I continued my frontal assault, hearing the pounding feet of the two other assailants coming up behind me. Then my opponent stumbled. As he went down flat on his back with a *whoof* sound as the breath went out of him, I seized the moment and ran like hell.

I ran over him, literally ran over him. I didn't care where my boots landed: kneecaps, groin, stomach, chest, face. I just used him as turf to get a good foothold, and like a sprinter starting from blocks, I pushed off and went flying toward Tenth Avenue, knowing that I was in the clear and not even the devil could catch me now.

I whizzed around the corner, banking, and there was the New York *Times* truck, unloading bundles of the Sunday edition, with vendors, merchants, customers crowding around: a pushing, shoving mob. It was lovely, noisy confusion, and I plunged right into the middle of it, sobbing to catch my breath. I was startled to find that not only was my body intact, but I was still clutching my copy of the Sunday *News* under my arm.

I waited until complete copies of the *Times* had been made up. I bought one, then waited a little longer until two other customers started down my street, carrying their papers. I followed them closely, looking about warily. But there was no sign of my attackers.

When I came to my brownstone, I had my keys ready. I darted up the steps, unlocked the door, ran up the stairs, fumbled my way into my apartment, locked and bolted the door. I put on all the lights and searched the apartment. I knew it was silly, but I did it. I even looked in the closet. I was shivering.

I poured myself a heavy brandy, but I didn't even taste it. I just sat there in my parka and watch cap, staring into the fireplace where there were now only a few pinpoints of red, winking like fireflies.

That black eyepatch I'd spotted under my assailant's ski mask haunted me.

A lot of men in New York wore black eyepatches, I supposed, and were of the same height and build as the young man I had seen at the Tentmakers Club on Carmine Street. Still . . .

Tippi Kipper had obviously reported to Knurr the details of our conversation. Perhaps she'd told him I'd mentioned the name of Martin Reape to her. Perhaps she'd said that I had asked prying questions, doubly suspicious coming from an attorney's clerk supposedly engaged only in making an inventory of her husband's estate.

So the two of them must have decided I had to be removed from the scene. Or, at least, warned off.

Was that the way of it?

I had to admit that I wasn't comfortable with that theory. If I knew the name of Martin Reape, then presumably my employers did too, and putting me in the hospital wouldn't stop an inquiry into the alleged bills of the private detective. And as for my "prying questions," I had asked nothing that could not be accounted for by sympathetic interest.

I didn't know why Godfrey Knurr had set up the attack on me. But I was convinced he had. It made me sad. I admired the man.

I looked at my watch. It was a little after ten o'clock. Perhaps if I went to Knurr's place on Carmine Street I could observe the three guttersnipes entering or leaving the club and thus confirm my suspicions.

Disregarding the dozen reasons why this was a foolish course of conduct, I turned off the lights, pulled my parka hood over my watch cap, made certain I had my warm gloves, and went out again into the darkness. It was not the easiest thing I have ever done in my life.

When a cab dropped me off on Carmine Street and Seventh Avenue, I found to my dismay that I had neglected to replenish my wallet. I had enough to pay and tip the driver but that would leave me with only about ten dollars in bills and change, just about enough to get me home again.

I walked east on Carmine Street, hooded head lowered, gloved hands thrust into capacious parka pockets. I walked on the opposite side of the street from the Reverend Knurr's club and inspected it as I passed.

At first I thought it was completely dark. But then, through the painted-over window, I saw a dull glow of light. That could have been nothing more than a night-light, of course. The club might be empty, the Pastor out somewhere, and I could be wasting my time.

But remembering Roscoe Dollworth's instructions on the need for ever-lasting patience on a stakeout, I continued down the block, then turned and retraced my steps. I must have paraded down that block a dozen times, up and down.

At that point, already wearying of my patrol, I took up a station in the shadowed doorway of a Chinese laundry, not exactly opposite the Tentmakers Club, but in a position where I could observe the entrance without being easily seen.

I continued this vigil for approximately an hour, huddling in the doorway, then walking up and down the street and back, always keeping Knurr's club in view. The street was not crowded, but it wasn't deserted either. None of the other pedestrians seemed interested in my activities, but I took advantage of passing groups by falling in closely behind them, giving the impression, or so I hoped, that I was part of a late dinner party.

I was back in the doorway, stamping my feet softly, when the light brightened behind the painted window of the Tentmakers Club. I drew farther back into the shadows. I waited. Finally the front door opened. A shaft of yellowish light beamed out onto the sidewalk.

Godfrey Knurr came out. There was no doubt it was he; I saw his features clearly, particularly the slaty beard, as he turned to close and lock the door. He was hatless but wearing a dark overcoat with the collar turned up.

He tried the door, put the keys in his trouser pocket, and then started walking east, toward Sixth Avenue. He strode at a brisk clip, and I moved along with him on the other side of the street, keeping well back and close to the deep shadows of the storefronts and buildings.

He crossed Sixth and stopped at the curb, looking southward. He would raise his hand when a cab approached, then let it fall when he saw it was occupied. I hurried south on Sixth, ending up a block below Knurr. Then I ran across the avenue and took up my station at the curb.

I got the first empty cab to come along.

"Where to?" the driver said.

"Start your meter and stay right here," I said. "I've got about ten dollars. When I owe you eight, tell me and I'll give you ten and get out of your cab. All right?"

"Why not?" he said agreeably. "Beats using gas. You got wife trouble?"

"Something like that," I said.

"Don't we all?" he offered mournfully, then was silent.

The name of the registration card said he was Abraham Pincus. He was a grizzle-haired, middle-aged man with a furrowed brow under his greasy cap and deep lines from the corners of his mouth slanting down to his chin, like a ventriloquist's dummy.

"Mind if I smoke?" he asked.

The passenger's compartment was plastered with signs: PLEASE DO NOT SMOKE and DRIVER ALLERGIC TO SMOKING and the like.

"What about these signs?" I said.

"That's the *day* driver," he said. "I'm the *night* driver."

I had been sitting forward on the rear seat, trying to peer through the bleared windshield to keep Reverend Knurr in sight. He had still not caught a cab. Finally, after about three minutes, one passed us with its roof lights on and began to pull into the curb where Knurr stood and signaled.

"All right," I said. "We're going to move now. Just drive north."

"Why not?" Mr. Pincus said equably, finishing lighting his cigar. "You're the boss. For eight dollars' worth."

I saw Knurr get into the taxi and start north on Sixth Avenue. Then my driver started up and we traveled north, keeping about a block behind Knurr's cab. At 14th Street, Knurr turned left.

"Turn left," I said to my driver.

"We following that cab ahead?" he asked.

"Yes."

"Why didn't you say so? All my life I been waiting for someone to get in my cab and say, 'Follow that car!' Like in the movies and TV—you know? This was my big chance and you blew it. He the guy that's fooling around with your tootsie?"

"That's the one," I said.

"I won't lose him," he promised. "Up to eight dollars, I won't lose him."

Knurr's cab zigzagged northward and westward, with us a block behind but sometimes closing up tighter when my driver feared he might be stopped by a traffic light. Finally we were on Eleventh Avenue, heading directly northward.

"You from New Jersey?" A. Pincus asked.

"No," I said. "Why?"

"I thought maybe he's heading for the George Washington Bridge and Jersey. You can't go there for eight bucks."

"No," I said, "I don't think he's going to New Jersey."

"Maybe you and your creampuff can get back together again," Mr. Pincus said. "As the old song goes, 'Try a little tenderness.' "

"Good advice," I said, hunching forward on my seat, watching the tail-lights of the cab ahead.

Then we were on West End Avenue, still speeding north.

"He's slowing," Pincus reported, then, "He's stopping."

I glanced at a street sign. We were at 66th Street.

"Go a block past him, please," I said. "Then let me out."

"Why not?" he said.

While I huddled down in my seat, we passed Knurr's halted cab and stopped a block farther north.

"You got about six bucks on the clock," my driver said. "Give or take. You want me to wait?"

"No," I said, "thank you. I'll get out here."

I gave him nine dollars, figuring I could take the bus or subway home.

"Lots of luck," Pincus said.

"Thank you," I said. "You've been very kind."

"Why not?" he said. His cab roared away.

I was on the east side of West End Avenue, on a tree-lined block bordering an enormous apartment development. There were towering buildings and wide stretches of lawn, shrubbery, and trees everywhere. It must have been pleasant in daylight. At that time of night, it was shadowed, deserted, and vaguely sinister.

I had been watching Knurr through the rear window of my cab as he waited for a break in the traffic to dash across the avenue. Now I walked rapidly back to where his cab had stopped.

As I scurried southward, I spotted him on the west side of West End. He was heading for the brightly lighted entrance of a public underground garage in the basement of one of the tall apartment houses bordering the river. There were large signs in front stating the parking rates by the hour, day, week, and month.

I positioned myself across the street from the garage, standing in the deep shadow of a thick-trunked plane tree. I watched Knurr walk rapidly into the bright entrance. As he approached the attendant's booth, a woman stepped out of the shadows, and she and the Reverend embraced briefly. Then an attendant appeared. He and Knurr spoke for a moment. The Pastor handed him something. The attendant turned and disappeared. Knurr and the woman remained where they were, close together, conversing, his arm about her shoulders.

She was wearing what I guessed to be a mink coat that came a little lower than calf-length. It was very full and had a hood that now covered her head, shadowing her features.

Finally, a long, heavy car came rolling into the lighted area of the garage entrance. It was a black Mercedes-Benz sedan, gleaming, solid, and very elegant. The garage attendant got out of the driver's side and handed something to Godfrey Knurr. The Reverend then gave something to the attendant.

Knurr opened the door on the passenger's side. He assisted the lady into her seat, then went around to the driver's side, got in, slammed the door—I heard it *chunk* from where I stood—and slowly, carefully, pulled out into West End Avenue. He turned north. I watched the taillights fade away.

I wasn't thinking about where he might be heading. I couldn't care less. I was too shocked.

For when he had helped the woman into the car, she had flung back the hood of her fur coat. Her features, for a brief moment, were revealed in the bright light. I saw her clearly.

It wasn't Tippi Kipper.

It was Glynis Stonehouse.

PART THREE

1

•

THAT NIGHT I AWOKE FREQUENTLY, DOZED OFF AS OFTEN, AND finally lost all ability to determine if I was fully conscious or dreaming. I vividly remember wondering if I had actually seen Glynis Stonehouse and Godfrey Knurr together.

My brain continued churning all night, and things were no better when I arose early Sunday morning, showered, dressed, and poked disconsolately at a bowl of sodden cornflakes. I simply didn't know what to do. It seemed to me I was in over my head and badly in need of wise counsel.

I hated to bother Percy Stilton, but what I had learned was of such moment that I wanted him to know at once. I dialed the only number I had for him and learned that he wouldn't be in the precinct until Monday morning.

"Couldn't you call him at home and ask him to contact me?" I tried to convey the urgency of the situation to the officer on the other end of the phone.

"Can't anyone else help you?" he asked, still reticent.

"No," I said firmly. "It's got to be Stilton. It's really very important, honest, to me and to him."

Silence.

"A case he's on?" he said finally.

"Yes," I said, lying valiantly. "Just call and ask him to call Joshua Bigg. As soon as possible."

A short silence again, then: "What was that name—Pigg?"

"Bigg. B-i-g-g. Joshua Bigg. Tell him it's a matter of life and death."

"I'll tell him that," the officer said.

I tried to read the Sunday papers. I watched TV for a while, but didn't see it. My phone finally rang shortly before noon.

"Hello?" I said breathlessly.

The voice was low, husky, soothing. "Mr. Bigg?"

"Yes."

"This is Maybelle Hawks," she said pleasantly. "I am Percy Stilton's consenting adult."

"Yes, ma'am."

"Mr. Bigg, Perce received your message, but he's really in no, ah, condition to speak intelligibly to you at the moment."

"Is he ill?" I asked anxiously.

"You might say that," she replied thoughtfully. "Nothing fatal. I would judge that he will recover, in time. But right now he's somewhat unhinged. It being Sunday morning. I do hope you understand."

"Yes, ma'am," I said miserably. "He's hungover."

"Oh, Mr. Bigg," she laughed gaily, "that *is* the understatement of the year. He's comatose, Mr. Bigg. *Com-a-tose.* He asked that I return your call and explain why it might be best if you call him at the precinct tomorrow."

"Miss Hawks," I said, "is—"

"Call me Belle," she said.

"Thank you. Belle, is there no chance of my seeing him today? It really is urgent. I wouldn't be bothering you if it wasn't. Surely Perce, and you too, of course, have to eat sometime today. It would give me great pleasure if you would both join me for dinner some place. Any place."

"Mr. Bigg, you sound to me like a sober, reasonable man."

"Yes, ma'am," I said, "I mean to be."

"Then you must realize that right now, this second, if I mention food to Percy Stilton, he's like to give me a shot in the chops."

"Oh no, ma'am," I said hastily. "Not right this minute. What I was thinking was that later this evening, say around six o'clock, he might be recovered sufficiently, and the both of you might be hungry enough to join me for dinner."

"Hmm," she said. "You're getting through to me, Mr. Bigg. All right, I'll see what I can do with the Incredible Hulk here. Where do you want to eat?"

We settled on Woody's at about 6:00 P.M.

I spent the rest of the afternoon leafing through the Sunday papers and then the Stonehouse file once again. I left my apartment at 5:30 and walked to Woody's. It wasn't dark yet, but still I scanned the street before I left the vestibule, and my head was on a swivel during my rapid walk to 23rd Street.

Nitchy greeted me after I had hung my hat and coat on the front rack.

"No princess tonight, Josh?" she said.

"Not tonight, Nitchy," I said.

"It'll happen," she said confidently. "One of these nights you'll waltz through that door with a princess on your arm. You'll see."

As usual she was looped with bangles, hoops, and amulets. Her black helmet of hair gleamed wickedly, and the heavy eye shadow and precisely painted lips accented her sorceress look. She gave me a table where I could watch the front door.

They weren't very late—not more than fifteen minutes. The moment

Maybelle Hawks entered the restaurant, and the heads of everyone in the front room began to turn, I realized who she was.

She was one of the most famous high-fashion models in Manhattan. Her classic features had adorned dozens of haute couture magazines, she had posed in the nude for many artists and photographers, and a scholarly art critic had written a much quoted monograph on her "Nefertiti-like beauty" and "ethereal sensuality." She towered over Stilton, who lurked behind her. I guessed her to be 6-4 or 6-5. She was wearing a supple black leather trench coat, mink-lined. It hung open, revealing a loose chemise-styled shift in soft, plum-colored wool. There was a fine gold chain about the strong stalk of her neck.

I could see why that art critic had thought of Nefertiti. Her head seemed elongated, drawn out in back so that it had the shape of a tilted egg. Her hair was a cap of tight black curls. Oriental eyes, Semitic lips, a thin scimitar of a nose. All of her features seemed carved, polished, oiled. Her teeth were unbelievably white.

They made it to my table and sat down. From close range, Percy wasn't looking so good. He was as elegantly clad as the first time I had seen him, but the eyes were sunk deeply and bagged. The whites were reddish and he blinked frequently. There was a sallow tinge to his cordovan skin.

Nitchy asked if we'd like a drink. Belle saw my glass of white wine and said that's what she'd have. Percy raised his bloodshot eyes to Maybelle Hawks.

"Please, babe," he croaked piteously.

"Nitchy," Belle said in tones that were more song than speech, "please bring this basket case a shot of cognac with about a quart of ice water for a chaser."

"Coming up," Nitchy said. She looked sympathetically at Perce. "Got the whim-whams?" she asked.

"Whim-whams?" Belle said with a scoffing laugh. "This is the guy who swore he could mix grass, martinis, wine, bourbon, and brandy stingers. 'I can handle it,' he said."

"Belle," Stilton implored. "Don't shout."

When our drinks were served, Perce sat there staring at his brandy. He took a deep breath. Then he bent forward so he had to lift the glass only a few inches to his lips. He took half of it in one gulp. Then he closed his eyes and clenched his teeth.

"Jesus!" he said finally. "Did you hear that hit?"

He took another deep breath, sat back in his chair, drained off his glass of ice water. Nitchy was there with a pitcher to fill it up again.

"Well, now," Percy Stilton said, looking at us with a weak grin. "This is what I should have done eight hours ago."

"I wanted you to suffer," Maybelle Hawks said.

Stilton finished his cognac and handed the empty glass to Nitchy. "Another plasma, please, nurse," he said.

By the time Belle and I had finished our wine, the detective seemed recovered, lighting a cigarette with steady fingers, laughing and joking, surveying his surroundings with interest.

"Nice, comfy place," he said, nodding. "How's the food?"

Nitchy was still hovering, proud at having Maybelle Hawks in her establishment. I had seen her boasting at other tables.

"For you," she said to Stilton, "I suggest a rare sirloin, a mixed green salad, and nothing else."

"Marry me," he said.

"I'll have the same, please," Belle said. "Oil and vinegar on the greens."

I ordered a hamburger and another round of drinks.

"All right, Josh," Percy said, "what's all this about?"

I glanced quickly toward Maybelle Hawks. Stilton caught it. "She knows everything. She thinks it's interesting."

"Fascinating," she said.

"You know all the people involved?" I asked her. "Tippi Kipper? Godfrey Knurr? Marty Reape?"

She nodded.

"Good," I said. "But what I have to say will be new to both of you. I've got a lot to tell."

"Talk away," Percy Stilton said. "We're listening."

I told them about the Stonehouse case: the arsenic poisoning, how I thought it had been done, the personalities of the people involved, how I was attempting to locate a cabdriver who might have picked up Professor Stonehouse on the night he disappeared. They listened intently.

When I told them about the attempted assault on me the previous evening, Detective Stilton paused, his last forkful of steak halfway to his mouth, and stared at me. Then he devoured the final bite, pushed his plate away, and reached for his cigarette case.

I told them how I had shadowed Godfrey Knurr, how he had traveled up to that West Side garage, met a woman, and how the two of them drove northward in a black Mercedes-Benz.

"But it wasn't Tippi Kipper," I said. "It was Glynis Stonehouse."

I finished my hamburger and looked up. Detective Percy Stilton had lighted his cigarette. He was puffing calmly, looking into the space over my head. Maybelle Hawks had also finished her dinner despite my earthshaking news. She was patting her lips delicately with her napkin.

"Good steak," was all she said.

Stilton's eyes came down slowly until he was staring at me.

"Roll me over," he sang softly, "in the clover. Roll me over, lay me down, and do it again."

"Coffee?" the waitress asked.

We agreed and added brandy to the order. Nothing was said until the waitress moved away. Then Detective Stilton struck the top of the table with his palm. Cutlery jumped.

"That fucker," Stilton cried. "That fucker!"

"Easy, babe," Maybelle Hawks said. "Don't get physical."

"You think . . . ?" I said.

"Sheet," the detective said disgustedly. "It's him. It's got to be him. I don't know how he managed the Kipper snuff or what he did with Stonehouse, but it's him, it's got to be him. And he thinks he's going to stroll, chuckling."

"He's doing all right so far," Belle said dryly.

"Yes," I said, nodding. "But it's all guesswork."

Stilton ground out his cigarette, half-smoked, and immediately lighted another.

"Uh-huh," he said. "Guesswork. No hard evidence. Right. Well, I'll tell you, Josh, sometimes it goes like that. You got the guy cold but you can't prove."

"What do you do then?"

He put his head far back, blew smoke at the ceiling.

"Well . . ." he said slowly, "I know a couple of guys who owe me. Not cops," he added hurriedly. "Just friends from my old neighborhood. They like to go hunting."

I looked at him, puzzled.

"They could take this Knurr hunting with them," he said. "In the forest. Lots of trees upstate. Accidents happen all the time. Hunting accidents."

"No," I said.

"Why not?" Stilton demanded harshly.

"Perce," I said, "I don't believe in brute force and brute morality. I don't believe they rule the world. I don't believe they're what make history and form the future. I just don't believe that. I *can't* believe that, Perce. Look at me. I'm a shrimp. If brute force is what it's all about, then I haven't got a chance, I'm dead already. Also, I don't *want* to believe it. If brute morality is the law of survival, then I want to be dead. I don't want to live in a world like that because it would just be nothing, without hope and without joy."

Stilton stared at me, his eyes wide.

"You're a pisser," he said finally.

"That's the way I feel," I said.

Maybelle Hawks reached across the table and put a hand on my arm.

"I'm with you, babe," she said softly.

The detective leaned back and lighted another cigarette.

"And the meek shall inherit the earth," he said tonelessly.

"I didn't say that," I told him angrily. "I want to nail Godfrey Knurr as much as you do. More maybe. He played me for a fool. I'm not meek about it at all. I'm not going to let him escape."

"And just how do you figure to nail him?"

"I've got a good brain—I know I have. Knurr isn't going to stroll away. Right now I can't tell you exactly how I'm going to nail him, but I know I will. Guile and cunning. That's what I'm going to use against him. Those are the only weapons of a persecuted minority. And that is how I consider myself: a member of the minority of shorts."

"All right, Josh," Stilton said. "We'll play it your way—for the time being. Tomorrow I'll see what the machine's got on the Reverend Godfrey Knurr."

"And Tippi Kipper," I reminded him.

"Right. You're going ahead with those posters?"

"First thing tomorrow."

"Take my advice: don't describe Stonehouse on the posters. If you do, you'll get a million calls from smart-asses. Just run his picture and give the address of his apartment house. Then, if you get any calls, you can check how legit they are by asking the caller to describe Stonehouse."

"That makes sense."

"Also," Stilton went on, "check out those chemical analyses Stonehouse had made. Go to the lab, blow some smoke. Get copies of the analyses. You think the arsenic was in the brandy, and you're probably right. But you need paper. Find that clinic where Glynis does volunteer work. See if they have any arsenic."

I was scrawling rapid memoranda in my little notebook. "Anything else?" I asked him.

"If the clinic doesn't work out, try to discover where she worked previously. Maybe they had arsenic."

"I don't even know how long ago she worked there," I said. "Maybe a year or two, or longer."

"So?" Percy Stilton said. "It's possible."

"Do you know when Glynis met Godfrey Knurr?" Maybelle Hawks asked.

"No, I don't," I confessed. "I'll try to find out."

"Uh-huh," Stilton said. "And while you're at it, try to get us a recent photograph of Glynis."

"What for?"

"Oh, I don't rightly know," he said lazily.

I made a note: *Gly foto.*

"Anything else?" I asked.

"I don't know how much time you can put in on this thing," Perce said, "but it would help if you could keep tabs on Knurr. Just to get some idea of the guy's schedule. Where he goes, who he sees. Especially where he goes when he and Glynis take off in that black Mercedes from the West Side garage. That's another thing: try to find out if it's his car."

"It's not. Knurr owns a battered VW," I said.

"Sure," Stilton said genially. "He would. Fits right in with his image of a poor-but-honest man of the cloth. He's probably got a portfolio of blue-chip stocks that would knock your eye out. Well, that's about all I can think of, Josh." He looked at Maybelle Hawks. "You think of anything else, babe?"

"Not at the moment," she said. "I'd feel a lot surer about this whole thing if we could figure out how Knurr and Tippi put Sol Kipper over that railing. Also the suicide note."

"You're a wise old fox," he told her. "Give it some thought. I'll bet you'll come up with something."

"I wish I could say the same about you," she murmured. "Tonight."

"Try me," he said.

"I intend to," she said. "Josh, many thanks for the dinner. And you just keep right on. You're going to crash this; I know you are."

"Thank you," I said. "Perce, would you be willing to give me your home telephone number?"

"Sure," he said immediately, and did.

I waited with them until they got a cab. Maybelle swooped to kiss my cheek.

"I want to see more of you, Josh," she said. "Promise?"

"Of course," I said.

"You'll come up and have dinner with us? I'm really a very good cook. Right, Perce?"

He flipped a palm back and forth.

"So-so," he said.

"Bastard," she said.

I walked home slowly, ashamed. I was embarrassed at confessing how I saw myself as a member of the persecuted minority of the short.

Still, it was true. You may believe I was obsessed by my size. Let me tell how I felt. I have already commented on the rewards society offers to men of physical stature. The tall are treated with respect; the short earn contempt or amusement. This is true only of men. "Five-foot-two, eyes of blue" is still an encomium for a female. Our language reflects this prejudice. A worthy person is said to be "A man you can look up to." An impecunious man is suffering from "the shorts." To be short-tempered is reprehensible. To short-circuit is to frustrate or impede. A shortfall is a deficiency.

Thus does our language reflect our prejudice. And the philosophy that I had in a moment of weakness divulged to Belle and Perce reflected my deepest feelings about being a midget. From my size, or lack of it, came my beliefs, dreams, ideas, emotions, fantasies, reactions. All of which would be put to the test whether I liked it or not, in the rocky week ahead.

2

•

I ARRIVED AT TORT THE NEXT MORNING BEFORE 9:00 A.M. MY IN basket was piled high with requests for investigations and research, but after shuffling through them, I decided that most could be handled by Mrs. Kletz and the rest could wait.

Shortly before ten, I phoned Gardner & Weiss, who did all the job printing for Tabatchnick, Orsini, Reilly, and Teitelbaum. I spoke directly to Mr. Weiss and explained what I wanted on the Stonehouse reward posters.

"No problem," he said. "I'll send a messenger for the photograph and copy. How many do you want?"

I had no idea. "A hundred," I said.

"Wednesday," he said.

"This afternoon," I said.

"Oh," he said sadly. "Oh, oh, oh."

"It's a rush job. We'll pay."

"Without saying," he told me. "You want to see a proof first?"

"No. I trust you."

"You do?" he said.

"By one o'clock this afternoon?"

"I'll try. Only because you said you trust me. The messenger's on his way."

I dug out the photograph of Professor Stonehouse and typed the copy for the poster: REWARD! *A generous cash award will be paid to any cabdriver who can prove he picked up this man in the vicinity of Central Park West and 70th Street on the night of January 10th, this year.* Then I added the TORT telephone number and my extension.

As usual, Thelma Potts was seated primly outside the office of Mr. Leopold Tabatchnick.

"Miss Potts!" I cried, "you're looking uncommonly lovely this morning."

"Oh-oh," she said. "You want something."

"Well, yes. I have a friend who needs legal advice. I wondered if I could have one of Mr. Tabatchnick's cards to give him."

"Liar," she said. "You want to pretend you're Mr. Tabatchnick."

I was astonished. "How did you know?" I asked her.

"How many do you need?" she asked, ignoring my question.

As I was leaving she dunned me for a dollar for the sick kit. I handed it over.

"Still betting on Hamish Hooter?" I asked her.

"I only bet on sure things," she said loftily.

When Gertrude Kletz came in I called her into my office and showed her the photograph of Professor Stonehouse and the reward copy. I explained that she should expect the posters to be delivered by Gardner & Weiss in the early afternoon. Meanwhile, she could begin compiling a list of taxi garages, which she could get from the Yellow Pages.

"Or from the Hack Bureau," she said.

I looked at her with admiration.

"Right," I said. I told her the posters would have to be hand-carried to the garages and, with the permission of the manager, displayed on walls or bulletin boards.

"I'll need sticky tape and thumbtacks," she said cheerfully. The Kipper file had hooked her; now the Stonehouse case had done the same. I could see it in her bright eyes. Her face was burning with eagerness.

I told her I was off to the lab to check into Stonehouse's tests, and that by the time I got back, she'd probably be out distributing the posters. I put on hat and coat, grabbed up my briefcase, and rushed out, waving at Yetta as I sailed past.

She was wearing the green sweater I had given her, but curiously this failed to stir me.

The chemical laboratory was on Eleventh Avenue near 55th Street. I took a cab over. Bommer & Son, Inc., was on the fourth floor of an unpretentious building set between a sailors' bar (BIG BOY DRINKS 75 CENTS DURING HAPPY HOUR. 9 TO 2 A.M.) and a gypsy fortune-teller (READINGS, PAST, PRESENT, FUTURE. SICKNESS). The elevator was labeled FREIGHT ONLY, so I climbed worn stairs to the fourth floor, the nose-crimping smell of chemicals becoming more intense as I ascended.

The receptionist in the outer office was typing away at Underwood's first model. She stopped.

"I'd like to speak to Mr. Bommer, please."

In a few moments a stoutish man wearing a stained white laboratory coat flung himself into the office.

"Yes?" he demanded in a reedy voice.

The receptionist pointed me out. He came close to me, peering suspiciously at my face. I thought him to be in the sixties—possibly the 1860s.

"Yes?"

"Mr. Waldo Bommer?"

"Yes."

I proffered Mr. Tabatchnick's card. He held it a few inches from his eyes and read it aloud: "Leopold H. Tabatchnick. Attorney-at-Law." He lowered the card. "Who's suing?" he asked me.

652 • LAWRENCE SANDERS •

"No one," I said. "I just want a moment of your time. I represent the estate of Professor Yale Stonehouse. Among his papers is a canceled check made out to Bommer & Son, with no accompanying voucher. The government is running a tax audit on the estate, and it would help if you could provide copies of the bill."

"Come with me," he said abruptly.

I followed him through a rear door into an enormous loft laboratory where five people, three men, two women, all elderly and all wearing stained laboratory coats, were seated on high stools before stone-topped workbenches. They seemed intent on what they were doing; none looked up as we passed through.

Mr. Waldo Bommer led the way to a private office tucked into one corner. He closed the door behind us.

"How do you stand it?" I asked him.

"Stand what?"

"The smell."

"What smell?" he said. He took in a deep breath through his nostrils. "Hydrogen sulfide, hypochlorous acid, sulfur dioxide, a little bit of this, a little bit of that. A smell? I love it. Smells are my bread and butter, mister. How do you think I do a chemical analysis? First, I smell. You see before you an educated nose."

He tapped the bridge of his nose. A small pugnose with trumpeting nostrils.

"An educated nose," he repeated proudly. "First, I smell. Sometimes that tells me all I have to know."

Suddenly he grabbed me by the shoulders and pulled me close. I thought he meant to kiss me. But he merely sniffed at my mouth and cheeks.

"You don't smoke," he said. "Right?"

"Right," I said, pulling back from his grasp.

"And this morning, for breakfast, you had coffee and a pastry. Something with fruit in it. Figs maybe."

"Prune Danish," I said.

"You see!" he said. "An educated nose. My father had the best nose in the business. He could tell you when you had changed your socks. Sit down."

Waldo Bommer shuffled through a drawer in a battered oak file.

"Stacy, Stone, Stonehouse," he intoned. "Here it is. Professor Yale Stonehouse. Two chemical analyses of unknown liquids. December 14th of last year."

"May I take a look?" I asked.

"Why not?"

I scanned the two carbon-copy reports. There were a lot of chemical terms; one of them included arsenic trioxide.

"Could you tell me what these liquids were, please?"

He snatched the papers from my hands and scanned them. "Simple. This one, plain cocoa. This one was brandy."

"The brandy has the arsenic trioxide in it?"

"Yes."

"Didn't you think that unusual?"

He shrugged.

"Mister, I just do the analysis. What's in it is none of my business. A week ago a woman brought in a tube of toothpaste loaded with strychnine."

"Toothpaste?" I cried. "How did they get it in?"

Again he shrugged. "Who knows? A hypo through the opening maybe. I couldn't care less. I just do the analysis."

"Could I get copies of these reports, Mr. Bommer? For the government. The tax thing . . ."

He thought a moment.

"I don't see why not," he said finally. "You say this Professor Stonehouse is dead?"

"Yes, sir. Deceased early this year."

"Then he can't sue me for giving out copies of his property."

Ten minutes later I was bouncing down the splintering stairs with photocopies in my briefcase. I had offered to pay for the copies, and Bommer had taken me up on it. I inhaled several deep breaths of fresh air, then went flying up Eleventh Avenue. There is no feeling on earth to match a hunch proved correct. I decided to press my luck. I stopped at the first unvandalized phone booth I came to.

"Yah?" Olga Eklund answered.

"Olga, this is Joshua Bigg."

"Yah?"

"Is Miss Glynis in?"

"No. She's at her clinic."

That was what I hoped to hear.

"But Mrs. Stonehouse is at home?"

"Yah."

"Well, maybe I'll drop by for a few moments. She's recovered from her, uh, indisposition?"

"Yah."

"Able to receive visitors?"

"Yah."

"I'll come right over. You might mention to her that I'll be stopping by for a minute or two."

I waited for her "Yah," but there was no answer; she had hung up. Shortly afterward Olga in the flesh was taking my coat in the Stonehouse hallway.

"I'm sorry Miss Glynis isn't at home," I said to Olga. "You think I might be able to call her at the clinic?"

"Oh yah," she said. "It's the Children's Eye, Ear, Nose and Throat Clinic. It's downtown, on the East Side."

"Thank you," I said gratefully. "I'll call her there."

Ula Stonehouse was half-reclining on the crushed velvet couch. She was beaming, holding a hand out to me. As usual, there was a wineglass and a bottle of sherry on the glass-topped table.

"How nice!" she warbled. "I was hoping for company and here you are!"

"Here I am, indeed, ma'am," I said, taking her limp hand. "I was sorry to hear you have been indisposed, but you look marvelously well now."

"Oh, I feel so *good,*" she said, patting the couch next to her. I sat down obediently. "My signs changed and now I feel like a new woman."

"I'm delighted to hear it."

I watched her reach forward to fill her glass with a tremulous hand. She straightened back slowly, took a sip, looking at me over the rim with those milk-glass eyes flickering. The mop of blond curls seemed frizzier than ever. She touched the tip of her nose as one might gently explore a bruise.

"Would you care for anything, Mr. Bigger?" she asked. "A drink? Coffee? Whatever?"

"Bigg, ma'am," I said. "Joshua Bigg. No, thank you. Nothing for me. Just a few minutes of your time if you're not busy."

"All the time in the world," she said, laughing gaily.

She was wearing a brightly printed shirtwaist dress with a wide, ribbon belt. The gown, the pumps, the makeup, the costume jewelry: all too young for her. And the flickering eyes, warbling voice, fluttery gestures gave a feverish impression: a woman under stress. I felt sure she was aware of what was going on.

"Mrs. Stonehouse," I said, "I wish I had good news to report about your husband, but I'm afraid I do not."

"Oh, let's not talk about that," she said. "What's done is done. Now tell me all about yourself."

She looked at me brightly, eyes widened. If she wasn't going to talk about her vanished husband, I was stymied. Still, for the moment, it seemed best to play along.

"What would you like to know about me, ma'am?"

"You're a Virgo, aren't you?"

"Pisces," I told her.

"Of course," she said, as if confirming her guess. "Are you married?"

"No, Mrs. Stonehouse, I am not."

"Oh, you must be," she said earnestly. "You *must* listen to me. And you must because I have been so happy in my own marriage, you see. A family is a little world. I have my husband and my son and my daughter. We are a very close, loving family, as you know."

I looked at her helplessly. She had deteriorated since I first met her; now she was almost totally out of it. I thought desperately how I might use her present mood to get what I wanted. "I'm an orphan, Mrs. Stonehouse," I said humbly. "My parents were killed in an accident when I was an infant."

Surprisingly, shockingly, tears welled up in those milky eyes. She stifled a sob, reached to grip my forearm. Her clutch was frantic.

"Poor tyke," she groaned, then lunged for her glass of sherry.

"I was raised by relatives," I went on. "Good people. I wasn't mistreated. But still . . . So when you speak of a close, loving family, a little world—I know nothing of all that. The memories."

"The memories," she said, nodding like a broken doll. "Oh yes, the memories . . ."

"Do you have a family album, Mrs. Stonehouse?" I asked softly, and, to my surprise, she responded by producing the album with unexpected rapidity.

What followed was a truly awful hour. We pored over those old photographs one by one while Ula Stonehouse provided running commentary, rife with pointless anecdotes. I murmured constant appreciation and made frequent noises of wonder and enjoyment.

Wedding Pictures: the tall, gaunt groom towering over the frilly doll-bride. An old home in Boston. Glynis, just born, naked on a bearskin rug. Childhood snapshots. Powell Stonehouse at ten, frowning seriously at the camera. Picnics. Outings. Friends. Then, gradually, the family groups, friends, picnics, outings—all disappearing. Formal photographs. Single portraits. Yale, Ula, Glynis, Powell. Lifeless eyes. A family moving toward dissolution.

When Mrs. Stonehouse leaned forward to refill her glass, I rapidly removed a recent snapshot of Glynis from the album and slipped it into my briefcase before she sat back again. "Remarkable," I said, as if I were riveted to the book. "Really remarkable. Happy times."

She looked at me, not seeing me.

"Oh yes," she said. "Happy times. Such good babies. Glynis never cried. Never. Powell did, but not Glynis. It's over."

I didn't dare ask what she meant by that.

"Emanations," she went on. "And visits beyond. I know it's over."

"Mrs. Stonehouse," I asked anxiously, "are you feeling well?"

"What?" she said. "Well," she said, passing a faltering hand across her brow, "perhaps I should lie down for a few moments. So many memories."

"Of course," I said, rising. "I'll call Olga."

I found her seated at the long dining room table, leafing through *Popular Mechanics*.

"Olga," I said, "I think Mrs. Stonehouse needs you. I think she'd like to rest for a while."

"Yah?" she said. She rose, yawned, and stretched. "I go."

In the kitchen Effie was at the enormous stove, stirring something with a long wooden spoon. Her porky face creased into a grin.

"Mr. Bigg!" she said. "How nice!"

She put the spoon aside, clapped a lid on the pot, and wiped her hands on her apron. She gestured toward the white enameled table and we both drew up chairs.

"Effie," I said, "how are you? It's good to see you again."

That was true, and it was a comfort to be honest again. She was such a jolly tub of a woman.

"Getting along," she said. "You look a little puffy around the gills. Not sick, are you?"

"No," I said, "I'm okay. But I've been talking to Mrs. Stonehouse. I'm a little shook."

"Yes," she said, wagging her head dolefully. "I know what you mean. Worse every day."

"Why?" I asked. "What's happening to her?"

She frowned. "I don't rightly know. Her husband disappearing, I guess. Powell moving out. And the way Glynis has been acting. I suppose it's just too much for her."

"How has Glynis been acting?"

"Strange," Effie said. "Snappish. Cold. Goes to her room and stays there. Never a smile."

"Is this recent?" I asked.

"Oh yes. Just since your last visit."

She looked at me shrewdly. I decided to plunge ahead. If she repeated what I was saying to Glynis, so much the better. So I told Effie what I knew about the arsenic. She listened closely, then nodded when I had finished.

"Are you a detective?" she asked.

"Sort of," I said. "Chief Investigator for the legal firm representing Professor Stonehouse."

"You don't suspect me of poisoning him, do you?"

"Never," I lied. "Not for a minute."

"Glynis?"

We stared at each other. I wondered if her silence was meant to imply consent, and decided to act as if it did.

"I must establish that Glynis had the means," I said. "You just can't go out and buy arsenic at Rexall's. And to do that, I need the name of the medical laboratory where she worked as a secretary."

"I'd rather not," she said quickly.

"I was going to ask Mrs. Stonehouse, but she's in no condition to answer questions. Effie, I need the name."

Once again we stared at each other.

"It's got to be done," I said.

"Yes," she agreed sadly.

After a while she got up and lumbered from the kitchen. She came back in a few minutes with a slip of paper. I glanced at it briefly. Atlantic Medical Research, with the address and phone number.

"I had it in my book," Effie explained, "in case we had to reach her at work."

"When did she stop working there?"

She thought a moment.

"Maybe June or July of last year."

About the time Professor Stonehouse became ill.

"Did she just quit or was she fired?"

"She quit, she told us. Said it was very boring work."

"Effie, did you ever hear her mention a man named Godfrey Knurr? He's a minister."

"Godfrey Knurr? No."

"Is Glynis a religious woman?"

"Not particularly. They're Episcopalian. But I never thought she was especially religious. But she's deep."

"Oh yes," I agreed, "she's deep all right. Before her father's disappearance, was she in a good mood?"

Mrs. Dark pondered that.

"I'd say so," she said finally. "She started changing after the Professor disappeared and in the last week she's gotten much worse."

"Me," I said. "I'm troubling her. I told her I knew her father had been poisoned."

"You didn't!"

"I did. Of course I didn't tell her I thought she had done it."

"What are you going to do now?"

"Dig deeper. Try to find out what happened to the Professor. Effie, what kind of a car do the Stonehouses own?"

"A Mercedes."

"Do they keep it in a garage over on 66th Street and West End?"

"Why, yes. The garage people bring it over when we need it. How did you know?"

"I've been looking around."

"You surely have," she said. "Have you found the will yet?"

"Not yet. But I think I know where it is."

"I don't see why it's so important," she said. "If he's dead and didn't leave a will, the money goes to his wife and children anyway, doesn't it?"

"Yes," I said, "but if he left a will, he might have disinherited one of them."

"Could he do that?"

"Probably. With good cause. Like attempted murder."

"Oh," she said softly, "I hadn't thought of that."

"Effie, can I count on your discretion about all this?"

She put a fat forefinger alongside a fatter nose.

"Mum's the word," she said.

I rose, then bent swiftly to kiss her apple cheek.

"Thank you," I said. "I know it's not pleasant. But we agreed, it's got to be done. One last question: will Miss Glynis be in tonight? Did she say?"

"She said she's going to the theater. She asked for an early dinner."

"Uh-huh. So she'll be leaving about when?"

"Seven-thirty," Mrs. Dark said. "At the latest."

"Thank you very much," I said. "You've been very kind." I had a Big Mac and a Coke before I returned to the office. Yetta Apatoff was on the phone when I entered the TORT building. She blew me a kiss. I'm afraid I responded with a feeble gesture. Her scarf had come awry and the diving neckline of the green sweater now revealed a succulent cleavage. I wondered nervously when Mr. Teitelbaum or Mr. Tabatchnick would instruct their respective secretaries to order Yetta to cover up.

Mrs. Kletz had left a note on my desk; she was indeed out distributing the reward posters to the taxi garages and had left me a copy of the poster. It looked perfect.

I spent the remainder of the afternoon typing out reports of my morning's activities and adding them to the Stonehouse file, along with the photocopies of the chemical analyses. Then I hacked away at routine inquiries until about 4:00 P.M., when I dialed the number of the Children's Eye, Ear, Nose and Throat Clinic in the Manhattan phone book and asked to speak to the director.

"Who is calling, please?" the receptionist asked.

"This is the Metropolitan Poison Control Board," I said solemnly. "It concerns your drug inventory."

A hearty voice came on the line almost instantly.

"Yes, sir!" he said. "How may I be of service?"

"This is Inspector Waldo Bommer of the Metropolitan Poison Control Board. In view of the recent rash of burglaries of doctors' offices, clinics, hospitals, laboratories, and so forth, we are attempting to make an inventory of the establishments that keep poisonous substances in stock."

"Narcotics?" he said. "We have nothing like that. This is a clinic for underprivileged youngsters."

"What we're interested in is poisons," I said. "Arsenic, strychnine, cyanide: things of that sort."

"Oh, heavens no!" he said, enormously relieved. "We have nothing like that in stock."

"Sorry to bother you," I said. "Thank you for your time."

My second call, to Atlantic Medical Research, was less successful. I went through my Poison Control Board routine, but the man said, "Surely you don't expect me to reveal that information on the phone to a complete stranger? If you care to come around with your identification, we'll be happy to cooperate."

He hung up.

It wasn't 5:00 P.M. yet, but I packed my briefcase with the Kipper and Stonehouse files, yanked on my hat and coat, and sallied forth. Yetta was not on the phone. She held out a hand to stop me.

"Josh," she said, pouting, "you didn't even *notice*."

"I certainly did notice," I said. "The sweater looks lovely, Yetta."

"You like?" she said, arching her chest.

"Fine," I said, swallowing. "And the scarf is just right."

"Oh, this old thing," she giggled, swinging it farther aside. "It just gets in my way when I type. I think I'll take it off."

Which she did. I looked about furtively. There were people in the corridor. Was I a prude? I may very well have been.

"Josh," she said eagerly, "you said we might, you know, go out some night together."

"Well, uh, we certainly shall," I said with more confidence than I felt. "Dinner, maybe the theater or ballet." The image of Yetta Apatoff at a performance of *Swan Lake* shriveled my soul. "But I've been so busy, Yetta. Not only during the day, but working at home in the evening as well."

"Uh-huh," she said speculatively. She was silent a moment as I stood there awkwardly, not knowing how to break away. It was clear she was summing me up and coming to a decision.

"Lunch maybe?" she said.

"Oh absolutely," I said. "I can manage lunch."

"Tomorrow," she said firmly.

"Tomorrow?" I said, thinking desperately of how I might get out of it. "Well, uh, yes. I'll have to check my schedule. I mean, let's figure on lunch, and if I have to postpone you'll understand, right?"

"Oh sure," she said.

Coolness there. Definite coolness.

I waved goodbye and stumbled out. I felt guilt. I had led her astray. And then I was angry at my own feeling of culpability. What, actually, had I done? Bought her a few lunches. Given her a birthday present. I assured myself that I had never given her any reason to believe I was . . . It was true that I frequently stared at her intently, but with her physical attributes and habit of wearing knitted suits a size too small, that was understandable.

Such were my roiling thoughts as I departed the office that Monday evening, picking up a barbecued chicken, potato salad, and a quart of Scotch on the way home. Back in Chelsea, I ate and drank with an eye on the clock. I had to be across the street from the Stonehouse apartment at 7:15 at the latest, and I intended to proceed to the Upper West Side at a less-frenzied pace than my recent forays.

Clad in my fleece-lined anorak, I made it there in plenty of time and assumed my station. It was a crisp night, crackling, the air filled with electricity. You get nights like that in New York, usually between winter and spring, or between summer and fall, when suddenly the city seems bursting with promise, the skyline a-sparkle with crystalline clarity.

As I walked up and down the block, always keeping the doorway of the Stonehouse apartment house in view, I could glimpse the twinkling towers of the East Side across the park, and the rosy glow of midtown. Rush of traffic, blare of horns, drone of airliners overhead. Everything seemed so *alive*. I kept reminding myself I was investigating what was fast emerging as a violent death, but it was difficult.

I had been waiting exactly twenty-three minutes when she came out, wearing the long, hooded mink coat I'd seen in the garage.

When she paused outside the lighted apartment lobby for a moment, I was able to see her clearly as she raised and adjusted her hood. Then she started off, walking briskly. I thought I knew where she was going; despite Mrs. Dark's information, it was not the theater. I went after her. Not too close, not too far. Just as Roscoe Dollworth had taught me, keeping to the other side of the street when possible, even moving ahead of her. It was an easy tail because as we walked west and south a few blocks, I became more and more certain that she was taking me back to that garage on West 66th Street.

Crossing Broadway, she went west on 69th Street, keeping to the shadowed paths of a housing development. A man coming toward her paused and said something, but she didn't give him a glance, or slow down her pace. When she crossed West End Avenue, heading toward the lighted garage, I hurried to catch up, staying on the other side of the street and moving about a half-block southward. I could see her waiting in the entrance of the garage. I stopped the first empty cab that came along.

"Where to?" the driver asked, picking up his trip sheet clamped to a clipboard. He was a middle-aged black.

"Nowhere," I said. "Please start your clock and we'll just wait."

He put the clipboard aside and turned to stare at me through the metal grille.

"What is this?" he said.

"See that woman over there? Across the street, ahead of us? In the fur coat?"

He peered.

"I see her," he said.

I had learned from my previous experience.

"My wife," I said. "I want to see where she's going. I think someone's going to pick her up."

"Uh-huh," he said. "There's not going to be any trouble, is there?"

"No," I said, "no trouble."

"Good," he said. "I got all I can handle right now."

We sat there, both of us staring at the figure of Glynis Stonehouse across the street. The meter ticked away.

Within three or four minutes Knurr arrived. I had expected him to pull up in a cab, then switch to the Mercedes, but instead he raced into the garage entrance, near where Glynis waited, and opened the passenger door of his old VW. As soon as she got in, he backed out fast, swung around, and headed northward again, shoving his way into traffic.

"Follow?" my driver said.

"Please," I said.

"That guy is some cowboy. He drives like he don't give a damn."

"I don't think he does," I said.

We tailed them north. Knurr made a left onto 79th Street, then began to circle the block.

"Looking for a place to park," the cabdriver commented knowledgeably. "If he pulls in, what do you want me to do?"

"Go down to the next corner and wait."

That's what happened. Knurr found a place to park on West 77th Street near Riverside Drive. We went past and pulled in close to the corner. Through the rear window, I watched them both get out and walk past. They passed by my parked cab, talking much too intently to notice me.

I let them turn north on the Drive before I paid and got out of the taxi.

"Thank you," I said to the driver.

"Don't do anything foolish," he said.

As I followed Glynis Stonehouse and Godfrey Knurr into Riverside Park, I noted with relief that a few joggers and groups of raucous teenagers still braved the darkened expanse. And yet my nervousness increased as we penetrated deeper along lonely, descending paths, heading westward. I lurked as best I could in the shadows of leafless trees, trying to tread lightly. But I was being overcautious, for the couple ahead of me walking arm-in-arm were so intent on their talk that they seemed innocent of the secret sharer padding along behind them.

They walked around the rotunda, a large circular fountain girdled by a walk that was in turn enclosed by a ring of archways vaguely Roman in feeling. The fountain had long since ceased to operate; the basin was dried and cracked. All the white light globes were now shattered and dark. The archways were sprayed with graffiti. Splintered glass and broken bits of masonry grated underfoot. The ground was crumbling.

I paused briefly, not wanting to follow Glynis and Godfrey into one of those echoing passages lest they hear my footfall. I waited until they were clear on the other side of the fountain before hurrying through.

Ahead was the molten river, a band of gently heaving mercury in the nightlight. Across were the flickering lights of the Jersey shore. Closer, the swell of black water. I searched frantically about until I spotted them again, approaching the boat basin at 79th Street. I kept well back in the shadows as Glynis and Knurr walked onto the planked pier. They stopped briefly to speak to someone who appeared to be a watchman. Then they continued along one of the slips until they stepped down carefully onto the foredeck of what looked like a houseboat.

Lights came on inside the craft. When I saw curtains drawn across the wide windows, I turned and hurried back the way I had come.

3

•

I ARRIVED AT THE TORT BUILDING BEFORE 9:00 A.M. ON TUESDAY morning. The night security guard was still on duty, sitting at Yetta Apatoff's desk.

"There was a telephone call for you about fifteen minutes ago, Mr. Bigg," he said. "The guy wouldn't leave a name or message, but said he'd call back."

"Thank you," I said, and went back to my office. My phone rang before I had a chance to take off my coat. I picked it up and said, "Hello?" A man's voice growled, "You the guy who put up the posters?" I said I was. He said, "How much is the reward?"

I hadn't even considered that. Fifty dollars seemed insufficient; a hundred might tempt a lot of fraudulent claims. But rather, I reasoned, too many replies than too few.

"A hundred dollars," I said.

"Shit," he said, and hung up.

The second call came in ten minutes later. Once again the first question asked was: "How much?"

"A hundred dollars," I said firmly.

"Yeah, well, I carried the guy. Picked him up on Central Park West and 70th Street the night of January 10th."

"What did he look like?"

"Well, you know, an average-sized guy. I didn't get a real good look at him, but I'd say he was average."

"Kind of short, fat, dumpish?"

"Yeah, you could say that."

"Wearing a sweater and jacket?"

"Yeah, that's the guy."

"No, it isn't," I said.

"Fuck you," he said, and hung up.

I sighed, finished my strawberry strudel and black coffee, and started mechanically answering some of the routine research and investigation requests. I wondered if I dared bother Percy Stilton with what I had discovered—the houseboat at 79th Street—and what I was beginning to guess about how Godfrey Knurr had murdered Sol Kipper.

Stilton solved the problem by calling me at about 10:00 A.M.

"Listen, Josh," he said, speaking rapidly, "I know you didn't want me to call you at your office, but this is important. I've only got a minute. Can you meet me in the lobby of the Newsweek building? 444 Madison? Between 49th and 50th?"

"Well, yes, sure," I said. "But I wanted—"

"About five minutes before four o'clock this afternoon."

"I'll be there, Perce," I said, making rapid notes on my scratchpad. "But here are a few things I—"

"Got to run," he said. "See you then."

The line went dead. I hung up slowly, bewildered. The phone rang again almost immediately and I plucked it up, hoping Stilton was calling back.

"Josh," Yetta Apatoff said, giggling, "you haven't forgotten our lunch today, have you?"

"Of course not," I lied bravely. "What time?"

"Noon," she said. "I've got a lot to tell you."

"Good," I said, my heart sinking.

Another call:

"Yeah, I picked up the guy on that night. A tall, skinny gink, right?"

"Could be," I said. "And where did you take him—to the Eastern Airlines ticket office on Fifth Avenue?"

"Yeah," he said, "you're right."

"Waited for him and then drove him back to Central Park West and 70th Street?"

"Uh . . . yeah."

"No," I said, "I don't think so."

He suggested an anatomical impossibility.

Inwardly cursing the venality of mankind, I hung up, then phoned the Kipper house. Chester Heavens answered.

We exchanged polite greetings, inquired as to the state of each other's health, and spoke gravely about the weather, which we agreed was both pleasant and bracing for that time of year.

"Chester," I said, "Mr. Kipper died on Wednesday, January 24th. Is that correct?"

"Oh yes, sah," he said somberly. "I shall never forget that date."

"I don't suppose you will. I know Mr. Godfrey Knurr arrived a few moments after the tragedy. Now my question is this: do you recall if he was at the house on Tuesday, January 23rd, the day before Mr. Kipper died?"

Silence. Then . . .

"I can't recall, sah. But if you'll be good enough to hang on a moment, I'll consult the book."

"Wait, wait!" I said hastily. "What book?"

"The house diary, sah," he said. "The first Mrs. Kipper insisted it be kept. It was one of my father's duties. After the first Mrs. Kipper and my father had both passed away, I kept it with the approval of the second Mrs. Kipper.

What it is, sah, is a diary or log of visitors, delivery of packages, repairs to the house, appointments, and so forth. Many large homes keep such a daily record, sah. It is invaluable when it becomes necessary to send Christmas cards, thank-you notes, invitations, or to question tradesmen about promised deliveries and things of that nature."

"Very efficient," I said, beginning to hope. "Could you consult the log, please, Chester, and see if the Reverend Knurr visited on Tuesday, January 23rd?"

"Just a moment, sah."

He was gone more than a moment. I had crossed all fingers of both hands and was trying to cross my toes within my shoes when the butler came back on the phone.

"Mr. Bigg?" he said. "Are you there?"

"I am here," I told him.

"Yes, sah, the diary shows that the Reverend Knurr visited on Tuesday, January 23rd. He arrived at approximately 3:30 P.M."

"Any record of when he left?"

"No, sah, there is no record of that."

"Thank you, Chester," I said gratefully, uncrossing my digits. "Just out of curiosity, where is this house diary kept?"

"In the kitchen, sah. In the back of one of the cutlery drawers."

"I wonder if you would do me a favor, Chester. I wonder if you would take the house diary to your apartment and conceal it carefully. I realize that is a strange request, but it is very important."

He didn't speak for a while. Then he said softly:

"Very well, Mr. Bigg, I shall do as you request."

"Thank you," I said.

"My pleasure, sah," he said.

My case was looking better and better. I thought I had Knurr cold, and I refused to worry about how I might begin to prove it.

"I'll check in later," I told Chester conspiratorially.

"I'll look forward to it, sah," he said, then rang off.

The high points of my long, dull morning were two more inconclusive calls from cabdrivers. A few minutes before noon I went into the men's room to freshen for lunch with Yetta. At an adjoining basin Hamish Hooter was combing his black, greasy locks sideways in a futile effort to conceal his growing tonsure.

He saw me reflected in the mirror and sucked his teeth noisily.

"See here, Bigg," he said, the voice reedy but not aggrieved; smug, in fact. "I understand you're having lunch with Yetta Apatoff today."

"You understand correctly," I said coldly.

He dried his hands busily on one paper towel. About a year previously, he had circulated a memo about the wasteful practice of using more than a single paper towel.

Hooter examined himself in the mirror with every evidence of approval. He passed a palm over his slicked-down hair. He attempted to straighten his rounded shoulders. He inhaled mightily, which caused his potbelly to disappear until he exhaled.

"Well," he said, turning to face me, "have a good time. Enjoy it while you can." Then he gave me a foxy grin and was gone.

When I walked out to meet Yetta, I saw at once that she was "dolled up" and looked especially glowing and attractive. I thought this was in anticipation of lunch with me, and I swelled with male satisfaction. At the same time I imagined how shattered she would be by the can't-we-be-friends speech I had in mind. Especially when she'd gone to so much trouble.

Instead of the usual knitted suit she was wearing a dress of some shimmering stuff with a metallic gleam.

About her blond curls was bound a light blue chiffon scarf. The electric combination of blue and green enhanced her creamy complexion, sweetly curved lips, and the look of innocence in those limpid brown eyes. Was I being too hasty in putting our relationship on a purely friendly basis?

We walked over to the Chinese restaurant, Yetta chattering briskly about a movie concerning creatures from outer space who descend to earth and turn everyone into toadstools. She assured me it had been one of the scariest movies she had ever seen.

"Also," she added, "it made you think."

Then she babbled on about a used car her brother was thinking of buying, and about a girl she went to high school with who had recently obtained a job with the telephone company. Even for Yetta it was a manic performance.

All became clear over the wonton soup.

"Josh," she said breathlessly, "I wouldn't hurt you for the world."

I stared at her, perplexed.

"First of all," she started, "I want it definitely understood that you and I can still be friends."

Naturally I resented that. It was *my* line.

"Second of all," Yetta went on, "I have really enjoyed knowing you and these lunches and everything. I will never forget you, Josh."

"What—" I began.

"And third of all," she said in a rush, "Hamish Hooter asked me to marry him and I said yes. I know that must be a real downer for you, Josh, but I want you to know that I think I'm doing the right thing, and I've given it a lot of thought. He's not as cute as you are, Josh, that I freely admit, but he says he loves me and he needs me. Josh, you don't need me. Do you?"

There was no answer to that. I stared down into my soup bowl, saw it whisked away and a Number Three Combination slid into its place.

"Josh, don't take it too hard," Yetta pleaded. "It's best for all of us."

Could I tell her that my heart was leaping upward like a demented stag?

"You have your work," she continued, "and I know how important it is to you. Will you pass the sweet-and-sour sauce, please? So I thought—Hamish and I thought—that this would be the best way to tell you, honestly and straight out. He wanted to be here, but I said it would be best if I told you myself . . . Josh," Yetta Apatoff continued, staring at me with those guileless eyes, "I hope you don't hate me?"

"Hate you?" I said, keeping any hint of glee out of my voice. "How could I? All I want is what makes you happy. Yetta, I wish you the best of everything. Hooter is a very lucky man."

"Oh, Josh," she said, sighing, "you're so nice and understanding. I knew you would be. I told Hammy—that's what I call him: Hammy—I said, 'Hammy, his heart may be broken, but he'll wish me the best of everything.' That's what I told Hammy. Josh, is your heart broken? Could I have the mustard, please?"

I resisted the urge to suggest to Yetta that we go Dutch, and the lunch hour passed reasonably amicably, all things considered.

My first visitor upon my return to TORT was Hamish Hooter. "See here, Bigg," he said. "I guess Yetta told you the news?"

"She did," I said, "and I want to wish the two of you the best of everything."

"Yes?" he said, surprised. "Well, uh, thanks."

"I hope you'll be very happy together," I went on enthusiastically. "I'm sure you will be. Congratulations."

"Uh, thanks," he said again. "Listen, Bigg, you're being very decent about this."

I made an "it's nothing" gesture.

"If there's anything I can do . . ." he went on lamely.

"Well, there is something. You know I've got an assistant now. Temporary at the moment, but my workload seems to increase every day. If a larger office becomes available, I'd appreciate it if you'd keep me in mind."

"Well, uh, sure," he said. "I'll certainly do that."

"Thank you," I said humbly. "And once again, I wish you every happiness."

Next I did what most TORT employees did when they had an intraoffice problem: I went to Thelma Potts.

The news had already spread; she greeted me with a sympathetic smile. "I'm sorry, Mr. Bigg," she said.

"The better man won," I said.

Then she said something so completely out of character that she left me openmouthed.

"Bullshit," Thelma Potts said. "You're well out of it. The girl is a moron. Not for you."

"Well . . ." I said, "at least you won."

"You did, too," she assured me with some asperity. "Did you come up here for sympathy?"

"Not exactly," I said. "I've got a problem. Nothing to do with Yetta," I added hastily.

"What's the problem?"

"I want to get together with Mr. Teitelbaum and Mr. Tabatchnick in a kind of conference. I have a lot to tell them, and it's very important, but I don't want to tell them separately. I was hoping you would speak to Ada Mondora and maybe the two of you might arrange something."

"It's that important?"

"It really is, Miss Potts. I wouldn't ask if it wasn't. It concerns a case each of them is handling, and the two cases have come together in a very peculiar fashion."

"Kipper and Stonehouse?" she asked.

"Miss Potts," I said, "is there anything you don't know?"

"Ada and I have lunch together almost every day," she said. "When do you want to meet with the two Mr. T's?"

"As soon as possible." I thought of my appointment with Detective Percy Stilton. "Not today, but tomorrow. If you can set it up."

"I'll talk to Ada," she said, "and we'll see what we can do. I'll let you know."

"Thank you," I said gratefully. "I don't know what we'd all do without you."

She sniffed.

I bent swiftly to kiss her soft cheek.

"Now that I've been jilted," I said, "I'm available."

"Oh *you!*" she said.

I returned to my office and took calls from two more cabdrivers, one of them drunk, then did routine stuff until it was time to leave for my meeting with Stilton. I packed my scruffy briefcase, put on hat and coat, and peeked cautiously out into the corridor.

Yetta Apatoff was seated at her receptionist's post, hands clasped primly on the desk. I ducked back into my office and waited a few moments. When I peeked out again, she was in the same position, still as a statue. I ducked back inside again. But the third time I peered out, she was busy on the phone, and I immediately sailed forth and gave her a sad smile and a resigned wave of my hand as I passed.

Cowardly conduct, I know.

I arrived early at the Newsweek building. A few minutes before 4:00 P.M., Percy Stilton came up behind me and stuck a hard forefinger in my ribs.

"Perce," I said, "I've got to tell you. I was—"

"Sure," he said, "but later. We've got a four o'clock appointment with Bishop Harley Oxman. He's in charge of personnel for the church the Reverend Godfrey Knurr belongs to. You just do as little talking as possible and follow my lead. In this scam, you play a lawyer."

"I've got Mr. Tabatchnick's business card," I offered.

"Beautiful," he said. "Flash it."

The church's personnel headquarters was a brightly lighted, brisk, efficient-appearing office in a five- or six-story commercial building on Forty-ninth between Madison and Park. The walls were painted a no-nonsense beige, the floors covered with practical vinyl tile; partitions between individual offices were steel. I saw no paintings of a religious nature on view. Typewriters clacked away merrily. Men and women moving along the corridors were all in mufti. Percy and I approached the matronly receptionist, and Perce identified himself. She didn't seem surprised that the Bishop would be meeting with a detective of the New York Police Department. She spoke briefly into an intercom, then gave us a wintry smile.

"You may go right in," she said. "Turn left outside, go to the end, and turn right. Last office."

We found the Bishop's office with no difficulty. The door was opened before we had a chance to knock. The man greeting us was tall and broad, though somewhat stooped and corpulent. He was wearing an old-fashioned suit of rusty cheviot and a gray doeskin waistcoat with white piping. His polka-dot bow tie was negligently knotted.

He had a very full, almost bloated face, ranging in hue from livid pink to deep purple. The full, moist, bright rose lips parted to reveal teeth of such startling whiteness, size, and regularity that they could only have been "store-bought." Set into this blood pudding of a face were sharp eyes of ice blue, the whites clear. And he had a great shock of steel-gray hair, combed sideways in rich billows.

"I am Bishop Oxman," he intoned in a deep resonant voice. "Won't you gentlemen come in?"

He ushered us into his office and seated us in leather armchairs in front of his glass-topped desk. Perce Stilton slid his identification across the desk without being asked, and I hastily dug in my wallet and did the same with Mr. Tabatchnick's business card.

While the Bishop was examining our bona fides slowly and with interest, I studied the bare office, its single bookcase, artificial rubber plant, and a framed photograph behind the Bishop. It appeared to be Bishop Oxman's seminary graduating class.

He returned our identification to us, sat back in his swivel chair, squirmed slightly to make himself more comfortable, then laced his pudgy fingers across his paunch. He wasted no time on pleasantries.

"Detective Stilton," he said in his rumbling bass-baritone, "when we spoke on the phone, you stated that a situation had arisen concerning one of our pastors that might best be handled by discussing it with me personally." He glanced briefly at me. "And privately."

"Yes, sir," Percy said firmly but with deference. "Before any official action is taken."

"Dear me," Bishop Oxman said with a cold smile, "that does sound ominous." But he didn't seem at all disturbed.

"It's something I think you should be aware of," Stilton went on, speaking with no hesitation. "Mr. Tabatchnick here represents a young woman who claims she was swindled out of her savings and an inheritance—slightly over ten thousand dollars—by the one of your clergymen who promised her he could double her money in six months."

"Oh my," Bishop Oxman murmured.

"This young lady further alleges that she was persuaded to hand over her money by the promise of the pastor that he would marry her as soon as her money increased."

"What is the young lady's name?" the Bishop asked.

"I don't believe that is germane to this discussion at the present time," Percy Stilton said.

"How old is the young lady? Surely you can tell me that?"

Stilton turned to me.

"Mr. Tabatchnick," he said, "how old is your client?"

"Twenty-three," I said promptly.

Oxman turned those piercing eyes on me.

"Has she been married before?"

"No, sir. Not to my knowledge."

The Bishop raised his two hands, pressed them together in an attitude of prayer, then put the two forefingers against his full lips. He appeared to be ruminating. Finally:

"Is your client pregnant, Mr. Tabatchnick?"

Stilton looked at me.

"Yes, sir," I said softly, "she is. I have seen the doctor's report. My client attempted to contact the clergyman to tell him, but was unsuccessful."

"She called the phone number he had given her," Stilton broke in, "a number she had previously used, but it had been disconnected. Both she and Mr. Tabatchnick went to his apartment, in the Murray Hill section of Manhattan, but apparently he had moved and left no forwarding address. Mr. Tabatchnick then reported the matter to the police, and I was assigned to the investigation. I have been unable to locate or contact the man. I felt—and Mr. Tabatchnick agreed—that it would be best to apprise you of the situation before more drastic steps were taken."

"And what is this clergyman's name?"

"The Reverend Godfrey Knurr," Percy said. "That's K-n-u-r-r."

The Bishop nodded and pulled his phone toward him. He dialed a three-digit number and waited. Then:

"Timmy? Would you see if you can find a file on Godfrey Knurr? That's K-n-u-r-r," he rumbled, then hung up. Speaking to us again, he announced with solemnity, "Unfortunately this is not a unique situation. But I must tell you that frequently the minister involved is entirely innocent. A young woman misinterprets sympathy and understanding. When the pastor tries to convince her that his interest is spiritual she becomes hysterical. In her disturbed state, she makes all kinds of wild accusations."

"Yes, sir," Stilton said, "I can imagine. But a complaint has been made and I've got to check it out."

"Dear me, of course! In any event I'm glad you came to me before pursuing the matter further. It's possible the clergyman in question is not a clergyman at all, but a con man acting the role and preying on lonely women."

But such was not to be the case. The Bishop had hardly ceased speaking when there was a light tap on the office door, it was opened, and a young man entered with a manila folder. He placed it carefully on Oxman's desk and turned to leave.

"Thank you, Timmy," the Bishop called. Then he picked up the folder and read the label on the tab. Then he looked at us. "Oh dear," he said dolefully, "I'm afraid he's one of ours. Godfrey Mark Knurr. Well, let's see what we've got . . ."

He began to scan the documents in the folder. We sat in silence, watching him. One of the things he looked at was a glossy photograph.

"Handsome man," he said.

We waited patiently while the Bishop went through all the papers. Then he shut the folder. "Oh dear, oh dear," he said with a thin smile, "it appears that Mr. Knurr has been a naughty boy again."

"*Again?*" Stilton said.

Bishop Oxman sighed. "Sometimes," he said, "I feel there should be limits to Christian charity. The Reverend Knurr came to us from Chicago where he served as assistant pastor. He seems to have been very popular with the congregation. It appears that he became, ah, intimate with the twenty-two-year-old daughter of one of the vestrymen. When her pregnancy could no longer be concealed, she named Mr. Knurr, claiming he had promised to marry her. In addition, she said, she had made several substantial loans to him. Loans which were never repaid, needless to say. The affair seems to have been hushed up. Knurr, who continued to protest his innocence despite some rather damning evidence against him, was banished from Chicago and sent here."

"Can they do that, sir?" I asked curiously. "Can the church of another city stick New York with one of their problems?"

"Well," the Bishop said, "Knurr may have been part of, ah, an exchange program, so to speak. One of their bad apples for one of ours. Of course there was no possibility of Knurr getting a church here. We are already burdened with a worrisome oversupply of clergymen, and their numbers are increasing every year. But I assure you that the great majority of our pastors are honorable, God-fearing men, deeply conscious of their duties and responsibilities."

THE TENTH COMMANDMENT • 671

"So what did you do with Knurr?" Stilton asked.

"He retained his collar," Oxman said, "and was allowed to make his own way, with the understanding that because of his record, assignment to a parish was out of the question. According to these records, our last communication from the Reverend Godfrey Knurr was a letter from him requesting permission to open a sort of social club for underprivileged youngsters in Greenwich Village. He felt he could raise the required funds on his own. Permission was granted. But there is nothing in his file to indicate if he actually followed through on his proposal. And, I am sorry to say, there is no current address or telephone number listed."

"Where was the letter sent from?" Detective Stilton asked. "The one that asked permission to open the social club?"

"Oh dear," he said. "No address given."

"How about next of kin?" Stilton asked. "Have you got that?"

"Yes, that I know we have," the Bishop said, digging through the papers. "Here it is. A sister, Goldie Knurr, living in Athens, Indiana. Would you like the address?"

"Please," the detective said.

Percy and I were the only ones in the elevator going down. "You did fine," Stilton said.

"Thank you."

"But I knew you would," he went on, "or I'd have made you rehearse. The scam was necessary, Josh, because if I had just waltzed in there and asked to see the file on Knurr, without a warrant or anything, the Bishop would have told me to go peddle my fish. He looks sleepy, but he's no dummy."

In the lobby, Stilton paused to light a cigarette.

"Perce," I said, "how did you get onto this office? I didn't even know which sect Knurr belongs to."

"I looked him up in the telephone book and got the address of that boys' club of his in Greenwich Village. Then I called Municipal Records downtown and got the name of the owner of the building. Then I went to see him and got a look at Knurr's lease for that storefront. Like I figured, when he signed the lease he had to give a permanent or former address. It was the headquarters of his church. I called them and they referred me to Bishop Oxman's personnel offices. So I called him."

I shook my head in wonderment.

"It's a lot easier," the detective assured me, "when you can flash your potsy." He looked at his watch. "I've got maybe a half hour. You have something to tell me? There's a bar around the corner. Let's have a beer and I'll listen."

In the corner of a small bar on East 48th Street I asked, "Perce, that story you dreamed up about Knurr swindling a girl in New York was almost word for word what he actually pulled out in Chicago. How did you know?"

He shrugged. "I didn't," he said. "Josh, the bad guys don't have *all* the luck. Sometimes we get lucky, too. I figured if we were right about him, that con about your client would be right in character. Now I'm wondering if we got enough on the guy for me to got to my lieutenant and ask that the Kipper case be reopened." He pondered a moment. "No, I guess not," he said finally. "What happened in Chicago a couple of years ago is just background. It's got fuck-all to do with how Sol Kipper died. You got things to tell me?"

I told him about the reward posters and the calls that had come in, and how I had obtained copies of the chemical analyses of Professor Stonehouse's brandy.

"Mmm," Stilton grunted. "Good. More paper."

I told him I had obtained a photograph of Glynis Stonehouse and the name of the clinic where she presently did volunteer work and the medical laboratory where she had been employed a year ago.

"I checked out the clinic on the phone," I said, "and they claim they don't stock poisons. It sounds logical; it's an eye, ear, nose and throat clinic for children. I got nowhere with the medical lab."

"Give me the name and address," the detective said. "I'll pay them a call."

He copied the information into his elegant little notebook.

Finally I told him about following Glynis Stonehouse to her rendezvous with Godfrey Knurr, and then tailing the two of them to the 79th Street boat basin.

"That's interesting," Stilton said thoughtfully. "You're doing fine, Josh."

"Thank you," I said. "I've saved the best till last. I think I know how he killed Sol Kipper."

The detective stared at me for a moment.

"Let's have another beer," he said.

"There's an old gentleman who lives in the apartment across the hall from me," I said. "He's confined in a wheelchair and he's been rather lonely. Sometimes when I come home from work, he's waiting for me in his chair on the landing. Just to talk, you know. Well, a few times in the past month I've gotten home early, and he didn't know I was already in my apartment, and when I came out later, there he was on the landing, waiting for me."

Stilton looked at me, puzzled.

"So?" he asked.

"That's what gave me the idea of how Knurr killed Sol Kipper. I was already inside the apartment."

He had started to take a gulp of beer, but suddenly put his full glass back on the bar and sat there, staring straight ahead.

"Yeah," he breathed. "That sucker! That's how he did it. Let me tell you: He was in the house all the time. Probably hiding in one of those empty rooms. Only Tippi knew he was there. She leaves her husband, comes downstairs. Knurr goes up to the master bedroom on the fifth floor and wastes Sol

Kipper. Maybe with one of those karate chops of his or with the famous blunt instrument—who knows? Then he carries—"

"No," I said, "that's no good. Sol Kipper wasn't a heavy man, but it would be a difficult task to carry him up that narrow rear staircase to the sixth floor. I think Knurr rang for the elevator and took Kipper's body up that way."

"Right," Stilton said decisively. "The first blues on the scene found the elevator on the sixth floor. All right, he gets Sol up on the terrace and throws him over. I mean literally *throws* him. That's why the body was so far from the base of the wall."

"Then Knurr goes down— How does he go down?"

"He takes the stairs. Because the elevator door on the main floor can be seen from the kitchen. And also, the elevator was found on the sixth floor by the first officers to arrive."

"Tippi fainted," I reminded him, "or pretended to."

"Sure. To give Knurr time to get downstairs. Then he goes out the front door, turns right around, rings the bell, and waits for the butler to let him in."

"Yes," I said, nodding, "I think so. You can't see the front door from the kitchen, so even if they were inside when he exited, he was safe. Perce, I think he stayed in the house overnight. The butler keeps a house diary of visitors, deliveries, and so forth. He has a record of the Reverend Godfrey Knurr arriving on Tuesday the 23rd, the day before Kipper died."

"Oh wow," Percy said, "that's beautiful. I hate to admit it, but I got to admire him for that. The balls!"

"Then you think that's how it was done?" I said eagerly.

"Got to be," Perce said. "*Got* to! Everything fits. It was just a matter of planning and timing. That guy is one cool cat. When we take him, I'm bringing along a regiment of marines. But what about the suicide note?"

"I can't explain it," I confessed. "Right now I can't. But I'm going to give it some thought."

"You do that," he said, patting my arm. "Give it some thought. I'm beginning to think Roscoe Dollworth knew exactly what he was doing when he got you the job. Chief Investigator? You better believe it! Josh, I think now I got enough to ask my loot to reopen the Kipper case. I'll lay out the whole shmeer for him, how it ties into the Stonehouse disappearance, and how—"

"Perce," I said, "could you hold off for just a day or two?"

"Well . . . sure, but why?"

"I'm trying to set up a conference with Mr. Tabatchnick and Mr. Teitelbaum. Teitelbaum's the senior partner who represents the Stonehouse family. I want to tell the two of them everything we've discovered and suggest how the two cases are connected. I want them to let me devote all my time to the investigation and stick to it no matter how long it takes. I'd like you to be there at the conference. They have some clout, don't they? Political clout?"

"I guess they do."

"Well, if we get them on our side first, won't it help you to get the Kipper case reopened and maybe be assigned to it full time?"

"Maybe it would," he said slowly. "Maybe it would at that." He ruffled my hair with his fingertips. "You're a brainy little runt," he said.

I didn't resent it at all.

We were back on the sidewalk, about ready to part, when Stilton snapped his fingers.

"Oh Jesus!" he said. "I forgot to tell you. There was nothing in Records on Knurr, which was why I pulled that scam at the church office. Just to get some background on the guy. But Tippi Kipper—she's another story. She's got a sheet. It goes back almost twenty years—but it's there."

"She's done time?" I said unbelievingly.

"Oh no," the detective said. "Just charged. No record of trial or disposition."

"Charged?" I said. "With what?"

"Loitering," he said, "for the purpose of prostitution."

4

•

BEFORE I LEFT FOR WORK EARLY WEDNESDAY MORNING, I SLID A note under Cleo's door: "Mr. Joshua Bigg respectfully requests the pleasure of Miss Cleo Hufnagel's company at dinner in Mr. Bigg's apartment tonight, Wednesday, at 8:00 P.M. Dress optional. RSVP."

I went off to work planning the menu.

I found a memo on my desk from Ada Mondora stating that Mr. Teitelbaum and Mr. Tabatchnick would meet with me in the library at 2:00 P.M. I called Percy, but he wasn't in. I left a message asking him to call back as soon as possible. I then started to type notes on our meeting with Bishop Harley Oxman for the Kipper file.

I was interrupted by a nervous call from Mrs. Gertrude Kletz. She had broken a tooth and the dentist could only take her at eleven o'clock. Would it be acceptable if she came in from twelve to four? I told her that would be fine. A cabdriver called who claimed to have picked up Professor Stonehouse on the night of January 10th. He described his passenger as being short, in his middle 40s, with a noticeable limp.

"Sorry," I said, "that's not the man."

"No harm in trying," he said cheerfully and hung up.

The next call was from Percy Stilton. I told him about the meeting with Teitelbaum and Tabatchnick at 2:00 P.M., and he said he'd do his best to make it. Then he told me that he had visited Glynis Stonehouse's former employer, Atlantic Medical Research, that morning.

"They stock enough poison to waste half of Manhattan," Stilton reported. "And they've got a very lax control system. The poison cabinet has a dime-store lock that could be opened with a heavy breath. The supervisor is the only one with a key, but he keeps it in plain view, hanging on a board on his wall, labeled. He's in and out of his office a hundred times a day. Anyone who works in the place could lift the key, use it, and replace it without being noticed. Every time a researcher takes some poison he's supposed to sign a register kept in the poison locker stating how much he took, the date, and his name. So I had the supervisor run a total on the arsenic trioxide withdrawn and check it against the amount they started with and how much was there this morning. Over two ounces is unaccounted for. He couldn't understand how that could happen."

"I can," I said. "Two ounces! She took enough to kill the old man ten times."

"Sounds like," Stilton agreed, "but no way to prove it. *Now* they're going to tighten up their poison control procedure. By the way, Glynis Stonehouse wasn't fired; she left voluntarily. Cleaned out her desk one Friday and called on Monday to say she wasn't coming in. Didn't even give them a reason or excuse; just quit cold. Well, I've got to run, Josh. I'm going to try to get over to the 79th Street boat basin around noon. And if possible, I'll see you at two o'clock."

I finished typing up my notes on the Bishop Oxman interview and began trying to compose a rough agenda for the meeting that afternoon with the two senior partners. I knew I would make a better impression if my presentation was organized, brief, succinct.

I was scribbling notes when the phone rang again. It was another cabdriver and the conversation followed the usual pattern:

"How much is the reward?" he asked in a gargling voice.

"A hundred dollars," I said automatically, continuing to make notes as I spoke.

"Well," he said, "it isn't much, but it's better than a stick up the nose. I think I picked up the guy. About January 10th. It *could* have been then. On Central Park West and maybe 70th or 71st. Around there."

"What time?"

"Oh, maybe nine o'clock at night. Like that. I was working nights then. I'm on day now."

"Do you remember what the weather was like?"

"That night? A bitch. Lousy driving. Sleety. I was ready to pack it in when this guy practically threw himself under my wheels, waving his arms."

"Do you remember what he looked like?"

"The only reason I remember, he gave me such a hard time. I wasn't driving fast enough. I was taking the long way. The back of the cab was littered and smelled. And so forth and so on. A real ball-breaker, if you know what I mean."

I put my pen aside and took a deep breath. It was beginning to sound encouraging.

"Can you describe him physically?"

"Hat, scarf, and overcoat," the cabdriver said. "An old geezer. Tall and skinny. Stooped over. Ordinarily I don't take a lot of notice of who rides my cab, but this guy was such a fucking asshole I remember him."

He was sounding better and better.

"And where did you take him?" I asked, closing my eyes and hoping.

"The 79th Street boat basin," the cabdriver said. "And he gives me a quarter tip. In weather like that! Can you beat it?"

I opened my eyes and let my breath out in a long sigh.

"Would you tell me your name, please?" I said.

"Bernie Baum."

"And where are you calling from now, Mr. Baum?"

"Gas station on Eleventh Avenue."

"We're on East 38th Street. If you'd be willing to come over and sign a short statement attesting to what you've just told me, you can pick up your hundred dollars."

"You mean that was the guy?" he said.

"That was the guy," I said.

"Well, yeah, sure," he said, "I'll sign a statement. It's the truth, ain't it? But listen, I wouldn't have to go to court or nothing like that, will I?"

"Oh no, no," I said hurriedly. "Nothing like that. It's just for our files."

Maybe someday he would have to repeat his statement in court, but I wasn't about to tell him that.

"Well, I want to grab some lunch first," he said, "but I'll be over right after."

"Fine," I said heartily. "Try to make it before one o'clock."

I gave him our address and told him to ask for Joshua Bigg. I hung up, grinning. Percy Stilton had been right; the bad guys didn't have *all* the luck.

I typed out a brief statement to be signed by Bernie Baum that said only that he had picked up a man he later identified from a photograph as Professor Yale Stonehouse at approximately 9:00 P.M. on the evening of January 10th in the vicinity of Central Park West and 70th Street and had delivered him to the 70th Street boat basin. I kept it as short and factual as possible.

Mrs. Kletz arrived while I was finishing up. She said her tooth was feeling better and she felt well enough to put in her four hours.

I told her about Bernie Baum and she was as pleased as I was.

"A lot has happened since you read the Kipper and Stonehouse files," I said. "Sit down for a moment and I'll bring you up to date."

She listened intently, sucking her breath in sharply when I told her about Glynis and Knurr.

"And that's where the cabdriver took Professor Stonehouse the night he disappeared," I finished triumphantly.

But she was thinking of something else. Those young eyes seemed to have taken on a thousand-yard stare.

"Do you suppose, Mr. Bigg," she said in her light, lilting voice, "do you suppose that either of the two women, Tippi Kipper or Glynis Stonehouse, knows of the other?"

I blinked at her. The question had never occurred to me, and I was angry with myself because it should have.

"I don't know, Mrs. Kletz," I confessed. "I'd say no, neither is aware of the other's existence. If there's anything Knurr doesn't need right now it's a jealous and vindictive woman."

She nodded thoughtfully. "I expect you're right, Mr. Bigg." She went back to her desk and began answering some of the routine requests. As for me, I ordered a pastrami on rye, kosher dill pickle, and tea from a Madison Avenue deli. Bernie Baum arrived and turned out to be a squat, middle-aged man with two days' growth of grizzled beard and a wet cigar. He was wearing a soiled plaid mackinaw and a black leather cap.

I handed him the statement I had prepared, and he took a pair of spectacles from his inside shirt pocket. One of the bows was missing and he had to hold the ramshackle glasses to his eyes to read.

Then he looked up at me.

"What'd this guy do?" he asked in his raspy, gargling voice. "Rob a bank?"

"Something like that," I said.

"It figures," he said, nodding. "Since I talked to you on the phone, I been trying to remember the guy better. I figure now he was nervous—you know? Something was bugging him and that's why he was bugging me."

"Could be," I said.

"Well," said Bernie Baum judiciously, "if he had a yacht stashed in that boat basin, he's probably in Hong Kong by now."

"That could be, too," I said. "Now if you'll just sign the statement, Mr. Baum, I'll get you your money."

He signed Bernard J. Baum, with his address, and I made out a petty cash voucher for $100. We shook hands and I sent him up to the business office with Mrs. Kletz. She was back in five minutes and told me Bernie Baum had received his cash reward and departed happily. She also told me that Hamish Hooter had okayed the request with no demur. In victory, magnanimous . . .

Percy Stilton showed up right on time, dressed, I was happy to see, very conservatively in navy blue suit, white shirt, black tie. No jewelry. No flash. He had judged his audience to a tee. I showed him the statement the cabdriver had signed.

Percy sat there a moment, knees crossed, pulling gently at his lower lip.

"Uh-huh," he said finally. "We're filling in the gaps—slowly. Know what I think? Professor Stonehouse is down in the mud at the bottom of the Hudson River at 79th Street with an anchor tied to his tootsies. That's what I think. I checked out the boat basin about an hour ago. There's a houseboat registered to a *Mister* Godfrey Knurr. Not reverend, but mister. It's a fifty-foot fiberglass Gibson, and the guy I talked to told me it's a floating palace. All the comforts of home and then some."

I sighed.

"It makes sense," I said. "It doesn't make sense to think a man like Knurr would be content to live in the back room of a dingy store down on Carmine Street."

Perce was silent, and I glanced nervously at my watch. We only had a few more minutes.

"Something bothering you?" I asked.

"Do you really think Knurr burned Kipper and Stonehouse?" he asked tonelessly.

"Kipper certainly," I said. "Probably Stonehouse."

"That's how I see it," he said, nodding somberly. "What's bothering me is this: we know of two. How many more are there we don't know about?"

I gathered up my notes and files and we took the elevator up to the library. Neither of us spoke during the ascent.

There was a note Scotch-taped to the library door: "Closed from 2:00 to 3:00 P.M." An effective notice to me that I would be allotted one hour, no more. Stilton and I went in and took adjoining leather-padded captain's chairs at the center of one of the table's long sides.

"Perce, can you get through this without smoking?" I asked him.

"Sure."

"Try," I said.

I arranged my files and papers in front of me. I went over my presentation notes. Then we sat in silence.

When Ignatz Teitelbaum and Leopold Tabatchnick entered together, at precisely 2:00 P.M., Stilton and I rose to our feet. I thought wildly that there should have been a fanfare of trumpets.

Both senior partners were wearing earth-colored vested suits, with shirts and ties of no particular style or distinction. But there the resemblance ended. Tabatchnick, with his brooding simian posture, towered over Teitelbaum, who appeared especially frail and shrunken in comparison.

I realized with a shock that these two men had lived a total of almost a century and a half, and shared a century of legal experience. It was a daunting perception, and it took me a few seconds to gather my courage and plunge ahead.

"Mr. Tabatchnick," I said, "I believe you've already met Detective Percy Stilton of the New York Police Department. Detective Stilton was involved in the initial inquiry into the death of Solomon Kipper."

Tabatchnick gave Percy a cold nod and me an angry glare as he realized I had disobeyed his injunction against sharing the results of my investigation with the police.

I introduced Percy to Mr. Teitelbaum. Again, there was an exchange of frosty nods. Neither of the partners had made any effort to sit down. My longed-for conference was getting off to a rocky start.

"Detective Stilton," Mr. Tabatchnick said in his most orotund voice, "are we to understand that you are present in an official capacity?"

"No, sir, I am not," the detective said steadily. "I am here as an interested observer, and perhaps to contribute what I can to the solution of a dilemma confronting you gentlemen."

I could have kissed him. Their eyebrows went up; they glanced at each other. Obviously they hadn't been aware they were confronted by a dilemma, and just as obviously wanted to hear more about it. They drew up chairs opposite us. I waited until everyone was seated and still.

"Gentlemen," I started, "it would save us all a great deal of time if you could tell me if each of you is aware of my investigation into the other's case. That is, Mr. Teitelbaum, have you been informed of the circumstances surrounding the death of Sol Kipper? And, Mr. Tabatchnick, are you—"

"Get on with it," Tabatchnick interrupted testily. "We're both aware of what's been going on."

"As of your last reports," Mr. Teitelbaum added, his leathery hands lying motionless on the table before him. "I presume you have something to add?"

"A great deal, sir," I said, and I began, using short declarative sentences and speaking as briskly as possible without garbling my words.

I was gratified to discover that I could speak extemporaneously and forcefully without consulting my notes. So I was able to meet the eyes of both men as I spoke, shifting my gaze from one to the other; depending on whether I was discussing matters relating to Kipper or Stonehouse.

It was like addressing two stone monoliths, as brooding and inexplicable as the Easter Island heads. Never once did they stir or change expression. Mr. Teitelbaum sat back in his chair, seemingly propped erect with stiff, spindly arms thrust out, splayed hands flat on the tabletop. Mr. Tabatchnick leaned forward, looming, his hunched shoulders over the table, heavy head half-lowered, the usual fierce scowl on his rubbery lips.

Up through my account of recognizing one of Knurr's street Arabs among my attackers, neither of the attorneys had asked any questions or indeed shown any great interest in my recital. But my telling of the meeting I had seen at the 66th Street garage changed all that.

First of all, both men switched positions suddenly: Tabatchnick leaned back, almost fell back into his chair as if with disbelief, and Teitelbaum suddenly jerked forward, leaning over the table.

"You're certain of that, Mr. Bigg?" he barked sharply. "The Reverend Godfrey Knurr met Glynis Stonehouse? No doubt about it at all?"

"None whatsoever, sir," I said decisively.

I explained that I had then requested a meeting with Detective Percy Stilton and told him everything that had occurred.

"It was necessary, gentlemen," I said earnestly, "because I needed Detective Stilton's cooperation to determine if anyone involved had prior criminal records. Detective Stilton will tell you the results of that investigation. To get back to your question, Mr. Teitelbaum—was I certain that Knurr met Glynis Stonehouse? Yes, I am certain, because I saw them together again two nights ago."

I then told them how I had shadowed Glynis Stonehouse to a rendezvous with Knurr and had tailed both of them to a houseboat at the 79th Street boat basin.

"Perce," I said, "will you take it from here?"

His recital was much shorter than mine, and delivered in toneless police officialese: "the alleged perpetrator" and "the suspect" and so forth. It was courtroom testimony, and both lawyers seemed completely familiar with the phrases and impressed by them.

He told them that he had never been completely satisfied with the suicide verdict in the Kipper case, and gave his reasons why. So, he explained, he had welcomed my independent inquiry and cooperated every way he could, especially since he was impressed by the thoroughness and imaginative skill of my investigation.

I ducked my head to stare at the table as he continued.

He said his hope was that I would uncover enough evidence so that the NYPD would be justified in reopening the Kipper case. To that end, he had run the names of Godfrey Knurr and Tippi Kipper through the computer and discovered Tippi's arrest record. He told them about our interview with Bishop Harley Oxman and the revelation of Knurr's prior offense in Chicago.

He had also, he said, after I had furnished the lead, determined what was probably the source of the arsenic used to poison Professor Stonehouse: a medical research laboratory where Glynis Stonehouse had been employed less than a year ago.

Finally, he had discovered that Godfrey Knurr owned a houseboat moored at the 79th Street boat basin.

Then Stilton turned to me and I told them that a cabdriver had come forward that morning who remembered driving Professor Stonehouse to the boat basin on the night he disappeared.

I slid Baum's statement across the table to the senior partners, but neither reached for it. Both men were staring at Percy.

"Detective Stilton," Mr. Tabatchnick boomed in his magisterial voice, "as a police officer with many years' experience, do you believe that Godfrey Knurr murdered Solomon Kipper?"

"Yes, sir, I do. With premeditation."

"But how?" Mr. Teitelbaum asked in a mild, dreamy tone.

"I'll let Josh tell you that," Percy said.

So I told them.

Mr. Tabatchnick was the first to turn back to me.

"And the suicide note?" he asked.

"No, sir," I said regretfully. "I haven't yet accounted for that. But I'm sure you'll admit, sir, that the wording of the note is subject to several interpretations. It is not necessarily a *suicide* note."

"And assuming the homicide occurred in the manner you suggest, you further assume that Tippi Kipper and the Reverend Godfrey Knurr were joined in criminal conspiracy? You assume that they planned and carried out the murder of Solomon Kipper because he had discovered, through the employment of Martin Reape, that his wife had been unfaithful to him with Godfrey Knurr and had decided to change his will to disinherit her to the extent allowed by law? You assume all that?"

"Yes, sir," I said finally.

But now it was Mr. Teitelbaum's turn.

"Do you further assume," he said in a silky voice, "that Professor Stonehouse, having discovered that his daughter had attempted to poison him, furthermore discovered that she was having an affair with Godfrey Knurr. And you assume that Stonehouse learned of the existence of Knurr's houseboat, by what means we know not, and resolved to confront his daughter and her paramour on the night he disappeared. And you suspect, with no evidence, that he may very well have been killed on that night. Is that your assumption?"

"Yes, sir," I said, fainter than before. "It is."

We all sat in silence. The quiet seemed to go on forever, although I suppose it was only a minute or two before Mr. Teitelbaum pushed himself from the table and leaned back in his chair.

"And what, precisely," he said in an unexpectedly strong voice, "do you suggest be done next in this unpleasant matter?"

"As far as I'm concerned," Percy Stilton said, "I'm going to tell my lieutenant the whole story and see if I can get the Kipper case reopened. You gentlemen might help me there—if you have any influence that can be brought to bear."

"What would be the advantage of reopening the case?" Leopold Tabatchnick asked.

"I would hope to get assigned to it full time," the detective said. "With more personnel assigned as needed. To keep a stakeout on that houseboat so Knurr doesn't take off. To dig deeper into the backgrounds and relationships of the people involved. To check Knurr's bank account, and so forth. All the things that would be done in a homicide investigation."

The two senior partners looked at each other again, and again I had the sense of communication between them.

"We are not totally without *some* influence," Ignatz Teitelbaum said cautiously. "We will do what we can to assist you in getting the Kipper case reopened. But I must tell you in all honesty that I am not optimistic about bringing this whole affair to a successful solution, even with the most rigorous homicide investigation."

"I concur," Mr. Tabatchnick rumbled.

Mr. Teitelbaum scraped his chair farther back from the table and, not without some difficulty, crossed his knees. He sat there a moment, staring into space between Percy and me, not really seeing us. He was, I thought, composing his summation to the jury.

"First of all," he said finally, "I would like to compliment you gentlemen—and especially you, Mr. Bigg—on your intelligence and persistence in this investigation."

"Imaginative," Mr. Tabatchnick said, nodding. "Creative."

"Exactly," Teitelbaum said. "You have offered a hypothesis that accounts for all known important facts."

"It may be accurate," Tabatchnick admitted almost grudgingly.

"It may very well be. Frankly, I believe it is. I believe your assumptions are correct," Teitelbaum concurred.

"But they are still assumptions," Tabatchnick persisted.

"You have little that is provable in a court of law," Teitelbaum persevered.

"Certainly nothing that might justify legal action." Tabatchnick was firm.

"No eyewitness, obviously. No weapons. In fact, no hard evidence of legal value." Teitelbaum was firmer.

"Merely thin circumstantial evidence in support of what is, essentially, a theory." Tabatchnick.

"We don't wish to be unduly pessimistic, but you have told us nothing to indicate that continued investigation would uncover evidence to justify a criminal indictment." Teitelbaum.

"You are dealing here with a criminal conspiracy." The judgment was from Tabatchnick, but the coup de grace was delivered by Teitelbaum as follows:

"Really two criminal conspiracies with one individual, Knurr, common to both."

Perce looked at them dazedly. I was shattered. I thought their rapid dialogue was a prelude to ordering me to drop the investigation. I glanced at Percy Stilton. He was staring intently at the two attorneys. He seemed entranced, as if he were hearing something I couldn't hear, as if he enjoyed being a tennis ball in the Jurisprudential Open.

"It is an unusual problem," Mr. Tabatchnick intoned, inspecting the spotted backs of his clumpy hands. "Sometimes unusual problems require unusual remedies."

"When more than one person is involved in a major criminal enterprise," Mr. Teitelbaum said, uncrossing his knees and carefully pinching the crease back into his trousers, "it is sometimes possible . . ."

His voice trailed away.

"You have shown such initiative thus far," Mr. Tabatchnick said, "surely the possibility exists that . . ."

His voice, too, faded into silence.

Then, to my astonishment, the lawyers glanced at each other, a signal was apparently passed, and they rose simultaneously to their feet. Percy and I stood up. They reached across the table and the two of us shook hands with both of them.

"I shall look forward to your progress," Tabatchnick said sternly.

"I have every confidence," Teitelbaum said in a more kindly tone.

Still stunned, I watched them move to the door. I was bewildered because I was sure they had told us something. What it was I did not know.

Mr. Teitelbaum had already opened the door to the corridor when he turned back to address me.

"Mr. Bigg," he said softly, "is Tippi Kipper older than Glynis Stonehouse?"

"What?" I croaked. "Oh yes, sir," I said, nodding madly. "By at least ten years. Probably more."

"That might be a possibility," he said pleasantly.

Then they were gone.

We sank back into our chairs. I waited as Percy lighted a cigarette, took two deep drags, and slumped down in his armchair. Clerks and paralegal assistants began to straggle into the library, heading for the stacks of law books.

I leaned toward Stilton. I spoke in a low voice.

"What," I asked him, still puzzled, "was that all about? Those last things they said? I didn't understand that at all. I'm lost."

Percy put his head far back and blew a perfect smoke ring toward the ceiling. Then, to demonstrate his expertise, he blew a large ring and puffed a smaller one within it.

"They're not lawyers," he said, almost dreamily, "they're pirates. *Pi-rates!*"

"What are you talking about?" I said.

"Incredible," he said, shaking his head. "Infuckingcredible. Teitelbaum and Tabatchnick. T and T. T'n'T. TNT. They're TNT all right. If I ever get racked up, I want those pirates on my side."

"Perce, will you please tell me what's going on?"

He straightened up in his chair, then hunched over toward me so our heads were close together.

"Josh, I think they're right. That's a hell of a plot you came up with about how Knurr offed Sol Kipper. Probably right on. But how are we going to prove it? Never. Unless we break Knurr or Tippi Kipper. Get one to spill on the other. And what have we got on Glynis Stonehouse? We can't even *prove* she tried to poison her father. She shacks up with Knurr on a houseboat. So what? It's not an indictable offense. Your bosses saw right away that the only way we're going to snap this thing is to get one of the main characters to sing."

"And how are we going to do that?"

"Oh, T and T were so *cute!*" he said, grinning and lighting another cigarette. "You notice that not once did either of them say anything that could be construed as an order or instructions to do anything illegal. All they did was pass out a few vague hints."

"But what *did* they say?" I cried desperately.

"Shh. Keep your voice down. They want us to run a game on Knurr. A scam. A con."

I looked at him, startled.

"How are we going to do that?"

"Spook him. Him and the ladies. Stir them up. Let them know they're suspects and are being watched. Play one against the other. Work on their nerves. Wear them down. Push them into making some stupid move. Guerrilla warfare. Mousetrap them. You think Knurr and Tippi and Glynis are smarter than we are? I don't. They got some nice games running, and so far they've worked. Well, we can run plots just as clever. More. That's what T and T were telling us. Run a game on these people and split them. They were right; it's the only way."

"I get it," I said. "Take the offensive."

"Right!"

"And that last thing Teitelbaum said about Tippi Kipper being older than Glynis Stonehouse?"

"He was suggesting that we let Tippi know about Glynis."

Before Perce and I took our leave of each other, we had decided on at least the first play of our revised game plan. I set about implementing it as soon as I got back to my office.

Mrs. Kletz and I sat down to compose a letter which Mrs. Kletz would then copy in her handwriting on plain paper. The finished missive reads as follows:

Dear Mrs. Kipper,

We have met casually several times, but I believe I know more about your private life than you are aware. You'll see that I am not signing this letter. Names are not important, and I don't wish to become further involved. I am writing only with the best of intentions, because I don't want you to know the pain I suffered in a comparable situation.

Mrs. Kipper, I happen to know how close your relationship is with the Reverend Godfrey Knurr. I hope you will forgive me when I tell you that your "affair" is common knowledge and a subject of sometimes malicious gossip in the circles in which we both move.

I regret to inform you that the Reverend is also currently carrying on a clandestine "affair" with a beautiful young woman, Glynis Stonehouse. Believe me when I tell you that I have irrefutable proof of their liaison which has existed for several months.

They have been seen together by witnesses whose word cannot be doubted. Their frequent trysts, always late at night, are held aboard his houseboat moored at the 79th Street boat basin. Were you aware that the Reverend Knurr owned a lavishly furnished houseboat and uses it for midnight meetings with this young beautiful woman? And possibly others?

As I said, Mrs. Kipper, I am writing only to spare you the agony I recently endured in a similar situation. I wish now that a concerned friend had written to me as I am writing to you, in time to prevent me from acting foolishly and deserting a loving husband and family for the sake of an unfaithful philanderer.

I have been able to obtain a photograph of the other woman, Glynis Stonehouse, which I am enclosing with this letter.

Forgive me for writing of matters which, I am sure, must prove painful to you. But I could not endure seeing a woman of your taste and refinement suffer as I suffered, and am suffering.

A FRIEND

When Mrs. Kletz finished copying the letter, we sealed it with the snapshot of Glynis Stonehouse in a plain manila envelope. Mrs. Kletz addressed it in her hand.

"Just ring the bell at the front gate," I instructed her, as I prepared to send her out on this important assignment. "The butler, a big man, will come out. Tell him you have a letter for Mrs. Kipper, give it to him, and walk away as quickly as you can."

"Don't worry, Mr. Bigg," she said. "I'll get out of there fast."

She put on her Tam O'Shanter and a loden coat as billowy as a tent and set out. A half hour later I locked the Kipper and Stonehouse files securely away and left the office. Uncharacteristically I took a cab home, so anxious was I to find a message from Cleo. I found it slipped under my door: "Miss Cleo Hufnagel accepts with pleasure Mr. Joshua Bigg's kind invitation to dinner tonight in his apartment at 8:00 P.M."

Smiling, I changed into parka and watch cap, and then checked my larder, refrigerator, and liquor supply. I made out a careful list of things I needed and then set forth with my two-wheeled shopping cart. It was a cold, misty evening, and I didn't dawdle. I bought two handsome club steaks; baking potatoes; sour cream already mixed with chives; butter (should she prefer it to the sour cream); a head of iceberg lettuce; a perfectly shaped, plasma-colored tomato; a cucumber the size of a tough, small U-boat, and just as slippery; a bottle of creamy garlic dressing; and a frozen blueberry cheesecake. I also purchased two small shrimp cocktails that came complete with sauce in small jars that could later be used as juice glasses. A paper tablecloth. Paper napkins. An onion.

I also bought a cold six-pack of Ballantine ale, two bottles of Chianti in raffia baskets, and a quart of California brandy. And two long red candles. On impulse I stopped at a florist's shop and bought a long-stemmed yellow rose.

She tapped on my door a few minutes after 8:00 and came in smiling. She bent swiftly to kiss my cheek. She had brought me a loaf of crusty sour rye from our local Jewish bakery. It was a perfect gift; I had forgotten all about bread. Fortunately I had butter.

I gave her the yellow rose, which came close to bringing tears to her eyes and earned me another cheek-kiss, warmer this time. I led her to my favorite armchair and asked her if she'd like a fire.

"Maybe later," she said.

I poured a glass of red wine for her and one for myself.

"Here's to you," I toasted.

"To us," she said.

I told her what we were having for dinner.

"Sounds marvelous," she said in her low, whispery voice. "I like every-thing."

Suddenly, due to her words or her voice or her smile, something struck me.

"What's wrong?" Cleo asked anxiously.

I sighed. "I bought a kite. And a ball of string and a winder. But I left them all at the office. I forgot to bring them home."

She laughed. "We weren't going to fly it tonight. But I'm glad you re-membered."

"It's a red kite," I told her. "Listen, I have to go into the kitchen and get things ready. You help yourself to the wine."

"Can't I come in with you?" she said softly. "I promise I won't get in the way."

I couldn't remember ever having been so content in my life. I think my feeling—in addition to the beamy effects of the food and wine—came from a realization of the sense of home. I had never known a real home. Not my own. And there we were in a tiny, messy kitchen, fragrant with cooking odors and the smoke of candles, quiet with our comfort, walled around and shielded.

It was a new experience for me, being with a woman I liked. Liked?

Well . . . wanted to be with. I didn't have to make conversation. She didn't have to. We could be happily silent together. That was something, wasn't it?

After dinner, she murmured that she'd help me clean up.

"Oh, let's just leave everything," I said, which was out of character for me, a very tidy man.

"You'll get roaches," she warned.

"I already have them," I said mournfully, and we both smiled. Her large, prominent teeth didn't offend me. I thought them charming.

We doused the candles and straggled back to the living room. We decided a blaze in the fireplace would be superfluous; the apartment was warm enough. She sat in the armchair. I sat on the floor at her feet. Her fingers stroked my hair idly. I stroked her long, prehensile toes. Her bare toes. She groaned with pleasure.

"Do you like me, Cleo?" I asked.

"Of course I like you."

"Then, if you like me, will you rise from your comfortable chair, find the bottle of brandy in the bar, open it, and pour us each a small glass of brandy? The glasses are in the kitchen cupboard."

"Your wish is my command, master," she said humbly.

She was back in a few moments with glasses of brandy, handed me one and, while she was bent over, kissed the top of my head. Then she resumed her sprawling position in the armchair, and I resumed stroking her toes.

"It was a wonderful dinner," she said, sighing.

"Thank you."

"I'm a virgin," she said in exactly the same tone of voice she had said, "It was a wonderful dinner."

What could I answer with but an equally casual, "Yes, you mentioned it last time."

"Did I also mention I don't want to be?" she added thoughtfully.

"Ah," I said, hoping desperately that I could eventually contribute something better than monosyllables. When it occurred to me almost at once that a lunge qualified as something better, the ice broke.

I have told you that she was tall. Very tall. And slender. Very slender. But I was not prepared for the sinuous elegance of her body, its lithe vigor. And the sweetness of her skin. She was a rope dipped in honey.

Initially, I think, there was a certain embarrassment, a reticence, on my part as well as hers. But this reserve soon vanished, to be replaced by a vigorous tumbling. She was experiencing new sensations, entering a new world, and wanted to know it all.

"What's this?" she asked eagerly. "And this?"

She was amazed that men had nipples capable of erection. She was delighted to learn that many of the things that aroused her, aroused me; that there could be as much (or more) pleasure in the giving as in the taking. She wanted to know everything at once, to explore, probe, understand.

"Am I doing this correctly?" she asked anxiously. And, "Is it all right if I do this?" and, "What must I do now?"

"Shut up," I replied.

We may have roared. We certainly cried out, both of us, and I dimly recall looking into a face transformed, ecstatic, and primitive. When it was over, we lay shuddering with bliss, so closely entwined that my arms ached with the strain of pulling her closer, as if to engulf her, and I felt the muscular tremor in those long, flexible legs locked about me.

"I love you," she said later.

"I love you," I said.

I buried my face in the soft hollow of neck and shoulder. My toes caressed her ivory shins.

I interrupted our idyll for business reasons only once that evening. Feeling I had to be honest, I informed Cleo that I had to call the floozie spotted earlier leaving my apartment by the evil Finkel. Further, I would seemingly be arranging a rendezvous, really an interrogation. Should Cleo mistakenly conclude I was growing bored with her, I would be glad to prove her wrong as soon as I completed the call. She laughed and kissed me merrily.

The phone rang three times before Perdita Schug answered.

"Yes?"

"Perdita?"

"Yes. Who's this?"

"Joshua Bigg."

"Josh!"

"I apologize for calling so late, Perdita. I hope I didn't wake you."

"Don't be silly. I just came up. We had a dinner for seven tonight. A lot of work."

"Oh? Was Mr. Knurr there?"

"No. Which was odd. First we were told there'd be eight. But he didn't show up. Usually he's here all the time. Are you going to come by Mother Tucker's tomorrow night?"

"I'm certainly going to try," I lied. "Listen, Perdita, I have an unusual question to ask you. When Sol Kipper was alive, did he ever write notes to his wife? You know, little short notes he'd leave where she'd find them?"

"Oh sure," she said promptly. "He was always writing her notes. She was running around so much, and then he'd go out and leave a note for her. I read a few of them. Love notes, some, or just messages."

"Did she keep them, do you think?"

"Tippi? I think she kept some of them. Yes, I know she did. I remember coming across a pile of them in a box of undies in her dressing room. Some of them were hilarious. The poor old man was really in love with her. She had him hooked. And you know how."

"Yes," I said. "Thank you very much, Perdita. Sorry to bother you."

"And I'll see you tomorrow night?"

"I'm certainly going to try." It was getting easier all the time.

5

•

THURSDAY MORNING: ALIVE, BUBBLING, LAUGHING ALOUD. CLEO hadn't wanted to upset her mother by staying the night, but I'd awakened steeped in her recent presence. I sang in the shower ("O Sole Mio"), looked out the window, and nodded approvingly at the pencil lines of rain slanting down steadily. Nothing could daunt my mood. I wore raincoat and rubbers to work, and carried my umbrella. It was the type of bumbershoot that extends with the press of a button in the handle. Very efficient, except that when a stiff wind was blowing, it cracked open and seemed to lift me a few inches off my feet.

However, I arrived at the TORT building without misadventure and set to work planning my day's activities.

My first call was to Glynis Stonehouse. She came to the phone, finally, and didn't sound too delighted to hear from me. I acted the young, innocent, optimistic, bouncy investigator, and I told her I had uncovered new information about her father's disappearance that I'd like to share with her. Grudgingly, she said that she could spare me an hour if I came immediately.

I thanked her effusively, ran out of TORT and, miraculously, given the weather, hailed a cab right in front of the building.

In the Stonehouse hallway the formidable Olga Eklund relieved me of hat, coat, rubbers, and umbrella, and herded me into that beige living room where Glynis Stonehouse reclined in one corner of the velvet sofa, idly leafing through a magazine. Nothing about her posture or manner suggested worry.

If she made an error, it was in her greeting.

"Oh," she said, "Mr. Bigg. Do sit down."

Too casual.

I sat down, opened my briefcase, and began to rummage through it.

"Miss Stonehouse," I said enthusiastically, "I think I'm making real progress. You'll recall that I told you I had discovered your father had been suffering from arsenic poisoning prior to his disappearance? Well, I've defi-

690 • LAWRENCE SANDERS •

nitely established how he was being poisoned. The arsenic was being added to his brandy!"

I handed her the copies of the chemical analyses. She looked at them. I don't believe she read them. I plucked them from her fingers and replaced them in my briefcase.

"Isn't that wonderful?" I burbled on. "What a break!"

"I suppose so," she said in her husky, low-pitched voice. "But what does it mean?"

"Well, it means we now know how the poison was administered."

"And what will you do next?"

"That's obvious, isn't it?" I said, laughing lightly. "Find the source of the poison. You can't buy arsenic at your local drugstore, you know. So I must check out everyone involved to see who had access to arsenic trioxide."

I stared at her. I thought there would be a reaction. There wasn't.

She sighed deeply.

"Yes," she said, "I suppose you will have to keep digging and digging until you discover the . . . what do the police call it? . . . the perpetrator? You'll never give up, will you, Mr. Bigg?"

"Oh no!" I said heartily. "I'm going to stick to it. Miss Stonehouse, may I speak to Effie Dark for a few moments? I'd like to find out who had access to your father's brandy."

She looked at me.

"Yes," she said dully, "talk to Mrs. Dark. That's all right."

I smiled my thanks, bent to reclasp my briefcase. Before I could stand, she said:

"Mr. Bigg, why are you doing this?"

I shook my head, pretending puzzlement.

"Doing what, Miss Stonehouse?"

"All these questions. This—this investigation."

"I'm trying to find your father."

Her body went slack. She melted. That's the only way I can describe it. Suddenly there was no complete outline around her. Not only in her face, which sagged, but in her limbs, her flesh. All of her became loose and without form. It was a frightening thing to see. A dissolution.

"He was a dreadful man," she said in a low voice.

I think I was angered then. I tried to hide it, but I'm not certain I succeeded.

"Yes," I said, "I'm sure he was. Everyone says so. An awful person. But that's not important, is it?"

She made a gesture. A wave of the hand. A small, graceful flip of dismissal. Of defeat.

Effie Dark was seated at the white enameled table, an emptied coffee cup before her. There was a redolence, and it took me a few seconds to identify it: the air smelled faintly of brandy.

She looked up listlessly as I entered, then smiled wanly.

"Mr. Bigg," she said, and pulled out a chair for me. "It's nice to see a cheerful face."

"What's wrong, Effie?" I asked, sitting down. "Problems?"

"Oh . . ." she said, sighing, "there's no light in this house anymore. The missus, she's taken to her bed and won't get out of it."

"She's ill?"

"Sherry-itis. And Miss Glynis is as down as I've ever seen her. I even called Powell, thinking a visit from him might help things. But he says he must avoid negative vibrations. That means he's scared misery might be catching. Well . . ." she said, sighing again, "I was figuring on retiring in a year or two. Maybe I'll do it sooner."

"What will you do, Effie?" I asked softly.

"Oh, I'll make do," she said, drawing a deep breath. "I have enough. It's not the money that worries me, it's the loneliness."

"Move somewhere pleasant," I suggested. "Warm, sunny weather. Maybe Florida or California. You'll make new friends."

Suddenly she perked up. Those little blueberry eyes twinkled in her muffin face. She lifted one plump arm and poked fingers into the wig of marcelled yellow-white hair. I could have sworn I heard her dentures clacking.

"I might even find myself a husband," she said, looking at me archly. "What do you think of *that*, Mr. Bigg. Think I'm too fat?"

" 'Pleasingly plump' is the expression, Effie. There are many men who appreciate well-endowed women."

"Well-endowed?" she spluttered. "How you do go on! You're medicine for me, Mr. Bigg, you truly are. See? I'm laughing for the first time in days. But I don't suppose you stopped by just to make a silly old woman happy. You need some help?"

"Thank you," I said gratefully. I lowered my voice. "Effie, is the door locked to Professor Stonehouse's study?"

She nodded, staring at me with bright eyes.

"You have a key?"

Again the nod.

I thought a moment. "What I'd like you to do is this: I'll wait here while you go out and unlock the door to the study and then come back. I'll go into the study. You'll be here, so you won't see me enter. I'll only be a few minutes. No more than five. I swear to you I will not remove anything from the study. Then I will come back here to say goodbye, and you can relock the study door. That way, if you're ever asked any questions, you can say truthfully that you never saw me in the study, didn't see me go in or come out."

She considered that for a while.

"Glynis is here," she said. "In the living room, I think. And the Sexy

Swede is wandering around someplace. Either of them could catch you in there."

"I know," I said.

"I hope I'm doing the right thing," she said.

When I was inside the study, I closed the door softly behind me. I went directly to the wall where the model ship hulls were displayed. I moved along the bottom row, rapping on the hulls gently with a knuckle. Some sounded solid, some hollow. I found the *Prince Royal* in the middle of the third row. I stood on tiptoe to lift the *Prince Royal* plaque off picture hooks nailed into the wall.

I carried the model hull to the desk and set it on top of the littered papers and maps. I switched on the desk lamp. I picked up a pencil and tapped the hull form twice. It sounded hollow. So far so good.

I grasped the hull and lifted gently. It came away. As easily as that. Just came right off. I was astonished, and looked to see what had been holding it to the plaque. Eight small magnets, inch-long bars, four inset into the hull and four in the plaque. They gripped firmly enough to hold the hull when the tablet was on the wall, but released with a slight tug.

Of course I was more interested in the papers folded inside. Most were thin, flimsy sheets, of the weight used for carbon copies. I unfolded them carefully, handling them by the corners. The top four sheets were not typed, but handwritten. It took me a while to read it through. The writing was as crabbed, mean, and twisted as the man himself.

I, Yale Emerson Stonehouse, being of sound mind and body . . .

It was all there: the holographic last will and testament of the missing Professor Stonehouse. He started by making specific cash bequests. Fifty thousand to his alma mater, and twenty thousand to Mrs. Effie Dark, which I was happy to see. Then there were a dozen cash bequests to cousins and distant relatives, none of whom was to receive more than a thousand dollars, and one of whom was to inherit five bucks. Olga Eklund got one hundred.

The bulk of his estate was to be divided equally between his wife, Ula Stonehouse, and his son, Powell Stonehouse. The will specifically forbade his daughter, Glynis Stonehouse, from sharing in his estate because she had "deliberately and with malice aforethought" attempted to cause his death by adding arsenic trioxide to his brandy. In proof of which, he was attaching to this will copies of chemical analyses made by Bommer & Son and a statement by Dr. Morris Stolowitz that Professor Stonehouse had indeed been suffering from arsenic poisoning.

In addition, the will continued, if the testator was found dead by violence or by what appeared to be an accident, he demanded the police conduct a thorough investigation into the circumstances of his demise, with the knowledge that his daughter had tried to murder him once and would quite possibly try again, with more success.

The will had been witnessed by Olga Eklund and Wanda Chard. I could understand the loopy maid signing anything the Professor handed her and promptly forgetting it. But Wanda Chard?

I carefully folded up the papers on their original creases, tucked them back into the hull of the *Prince Royal,* reattached hull to plaque, and wiped both with my handkerchief. Then, holding the tablet by the edges with my fingertips, I rehung it on the wall, adjusted it so it was level, and returned to the kitchen.

"Thank you, Effie," I said, bending to kiss her cheek.

She looked up at me. I thought I saw tears welling.

"It's the end of everything, isn't it?" she asked.

I couldn't lie to her.

"Close to it," I said.

I went back into the living room. Glynis Stonehouse was standing at one of the high windows, staring down at the rain-lashed street. She turned when she heard me come into the room.

"Finished?" she asked.

"Finished," I said. "Mrs. Dark tells me your mother isn't feeling well. I'm sorry to hear that, Miss Stonehouse. Please convey to her my best wishes and hope for her quick recovery."

"Thank you," she said.

She stood tall and erect. She had recovered her composure. She looked at me steadily, and there was nothing in her appearance to suggest that she knew how close she was to disaster.

"I'll keep you informed of the progress of my investigation, Miss Stonehouse."

"Yes," she said levelly, "you do that."

She was so strong. Oh, but she was strong! If she had weakened, briefly, that weakness was gone now; she was resolute, determined to see it through. I admired her. She was a woman of intelligence and must have known she was in danger, walking the edge. I bade her a dignified good day, then hightailed it across town to the Kipper manse.

Chester Heavens greeted me with his usual aplomb, but I sensed a certain reticence, almost a nervousness in his replies to my chatter about his health, the weather, etc. We were standing in the echoing entrance hall when I became aware of raised voices coming from behind the closed doors of the sitting room.

"Mom is at home, sah," the butler informed me gravely, looking over my head.

"So I hear," I said. "And Mr. Knurr?"

He nodded slowly.

I hid my pleasure.

"Chester," I said, "I won't stay long. This may be my last visit."

"Oh?" he said. "I am sorry to hear that, sah."

"Just a few little things to check out," I told him.

He bowed slightly and moved away toward the kitchen. I stood at the front door and looked toward the rear of the house. The doorway could not be seen from the kitchen. Then I moved to the elevator. That was in plain view of anyone in the kitchen or pantry.

I saw Mrs. Bertha Neckin standing at the sink. She glanced up and I waved to her, but she didn't respond.

I took the elevator up to the fifth floor and went swiftly into Tippi Kipper's dressing room. I set down my briefcase and began searching. It wasn't hard to find: a cedar-smelling box of filigreed wood with brass corners. It appeared to be of Indian handicraft. It was tucked under a stack of filmy lingerie in a bottom dresser drawer. I may have blushed when I handled those gossamer garments.

The box was unlocked and filled with a carelessly tossed pile of notes. There were jottings on his personal stationery, on sheets from notepads, on raggedly torn scrap paper, and one on a personal check of Solomon A. Kipper, made out to Tippi Kipper in the amount of "Ten zillion dollars and all my love" and signed "Your Sol."

I scanned the notes quickly. My heart cringed. Most were love letters from an old man obviously obsessed to the point of dementia by a much younger woman whose seductive skills those notes spelled out in explicit detail.

And there were notes of apology.

"I am sorry, babe, if I upset you." Wasn't so bad for starters, but then I came across "Please forgive me for the way I acted last night. I realize you had a headache, but I couldn't help myself, you looked so beautiful." As I read on, a pattern of increasing desperation, dependence, and humiliation emerged.

"Can you ever forgive me?" Then, "Here is a little something for you to make up for what I said last night. Am I forgiven?"

It was punishment, reading those revelations of a dead man. I stole two of them:

"Tippi, I hope you will pardon me for the pain I caused you." And, "My loving wife, please forgive me for all the trouble I made. I promise you that you'll never again have any reason to doubt my everlasting love for you."

Those two, I thought, would serve as suicide notes as well as the one found prominently displayed in the master bedroom after Sol Kipper's plunge.

I tucked the two notes into my briefcase, closed and replaced the box, and then went up the rear staircase to the sixth floor. I entered the party room, went over and stood with my back against the locked French doors leading to the terrace.

I looked at my watch. I allowed fifteen seconds for the act of throwing Kipper over the wall. Then I started running. I went down the rear staircase as fast as I could. I dashed along the fifth-floor corridor to the main staircase. I went bounding down rapidly, swinging wildly around the turns. I came down to the entrance hall, rushed over to the front door. I looked at my watch, gasping. About ninety seconds. He could have made it. Easily.

There was no one about, and no sounds from the sitting room. I found my outer garments and donned them and went out into the chill rain without saying goodbye to Chester. I walked toward Fifth Avenue, intending to catch a cab. I was almost there when who should fall into step alongside but the Reverend Godfrey Knurr.

"Joshua!" he said, moving under the shelter of my umbrella. "This *is* nice. Chester told us you were about. If you say this is good weather for ducks, I may kick you!"

He was bright again, his manner jaunty.

I didn't panic. I knew he had been waiting for me, but in a way I couldn't understand, I welcomed the confrontation. Maybe I thought of it as a challenge.

"Pastor," I said, "good to see you again. I didn't want to interrupt you and Mrs. Kipper."

He rolled his eyes in burlesque dismay.

"What an argument that was," he said carefully, taking my arm. "Want to hear about it?"

"Sure."

He looked about.

"Around the corner," he said. "Down a block or so. Posh hotel. Nice cocktail lounge. Quiet. We can talk—and keep dry. On the outside, at least."

A few minutes later we were standing at the black vinyl, padded bar in the cozy lounge of the Stanhope, the room dimmed by rain-streaked windows in which the Metropolitan Museum shimmered like a Monet. We were the only customers, and the place was infused with that secret ambience of a Manhattan bar on a rainy day, comfortably closed in and begging for quiet confessions.

Knurr ordered a dry Beefeater martini up, with lemon peel. I asked for a bottle of domestic beer. When our drinks were served, he glanced around the empty room. "Let's take a table," he said.

He picked up his drink and led the way to a small table in a far corner. I followed with my bottle of beer and a glass.

That was the difference between us: I would have asked the bartender, "Is it all right if we take a table?"

I must admit it was more comfortable sitting in the soft chairs, walls at our backs. We sat at right angles to each other, but we turned slightly so we were facing each other more casually.

Knurr rattled on for a while, gabbing mostly about inconsequential things like the weather, a cold he was trying to shake, how every year at this time he began to yearn for warmer climes, a hot sun, a sandy beach, etc.

I looked into his eyes as he spoke. I nodded occasionally. Smiled. It was the oddest feeling in the world—sitting drinking, exchanging idle talk, with a murderer.

How had I thought a killer would be different—disfigured with a mark perhaps? That would be too easy. As it was, I had to keep reminding myself of who Knurr was and what he had done. But all I was conscious of was the normality of our conversation, its banality. "A miserable day." "Oh yes, but they say it may clear tonight."

Finally he stopped chattering. He put both elbows on the table, scrubbed his face with his palms. He sighed and looked off into the emptiness of the room.

"I counsel a great many people," he said, talking to the air. "As I told you, mostly women. Occasionally they come to feel that my interest in them is not purely in their immortal souls. They assume I have, uh, a more personal interest. You understand?"

"Of course," I said. "It must lead to difficulties."

"It does indeed," he said, sighing. "All kinds of difficulties. For instance, they demand more of my time than I am willing to give, or *can* give, for that matter."

I made sympathetic noises.

"Would you believe," he went on, "that some of my—well, I was about to say patrons, but not all of them are that. For want of a better word, let's call them clients."

"How about dependents?" I suggested.

He looked at me sharply to see if I was being sarcastic. I was not. He punched my upper arm lightly.

"*Very* good, Joshua," he said. "Dependents. I like that. Much better than clients. Well, as I was saying, occasionally some of my dependents become jealous of others, believing I am devoting too much time to them. I don't mean to imply selfishness on their part, but I have found that most unhappy people, women *and* men, are inclined to be self-centered, and when sympathetic interest is expressed, they want more and more. Sympathy becomes an addiction, and they resent it when others share. That's what my disagreement with Mrs. Kipper was about. I am currently counseling other women, of course, and she felt I was not devoting enough time to her and her problems."

It wasn't a clumsy lie, but it seemed to me unnecessarily complex. There was no need for him to explain at all. But having started, he should have kept it simple.

I looked at him as he signaled the bartender for another round of drinks. He did have an imperious way about him, lifting a hand and gesturing curtly.

"How is your social club coming along?" I asked.

"What?" he said vaguely. "Oh, fine, fine. The barkeep put a shade too much vermouth in that last martini. I hope this one will be drier."

The bartender himself brought the drinks over to our table, but did not hover. Knurr sipped eagerly.

"*Much* better," he smiled with satisfaction, relaxing and sliding down a bit in his chair. "Dry as dust."

He was certainly a craggily handsome man, brooding and intense. I could understand why women were attracted to him; he radiated vigor and surety. The slightly bent nose and steady brown eyes gave the appearance of what is known as "a man's man." But the slaty beard framed rosy, almost tender lips that hinted of a soft vulnerability.

"I hope you and Mrs. Kipper parted friends," I said.

He gave a short bark of hard laughter. "Oh, I think I persuaded the lady," he said with a smile.

I didn't like that smile; it was almost a smirk. Did it mean that the photo of Glynis Stonehouse and the Mrs. Kletz letter had gone for naught?

I considered what he knew about me—or guessed. I thought my cover in the Kipper case was still intact, that he accepted my role of law clerk making a preliminary inventory of the estate. In the Stonehouse matter, Glynis would have told him of my investigation into her father's disappearance. He knew that I had uncovered the arsenic poisoning. What he did not know, I felt sure, was that I was aware of his intimate relationship with Glynis.

"That was my last visit to the Kipper home," I offered. "The expert appraisers will take over now."

"Oh?" he said in a tone of great disinterest. "Well, I suppose you have plenty of other things to keep you busy."

"I certainly do," I said enthusiastically. "I've been ordered to devote all my time to a case involving a man who disappeared without leaving a will."

"That sounds interesting," he said casually, taking a sip of his martini. "Tell me about it."

I imagined that was what fencing must be like: lunge, parry, thrust.

"There's not much to tell," I said. "Just what I've said: a man disappeared—it's been two months now—and no will has been found. The legal ramifications are what make the case so fascinating. All the assets are in his name alone. So it will require a petition to the court to free living expenses for his family."

"And if he never shows up again?"

"That's the rub," I said, laughing ruefully as I tried to recall what Mr. Teitelbaum had told me about applicable law. "I think that five years must elapse before a missing person's estate can go to probate."

"Five years!" he exclaimed.

"Minimum," I said. I laughed merrily. "It would be a lot simpler if the missing man's body turned up. If he is, indeed, dead, as everyone is beginning to suspect. But I'm boring you with all this."

"Not at all," he said genially. "Good talk for a rainy afternoon. So if the missing man turned up dead, his estate could be distributed to his legal heirs at once?"

Got him, I thought with some satisfaction.

"That's right," I said airily. "Once proof of death is definitely established, the man's will goes to probate."

"And if no will exists—or can be found?"

"Then the estate is divided under the laws of intestacy. In this case, it would go to his wife, daughter, and son."

"Is it a sizable estate?" he asked slowly.

Greedy bugger.

"I believe it is," I said, nodding. "I have no idea of the exact dollar amount involved, but I understand it's quite sizable."

He pulled pipe and tobacco pouch from his jacket pocket. He held them up to me.

"You don't mind?"

"Not at all," I said. "Go right ahead."

I watched and waited while he went through the deliberate ceremony of filling his pipe, tamping the tobacco down with a blunt forefinger, lighting up, tilting back his head and blowing a long plume of smoke at the ceiling.

"The law is a wonderful thing," he said with a tight smile. "A lot of money there. I mean in the practice of law."

"Yes, sir, there certainly is."

"Sometimes I think justice is an impossible concept," he went on, puffing away. "For instance, in the case you were describing, I would think the very fact of the man's disappearance for two months would be enough to allow his family to share in his estate. He left voluntarily?"

"As far as we know."

"No letter or message to his lawyer?"

"No, nothing like that. And no evidence of foul play. No evidence at all. He may still be alive for all we know. That's why the law requires a diligent search and a five-year grace period. Still, it's murder on the family." I couldn't resist, but, then, neither could he.

"It surely is," he murmured, a wee bit too fervently.

"However," I said, sinking the hook as deeply as I could, "if the body is discovered, regardless of whether he died a natural death or was a victim of accident or foul play, the estate goes to probate." I thought I had said enough and changed the subject abruptly. "Pastor, did you tell me you were from Chicago originally?"

"Not the city itself," he said, meeting my gaze. "A suburb. Why do you ask?"

"I have a cousin who lives there, and he's invited me out for a visit. I've never been in Chicago and wondered if I'd like it."

"You'll find a lot to do there," he said tonelessly.

"Did you like it?" I persisted.

"For a while," he said. "I must confess, Joshua, I get bored easily. So I came on to New York."

"New worlds to conquer?" I asked.

"Exactly," he said with a wry grin.

"And you haven't regretted it?"

"Once or twice," he said, still grinning, "at three in the morning."

I found it difficult to resist the man's charm. For one brief instant I doubted all I had learned about him, all I had imagined.

I tried to analyze why this should be so, why I was fighting an admiration for the man. Most of it, I thought, was due to his physical presence. He was big, strong, stalwart: everything I was not. And he was decisive, daring, resolute.

More than that, he really did possess an elemental power. Behind the bright laugh, the bonhomie, the intelligence and wit, there was naked force, brute force. I realized then how much I wanted him to like me.

Which meant that I feared him. It was not a comforting realization.

We finished our drinks without again alluding to either the Kipper or Stonehouse matters. Knurr insisted on paying for the drinks. He left a niggardly tip.

He said he had an appointment uptown, and since I was returning to the TORT building, we parted company under the hotel marquee. We shook hands and said we'd be in touch.

I watched him stride away up Fifth Avenue, erect in the rain. He seemed indomitable. I tried to get a cab, then gave up and took a downtown bus. It was crowded, damp, and smelled of mothballs. I got back to my office a little after one o'clock and stripped off wet hat, coat, and rubbers. I stuck my dripping umbrella in the wastebasket.

I called Stilton's office and was told he couldn't come to the phone at the moment. I left my number, asking that he call back. Then I sat staring at the blank wall and ignoring the investigation requests filling my In basket.

I was still thinking about the Reverend Godfrey Knurr. I acknowledged that the resentment I felt toward him could be traced to my feeling that he took me lightly, that he patronized me. The glib lies and little arm punches, the genial pats on shoulder and knee, and that bright, insolent laugh. That he considered me a lightweight, a nuisance perhaps, but of no consequence bore out my worst fears about myself. I strove to keep in mind that by attacking my self-esteem, he was attempting to gain control over me.

I opened the Kipper and Stonehouse files and reread only those notes pertaining to Godfrey Knurr. He seemed to move through both affairs like a wraith. I suspected him to be the prime mover, the source, the instigator of all the desperate events that had occurred. I had enough notes *about* the man: his strength, determination, charm, etc. I even had a few tidbits on his background.

But I knew almost nothing about the man himself, who he *was,* what drove him, what gave him pleasure, what gave him pain. He was a shadow. I had no handle on him. I could not explain what he had done yesterday or predict what he might do tomorrow.

I was looking for a label for him and could not find it. And realizing that, I was increasingly doubtful of ensnaring him with our cute tricks and sly games. He was neither a cheap crook nor a cynical confidence man. What he was, I simply did not know. Yet.

My reverie was broken by Percy Stilton returning my call. He was speaking rapidly, almost angrily.

"The Kipper case hasn't been reopened," he said. "Not yet it hasn't. The loot didn't think I had enough, and bucked it to the Captain. God only knows who he'll take it to, but I don't expect any decision until tomorrow at the earliest. I hope your bosses are using their juice. I had my partner call Knurr last night and pretend he was the cabdriver who drove Stonehouse to the boat basin. Knurr wouldn't bite. Hung up, as a matter of fact. He's toughing it out."

"Yes," I said, "I'm beginning to think we're not going to panic him."

I told Stilton about my unearthing the Stonehouse will, then detailed the contents.

"Nice," he said. "That wraps up Glynis. But Jesus, you didn't lift the will, did you? That would ruin it as evidence."

"No," I assured him, "I left it where it was. But I did steal something else."

I described the notes Sol Kipper had written to his wife, and how the two I had purloined could perfectly well have served as suicide notes.

"Good work, Josh," Percy said. "You're really doing a professional job on this—tying up all the loose ends."

I was pleased by his praise.

"Something else," I said. "I had a long talk with Knurr. We had a couple of drinks together."

I reported the substance of our conversation.

"I don't think that photo of Glynis Stonehouse and the poison-pen letter did a bit of good."

"No," Stilton said, "I don't think so either. He got Tippi calmed down and he's going his merry way."

"Another thing . . ." I said, and told the detective how I had fed Knurr information about laws regarding the disposition of the estate of a missing man.

"Uh-huh," Percy said. "You figure that will get him to dump the body? If he's got it?"

"That's what I hoped," I said. "Now I'm not so sure he's going to react the way we want him to. Perce, Knurr is a mystery man. I'm not certain we can manipulate him."

"Yeah," he said, sighing. "If he doesn't spook, and if he can keep his women in line, we're dead."

"There's one possibility," I said. "A long shot."

"What's that?"

"I've been going through all my notes on Knurr. Remember that interview we had with Bishop Oxman? He gave us the name of Knurr's next of kin. Goldie Knurr. A sister."

"And?"

"What if she's not his sister? What if she's his wife?"

Silence for a moment.

"You're right," Stilton said finally. "A long shot."

"We've got to try it," I insisted. "You've got the address? I think it was in Athens, Indiana."

He found it in his notebook and I carefully copied it down as he read it to me.

"You going to give her a call?" Percy asked.

"That wouldn't do any good," I said. "If he listed her as a sister, she probably has orders to back him up if anyone inquires."

"So?"

"So," I said, making up my mind at that precise instant, "I think I better go out there and talk to the lady."

That was what I had to do. I knew it on the spur of the moment. I booked a seat on American to Chicago through the office agency. I had no time to ask permission of Teitelbaum or Tabatchnick. I had no time to listen to Orsini as I tore out of the building.

As luck had it, he was coming in as I left, surrounded by his entourage. I attempted to sneak by, but Orsini's glittering eyes saw everything. A hand shot out and clamped my arm. I looked at the diamond flashing on his pinkie. I looked at the glossy manicured fingernails. My eyes rose to note the miniature orchid in his lapel: an exquisite flower of speckled lavender.

"Josh!" he cried gaily. "Just the man I wanted to see! I've got a joke you're going to love."

He glanced smilingly around his circle of sycophants, and they drew closer, already composing their features into expressions of unendurable mirth.

"There's this little guy," Romeo Orsini said, "and he goes up to this tall, beautiful, statuesque blonde. And he says to her, 'I'm going to screw you.' And she says—"

"Heard it," I snapped. "It's an old joke and not very good."

I jerked my arm from his grip, pushed my way through the circle of aides, and stalked from the building. I didn't look back, but I was conscious of the thunderous silence I had left behind.

I wasted no time in wondering why I had dealt so rudely with Orsini or how it would affect my career at TORT. I was too intent on reaching my bank before it closed, on trying to estimate the balance in my account and how much cash would be required for my trip to Chicago. Luckily, I was covered, and soon was in a cab heading through the Midtown Tunnel toward Kennedy after a hurried trip home to pack.

The flight to Chicago was the only chance to relax in much too long, and I decided to enjoy it. I even laughed at the terrible movie and wolfed down the mystery meat. We touched down in Chicago without incident and, as I walked into the terminal, I found O'Hare Airport to be crowded, noisy, and frantic as Mother Tucker's on East 69th Street in Manhattan. Where, I thought with rueful longing, even at that moment Perdita Schug and Colonel Clyde Manila were probably well along on their Walpurgisnacht.

I wandered about the terminal for a while, continually touching my newly fattened wallet and feeling for my return ticket at irregular intervals. I finally found my way to where cabs, limousines, and buses were available. Obviously a cab to Athens would cost too much. I approached a uniformed chauffeur leaning against the fender of a black behemoth which seemed to have twice as many windows as any gas-driven vehicle deserved.

The driver looked at me without interest, his sleepy eyes taking in my wrinkled overcoat, shapeless hat, and the sodden suitcase pressed under my arm. His only reaction was to switch a toothpick from the right corner of his mouth to the left.

"Do you go to Athens?" I asked.

"Where?"

"Athens. It's in Indiana." I had looked it up in the office atlas.

"Never heard of it," he said.

"It's between Gary and Hammond."

"*Where* between Gary and Hammond?"

"I don't know," I confessed.

"Then I don't go there," he said.

The toothpick switched back again. I know when I've been dismissed. I wandered over to the bus area. There was a uniformed driver leaning against a bus marked Gary-Hammond, gazing about with total disinterest. I decided I'd like to have the toothpick concession at O'Hare Airport, but at least he didn't shift it when I addressed him:

"Could you tell me if I can take this bus to Athens?"

"Where?"

"Athens, Indiana."

"Where is that?"

"Between Gary and Hammond. It's an incorporated village."

He looked at me doubtfully.

"Population 3,079 in 1939," I added helpfully.

"No shit?" he said. "Between Gary and Hammond?"

I nodded.

"You stand right there," he told me. "Don't move. Someone's liable to steal you. I'll be right back."

He went over to the dispatcher's desk and talked to a man chewing a toothpick. The bus driver gestured. Both men turned to stare at me. Then the dispatcher unfolded a map. They both bent over it. Another uniformed bus driver came along, then another, and another. Finally there were five men consulting the map, waving their arms, arguing in loud voices, their toothpicks waggling like mad.

The driver came back to me.

"Yeah," he said, "I go to Athens."

"You learn something every day," I said cheerfully.

"Nothing important," he said.

An hour later I was trying to peer through a misted window as the bus hurtled southeastward. I saw mostly darkness, a few clumps of lights, flickering neon signs. And then, as we crossed the state line into Indiana, there were rosy glows in the sky, sudden flares, views of lighted factories and mills, and one stretch of highway seemingly lined with nothing but taverns, junkyards, and adult book stores.

About ninety minutes after leaving O'Hare Airport, with frequent stops to discharge passengers, we pulled off the road at a street that seemed devoid of lighting or habitation.

"Athens," the driver called.

I struggled from my seat, lifted my suitcase from the overhead rack, and staggered down the aisle to the door.

I bent to look out.

"This is Athens?" I asked the driver.

"This is it," he said. "Guaranteed."

"Thank you," I said.

"You're welcome," he said.

I stood on a dark corner and watched the bus pull away, splashing me from the knees downward. All I could feel was regret at not staying aboard that bus to the end of the line, riding it back to O'Hare, and returning to Manhattan by the earliest available flight. Cold, wet, miserable.

After a long despairing wander I came to what might be called, with mercy, a business district. Most of the stores were closed, with steel shutters in place. But I passed a drugstore that was open, a mom-and-pop grocery store, and at last—O Lord, I gave thanks!—a liquor store.

"A pint of brandy, please," I said to the black clerk.

He inspected me.

"Domestic?" he said.

"Anything," I said. "Anything at all."

He was counting out my change when I asked if there were any hotels in the immediate area.

"One block down," he said, pointing. "Then two blocks to the right. The New Frontier Bar and Grill."

"It's a hotel?"

"Sure," he said. "Up above. You want to sleep there tonight?"

"Of course."

"Crazy," he said, shaking his head.

I followed his directions to the New Frontier Bar and Grill. It was a frowsy beer joint with a dirty front window, a few customers at the bar with blue faces from the TV set, and a small back room with tables.

The bartender came right over; it was downhill. The whole floor seemed to slope toward the street.

"Scotch and water, please," I said.

"Bar scotch?"

"All right."

He poured me what I thought was an enormous portion until I realized the bottom of the shot glass was solid and at least a half-inch thick.

"I understand you have a hotel here," I said.

He looked at me, then bent over the bar to inspect me closely, paying particular attention to my shoes.

"A hotel?" he said. "You might call it that."

"Could you tell me your rates?"

He looked off into the middle distance.

"Five bucks," he said.

"That seems reasonable," I said.

"It's right next door. Up one flight. The owner's on the desk. Tell him Lou sent you."

I quaffed my Scotch in one meager gulp, paid, walked outside, and climbed the narrow flight of stairs next door. The owner-clerk, also black, was seated behind a desk enclosed in wire mesh. There was a small hinged judas window in front.

He was a husky man in his fifties, I judged, wearing a T-shirt with a portrait of Beethoven printed on the front. He was working a crossword puzzle in a folded newspaper. He didn't look up. "Five bucks an hour," he said. "Clean sheets and running water. Payable in advance."

"I'd like to stay the night," I said. "To sleep. Lou sent me."

He wouldn't look up. "What's an ox with three letters?" he said. "With a long tail and short mane."

"Gnu," I said. "G-n-u."

Then he looked up at me.

"Yeah," he said, "that fits. Thanks. Twenty for the night. Payable in advance."

He opened the window to take the bill and slide a key on a brass medallion across to me.

"Two-oh-nine," he said. "Right down the hall. You're not going to do the dutch, are you?"

"Do the dutch?"

"Commit suicide?"

"Oh no," I protested. "Nothing like that."

"Good," he said. "What's a four-letter word meaning a small child?"

"Tyke," I suggested.

Oh, what a dreadful room that was! So bleak, so tawdry. It was about ten feet square with an iron bed that had once been painted white. It appeared to have the promised clean sheets—threadbare but clean—but on the lower third of the bed, the sheet and a sleazy cotton blanket had been covered with a strip of black oilcloth. It took me a while to puzzle that out. It was for customers too drunk or too frantic to remove their shoes.

I immediately ascertained that the door could be double-locked from the inside and that there was a bolt, albeit a cheap one. There was a stained sink in one corner, one straight-backed kitchen chair and a small maple table, the top scarred with cigarette burns. There was no closet, but hooks had been screwed into the walls to compensate, and a few wire coat hangers depended from them.

I went into the corridor to prowl. I found a bathroom smelling achingly of disinfectant. There was a toilet, sink, bathtub with shower. I used the toilet after latching the door with the dimestore hook-and-eye provided, but I resolved to shun the sink and tub.

I went back to my room and hung up my hat and overcoat on a couple of the hooks. After a great deal of struggling, I opened the single window. A chill, moist breeze came billowing in, still tainted with sulfur. It didn't take long to realize that there was no point in sitting around in such squalor, and soon I had reclaimed my hat and coat and headed back downstairs.

"Going to get something to eat," I said to the owner-clerk, trying to be hearty and cool simultaneously.

"A monkey-type creature," he said. "Five letters."

"Lemur," I said.

The New Frontier Bar and Grill had gained patrons during my absence; most of the barstools were occupied, and there were several couples, including a few whites, at tables in the back room. All the men were big, wide, powerfully built, with rough hands, raucous laughs, and thundering angers that seemed to subside as soon as they flared.

I was pleased to note the bartender remembered what I drank.

"Scotch?" he asked as if it were a statement of fact.

"Please. With water on the side."

When he brought my drink, I asked him about the possibility of getting sandwiches and a bag of potato chips.

"I'm a little fandangoed at the moment," he said. "When I get a chance, I'll make them up for you—okay?"

"Fine," I said. "No rush."

I looked around, sipping my shot glass of whiskey. The monsters on both sides of me were drinking boilermakers, silently and intently, staring into the streaked mirror behind the bar. I did not attempt conversation; they looked like men with grievances.

I turned back to my own drink and in a moment felt a heavy arm slide across my shoulders.

"Hi, sonny," a woman's voice said breezily.

"Good evening," I said, standing. "Would you care to sit down?"

"Sit here, Sal," the man next to me offered. "I got it all warmed up for you. I'm going home."

"You do that, Joe," said the woman, and a lot of woman she was, too, "for a change."

They both laughed. Joe winked at me and departed.

"Buy a girl a drink?" Ms. Sal asked, swinging a weighty haunch expertly atop the barstool.

"A pleasure," I said.

"Can I have a shot?" she asked.

"Whatever you like."

"A shot. Beer makes me fart."

I nodded sympathetically.

"Lou!" she screamed, so loudly and so suddenly that I leaped. "The usual. I've got a live one here."

She dug a crumpled pack of cigarettes from a stuffed purse. I struck a match for her.

"Thanks, sonny," she said. She took a deep inhalation and the smoke just disappeared. I mean, I didn't see it come out *anywhere*.

She was a swollen, bloated woman in her middle forties. She looked like the kind of girl who could never be surprised, shocked, or hurt; she had seen it all—twice at least.

The bartender brought her drink: a whiskey with a small beer chaser.

Sal looked me up and down.

"You work in the steel mills, sonny?"

"That Sal," the bartender said to me, "she's a card."

"Oh no," I said to her. "I'm not from around here. I'm from New York."

"You could have fooled me," she said. "I would have sworn you were a puddler."

"Come on, Sal," the bartender said.

"That's all right," I told him. "I know the lady is pulling my leg. I don't mind."

She smacked me on the back, almost knocking me off the stool.

"You're okay, sonny," she said in a growly voice. "I like you."

"Thank you," I said.

"What the hell you doing in Gary?"

"Gary?" I said, fear soaring. "I thought this was Athens. Isn't this Athens, Indiana?"

"Athens?" she said. She laughed uproariously, rocking back and forth on her barstool so violently that I put out an arm to assist her in case she should topple backward.

"Jesus Christ, sonny," she said, wiping her eyes with the back of her hand, "this place hasn't been called Athens in years. It was absorbed by Gary a long time ago."

"But it *was* Athens?" I insisted.

"Oh sure. It was Athens when I was a kid, more years ago than I want to remember. What the hell you doing in Athens?"

"I work for a law firm in New York," I said. "It's a matter of a will. I'm trying to locate a beneficiary whose last address was given as Athens, Indiana."

"No shit?" she said, interested. "An inheritance?"

"Oh yes."

"A lot of money?"

"It depends on what you mean by a lot of money," I said cautiously.

"To me," she said, "anything over twenty bucks is a lot of money."

"It's more than twenty bucks."

"What's the name?"

"Knurr," I said. "K-n-u-r-r. A woman. Goldie Knurr."

"Goldie Knurr?" she repeated. "No," she said, shaking her head, "never heard of her. Lou!" she screamed. When the bartender came over, she asked, "Ever hear of a woman named Goldie Knurr?"

He pondered a moment, frowning.

"Can't say as I have," he said.

"Buy me a double," Sal said to me, "and I'll ask around for you."

When she returned she slid onto the barstool again, spanked her empty glass on the bar.

"What the hell's your name?" she demanded.

"Josh."

"My name's Sal."

"I know. May I buy you another drink, Sal?"

She pretended to consider the offer.

"Well . . . all right, if you insist." She signaled the bartender, holding up two fingers. "Bingo," she said. "I found a guy who knows Goldie Knurr. Or says he does. See that old swart in the back room? The gray-hair, frizzy-haired guy sitting by himself?"

I turned. "I see him," I said.

"That's Ulysses Tecumseh Jones," she said. "Esquire. One year younger than God. He's been around here since there was a here. He says he knew the Knurr family."

"You think he'll talk to me?" I asked.

"Why not?" she said. "He's drinking beer."

"Mr. Jones?" I said, standing alongside his table with my drink in one hand, a stein of beer in the other.

He looked up at me slowly. Sal had been right: he had to be ninety, at least. A mummy without wrappings. Skin of wrinkled tar paper, rheumy eyes, hands that looked like something tossed up by the sea and dried on hot sands.

"Suh?" he said dimly.

"Mr. Jones," I said, "my name is Joshua Bigg and I—"

"Joshua," he said. "Fit the battle of Jericho."

"Yes, sir," I said, "and I would appreciate it if we could share a drink and I might speak to you for a few moments."

I proffered the stein of beer.

"I take that kindly," he said, reaching. "Set. Sal says you asking about the Knurrs?"

"Yes, sir," I said, sliding onto the banquette next to him. The ancient sipped his beer. He told me a story about his old army sergeant. He cackled.

"What war was that, sir?" I asked.

"Oh . . ." he said vaguely. "This or that."

"About the Knurrs?" I prompted him.

"It was about '58," he said, not bothering to tell me which century. "On Sherman Street that was. Am I right? Sherman Street?"

"You're exactly right, sir," I said. "That's the address I have. One-thirteen Sherman Street."

"If nominated, I will not run," he recited. "If elected, I will not serve."

"That's wonderful," I marveled. "That you remember."

"I still got all my nuts," he said, nodding with satisfaction. He suddenly grinned. No teeth. No dentures. Just pink gums.

"This was in 1958?"

"Nineteen and fifty-eight," he said. "Maybe long before. I tell you something funny about that family, suh. They was all G's. Everybody in that family had a name with a G."

"Goldie Knurr," I said. "Godfrey Knurr."

"Zactly," he said. "The father, George Knurr. The mother, Gertrude Knurr. Three other tads. Two sons: Gaylord Knurr and Gordon Knurr. Another daughter: Grace Knurr."

"You've got an incredible memory, sir."

"I sure do," he said. "Ain't nothing wrong with my nuts."

"What happened to them?" I asked. "The Knurr family?"

"Oh . . ." he said, "the old folks, George and Gertrude, they died, as might be expected. The kids, they all went away, also as might be expected. Goldie, I hear tell, is the only one around still."

It was not good news. If this old man's memory was accurate, Goldie Knurr was indeed the sister of my target.

"Mr. Jones," I said, "how is it you know so much about the Knurr family?"

"Oh," he said slowly, "I used to do this and that around their house. Little jobs, you know. And my third wife, Emily that was—no, Wanda; yes, the third was Wanda—she was like a mother to the kids."

"You don't recall anything about Godfrey Knurr, do you, Mr. Jones?" I asked. "One of the sons?"

"Godfrey Knurr?" he repeated, his eyes clouding. "That would be the middle boy. Became a preacher man, he did. Left town. Can't blame him for that."

"No indeed," I said fervently, "I really can't. You don't remember anything else about Godfrey? Anything special?"

"Smart young one," he said. "Big and strong. Liked the girls. Played football. Something . . ."

He stopped suddenly.

"Something?" I prompted.

"I don't rightly recall."

"Something good or something bad?"

He stared at me with eyes suddenly clear and piercing and steady.

"I don't rightly recall," he repeated.

6

•

I OPENED MY EYES FRIDAY MORNING, BEWILDERED FOR AN IN-stant before I recalled where I was. I rose, did a few halfhearted stretching exercises. I looked in vain for soap, washcloth, towel. I made do by sponging myself with a handkerchief dipped in water from my corner sink. As promised, it was running water. Cold. But invigorating.

I then dressed. My suit, of course, was badly wrinkled, but that seemed a minor consideration.

The owner-clerk was still in his wire mesh cage, drinking coffee from a cardboard container and reading a copy of *Architectural Digest*.

"When is checkout time, please?" I asked.

"Every hour on the hour," he said. "Oh, it's you. Checkout time for you will be around eight or nine tonight."

I stepped outside to find the rain had ceased, but the sun was hidden behind an oysterish sky. It put a dull tarnish on the world. I walked a few blocks. It took all my optimism to keep my spirits from drooping: block after block of mean row houses, a few scrubby trees.

I finally found a luncheonette that seemed to be doing a thriving business, went in, and had a reasonably edible breakfast. When I paid my bill, I got directions to Sherman Street.

Sherman Street was absolutely no different from any other in Athens: a solid culvert of row houses, jammed together, all of the same uninspired design, all three stories high, either clapboard or covered with counterfeit brick siding.

I found 113 Sherman Street. I climbed the three steps to the stoop, pushed the bell, heard it ring inside the house, and waited.

The door opened a cautious crack.

"Miss Goldie Knurr?" I asked, taking off my hat.

"I'm not buying anything," she said sharply.

"I don't blame you, ma'am," I said, smiling so widely that my face ached. "Prices being the way they are. But I'm not selling anything. It's about your brother, Godfrey Knurr."

The door was flung open.

"He's dead!" the woman wailed.

"Oh no," I said hastily. "No, no, no. Nothing like that. I saw him, uh, yesterday, and he's healthy and, uh, in fine shape."

"Law," she said, pressing a fist into her soft bosom, "you gave me such a start. Come in, sir."

She let me into a hallway, paused to lock, chain, and bolt the door, then turned to face me.

"You saw Godfrey yesterday?" she said in a voice of marvel: Robert Browning asking, "Ah, did you once see Shelley plain . . . ?"

"I did indeed, ma'am."

"And he's all right?"

"As far as I could tell, he's in excellent health. He has a beard now. Did you know?"

"A beard?" she cried. "Think of that! Did he give you a message for me?"

"Ah . . . no," I said softly. "But only because I didn't tell him I was coming to see you. May I tell you about it?"

"Of course you may!" she said loudly, recalling her duties as a hostess with a guest in the house. "Here, let me take your coat and hat, and you come into the parlor and we'll have a nice chat. A cup of tea? Would you like a nice cup of tea?"

"Thank you, ma'am, but no. I just finished my breakfast."

I waited while she hung my hat and coat on brass hooks projecting from an oak Victorian rack with a long, silvered mirror, lidded bench, and places for umbrellas with shallow pans to catch the dripping. Then I proffered my business card.

"Leopold Tabatchnick, ma'am," I said, "of New York. Attorney-at-law."

"He's not in any trouble, is he?" she asked anxiously, scarcely glancing at the card.

"None whatsoever," I assured her, reclaiming my card. "Please let me tell you what this is all about."

"Oh, law," she said, pressing a fist into her bosom again, "I'm just so discombobulated. It's been so long since I've heard from Godfrey. Do come in and sit down, Mr.—what was that name?"

"Tabatchnick. Leopold Tabatchnick."

"Well, you just come in and sit down, Mr. Leopold," she said, "and tell me what brings you to Gary."

She led the way into the parlor. There were the bright colors missing from outdoor Gary. Red, green, blue, yellow, purple, pink, orange, violet: all in chintz run wild. The sofa, chairs, pillows, even the tablecloths were flowers and birds, butterflies and sunrises. Parrots on the rug and peonies in the wallpaper. Everything blazing and crashing. Overstuffed and overwhelming. The room stunned the eye, shocked the senses: a funhouse of snapping hues in prints, stripes, checks, plaids. It was hard to breathe.

Goldie Knurr was just as overstuffed and overwhelming. Not fat, but a big, solid-soft woman, as tall as Godfrey and just as husky. She was dressed for a garden party in a flowing gown of pleats and flounces, all in a print of cherry clumps that made her seem twice as large and twice as imposing.

Sixty-five at least, I guessed, with that rosy, downy complexion some matrons are blessed with: the glow that never disappears until the lid is nailed down. I saw the family resemblance; she had Godfrey's full, tender lips, his steady, no-nonsense brown eyes, even the masculine cragginess of his features.

Her figure was almost as broad-shouldered as her brother's, but softened, plumpish. Her hands were chubby. The hair, which might have been a wig— although I suspected she might call it a "transformation"—was bluish-white, elaborately set, and covered with a scarcely discernible net.

She sat me down in an armchair so soft that I felt swallowed. When she came close, I smelled lavender sachet, sweetly cloying. I hoped she wouldn't take a chair too near, but she did. She sat upright, spine straight, ankles crossed, hands clasped in her lap.

"Yes, Mr. Leopold?" she said, beaming.

"Tabatchnick, ma'am," I murmured. "Leopold Tabatchnick. Miss Knurr, I represent a legal firm on retainer to the Stilton Foundation of New York. You've heard of the Stilton Foundation, of course?"

"Of course," she said, still beaming. Her voice was warm, burbling, full of aspirates. A very young, hopeful voice.

"Well, as you probably know, the Stilton Foundation makes frequent grants of large sums of money to qualified applicants in the social sciences for projects we feel will benefit humanity. Your brother, the Reverend Godfrey Knurr, has applied for such a grant. He desires to investigate the causes of and cures for juvenile delinquency. He seems well qualified to conduct such a research project, but because the amount of money involved is considerable,

712 • L A W R E N C E   S A N D E R S •

we naturally must make every effort to investigate the background, compe-
tence, and character of the applicant. And that is why I am here today."

She was dazzled. I was not sure she had quite understood everything I had
thrown at her, but she did grasp the fact that her brother might be granted a
great deal of money if this funny little man in the wrinkled suit lost in her
best armchair gave him a good report.

"Of course," she gasped. "Any way I can help . . ."

"I understand yours was a large family, Miss Knurr. Five children,
and—"

"Five *happy* children," she interrupted. "And five *successful* children. Not
one of us on welfare!"

"Most commendable," I murmured. "About Godfrey, could you tell me
if—"

"The best," she said firmly. "Absolutely the best! We all knew it. There
was no jealousy, you understand. We were all so proud of him. He was the
tallest and strongest and most handsome of the boys. Star of the football team,
president of his high school class, captain of the debating team, good marks
in every subject. Everyone loved him—and not just the family. *Everyone!*
You'll find that no one has a bad word to say about Godfrey Knurr. We all
knew that he was destined for great things, and that's just the way it turned
out."

She sat back, smiling, nodding, panting slightly, pleased with the panegyric
she had just delivered.

But I couldn't let it go at that. This was the woman who instinctively
suspected sudden death when her brother's name was first mentioned, who
asked if he was in trouble when she learned I was a lawyer, who apparently
hadn't seen or heard from the favored brother in years. It didn't jibe with the
dream she had recalled.

"Then he was never in any, ah, trouble as a boy?"

"Absolutely not!" she said definitely, then decided to amend that. "Oh,
there were a few little things you might expect from a high-spirited youngster.
But nothing serious, I do assure you."

"He had friends?"

"Many! Many! Godfrey was very popular."

"With his teachers as well as his peers?"

"Oh, law, yes," she said enthusiastically. "He was such a good student,
you see. So quick to learn. The other boys, they talked about going into the
mills and things like that. But Godfrey would never be satisfied with that.
He aimed for higher things. That boy had ambition."

It was the unreserved love of a sister for a handsome, talented younger
brother. I found it hard to break through that worship.

"Miss Knurr," I said, "about Godfrey's choice of the ministry as a career—
was he very religious as a boy?"

Lucky shot. Up to that point her answers had been prompt and glib. Now she paused before answering. She was obviously giving some thought to framing her reply, and when she spoke the timbre of her voice had changed. I thought her uncertain, if not fearful.

"Well . . ." she said finally, "ours was a God-fearing family. Church every Sunday morning without fail, I can tell you! I can't say that Godfrey was any different from the rest of us children as far as religion was concerned. But when he announced he was going to study for the ministry, we were all very happy. Naturally."

"Naturally," I said. "And the other boys, Godfrey's brothers, did they really go into the mills?"

"No," she said shortly, "they never did. They were both drafted, of course, and Gaylord decided to stay in the army. Gordon owns a gas station in Kentucky."

"And Godfrey became a minister," I said encouragingly. "Your church is in the neighborhood?"

"Two blocks south on Versailles Street," she said, pronouncing it "Versales." "It's St. Paul's. The pastor then was the Reverend Stokes. He's retired now."

"And who took his place?" I asked.

"Reverend Dix," she said stonily. "A black." Then she brightened. "Would you like to see our family album? Pictures of all of us?" She rose briefly, left the room, and returned with the album. Then she sat down on a posy-covered sofa and motioned me to sit beside her.

What is it about old snapshots that is so sad? Those moments in sunshine caught forever should inspire happiness and fond memories. But they don't. There is a dread about them. The snapshots of the Knurr family weren't photographs so much as memento mori.

We finished the album and I turned back to the section devoted to photographs of Godfrey.

"Who is this he's with?" I pointed at a snapshot of two stalwart youths in football uniforms standing side by side, legs spread, hands on hips. The boy alongside Godfrey Knurr was a black.

"Oh, that's Jesse Karp," she said, and I thought she sniffed. "He's principal of our high school now—would you believe it?"

"They were close friends?"

"Well . . . they were friends, I guess."

"And this priest with Godfrey—is he the Reverend Stokes?"

"That's right. He helped Godfrey get into the seminary. He helped Godfrey in so many ways. The poor man . . ."

I looked up.

"I thought you said he's retired?"

"Oh, he is. But doing, ah, poorly."

"I'm sorry to hear it."

"You're not planning to talk to him, are you?"

"I wasn't planning to, no, ma'am."

"Well, he's not all there—if you know what I mean."

"Ah. Too bad. Senile?"

"Not exactly," she said, examining the pink nails on her plump fingers. "I'm afraid the Reverend Stokes drinks a little more than is good for him."

"What a shame," I said.

"Isn't it?" she said earnestly. "And he was such a *fine* man. To end his days like that . . . So if you *do* talk to him, Mr. Leopold, please keep that in mind."

"Tabatchnick," I murmured. "I certainly shall."

I turned to a page of six snapshots, each showing a young, confident Godfrey with a muscular arm about the shoulders of a different and pretty girl. The posture was possessive.

"He seems to have been popular with girls," I observed.

"Oh law!" she cried. "You have no idea! Calling him at all hours. Hanging around outside the house. Sending him notes and all. Popular? I should say! No flies on Godfrey Knurr."

One of the six photos showed Godfrey with a girl shorter and younger than the others. Long, long flaxen hair fell to her waist. Even in the slightly out-of-focus snapshot she looked terribly vulnerable, unbearably fragile. I looked closer. One of her legs was encased in a heavy iron brace.

"Who is this girl?" I asked casually, pointing.

"Her?" Goldie Knurr said too quickly. "Just one of Godfrey's friends. I don't recall her name."

It was the first time she had actually lied to me. She was not a woman experienced in lying, and something happened to her voice; it weakened, became just a bit tremulous.

I closed the album.

"Well!" I said heartily. "That was certainly interesting, and I thank you very much, Miss Knurr, for your kind cooperation. I think I've learned what I need."

"And Godfrey will get the money?" she asked anxiously.

"Oh, that isn't my decision to make, Miss Knurr. But I've certainly discovered nothing today that will rule against it. Thank you for your time and hospitality."

She helped me on with my coat, handed me my hat, went through the rigmarole of unlocking the door. Just before I left, she said . . .

"If you see Godfrey again, Mr. Leopold . . ."

"Yes?"

"Tell him that he owes me a letter," she said, laughing gaily.

I went next to McKinley High School. It occupied an entire block with its playgrounds and basketball courts. As I marched up the front steps, the plate glass door opened and a black security guard, uniformed and armed with a nightstick, came out to confront me.

"Yes?" he said.

"Could you tell me if Mr. Jesse Karp is principal of this school?" I asked.

"That's right."

"I'd like to talk to him if I could."

"You have an appointment?"

"No, I don't," I admitted.

"Better call or write for an appointment," he advised. "Then they know you're coming—see? And you go right in."

"This is about the record of a former student of McKinley High," I said desperately. "Couldn't you ask?"

He stared at me. Sometimes it's an advantage to be diminutive; I obviously represented no threat to him.

"I'll call up," he said. "You stay here."

He went back inside, used a small telephone fixed to the wall. He was out again in a moment.

"They say to write a letter," he reported. "Records of former students will be forwarded—if you have a good reason for wanting them. Please enclose a stamped, self-addressed envelope."

I sighed.

"Look," I said, "I know this is an imposition and I apologize for it. But could you make another call? Please? Try to talk to Mr. Karp or his assistant or his secretary. The student I want to ask about is Godfrey Knurr. That's K-n-u-r-r. I'd like to talk to Mr. Karp personally about Godfrey Knurr. Please try just one more time."

"Oh man," he said, "you're pushing it."

"If they say no, then I'll go away and write a letter. I promise."

He took a deep breath, then made up his mind and went back to the inside telephone. This time the conversation took longer and I could see him waiting as he was switched from phone to phone. Finally he hung up and came out to me.

"Looks like you clicked," he said.

A few moments later, through the glass door, I saw a tall skinny lady striding toward us. The guard opened the door to let me enter just as she came up.

"To see Mr. Karp?" she snapped.

"Yes, ma'am," I said, taking off my hat. "I'd like to—"

"Follow me," she commanded.

The guard winked and I trailed after that erect spine down a waxed linoleum corridor and up two flights of stairs. Not a word was spoken. From somewhere I heard a ragged chorus of young voices singing "Frère Jacques."

We entered a large room with a frosted glass door bearing the legend: PRINCIPAL'S OFFICE. My conductress led the way past three secretaries, typing away like mad, and ushered me to the doorway of an inner office. The man inside, standing behind a desk piled high with ledgers and papers, looked up slowly.

"Mr. Karp?" I said.

"That's right," he said. "And you?"

I had my business card ready.

"Leopold Tabatchnick, sir," I sang out. "Attorney-at-law. New York City."

He took the proffered card, inspected it closely. "And you want information about Godfrey Knurr?"

"That's correct, sir."

I launched into the Stilton Foundation spiel. Through it all he stared at me steadily. Then he said:

"He's in trouble, isn't he?"

I almost collapsed. But I should have known it had to happen eventually. "Yes," I said, nodding dumbly, "he's in trouble."

"Bad?"

"Bad enough," I said.

"Had to happen," he said.

He went to the door of his office and closed it. He took my hat and coat, hung them on an old-fashioned bentwood coat tree. He gestured me to the worn oak armchair, then sat down in a creaking swivel chair behind his jumbled desk. He leaned back, hands clasped behind his head, and regarded me gravely.

"What's your real name?" he asked.

I decided to stop playing games.

"Joshua Bigg," I said. "I'm not a lawyer, but I really do work for that legal firm on the card. I'm the Chief Investigator."

"Chief Investigator," he repeated, nodding. "Must be important to send you all the way out from New York. What's the problem with Godfrey Knurr?"

"Uh, it involves women."

"It would," he said. "And money?"

"Yes," I said, "and money. Mr. Karp, if you insist, I will tell you in detail what the Reverend Godfrey Knurr is implicated in, and what he is suspected of having done. But, because of the laws of slander, I'd rather not. He has not been charged with any crimes. As yet."

"Crimes?" he echoed. "It's come to that, has it? No, Mr. Bigg, I really don't want to know. You wouldn't be here if it wasn't serious. Well . . . what can I tell you?"

"Anything about the man that will help me understand him."

"Understand Godfrey Knurr?" he said, with a hard grin that had no mirth to it. "No way! Besides, I can't tell you about the *man*. We lost touch when he went away to the seminary."

"And you haven't seen him since?"

"Once," he said. "When he came back to visit his sister years and years ago. He looked me up and we had a few drinks together. It was not what you'd call a joyous reunion."

"Well, can you tell me about the boy? Maybe it would help me understand what he's become."

"Maybe," he said doubtfully. "Mr. Bigg, when my family came up here from Mississippi, we were one of the first colored families in the neighborhood. It wasn't easy, I do assure you. But my daddy and older brothers got jobs in the mills, so we were eating. That was something. They put me in grade school here. Mostly Irish, Polish, and Ukrainian kids. I was the only black in my class. It would have been worse if it hadn't been for Godfrey Knurr."

I must have looked surprised.

"Oh yes," he said. "He saved my ass more than once, I do assure you. This was in the eighth grade, and he was the biggest, strongest, smartest, best-looking boy in school. The teachers loved him. Girls followed him down the street, passed him notes, gave him the cookies they baked in home economics class. I guess you could say he was the school hero."

"Is that how you saw him?"

"Oh yes," he said seriously, "I do assure you. He was my hero, too. Protected me. Showed me around. Took me under his wing, you might say. I thought I was the luckiest kid in the world to have a friend like Godfrey Knurr. I worshiped him."

"And then . . . ?" I asked.

"Then we went to high school together—right here in dear old McKinley—and Godfrey began to call in my markers. Do you know what that means?"

"I know."

"It started gradually. Like we'd have to turn in a theme, and he'd ask me to write one for him because he had put it off to the last minute and he wanted to take a girl to the movies. He was something with the girls. Or maybe we'd be taking a math test, and he'd make sure to sit next to me so that I could slip him the answers if he got stuck."

"I thought you said he was smart?"

"He was. The smartest. If he had applied himself, and studied, he could have sailed through high school, just *sailed,* and ended up first in his class. But he had no discipline. There were always a dozen things he'd rather be doing than homework—mooning around with girls, playing a game of stickball in a vacant lot, going into Chicago to see a parade—whatever. So he began to lean on me more and more until I was practically carrying him."

"You didn't object to this?"

Jesse Karp swung his creaking swivel chair around until he was looking out a window. I saw him in profile. A great brown bald dome. A hard, brooding expression.

"I didn't object," he said in a rumbling, ponderous voice. "At first. But then I began to grow up. Physically, I mean. I really sprouted. In the tenth grade alone I put on four inches and almost thirty pounds. After a while I was as tall as Godfrey, as strong, and I was faster. Also, I was getting wiser. I realized how he was using me. I still went along with him, but it bothered me. I didn't want to get caught helping him cheat. I didn't want to lie for him anymore. I didn't want to do his homework or lend him my notes or write his themes. I began to resent his demands."

"Do you think . . ." I said hesitantly, "do you think that when you first came up here from the south, and he took you under his wing, as you said, do you think that right from the start, the both of you just kids, that he saw someone he could use? Maybe not right then, but in the future?"

Jesse Karp swung around to face me, to stare at me somberly.

"You weren't raised to be an idiot, were you?" he said. "I gave that question a lot of thought, and yes, I think he did exactly that. He had a gift—if you can call it that—of selecting friends he could use. If not immediately, then in the future. He *banked* people. Just like a savings account that he could draw on when he was in need. It hurt me when I realized it. Now, after all these years, it still hurts. I thought he liked me. For myself, I mean."

"He probably did," I assured him. "Probably in his own mind he doesn't know the difference. He only likes people he can use. The two are inseparable."

"What you're saying is that he's not doing it deliberately? That he's not consciously plotting?"

"I think it's more like an instinct."

"Maybe," he said. "Anyway, after I realized what he was doing, I decided against a sudden break. I didn't want to confront him or fight him or anything like that. But I gradually cooled it, gradually got out from under."

"How did he take that?"

"Just fine. We stayed friends, I do assure you. But he got the message. Stopped asking me to do his themes and slip him the answers on exams. It didn't make any difference. By that time he had a dozen other close friends, some boys but mostly girls, who were delighted to help him. He had so much *charm*. Even as a boy, he had so damned much charm, you wouldn't believe."

"I'd believe," I said. "He's still got it."

"Yes? Well, in our senior year, a couple of things happened that made me realize he was really bad news. He had a job for an hour after school every day working in a local drugstore. Jerking sodas and making deliveries—like that. He worked for maybe a month and then he was canned. There were rumors that he had been caught dipping into the till. That may or may not have been true. Knowing Godfrey, I'd say it was probably true. Then, we were both on the high school football team. Competitors, you might say, because we both wanted to play quarterback, although sometimes the coach played us both at the same time with one of us at halfback. But still, we both wanted to call the plays. Anyway, in our last season, three days before the big game with Edison High, someone pushed me down the cement steps to the locker room. I never saw who did it, so I can't swear to it, but I'll go to my grave believing it was Godfrey Knurr. All I got out of it, thank God, was a broken ankle."

"But he played quarterback in the big game?"

"That's right."

"Did McKinley High win?"

"No," Jesse Karp said with grim satisfaction, "we lost."

"And who ended up first in the class? Scholastically?"

"I did," he said. "But I do assure you, if Godfrey Knurr had applied himself, had shown some discipline, there is no way I could have topped him. He was brilliant. No other word for it; he was just brilliant."

"What does he *want?*" I cried desperately. "Why does he do these things? What's his motive?"

The principal fiddled with an ebony letter opener on his desk, looking down at it, turning it this way and that.

"What does he want?" he said ruminatively. "He wants money and beautiful women and the good things of this world. You and I probably want exactly the same, but Godfrey wants them the easy way. For him, that means a kind of animal force. Rob a drugstore cash register. Push a competitor down a flight of cement steps. Make love to innocent women so they'll do what you want. What you *need*. He goes bulling his way through life, all shoulders and elbows. And God help you if you get in his way. He has a short fuse—did you know that? A really violent temper. He learned to keep it under control, but I once saw what he did to a kid in scrimmage. This kid had made Godfrey look bad on a pass play. The next time we had a pileup, I saw Godfrey go after him. It was just naked violence; that's the only way I can describe it. Really vicious stuff. That kid was lucky to come out alive."

I was silent, thinking of Solomon Kipper and Professor Yale Stonehouse. They hadn't come out of the pileup.

"What does he want?" Jesse Karp repeated reflectively. "I'll tell you something odd. When Godfrey and I were kids, almost everyone collected baseball cards. You know—those pictures of players you got in a package of bubble gum. Godfrey never collected them. You know what he saved? He showed me his collection once. Models and movie stars. Yachts and mansions. Jewelry and antiques. Paintings and sculpture. He wanted to own it all."

"The American dream?" I asked.

"Well . . ." he said, "maybe. But skewed. Gone bad. He wanted it all *right now*."

"Why did he go into the ministry?" I asked.

He lifted his eyes to stare at me. "Why do you think?"

"To avoid the draft?"

"That's my guess," Jesse Karp said, shrugging. "I could be wrong."

"Was Knurr ever married?"

"Not to my knowledge," he said too quickly.

"I understand there is a Reverend Stokes who helped him?"

"That's right. The Reverend Ludwig Stokes. He's retired now."

"Goldie Knurr hinted that he's fuddled, that he drinks too much."

"He's an old, old man," Jesse Karp said stonily. "He's entitled."

"Could you tell me where I might find him?"

"The last I heard he was living in a white frame house two doors south of St. Paul's on Versailles."

He glanced obviously at his wristwatch and I rose immediately to my feet. I thanked him for his kind cooperation. He helped me on with my coat and walked me to the door.

"I'll let you know how it all comes out," I told him.

"Don't bother," he said coldly. "I really don't want to know."

I was saddened by the bitterness in his voice. It had all happened so many years ago, but he still carried the scars. He had been duped and made a fool of. He had thought he had a friend who liked him for what he was. The friend had turned out to be just another white exploiter. I wondered how that discovery had changed Jesse Karp's life.

At the doorway, I thought of something else and turned to him.

"Do you remember a girl Knurr dated, probably in high school—a short, lovely girl with long blond hair? She had a heavy metal brace on one leg. Maybe polio."

He stared at me, through me, his high brow rippling.

"Yes," he said slowly, "I do remember. She limped badly. Very slender."

"Fragile looking," I said. "Wistful."

"Yes, I remember. But I can't recall her name. Wait a minute."

He went back to the glass-enclosed bookcase set against the far wall. He opened one of the shelf doors, searched, withdrew a volume bound in maroon. Plastic stamped to look like leather.

"Our yearbook," he said, smiling shyly. "The year Godfrey and I graduated. I still keep it."

I liked him very much then.

I stood at his side as he balanced the wide volume atop the mess at his desk and flipped through the pages rapidly. He found the section with small, individual photographs of graduating seniors, head-and-shoulder shots. Then Jesse Karp turned the pages slowly, a broad forefinger running down the columns of pictures, names, school biographies.

"Here I am," he said, laughing. "God, what a beast!"

I learned to look: Jesse Karp, not a beast, but an earnest, self-conscious kid in a stiff white collar and a tie in a horrendous pattern. Most of the other boys were wearing suit jackets, but Karp wasn't. I didn't remark on it.

"Not so bad," I said, looking at the features not yet pulled with age. "You look like it was the most solemn moment of your life."

"It was," he said, staring down at the book. "I was the first of my family to be graduated from high school. It was *something*. And here's Godfrey."

Directly below Karp's photograph was that of Knurr, wearing a sharply patterned sport jacket. He was smiling at the camera, his chin lifted. Handsome, strong, arrogant. A Golden Boy. He had written an inscription in the yearbook directly below Karp's biography: "To Jesse, my very best friend ever. Godfrey Knurr." I guessed he had written that same sentiment in many McKinley High yearbooks.

Each student had a pithy motto or prediction printed in italic type below his biography. Jesse Karp's said: *A slow but sure winner.*

Godfrey Knurr's was: *We'll be hearing of him for many years to come.*

The principal continued flipping through the pages of stamp-sized portraits. Finally his finger stopped.

"This one?" he said, looking at me.

I glanced down. It was the same girl I had seen in Goldie Knurr's photo album. The same pale gold beauty, the same soft vulnerability.

"Yes," I said, reading her name. "Sylvia Wiesenfeld. Do you know anything about her?"

He closed the yearbook with his two hands, slapping the volume with what I thought was unusual vehemence. He went back to the bookcase to restore the book to its place and close the glass door.

"Why are you asking about her?" he demanded, his back to me. I thought something new had come into his voice: a note of hostility.

"Just curious," I said. "She's so beautiful."

"Her father owned a drugstore," he said grudgingly. "He's dead now—the father. I don't know what happened to her."

"Was this the drugstore where Godfrey Knurr worked after school?"

"Yes," he said shortly.

He insisted on personally accompanying me through the outer offices, down the hallways and staircases to the front entrance of McKinley High School. I didn't know if he was being polite or wanted to make certain I didn't loiter about the premises.

I thanked him again for his kindness and he sent me on my way. He didn't exactly push me out the door, but he made certain I exited. I didn't think he regretted what he had told me about Godfrey Knurr. I thought he was ashamed and angry at what he had revealed about himself. I had set the old wounds throbbing.

On the sidewalk, I turned and looked back at the high school, a pile of red brick so ugly it was impressive. I had brief and sententious thoughts of the thousands—maybe millions!—of young students who had walked those gloomy corridors, sat at those worn desks, who had laughed, wept, frolicked, and discovered despair.

I found the white frame house two doors south of St. Paul's on Versailles Street. Perhaps it had once been white, but now it was a powdery gray, lashed by rain and wind, scoured by the sun. It looked at the world with blind eyes: uncurtained windows with torn green shades drawn at various levels. The cast-iron fence was rusted, the tiny front yard scabby with refuse. It was a sad, sad habitation for a retired preacher, and I could only wonder how his parishioners could allow their former pastor's home to fall into such decrepitude.

I went cautiously up the front steps and searched for a bell. There was none, although I discovered four stained screwholes in the doorjamb, a larger drilled hole in the middle, and the faint scarred mark of a square enclosing them all. Apparently a bell had once existed but had been removed.

I rapped sharply on the peeling door and waited. No answer. I knocked again. Still no reply.

"Keep trying," someone called in a cackling voice. "He's in there all right."

I turned. On the sidewalk was an ancient black man wearing a holey wool cap and fingerless gloves. He seemed inordinately swollen until I realized he was wearing at least three coats and what appeared to be several sweaters and pairs of trousers. He was pushing a splintered baby carriage filled with newspapers and bottles, cans, an old coffee percolator, tattered magazines, two bent umbrellas, and other things.

"Is this the home of the Reverend Stokes?" I asked him.

"Yeah, yeah, that's it," he said, nodding vigorously and showing a mouthful of yellow stumps. "What you do is you keep pounding. He's in there all right. He don't never go out now. Just keep pounding and pounding. He'll come to the door by and by."

"Thank you," I called, but he was already shuffling down the street, a strange apparition.

So I pounded and pounded on that weathered door. It seemed at least five minutes before I heard a quavery voice from inside: "Who is there?"

"Reverend Stokes?" I shouted. "Could I speak to you for a moment, sir? Please?"

There was a long pause and I thought I had lost him. But then I heard the sounds of a bolt being drawn, the door unlocked. It swung open.

I was confronted by a wild bird of a man. In his late seventies, I guessed. He was actually a few inches taller than I, but his clothes seemed too big for him so he appeared to have shrunk, in weight and height, to a frail diminutiveness.

His hair was an uncombed mess of gray feathers, and on his hollow cheeks was at least three days' growth of beard: a whitish plush. His temples were sunken, the skin on his brow so thin and transparent that I could see the course of blood vessels. Rheumy eyes tried to stare at me, but the focus wavered. The nose was a bone.

He was wearing what had once been a stylish velvet smoking jacket, but now the nap was worn down to the backing, and the elbows shone greasily.

Beneath the unbuttoned jacket was a soiled blue workman's shirt, tieless, the collar open to reveal a scrawny chicken neck. His creaseless trousers were some black, glistening stuff, with darker stains and a tear in one knee. His fly was open. He was wearing threadbare carpet slippers, the heels broken and folded under. His bare ankles were not clean.

I was standing outside on the porch, he inside the house. Yet even at that distance I caught the odor: of him, his home, or both. It was the sour smell of unwashed age, of mustiness, spilled liquor, unmade beds and unaired linen, and a whiff of incense as rancid as all the rest.

"Reverend Stokes?" I asked.

The bird head nodded, pecking forward.

"My name is Joshua Bigg," I said briskly. "I'm not trying to sell you anything. I'd just like to talk to you for a few minutes, sir."

"About what?" he asked. The voice was a creak.

"About a former parishioner of yours, now an ordained minister himself. Godfrey Knurr."

What occurred next was totally unexpected and unnerving.

"Nothing happened!" he screamed at me and reached to slam the door in my face. But a greenish pallor suffused his face, his hand slipped down the edge of the door, and he began to fall, to sag slowly downward, his bony knees buckling, shoulders slumping, the old body folding like a melted candle.

I sprang forward and caught him under the arms. He weighed no more than a child, and I was able to support him while I kicked the door shut with my heel. Then I half-carried, half-dragged him back into that dim, malodorous house.

I pulled him into a room that had obviously once been an attractive parlor. I put him down on a worn chesterfield, the brown leather now crackled and split. I propped his head on one of the armrests and lifted his legs and feet so he lay flat.

I straightened up, breathing through my mouth so I didn't have to smell him or the house. I stared down at him, hands on my hips, puzzling frantically what to do.

His eyes were closed, his respiration shallow but steady. I thought his face was losing some of that greenish hue that had frightened me. I decided not to call the police or paramedics. I took off my hat and coat and placed them gingerly on a club chair with a brown corduroy slipcover discolored with an enormous red stain on the seat cushion. Wine or blood.

I wandered back into the house. I found a small kitchen from which most of the odors seemed to be emanating. And no wonder; it was a swamp. I picked a soiled dishtowel off the floor and held it under the cold water tap in the scummed sink. Pipes knocked, the water ran rusty, then cleared, and I soaked the towel, wrung it out, soaked it again, wrung it out again.

I carried it back to the parlor. I pulled a straight chair alongside the chesterfield. I sat down and bent over the Reverend Stokes. I wiped his face gently with the dampened towel. His eyes opened suddenly. He stared at me dazedly. His eyes were spoiled milk, curdled and cloudy.

A clawed hand came up and pushed the towel aside. I folded it and laid it across his parchment brow. He let me do that and let the towel remain.

"I fainted?" he said in a wispy voice.

"Something like that," I said, nodding. "You started to go down. I caught you and brought you in here."

"In the study," he whispered, "across the hall, a bottle of whiskey, a half-filled glass. Bring them in here."

I looked at him, troubled.

"Please," he breathed.

I went into the study, a shadowed chamber littered with books, journals, magazines: none of them new. The room was dominated by a large walnut desk topped with scarred and ripped maroon leather. The whiskey and glass were on the desk. I took them and started out.

On a small marble-topped smoking stand near the door was a white plaster replica of Michelangelo's "David." It was the only clean, shining, lovely object I had seen in that decaying house. I had seen nothing of a religious nature—no pictures, paintings, icons, statuary, crucifixes, etc.

I brought him the whiskey. He raised a trembly hand and I held the glass to his lips. He gulped greedily and closed his eyes. After a moment he opened his eyes again, flung the towel from his brow onto the floor. He took the glass from my hand. Our fingers touched. His skin had the chill of death.

"There's another glass," he said. "In the kitchen."

His voice was stronger but it still creaked. It had an unused sound: harsh and croaky.

"Thank you, no," I said. "It's a little early for me."

"Is it?" he said without interest.

I sat down in the straight chair again and watched him finish the tumbler of whiskey. He filled it again from the bottle on the floor. I didn't recognize the label. It looked like a cheap blend.

"You told me your name?" he asked.

"Yes, sir. Joshua Bigg."

"Now I remember. Joshua Bigg. I don't recognize you, Mr. Bigg. Where are you from?"

"New York City, sir."

"New York," he repeated, and then with a pathetic attempt at gaiety, he said, "East Side, West Side, all around the town."

He tried to smile at me. When his thin, whitish lips parted, I could see his stained dentures. His gums seemed to have shrunk, for the false teeth fitted loosely and he had to clench his jaws frequently to jam them back into place. It was like a pained grimace.

"I was in New York once," he said dreamily. "Years and years ago. I went to the theater. A musical play. What could it have been? I'll remember in a moment."

"Yes, sir."

"And what brings you to our fair city, Mr. Bigg?"

I was afraid of saying the name again. I feared he might have the same reaction. But I had to try it.

"I wanted to talk to you about the Reverend Godfrey Knurr, Pastor," I said softly.

His eyes closed again. "Godfrey Knurr?" Stokes repeated. "No, I can't recall the name. My memory . . ."

I wasn't going to let him get away with that.

"It's odd you shouldn't remember," I said. "I spoke to his sister, Miss Goldie Knurr, and she told me you helped him get into the seminary, that you helped him in so many ways. And I saw a photograph of you with young Godfrey."

Suddenly he was crying. It was awful. Cloudy tears slid from those milky eyes. They slipped sideways into his sunken temples, then into his feathered hair.

"Is he dead?" he gasped.

First Goldie Knurr and now the Reverend Stokes. Was the question asked hopefully? Did they wish him dead?

I turned my eyes away, not wanting to sit there and watch this shattered man weep. After a while I heard him snuffle a few times and take a gulp from the glass he held on his thin chest. Then I looked at him again.

"No, sir," I said, "he is not dead. But he's in trouble, deep trouble. I represent a legal firm. A client intends to bring very serious charges against the Reverend Knurr. I am here to make a preliminary investigation . . ."

My voice trailed away; he wasn't listening to me. His lips were moving and I leaned close to hear what he was saying.

"Evil," the Reverend Ludwig Stokes was breathing. "Evil, evil, evil, evil . . ."

I sat back. It seemed a hopeless task to attempt to elicit information from this old man. Goldie Knurr had been right; he was fuddled.

But then he spoke clearly and intelligibly.

"Do you know him?" he asked. "Have you seen him?"

"Yes, sir," I said. "I spoke to him yesterday. He seems to be in good health. He has a beard now. He runs a kind of social club in Greenwich Village for poor boys and he also counsels individual, uh, dependents. Mostly wealthy women."

His face twisted and he clenched his jaw to press his dentures back into place. A thin rivulet of whiskey ran from the corner of his mouth and he wiped it away slowly with the back of one hand.

"Wealthy women," he repeated, his voice dull. "Yes, yes, that would be Godfrey."

"Reverend Stokes," I said, "I'm curious as to why Knurr selected the ministry as his career. I can find nothing in his boyhood that indicates any great religiosity." I paused, stared at him. "Was it to avoid the draft?" I asked bluntly.

"Partly that," he said in a low voice. "If his family had had the money, he would have wished to go to a fashionable eastern college. That was his preference, but it was impossible. Even I didn't have that kind of money."

"He asked for it? From you?"

He didn't answer.

"I understand he had good marks in high school," I went on. "Perhaps he could have obtained a scholarship, worked to help support himself?"

"It wasn't his way," he said.

"Then he could have gone to a low-tuition, state-supported college. Why the ministry?"

"Opportunity," the Reverend Stokes said without expression.

"Opportunity?" I echoed. "To save souls? I can't believe that of Godfrey Knurr. And surely not the monetary rewards of being an ordained minister."

"Opportunity," he repeated stubbornly. "That's how he saw it."

I thought about that, trying to see it as a young ambitious Godfrey Knurr had.

"Wealthy parishioners?" I guessed. "Particularly wealthy female parishioners? Maybe widows and divorcées? Was that how his mind worked?"

Again he didn't answer. He emptied the bottle into his tumbler and drained it in two gulps.

"There's another in the kitchen," he told me. "In the cupboard under the sink."

I found the bottle. I also found a reasonably clean glass for myself and rinsed it several times, scrubbing the inside with my fingers. I brought bottle and glass back to the parlor, sat down again, and poured him half a tumbler and myself a small dollop.

"Your health, sir," I said, raising my glass. I barely wet my lips.

"He was a handsome boy?" I asked, coughing. "Godfrey Knurr?"

He made a sound.

"Yes," he said in his creaky voice, "very handsome. And strong. A beautiful boy. Physically."

I caught him up on that.

"Physically?" I said. "But what of his personality, his character?"

Another of his maddening silences.

"Charm," he said, then buried his nose in his glass. After he swallowed he repeated, "Charm. A very special charm. There was a golden glow about him."

"He must have been very popular," I said, hoping to keep his reminiscences flowing.

"You had to love him," he said, sighing. "In his presence you felt happy. More alive. He promised everything."

"Promised?" I said, not understanding.

"I felt younger," he said, voice low. "More hopeful. Life seemed brighter. Just having him near."

"Did he ever visit you here, in your home?"

Again he began to weep, and I despaired of learning anything of significance from this riven man.

I waited until his eyes stopped leaking. This time he didn't bother wiping the tears away. The wet glistened like oil on his withered face. He drank deeply, finished his whiskey. His trembling hand pawed feebly for the full bottle on the floor. I served him. I had never before seen a man drink with such maniacal determination, as if unconsciousness could not come soon enough.

He lay there, wax fingers clamped around the glass on his bony chest. He stared unblinking at the ceiling. I felt I was sitting up with a corpse, waiting for the undertaker's men to come and take their burden away.

"I understand he was in trouble as a boy," I continued determinedly. "In a drugstore where he worked. He was accused of stealing."

"He made restitution," the old man said, his thin lips hardly moving. "Paid it all back."

"You gave him the money for that?" I guessed.

I hardly heard his faint, "Yes." Then . . .

"I gave him so much!" he howled in a voice so loud it startled me. "Not only money, but myself. I gave him *myself!* I taught him about poetry and beauty. Love. He said he understood, but he didn't. He was playing with me. He teased me. All the time he was teasing me, and it gave him pleasure."

I felt suddenly ill as I began to glimpse the proportions of this tragedy. Now I could understand that screeched, *"Nothing happened!"* And the statue of David. And the whispered, "Evil, evil, evil . . ."

"You loved him?" I asked gently.

"So much," he said in a harrowed voice. "So much . . ."

He lifted his head to drain his tumbler, then held it out to me in a quavery hand. I filled it without compunction.

"You never married, Reverend?" I asked.

"No. Never." He was staring at the ceiling again, seeing things that weren't there.

"Did you tell Godfrey how you felt about him?"

"He knew."

"And?"

"He used me. *Used* me! Laughing. The devil incarnate. All I saw was the golden glow. And then the darkness beneath."

"Knowing that, Pastor, why did you help him become a man of God?"

"Weakness. I did not have the strength of soul to withstand him. He threatened me."

"Threatened you? How? You said that nothing happened."

"Nothing did. But I had written him. Notes. Poems. They would have ruined me. The church . . ."

Notes again. I was engulfed in notes, false and true . . .

I took a deep breath, trying to comprehend the extent of such perfidy. The pattern of Godfrey Knurr's life was becoming plainer. An ambition too large for his discipline to contain was the motive for trading on his charm. He moved grinning from treachery to treachery, leaving behind him a trail of scars, wounds, broken lives.

And finally, I was convinced, two murders that meant no more to him than a rifled cash register or this betrayed wreck of a man.

"So you did whatever he demanded?" I said, nailing it down. "Got him out of scrapes, got him into the seminary? Gave him money?"

"All," he said. "All. I gave him everything. My soul. My poor little shriveled soul."

His words "shriveled soul" came out slurred and garbled, almost lost between his whiskey-loosened tongue and those ill-fitting dentures. I did not think he was far from the temporary oblivion he sought.

"Sylvia Wiesenfeld," I said. "You knew her?"

He didn't answer.

"You did," I told him. "Her father owned the drugstore where Godfrey stole the money. A lovely girl. So vulnerable. So willing. I saw her picture. Did she love Godfrey, too?"

His eyes were closed again. But his lips were moving faintly, fluttering. I rose, bent over him, put my ear close to his mouth, as if trying to determine if a dying man still breathed.

"What?" I said sharply. "I didn't hear that. Please repeat it."

This time I heard.

"I married them," he said.

I straightened up, took a deep breath. I looked down at the shrunken, defenseless hulk. All I could think of was: Godfrey Knurr did that.

I took the whiskey glass from his strengthless fingers and set it on the floor alongside the couch. He seemed to be breathing slowly but regularly. The tears had dried on his face, but whitish matter had collected in the corners of his eyes and mouth. Occasionally his body twitched, little moans escaped his lips like gas released from something corrupt.

I wandered about the lower floor of the house. I found a knitted afghan in the hall closet, brought it back to the parlor, and covered the Reverend Ludwig Stokes, a bright shroud for a gray man.

Then I went back into his study and poked about. I finally found a telephone directory in the lowest drawer of the old walnut desk. There was an S. Wiesenfeld on Sherman Street, not too far from the home of Goldie Knurr.

It seemed strange that such tumultuous events had occurred in such a small neighborhood.

The woman who answered my ring was certainly not Sylvia Wiesenfeld; she was a gargantuan black woman, not so tall but remarkable in girth. Her features, I thought, might be pleasant in repose, but when she opened the door, she was scowling and banging an iron frying pan against one redwood thigh. She looked down at me.

"We ain't buying," she said.

"Oh, I'm not selling anything," I hurriedly assured her. "My name is Joshua Bigg. I represent a legal firm in New York City. I've been sent out to make inquiries into the background of Godfrey Knurr. I was hoping to have a few minutes' conversation with Miss Wiesenfeld."

She looked at me suspiciously.

"You *who?*" she said. "You New York folks talk so fast."

"Joshua Bigg," I answered slowly. "That's my name. I'm trying to obtain information about Godfrey Knurr. I'd like to talk to Sylvia Wiesenfeld for a few moments."

"You the law?" she demanded.

"No," I said, "not exactly. I represent attorneys who, in turn, represent a client who is bringing suit against the Reverend Godfrey Knurr. I'm just making a preliminary investigation, that's all."

"You going to hang him?" she demanded. "I hope."

I tried to smile.

"Well . . . ah . . ." I said, "I'm sure our client would like to. May I speak to Miss Wiesenfeld for a few moments?"

She glared at me, making up her mind. That heavy cast-iron frying pan kept banging against her bulging thigh. I was very conscious of it.

"Well . . ." she said finally, "all right." Then she added fiercely, "You get my honey upset, I break yo' ass!"

"No, no," I said hastily, "I won't upset her, I promise."

She stared down at me again.

"You and me," she said menacingly, "we come to it, I figure I come out on top."

"Absolutely," I assured her. "No doubt about it. I'll behave; I really will."

Suddenly she grinned: a marvelous *human* grin of warmth and understanding.

"I do believe," she said. "Come on in, lawyer-man."

She led me into a neat entrance hall, hung my coat and hat on an oak hall rack exactly like the one in Miss Goldie Knurr's home.

"May I know your name, please, ma'am?" I asked her.

"Mrs. Harriet Lee Livingston," she said in a rich contralto voice. "I makes do for Miz Sylvia."

"How long have you been with her?"

"Longer than you been breathin'," she said.

The enormous bulk of the woman was awesome. That had to be the largest behind I had ever seen on a human being, and the other parts of her were in proportion: arms and legs like waists, and a neck that seemed as big around as her head.

But her features were surprisingly clear and delicate, with slanty eyes, a nice mouth, and a firm chin that had a deep cleft precisely in the center. You could have inserted a dime in that cleft. Her hands and feet were unexpectedly dainty, and she moved lightly, with grace.

Her color was a briar brown. She wore a voluminous shift, a shapeless tent with pockets. It was a kaleidoscope of hues: splashes of red, yellow, purple, blue, green—all in a jangling pattern that dazzled the eye.

"You stand right here," she said sternly. "Right on this spot. I'll tell Miz Sylvia she's got a visitor. I takes you in without warning, she's liable to get upset."

"I won't move," I promised.

She opened sliding wooden doors, squeezed through, closed the two doors behind her. I hadn't seen doors like that since I left my uncle's home in Iowa. They were paneled, waxed to a high gloss, fitted with brass hardware: amenities of a bygone era.

The doors slid open again and Mrs. Livingston beckoned me forward.

"Speak nice," she whispered.

"I will," I vowed.

"I be right here to make sure you do," she said grimly.

The woman facing me from across the living room was small, slight, with long silvered blond hair giving her a girlish appearance, although I knew she had to be at least forty. I could not see a leg brace; she wore a collarless gown of bottle-green velvet, a lounging or hostess gown, that fell to her ankles.

She was a thin little thing, still with that look of tremulous vulnerability that had caught my eye in the photos in the Knurr family album and Jesse Karp's yearbook. She seemed physically frail, or at least fragile, with narrow wrists, a white stalk of a neck, a head that appeared to be pulled backward, chin uptilted, by the weight of her hair.

She had a luminous quality: pale complexion, big eyes of bluish-green (they looked like agates), and lips sweetly bowed. I saw no wrinkles, no crow's-feet, no furrows—nothing in her face to mark the passage of years. If she had been wounded, it did not show. The smooth brow was serene, the dim smile placid.

But there was a dissonance about her that disturbed. She seemed removed. The lovely eyes were vacant, or focused on something no one else could see. That half-smile was, I soon realized, her normal expression; it meant nothing.

I recognized Ophelia, looking for her stream.

"Mr. Bigg?" she said. Her voice was young, utterly without timbre. A child's voice.

"Miss Wiesenfeld," I said, bowing, "I know this is an intrusion, and I appreciate your willingness to grant me a few moments of your time."

"Oh la!" she said with a giggling laugh. "How pretty you do talk. Doesn't he talk pretty, Harriet?"

"Yeah," Mrs. Livingston said heavily. "Pretty. Mr. Bigg, you sit in that armchair there. I sits on the couch here. Honey, you want to rest yourself?"

"No," the lady said, "I prefer to remain standing."

I seated myself nervously. My armchair was close to the corner of the big davenport where Mrs. Livingston perched, not leaning back but balancing her bulk on the edge. She was ready, I was certain, to lunge for my throat if I dared upset her honey.

"Miss Wiesenfeld," I started, "I have no desire to rake up old memories that may cause you pain. If I pose a question you don't wish to answer, please tell me so, and I will not persist. But this is a matter of some importance. It concerns the Reverend Godfrey Knurr. I represent a legal firm in New York City. One of our clients, a young woman, wishes to bring serious charges against Reverend Knurr. I am making a preliminary investigation in an attempt to discover if Knurr has a past history of the type of, ah, activities of which he is accused."

"Pretty," she murmured. "So pretty. It's nice to meet someone who speaks in complete sentences. Subject, verb, object. Do all your sentences parse, Mr. Bigg?"

She said that quite seriously. I laughed.

"I would like to think so," I said. "But I'm afraid I can't make that claim."

She began moving across the room in front of me. I saw then that she limped badly, dragging her left leg. Below the hostess gown I could see the foot bound in the stirrup of a metal brace.

She went close to a birdcage suspended from a brass stand. Within the cage, a yellow canary hopped from perch to perch as she approached.

"Chickie," she said softly. "Dear, sweet Chickie. How are you today, Chickie? Will you chirp for our guest? Will you sing a lovely song? How did you find me, Mr. Bigg?"

The abrupt question startled me.

"I saw your photograph in the Knurr family album, ma'am. With Godfrey. Mr. Jesse Karp supplied your name. The Reverend Ludwig Stokes provided more information."

"You have been busy, Mr. Bigg."

"Yes, ma'am," I said humbly.

"The busy Mr. Bigg," she said with her giggling laugh. "Busy Bigg." She poked a pale finger through the bars of the cage. "Sing for Busy Bigg, Chickie. What is Godfrey accused of?"

I had determined to use Percy Stilton's scam. The one that had worked with Bishop Oxman.

"He is accused of allegedly defrauding a young woman of her life's savings by promising to double her money."

"And promising to marry her?" Sylvia Wiesenfeld asked.

"Yes," I said.

"He is guilty," she said calmly. "He did exactly that."

A low growl came from Mrs. Livingston.

"I'd like to have him right here," she said in her furred contralto. "In my hands."

"Miss Wiesenfeld," I said, "may I ask you this: were you married to Godfrey Knurr?"

"Chickie," she said to the bird, "why aren't you chirping? Aren't you feeling well, Chickie?"

She left the cage, came back to the long davenport. The housekeeper heaved her bulk and assisted Sylvia to sit in the corner, the left leg extended, covered with the skirt of her long gown. Mrs. Livingston reached out, tenderly smoothed back strands of blond hair that had fallen about her mistress's pale face.

"Oh la!" Miss Wiesenfeld said. "A long time ago. Where are the snows of yesteryear? Reverend Stokes told you that?"

"Yes, ma'am."

"It happened in another world," she said. "In another time."

Her beautiful eyes looked at me, but she was detached, off somewhere.

"But you were married?" I persisted. "Legally?"

"Legally," she said. "A piece of paper. I have it."

"How long were you married, Miss Wiesenfeld?"

She turned those vacant eyes on the enormous black woman.

"Harriet?" she said.

"Fourteen months," Mrs. Livingston said. "Give or take."

"And then?" I asked.

"And then?" she repeated my question, perplexed.

"Did you separate? Divorce?"

"Harriet?" she asked again.

"He cleared out," Mrs. Livingston told me furiously. "Just took off. With everything of my honey's he could get his hands on. But her daddy was too smart for him. He left my honey some kind of a fund that cur couldn't touch."

I tried to remember when I had last heard a man called a "cur." I could not recall ever hearing it.

"So you are still married to Godfrey Knurr?" I asked softly.

"Oh no," Sylvia Wiesenfeld said with her disturbingly childish laugh. "No, no, no. I have a paper. Don't I, Harriet? So much paper. Paper, paper, paper."

I looked beseechingly at Mrs. Livingston.

"We got us a letter from a lawyer-man in Mexico," she said disgustedly. "It said Godfrey Knurr had been granted a divorce from his wife Sylvia."

I turned to Miss Wiesenfeld in outrage.

"Surely you went to an attorney, ma'am?" I said. "I don't know divorce law all that well, but the letter may have been fraudulent. Or Mexican divorces without the consent of both parties might not have been recognized in the state in which you were married. I hope you sought legal advice?"

She looked at me, eyes rounding.

"Whatever for?" she asked in astonishment. "I wanted him gone. I wanted him dead. He hurt me."

I swallowed.

"Physically, ma'am?" I said gently.

"Once," Mrs. Livingston said in a deadly voice. "I told him he puts hands to her again, I kill him. I told him that. But that's not what she means when she says he hurt her. He broke my honey's heart."

She was speaking of her mistress as if she was not present. But Miss Wiesenfeld did not object. She just kept smiling emptily, face untroubled, eyes staring into the middle distance.

"Oh la!" she said. "Broke poor Sylvia's heart."

I was not certain of the depth of her dementia. She seemed to flick in and out, sometimes in the same sentence. She was lucid in speech and controlled in manner, and then suddenly she was gone, flying.

"Ma'am," I said, hating myself, "what did Godfrey Knurr do with your money? When you were married?"

"Ohh," she said, "bought things. Pretty things."

Mrs. Livingston leaned toward me.

"Women," she said throatily. "High living. He just pissed it away."

That "pissed" shocked me. It was hissed with such venom that I thought Godfrey Knurr fortunate to have escaped the vengeance of Mrs. Harriet Lee Livingston. She would have massacred him.

"Harriet," Sylvia said in a petulant, spoiled child's voice, "I want to get up again."

"Sure, honey," the housekeeper said equably, lurching to her feet. She helped her mistress stand. Miss Wiesenfeld dragged her leg back to the birdcage.

"Chickie?" she said. "Chirp for me?"

There were other questions I wanted to ask. I wanted to probe deeper, explore the relationship between Sylvia and Knurr, discover how the marriage had come about, when, and why it had dissolved. But I simply didn't have the stomach for it.

It seemed to me that all day I had been poking through the human detritus Godfrey Knurr had left in his wake. I was certain Roscoe Dollworth would have persevered in this investigation, but I lacked the ruthlessness. He had told me never to let my personal feelings interfere with the job, but I couldn't help it. I *liked* all these victims, shared their misery, their sad memories, and

I had heard just about all I could endure. Probing old wounds was not, really, a noble calling.

When I departed from the living room, Sylvia Wiesenfeld was still at the birdcage. Her forefinger was reaching through the bars. "Chickie?" she was saying. "Dear, sweet Chickie, sing me a song."

I didn't even thank her or say goodbye.

Out in the hallway, Mrs. Livingston helped me on with my coat.

"You going to mash him?" she demanded.

I stared at her a moment.

"Will you help?" I asked.

"Any way I can."

"I need that marriage license," I said. "And the letter from the Mexican lawyer, if you can find it. But the marriage license is most important. I'll try to get copies made this afternoon and bring the originals back to you. If I can't get copies made, I want to take the originals to New York with me. I'll return them; I swear it."

"How do I know?" she said mistrustfully.

"I'll give you money," I said. "I'll leave fifty dollars with you. When I return the license, you return the money."

"Money don't mean nothing," she said. "You got a pawn that means something to you?"

I looked down at myself.

"My wristwatch!" I said. "My aunt and uncle gave it to me when I was graduated from school. It means a lot to me. But it's a cheap watch. Not worth even fifty dollars."

"I'll take it," she said. "You bring the marriage license back, or mail it back, and you gets your watch back."

I agreed eagerly and slipped the expansion band off my wrist. She dropped the watch into one of her capacious pockets.

"You wait right here," she commanded. "Don't move a step."

"I won't," I said, and I didn't as I watched her climb the carpeted steps to the second floor. That was really a leviathan behind.

She came stepping down in a few minutes, carrying two folded documents. I took a quick look at them. A marriage license issued to Sylvia Wiesenfeld and Godfrey Knurr by the State of Indiana, dated February 6, 1959, and a letter from a Mexican attorney dated fourteen months later, informing Sylvia that a divorce had been granted to Knurr. I refolded both documents, slid them into my inside jacket pocket.

"You'll get them back," I promised once more.

"I got your watch," she said, and then grinned again at me: that marvelous, warm, human smile of complicity.

"Thank you for all your help," I said.

"I don't know why," she said, "but I trusts you. You play me false, don't never come back here again—I tear you apart."

• • •

ON THE EARLY evening New York–bound airliner, a Scotch-and-water in my hand, I relaxed gratefully. The seats on both sides of me were empty, and I could sprawl in comfort. I emulated the passenger across the aisle and removed my shoes. I wiggled my stockinged toes, a pleasurable sensation at 33,000 feet, and planned the defeat of Godfrey Knurr.

It seemed to me that our original assessment of the situation had been correct; in the absence of adequate physical evidence the only hope of bringing the Kipper and Stonehouse cases to satisfactory solutions was to take advantage of the individual weaknesses of the guilty participants. If we had failed so far in trying to "run a game" on them, it was because we did not have sufficient leverage to stir them, set one against the other, find the weakest link and twist that until it snapped.

By the time we started our descent for LaGuardia Airport in New York, I thought I had worked out a way in which it might be done. It would be a gamble, but not as dangerous as the risks Godfrey Knurr had run.

Also, it would require that I mislead several people, including Detective Percy Stilton.

I was sorry for that, but consoled myself by recalling that at our first meeting he had given me valuable tips on how to be a successful liar. Surely he could not object if I followed his advice.

I arrived home at my apartment in Chelsea shortly after 11:00 P.M. It looked good to me. I was desperately hungry, and longing for a hot shower. But first I wanted to contact Percy Stilton while my resolve was still hot. I had rehearsed my role shamelessly, and knew I must be definite, optimistic, enthusiastic. I must convince him, since as an officer of the law he could add the weight of his position to trickery that would surely flounder if I tried it by myself.

I called his office, but they told me he was not on duty. I then called his home. No answer. Finally I dialed the number of Maybelle Hawks's apartment. She answered:

"Hello?"

"Miss Hawks?"

"Yes. Who is this?"

"Joshua Bigg."

A short pause, then:

"Josh! So good to hear from you. How are you, babe?"

"Very well, thank you. And you?"

"Full of beans," she said. "Literally. We just finished a pot of chili. Perce said you went to Chicago. You calling from there?"

"No, I'm back in New York. Miss Hawks. I—"

"Belle," she said.

"Belle, I apologize for calling at this hour, but I'm trying to locate Percy. Is he—"

"Sure," she said breezily, "his majesty is here. You got something to tell him about those cases?"

"I certainly do," I said heartily.

"I'll put him on," she said. "Mind if I listen on the extension?"

"Not at all," I said. "It's good news."

"Great," she said. "Just a minute . . ."

There was a banging of phones, voices in the background, then Stilton came on the line.

"Josh?" he said. "How you doing?"

"Just fine. Sorry to disturb you."

"I'm glad you did. Lousy dinner. Dull broad."

"Up yours," Maybelle Hawks said on the extension.

"Got some good news for you, Josh. They reopened the Kipper case. Your bosses swung some heavy clout."

"Good," I said happily. "Glad to hear it. Now listen to what I've got . . ."

I kept my report as short and succinct as I could. I told him Goldie Knurr really was Godfrey's sister. I gave a brief account of my meeting with Jesse Karp and what he had told me of the boyhood of Godfrey Knurr. I went into more detail in describing the interviews with the Reverend Ludwig Stokes and Sylvia Wiesenfeld. I told Stilton I had returned with the original marriage license. I did not mention the letter from the Mexican attorney.

They didn't interrupt my report, except once when I was describing Knurr's physical abuse of Sylvia Wiesenfeld, which I exaggerated. Maybelle Hawks broke in with a furious "That bastard!"

When I finished, I waited for Stilton's questions. They came rapidly.

"Let's take it from the top," he said. "This priest—he's how old?"

"About seventy-five. Around there."

"And Knurr has been blackmailing him for twenty-five years?"

"About."

"Why didn't he blow the whistle before this?"

"Personal shame. And what it would do to his church."

"What did Knurr take him for?"

"I don't know the exact dollar amount. A lot of money. Plus getting Knurr into the seminary. And performing the marriage ceremony, probably without the bride's father's knowledge."

"And you say this Stokes is willing to bring charges now?"

"He says so. He says he's an old man and wants to make his peace with God."

"Uh-huh. What kind of a guy is he? Got all his marbles?"

"Oh yes," I said, and found myself crossing my fingers, a childish gesture. "He's a dignified old gentleman, very scholarly, who lives alone and has plenty of time to think about his past life. He says he wants to atone for his sins."

"He may get a chance. All right, now about the wife . . . The marriage license is legit?"

"Absolutely."

"No record of a divorce, legal separation—nothing like that?"

"She says no. She's living on a trust fund her father left her. After the way Knurr treated her, she was glad to get rid of him and assume her maiden name."

"He deserted her?"

"Right," I said definitely. "She was happy to find out where he is. I don't think it would take much to convince her to bring charges. The reasons are economic. That trust fund that seemed like a lot of money twenty years ago doesn't amount to much now. She's hurting."

"And what kind of a woman is she? A whacko?"

"Oh no," I protested. "A very mature, intelligent woman."

There was silence awhile. Then Detective Stilton said: "What we've got are two out-of-state possibles. Charges would have to be brought in Indiana, then we have extradition. If that goes through, we've lost him on the homicides."

"Correct," I agreed. "The blackmail and desertion charges are just small ammunition. But the big guns are that marriage license—and his affair with Glynis Stonehouse."

He knew at once what I meant.

"You want to brace Tippi Kipper?" he said.

"That's right, Perce. Be absolutely honest with her. Lay out all we've got. Show her the marriage license. I think she'll make a deal."

"Mmm," he said. "Maybe. Belle, what do you think? Will it work?"

"A good chance," she said on the extension. "I'll bet my left tit he never told her he was married. A guy like him wouldn't be that stupid. And when you tell her about Glynis Stonehouse, it'll just confirm what she read in that poison-pen letter Josh sent her. She'll be burning. He played her for a sucker. She's a woman who's been around the block twice. Her ego's not going to let him make her a patsy. I'm betting she'll pull the rug on him."

"Yeah," Stilton said slowly. "And we can always try the publicity angle on her, just happen to mention we know about her prostitution arrest. She's a grand lady now; she'd die if that got in the papers."

"Let's go after her," I urged. "Really twist."

He made up his mind.

"Right," he said, "we'll do it. Go in early before she's had a chance to put herself together. Josh, I'll meet you outside the Kipper place at nine o'clock tomorrow morning. Got that? Bring all the paper, especially that marriage license."

"I'll be there," I promised.

"We'll break her," he said, beginning to get excited by the prospect. "No rough stuff. Kid gloves. Very sincere and low-key. Treat a whore like a lady and a lady like a whore. Who said that, Josh?"

"I'm not sure. It sounds like Lord Chesterfield."

"Whoever," he said.

"If you believe that, Perce," Maybelle Hawks said, "it makes me a lady."

We all laughed, talked for a moment of how we should dress for our confrontation with Tippi Kipper, and then said goodnight.

I went immediately to my kitchen and began to eat ravenously. I cleaned out the refrigerator. I had three fried eggs, a sardine and onion sandwich, almost a quart of milk, a pint of chocolate ice cream. Then, still hungry, I heated up a can of noodle soup and had that with two vanilla cupcakes and half a cucumber.

Belching, I undressed and went into the shower. The water was blessedly hot. I soaped and rinsed three times, washed my hair, shaved, and doused myself with cologne.

Groaning with contentment, I rolled into bed about 1:00 A.M. It may have been my excitement, or perhaps that sardine and onion sandwich, but I did not fall asleep immediately. I lay on my back, thinking of what we would do in the morning, what we would say to Tippi Kipper, how important it was that we should break her.

I did not pray to God because, although I am a religious man, I did not much believe in prayer. What was the point—since God must know what is in our hearts? But I felt my lies and low cunning would be pardoned if they succeeded in bringing down Godfrey Knurr.

He was an abomination. As Jesse Karp had said, Knurr went bulling his way through life, all shoulders and elbows. He just didn't *care;* that was what I could not forgive. He exemplified brute force and brute morality. I felt no guilt for what I was trying to do to him.

Just before I fell asleep, I remembered Cleo Hufnagel. I realized, groaning, that she had been out of my thoughts for days. I felt guilt about *that.*

7

•

ON SATURDAY, THE MARCH SKY WAS HARD, AN ICY BLUE WHITened by a blurry sun, and in the west a faded wedge of morning moon. Not a cloud. But an angry wind came steadily and swirled the streets.

I took a cab uptown and marveled at how sharp the city looked, chopped out, everything standing clear. The air was washed clean, and pierced.

I was wearing my good pinstripe suit, vested, with a white shirt and dull tie. Stilton and I had agreed to dress like undertakers: conservative, solemn, but sympathetic. Men to be trusted.

A dusty-blue Plymouth was parked in front of the Kipper townhouse. Behind the wheel was a carelessly dressed giant of a man with a scraggly blond mustache that covered his mouth. Percy sat beside him, looking like a judge. He motioned me into the backseat. I climbed in, closed the door. I held my scruffy briefcase on my lap.

"Josh," Perce said, "this slob is Lou, my partner."

"Good morning, Lou," I said.

"Got all the paper?" Stilton asked.

"Everything," I said, feeling slightly ill.

"Good," he said. "When we get inside, let me do the spiel. You follow my lead. Just nod. You're the shill. Got that?"

"I understand."

"Act sincere," he said. "You can act sincere, can't you?"

"Of course," I said in a low voice.

"Sure you can," he said. I knew he was trying to encourage me and I appreciated it. "Don't worry, Josh, this is going down. This is going to be the greatest hustle known to living man. A classic."

Lou spoke for the first time.

"The world is composed of five elements," he stated. "Earth, air, fire, water, and bullshit."

"You're singing our song, baby," Percy told him. "Okay, Josh, let's *do* it."

Chester Heavens came to the door.

"Gentlemen?" he said somberly.

"Good morning, Chester," I mumbled.

"Morning," Percy said briskly. "I am Detective Percy Stilton of the New

York Police Department. I believe we've met before. Here is my identification."

He flipped open his leather, held it up. Heavens peered at it.

"Yes, sah," he said. "I remember. How may I be of service?"

"It's important we see Mrs. Kipper," Stilton said. "As soon as possible. She's home?"

Chester hesitated a moment, then surrendered.

"Please to step in," he said. "I'll speak with mom."

We waited in that towering entrance hall. Heavens had disappeared into the dining room and closed the door. We waited for what I thought was a long time. I fidgeted, but Stilton stood stolidly. Finally Chester returned.

"Mom will see you now," he said, expressionless. "She is at breakfast. May I take your things?"

He took our coats and hats, hung them away. He opened the door to the dining room, stood aside. Percy entered first. As I was about to go in, Chester put a soft hand on my arm.

"Bad, sah?" he whispered.

I nodded.

He nodded, too. Sorrowfully.

She was seated at the head of that long, shining table. Regal. Wearing a flowing, lettuce-green peignoir. But her hair was down and not too tidy. Moreover, as I drew closer, I saw her face was slightly distorted, puffy. Staring, I saw that the left cheek from eye to chin was swollen, discolored. She had attempted to cover the bruise with pancake makeup, but it was there.

Then I understood Godfrey Knurr's smarmy comment: "I think I persuaded the lady."

Stilton and I stood side by side. She stared at us, unblinking. She did not ask us to sit down.

"Ma'am," Percy said humbly, "I am Detective—"

"I know who you are," she said sharply. "We've met. What do you want?"

"I am engaged in an official investigation of the Reverend Godfrey Knurr," Stilton said, still apologetic. "I hoped you would be willing to cooperate with the New York Police Department and furnish what information you can."

She turned her eyes to me.

"And what are you doing here?" she demanded.

"Mr. Bigg asked to come along, ma'am," Percy said swiftly. "The request for an investigation originated with his legal firm."

She thought about that. She didn't quite believe, but she didn't *not* believe. She wanted to learn more.

"Sit down, then," she said coldly. "Both of you. Coffee?"

"Not for me," Perce said, "thank you, Mrs. Kipper. You, Mr. Bigg?"

"Thank you, no," I said.

We drew up chairs, Stilton on her right, me on her left. We had her surrounded, hemmed in. I don't think she expected that.

She shook a cigarette from an almost empty pack. Stilton was there with his lighter before I could make a move. I think his courtesy reassured her. She blew smoke at the ceiling.

"Well," she said, "what's this all about?"

"Ma'am," Stilton said, hunching forward earnestly, "it's a rather involved story, so I hope you'll bear with me. About two weeks ago the NYPD received a request from the police department of Gary, Indiana, asking us to determine if the Reverend Godfrey Knurr was in our area. A warrant had been issued for his arrest. Two warrants, actually."

"Arrest?" she cried. "What for?"

"One was for blackmail, Mrs. Kipper. Allegedly, for a period of many years, Knurr has been blackmailing an elderly clergyman in the neighborhood where he grew up. The other warrant was for desertion."

We were both watching closely. She may have been an actress, but she couldn't conceal her reaction to that. The hand that held the cigarette began to quiver; she put her wrist on the table to steady it. Her face paled; the bruise stood out, a nasty blue. She leaned forward to pour herself more coffee.

Maybelle Hawks had been right; she hadn't known.

"Desertion?" she asked casually, and I noted that the charge of blackmail hadn't stirred her at all.

"Oh yes," Detective Stilton said. "Knurr was married about twenty years ago and has never been divorced or legally separated. Mr. Bigg, do you have the license?"

I plucked it from my briefcase and held it up before Tippi Kipper, making certain it did not leave my hands. She leaned forward to read it.

"Yes," she said dully, "I see."

Percy leaned back in his chair and folded his hands comfortably on the tabletop.

"Well," he said, "the request from the Gary, Indiana, police was circulated, and a copy came across my desk. Ordinarily I would just file it and forget it. I'm sure you appreciate how busy we are, ma'am, and how an out-of-state request gets a very low priority on our schedule. You can understand that, Mrs. Kipper?"

I admired the way he was taking her into his confidence—even confessing a little weakness with a small chuckle.

"Oh sure," she said, still stunned. "I can understand that."

"But the name caught my eye," Detective Stilton went on. "Only because I had interviewed Godfrey Knurr in connection with your husband's unfortunate death. So I knew who he was and where I could find him."

She didn't say anything. She was pulling herself together, sipping her coffee and lighting another cigarette. Fussing. Doing anything to keep from looking at us.

"Then," Stilton continued, speaking gently and almost reflectively, "before we had a chance to reply to the request from the Gary police, Mr. Bigg came to us, representing the attorneys he works for. They wanted us to dig deeper into the case of a missing client of theirs. A Professor Yale Stonehouse. He had disappeared under mysterious circumstances. Well, we looked into it and discovered that prior to his disappearance he had been the victim of arsenic poisoning. Mr. Bigg?"

I whipped out the chemical analyses and held them up before her eyes. I don't think she even read them, but she was impressed. They were official documents. I began to appreciate Detective Stilton's insistence on such evidence. They could be true or false, but printed foolscap carried weight.

"So," Percy went on, sighing, "we dug deeper and discovered that the poison had apparently been administered by Glynis Stonehouse, the daughter of the missing man. In addition, we found out that Glynis has been having an affair, is still having an affair, with the Reverend Godfrey Knurr. We do not know for sure, but we suspect that Professor Stonehouse has been murdered and that Knurr is deeply involved. So we are here, Mrs. Kipper, to ask you to help by telling us what you can about this man. He's already charged with blackmail and wife desertion. It's only a matter of time before we can bring a first-degree homicide charge against him."

For a moment I thought we had her. She stood up, circled her chair, started to sit down again. Then she stalked off to a far corner of the room, twisting her hands. We watched her. She stood, facing a blank wall, then turned and came back. The air vibrated; you could feel it.

I had to admire her. She had been rocked, there was no doubt of that, but she rallied. I thought of the word "spunk."

She sat down again, carelessly this time, sprawled. No longer the queen. She dug a last cigarette from the crumpled pack. Percy Stilton was there with his lighter. She inhaled deeply, let the smoke escape lazily from her nostrils.

The silver-blond hair was damp and tangled. The profile had lost its crispness; the bruise bulged an entire side of her face. The eyes seemed muddy, the thin lips were tightened and drawn. The chin she once carried so high had come down; there was soil in the wrinkles of her neck. Her body had slackened; the breasts sagged under the peignoir, the thighs had flattened.

Is it possible to suffer from an excess of sympathy? At that moment I felt sorry for her. She was being buffeted cruelly, but was far from surrender.

"This is very, uh, distressing," she said finally.

"I can imagine," Detective Stilton said.

I nodded madly.

We stared at her, silent again.

"All right," she burst out, "the man was a—a—"

"Close friend of yours?" Percy suggested.

"Not exactly," she said quickly, already cutting her losses. "More like a— a—"

"Spiritual adviser?" I said innocently.

She looked at me sharply.

"Yeah," she said, "spiritual adviser. For a few years. All right—bad news. Now he turns out to be a bummer. He's wanted. But what's it got to do with me?"

The use of the slang—the "yeah" and the "bummer"—was the first indication I had that she was slipping back to her origins. The grand lady was fading.

Stilton, the gentleman, still treated her with soft politesse, leaning toward her with a manner of great solicitude.

"Let me tell you what we've got, Mrs. Kipper," he said. "Warrants have been issued for Knurr's arrest and the arrest of his paramour, Glynis Stonehouse. In addition, we have search warrants for her home, his home, and his houseboat. Sooner or later we're going to pick him up."

"So?" she said. "Pick him up. It's got nothing to do with me."

Percy sat back, crossed his knees, selected a cigarette from his case and lighted it with slow deliberation.

"I think it does," he said, looking at her steadily. "I think it has a great deal to do with you. In addition to the out-of-state charges and complicity in the disappearance of Professor Stonehouse, the Reverend Godfrey Knurr will also be charged with the murder of Martin Reape."

"Who?" she croaked. "Never heard of him."

"No?" Stilton said. "Your late husband employed him." He motioned toward me. "Mr. Bigg, the canceled checks, please."

I dug into my briefcase, came up with copies of Martin Reape's bills and the canceled checks. I showed them to her. She looked at them with smoky eyes.

"Martin Reape was a private detective," Stilton went on inexorably. "He was pushed to his death beneath the wheels of a subway train. We have the testimony of two eyewitnesses placing the Reverend Godfrey Knurr at the scene of the homicide at the time it occurred. Reape's widow was also murdered. We have evidence proving Knurr's complicity in that homicide as well."

He lied so skillfully I could hardly believe it. His lies were "throwaway" lines, spoken casually, as unemphasized as if he had mentioned "Chilly out today." They were absolutely believable. He was stating falsehoods and giving them no importance. He was saying, "These things exist; everyone knows it."

Tippi Kipper had gone rigid. She was motionless. Frozen. I think that if I had flicked her flesh, it would have pinged. She was in an almost catatonic state. Every time she had adjusted to a blow, thought she had countered it, Stilton had jolted her again. He kept after her, feeding her confusion.

"So," he said, "on the basis of this and other evidence, the investigation into the circumstances of your husband's death has been reopened, Mrs. Kipper. If you doubt that, I suggest you call the New York Police Department and verify what I am saying. We now believe your husband was murdered.''

"Murdered?" she cried. "Impossible! He left a suicide note."

Detective Stilton held out a hand. I gave him the notes I had taken from Tippi Kipper's dressing room. Percy held them up before her.

"Like these?" he asked stonily.

She glanced at them. Her face fell apart.

"Where did you get those?" she yelled.

"I, uh, obtained them," I said.

She whirled and glared at me.

"You little prick!" she said.

I bowed my head.

"As I said," Percy went on relentlessly, "the investigation into your husband's murder has been reopened. We know how it was done: Knurr staying in an empty room overnight, going upstairs, killing the victim, running downstairs, going out the door only to turn around and ring the bell, coming right back in again while all of you were at the body in the backyard."

"Ridiculous," she said. "You'll never prove it."

"Oh, I think we will," Stilton said. "We've filed for a search warrant for these premises. On the basis of what we've got, I think it will be granted. We'll come in here and tear the place apart. The lab boys will vacuum every inch. They'll find evidence of Godfrey Knurr spending the night in an upstairs room. Dust from his shoes, a partial fingerprint, a thread or crumbs of his pipe tobacco, maybe the weapon he used. Maybe just a hair or two. It's impossible for a man to sleep somewhere overnight without leaving some evidence of his presence. And we'll confiscate that house diary the butler keeps. It shows Godfrey Knurr arrived the afternoon before the day your husband was killed, with no record of his departure. Oh yes, I think we have enough for an indictment, Mrs. Kipper. Godfrey Knurr for homicide and you as accomplice. Both of you are going down the tube."

She made gulping sounds. Stilton continued lecturing.

"And even if we can't make it stick," he said tonelessly, "there's the publicity. Tabloids, radio, TV. The fashionable Mrs. Tippi Kipper, active in social and charitable affairs, with a prior arrest record for prostitution."

I could barely hear. Her head was down. But she was saying, "Bastard, bastard, bastard . . ."

Percy Stilton looked around. He spotted the handsome, marble-topped sideboard with a display of crystal decanters. He went over, inspected the offerings, selected a captain's decanter bearing a porcelain label: BRANDY. He brought it back to the dining room table, poured a healthy wallop into the dregs of Tippi Kipper's coffee cup.

"Drink up," he ordered.

She drained it, holding the cup with trembling hands. He poured in another shot, set the bottle on the table close to her. She dug, fumbling, into her empty cigarette pack. Percy offered his case, then held his lighter for her again. He didn't look at me. There was no triumph in his manner.

"Mrs. Kipper," he said, "I've been as honest with you as I know how. As of this moment there is no warrant out for *your* arrest. But I think it's time we talked about you, your legal position, and your future."

"Now comes the crunch," she said bitterly.

"Correct," he said equably. "Now comes the crunch. We're going to pick up Godfrey Knurr; you know that. We're going to lean on him. Do you really think he's going to remain steadfast and true? Come on, Mrs. Kipper, you know better than that. He's going to sing his rotten little heart out. Before he's through, the whole thing will be *your* idea. *You* seduced him, *you* planned the murder of your husband; he was just the innocent bystander. You *know* that's how he's going to play it. That's the kind of man he is."

She rose abruptly, scraping her chair back on the polished parquet floor. She stood leaning forward, knuckles on the table: a chairman of the board addressing a meeting of hostile executives. But she was not looking at us. She was staring between us, down the length of that gleaming table, the translucent china, the silver candelabrum. Wealth. Gentility. Security.

"The first one in line makes the best deal," Detective Percy Stilton said softly.

Her eyes came back to him slowly.

"Talk business," she said harshly.

We had her then, I knew, but Perce didn't change expression or vary his polite, solicitous manner.

"This is how I suggest it be done," he said. "We didn't come to you; you came to us. You called Mr. Bigg at the law firm that represented your late husband, and Mr. Bigg then contacted me. But you made the initial move. You volunteered. Mr. Bigg and I will so testify."

He looked at me. I nodded violently.

"What was my motive for calling in the cops?" she asked.

"You wanted to see justice done," Stilton said.

She shook her head. "It won't wash," she said.

"Duress," I said. "Physical assault. Knurr threatened you. So you went along with his plan. But now you're afraid for your life."

Percy looked at me admiringly.

"Yeah," Tippi Kipper said, "that's just how it was. He said he'd kill me if I didn't go along. I'll take off my makeup and you can get a color picture of this." She pointed at the puffy bruise on her cheek. "He punched me out," she said furiously. "He has a wicked temper, and that's the truth. I was afraid for my life."

"Beautiful," Percy said. "It fits."

"You think the DA will believe it?" she asked anxiously.

Stilton leaned back, crossed his knees again, lighted another cigarette.

"Of course not," he said. "he's no dummy. But he'll go along. You're going to be his star witness, clearing up three homicides and probably four. So he'll play ball. We're giving him *something*."

"What do you think I'll draw?" she asked him.

"*Bupkes*," he said. "Time suspended and probation. You'll walk."

"And the prostitution arrest?" she demanded.

"Buried," Stilton said. "Nothing to the press. You have my word on that."

She took a deep breath, looked around that lovely room as if she might never see it again.

"Well . . ." she said, "I guess we better get the show on the road. Can I get dressed?"

"Of course," Percy said, "but I'll have to go upstairs with you. I hope you understand."

We all moved out into the entrance hall. Chester Heavens, Perdita Schug, and Mrs. Neckin were gathered in a tight little group in the corridor to the kitchen. They watched, shocked, as their mistress and the detective entered the elevator. I retrieved my hat and coat and left hurriedly. I didn't want to answer their questions.

Lou, behind the wheel of the blue Plymouth, saw me coming. He leaned across to the passenger's side and rolled down the window.

"How'd it go?" he asked.

"Fine," I said. "They'll be coming out soon."

"Is she going to spill?"

I nodded.

"It figures," he said. "That Perce, he's something. I'm glad we're on the same side. If he was on the wrong, he'd end up owning the city."

Then we waited in silence. I didn't want to get into the car. I wanted to look at that pure sky, breathe deeply in the sharp, tangy air. I didn't want to think about what had just happened. I wanted to savor the wide, wide world.

They came out in about fifteen minutes. Tippi Kipper was wearing a belted mink coat that seemed to go around her three times. She was hatless, carrying an oversized black alligator purse. She had removed her makeup. The bruise was hideous. Percy Stilton was carrying a small overnight case of buttery pigskin.

He opened the back door of the Plymouth for her. She climbed in without looking at me. Perce put the little suitcase in the front seat. Then he took me by the elbow, led me aside.

"End of the line for you, Josh," he said.

"Can't I—" I started, but he shook his head regretfully and interrupted.

"It's all official from now on," he said. "I'll call you as soon as we get something. Where will you be?"

"Either at the office or home. Perce, promise you'll call."

"Absolutely," he vowed. "I'll keep you up on things. You deserve all the credit."

"Thank you," I said faintly.

He looked at me narrowly.

"They were divorced, weren't they?" he said. "Knurr and that Sylvia? And she and the old priest are a couple of whackos. Am I right?"

I nodded miserably.

He laughed and clapped me on the shoulder.

"You're good," he said, "but not *that* good. Never try to scam a scammer."

I watched the Plymouth pull away. Stilton sitting next to Tippi Kipper in the backseat. When the car had turned the corner and disappeared, I walked over to Fifth Avenue and headed south. I decided to walk down to the TORT building.

I should have been exultant but I wasn't. It was the morality of what I had done that was bothering me. All that chicanery and deceit. I would have committed almost any sin to demolish Godfrey Knurr, but conniving in the escape of Tippi Kipper from justice was more than I had bargained for. And I *had* connived. I had worked almost as hard as Percy Stilton to convince her to betray Knurr. It had to be done. But as Perce had said, she was going to walk. An accomplice to murder. Was that fair? Was that justice?

I realized I didn't really know what "justice" meant. It was not an absolute. It was not a color, a mineral, a species. It was a human concept (what do animals know of justice?) and subject to all the vagaries and contradictions of any human hope. How can you define justice? It seemed to me that it was constant compromise, molded by circumstance.

I would make a terrible judge.

The brisk walk downtown refreshed my spirits. The sharp air and exercise were cleansing. By the time I signed in with the security guard at the TORT building, I had come to terms with what I had done. I was still regretful, but guilt was fading. I reckoned that if all went well, in a few weeks I would be proud of my role in bringing the Reverend Godfrey Knurr to justice—whatever that was.

Mrs. Gertrude Kletz had left me a sheaf of notes and a stack of requests for investigations and research. I set to work with pleasure, resolutely turning my mind from the Kipper and Stonehouse cases and concentrating on my desk work.

I labored all afternoon with no breaks except to rise occasionally to stretch, walk into the corridor to loosen my knees. I accomplished a great deal, clearing my desk of most of the routine matters and making a neat list of those that would require personal investigation.

Shortly before 5:00 P.M., after trying to resist the urge, I called Percy Stilton's office. I was told he was "in conference" and could not come to the phone, so I assumed the interrogation of Tippi Kipper was continuing.

I put away the Kipper and Stonehouse files, emptying my cruddy briefcase. I considered buying a new one. Perhaps an attaché case, slender and smart.

But that battered briefcase had been left to me by Roscoe Dollworth and I was superstitious enough to believe it had magical properties: good luck and wisdom.

I left the TORT building at about 5:50, remembering to take with me the wrapped red kite, string, and winder. I signed out, walked over to Broadway and took a bus down to West 23rd Street. I went directly to Woody's Restaurant, trying to recall how long it had been since I had enjoyed a decent dinner.

As usual, Nitchy was on duty, looking especially attractive in her exotic, gypsy way. I told her so and she tapped her fingers against my cheek.

"No princess tonight, Josh?" she asked.

"Not tonight," I said, smiling tiredly.

I think she caught my mood, because she ushered me to a small table in a quiet corner and left me alone. I had two Scotch-and-waters, a club steak, baked potato, string beans, salad, a bottle of beer, coffee and brandy.

When I left, I was subdued, thoughtful, content. I carried the kite back to my apartment and settled in to wait. I tried to read but ended up with a copy of *Silas Marner* on my lap, staring into the cold fireplace and trying to make sense of everything that had happened in the last month.

I came to no great conclusions, was subject to no great revelations. I tried to understand what motives, what passions, might drive apparently sane men and women to commit the act of murder. I could not comprehend it, and feared the fault was mine: I was not emotional enough, not *feeling* enough to grasp how others of hotter blood, of stronger desires, might be driven to kill.

I was a mild little man, temperate, reflective. Nothing in my life was dramatic except what was contributed by others. It seemed incredible that I could survive in a world of such fiery wants and insatiable appetites.

When the phone rang at about 8:20, I did not leap to answer it, but moved slowly, calmly. I think I may have been dreading what I expected to hear.

"Josh?" Stilton's voice.

"Yes."

"Percy. She spilled. Everything. It went down the way you figured. She doesn't know exactly how he did it—a karate chop or a hunk of pipe. She didn't ask. She didn't want to know. Ditto Martin Reape and his wife. Knurr just told her not to worry, he'd take care of everything."

"And he did," I said.

"Yes," Perce said. "Jesus, I'm tired. Anyway, we're organized now. There's a team up at the Stonehouse apartment, looking for the will. Another at Knurr's place in the Village. And another staked out at his houseboat. We're also going into the Kipper townhouse. I don't think they'll find anything there, but you never can tell."

"No hairs?" I said. "Dust? Crumbs of tobacco?"

"Come on," Stilton said, laughing. "You know that was all bullshit."

"Yes," I said.

"Anyway, we've got a fistful of warrants. Lou and I are going up to the houseboat. Want to drag along?"

I came alive.

"I certainly do," I said.

"Pick you up at your place," Percy said. "Josh, do us a favor?"

"Of course. Anything."

"We're starved. Get us some sandwiches, will you? And maybe a six-pack?"

"That's easy," I said. "What kind of sandwiches?"

"Anything. We'll pay you."

"Nonsense. This will be on Tabatchnick, Orsini, Reilly, and Teitelbaum."

"You're sure?"

"Absolutely."

"We'll be outside your place in half an hour."

I had secured the sandwiches and was waiting on the sidewalk when the dusty-blue Plymouth pulled up, Lou driving. I climbed into the backseat. I handed the brown paper bag to Stilton, up front.

"I got them at a deli on Tenth Avenue," I said. "Roast beef on white with mayonnaise, and bologna on rye with mustard. Two of each. And a cold six-pack of Miller's. Is that all right?"

"Plasma," Lou groaned. "Plasma!"

They dived into the bag and ripped tabs from the beer cans. Percy turned sideways, talking to me as he ate.

"We got the Stonehouse will," he said. "They're going through Glynis's personal stuff now. She wasn't there. Her mother says she went to a matinee this afternoon. She's probably with Knurr. No sign of the two of them yet. If we haven't picked them up by midnight, we'll put out an all-precincts, then gradually expand it if needed."

"They're searching Knurr's social club on Carmine Street?" I asked.

"Oh sure," Stilton said. "Found a lot of official records. He was doing all right. How does half a mil grab you?"

"Incredible," I said.

"Ah well," Lou mumbled, starting another half-sandwich, "he was a hard worker."

"What about Chester Heavens's house diary?"

"Got it," Percy said. "Also Tippi's collection of notes her husband wrote her. Josh, the DA will want all the paper you're holding. Monday morning will be time enough."

"Does Tippi have legal counsel?"

"She does now," he said. "Not from your firm. Some hotshot criminal lawyer. He and the DA's man are kicking it around right now, sewing up the deal. Lots of screaming."

"Do you really think she'll go free?"

"Probably," he said without interest. Then he looked at me closely. "Josh, it happens all the time. You give a little, take a little. That's how the system works."

They finished the sandwiches and four of the beers.

"Dee-licious," Lou said, scrubbing his mustache with a paper napkin. "Now I'm ready for a fight or a frolic. Thanks, pal."

"We're going up to the boat basin," Stilton told me. "We've got a search warrant for the houseboat. There's a car with two men on Riverside Drive at 79th Street and one guy on the dock. The three of us are going into the boat. We'll be in touch with the others by walkie-talkie in case Knurr shows up. If the radios work."

"They won't," Lou said casually. "Let's go."

We drove north on Tenth Avenue, into Amsterdam, and turned west on 79th Street. The two detectives talked baseball for most of the trip. I didn't contribute anything.

We parked in a bus-loading zone near West End Avenue. We got out of the car, Percy and Lou taking their radios in leather cases. They didn't look around for the stakeout car. We walked across the park, down a dirt path. We came to the paved area and the rotunda.

It was a ghostly place, deserted at that hour. I thought again of an archaeological dig: chipped columns, dried and cracking foundation, shadowed corridor leading to the murky river. It was all so broken and crumbling. Ancient graffiti. Splits in the stone. A world coming apart.

We walked down the steps to the promenade by the river. A few late-hour joggers, pairs of lovers tightly wrapped, solitary gays on benches, an older man frisking with his fox terrier, several roller skaters doing arabesques, a few cyclists. Not crowded, but not empty either.

Stilton rattled the gate, calling, and when the marina manager came out from his shed to meet us, Percy and Lou showed their identification. Stilton held up the search warrant for the man to read through the fence. He let us in, pointing out Godfrey Knurr's houseboat south of the entrance.

We paced cautiously down planked walkways floating on pontoons. They pitched gently under our tread.

"You said you've got a man on the dock?" I asked anxiously.

The detectives laughed.

"The guy with the dog," Lou said.

"Al Irving," Stilton said. "He always takes his mutt along on a stakeout. Who's going to figure a guy with a dog is a cop? That hound's got the best assist record in the Department."

We stepped down from the wharf onto the foredeck of Knurr's long fiberglass houseboat. There was a thick cable leading to an electric meter on the dock. The sliding doors to the cabin were locked. Lou bent to examine them.

"Piece of cake," he said.

He took a leather case of picklocks from his jacket pocket. He fiddled a moment, pushed the door open. He stood aside.

"Be my guests," he said.

But I noticed he had unbuttoned his coat and jacket and his hand was on his hip holster. Percy Stilton went in first. His revolver was in his hand, dangling at his side. He found the switch and turned on the lights.

"Beautiful," he said.

And it was. We went prowling through. Chairs, tables, couches. Drapes and upholstery in cheery plaid. Plenty of headroom. Overhead lights. Tub and shower. Hot water heater. Toilet. Lockers and cabinets. Wall-to-wall carpeting. Beds, sinks. Larger than my apartment, and more luxurious. A floating home.

We searched all through the houseboat, stared at the twin engines, bilge pump, climbed to the sundeck, marveled at the forward stateroom and the instrument panel in the pilothouse. We ended up in the galley, looking at an electric range/oven and an upright refrigerator.

And a horizontal chest freezer.

It didn't look like standard equipment. It had been jammed into one corner, tight against a bulkhead and the refrigerator. The lid was secured with a cheap hasp and small padlock.

The two detectives looked at each other.

"Wanna bet?" Lou asked.

"No bet," Percy said.

Lou leaned down to examine the padlock.

"Five-and-dime," he reported. "I saw some tools in the engine room."

We waited, silent. Lou was back in a minute with a small claw bar. He hooked the curved end into the loop of the padlock and yanked upward. It popped with a screech of metal.

"Cheese," Lou said, flipping open the hasp. He gestured toward Percy. "Your treat," he said.

Stilton stepped forward and threw back the lid of the freezer.

We all craned forward. He was in there, wrapped in what appeared to be dry cleaner's bags. I could make out the lettering: THIS BAG IS NOT A TOY.

He had been jammed in, arms folded, knees drawn up. Plastic had frozen tightly around his head. I could see the face, dim and frosted. A long, sunken face, boned, gaunt, furious.

"Professor Stonehouse, I presume," Percy Stilton said, tipping his hat.

"Shut the goddamn lid," Lou said, "before he thaws."

I turned away, fighting nausea. Percy was on his walkie-talkie, trying to contact the team on Riverside Drive and the man on the dock. All he got in return was ear-ripping static.

"Shit," he said.

"I told you," Lou said. "They're great until you need them."

We were standing there discussing who would go to the nearest telephone when we heard the thump of feet on the outside deck and the houseboat rocked gently. Before I knew what was happening, the two detectives were crouched by the galley door, guns drawn.

"Josh," Stilton hissed, "*drop!*"

I went down on all fours, huddled near that dreadful freezer. Percy peered cautiously around the door frame. He smiled, rose, motioned us up.

"In here," Stilton shouted to someone outside.

Glynis Stonehouse entered slowly. She was wearing her long fur coat, the hood thrown back to rest on her shoulders. Following her came the Reverend Godfrey Knurr, dressed like a dandy: fitted topcoat, wide-collared shirt with a brocaded cravat tied in a Windsor knot, a black bowler tilted atop his head.

After them came Al Irving, grinning. He was holding his fox terrier on a leash. In his other hand was a snub-nosed revolver. The dog was growling: low, rumbling sounds.

"Look what I got," Detective Irving said. "They walked into my arms, pretty as you please. I tried to contact you. These new radios suck."

"What is the meaning of this?" Godfrey Knurr thundered.

It was such a banal, melodramatic statement that I was ashamed for him.

Percy Stilton gave him a death's-head grin and took two quick steps to the freezer. He threw back the lid.

"What is the meaning of *this?*" he demanded.

Then nobody had anything to say. We were all caught, congealed in a theatrical tableau. Staring at each other.

Only the pallor of her face marked Glynis Stonehouse's agitation. Her hands did not tremble; her glance was steady and cool. Did nothing dent her? She stood erect, aloof and withdrawn. Her father lay there, frozen in plastic, a supermarket package of meat, and she was still complete, looking at all of us with a curious disdain.

Godfrey Knurr was feeling more—or at least displaying more. His eyes flickered about, his mouth worked. Nervous fingers plucked at the buttons of his coat. His body slumped slightly until he seemed to be standing in a half-crouch, almost simian, taut and quivering.

His stare settled on me. So indignant, so furious. He looked me up and down, disbelieving that such a meek, puny creature could be responsible for his downfall. He made a sound. Like a groan. But not quite a groan. A protest. A sound that said, "It isn't fair . . ."

"Listen, Joshua," he said hoarsely, "I want you to know something . . ."

None of us moved, intent on what he was saying, waiting to hear what he wanted me to know.

"I think you—" he said, then suddenly whirled into action.

He was so fast, so *fast!*

He pivoted on his left foot, turned, clubbed down with the edge of one hand on Detective Al Irving's gun arm. We all heard the crack of bone. Knurr completed a full turn, a blur, and bulled his way past Glynis and Lou, all shoulders and elbows.

Then he was into the main cabin, running.

Stilton was the first to recover.

"Watch the woman," he yelled at Lou, and took up the chase.

I went rushing along at his heels.

Godfrey Knurr hurtled down the wharf, swerved left onto the pontooned walkway. It tilted and rocked under his pounding feet.

A young couple was approaching, chatting and laughing. He simply ran into them, through them, over them. They were flung wailing into the fetid water.

Stilton and I charged after him. I didn't know what I was doing, except that I didn't want Percy to be alone.

Knurr smashed through the gate and headed for the south staircase leading up to the rotunda. Stilton had his gun in his hand, but there were people on the promenade, strollers and cyclists. They scattered when they saw us coming, but Percy didn't want to risk a shot.

Godfrey Knurr went leaping up the steps, two at a time. I remember that his derby flew off and came bouncing down. By then we were straining up the stairs. I thought I was fast, but Percy was stronger; he was closing on Knurr and I was falling behind.

We all, the three of us, went thundering through the arched corridor, a crypt. Two pedestrians, hearing and seeing us coming, flattened themselves in terror against the stained wall.

We came into the rotunda. Knurr circled to his left, running frantically, hoping to gain the exit. His unbuttoned coat flapped out behind him.

Now Percy Stilton had a clear field of fire. He stopped, flexed his knees, grasped his massive revolver with both hands, arms extended, elbows slightly bent.

"Hold it right there!" he yelled.

Suddenly, unexpectedly, Knurr rounded the fountain basin and came racing back toward us. His hair was flying, the bearded face twisted, bright with rage.

"Hah!" he shouted, raising one hand high in a classic karate position, fingers together, the palm edge a cleaver.

"Oh for God's sake!" Percy Stilton said disgustedly, sighted carefully, and shot the Reverend Godfrey Knurr in the right leg. I saw the heavy slug pucker the trouser a few inches above the knee.

The blow spun Knurr around. He pirouetted as gracefully as a ballet dancer. His momentum and the force of the bullet kept him turning. His arms flung wide. A look of astonishment came to his contorted features.

He whirled, tilting, and fell backward over the rim of the ruined fountain.

He went down heavily. I heard the sound of his head smacking cracked cement. His legs and feet remained propped up on the basin rim. His head, shoulders, and torso were flat within.

We walked up to him cautiously, Stilton with his gun extended. Knurr was beginning to bleed, from the wound in his leg and from a head injury. He looked up at us dazedly.

"Idiot!" Stilton screamed at him. "You fucking idiot!"

Godfrey Knurr's vision cleared.

He glared at me.

I turned away, walked away, went over to one of the scarred pillars and pressed my forehead against the cold concrete.

After a moment Percy came over to me, put an arm across my shoulders.

"Josh," he said gently, "he wasn't a nice man."

"I know," I said dully. "Still . . ."

8

•

THERE WAS A PARTY AT THE HOUSE IN CHELSEA. THE LAST HAD been such a success they all wanted another.

It was a marvelous party. All the tenants were there, of course, and a boisterous bunch from the music world, Madame Zora Kadinsky's friends. Captain Bramwell Shank had invited a few cronies from his seafaring days aboard the Staten Island ferry. They were cantankerous old coots who spent most of their time at the two card tables set with food and drink.

The party was well begun, noisy with talk and laughter, when I arrived. At the last minute I had run out and bought a two-pound box of chocolate-covered cherries at the local drugstore. I presented it to Mrs. Hufnagel and got a warm kiss on my cheek in return. Madame Kadinsky insisted on introducing me to all her friends. I didn't remember any of their names, which seemed to be composed solely of consonants.

As we moved about the apartment, my eyes were searching for Cleo. After the introductions were finished, I finally saw her in the kitchen, talking to Adolph Finkel. Or rather, he was talking and she was listening, a bemused expression on her face. They both held paper cups of wine.

I observed her a few moments before I approached. She looked so *clean* to me. Physically clean, of course, but more than that. There was an innocent purity about her. She seemed untouched by violence, or even by evil. I could not conceive of her acting through malice or hate, greed or envy.

She was wearing a loose chemise of challis wool in a sort of forested print. She was without makeup; her face was clear and serene. How could I ever have thought her plain? She was beautiful! That high, noble brow; the lovely hazel eyes; a dream of a nose; lips delicately sculpted. Her teeth were not large and prominent at all; they were jewels, sparkling. The chestnut hair fell free, gleaming. And when I remembered that elegantly slender body, now hidden within the billowing chemise, I felt a surge of blood to my face, my breath caught, my knees turned to water.

I waited a moment longer, until my respiration had returned to normal, then I went toward the kitchen. Cleo looked up, saw me approaching. Her eyes widened, her face became animated, she glowed.

"Josh!" she cried happily, "Where have you *been?*"

"Out of town," I said. "How are you, Cleo? Finkel, good to see you again."

"Bigg," he said.

Cleo, speaking in her soft, shy whisper, began telling me how concerned she had been—all the tenants had been concerned—because no one had seen me or heard me moving about since Thursday morning, and they feared I had met with some misadventure.

I assured her I was in good health, all was well, and I had a great deal to tell her about matters we had previously discussed.

Adolph Finkel had listened to this intimate dialogue with some discomfiture, his pallid features becoming more and more woebegone. I thought tears might flow from those weak eyes. He looked mousier than ever, the dull hair a tangle, a doomed smile revealing the discolored tombstone teeth.

"Well, Bigg," he broke in suddenly, "I guess the best man won."

He drained off his paper cup of wine, gave us a look of such martyrdom that I wanted to kick his shins, and shambled away, shoulders slumping. We looked after him with astonishment. I turned back to Cleo.

"The best man?" I said, remembering Hamish Hooter and Yetta Apatoff.

Then Cleo and I were giggling, leaning toward each other, our heads touching.

"Listen," I said, "can we leave as soon as possible? There's so much I want to tell you."

She looked at me steadily.

"Where do you want to go?" she asked.

I took a deep breath.

"There's a nice restaurant on 23rd Street," I said casually. "Woody's. It's open on Sundays. Good food. I know the woman who runs the place. We can have dinner and drinks in real glasses."

"You're sure you want to go out with me?" she said, still looking into my eyes. She knew I had been afraid of being seen with her. Mutt and Jeff.

"Positive," I said stoutly.

"I'd love to go to Woody's with you," she said, smiling.

I eased out the door, took my hat and coat, and waited for Cleo in the entrance hall. She came flying down a few moments later in a coat and tam and we set out.

It was a hard, brilliant day, flooded with sunshine. But the wind was gusting strongly, whipping our coats, tingling our cheeks. Cleo took my arm, and I looked nervously at passersby, watching for signs of amusement when they saw this tall, willowy woman with her runty escort.

But no one gave us a glance, and after a while I stopped caring what people might think.

"I brought the kite home," I told Cleo. "And the string and winder."

"Too windy today," she said. "But we'll fly it another day."

"Sure we will," I said.

We hung coats and hats on the rack just inside the door of Woody's. We waited a moment, and then Nitchy came toward us from the back dining room.

"Cleo," I said, "I'd like you to meet Nitchy, a good friend. Nitchy, meet Cleo."

The two women shook hands. Nitchy looked up searchingly at Cleo's face. Then she turned to me, smiling. She put a soft hand on my arm.

"At last!" she said.